D0052464

Snow Angel Season

Christmas in Eternity Springs
The Christmas Wishing Tree

TWO NOVELS IN ONE

EMILY MARCH

St. Martin's Paperbacks

This is a work of fiction. All of the characters, organizations, and events portrayed in this novel are either products of the author's imagination or are used fictitiously.

First published in the United States by St. Martin's Paperbacks, an imprint of St. Martin's Publishing Group.

SNOW ANGEL SEASON: CHRISTMAS IN ETERNITY SPRINGS copyright © 2016 by Geralyn Dawson Williams and THE CHRISTMAS WISHING TREE copyright © 2018 by Geralyn Dawson Williams.

For information, address St. Martin's Publishing Group, 120 Broadway, New York, NY 10271.

www.stmartins.com

ISBN: 978-1-250-76640-3

Our books may be purchased in bulk for promotional, educational, or business use. Please contact your local bookseller or the Macmillan Corporate and Premium Sales Department at 1-800-221-7945, ext. 5442, or by email at MacmillanSpecialMarkets@macmillan.com.

Printed in the United States of America

St. Martin's Paperbacks edition 2020

10 9 8 7 6 5 4 3 2 1

Christmas in
Eternity Springs

*To the members of the Emily March Fans group
(I want to call it a sisterhood) on Goodreads,
led by the most fabulous Paula Radell.
You women warm my heart.
Merry Christmas!*

Acknowledgments

I want to thank the outstanding team at St. Martin's Press for their enthusiastic support of all things Eternity Springs, in particular my editor, Rose Hilliard. It's a pleasure to work with you. To my agents, Meg Ruley and Christina Hogrebe at the Jane Rotrosen Agency, your professionalism and support are beyond compare. To my personal support team: Mary Dickerson, Christina Dodd, Nicole Burnham, Susan Sizemore, Mary Lou Jarrell, Caitlin Williams and Steve Williams, maybe by book 50 I'll figure out how not to be quite so crazy at deadline time. But probably not. I love you guys dearly.

Prologue

DECEMBER
DALLAS, TEXAS

The fragrance of Christmas swept into the house along with the tree that the garden center's deliverymen carried inside. As they placed the twelve-foot-tall blue spruce into the stand she'd positioned in front of the living room picture window, Claire Branham allowed herself to reflect on the once-upon-a-time memories triggered by the scent.

Days of Christmas Past. Such happy times —laughter and excitement and family traditions. A home filled with love. All lost, wiped away by the reality of illness and death and broken hearts.

As she watched the workers secure the tree to the stand, she reflected upon what a momentous occasion this was for her. She hadn't put up a Christmas tree in a very long time. For Claire, Black Friday didn't represent the beginning of the holiday shopping season. It signified the day the doctor's office called and changed the lives of everyone she loved.

Fifteen Christmases had passed since that first life-altering year. Some years, she'd gone through the motions of participation, even though her heart wasn't in it. Other years, she did her best to ignore it entirely. Mostly, she'd muddled through, grumpy and unhappy and counting the days until the season was over for another year.

"That should do it," said one of the deliverymen, stepping back from the tree. He handed Claire a little green bottle of preservative. "Mix this with water according to the directions. Add water as needed. Doesn't hurt to check it every day, but it needs to be watered at least every other day."

"Thank you."

"You picked a pretty one, Ms. Branham. You have a perfect spot for a tree in this home. Now . . ." He flipped a page on his clipboard. "Are we decorating the tree, too, or just doing the outdoor lighting and decorations?"

"You're hanging the outdoor lights and helping with the high things inside the house. I'm saving the tree to decorate until my fiancé gets home from a business trip tomorrow."

Claire showed him the outdoor decorations in her garage, then went back inside to begin draping garland on the staircase. Anticipation made her feel like a child on Christmas morning. It had been years since she'd decorated a tree, and she couldn't wait to do it again. This year, Claire wasn't spending her holiday season with her Grinch on. She was going all Elf. Because for the first time in forever, the thought of the holiday season made Claire happy.

It started on Black Friday. Rather than launching her usual month-long depression, Black Friday this year got Claire off to a joyful holiday start. After she and Landon ran the Turkey Trot 10K on Thanksgiving morning, she'd sent him off to the airport with a kiss and a turkey sandwich so he could make his early afternoon flight to the West Coast where he had meetings scheduled with movie executives. Friday morning, rather than lie in bed with her covers over her head as in years past, Claire had bounded out of bed early, joined the shopping hoards, and had a ball doing it.

It set the tone for her days as she anticipated Landon's return. Claire was happy and excited and joyful. With Landon's help, she had climbed her way out of the valley of loss and loneliness and found her happiness. Now, she was finding her Christmas spirit again.

She had volunteer work to thank for it, since that's how she'd met the love of her life. Volunteer work and a book that was special to her heart. There was a lesson there, one she intended to honor for the rest of her days, because from that relatively simple act of generosity, dreams beyond her wildest imaginings were coming true.

Tomorrow would be yet another milestone. She and Landon would be celebrating their first Christmas in their new home, so the time had come to begin making their own family traditions. She had it all planned. She'd have carols playing softly on the stereo system, a fire in the fireplace, and mulled wine simmering on the stove.

She'd be wearing a little something special from Victoria's Secret.

She simply couldn't wait. She'd had a ridiculous amount of fun shopping for the lights and ornaments and decorations for the tree. She'd even bought and worn a Santa hat while she went about it.

She made their bed with the holiday sheets and comforter, hung holiday towels in the bathroom. She dressed the dining room table with a crimson and gold table runner, and as a centerpiece, used glass ornaments in a crystal bowl. By mid-afternoon, the lights were strung, wreaths hung, and stockings lay draped across the easy chair. Stocking hanging would be one of their traditions, she'd decided. Together, they'd hang the stockings and decorate the tree, ending with the most special Christmas tradition of all—placing her precious Christmas angel named Gardenia atop their tree.

Claire was excited, so excited in fact, that she didn't want to spend the evening home alone and watching a movie like she'd originally planned. She could dive into the holiday baking she intended to do. She'd bought ingredients for her mother's traditional Christmas fudge, three different kinds of her favorite Christmas cookies, and a cake she wanted to try.

She debated the idea for a long moment, then shook her head. Her mother used to say that baking was best done in the mornings.

Maybe she'd do a little more shopping or, even better, a lot of shopping. She could afford it, couldn't she? She'd been meaning to make a run over to Cook Children's Hospital in Fort Worth to check out the waiting rooms and see what was on their wish lists. Why not go today? She could visit the hospitals and maybe have dinner at one of the restaurants on the square downtown. She'd heard the Christmas decorations there were lovely. After dinner, she could stop in at the Texas Ranger baseball shop and pick up another gift for Landon. The man was such a huge Ranger fan. He loved baseball, the law, and her.

Liking the idea, she changed clothes, loaded up her wallet with cash, checks, and cards, and started out the door. At the threshold, she hesitated. She was going to Cook Children's. Maybe she should go prepared. What would be more appropriate than spending a few hours doing the thing that led her to Landon and to all of her happiness today?

Decision made, she grabbed her book tote, checked the contents, then detoured to the family room where Gardenia awaited her big moment the following day. Claire tucked her gently into the bag, then did a slow turn around to soak in the joy of having her home spruced up for Christmas. "It's good. I've missed this. I shouldn't have let it go."

She gave the jingle bells hanging on her door a little shake, then left her north Dallas home. Traffic was light, and the drive to Fort Worth took a little over half an hour. She made her way to the volunteer office at the children's hospital where she gave the receptionist a little of her history and explained what she wanted to do.

"Oh, that's just wonderful," a middle-aged woman dressed in slacks, a white shirt, and pink vest said. "So generous! My name is Lisa Norris and I'm happy to show you around, but you really need to speak with our coordinator, Stella Hewitt. The Jewel Charity Ball is tonight—Cook's is the beneficiary—and she's meeting with the chairpersons. Stella will know what needs are being met and what wishes are still on our list, but I'm not sure she has time in her schedule to meet with you."

"That's okay. We can do that over the phone another time. I'd like to look at the waiting rooms while I'm here."

"Of course." Smiling, Lisa said, "Follow me. We will start in orthopedics."

Claire stepped out into the hall to wait for her escort. The woman gave a brief history of the hospital while she led Claire to waiting rooms on the first and second floors. Claire took a notebook from her purse and began to sketch ideas. After viewing a waiting room on the third floor, she had her head down looking at her notes when her escort stopped.

"This is handy," Lisa said. She raised her voice. "Stella? Do you have a moment?"

Claire glanced up with a smile on her face. She saw an attractive woman in her early sixties exiting a boardroom followed by a younger couple. Claire's steps slowed. Her smile faltered. Landon? What was he doing here?

And why was that tall, leggy blonde wrapped around him?

Lisa said, "Stella, I know you're frightfully busy, but I'd like to introduce you to Claire Branham. She wants to make a directed donation to outfit our waiting rooms here. Would you have a few moments to visit with her?"

"Of course," the older woman said. She approached Claire, her hand extended. "I'm Stella Hewitt. These are two of the chairpersons for tonight's Jewel Ball, Jennifer Perryman and her husband, Landon."

Her husband, Landon Perryman. Her husband.

My fiancé.

The man wearing a two-thousand-dollar suit and an "oh shit" look on his face.

As the room began to spin, she gazed back at Landon. She could almost see his calculating brain at work. He took a half step toward her, the clingy blonde in tow. "Claire."

She shook her head, lifted her hand palm out to fend off anything he might try to say. She brought her left hand up and placed it over her breaking heart. "Excuse me, I'm going to be sick."

There was a door to the ladies' room ten steps beyond him. Her stomach churning, she started forward. The bile rose and when she was a mere step away, she caught a whiff of his familiar aftershave.

She vomited on his Italian suit and loafers, then giggled a bit hysterically all the way to her car.

Chapter One

In her second-floor apartment above her shop, Forever Christmas, Claire eyed the express delivery envelope lying on her kitchen table as if it were a snake. A six-foot-long rattlesnake. Or, maybe a python. Pythons squeezed the life out of their prey, didn't they? The contents of that envelope were sure to wring the peace right out of her day.

She could see it now. She'd tear open the envelope and a snake with blue eyes and a forked tongue would slither out and wind its way along her arm, climbing up to twine around her neck and—*Clang!*

She jumped at the sound of a wrench hitting a metal pipe.

"Earth to Claire," came a male voice from beneath her sink. "You still there? You zoned out again, didn't you?"

"Sorry." She had a tendency to let her mind wander, especially when she was nervous. "Do you need something?"

"Try the water again."

She leaned over the long, jeans-clad legs and twisted on the cold water. A moment later, Brick Callahan said, "That's got it. You're good to go."

Claire switched off the water and stepped backward as the man dressed in worn jeans, a Stardance Ranch

T-shirt, and hiking boots scooted out from beneath the sink. "Thank you, Brick. I just didn't have the hand strength to get it tight enough."

"Hey, no problem." A teasing glint entered his forest-green eyes as he flexed his muscles and grinned. "I'm always happy to show off my guns."

Claire gave an exaggerated huff. "Do you ever *not* flirt?"

Innocence echoed in his voice. "Hey, you're a gorgeous single woman about my age, and a redhead to boot. I've always had a thing for redheads. Why *wouldn't* I flirt with you?"

"I saw you flirt with Elaine Hanks at the Trading Post last week," Claire challenged. "She's seventy if she's a day."

He shrugged. "I like women. What can I say?"

"And women like you, too, don't they?"

"It's my cross to bear." He rolled to his feet and studied her. "One of these days when you're ready, I'd like to hear about the jerk who hurt you."

Claire shook her head at him in bemusement. He'd asked her on a date after they'd met at the Chamber of Commerce last spring. She'd thanked him, then explained that she had no desire to date in the wake of a recent bad breakup. "Why would you want to listen to my sorry tale of woe?

"Because I like you. We're friends. And sometimes you get a Bambi look going on that makes me want to find the SOB and knock him on his ass."

"You're a knight in shining armor," she said, her heart warming. He'd make someone a great catch. Just not her.

Never her. Never again.

Had she not been watching him closely, she'd have missed the shadow that flitted across his face. "Not always, sweetheart. Not always."

The note of regret in his voice intrigued Claire. She wasn't the only one with baggage and regrets, apparently. Brick Callahan was a mystery. Handsome, witty, nice, and a hard worker—why *hadn't* someone snapped him up already?

As it was wont to do, her imagination took flight. There was a woman in Brick's past. Who was she? A driven city girl who didn't like the slow pace of mountain life? Or maybe she was an entertainer, a country music singer. A girl who dreamed of stadiums filled with adoring fans. Perhaps she—

"So," Brick said. "Anything else I need to fix while I'm here?"

Claire crashed back to reality and her gaze shifted to the envelope on the kitchen table. *If only.* "No. That takes care of it. Thanks a million, Brick. I really appreciate the help."

"Not a problem. It's the least I could do after you kept the shop open late so I could get a last-minute birthday present for my aunt Maddie."

She glanced at the clock. "Speaking of last minutes, this took longer than I expected. You'd better get moving or you'll miss the party."

"Not a Callahan party." Brick set the wrench down on her countertop. "We start early and finish late. Sure I can't talk you into going with me?" He held up a hand to ward off her immediate refusal and added, "Friends, Claire. Just friends."

Claire hesitated. She sensed that he meant it. Not all men were liars, cheats, and thieves. Brick Callahan wasn't just saying what he thought she wanted to hear.

Maybe. Probably.

But she couldn't be sure. She'd learned the hard way that she dare not trust her instincts where men were concerned. She wasn't about to trust, period. "Thanks, but not tonight. I'm exhausted. It's been a long week."

He washed his hands in the kitchen sink, and she handed him a dishtowel so he could dry them. "If you change your mind, come on out. You know where our place is on Hummingbird Lake?"

"I do." She handed him the gift box she'd wrapped while he worked on her leaky faucet, then led him downstairs and through the shop. She flipped the lock on the front door. Jingle bells on the wreath chimed as she opened it. "Enjoy your evening, Brick. I hope Maddie likes the tree topper."

"I know she will. Uncle Luke might have been deaf to her hints, but not me."

"Tell her I said happy birthday."

"Will do." Then, because Brick liked to kiss women as much as he liked to flirt, he leaned down and kissed her cheek. "G'night, Claire. I'm glad you moved to Eternity Springs."

She beamed a smile at him. "That's nice of you to say. Thank you. I love it here."

It was true, she thought as she locked the door behind him and gazed around her shop. Her Christmas shop. She would admit that her spur-of-the-moment decision to open a Christmas shop in the middle of Nowhere, Colorado, based on the recommendation of a twinkling-eyed stranger riding a motorcycle could make a decent case study for a psych professor.

However, the town suited her. She was making friends. She was operating her business in the black. Sure, she had issues, but she was working on them, wasn't she? She didn't *want* to hate Christmas. She was tackling one of her biggest demons. And she got points for creating an Angel Room in Forever Christmas, didn't she?

Her gaze drifted toward said Angel Room, where the tree central to the entire display stood with a naked top. A flurry of sales in the past two days had depleted her inventory and she'd been forced to use her sample to fill Brick's request. "Bonus points if you go ahead and put a different angel on top of that tree tonight," she challenged herself.

If she faced the Angel Room and that envelope in the same day, she'd deserve more than just bonus points. She'd deserve ice cream. Two scoops.

Because Claire and Christmas weren't exactly on the best terms. She associated Bad Things with Christmas. Things like illness and death, and more recently, betrayal. She couldn't help it. All of it had happened. Before the Lying Lizard Louse, the holiday season had depressed her. Made her sad. Made her heart ache. Since him, she'd connected Christmas with the molten anger boiling inside her.

And dang it, she was going to change that. Despite the larcenous liar, she was going to learn to love Christmas again. Love the scents and the tastes and the sounds and the colors of Christmas. Love the snowmen and ornaments and peppermints. Love the angels.

The angels. She'd love every freaking sparkling feathery angel. Even if it killed her.

Well, except for Starlina. That was asking too much. Claire still had her pride.

She blew out a breath, mentally reviewed her inventory, and decided on a new angel to crown the centerpiece tree. She carried her ladder from the supply room and positioned it. As she removed a simple white porcelain topper from the box, her gaze stole toward an angel with a tattered dress and a broken wing sitting mostly hidden behind a trio of bright, shiny, beautiful angels. Gardenia.

Emotion roiled within her. With her gaze focused on the bedraggled angel, she thought of the envelope upstairs. Almost against her will, she glanced down at the empty third finger of her left hand. The tears that stung the back of her eyes annoyed her, so she stomped her feet just a little bit as she climbed the ladder.

Claire's petite form came with short arms. Ordinarily when she trimmed a tall tree, she used an extension tool to help her place decorations. She'd already climbed the ladder when she realized she'd forgotten it. Impatient with herself on many levels, she wanted the task over and done with. She climbed another rung of the ladder, extended her arm, and reached for the tip of the tree with the angel topper. And reached. Leaned a little farther. Stretched . . .

"Ow!" Pain sliced through her shoulder as she slid the angel on the treetop. She'd tweaked an old rotator-cuff injury. "This day just keeps getting better and better."

She couldn't even dull the ache with nice glass of cabernet since she still had two days of antibiotics to take after having an emergency root canal on Monday. As she descended the ladder, she grumbled aloud, "A great day in a spectacular week."

Root canal. Flat tire. Shattered phone screen.

Contact from the past she'd run from but could never escape.

Claire exhaled a heavy sigh, put away her ladder, then turned off the shop lights and climbed the stairs to her apartment. Unfortunately, the envelope hadn't slithered off her kitchen table in her absence.

She pulled a bottle of ibuprofen from a cabinet and tossed two into her mouth, chasing the pills with a full glass of water. She set down the empty glass and focused on the delivery envelope. Focused on her name and address. Did her best to ignore the name of the law firm in the upper left-hand corner of the label.

"Do it," she muttered to herself. "Just do it. Get it over with."

Heart pounding, her mouth sandpaper dry, she picked up the envelope, pulled the tab, and looked inside. A black binder clip secured a stack of papers over an inch thick. She took a deep breath and yanked the paperwork from the envelope.

The check fell onto her table printed side down. Claire flipped it over and read the amount. She stumbled back against the wall. "Sweet baby Jesus in a manger."

Her knees buckled and she melted onto her kitchen floor.

As the sun began to dip below a craggy mountain peak to the west, Jax Lancaster pushed open the gate to the hot springs pools at Angel's Rest Healing Center and Spa. He turned away from a section of the small park where families congregated and chose an isolated pool that offered a great view of the spectacular orange and gold rays framing a purple mountain. Jax appreciated sunrises and sunsets in a way that only a man who'd gone months at a time for years in a row without seeing them could do. He pulled his U.S. Navy T-shirt over his head and tossed it aside before easing his aching body into the steaming waters of the mineral springs.

As welcome warmth seeped into his bones, Jax exhaled a heavy sigh and tried to relax and enjoy the view. Ten days of nonstop travel had taken its toll on his body. Eighteen months of constant worry about his son had worn upon his soul.

The fact that he was dead broke and out of work didn't help matters. Divorce and a custody battle had eaten up his savings, and then ten days ago, he'd walked away from a career he'd loved. He didn't regret the decision. He'd had no choice. Bottom line was Nicholas needed his father.

Whether the boy recognized it or not.

The gate hinges squeaked again and Jax glanced toward the sound. He gave the redheaded woman with a short but sexy pair of legs a quick once-over as she stepped into the pool area. Very nice, he thought. He'd always had a thing for redheads. She wore a black swimsuit cover-up and carried a long beach towel in shades of red and green draped over her left shoulder. In her right hand, she carried a large tote bag with a cartoon character on the side. Rudolph? In July?

When she turned toward the families, he returned his attention to the sunset and his troubles. He'd checked his e-mail after arriving at the resort, but the good news he'd hoped to find waiting for him had not materialized. Jax tried not to brood about the goose egg in his job-offer in-box. He needed to give it some time. Seattle was a big, fast-growing city with a hot economy. Something would come along. Hadn't he been told by more than one potential employer to reach out to them again after his discharge was official? In the meantime, well, he had an offer on the table that would pay the basic bills, didn't he?

Never mind that he'd almost rather panhandle on the streets than work for his ex-father-in-law's chain of independent bookstores.

Jax sank farther into the water and rolled his shoulders. If he had to work for Lara's dad in order to put a roof over Nicholas's head, keep Cheerios in his breakfast bowl, and ensure that the checks to the child psychologist didn't bounce, then that's what he'd do. The boy came first.

An explosion of laughter erupted from the other side of the park. Jax tried to remember the last time he'd laughed like that. Before the accident, certainly.

The accident. What a mild term for such a life-altering event.

Spying movement in his peripheral vision, he turned his head to see the redhead approach. She stepped into a beam of sunshine and the fire in her hair glistened. It was as if the sunset walked right out of the sky and up to the edge of the mineral springs pool where he sat. "Excuse me," she said. "There's a water world war going on in the other pools. Mind if I share your little Switzerland?"

He smiled. "Not at all. *Mi Switzerland es tu Switzerland.*"

"Thanks." She kicked off her sandals, then swiftly unbuttoned her cover-up—no wedding ring on her left hand, he noticed—and pulled it off to reveal a modest black swimsuit. Since her curves were as appealing as her legs, Jax had to force himself to look away.

He heard the splash and then a feminine cough. "Mercy. This is my first time to visit the mineral springs. I hadn't realized exactly how bad they smell."

"You'll get accustomed to it after a couple of minutes. Now, you might not smell anything else for two days afterward, but your sense of smell will return."

"I'll take your word for it. Soaking in a mineral spring is supposed to have health benefits, right? Like soothing sore muscles?"

Jax nodded. "Yes, although I don't know how effective it is. Still, mineral springs have attracted people all across the world throughout history, so on that basis alone, I think there must be something to it. Personally, I like it here because I find this relaxing."

"And I'm interrupting your peace with my chatter. I apologize."

"No need. I'm always happy to . . ." Jax bit back the words "share my tub with a beautiful lady" and settled for something that sounded less like a come-on. "Meet new people. I'm Jax Lancaster."

"Claire Branham. I've recently moved to Eternity Springs and opened a business, which is keeping me busy and is why I haven't visited these pools before tonight. Are you a guest at Angel's Rest, Jax?"

"I am. I'm here for a couple of days to pick up my son from the Rocking L summer camp."

"Oh." The note of sympathy and understanding she managed to insert into the tone of that one short word revealed that she knew the Rocking L wasn't an ordinary camp. "The Rocking L program is fabulous. I know the children who get to attend are thrilled with the experience. How old is your son?"

"Nicholas is eight." Jax hesitated, then because he was curious to get another perspective on the Rocking L program, he added, "He's been having a rough time of it. He was with his mother when she died a year and a half ago, and it damaged him. I'm hoping the weeks he's spent at camp will kick-start his recovery."

"I'm so sorry for your loss."

"His loss, not mine," Jax clarified. Then he winced. "That sounds terrible, doesn't it? That's not what I intended. We were divorced. His mother and I were divorced. Acrimoniously. Ugly custody battle. I've been in the navy and they don't always just let you quit when you want, so Nicholas has been living with her parents and I'm babbling. Sorry. Too much traveling through too many time zones and I'm punch-drunk and nervous about picking him up tomorrow."

"Don't worry about it. I've been known to babble, myself. Frequently. So where did you begin your travels?"

The specific information was classified. Jax picked a point in the middle. "Seventy-two hours ago I was in Dubai."

"Whoa. I'll bet the jet lag is brutal."

His mouth twisted in a rueful grin. "I don't ordinarily spill my guts to strangers. I've embarrassed myself. I'll shut up now."

"Oh, don't be embarrassed. Sometimes sharing a burden

makes it easier to carry. And doing so with a stranger instead of a friend protects against potential blowback."

"Blowback?"

"Haven't you ever been a little too honest with friends or family and it comes back to haunt you?"

He thought of the conversation with Lara right before he left on the deployment that doomed his marriage. Oh, yeah. He understood the risk of too much honesty. Been there, done that, got the divorce. However, not even his jet-lagged tongue was loose enough to go there, so he stuck with something lighter. "You mean like telling my ex that those yellow slacks did indeed make her butt look big?"

Claire snorted. "You didn't."

"We started dating our freshman year in college. I was very young and stupid at the time, but I did learn." *Just not fast enough.* Wanting to direct the conversation away from himself, Jax asked, "How about you, Claire? Has honesty come back to haunt you with a significant other?"

"I'm not married. I ended a relationship not long ago, but it wasn't due to too much honesty." Her tone turned bitter as she added, "Just the opposite, in fact."

"Sounds like you have a burden to unload, yourself. Go for it. You won't get any blowback from me."

"Hmm . . ." She shot him a narrow-eyed look. "You said you're only in town for a couple of days?"

"We leave the day after tomorrow for San Diego. I'll pack up my place there, and then it's on to Seattle where Nicholas has been living."

Claire shifted her position in the pool so that she faced the sunset rather than Jax. A full minute of silence ticked by before she spoke again. "I should be celebrating tonight. I should be drinking champagne and having wild sex with a ski instructor named Stamina Sven. Instead

I'm soaking an old softball injury in a stinky, steamy pool while drinking sparkling water and spilling my secrets to a stranger."

Jax's brows arched. *Stamina Sven?* "It's obvious you have a shoulder injury when you throw a hanging curve ball like that one."

"Let me guess," she drawled. "Your middle name is Sven."

He waggled his brows. "You can call me Stamina for short. And I understand that room service delivers out here. I'm happy to order a bottle of bubbly."

"Thanks, but no."

"So what are we not celebrating?"

She sighed heavily. "Lawyers."

Jax lifted an imaginary champagne goblet in toast. "I can definitely drink to that."

"And Christmas."

"Christmas? Well, it is July."

"Forever Christmas. My shop. It's doing great. It's on the corner of Cottonwood and Third. I opened it this spring and this month I'm going to finish in the black. By a kitten's whisker, but black is black, right?"

"Right." A Christmas store. Guess that accounted for the Rudolph tote bag.

"I'm trying hard to take pleasure in my shop. I'm giving myself a pass on the angels, although I'm trying very hard to hold on to the rest of my joy, but it's hanging by a strand of tinsel. See, I'd lost it, then I found it, but I discovered it was a lie. Well, he was a lie. What I felt wasn't a lie."

"You loved him."

"Yes, I loved him. I loved the thought of making a life with him, of having Christmas with him. After all those years of missing it, hating it, wishing I could go to a deserted island from Black Friday to January second, I put up a tree in my house and even bought silly holiday towels! He ruined it with his lies, but I'm not letting him ruin anything else. No way. That's what I'm trying to hold on to. I won't let him steal it from me. It's bad enough that I was stupid enough to be fooled by a dirty rotten lying lawyer, that I let him break my heart. I won't allow him to steal my joy."

Jax wondered what sort of problem she had with angels, but he didn't interrupt to ask. She was on a roll.

"I tell everyone that the reason I moved to Eternity Springs was because I saw a business opportunity, but that's not really true. I was running away. From him. From reminders of him. From reality. Eternity Springs was my place to hide and to heal. I thought I was doing a pretty decent job of it. I'm making friends. I'm becoming involved in town life. Forever Christmas is an in-your-face declaration that he's not going to win. It's good. I'm tooling along, getting along, thinking maybe I've got this thing whipped, when today . . . *boom!*" She clapped her hands. "The lousy lawyer and his great big lie followed me home."

Jax sat up straight. Every protective instinct he possessed went into full alert. "This jerk is stalking you?"

Chapter Two

"Stalking me?" she repeated. She lifted her gaze toward the mountains as she considered the question a moment before speaking. "No. Not in person, anyway. I feel as if I'm being hunted, because he did hire a private detective to find me so he's been making constant attempts to contact me, but that can't be termed stalking. He's sending paperwork."

"Paperwork?"

"Paperwork. It's a legal thing I can't sever right now. And whenever I receive communication from him, I can't help but get my Grinch on."

"Ah." Jax relaxed back down into the water.

She gave her head a shake. "But enough talk of lizards. Let's talk about something happier. Tell me about your son. He's eight, you said? What's he like? Is Nicholas adventurous and strong-willed? Talkative and imaginative? Thoughtful and diplomatic?"

Jax tore his gaze away from the glistening sunset of her hair. He didn't want to admit that he didn't know his son well enough to answer her question. "Nicholas has always been detailed and orderly. When he was just a toddler, he spent hours stacking blocks. They had to be color coordinated and positioned exactly so."

The corners of Jax's mouth lifted. *My little engineer,* he remembered thinking. "Before his mother died . . ."—*before our divorce*—"Nicholas was lively and talkative. I'm hopeful his time at this summer camp will put us on the road to finding that happy little boy again."

She encouraged him with a smile. "Well, from everything I hear about the Rocking L, you couldn't ask for a more dedicated staff."

"Do you know any of them personally? Anything you can tell me about the camp from a local point of view?"

"Well, hmm." She considered a few moments, then said, "Like I said, I'm a relative newcomer to town, myself. I don't believe I've met any of the staff. I have met the camp's benefactors, the Davenports, and I like them very much. I also know a couple of the people from town who volunteer up there—the local vet and the owner here at Angel's Rest, Celeste Blessing."

"I met Celeste when I checked in. She told me she leads nature hikes up at the camp."

"I've heard they are fabulous. She seems to have extraordinary luck when it comes to sighting wildlife."

"According to her, my boy has had a great time."

"If Celeste said it, you can believe it. She has her fingers on the pulse of everything that happens in this valley. Plus, she's very . . . well . . . I guess I'd call it intuitive. She has an uncanny ability to say exactly what I need to hear when I need to hear it." She gave a soft, self-deprecating laugh then added, "Unfortunately, she didn't stop by the store today."

"She's quite the ambassador for Eternity Springs," Jax said. "I asked what Nicholas and I should do tomorrow afternoon, and she gave me a list that would take two weeks to complete. Do you have any ideas for me?"

Claire offered her suggestions for afternoon activities in and around Eternity Springs, and after that discussion, conversation naturally paused as they both watched in silent appreciation as a full moon rose over the Rockies.

"It's beautiful here," Jax said.

"Yes, it is. Eternity Springs is a good place. It has good energy. Positive energy."

Jax thought of what lay before him and observed, "I wish there was a way to bottle it up and take it with me."

"You should ask Celeste."

A voice rang out of the shadows behind Jax. "Ask me what?"

Jax glanced over his shoulder to see Celeste Blessing approach, carrying a tray holding a bucket of champagne and two flutes. "I didn't order champagne," he murmured.

"It's for the newlyweds in our honeymoon cottage," Celeste explained. "I noticed Claire headed this way earlier, and I wanted to ask her if she has any news about my special order."

"The Lalique angel? No, I'm afraid not. I called about it this afternoon, and they've promised me a firm ship date tomorrow. If I haven't heard from them by noon, I'll give them another call."

"Lovely. Thank you, dear. Now, Mr. Lancaster, what question may I answer for you?"

Embarrassment turned his smile bashful. "We were just talking about Eternity Springs."

"Jax wished there was a way to bottle up the valley's positive energy to take with him when he leaves," Claire added. "If anyone knows a way to do it, you would, Celeste."

The older woman laughed with delight. "Well, of course I do. That's easy enough."

"I don't think they'll let me on an airplane with bottles of mineral water," Jax observed.

"Oh, it's not the mineral water. It's the basic state of mind. A positive thought in the morning sets the tone for your entire day."

Jax was fairly certain he'd seen that platitude on a T-shirt.

However, Celeste took it a step further. "Now, the key to having that positive thought each morning starts the night before. I suggest that each night before you go to sleep, you make note of one positive thing that happened in your day. Even the darkest of days will have one moment of light. Make note of it. Write it down. Use it to jump-start your day the following morning. It's like a cup of coffee for your attitude."

"I like it," Claire said.

"Thank you, dear. Now, if you'll excuse me, I need to get this champagne to our honeymooners. Enjoy the rest of your evening and think of something positive that happened today when you go to sleep tonight."

Celeste's words hung in the air long after her departure. Claire twisted her head around to meet Jax's gaze. "See what I mean? She's a wise woman. That's a commonsense idea and it makes so much sense to me."

"It's simplistic," Jax cautioned. "Life seldom is."

"True. Maybe that's the problem. Maybe that's part of what makes Eternity Springs special. I think it's possible to live a somewhat simple life here."

"Because it's a small town?"

"No. More because Eternity Springs had a near-death experience, and it changed the outlook of those who live here."

An easy gust of summer breeze swept petals from the nearby rose garden into the hot springs. Jax idly watched the yellow petals float in lazy circles on the moonlit surface of the pool as Claire told him how the little town had been on the brink of financial failure when Celeste decided to open Angel's Rest, which led to the rebirth of Eternity Springs.

"I studied the stats before I decided to move here,"

she said. "Since the resort opened, the town has added over three hundred permanent residents and half again as many permanent seasonal residents. The only thing holding back even stronger summer tourism is a shortage of rooms to rent."

"I noticed lots of No Vacancy signs around town."

"We're having a great summer tourist season. I think the change from a bleak economic outlook to a positive one has taken a big burden off the shoulders of people who live here. Life is easier now. People are happier. They have more time and treasure to devote to what matters to them. Here in Eternity Springs, that tends to be friends and family and faith—the recipe for a basic, simple life."

"I dunno, Claire. In my experience, family is the most complicated thing on earth."

Claire smiled ruefully and sadness dimmed her eyes. "I won't argue that, but I think Celeste would say there's a lesson there."

"What lesson is that?"

"Actually . . . I haven't a clue. I'm just certain Celeste would point one out."

The two shared a grin, then Jax said, "I concede you have a point. I've seen how close calls can change an individual's outlook on life. I can imagine that it would work similarly for a community, too. So, if you decided to brew a pot of her attitudinal coffee, what positive thing would you write down about today for tomorrow morning?"

"Hmm . . . that's actually a difficult question. I have a number of positive things that happened today from which to choose."

She stilled and an expression of wonder stole across her face. "Wow. It worked. I was all Grinchy Grouch when I arrived here tonight, but now my mind is filled with good things. That's kinda cool. Your turn, Jax. What was your moment of light today?"

The answer was easy. "You. I met you. You've been my ray of sunshine today."

"Why, thank you." She beamed like the moonlight. "That's the nicest thing someone has said to me in a long time." She glanced toward the west where the glow of sunset faded to night. "I also think it's a good note on which to take my leave."

Claire stood and as she climbed out of the pool and reached for her towel, Jax took advantage of her momentary inattention to ogle her shapely figure. Lots of curves in a compact form. She swiped her towel over her arms and legs before wrapping it around her torso. "I am glad we met, Jax Lancaster. I hope you and Nicholas have a wonderful reunion tomorrow and a fabulous trip home."

"Thank you. I am glad we met, too, Claire Branham." He was sorry to see her go. "I wish you a quick recovery from your shoulder injury, continued success with Forever Christmas, and a life free from lawyers for as long as you'd like."

"Amen to that," she declared. "Good night and safe journey."

"Good night."

As Claire walked off into the shadows, Jax stretched out his legs, laced his fingers behind his head, and tried to recall the last time he'd shared such a pleasant conversation with a woman. Throughout the exchange, an undercurrent of mild flirtation had hummed between them and he'd enjoyed it.

At least, he thought that's what had been going on. He was rusty in that respect. He'd been faithful to his wife, and deployed almost continuously since the divorce, so the opportunities to indulge in flirtation to any degree had been few and far between.

That situation wouldn't be changing anytime soon,

either. Nicholas had to be his first, his only, priority for the time being.

Wonder what would have happened if he'd amped things up, if he'd come out and hit on her? Jax didn't pick up women in bars—or mineral pools—as a rule, and she certainly hadn't seemed to be on the prowl herself. And yet, he'd sensed that she was lonely like him. And she *had* mentioned Stamina Sven.

"Jax?"

He lowered his arms at the sound of her voice and sat up straight. His heart began to pound. "Did you forget something?"

"Not really. I had an idea. It's probably really stupid and I can't believe I'm going to suggest it, but what the heck. I think we should do it."

His eyes widened. Sex? She wanted sex? Had he misread her? Had she come back to pick him up?

"See, I think Celeste's suggestion is spot-on," she continued. "I believe in the power of positive thinking, but I also believe in running two miles a day. I'm a pitiful self-motivator. If I have a running buddy, I'm much more successful at dragging myself out of bed and lacing on my shoes. That's where you come in."

Something tells me she's not talking about me dragging myself out of bed with her.

"If I've made a promise to someone, I keep it. So, here's your chance to bottle up the positive energy of Eternity Springs and take it with you to the West Coast, Jax. Want to be my affirmative attitude buddy?"

"Affirmative attitude" isn't the type of "buddy" I'm wanting tonight. Cautiously, he asked, "What would be involved?"

"Well, we could both keep journals, but it needn't be that formal. It can be as simple as promising that each night, you'll make a mental note of something positive that happened that day."

"That's it?"

"Sure. Unless . . . I guess we could pick an amount of time we will commit to doing it. Probably shouldn't leave it open-ended."

"But no accountability between the two of us?"

Claire shrugged. "It's the guilt that works with me. If I say I'll do it, and I think you are doing it too, well, I can't slack off. So, how about it?"

She was so darned cute. So appealing. He felt the urge to tease her. "I don't know, Claire. It has a bit of a girly, 'Dear Diary' feel."

She folded her arms and sniffed with disdain. "Now, that's just wrong. Didn't you tell me you just got out of the navy? I'll bet you made notations in some sort of chart or report every day, didn't you?"

"Well, yes."

"So think of this as a charting. Or, keeping your log-book."

Jax arched an amused brow. "Be captain of my own life?"

"Why not?"

"Why not?" he repeated. "Sure, Claire. I'll play."

"Excellent. Do you want to commit to a time period?"

He rubbed his chin and considered. "How about three months? That's long enough to give it a fair shot and see if it actually works."

"Perfect. And at the end of those three months, if you're so inclined, reach out to me and let me know how it's worked for you. You can always contact me through my Web site. It's www.ForeverChristmasinColorado .com. Or, if you have a chance tomorrow, stop by and I'll give you a card with my info on it. Your son will enjoy the shop. All children do."

No, not my Nicholas. His son would be the exception.

Claire continued, "I'm so glad I came back and asked you to do this with me. Thanks, Jax. This makes me happy. I have a feeling this will be good for both of us."

They exchanged good nights once again, and she departed. Jax listened until the gate squeaked open and then closed.

"Well, that was an interesting encounter," he murmured. And now rather than relaxing, the hot springs pools felt lonely to him.

He rolled his shoulders, then stood and reached for his towel. He figured he'd head to his room, shower, and go down to dinner. Since a gorgeous redhead didn't appear to be on the menu for tonight, he'd settle for a steak and a nice glass of wine.

Who knows, he might even wander into the Angel's Rest gift shop and buy a notebook.

As he walked back toward the resort, his thoughts shifted to tomorrow. His schedule was packed. He had a phone appointment first thing in the morning with Nicholas's psychologist in Seattle, then a second phone appointment with the woman who'd been his teacher. Also, he'd been invited to a parents' luncheon at Eagle's Way, Jack and Cat Davenport's estate. No way was he missing that. He was glad to have the opportunity to personally thank the Davenports for their generosity toward Nicholas and all the campers.

Pickup time at the Rocking L was one o'clock. Jax intended to be there on the dot. Though he was nervous about what the future held, he couldn't wait to hold his boy once again. He'd missed him terribly.

Tomorrow afternoon, he would like to take his son fishing at Hummingbird Lake. Maybe canoeing, too, if

Nicholas would like that. Anything that might help them get beyond the awkwardness he fully expected to encounter during the first few hours they spent together.

Hours, hell. More likely days. Probably even weeks. Could be months. Who knew what sort of things Lara's parents had been saying about Jax to the boy? Nothing good, based on past experience.

Jax sighed heavily as the tension that he'd soaked away in the mineral springs came flooding back. He very much feared that he and Nicholas had a tall mountain to climb to establish a comfortable father-son relationship. Then he glanced up at the big Victorian house that served as the central building at Angel's Rest Healing Center and Spa, and he heard the echo of Celeste Blessing's advice in his mind. *Even the darkest day has a moment of light. Write it down. Use it to jump-start your day the following morning. It's like a cup of coffee for your attitude.*

He thought about Claire Branham and her challenge, and damned if he didn't feel a little more positive. He could do it. *They* would do it.

Tomorrow was the start of the Lancaster men's fresh beginning. Tomorrow he and Nicholas would begin to forge new bonds in a new version of their family. Shoot, maybe the boy's time at camp in this special little valley might actually help heal some of the wounds upon his poor heart.

How cool would it be if he could take his son shopping at Forever Christmas tomorrow afternoon?

Because ever since his mother's death and the traumatic events surrounding it, Jax's boy—his precious little Nicholas—was afraid of the trappings of Christmas. Deeply, deathly afraid.

The nightmare had started before Thanksgiving last year when his grandmother took him to a mall and continued through the end of the year when the decorations finally came down. He froze at the sight of gift-wrapped packages. The scents of cinnamon and peppermint and fir trees made him sick to his stomach. The sound of Christmas carols sent him into a terrorized stupor.

Unfortunately, Jax's sub had been beneath the Indian Ocean at the time and Lara's parents had taken a "tough love" stance, thinking Nicholas simply needed more exposure to all things holiday in order to get over his fears. It had been a disastrous approach, and by the time Jax learned of it, the damage had been done.

"And you need to manage your expectations, Dad," Jax murmured to himself. Tomorrow, his goal was to get a hug from his son. Beyond that, well, Christmas was still five months away.

Tonight he'd go up to his room and write down his bright moment and do his best to bottle some of this valley's positive mojo.

Too bad they didn't do miracles here in Eternity Springs.

Chapter Three

Hugs are even better than I remembered.
—JAX

Claire deposited a satisfyingly long receipt into the gold shopping bag that bore her store's logo. Wearing a friendly smile, she walked around the end of the antique wood counter and handed two bulging bags to her customer, a lovely sixty-something woman from New Mexico vacationing in Colorado with her husband and two other couples. "Thank you for shopping at Forever Christmas."

"Thank you, Claire!" the customer replied, snapping her wallet closed. "We had so much fun. The display of ornaments and gifts for family members is the most creative thing I've seen in a long time. I can't wait to give my sister the ornament I bought for her. So clever."

"I love the Angel Room," her companion said. "It's easy to imagine that you're being surrounded by love when you walk into that room."

Claire went to work ringing up the second customer's purchases, which were heavy on angels, she noticed. "Are you staying at our local resort, Angel's Rest?"

"No, we're guests of a fellow church member who owns cabins in a little valley not far from here," the first woman said. "It's a fabulous place. There are three cabins—although 'cabin' doesn't quite describe them because they are quite luxurious. And the way each is decorated is just precious. I've never seen such fabulous tile work as the mosaics in the kitchen and baths and on the fireplaces. They tell the story of the settling of this part of Colorado. So creative."

"We love it there," her companion agreed. "Eternity Springs is just darling. We've heard that Angel's Rest is wonderful, too. We have reservations for high tea there this afternoon."

"In that case, be sure to take a peek into the parlor," Claire suggested. "The owner has an exquisite collection of angels on display there."

Once the sale was completed and her visitors departed, Claire made a quick pass through Forever Christmas. For the first time since shortly after she'd flipped the CLOSED sign to OPEN five hours ago, she had a lull in customers.

Good. She could stand to get off her feet for a few minutes. Her choice of footwear this morning had been a mistake. She knew better than to wear heels at the shop. Ordinarily she wore sneakers with slacks, a white shirt, and a Forever Christmas apron. Today for some strange reason, she'd pulled on a sundress from her closet and slipped her feet into darling strappy sandals. The same sandals she wanted to kick off asap.

She detoured into the back room long enough to grab her tablet, thinking she'd use the time to catch up on e-mail. She took a seat on the tall wooden stool behind her checkout counter, which gave her an excellent view of the street.

All day long she'd watched the front door with more attention than customary. Would Jax Lancaster stop by? Why did she care? And why in the world had she worn heels just in case he showed up?

Claire let one shoe dangle from her foot and fall to the floor. Her gaze stole to the shelf below the cash register where she'd set the brown leather-bound journal embossed with the word "Believe" on the front. Simple and masculine, it was perfect for Jax and this particular project. If he stopped by, she planned to give it to him.

Why she cared whether or not he brought his son by the shop, she couldn't say. Seriously, she'd spent a whopping hour with the man. Half of that time, she'd been blabbering on, making a fool of herself. Why in the world did she want to see him again? Yes, he'd been easy on the eyes—very easy—but she'd learned that particular lesson, hadn't she?

Maybe because he'd blabbered on, too?

He'd seemed so genuinely worried about his son. He'd seemed so genuine, period. Maybe she'd needed to be reminded that genuine men do exist after Landon the Louse invaded her world yesterday.

"Genuine men do still exist" had been the message she'd written in the journal she'd chosen for herself last night—a fabric-covered, spiral-bound notebook with a hand-painted star on the cover.

Claire responded to a half-dozen e-mails before both her attention and her gaze wandered. Traffic on Third Street was beginning to pick up.

Jax would have picked his son up by now. Had he said what activity he had settled on for the afternoon? She couldn't recall.

The arrival of a new group of shoppers followed by the UPS truck provided a welcome distraction. She used paint pens to personalize seven ornaments for a grandmother from Denver and sold three Advent calendars, two snow globes, and a beautifully illustrated copy of *'Twas the Night Before Christmas*. When she checked in the delivery items, she discovered that Celeste's special order had arrived.

Jax Lancaster and his son never did.

At five o'clock, she flipped her OPEN sign and locked

the front door. Bookkeeping and housekeeping took her another half an hour, and when she was ready to turn out the lights, she hesitated.

Celeste would be thrilled if Claire delivered the Lalique to Angel's Rest. It would be good business. While she was there, she could drop off the journal for Jax. She wouldn't ask to see him or anything. She didn't want to be a creeper. Thinking that he might use her journal each night gave the project more substance in her imaginings. And the whole thing was about imaginings, right?

She'd do it. She'd wrap it up and leave it for him.

And if part of her was aware that fussing over journals and strangers and gifts was her way to avoid dealing with the paperwork that remained on her kitchen table upstairs, well, okay. Avoidance wasn't a crime.

She wrapped the journal in the gift-wrap paper that was printed in Forever Christmas's logo—Claire was a big believer in branding—and debated a full minute over what to write on the gift tag. Finally, she signed the words "Think positive!" and her name.

Before she could second-guess herself, Claire collected the box for Celeste, deposited it and the journal into a shopping bag, and headed for Angel's Rest.

It was another beautiful midsummer evening and pleasure hummed through Claire's veins as she made her way along Cottonwood toward the footbridge that spanned Angel Creek. She felt energized and upbeat and, amazingly, her feet no longer hurt. Maybe after her errand, she'd treat herself to dinner at the Yellow Kitchen. After a plate of pasta and a couple glasses of nice wine, she might even be up to reading the contract awaiting her signature that was part of yesterday's package.

She waved at Nic Callahan, who was out taking her daily walk, sporting a growing baby bump. Nic waved back, then as she rested a maternal hand atop her belly, Claire's heart gave a little twist. She adored children and she'd always wanted a big family. Landon had told her too many lies to count, but his oft-stated desire to start a family right after the wedding had been one of the worst.

At thirty-one, Claire's biological clock was ticking and some days it sounded louder than a bass drum. She hadn't given up on her dream of having a family, but as with everything else in her life, she was in the midst of read-justing her expectations. After the debacle with Landon, she couldn't imagine ever getting married, so her dream of having a husband and three or four or even five kids wasn't in the cards.

That didn't mean she couldn't still have a family, Claire knew. A traditional family wasn't the only option available. Hadn't her childhood best friend's mother been a single mom? Mary Elizabeth Sanders had been a great mother to Claire's friend Penny, though her path had not been an easy one. Money always had been tight for the Sanderses, and it was why, when she'd been offered a pro-motion that required a transfer to Atlanta, Mrs. Sanders had taken the job. Penny and Claire had both been dev-astated. They'd promised to stay in touch with one an-other and to visit each other. For a time, they'd followed through.

Then six months after Penny moved, Michelle got sick. Claire had lost touch with Penny as life as she'd known it changed.

Wonder how life might have been different had she had a friend to talk to during those awful months and years? She'd been alone. Too alone, for too long.

Then, she'd picked Landon the Lizard.

"Stop thinking about him," she muttered to herself. It was too beautiful an evening and the goal here was to focus on the positive. Right?

"Absolutely."

So when she caught a whiff of fragrance drifting on the evening air, she decided to take the long way to her destination and stop and smell the roses. Literally. It would give her something positive to write in her journal, and besides, she was a sucker for flowers.

Angel's Rest boasted an extensive rose garden with one section of Peace roses designated as a memorial garden. A fabulous carved wooden bench provided a place to sit and bask in the beauty and tranquility of the spot, and Claire might have done just that had she not spied Jax Lancaster standing beside the creek, his hands shoved into his pockets. A pair of fishing poles lay at his feet. A young boy—Nicholas, she assumed—stood about ten feet away, his position a copy of his father's. Neither one appeared too comfortable.

Claire hesitated. Maybe she should pretend she hadn't seen them and go on up to the house and drop off her packages. She didn't want him to think she was stalking him.

Even as she prepared to turn and continue along her way, Jax's head swiveled around. He wore sunglasses, so she couldn't see his eyes. Nevertheless, she sensed that his gaze had locked onto hers. He smiled and waved at her to join him. A bit desperately, she thought.

"Claire!" he called. "This is a nice surprise."

The boy looked around. Dressed in jeans and a red Rocking L Summer Camp T-shirt, he wore black-framed glasses with thick lenses and his blond hair could use a trim. The owlish glasses and slight physique gave him a nerdy look that Claire found endearing, but the scuffs on his sneakers and grime on his jeans declared he was all boy.

He glanced from Claire back to his father and narrowed his eyes suspiciously. Jax didn't seem to notice.

"Claire, come meet my son, Nicholas. Son, this is Ms. . . . Branham, wasn't it?"

"Yes." She stepped forward and offered Nicholas her hand. "It's very nice to meet you, Nicholas. Your father told me you've been a camper at the Rocking L. I hear it's a wonderful place. My neighbor is our veterinarian here in town and she volunteers up there. Have you met Dr. Murphy?"

"Dr. Lori?" His expression brightened, chasing away the suspicion. He held out his hand and shook hers politely. "I love Dr. Lori. She's the nicest person. She knows everything about dogs." His little brow wrinkled as a thought occurred to him. "She's your neighbor? You didn't come here with my dad? You're not his girlfriend?"

"Girlfriend?" Claire repeated, confused.

"My mom had a boyfriend and then she married my stepdad. He didn't want me."

Oh. Claire wanted to wrap her arms around the little guy and give him a hard hug.

"I don't have a girlfriend, Nicholas," Jax said, a sharp note to his voice. "I met Ms. Branham after I arrived in Eternity Springs last night."

"Oh. Okay." The boy shuffled in embarrassment as an awkward silence fell.

Claire spoke up brightly. "I live in Eternity Springs, Nicholas. I run a Christmas shop. See?" She help up her bag and gave it a little shake. "Forever Christmas. In fact I'm bringing a gift to . . ."

Claire's voice trailed off when she saw Nicholas's gaze lock on the bag, his eyes going round as ornament balls on one of her trees, his complexion draining of color. "Oh." He took a step backward. "Oh. I . . . I . . ." He took another step back. "I gotta . . . gotta . . . I'm outta worms. Dad, I'm gonna go dig for more worms, okay?"

Without waiting for his father's permission, he turned

and ran. Claire stood staring after him, her jaw agape. Jax raked his fingers through his hair as he watched his son flee, his expression stark and a little lost. "What just happened?" Claire asked. "I scared him. How did I scare him?"

"It wasn't you," Jax responded, a heavy sigh in his voice. "It was the bag."

"It's a paper bag. What does he think is in it?" Claire had a vivid imagination, and now it took off, bringing her to an ugly place. Jax had told her his ex-wife had died. That losing her had damaged their son. What if he'd meant it literally? What if Nicholas had been with his mother when it happened? What if the former Mrs. Lancaster had been a victim of violence?

She could see it now.

The beautiful blonde—because a hottie like Jax Lancaster would marry a beautiful blonde—walks through the mall, holding her son's hand. They've just left the food court where she treated Nicholas to a rare soft drink and he slurps from the straw as he attempts to wring every last bit of sweetness from the cup. Then, suddenly, his mother gasps. He looks up to see two men dressed all in black. The first man is pointed away from Nicholas. He's holding a shopping bag that suddenly drops to the floor.

The second man faces mother and son. He pulls something long and dark from his shopping bag. A gun. He points it toward the Lancasters. The beautiful blonde steps in front of her son as shots ring out.

Jax's voice interrupted her imaginings. "It's not the inside of the bag. It's what's on the outside."

Claire studied the shopping bag she carried. It was the store's usual printed bag. Nothing had spilled on it. "I don't understand."

"It's Christmas."

"Forever Christmas," she corrected. "My logo."

"It's a great logo. Great design. I'll bet people use your shopping bags as gift bags. Great advertising for you, I'm sure."

"I scared Nicholas with a logo?"

"The gift bag. Red and green gift bags are a part of Nicholas's nightmare." Jax kept his gaze trained on his son as he rubbed the back of his neck. "The kid suffered a seriously traumatic experience when his mother died. It's a long story and not a pretty one, but the bottom line is that Nicholas associates his terror with Christmas. All things Christmas. 'Festivalisophobia' is a term sometimes used. The slightest thing can set him off."

"Oh. Oh, no. That's horrible. So the sights and sounds of the holidays . . ."

"Trigger his fears."

The repercussions of such a scenario spun through her head. "December must be miserable for him."

"Not just December. Stores start rolling out the ribbon and wrapping and music earlier every year. Nicholas's grandfather told me he took the boy into a big-box hardware store in September and walked right into an inflatable Santa Claus. He fainted, Claire. Passed out in front of the paint counter."

"Oh, that's heartbreaking. What can you do to help him?"

"I'm willing to try anything and everything. He's working with the best child psychologist in Seattle. He'll be going to private school this fall in a setting where we can control what he's exposed to. The hope is that with another year of counseling, he'll overcome the aversion before it's time to start school in September of next year."

Claire followed the path of Jax's gaze to the spot some fifty feet or so away where Nicholas was down on his knees digging with a garden trowel. Poor little guy. "That must be so hard."

"He breaks my heart. It hasn't helped that my obligation to the navy kept me from being there for Nicholas when he needed me. I'm hoping that now that I'm able to be a full-time father, he'll feel more secure, and that will help. He did make some excellent progress while he was here at summer camp."

"It's Eternity Springs. I'm telling you, it's a magical place."

"Well, you said the magic word when you mentioned your veterinarian's name. She and the swim instructor—a guy named Chase—worked wonders with my son. They helped Nicholas overcome his cynophobia."

"I don't know what that is."

"Fear of dogs. That has been another issue—all arising from the same event." Sighing, he added, "He's been so happy here that I'm afraid he doesn't want to leave. We had a . . . discussion . . . about it shortly before you arrived."

Hence the fists shoved into pants pockets, she deduced. "I think there is another, shorter session of camp coming up. Some of the local kiddos attend it as day camp. If the Rocking L has been that beneficial for Nicholas, perhaps the Davenports would make a spot for him."

Jax's mouth twisted in a wry smile. "I'm afraid Nicholas is thinking longer than a week or two. He wants to move to Eternity Springs."

Claire blinked. Her heart leaped, followed almost immediately by panic. *Wait one minute. Jax Lancaster can't move here. He's my fantasy man. The guy who's honorable and sexy and a good family man. He's supposed to be safe! Safe and far away. So I can fantasize about him.*

Maybe she should discourage him. She could say something bad about the town. What might work?

While Claire's mind was busy drawing a blank, Jax continued, "Celeste didn't help matters any when she mentioned that there's a town ordinance forbidding the public display of Christmas decorations until after Thanksgiving."

"That's true," Claire said. "I had to appeal to the city council for an exception to the no-decorating rule when I decided to open my shop."

"I tried to use Forever Christmas in my arguments with Nicholas. He knows about your shop. He said a person can avoid that part of the street in a town this small."

"He has a point." Claire's gaze stole toward the boy. "Eternity Springs is very traditional. Here, they don't do Black Friday. It's Deck the Halls Friday, and it's an official town festival. This town loves its festivals. Once the decorating begins, they go all out. Nicholas won't be able to avoid it."

Jax's expression went tight with sadness and frustration. "He thinks if he lives in Eternity Springs, he'll be better by then."

She bit her bottom lip. A boy's needs trumped her fantasies. She'd just have to let Jax Lancaster go and return to mooning over fictional characters like Nora Roberts's Roark. "In that case, maybe you should consider it."

"Even if I wanted to move him, I can't. He's in therapy in Seattle and I need a job. My skill set is specialized. I doubt I could find work in Eternity Springs."

"You might be surprised. What did you do in the navy?"

His mouth twisted. "I was a nuclear engineer on a sub."

"Oh. Hmm. That *is* specialized."

"So is the treatment plan for Nicholas, and I won't do anything to put his recovery in jeopardy." He shoved his hands back into his pants pockets. "I just wish he and I hadn't gotten off to such a rocky start today. It's not what I'd hoped for when I got up this morning."

"Which reminds me." Claire reached into her shopping bag and pulled out her gift to him, careful to position herself to block Nicholas's view. "I was going to leave this at the desk for you. Luckily, it's not overtly Christmasy so if you go ahead and open it quickly, I don't think it should pose a problem for Nicholas."

Jax gave her an unreadable look, then stripped away the wrapping paper to reveal the brown leather journal. As his lips lifted in a slow smile, Claire took the crumpled pieces of paper from his hand and shoved them into her bag. He traced the embossed star with the pad of his thumb as his mouth silently formed the word "Believe." "This is really nice, Claire. Really thoughtful. Thank you."

Then in a move as natural as a sunrise, he leaned over and kissed her cheek.

It was as perfect a moment as Claire could have imagined—and she had quite an imagination.

"You're welcome. Good luck to you, Jax. Don't forget to think positive."

"Every morning," he replied, and it sounded almost like a vow.

Claire's smile bloomed like the roses in the garden. She shifted the shopping bag behind her back, shielding it from Nicholas's view, and called out, "I'm glad to have met you, Nicholas. I hope you catch lots of fish."

The boy shot her a cautious glance, and upon judging that it was safe, stood and faced her. "I found sixteen worms."

"A treasure trove," she solemnly replied.

"The trout steal a lot."

"Trout are tricky that way."

The boy took a few steps toward her. "I'm sorry I ran away from you. I'm phobic. Certain triggers cause me irrational fear."

Claire's heart melted as she heard the adult terms coming from an eight-year-old's mouth. She cut a quick glance toward Jax, who silently mouthed, *Damn therapists.*

"Don't fret, Nicholas. Everyone has things that scare him. Personally, I'm a bit creeped out by worms."

He showed her a shy grin, then said, "My friend Dr. Lori told me about you."

Surprised, Claire said, "Oh?"

"She said you're putting Mortimer on a Christmas ornament."

"Mortimer?" Jax repeated. "Isn't that the name of that dog who was up at the camp this morning?"

Nicholas nodded. "The really ugly one."

"You're putting that dog on a Christmas ornament?" Jax asked, his tone incredulous. "The one with the . . ." He waved his hand, searching for words.

"Bug eyes and pronounced underbite?" Claire laughed. "That's Mortimer. He's so ugly that he's quite darling. I think our Mortimer ornaments will sell like crazy. Face it, the dog makes you laugh, and anything that makes the customer laugh is good for sales. I'm doing a limited-edition set: the Twelve Dogs of Christmas. They're all dogs owned by people here in Eternity Springs, and we're selling them as a fund-raiser for . . ." She hesitated. Proceeds were to be used to purchase new Christmas decorations for the town. Instead of providing that detail, Claire kept it general. "The Chamber of Commerce."

"That's a clever idea."

"Thank you. I'm hopeful that it will be successful. People do like their pets, and we will have a good representation of different breeds available. One of our residents is a famous artist, and she's doing the drawings."

Nicholas drew back his sneaker and kicked a stone into the creek. "What about Captain, miss? Will he get an ornament, too? Are you going to use Captain?"

"Yes, I am."

"Which one is Captain?" Jax asked.

"He's Mr. Chase's dog, Dad. He's a golden retriever and he's the best dog ever." Nicholas turned imploring eyes toward Claire. "How much do they cost?"

"The ornaments?" At Nicholas's nod, Claire said, "Twenty dollars. We are selling them for twenty dollars apiece or two hundred twenty-five dollars for the entire set of twelve."

"Okay. Okay, then." Nicholas sucked in a deep, bracing breath, then asked, "Maybe . . . do you think . . . maybe you could save one for me? A Captain ornament?" He glanced at his father and added, "For when I'm better."

Jax opened his mouth to speak, but Claire stilled him by holding up her hand, palm out. "I've been thinking about establishing a layaway program for my shop. This would be the perfect opportunity for me to put that idea into motion. Would you like to put a Captain ornament on layaway?"

The boy narrowed his eyes. "How do I do that?"

"Well, it's a little like a loan, a little like a promise. If you put a Captain ornament on layaway, then you give me a deposit of . . . say . . . a dollar. I take it out of my sales stock, and I keep it in a special section of my shop with your name on it. Every month, you send me another payment and I mark it down in my layaway book. When you have paid the entire twenty dollars, I send the ornament to you."

"Twenty dollars?"

"Yes."

"So if I paid you two dollars a month, I could get it in ten months?"

"Yes. Of course, you can pay it off early. There's no penalty for that. Also, the Twelve Dogs of Christmas ornaments aren't due to arrive until October, so you could delay the start of your payments until then."

"What if I'm not ready for it once I've paid you the whole twenty dollars?"

"I can continue to hold it for you."

"For how long?"

"As long as you need me to hold it."

"Really? What if it takes me a really long time . . . like until I'm a grown-up? What if your store goes out of business or you die?"

"Jeez, Nicholas," his father said.

"I need to know, Dad!"

"He's right," Claire said. "We are entering into a business agreement, and it's always best to iron out any potential problems at the outset."

Nicholas shot his father a triumphant glare as Claire tapped her index finger against her lip in a show of considering the issue at hand. "I probably shouldn't commit to storing your purchase indefinitely because you're right, the business could fail or something bad could happen to me. Something good could happen, too. I could decide to move to Bora Bora."

"Where's that?"

"The South Pacific."

"Are you thinking about moving to Bora Bora?" Jax asked, his eyes gleaming with amusement.

"Not right now, but like Nicholas, I do like to keep my options open." To the boy, she said, "I have an idea. If you're not ready for me to send you the Captain ornament when you make the final payment, I could always send it to your dad to keep for you until you're ready."

"He's the one who goes away all the time."

Jax closed his eyes and sighed. Then he ruffled his son's hair. "Not anymore, son. You're stuck with me. And one more thing. Based on what I saw earlier today up at the Rocking L, I'm convinced you're not going to need to leave your dog ornament in layaway for a long time."

Nicholas looked up at his father with hope beaming in his eyes. "Really? Do you really think so? Are we going to move to Eternity Springs?"

"Yes, I really think so, Nicholas. And no, we're not going to move to Eternity Springs. I don't think you need to move. I think you're doing great now, and you'll continue to do great once you're back in Seattle. I have every confidence that you're going to want to hang your Captain ornament on our very own tree this coming holiday season."

Behind the thick lenses of his black-rimmed glasses, Nicholas's owl eyes blinked back tears. Solemnly, he said, "Maybe I can. Miss Celeste says that if you want something bad enough to tell the angel inside you. She says 'From your mouth to an angel's ears.'"

"An angel's ears?" his father repeated.

Claire thought of Celeste and of her own angel room where precious little Gardenia sat upon a shelf. Reaching out, she touched Nicholas's shoulder. "This is Eternity Springs. Angels are our specialty."

Chapter Four

Autumn colors in the mountains make my heart sing.
—CLAIRE

SEPTEMBER
SEATTLE, WASHINGTON

Jax opened the box of books and grimaced. If he had to look at one more bare-chested cowboy, he swore he might just hurl. He couldn't believe the way those paperback books flew off the shelves. To hear Nicholas's grandfather talk, nobody was reading anymore and those who were downloaded their books from pirate sites on the Internet.

After six weeks at this suburban strip-mall store "training from the bottom up" per his ex-father-in-law's requirements, Jax was just about ready to call bull on that. This store was as busy as a brothel during Fleet Week. If even half of the twenty-seven locations of Hardcastle Books had this sort of traffic, this amount of sales, then the old family business was doing just fine—despite Brian's dour proclamations.

Jax acknowledged that Brian Hardcastle was a brilliant businessman. He had successfully guided his privately held company through the contraction in the industry and the digital revolution, and now the stores were thriving. By all outward appearances, he was a decent man, too. He loved his wife and had all but worshiped his only child. Now he focused all that adoration on Nicholas.

His interference was giving Jax fits.

Brian didn't hesitate to show the passive-aggressive side of his nature to Jax. He'd always been outwardly friendly, but from the moment Lara had introduced them, Jax had never doubted that Brian believed the navy man wasn't good enough for his little girl. While Jax certainly didn't lay blame for the failure of his marriage at his in-laws' feet, he knew in his bones that they—his father-in-law, in particular—hadn't helped the situation, either.

How it galled him to be dependent on the man. He'd like nothing better than to tell Brian Hardcastle to take a flying leap, but he couldn't do it. Not because he wanted this job, certainly. (Seriously, what did women see in kilts, anyway?) No, he had to play nice with Brian and Linda because of Nicholas.

The psychologist told him so.

Nicholas's schoolteacher told him so.

Hell, even his old shipmate and friend to whom he'd poured out his troubles along with half a bottle of good Kentucky malt during the man's twenty-hour layover on his way home for a two-week R & R had agreed. For Nicholas's sake, for the time being, Jax had to put up and shut up with Brian Hardass Hardcastle.

"Young man? Excuse me, young man?"

Jax turned to see a woman who was the stereotypical little old lady. "Yes, ma'am. May I help you?"

"I'm looking for the new Mallory Hart. The one that has the handcuffs and pearls on the cover? Today is its release day and I don't see it anywhere."

Jax blinked hard. Mallory Hart, he'd recently learned, wrote erotica. Seriously down-and-dirty stuff. Granny and handcuffs? He did not want to think about it. "Um . . . it's over here."

He led the customer to the end cap where he'd stocked the shelves after closing last night and stopped abruptly.

The shelves were totally bare. Huh. "Looks like we sold out. Let me check stock in the back."

"Thank you, dear. I preordered my digital copy and read it first thing this morning, but I want a hard copy, too. It's a wonderful story. Have you read it?"

Wonderful story? Damn, he thought, as his cheeks grew warm. Was he blushing? Was he a submariner or a schoolgirl? He'd been to the flesh pits of the Orient. Hell, he'd *sampled* the flesh pits of the Orient. Now a little old lady was making him blush in the aisle of his father-in-law's suburban Washington bookstore? *Dorothy, you're not in Kansas anymore.*

"Um, no, ma'am."

"Well, you should. I imagine even a big, good-looking fella like yourself can learn a few new tricks."

"Uh. Yes. Well. Excuse me, I'll go check for your book." Jax beat a hasty retreat to the stockroom. By noon, Hardcastle's had burned through its entire stock of Mallory Hart's newest novel and he'd fielded seven . . . *seven!* . . . come-ons from strangers of both sexes. It even outsold *The Christmas Angel Waiting Room,* which was flying out the door due to the promo blitz for the upcoming animated movie based on the story.

Fighting the traffic home at the end of a very long day, he muttered, "If one more person asks me if I'm a cover model, I swear I'll kick a kitten."

As uncomfortable as the situation made him, it at least served as a temporary distraction from his worries, and he didn't have an opportunity to brood further until the drive home.

Nicholas wasn't improving. If anything, since Jax's return he seemed to be regressing.

Their trip from Eternity Springs to San Diego and on to Seattle had gone well, and Jax had high hopes as they settled into their new reality. In hindsight, his first mistake had been agreeing to spend even one night in the Hardcastle home. Once Linda Hardcastle saw her grandson returned to the bedroom where he'd lived ever since his mother's death, she'd wanted him to stay put. Jax had had a helluva time prying him away, but in that at least he'd stood his ground and moved the boy to an apartment. He might be the world's most insecure dad, but he knew in his bones how important it was for him and his son to begin to forge a family. They'd never do that as long as they were both living beneath Brian and Linda's roof.

Not that Jax didn't appreciate the help the Hardcastles continued to give him with Nicholas. He owed them bigtime. If they hadn't stepped up when the navy had refused Jax's discharge request, Jax didn't know what he would have done. They truly loved the boy and, heaven knows, that was important.

But Jax was Nicholas's father. He needed to *be* his father—a decision-maker, an authority figure, a disciplinarian. Wresting that job away from Brian was proving to be a challenge. It'd be so much easier to manage if Jax didn't second-guess everything where Nicholas was concerned.

The fact that he was so dependent on Brian didn't help matters at all. With any luck, he'd get good news about the job with Boeing soon. They'd led him to believe he'd hear by the end of the month, and the salary they floated would go a long way toward allowing him to snip some of the more uncomfortable strings.

Who knows? If the job panned out, maybe he'd be able to buy a house.

Jax had that dream for Nicholas. Not a big, fourteen-room mansion filled with leather and crystal and brocade draperies. He wanted a basketball goal on the garage. He wanted a house that a kid could run through. He wanted a sidewalk where Nicholas could ride his bike.

And maybe someday in the not too distant future, a backyard for a dog.

"Hey, nothing wrong with positive thinking," he murmured aloud as he accelerated onto the interstate.

Then, upon realizing what he'd said, Jax lifted his lips in a wry smile. The image of pretty little Claire Branham drifted through his mind—and not for the first time. He found he liked fantasizing about his chance encounter with the shopkeeper from Eternity Springs.

Wonder what she thought about cover models?

His cell phone rang, distracting him from his musings. He checked the number. "Hello, Brian. What's up?"

He expected to hear something about the day's record sales—Brian loved talking about business winners—but something about the pause before his son's grandfather spoke made the hackles rise on the back of Jax's neck.

"It's Nicholas. He's at Seattle Children's."

The hospital? Nicholas was at the hospital? Everything inside Jax went cold.

"He'll be fine, but we'll be here overnight."

"Why?" Jax's gaze flicked to the rearview mirror, and then he engaged the blinker and cut across two lanes of traffic in order to make the next exit and turn around.

"There was an incident at the therapist's today. He's been sedated."

"Today? His appointment is for tomorrow."

"We moved it."

Jax ground his teeth. He had arranged his work schedule so he could take Nicholas to his therapy appointment.

He bit back a caustic comment—he'd address the high-handed move later. "So what happened?"

"She tried hypnosis and—"

"Without my permission?" Jax shot his words like bullets.

Brian drew in an audible breath, then spoke calmly. "Technically, his grandmother and I are his guardians of record at Dr. Meacham's practice. You signed a power of attorney."

Well, that sure as hell is gonna change.

"Linda and I discussed it with Dr. Meacham at length, and we agreed it was time. Nicholas hasn't been progressing, and the Christmas season soon will be upon us."

Jax gripped the steering wheel so hard that his knuckles went white.

Brian continued, "Actually, there wouldn't have been a problem had Nicholas not hit his head upon coming out of it. The cut only needed five stitches, but you know head wounds bleed. The blood set off his panic attack."

Jax's lips formed a silent curse fitting of his navy background before firing off a round of questions. "When did this happen? How long has he been out?"

"The appointment was at one-thirty this afternoon. We arrived at the hospital around two-fifteen or two-thirty. They tell us he's not 'out' at this point, but sleeping."

"Two-fifteen." Jax held on to his temper by the thinnest of threads. It was after five. In a measured tone, he said, "You're just now calling me?"

"I knew your work schedule. Linda and I had it handled."

If Brian Hardcastle had been within arm's reach, Jax would have decked him. "What room is Nicholas in?"

"Seven twenty-one."

"If he wakes up before I get there, please tell him I'm on my way." Jax disconnected the call without waiting for a response from Brian. He stewed and broke the speed limit the rest of the way to the hospital. He parked illegally and didn't give a damn.

Getting to room 721 meant navigating a rabbit warren of hallways, and he took two frustratingly wrong turns before he found his way to his son's room. The door was open. Jax stepped inside. His gaze zeroed in on the boy in the bed, and his heart broke. It split right in two.

His little boy lay still and sleeping in the hospital bed, a big white bandage on his head and an IV hooked up to his arm. His complexion was pasty and pale. Vulnerable and younger than eight years old.

A whale-sized lump lodged in Jax's throat. When he finally looked up at Brian and Linda, it took every ounce of discipline he possessed to refrain from lashing out. The former naval officer managed a calm, even voice as he asked, "Did he wake up?"

"No," Linda said, her gaze soft with love as she watched her grandson. "He's been sleeping peacefully."

"I want to speak to his doctors."

"Dr. Meachum has already visited tonight. She said she'll be back in the morning."

"She's a psychologist. Who is treating the head injury?"

"I wouldn't call it a head injury," Brian began. His voice trailed off when the flutter of Nicholas's eyelids attracted everyone's attention. The boy started to sit up, but when he moved his head a grimace contorted his face. He croaked out an "Ow! It hurts!"

Linda and Brian both moved toward Nicholas. A week ago, Jax would have let them direct this little tableau. Hell, an hour ago he'd have held back and waited to greet his son. Now he stepped right in front of his boss. He brushed his boy's bangs away from his eyes and asked, "Hey, buddy. How ya doin'?"

"Where am I?"

"You're in the hospital, son."

"Am I gonna die?"

Jax said a definitive, "No!"

Brian said, "Don't be silly."

Because Jax believed that information was power, he

added, "You have a cut on your head, and you needed rest so that your body could recover from the effects of the hypnosis."

Nicholas brought his hand up to his forehead and tears filled his eyes. "Daddy, it hurts!"

"I imagine so. I hear you got five whole stitches. The guys at school are gonna be impressed."

"Is five a lot?"

"Darn sure is. Want to sit up taller? You can raise the bed without moving your head too much by pressing the up arrow on this." He handed his son the hospital bed's remote control and guided his thumb to the up button.

As Nicholas and Jax searched for the sweet spot on the mattress incline, Brian and Linda both moved around to the other side of the bed. Linda took the boy's hand in hers. Brian set his manicured hand on his grandson's shoulder. "Nicholas," he said, his tone gruff with emotion. "I know that your Mimi sure would like to see one of your smiles. Think you could manage one for her?"

Nicholas's gaze shifted to his grandparents. He gave half a nod, froze, winced, then bravely showed a smile.

"Oh, baby." Linda's eyes filled with tears. "Look at you. Aren't you the sweetest little boy in the whole wide world? You had us so worried."

The smile fell off Nicholas's face, and his eyes grew round. Fear added a squeak to his voice as he asked, "Why? I am gonna die, aren't I?"

"No, sweetheart," his grandmother said. "You know me. I always get worried."

Nicholas must have accepted that as fact, because he turned his gaze back toward his father. "So I can go home to Granddad's house, then?"

"Tomorrow," Jax said. "You and I are bunking here at the hospital tonight."

"We'll stay," Linda began.

Firmly, Jax said, "No. Thank you. You've done more than enough today. I have this covered."

Linda got that mulish look on her face that always reminded Jax of Lara. He'd learned shortly after joining the family that despite Brian's commanding personality, the women of the family usually got their way. Linda said, "Jax, I don't think that's a good idea. Women do better with this type of thing. You go home and—"

"No. Thank you, but no."

"I'm his grandmother."

With that, Jax had had enough. He threw down the gauntlet. "And I'm. His. Father."

Chapter Five

*A warm blanket in the middle of the night makes
a hospital stay bearable.*

—JAX

His declaration hung in the air and, based on the expressions on Brian's and Linda's faces, totally shocked them. When was the last time that someone had stood up to them?

I damn sure haven't done it before.

Frustration seasoned with a dash of self-disgust rolled through him as he waited for their response. How had they gotten to this place? That was pretty easy to figure. He'd let these people run right over him ever since he'd set foot in Seattle.

No more. Certainly no more tonight.

He realized he'd won the skirmish when Linda lifted her chin with regal disdain. He recognized that snippy, I'm-seriously-not-happy expression, too. Lara had given him that look often.

Linda dismissed him by turning her attention back to Nicholas. "I guess Granddad and I will go home, sweetheart, but we'll be back first thing in the morning."

Jax shot a look toward Brian. "Isn't the plan for Nicholas to go home tomorrow?"

"What about school? Am I going to miss school tomorrow?"

"I expect so," Linda replied, leaning over to kiss her

grandson's cheek. "Hospital discharge often takes longer than one would think."

"Oh." Nicholas exhaled loudly and appeared to wilt with relief.

Jax frowned. What was up with that? Nicholas loved school. At least, he used to. Jax realized he hadn't been chattering about school as much the last week or so. Not like he'd done the first week of the school year. *I should have noticed.*

He needed to bring up the subject once they were alone. His teacher had assured Jax that the boy was settling in just fine with the new school year, but maybe he should probe a little bit.

It took the Hardcastles another five minutes to clear out, and when Jax and Nicholas were finally alone, it was Jax's turn to sigh in relief. He took the smaller chair in which Linda had been sitting and moved it closer to Nicholas, flipped it around, and straddled it. "Can I get you anything, buddy? You hungry?"

"Where are my glasses? I need my glasses. And yeah, I'm hungry . . ."

Following a short debate and consultation with a nurse about available options, Jax called out for a pizza. He decided questions could wait until after his son had his supper, so he showed Nicholas how to work the TV. They found an old black-and-white episode of *The Andy Griffith Show,* which for some weird reason was one of Nicholas's favorites.

The pizza arrived just as the closing credits began to roll. Nicholas sighed and said, "I like Mayberry. Maybe we should move there."

Jax explained that Mayberry was a fictional place.

"People seem nice there. It makes me think of camp. Camp was the best thing ever."

Ah. Now I understand. Jax paid the pizza guy, requested

extra napkins, then set the box on Nicholas's tray. He was pleased to see his son sitting up straight. Looked like the smell of pizza had made him forget about his headache. As they both helped themselves to slices, he suggested, "Maybe we can find a camp for you to attend next summer."

"Nah," Nicholas said, his mouth full. "It wouldn't be the same." He chewed, swallowed, then looked up at his dad. "Unless . . . is there another summer camp in Eternity Springs?"

"I don't know. But Nicholas, why would it matter where the camp was located as long as it had horseback riding and canoeing and mountain climbing?"

"Swimming, too."

Jax grinned at that. When Nicholas first went to the Rocking L summer camp, he couldn't swim. "Swimming, too. So tell me why it would matter?"

"It makes me feel better."

"What makes you feel better?" Jax took a bite of pizza and the spicy taste of pepperoni exploded in his mouth.

"Eternity Springs."

"Hmm. Well, then . . . let's see." He pulled out his phone and connected to the Internet. He couldn't fork out the money for camp today, but if he hadn't found a job that paid well enough to send Nicholas by next summer, well . . . hell . . . he'd swallow his pride and ask Brian to fund it.

"Okay," he said a few minutes later. "I see one camp. Stardance Ranch, but I don't think it's the right kind. What the heck is a glam camp, anyway?"

"That's Mr. Brick's camp. Dr. Lori said his camp is for adults only."

Adults only! "What do they do—never mind. Who's Mr. Brick?"

"He's Dr. Lori's friend. Not her boyfriend. Mr. Chase

is her boyfriend. Maybe her husband. Trevor told me they're getting married, but I don't know when."

Trevor was Nicholas's friend from camp. He lived in Florida, and every so often, Trevor's parents and Jax allowed the boys to talk on the phone. Listening to them was a hoot. Trevor was a little wild man. Jax knew he should be glad that the kid lived on the other side of the country, but the look of happy anticipation Nicholas displayed prior to every phone call made him wish the boys lived closer. The loneliness in his son's expression when the boys hung up hurt Jax's heart.

"I see. Well, buddy, I'm afraid that except for the Rocking L, I'm not finding any kid camps in that area. I think I should point out that we didn't know Eternity Springs was special until we visited. Maybe we should give other places a try. We might find another camp, another town just as good, if we looked."

Nicholas shook his head and spoke in a doleful tone. "There's only one Eternity Springs."

Jax didn't have a response for that, so he took another piece of pizza and polished it off. When Nicholas reached for his fourth piece of pizza, Jax quirked a grin. "Better watch out, kiddo. You eat that and you're liable to have to stay here another day because of a bellyache."

Nicholas froze with the pizza halfway to his mouth. His big blue eyes filled with fright as he stared up at his father. "Will I die?"

Three times? Jeeze. "No, buddy. No! I was kidding you. I'm glad to see you eat so much."

"Pizza is bad for you. Mimi says so."

The Lancaster boys had pizza once a week. Leave it to Mimi to always find a way to get in her digs. "Sure tastes good, though, doesn't it?"

"It's my favorite."

"I know, bud." They might just start having it for

supper twice a week. "If you want that piece of pizza, have at it." Deliberately, he added, "A bellyache won't kill you."

Nicholas flicked a measuring gaze up at Jax, then took another huge bite. He ate all but the crust of his fourth piece of pizza, and when he settled back against his pillow, Jax decided his questions could keep no longer.

However, he wanted to work his way up to the tough ones slowly. Keeping a close eye on his son, he said, "So, Nicholas. You looked really happy when your grandmother said you wouldn't be going to school tomorrow. What's up with that? I thought you loved school."

His son's head dipped, and he shrugged. "I dunno."

Well, hell. Obviously, something was going on. How had he missed it? "So what's going on? You having a problem I need to know about?"

A second shrug. An added pout. "I dunno."

"Please tell me."

Silence dragged. Nicholas bit at a hangnail. He picked at the blanket on his bed. Although Jax felt the urge to speak and fill the void, he refrained. Recent experience had taught him that Nicholas would eventually respond. He was a boy who rather desperately wanted to please— something else that destroyed Jax.

Finally, Nicholas's eyes began to blink rapidly and Jax felt his desire for answers wane. He didn't want to make his son cry. It would kill him to make his son cry. At the end of his last R & R when he'd had to return to his assignment, the boy had stood at the Hardcastles' front door with big fat silent tears rolling down his face, and it had ripped Jax's heart in two. Climbing into the waiting cab, he'd promised himself never again. At least, not until his son had defeated the demons that his mother's death had brought into his world.

Even as the words "never mind" formed on Jax's lips,

Nicholas swiped his hand across his eyes and declared, "I don't like school."

Well, this is new. "Why not? What happened?"

"If I miss school tomorrow it'll only make it worse."

"Are you behind, Nicholas?"

"Behind what?"

"I mean, are you not doing well with your schoolwork?"

"I'm smart."

"I know you're smart. 'Smart' doesn't always matter where grades are concerned."

Nicholas plopped back against his pillow. "I did make a ninety-eight on a math paper last week. Miss Kelly took off two points because my eight looked too much like a three. But all my other papers are one hundreds."

The way he flung himself around his bed demonstrated to Jax that at least Nicholas's head felt better. "So it's not your grades. What has happened to make you not like school, son?"

The tears returned to his eyes. He folded his arms and accused, "They're mean!"

Okay. Now we're getting somewhere. "Who's mean?"

"Aiden. Jackson and Brayden, too, but mostly Aiden."

"What did they do?"

Jax expected to hear that they made fun of his glasses or his small stature or that they called him Brainiac. What Nicholas said floored him.

"They found out about me and Christmas. They bring stuff to school and surprise me with it."

The little bastards. "They're jerks. Bullies. Don't worry, Nicholas. I'll put a stop to that."

"No! Don't! You can't!" Nicholas said with a screech in his tone. "That will just make things worse. Promise me, Dad. Please! You can't say anything to anybody. Please!"

Jax panicked a little bit himself. If he were responsible

for bringing on another panic attack, he'd never forgive himself. "Okay. Okay. I won't say anything."

"You promise?"

"I promise."

"Good." Nicholas visibly relaxed.

Jax reached up and rubbed the back of his neck. Great. Just great. Now what did he do? He couldn't let this kind of bs continue. But he'd made a promise to his kid. One hard-and-fast rule he'd made for himself during the debacle of the divorce was that he would never, under any circumstances, break a promise he made to his son.

So what the hell did he do now?

He went with his instincts. "So, I guess if I don't stop this nonsense from happening, we need to figure out a way for you to do it."

"Me?"

"Yep. We need a plan. Those guys are being bullies, Nicholas. Everyone has to deal with a bully at some point in their lives—"

"Even you?"

"Even me," Jax replied as the image of Brian Hardcastle flashed in his mind. "Learning how to deal with a bully is part of growing up. Let me think on it a bit, and we'll make it happen."

"Think fast, Dad."

Jax reached out and ruffled Nicholas's hair. "We'll have it in place before you go back to Northwest Academy."

The hope in Nicholas's eyes all but did Jax in. He wanted a distraction before the kid asked him any more questions about this imaginary plan. Things were different in schools now than when he was growing up. His own father's advice to Jax about dealing with a bully simply wouldn't do.

Tackling kids and throwing punches on the playground led to expulsion in this day and age.

"I'm going to duck out real quick and see if the nurse can score me some sheets for my bed. Why don't you see what's on TV?" No way was he going to ask Nicholas about today's doctor's visit after seeing his reaction to Jax's "easy" question.

"Okay."

When he returned a few minutes later with sheets and a pillow for the foldout bed, Nicholas was watching cartoons. Jax bit back a sigh. Wonder how much this episode of *Paw Patrol* was going to cost him? Wonder how good the employee insurance at Hardcastle Books was?

Fatigue suddenly hit him like an eighteen-wheeler. He kicked off his shoes, stripped down to his T-shirt and slacks, then took a seat in the room's recliner with his feet up, ready to watch Rubble and Tracer and Rocky while yearning for some good old Donald Duck.

Immediately, his thoughts turned to his in-laws. He had two plans to concoct before morning. He simply could not allow their actions today to go unchallenged. Everything from changing the day of the appointment to making a decision about the treatment to trying to oust Jax from his son's hospital room—they'd not only crossed the line, they'd obliterated it. They'd refused to recognize Jax's authority and, frankly, his rights. This couldn't go on. It simply couldn't. Otherwise, things were bound to get ugly between Jax and the Hardcastles, and that wouldn't be good for Nicholas.

Anger that had simmered inside him all evening flared to a raging flame. No one could make him crazy like a Hardcastle. This was the second angriest he'd been in his life.

Lara still held the number one position, and he hoped like hell that nothing ever knocked her out of her spot. If anything ever happened that made him angrier than learning that his wife had run off with then six-year-old

Nicholas rather than let Jax have him for Christmas—per their bank-breaking custody agreement—then he feared he was likely to stroke out.

So what are you going to do about it?

Bottom line? Whatever was best for Nicholas.

He needed a job—one independent of Brian Hardcastle. He needed to assert himself when dealing with the Hardcastles. He needed to—

"Dad?"

"Yeah, buddy?"

"I don't think I'm getting any better."

Jax sat up. He leaned forward, his elbows resting on his thighs, as he studied his son. Nicholas stared straight at the cartoon, but Jax sensed he wasn't seeing the TV at all. "Because of what happened today?"

"I liked Dr. McDermott a lot better."

Dr. McDermott. Jax mentally ran his finger down the long list of doctors his son had seen during the past two years. "Your doctor at summer camp?"

"Yeah."

Dr. McDermott. What did Jax recall about him? Wasn't he the guy Jack Davenport had brought in who'd worked at Walter Reed with veterans suffering from PTSD? "He's older than Dr. Meacham."

"He's old. He's retired."

The seed of an idea that had just begun to form blew away in the wind of Nicholas's words.

"He told me he liked Eternity Springs so much he was going to move there."

"He did, did he?"

The seed blew back and planted itself in the once barren soil of Jax's wishes and desires, now fertilized by the manure supplied by Nicholas's grandparents.

By the time he made up his bed, kissed Nicholas good night, and turned off the light, Jax knew how to handle the bully situation. He knew how to deal with Brian and Linda. He just needed a few things to fall together. He'd start making calls first thing in the morning. By the time he drifted off to sleep, the seed had sprouted into a fully formed plan.

He dreamed of a field of red and green lollipops planted like corn. A puffy white cloud floated in a heavenly blue sky. From it rained sparkling, nourishing, healing . . . angel dust.

Chapter Six

Fantasies enrich your life.
—CLAIRE

Claire awoke in a full Grinch mood. Probably because she'd dreamed about lawyers last night. A lawyer. The lawyer.

She was lonely.

She didn't want to get out of the bed. She wanted to lie there with the covers pulled over her head and indulge in a pity party. Even as she contemplated doing just that—at least for a few minutes—her gaze fell upon the journal on the nightstand beside her bed. "Positive thoughts," she murmured. "Think positive thoughts and positive things will happen."

Maybe.

Probably not.

Life wasn't fiction. Grinches stay Grinched and Scrooges don't change.

Lawyers live.

"Now how's that for positive thinking. Not." She threw back the covers and climbed out of bed. She needed to do something to shake off her blue mood. Today was Tuesday. Nothing much was going on in town right now. The next conference booked into Angel's Rest didn't begin until Thursday. Traffic in the store would be light today. Maybe she'd close down for a few hours and go for a walk around the lake. Autumn leaves were glorious right now. The golden leaves on the white-barked aspen made the hills literally glow. Snow had yet to make it to the valley, but Murphy Mountain now wore a top hat of white. The Deck the Halls Festival would be here before she knew it.

Thinking of the festival made her think about little Nicholas Lancaster. She wondered how he was doing. She'd received another two dollars in the mail for his layaway last week. She wished he'd said something more than "For my Captain ornament" in the note he'd sent along with it. Maybe when she sent his receipt back she'd include a little note of her own for Jax. That wouldn't hurt anything, would it? Just being friendly. Friendly was the Eternity Springs way.

She wouldn't have to tell him that he was the star of her fantasy life. Her very active fantasy life. After all, Claire was a girl with a vivid imagination.

She could see it now. *She'd be dressed in something filmy and flowing. Emerald green. Seated at a Queen Anne writing desk, a fountain pen in hand. In front of her, the same stationery that the Duchess of Something uses, a cream color with her name in robin's-egg blue. Dear Jax, she'd write in beautiful, flowing handwriting . . . poof!*

That was too much fantasy for even her imagination. Claire had never had pretty handwriting, much to her despair.

Amused at herself, she threw back the covers and climbed out of bed, feeling somewhat more positive about the day. She made coffee, then showered, dressed, and walked downstairs to open Forever Christmas.

The delivery driver arrived a few minutes after nine. Will Brodsky greeted her and added, "I have a truckload for you, Claire. Literally."

"Oh." Concern washed through her. "My market orders must have arrived."

"You obviously made lots of salespeople happy."

Claire recalled her spending spree at Market Hall in Dallas in March when she'd returned to town to deal with the sale of her house. She'd made a lot of salespeople delirious during her frenzied, emotionally fueled shopping spree.

The delivery driver went to work hauling in boxes and Claire tackled making room in her stockroom. It quickly became obvious that no matter how hard she tried, she couldn't find a place for everything.

Will pulled the plate of the dolly from beneath a stack of boxes taller than he was and surveyed the stockroom. "Sorry, Claire. That's about all that's going to fit back here. Is there somewhere else you want me to drop stuff off?"

She didn't have anywhere else. She bit at her bottom lip as she shook her head in dismay at the mountain of boxes yet to find a home. What in the world had she been thinking?

She hadn't been thinking. She'd been fury shopping.

What was she going to do with all of this stuff?

"I don't have anywhere else, Will," she told the deliveryman. "Just stick boxes wherever you can find a spot. I'll figure something out."

"I'll do what I can, Claire. Maybe if we stack them to the ceiling, you'll at least have clear aisles."

"Thanks, Will. I have faith you can make them all fit. You did a masterful job fitting as much into the storeroom as you did. You're a geometrical genius."

"Thanks." The twenty-something deliveryman shot her a grin. "I'm gonna tell my wife you said that. Just this morning she called me an idiot."

He spoke in a tone that combined offense and sheepishness. Claire took his measure and asked, "What did you do?"

"Accidentally left the milk out after my middle-of-the-night kitchen raid. I tried to tell her it was her fault for baking such a delicious cake that lured me out of our bed."

"Good try."

"It's true. Now I can't wait to get home and tell her I'm a genius. Of course, I darn well better not forget to stop and buy a gallon of milk on my way." He handed her his signature pad to sign, then wheeled his dolly toward the door, saying, "See you soon, I imagine."

"Yes, I'm afraid this is only part of my order." Claire sighed as her gaze returned to the boxes. She braced her hands on her hips and tried to figure out what to do with them. She'd bought enough stock to fill a store twice this size. *Real bright, Branham.*

Her first mistake had been going by the house. She could have—she should have—hired somebody to empty the house in preparation for the sale, but she'd had a few mementoes she'd wanted to be sure didn't get lost. If she ever found out just which of her busybody neighbors had ratted her out to Landon in time for him to show up as she loaded the last box into her rental car, she'd take up voodoo and name a doll after them.

The scene still haunted her.

"Claire, honey. Where have you been? I've been so worried. We have to talk. I know it looked bad but—"

"No! Don't go there. Do *not* go there."

She would need to read her positive-thoughts journal for two days straight to shake off the funk of that particular memory.

She turned around, intending to head to her checkout counter, and tripped over a stack of boxes, catching one just before it crashed onto the floor.

"Stupid. Stupid. Stupid, Claire."

She'd have to rent a warehouse for all this stuff. Did Eternity Springs even have a warehouse?

She started to laugh, a small giggle that rose in volume and pitch that bordered on hysteria. Seriously, was there anything in Market Hall that day that she hadn't purchased for Forever Christmas?

Um, yes. You didn't spend a penny on Starlina, now did you?

Claire had enough self-awareness to recognize that her run-in with Landon wasn't the only reason she'd overbought. Oh, no. She'd gone more than a little crazy at Dallas Market Hall because every time she'd turned around, angels had accosted her.

Live, costumed "angels." Angels in every shape, size, and style imaginable.

Claire had learned firsthand that it was one thing to tell herself she was taking back her Christmas joy and another thing to actually confront the angels and do it.

One certain pink-cheeked, blond-haired, sparkling and courageous and faithful angel, in particular.

She'd responded by whipping out her credit card and buying anything and everything that appealed to her. Now her sins had come home to roost in the aisles of Forever Christmas. Heaven knows it would take forever to sell all this stuff.

She turned at the sound of her door chime. Sneakers squeaked against the wood floor, and Claire heard Celeste Blessing laugh. "Oh, my."

"I sure hope nobody cancels Christmas anytime soon," Claire said glumly. "Not in the next three years, at least."

"Three years? More like five."

"It's pitiful. I knew I went a little crazy at market, but this . . ."

"In my experience, show specials are irresistible," Celeste said. "Sometimes I just lose control."

"Oh, I do know that feeling. What am I going to do with all of this stuff, Celeste?"

"Well, that's easy. You should convert your apartment to retail space and find somewhere else to live."

Claire shot her an intent look. Now, there was an idea. Considering the battle she'd been fighting with her Grinch lately, it might do her good to get away from Christmas 24/7. She couldn't deny that her determination to hold on to her Christmas joy was flagging. She'd just about had her fill of the holiday—and that's before she tackled any of today's arrivals.

"I recently did something similar at Angel's Rest," Celeste continued. "We built the little cottage where I live now last year after demand for rooms in the main house grew so fierce. I must say I do enjoy having a nest that is completely separate from my work space."

"I don't know," Claire said, despite the immediate appeal of the idea. Wouldn't decamping from her apartment be running away? Hadn't she sworn she was done with letting the Lying Lizard Louse send her scurrying? Wouldn't moving away from the shop be letting him win again?

No, stupid. He wins if you let him steal your joy.

Celeste took a seat on one of the boxes and crossed her legs. Claire noted that her canvas shoes were decorated with angel wings. "Correct me if I'm wrong, but last summer when we were discussing the Twelve Dogs of Christmas, didn't you mention that you'd like to have a dog, but that having one while you lived in an apartment wasn't your cuppa? If you lived in a house, you'd have a yard. You could get that dog you want."

Yearning washed through Claire. She had lost her beloved collie, Buttercup, the week before she'd discovered the truth about the Lying Lizard Louse. She did miss having a pet, but they were a commitment. Did she feel settled enough now to adopt a dog?

Maybe. And if she moved in order to have a yard for

a dog, that took care of the whole running argument, didn't it?

You're arguing with yourself, Claire. Get over it.

Yet, she felt compelled to make one final argument. "Buying a house and getting a dog are big steps. I don't know if I'm ready for that."

"Actually, I know of a place you could rent short-term that would be perfect for you—plus, having you there would do my friend a big favor. Bob Hamilton owns three wonderful cabins in a fabulous little private valley a short drive from Eternity Springs. He's named them the Three Bears, and the valley is meant to be a family retreat. Bob lives in New Mexico and his family is spread all over.

"He called me just yesterday to ask if I knew of anyone looking for a place to live until spring break. Apparently babies due to be born and a family wedding mean the cabins won't get any use from now until then. He'd like to have a caretaker there over the winter. I suspect he won't even charge you rent."

"I can pay rent," Claire murmured. It sounded wonderful. It sounded like a perfect solution. "Maybe Lori Murphy can help me find a dog."

Celeste's blue eyes twinkled. "What do you think about a collie? I believe that the Mellingers still have one puppy available from the litter their Primrose gave birth to nine weeks ago."

A collie? "You are unbelievable, Celeste."

Celeste put her hand on her chest and drawled, "Me? But I try so hard to be believable."

Believe. That comment triggered the memory of the journal she'd given to Jax with its embossed "Believe." She wondered if he ever used it. She wondered what his handwriting looked like.

And why in the world was he on her mind so much today?

Because he's the fantasy and you don't feel quite so Scrooged when you're fantasizing, that's why.

Celeste patted her arm. "Tell you what. Why don't you humor an old woman and drive out to Three Bears with me this afternoon and take a look. I have a set of keys in case of emergency. No sense fretting over your delivery today if it's not necessary. If the Three Bears appeals to you, we can stop by the Mellingers' house and look at the puppy."

The temptation of a puppy sold her. "That sounds like an excellent idea."

"It's a nice, sunny day today. Would you like to ride out on my Gold Wing or should we take my Jeep?"

Claire had never ridden a motorcycle. Well, when in Rome . . . or Eternity Springs . . . "Sure. Let's take the Gold Wing."

"Fabulous!" Celeste's sunbeam smile lit up the morning. "Shall we make it two o'clock?"

"Sounds great."

So shortly after two P.M., Claire pulled on the helmet the older woman handed to her and climbed on the back of the Gold Wing. Fifteen minutes into the trip at the apex of a hill, Celeste turned onto a road marked PRIVATE and drove around a curve. Claire caught her breath.

Wearing a crown of autumn color, the valley was right off the page of a tourist brochure. It was not much bigger than a football field and a frothy, sparkling creek ran through its center. Three log cabins nestled up against the mountain. All they lacked was welcoming light in the windows and smoke rising from the chimneys. "It's gorgeous here," Claire said when Celeste switched off the motorcycle engine. "Beautiful . . . but cozy."

"I know. I adore this valley. I have to tell you I was anything but happy when I discovered that it had been for sale and Bob Hamilton beat me to it. Wait until you see the insides of the cabins. Shannon Garrett did tile mosaics. They're works of art."

That jogged a memory. "I think I had customers who were guests out here. They talked about the mosaics."

"Let's start with Papa Bear, shall we?"

They oohed their way through Papa Bear, then aahed as they toured Mama Bear. When Claire began dithering between which kitchen she could most easily picture herself in, she knew she was on the verge of becoming a commuter. If one could call a twenty-minute drive a commute.

Then they walked into Baby Bear. It was a dollhouse, a dream cottage with a luxurious bathroom and a bed fit for a princess. "Oh, wow," Claire said with a sigh.

"You love it, don't you?"

"To quote Goldilocks, it's just right."

"So you'll do it?"

"I can't say no."

Celeste bent her fingers, blew on her knuckles, then rubbed them against her shoulder. "Am I good or what?"

The two women shared a look and laughed.

"I'll call Bob this evening. He'll be so pleased. Shall I tell him you'll move in right away? You can take care of the lease through e-mail. Bob uses the same one that I use for my rental properties. I can assure you that you won't find any surprises."

Claire thought of the boxes stacked in Forever Christmas and her mind began to spin. "Yes. The sooner the better, I guess. It'll take me a while to decide on a display plan for expanding the shop, but at least I can get the boxes out of way. What will I do with my furniture? I don't have all that much, but what I do have I want to keep."

"You're welcome to store your things in the Angel's Rest storage room. We have lots of space."

"Thank you. It won't be much. I imagine I'll use some of it as display space." As ideas started flowing through her mind, excitement began to hum in her blood. The smile that spread across her face was as bright as one of Celeste's Impulsively, she reached over and hugged her friend. "Thank you, Celeste. This was a great idea. I'm really excited."

"Excellent. So, shall we stop by the Mellingers on our way back?"

A dog. A puppy. A collie.

A commitment.

Was she ready?

Claire nibbled at her lower lip. "Do you know if the puppy is a boy or a girl? Is it healthy? Are its parents well behaved?"

"I don't know the answer to any of those questions, but I know someone who does." She pulled her cell phone from her wallet and scrolled through her contacts list. When the call connected, she said, "Hello, Lori dear. I know you're a busy beaver with the wedding in just a few weeks, but would you have a few minutes to meet us at the Mellingers'? I think Claire is considering adopting their last pup, and she has a few questions." She paused and listened for a few moments. "Wonderful. Just wonderful. See you shortly."

When Celeste hung up, Claire spoke with a touch of panic in her tone. "Wait! I didn't say I wanted the dog."

"You haven't committed to anything. We'll just stop by to visit."

"The Mellingers might not be home."

"Barbara Mellinger will be there. Today is her laundry day. Her husband changes shirts twice a day and she still irons. She'll be glad to have an excuse to take a break. Trust me."

Claire thought that Celeste Blessing might be just

about the one person in the world whom she could trust without hesitation.

"However, I'll give her a quick call just to make sure."

Second thoughts began to plague Claire as they made the ride into town. Not about moving to Three Bears Valley. That she knew was right for her. Her hesitation had to do with a dog.

She barely could manage her own life. How could she possibly give a dog all the love and attention that it would need? Yes, she would plan to take her puppy to Forever Christmas with her, but there were times when she'd be busy. Times when the dog would have to be crated. Especially a puppy! And frankly, was Baby Bear any better than an apartment for a dog? Long runs through a mountain meadow were six or maybe even eight months away. Winter was right around the corner.

Buttercup had loved the snow.

But think about all that fur. *You've been furless for a while. Do you really want to go back to dog-hair hell?*

So get her groomed. Daily. You can afford it.

At that thought, she snickered a little darkly.

She spent the rest of the ride testing the feel of possible puppy names on her tongue.

They arrived at the Mellingers' house at the same time that Lori Murphy pulled up in her fiancé's Jeep. The town's veterinarian, Lori was the descendant of two of Eternity Spring's founding fathers. Since her fiancé, Chase Timberlake, was a descendant of the third, their marriage would be a uniting of the royal houses, so to speak.

As Lori bounded out of the Jeep, happiness enveloped her like Pigpen's cloud. Her smile beamed, her eyes sparkled. A unflattering wave of jealousy rolled through Claire. She liked Lori very much. They were close in age and well on their way to becoming friends. But oh, how she envied Lori her relationship home run.

Not that Lori and Chase hadn't faced their share of serious obstacles. They'd overcome great odds—and a former fiancée—on the way to their happy ending, set to occur on the fifteenth of October.

Today the bride-to-be sauntered toward Celeste and Claire wearing jeans, a flannel shirt, and a smirk. "Okay, Branham. What's the deal here? When I tried to talk you into adopting a puppy from our shelter you weren't hearing anything about it. What does Celeste have that I don't?"

"Bears."

At Lori's blank look, Celeste laughed and explained about the new living arrangement. Unbelievably, Lori's eyes brightened even more. "You get to live in Baby Bear? Color me green. Baby Bear even beats Heartsong Cottage for cuteness. I guess the trade-off is we get double the Christmas cheer. This is going to make my mother very happy. She's a decorating fool. And then there's . . ." Lori tilted her head in Celeste's direction. "Is there an angel made that she doesn't own?"

"I'll have you know that just this morning I saw one that I simply must have in a new catalogue," Celeste said. "But enough chitchat. Let's get down to business before Barbara begins to wonder if we got lost. Claire, do you have questions for Lori before we go inside?"

She did. She asked Lori what she knew about the pup's sire and dam, their health history, and any behavior issues they might have.

"They are both good dogs, both AKC registered," Lori told her. "This is Primrose's first litter and it will be her last. The Mellinger children wanted to raise one of Primrose's babies so they waited to have her spayed. And they put a lot of thought and research into their choice of sire. I honestly think that if you want purebred collie, you won't do better than this little girl."

"Why is she still available?"

"I know this answer," Celeste said. "Barbara promised her to the Coleman family, but then Crystal learned she was expecting. Surprise, surprise. You'd think after four she'd know the signs, but this time, she thought it was menopause. Anyway, they decided they don't need a puppy and a baby."

"Isn't her oldest daughter pregnant, too?"

"Yes. It's their own real-life movie—*Father of the Bride II*."

"Loved that movie," Lori observed. She flashed a wicked grin and added, "I wonder if Mom knows about Crystal? Chase and I want to start a family right away, and I know Dad thinks Michael needs a sibling close to his own age."

"Nic would love that. I know she's been bugging her friends to give little John Gabriel a playmate or two."

Puppies and babies, Claire thought. This conversation was so Eternity Springs—and she loved it.

She opened her mouth to ask how the new mother was doing when the squeak of door hinges distracted her. She glanced around toward the Mellingers' front porch—and fell in love.

Barbara Mellinger walked out of her front door carrying the cutest little bundle of fur Claire had ever seen. "I'm toast."

"I expected you would be," Celeste said.

Barbara approached and said, "Hello, dears. Claire, I was so excited when Celeste told me you are a collie person, too. We are picky about who we'll let have our dogs. I know you'll give this precious little girl a wonderful home."

Claire started to open her mouth to say she hadn't committed to taking the pup yet, but she knew that would be a lie. She'd committed her heart the moment she saw those big brown eyes.

"She's meant to be yours," Celeste told her, the look in her sky-blue eyes warm, her tone filled with certainty.

"I think you may be right." When she took the little bundle of cuteness in her arms and stared down into big, soulful eyes, certainty filled her.

This was right. The whole thing. She finally felt as if she were ready to put Landon and his lies behind her and move forward. It was time to kick her Grinch to the curb for good and dive headlong into a fresh start—a new dog, a new place to live, a new . . . everything. Who knows, maybe someday she might be ready for a new man, too? The real, flesh-and-blood kind.

It could happen. Wasn't Eternity Springs the place where broken hearts came to heal? Maybe it was working its mojo on her! "I'd love to have her."

"Then she's yours." Barbara gave the pup a scratch behind the ears. "Would you ladies like to come inside? I have a fresh pot of coffee brewing and a coffee cake still warm from the oven. Not as good as your mom's, Lori, but not half bad, either."

"I'll have coffee, but don't tempt me with cake, Barbara. I'm on a diet until W-day."

"I can be tempted," Celeste said.

"Claire?" Barbara asked.

"Why not? It seems to be my day for indulgences."

Lori's wedding was the thoroughly enjoyable main topic of discussion during the twenty-minute coffee break.

Claire couldn't stop smiling as she departed the Mellinger house with a puppy in her arms. What a day this had been! When she climbed out of bed this morning, little did she think that she'd end the day with both a new place to live and a bundle of four-legged love to mother.

Shoot. Today she was the poster child for the power of positive thinking!

"And . . ." she said dramatically to the precious bundle in her arms, "the day's not over yet. Who knows? Maybe I'll run into Mr. Flesh-and-Blood before dinner."

The puppy—who needed a name—stared up at her with chastising eyes. At least, Claire decided to interpret them as chastising. "I get to do that because I'm your mommy now."

Her focus on the puppy, she turned a corner without looking where she was going and barreled right into another pedestrian.

Muscular, flesh-and-blood arms came around her and her gaze flickered up to meet hauntingly familiar eyes.

Her fantasy just got real.

Chapter Seven

I am my own boss.
—JAX

As Jax approached the intersection of Third and Pinion, he had his hands full. He had a stack full of files in his arms, a ringing cell phone—Brian, oh shock of shocks—and Nicholas was dragging his feet. They had an appointment at the medical clinic in twenty minutes to get Nicholas set up with a new GP, and after the events of last week, his son had decided he'd had enough of doctors. Jax couldn't blame the boy, but he wanted to get all these arrangements made before Nicholas started his new school tomorrow.

After all, it wouldn't do for anyone to be able to say he wasn't properly caring for his son.

Along those lines, his next priority needed to be finding a job that would give him enough jingle in his pocket to provide an upgrade in lodging from the Elkhorn Lodge.

"Dad, I don't wanna go to the doctor. I don't need to go to the doctor."

"Buddy, I told you Dr. Cicero won't do an exam today. This is just a get-to-know-you meeting and to get you signed up as a patient in case you stick a marble up your nose."

"Why would I stick a marble up my nose?"

"Why do kids do anything?"

He looked down at his son just as they reached the intersection, so he didn't notice the woman rounding the corner until she slammed right into him. Reacting instinctively, he dropped the files and caught her in his arms.

"Oh. I'm so sorry," she said.

He held her just a little longer than he absolutely needed to, and only released her when the puppy in her arms began to squirm. Her name rolled off his tongue like a song. "Claire Branham."

"Jax," she said, her luminous, cinnamon-colored eyes becoming round. "Jax Lancaster? You're here? Seriously? Today of all days I run into you on a street corner in Eternity Springs?"

Today of all days? What did that mean? Did she want to run into him? More importantly, did he care if she had? "Why 'today of all days'?" he asked.

"Oh. Never mind." Color stained her cheeks. "I'm babbling. Why do I always babble around you? Honestly, I'm not a babbling sort of woman! I haven't babbled since the last time you visited Eternity Springs."

She made him smile. Something about this woman simply lifted his spirits. "Well, that could be a problem for you," he teased. "Nicholas and I have moved to town."

A look he couldn't quite define entered her lovely eyes before she took another step away.

"Wow. That is big news." She shifted her gaze toward his son. "Hello, Nicholas. People around here are going to be so excited to hear you're back. You made a lot of friends around town when you were here at camp."

"Grown-up friends," he said with a shrug. "I wish Trevor lived here instead of in Florida. Is that your dog?"

"Yes. She is."

"What's her name?"

"Well, she doesn't have one yet. I didn't know I was going to adopt her until just a little while ago. I haven't had time to come up with the perfect name for her yet." She paused, tilted her head, and studied the boy for a moment before she asked, "Names are very important. Want to help me decide on one for her?"

Nicholas pushed his glasses up on his nose and stared up at Claire, his expression deadly serious as he asked, "How?"

"Well, I think a name should appropriately reflect a dog's personality. For example, I know you met Mortimer last summer. It wouldn't fit him at all to be named 'Serenity.'"

Jax remembered Mortimer very well. What had to be the ugliest Boston terrier on the planet held a special place in his heart because he'd been the star of a presentation Nicholas had made to demonstrate to Jax that for the most part, he'd overcome his cynophobia.

"Dr. Lori said he'd eat anything. She said that one time he ate a whole plastic picture frame."

"Mortimer does have a reputation around town," Claire agreed.

"He shouldn't be Beauty, either. More like Beast . . . You know, from the movie?"

Her laugh rose on the crisp autumn air, and when Nicholas joined in, Jax thought it the sweetest sound he'd heard in months. "So true."

"What kind of personality does your puppy have?"

"Well, I don't know yet. We'll have to spend some time with her."

"Me, too?" The boy's eyes bugged out a little, like Mortimer's.

Claire studied him closely to judge whether it was fear or excitement that she saw in his expression. Excitement, she decided. "If you want to help pick her name, then yes, you, too."

Nicholas shot a hopeful glance toward his father. "Can I, Dad?"

"Sure." Jax took it as a good sign. During the past week they'd discovered that Nicholas's progress had done some backsliding since the hypnosis debacle. Not so much that he feared dogs like he had before Chase Timberlake and Lori Murphy worked with him at the Rocking L summer camp, but he was cautious now.

"When?" Nicholas asked. "When can I play with her? Can I play with her today? She needs a name. A dog shouldn't go without a name."

Claire glanced up at Jax, the question in her eyes. As happy as he was to see a spark in Nicholas's eyes because of a puppy, he still had to be a parent. "We have a doctor's appointment we need to be getting to."

"And I have a full afternoon myself."

"How about dinner?" Jax suggested. "Nicholas and I have had our hearts set on one of the burgers they sell at Murphy's. I recall that their patio is dog friendly. Would you and the little one like to join us?"

"That's a great idea. Thank you, I'd love that."

"What time works for you?"

Following a moment's consideration, she said, "Seven-ish is probably best for me, but I'm flexible."

"Seven it is." Jax smiled at her, then checked his watch. "Whoa. We'd better get moving or we'll be late for our appointment. Ready, buddy?"

"Just a second." Tentatively, Nicholas lifted his hand, reaching for the dog. He scratched the puppy behind her little ears and actually giggled when she licked him and nipped at his fingers.

The last doubt that Jax had harbored since making the decision to move to Eternity Springs disappeared.

"I'm glad you ran into us, Miss Claire," Nicholas said.

"Me, too!" she declared.

"We really need to go," Jax reluctantly said to both woman and boy.

Nicholas rolled his eyes. "Dad hates to be late ever."

"I do, too. I'll tell you a shortcut to the clinic from here." She pointed toward an alley halfway up the street. "Cut through that alley to Cottonwood. The clinic will be there on your right."

"Thanks," Jax said. "See you tonight, Claire."

"We'll be there with bells on."

"Bells?" Nicholas asked, worry clouding his tone. "Like 'Jingle Bells'?"

Claire's expression went soft. In a gentle voice, she explained. "No, we won't be wearing bells. That's just an expression. It means we will be happy to be there."

"Oh. Okay. That's good. I thought . . . well . . . you're the Christmas lady."

She lifted her hand, and for a moment, Jax thought she might tousle Nicholas's hair—something he hated strangers to do. Instead, she rested it briefly on his shoulder. "Nope. I'm not the jingle-bell-wearing type."

"Come on, Nicholas," Jax said, giving the boy's shirt a tug, then Claire one more wave. As they entered the alley, Nicholas began to chatter, as animated as he'd been about anything in a very long time.

Jax understood the boy's enthusiasm. He was plenty excited, himself. He had a dinner date with a beautiful woman.

Except, it wasn't a date. Not a "date" date. He'd have his kid along and she would have her dog and there wouldn't be a good-night kiss involved, much less sex. It was not a date.

Wonder if I'll have time to wash a shirt?

"It's not a date," Claire told the pup, who lay plopped in the middle of her bedroom floor, chewing on the dog toy that was part of the welcome-to-pet-ownership kit that Lori had dropped off earlier. "That's a good thing, too.

Dreaming about Mr. Flesh-and-Blood is one thing, but acting on it is something else entirely. I don't need to bite off more than I can chew. I'm better off approaching this fresh start with puppy steps. Romance is the very last thing I need in my life right now!!!"

If she said it with enough exclamation points, maybe she'd actually mean it.

She couldn't believe the star of her fantasy life had moved to town. Claire was dying to know why. Surely she'd find out at least part of the story tonight.

Celeste probably knew. Celeste seemed to know everything that happened around town. Curious, though, that she hadn't mentioned new residents to Claire this morning. That was the sort of news that interested everyone in town.

Bet the reason he was back had something to do with Nicholas. That poor little guy. She'd thought about him often, too. She'd even snooped around a bit, trying to learn more details about his situation. The last time Cat Davenport had shopped at Forever Christmas, Claire had brought up Nicholas Lancaster.

"I can't disclose anything from his file," Cat had told her. "However, much of it is public information. A reporter interviewed Nicholas's grandmother shortly after the tragedy. If you're curious, Google 'Hardcastle Books heiress.'"

Claire had heard of Hardcastle Books, of course. That night after closing up the shop, she'd indulged her curiosity. The news articles written about the tragedy had been plentiful and heartbreaking. What Claire learned was enough to give *her* nightmares—much less a six-year-old boy.

None of them did more than mention in passing that the woman's ex-husband served in the navy.

The puppy gave out a little yelp, and Claire looked away from her closet to check into what her new pet was doing. "Hey, little girl," she said as she scooped the puppy up and set her on the floor away from the bed. Handing her a different chew toy, she scolded, "Don't chew on the furniture!"

She turned her attention back to her closet. What should she wear? Something casual, certainly. She didn't want to dress as if this were a date. Because it wasn't a date. She'd let him buy dinner, but she'd spring for a welcome-to-town brew. She was being neighborly. That's what people did here in Eternity Springs.

She'd wear a sweater and jeans. "That says after-work casual, right?"

The puppy didn't pause in her mauling of the rubber toy. Grinning, Claire realized that when she wrote in her positive-thoughts journal tonight, she needed to include the fact that she'd no longer need to feel bad about her habit of talking to herself. From here on out, she'd be talking to the dog. "It's the little things in life that can make your day brighter, right? And talking to you will be even easier once you have a name."

She'd surprised herself with her offer to Nicholas, but the moment she'd asked the question, she'd known it was the right thing to do. He was such a sad little boy, full of yearning and fear. She sensed he might have suffered a setback of some sort in the weeks since he'd left Eternity Springs.

Maybe that's why the Lancasters had returned. Maybe they were looking for some more of that Eternity Springs magic.

"If so, then we need to do our best to give it to them," she informed the dog.

Claire believed in the magic of her adopted town. Of course, she'd believed in Santa Claus until she was eight, too, so go figure. Still, hadn't she come a long way herself since moving to Eternity Springs? Tonight was a prime example. A year ago, she'd no sooner have accepted a not-a-date with a drop-dead-gorgeous fantasy man than she would have gone out and bought a copy of that damned book. She might not be ready to trot herself into the cineplex in Gunnison, throw down money for buttered popcorn, and settle down to watch the most popular children's movie in America, but she darn well was ready to manage a nondate with Jax Lancaster!

Except, she wasn't ready. She was standing in front of her closet in her bra and panties. "Better get moving. You know the man will be punctual."

She debated between two V-necked cashmere sweaters, one red, one brown. The red one flattered her skin tone and hair color—she was one of those redheads who could wear red. The brown sweater matched her eyes and fit a little looser. "What do you think?"

The puppy just looked at her. Wonder if she could train the little dear to bark when she asked a question?

"The brown is probably a better choice. Not as datey."

Ten minutes later, she went downstairs carrying her new pup and wearing the red sweater, jeans, and her favorite red leather cowboy boots. She arrived precisely at seven and found Jax and Nicholas already there, hanging up their jackets on the coat pegs on the wall beside the door. Both males turned when she opened the door. Both smiled identical smiles when they identified her as the new arrival.

It did Claire's heart good.

Of course, Nicholas wasn't really grinning at her. He was grinning at the puppy. That made Claire's heart happy, too. "Hello, you two."

"Hi, Claire."

"Hi, Miss Claire. How is she doing?"

"She's great. We had a fun afternoon."

Nicholas frowned. "She's wearing a pink collar."

Unfortunately, that was true. Claire stocked dog collars at Forever Christmas, but they were all Christmas themed. Under the circumstances, she wouldn't have put one of those on her dog. She'd had to pick one up at Lori's, and sadly, her choice had been pink or pink. "It's temporary. I'm going to order one that suits her better once we've figured out her name."

Nicholas nodded sagely.

It took them a good five minutes to make their way out to the patio because the patrons of Murphy's Pub all wanted to see the puppy. In keeping with her plan, Claire declared the first round on her as a welcome to Eternity Springs. Jax carried the beers outside when they finally made it to their picnic bench.

Claire put down the dog and offered Nicholas the leash. "Would you like to be in charge of this?"

"Yes, please."

She ceremoniously handed over the leash and a bag of toys to a tentative Nicholas. The two adults didn't speak as they watched the boy and puppy grow accustomed to one another. When within just a few minutes, Nicholas got down on the floor to play with the puppy, Claire and Jax shared a happy smile. He lifted his pint in toast. "Thank you, Claire."

She clinked glasses with him. "You are very welcome, Jax."

"Pretty risky thing for you to do, you know. What if he chooses a name you hate?"

"I don't think that will be a problem. I'm pretty open-minded, and Nicholas doesn't strike me as someone who'd set his heart on something unfortunate. Besides, I'm an excellent negotiator. I feel certain that if necessary, I'll be able to talk him around to my way of thinking."

Jax snorted. "Don't have much experience with eight-year-olds, do you?"

"Is that a warning?"

"Let's just say you'd better bring your A game."

A giggle from the floor caught their attention, and

Claire turned toward the sound. Nicholas sat cross-legged on the ground, his glasses askew, and his arms full of puppy. She was up on her haunches, licking his face.

"I cannot tell you how happy it makes me to see this. It's as if a thousand-pound burden has been lifted from my shoulders."

"Something happened since July?"

He hesitated, giving her the impression that he was deciding just how much to say.

Finally, in a tone low enough that the boy couldn't overhear, he confided, "Nicholas's therapist tried a new direction in his treatment that backfired. His grandparents and I disagree about his care, and the power struggle between us wasn't helpful for my son." His mouth flattened in a grim smile and he added, "At all."

"But you're his father. You get to make decisions about your son."

"Absolutely. But in their defense, they took care of him and made those decisions for more than a year while I was trying to get out of the navy. I understand how they found it difficult to let go, but it reached a point where I had to say 'enough.'"

She studied him over the top of her beer. "Let me guess. They didn't take your decision well."

He snorted. "Not by a long shot. Remaining in Seattle became untenable, and Nicholas thought Eternity Springs would be a great place to go to third grade, so we decided we are going to take a bit of a breather here and figure out what is the best thing for our little family of two."

So it wasn't a permanent move. Okay. That was even better for her. She didn't have to wrestle with the question of whether or not her own heart had healed enough to venture out into relationship waters again. Knowing that Jax's stay in town was temporary made it possible for her to dip her toes back into the water, so to speak, should he ask her on a date.

Because this was not a date.

Never mind the fact that she'd spent nearly half an hour deciding what to wear. And it did appear that he had shaved since their collision earlier that afternoon.

"Enough of my woes. Let's order dinner, shall we? Then you can tell me what's been happening in your world since July."

They all ordered the Murphy's special burger. Claire subbed a side salad for fries, and Jax requested another beer. "So, Claire, beyond a new puppy, what's new?"

Just then Nicholas let out another laugh. She shared another grin with Jax, then said, "The biggest news is that I'm expanding Forever Christmas."

She told him about her storage problem and the solution Celeste had suggested. That led to discussion about Celeste's angel collection and other general town gossip. Jax mentioned he had a meeting with the owner of the lumberyard the following morning.

"I need work while we're living here," Jax said. "Since I doubt there's much of a market for nuclear engineers in Eternity Springs, I'm going to try to get on with a construction crew."

"Oh? Have you done that type of work in the past?"

"Yes. My father was a contractor, and I grew up working in construction. I can do a little of everything. I like working with my hands." He shrugged. "Frankly, the idea of doing this type of work for the next ten months appeals to me. I'm hoping Larry will give me the inside scoop on who to approach."

Just then the door between the pub and the patio swung open and the Callahan twins ran outside. Eight-year-old Meg and Cari had their strawberry-blond hair pulled up into ponytails, and they carried big fat sticks of sidewalk chalk in their hands, their focus on the section of concrete floor set aside for outdoor games. Upon seeing Nicholas with the puppy, they came to an abrupt halt.

"Puppy!" Meg squealed.

Cari pivoted toward Nicholas. "Can I hold her?"

"She's not my dog," Nicholas replied, holding the pup protectively.

Claire knew a prime opportunity when she saw one. Tomorrow, these three children would be in the same class. The Callahan girls were live wires, but they had kind hearts. Nicholas's introduction to a new school would go just a little bit easier if he made friends with them today. Standing, she said, "It's okay, Nicholas. I know these girls. Their mother is a veterinarian like Miss Lori. They are always kind to animals."

"Is this your puppy, Miss Claire?"

"She is."

"What's her name?"

"Nicholas and I are working on that. He's going to help me name the puppy. Girls, I want you to meet Nicholas. He'll be joining your class at school tomorrow. Nicholas, this is Meg and Cari."

"You look just alike," he said, his gaze shifting from one girl to the other. "Except your freckles are different."

Cari nodded twice. "We're identical. You're the first kid who noticed our freckles. Our daddy says that's how he tells us apart."

"My mom called freckles 'angel kisses,'" Nicholas said.

Cari grinned at him. "Miss Celeste says that, too. Can I hold the puppy?"

Nicholas hesitated only a moment before handing the dog over.

"Whew," Jax said in a near whisper. "I was worried about that for a minute. Eight-year-olds aren't always great about sharing."

Claire opened her mouth to reply, then gave up when the girls' squeals went to fire alarm level.

"Whoa, there." Brick Callahan sauntered onto the patio carrying a beer and two soft drinks. "Put a lid on it, squirts. Our eardrums are about to blow." Then, catching sight of the puppy, he added, "Whoa. If that picture's not too full of cute. Whatcha got there, Little Bit?"

"My new puppy," Claire offered.

Brick turned to her with a grin. "Well, well, well. A new puppy. A fluffy one at that. Cool. You won't have to use fake snow anymore in your displays at the shop. You can repurpose dog hair."

She rolled her eyes and gestured for him to join her and Jax. "Jax Lancaster, meet Brick Callahan. He owns Stardance Ranch, which isn't really a ranch, but a combination campground and resort."

"Glamping. I read your Web site. It's an interesting concept."

"It fills a void in the market," Brick replied.

Claire added, "Stardance isn't far from the Rocking L. Brick, you met Nicholas last summer, didn't you? Jax is his dad, and they're the newest residents of Eternity Springs."

"Oh, yeah? In that case, welcome."

"Thanks," Jax said, as the two men shook hands.

"Sunday night is your usual date night with the twins. Is something happening on the baby front?" Addressing Jax, she explained her question. "The twins' parents are expecting a baby any time now. Gabe Callahan is Brick's uncle."

Brick shook his head. "Nope, no baby news, but Nic is as cranky as Mortimer on bath day. Being the spectacular family member that I am, I sent them over to the Yellow Kitchen for a really nice dinner, and told them I'd have the girls to my place for a sleepover."

"We're having pizza and Coke for supper!" Meg called.

"And chocolate cake for dessert!" Cari added.

Claire scolded Brick with a look. He replied, "Am I a great cousin or what?"

"Can I have chocolate cake and Coke, too, Dad?" Nicholas asked.

"Sure. Why not?" When Claire included him in her scolding look, Jax shrugged. "Peer pressure gets me every time."

"Are we talking about them"—Claire nodded toward the twins—"or him?" she finished, jerking her thumb toward Brick.

Jax grinned mischievously, and Claire's heart went pit-a-pat.

She cleared her throat and changed the subject. "Brick has done some building up at Stardance, Jax. He might know something about contractors in the area."

Jax's interest perked up. "You know of any crews that can use help?"

"What do you do?"

"A little of everything. I grew up in the business."

"Right now, all the contractors who work the area are based out of Gunnison, but I don't think you need to sign onto a crew. Eternity Springs needs a general handyman. Ask people to spread the word that you're available. If you're good and dependable, you'll find all the work you want, and you'll earn more doing it, too."

"That's good news. Thanks for the tip."

"Glad to help." Brick rose and picked up his drink. "Since the urchins are occupied, and I don't want to horn in on your date any longer, I'll take my beer inside and see if I can't hustle up a game of eight ball."

"It's not a date!" Claire and Jax said simultaneously with similar alarm in their voices.

"Uh-huh." Brick rolled his tongue around his mouth, then said, "Nice sweater, Claire."

She sensed the warmth of a flush on her cheeks and decided she'd find a way to pay Brick back another time.

Jax picked up his glass and met and held her gaze with a steamy one of his own as he took a long sip. "It *is* a very nice sweater, Claire, and I want you to know something. When I take you out on our first date, it'll be for something better than burgers, and I won't bring my kid along."

Oh, my. The pitter-patter of her heart turned into a *thump, thump, thump.* Thankfully, Nicholas threw her a lifeline when he stood up and approached their table. "Miss Claire?"

She wanted to hug him for the interruption. "I have an idea."

"I like ideas. What is yours?"

"About her name. What it should be."

"Oh? Well, let's hear it."

"My new friends Meg and Cari call you Miss Christmas."

"Yes, they do." She darted a glance toward Jax. Would this be a problem for Nicholas?

"I think you should name her something Christmasy."

"You do?" The suggestion both surprised and delighted her. It had to be a good sign for the boy that he would suggest such a thing, didn't it? "Do you have something in mind?"

He nodded and his glasses slipped down the bridge of his nose. He pushed them back up. "She's bright and shiny and soft and she makes people happy. You could call her Tinsel."

"Hmm . . ." Claire folded her arms and considered.

In an obvious effort to buy her time, Jax repeated, "Tinsel makes people happy? Does it make you happy, Nicholas?"

"I remember when it did."

"Oh, yeah? When?"

"That one time the navy let you come home for Christmas. Remember? We decorated a tree and you bought boxes of tinsel and Mom called them icicles and you said it was tinsel and she said icicles and she threw a piece at you and you threw some back and we had a tinsel war?"

Jax slowly grinned. "I do remember that."

"Everybody laughed. It was fun, Dad."

"Yes, it was. We were all happy that day."

Listening to the Lancasters share a memory of a happy Christmas past, Claire's heart melted. When Nicholas turned back toward her, she said, "I happen to know that tinsel comes from the French word *étincelle,* which means 'spark' or 'glitter.' I think you're right, Nicholas. Tinsel is a perfect name for her."

The boy's face lit up like a Christmas tree. "You really think so?"

"I really think so. Meg, may I borrow the puppy for a minute?"

The little girl rose gracefully to her feet and carried the pup over to Claire. Claire snuggled the dog against her for a moment, lifted her to her face for a little nuzzle, then stared into those liquid brown eyes and said, "Puppy mine, I hereby christen you Tinsel."

Claire thought she would probably remember the look of delight on Nicholas's face forever. The look on Jax's face was more difficult to interpret. Approval, yes. Gratitude, certainly. But also, something more. Something that sparkled like tinsel on a Christmas tree.

It warmed her clear down to her toes.

Chapter Eight

A puppy's kiss is sweeter than honey.
—CLAIRE

Jax's heart gave a little twist when he delivered Nicholas to Eternity Springs Community School for his second first day of third grade. Unlike the first day of school in Seattle, his son didn't drag his feet. Meeting Cari and Meg last night had made a world of difference to the boy, especially after they told him he could be friends with the Cicero family boys, Keenan and Galen. "They'll be so happy a boy close to their age moved to town," Cari had assured Nicholas. "Third grade has tons of girls."

So now, today, he hopped out of the car and ran toward the front door with barely a "See you later, Dad."

As happy as it made Jax to see the boy so excited about school, a little part of him did miss the "us against the world" closeness they'd shared since Jax had told the Hardcastles they were moving to Eternity Springs.

Watching his boy disappear through the school's front doors, it occurred to him that maybe he'd been depending on Nicholas as much as his son depended on him.

Jax continued to feel rudderless in this new world of his. Being career military, he'd had a clear picture of his course for a very long time. Now, he drifted at the mercy of the wind and unfamiliar currents.

Keep in mind that it's temporary, he told himself.

These months were his breather, his time to reset. His time to figure out how he wanted to best use his education, training, and experience. His time to forge a bond with Nicholas that would last for the rest of his life.

There's your rudder for the next nine or ten months. Remember that.

He walked into his meeting with Larry Wilson with his self-confidence restored, and when he left the lumberyard an hour later, he had a course ready to chart.

And a reward waiting because of it.

He strolled up Aspen to Third and headed for Forever Christmas. He'd been curious about Claire Branham's shop since July, and he finally had the opportunity—and excuse—to take a tour.

He knew the address. He'd looked it up so he could avoid the block when he had Nicholas with him.

He spied Claire's store easily. Other merchants had pots of red geraniums and purple petunias and yellow daisies hanging on to summer lining the sidewalk in front of their stores. The pots in front of Forever Christmas sported Christmas trees complete with lights. The awning above the shop's red door was striped like a candy cane.

Drawing closer, he spied bows and wreaths and window displays worthy of Macy's in New York. Strings of lights lit the place up like . . . well, like Christmas. Jax wasn't much of a shopper, but Forever Christmas even beckoned to him.

"She has a talent for this," he murmured as he reached for the doorknob.

Hmm. His gaze flicked to the store hours posted on the door. The door chimes played the opening notes of "Frosty the Snowman" as Jax stepped inside. His gaze found her immediately.

She wore a Christmas-green apron embroidered with

the Forever Christmas logo over a Christmas-red blouse and black slacks. The combs in her glorious hair were made of silver and matched her star-shaped earrings. She stood surrounded by boxes. "Good morning, Miss Christmas."

The smile she turned his way warmed him like hot apple cider on a snowy day. "Hello, Jax. How are you this morning?"

"I'm doing just great, thanks. Nicholas couldn't wait to go to school this morning and my business with Larry went well. He agreed with Callahan that I can keep as busy as I want to be working as a handyman."

"That's excellent news."

"Yeah." He shook his head and repeated, "Yeah. It's a good solution. Not something I figured to do again after college." Dinged his pride a bit, to be honest. "But sometimes it can be good to go back to your roots, right?"

"Absolutely. Falling back to your roots can give you time to figure out which direction to grow next."

"I like that. So, care to show me around your shop, Miss Christmas?"

"I'd love to. But I have to warn you to be careful of the boxes. They're stacked everywhere. I've decided to close down for a couple of days while I knock this project out."

"That's probably a good idea."

"So, Nicholas wasn't nervous about meeting new classmates?"

"Apparently not." Jax shoved his hands in the back pockets of his jeans. "He wouldn't let me walk him inside today. Just ran off and left me behind like an afterthought."

"Good for him."

"I figure the big test will be tomorrow. If he drags his feet in the morning I'll know today didn't go as well as we both have hoped. Enough about us. Show me your place."

Claire made a flourishing gesture with her arm and

said, "Welcome to Forever Christmas. Honestly, the best way to see it is to explore at your own pace. My customers tell me that wandering through the shop is like a treasure hunt. I do have items grouped by subject, but right now I only have one dedicated room, though that's going to change. I sell lots of Baby's First Christmas ornaments and decorations. When I expand upstairs, I'm going to make one of the bedrooms into a nursery. I have plenty of merchandise to keep it stocked."

Jax listened to her words, but what captivated him was her enthusiasm. This was a woman who loved her work. She sparkled with it. He looked at her and thought of champagne. A champagne toast after midnight mass on Christmas Eve.

Beneath a ball of mistletoe. Mistletoe adorned with glittering tinsel.

When he realized that she now looked at him expectantly, he cleared his throat. "That's a great idea."

She beamed. "Thank you. I thought so, too. Why don't you look around a little bit. You'll see that I have merchandise stuffed—I mean displayed—in every nook and cranny in the place. I need to make two phone calls to let customers know that their orders have arrived, but then I'm flipping my sign to CLOSED and going into move mode."

"Need some help? I don't have anything else on my docket until it's time to pick Nicholas up from school."

"Only a fool would refuse moving muscle. Thank you. I don't have all that much. No heavy furniture. Just boxes. Though I should warn you there are stairs involved."

"Stairs don't scare me. Pianos scare me."

"No pianos," she promised with a laugh.

Jax tore his gaze away from her smiling lips and turned his attention toward her shop. He honestly enjoyed exploring Forever Christmas. She had created a homey world with evocative scents and sounds that tugged memories of Christmases past from the recesses of his mind. She stocked everything from high-dollar collectibles to low priced impulse items. Christmas china and linens set a sparkling holiday dining table. She'd arranged soft goods—towels and bedding—in visually pleasing blocks of color along one wall.

The woman had some money invested in this place.

With that realization came a faint niggle of unease. The last thing he needed was to get involved with another wealthy woman. He'd learned that lesson the hard way.

Not that he planned on getting involved with Claire Branham or any other woman, for that matter, while he was here in Eternity Springs. Nicholas needed to be Jax's only focus for a while. He'd have time enough to dip his toes into the relationship department once they settled somewhere permanently. Besides, it wouldn't be fair to anyone to start something that could never move beyond casual.

Unless all she wants is casual.

A uniquely lit display of glass ornaments caught his notice and he paused and read the sign. "HANDMADE IN ETERNITY SPRINGS. Visit Whimsies to see a larger selection of beautiful art glass." Jax tugged a four-color brochure from an acrylic holder and flipped through it. He wasn't much of an art connoisseur overall and he knew nothing about glass art or artists, but being married to Lara Hardcastle had educated him to some extent. He liked this Cicero guy's work. The pieces in this brochure were cool.

Hearing Claire come up behind him, he glanced over his shoulder. "It's nice that you advertise for other businesses in town."

"It's the Eternity Springs way. They advertise for me, too."

"I like your shop, Claire. It's festive."

"Thank you. I'm proud of it."

"It shows." Not just in the shop, but in her countenance. The woman glowed.

"Just wait until I've thinned it out a bit down here and have the upstairs the way I want it. It's going to be fabulous."

"Speaking of upstairs, want to show me what we'll be moving? Larry Wilson has a trailer we can use if we need it."

"That's nice of him," Claire said as she walked toward the stairs. "I can't begin to tell you how much I appreciate your help, Jax."

"Glad to . . ." His voice trailed off as they walked past the Angel Room. *It's a cross between Christmas and heaven,* Jax thought. Without making a conscious decision, he veered inside.

Angels, angels everywhere. The colors in the room were predominantly gold, silver, and a celestial blue. "It's like the parlor at Angel's Rest, only . . . more."

"Celeste is my best customer. I swear if I didn't have another customer until the end of the year, she'd do enough business to keep me afloat."

"It's magical."

"Thanks."

He folded his arms and studied her. "Do you believe in angels? Believe that they're real?"

For a long moment, she didn't respond. Her gaze drifted around the Angel Room. Finally, she nodded. "I do. Everyone should believe in angels because no one can deny that they walk among us. They're the people who nurse the sick and feed the poor and offer that kind word when it's needed. They're people like Celeste Blessing whose unbounded generosity is motivated by love. They are the people who bring light into the dark places."

"That's a broad definition of angels, but I get your point." He waited a beat, then asked, "So what about the spiritual angels? Do you believe in them?"

"I do." She gave him a curious look. "You don't?"

"I did. I was raised in a religious family. When I was a kid I used to make quick glances into mirrors thinking I might be fast enough to catch a glimpse of my guardian angel."

"What made you stop believing?"

Jax thought of that god-awful day and that terrifying phone call. "If guardian angels exist, where the hell was Nicholas's when he needed one?"

Claire reached out and touched Jax on the arm. "I'm so sorry. I don't know all the details, but what I know of the accident is heartbreaking."

"I need to be drinking to tell that story. Suffice to say I've lost my faith in angels."

"Don't let Celeste hear you say that," Claire warned. "She'll make you her next project."

Jax's lips twitched. "I dunno. That might not be a bad thing." As Claire laughed, he gave the Angel Room one final scan, until his gaze snagged on something almost totally hidden behind an elaborate tree topper on a shelf.

"What's this?" he asked. He stepped into the room in order to see it better. Though she was hidden, one angel stood apart from every other angel in the room. She was a tree topper . . . and not a new one. Both the burlap overskirt and glittery silver underskirt sported a tear. Her silver pipe-cleaner halo was bent. One dingy white-feathered wing was broken in half. She was one bedraggled Christmas-tree angel—and the sight of her made Jax smile.

"I see what you've done here." When she returned a blank look, Jax nodded toward the angel. "You've created your very own *Christmas Angel Waiting Room*. She's

Starlina. I worked in a bookstore for the past few weeks so I am up-to-date on my movie tie-ins. Clever marketing, though. Consumers are bombarded with Starlina everywhere they go. Your approach is subtle. You bring people right into the pages of the storybook. Bet you sell a truckload of those little angels."

"No!" Claire snapped. "She's not for sale and her name is not Starlina. She's Gardenia."

Jax could tell he'd touched a nerve, but he didn't know how. He lifted his hands in surrender. "Oh. Okay. Sorry."

She grimaced and gave her own head a little slap. "No. I'm sorry. My bad. I have this . . . thing . . . about that book."

"Apparently," he drawled.

She blushed, closed her eyes, and gave her head a little shake before attempting to explain further. "Gardenia is a family heirloom. I keep her there as a reminder to myself of the reasons I chose to move to Eternity Springs and open Forever Christmas."

Jax sensed some complexity in those reasons.

Claire continued, "Also, the commercialization of the book rubs me the wrong way."

"You don't stock it at all? I noticed you have a section of the shop dedicated to books."

"People can buy that book everywhere so, no, I don't stock it. I offer my customers the unusual and the unique, items that stand the test of time. The vast majority of my inventory is made in America, Germany, or Italy. A little in England and Ireland. I want to be the source for my customers' next family heirloom. Stuffed Starlina dolls are manufactured in the sweatshops of China and aren't future heirlooms!"

Jax thought it advisable not to mention the manufacturing origins of the Pez candy containers by her checkout counter, though even if he'd wanted to, she didn't give him a chance. Claire Branham was on a roll.

"And Starlina. What they've done to that character. The way she's drawn with those exaggerated eyes . . . you'd think she was a sci-fi character instead of an angel. And the clothes they put her in for her adventures aren't right at all. Something different every page. You know why they did that? Not because the story required it. Because it enhanced the merchandizing opportunities. Now they can sell tutus and leotards and ballet shoes *and* cowboy boots and hats and flannel shirts. Flannel shirts! Who ever heard of an angel wearing a flannel shirt?"

Her snit amused Jax. Obviously, Claire Branham felt passionate about angels. He couldn't help but tease. "Well, what about those earthly angels you spoke of earlier? I'll bet Celeste has worn a flannel shirt a time or two."

Claire waved it away. "I'm talking about Christmas angels. Two different things."

"Ah."

"As a small-business owner, I have the freedom to sell what I choose, and I choose not to support that book. I will encourage my customers to try other Christmas classics that haven't been ruined by commercialization. *The Polar Express* is a perfect example. It hit big. It had a movie. It's still a charming story, unlike the Starlina show."

Another time, Jax might have argued with her. *The Christmas Angel Waiting Room was* charming. The message about the key to Christmas was subtle and sweet and appealing to both children and adults. That's what had made it so successful. Well, that and a kick-ass title.

Instead of challenging her, he tried to calm the waters. "I think a lot of people dream of owning their own business due in part to reasons like that. It's basic nature to resist giving up control, but when you work for someone else, that's exactly what you do. There's power in being the decision-maker."

"Yes, there is. Of course, along with the power comes the burden of responsibility. And I'm not the only decision-maker where Forever Christmas is concerned." She ticked off names on fingers. "There's the banker, the tax man, the landlord, the city and its restrictions . . . I can go on and on."

"But you love it, don't you?"

Claire's gaze stole to the bedraggled Christmas angel hidden on the shelf. "Not always, no. Sometimes I can be a real Grooge."

"Grooge?"

"A combination of Scrooge and the Grinch."

"Ah."

"But I'm trying," she hastened to say. "I really am. And you're right, more often than not, I do love it." Then she gave a little laugh and added, "I'll love it even more once I get this move behind me."

"Then let's get to it, shall we?"

He followed her upstairs, enjoying how her slacks pulled tight against her shapely ass as she climbed the steps. He didn't feel a speck of guilt about his licentiousness. Helping her move should have some perks, shouldn't it?

In her apartment, he discovered she'd been busy since making the decision to move to Three Bears Valley. "That's a lot of boxes."

"I know. I'm not quite sure how I've accumulated so much stuff. My closets aren't that big. Of course, most of the boxes are filled with books."

"That sound is my back groaning."

She glanced at him in alarm. "You don't have to help, Jax. I planned to hire some—"

He cut off her protest by placing his index finger against her lips. Her full, soft, cherry-red lips. His voice rough, he said, "I was teasing."

She'd gone still. The pulse at her neck visibly fluttered.

Jax recognized that he'd made a mistake by touching her. However, now that he'd done it, he couldn't seem to stop.

He allowed his finger to slide, stroking her bottom lip back and forth. Her mouth fell open. Back and forth. "Do you like to be teased, Miss Christmas?"

"No. Yes. It depends," she replied, her voice low and breathy.

Jax chuckled softly. "You're quite a tease yourself."

"Why do you say that?"

Had she swayed toward him as she spoke? Maybe so. "You have mistletoe hung from every doorway in the building."

"That's not t-t-teasing. It's marketing." Her gaze was locked on his mouth. "Customers who shop with their significant others tend to love it. They linger."

He lifted his free hand to her waist. "I like to linger."

"You do?"

"Oh, yeah." He pulled her closer. "I've been thinking about lingering since last July."

"You have?"

"You ask a lot of questions, Miss Christmas."

"I'm curious."

"You're delicious."

"How do you know?" she challenged. "You haven't kissed me."

"Now, you have a point right there. But like I said, I like to linger."

He tilted her face up to him and finally . . . finally . . . lowered his mouth to hers.

Jax hadn't kissed a woman in a very long time, and he

wanted to savor the experience, so he lingered as promised. He nipped and nibbled and leisurely explored, banking the rising heat her response triggered and keeping the moment within the bounds of a totally appropriate first kiss.

So when it suddenly caught fire, it caught him by surprise.

He wasn't aware of backing her against the wall. He didn't consciously tug the tie of her apron and free the knot, then slip his hand beneath her blouse to skim across the downy softness of her skin. She tasted of peppermint—*of course she does, she's Miss Christmas*—and smelled of cinnamon and made him ache. For sex, oh, yeah, definitely for sex, but also for something more.

For home.

For hearth.

For love.

Whoa. That last was just what he needed to shock himself out of the sensual haze into which he'd fallen. He shifted his hands back to safer territory and broke the kiss, lifting his head and gazing down into her upturned face.

The vision of her lips pink and wet and swollen from his kiss proved irresistible. He needed one more taste, so he dove in again.

The one more taste became a second taste and then a third. Only when it threatened to flare out of control completely was he able to release her and take a step back. For a long minute, they gazed at one another in a bit of a daze. When Jax finally found his voice, he said, "Wow. You pack a punch, Miss Christmas."

The slow smile that spread across her face was as sweet as a candy cane. "That's the nicest thing anyone has said to me in a very long time."

"That kiss is the nicest thing I've shared with anyone in a very long time," he responded honestly.

She opened her mouth to speak, but hesitated. A shadow crossed her face and her teeth nibbled at that sweet lower lip. "What's wrong?" Jax asked.

"I just . . . well . . . this is probably the absolutely wrong thing to say. Way too presumptive. But . . . after my last romantic disaster, I promised myself . . . you see . . . expectations are a dangerous thing. I don't ever want anyone to think . . . I don't want you to think . . ."

"Spit it out, Claire."

"I like you, Jax. I really, really like you. And Nicholas, too. Like I said, I know this is presumptive, but I'd like to spend time with you. I'd like to share more . . ." She waved her hand about, obviously searching for a word. "More. But I'm not in the market for a relationship, and I want to be up-front about that."

"A point of clarification. Define 'relationship.' And maybe 'more,' too."

An embarrassed flush crossed her face. She looked so adorable that he wanted to kiss her again.

"This is so not me," she muttered. "My definition of relationship is the kind that leads to a ring. I don't want a ring. Been there, done that, had my heart broken."

"We are on the same page there. Nicholas and I will be moving on next summer."

"I know. That's what makes you perfect."

"For . . . more?"

"Yes!"

"I think you're definitely going to need to tell me what 'more' means to you." If she was about to tell him that "more" didn't include sex like he feared, he might just break down and cry.

"An affair! Sex!"

God bless Eternity Springs. "You want to have a fling?"

Her flush deepened and she nervously twisted her hands. "Well, if the idea appeals to you, then it's probably something . . . okay, it's definitely something . . . I'd be interested in."

"Okay, then."

She held up her hand, the universal signal for stop, and quickly clarified. "Not today or anything. We'd have to work up to it. But if it doesn't appeal to you, that's perfectly fine and I still want to be your friend and I don't want it to be weird between—"

For the second time that day, Jax stopped her by placing his finger against her mouth. He followed that with a quick hard kiss. "No wonder they call you Miss Christmas. You've just given me the best gift I can imagine. I'm definitely on board with the idea and to make it official . . ."

He took two steps toward the nearest doorway, reached up, and snagged a sprig of mistletoe. Then he laid it in the palm of her hand and folded her fingers around it. He brought her hand to his lips, kissed it, and asked, "Claire Branham, will you do me the honor of being my mistletoe fling?"

Chapter Nine

*A positive thought? I'll give you
a positive thought. Sex!*
—JAX

Claire's pulse raced like a mountain biker's descending Sinner's Prayer Pass. She couldn't believe that she was doing this. Never had she been so precipitous and presumptive. Never in her life had she been so bold. The only explanation had to be that the man's kiss had short-circuited both her modesty and her sense of caution.

Yet, she had hung on to at least a thread of the latter because she managed to ask, "What is a mistletoe fling?"

"Whatever we want to make it." He nibbled her finger and sent a shiver racing up her spine. "Though, since it is mistletoe, I think we should include kissing."

"Okay." Her cheeks grew warm.

His blue eyes glittered. "Lots of kissing."

Heat flushed her entire body. "Okay."

"I really like the way you kiss, Miss Christmas."

Claire was foundering. She'd didn't have experience with this sort of . . . frankness . . . and it seemed that her brazenness had evaporated. Landon had been her first serious relationship since college, and he'd been Mr. Smooth Seduction, not Mr. Circling-Like-a-Shark while flashing a grin that telegraphed the message that he was waiting for the perfect moment to take a bite.

"You're a flirt, Mr. Lancaster."

"Not usually, no. You bring it out in me. You're fun to tease. You get the prettiest embarrassed flush on your face. Lovely color against that alabaster skin of yours. Makes me wonder if you flush like that all over. I can't wait to see."

She closed her eyes and swallowed a groan, then ducked out from beneath him and said, "I think maybe that's enough for now. It's work hours, not playtime."

Her thundering heartbeat pounded out the seconds as she waited to see how he'd react. She couldn't have said whether she was relieved or disappointed when he nodded and took a step back. "I respect a taskmaster. Where do you want me to start?"

She opened her mouth to say "the bedroom" but better sense prevailed. "The kitchen, please."

It was the easiest, most enjoyable move she'd ever made. They debated playlists for the worst music of the nineties and argued the merits or lack thereof of television sitcoms. Jax carried the larger, heavier boxes, and asserted his masculinity by fussing at her when she lifted something he judged to be too heavy. She tried not to ogle his muscles after he stripped off the flannel shirt he wore to reveal a plain white T-shirt, but doing so proved difficult. The man was built. Some of his time on the submarine must have been spent in a weight room.

She rode with Jax on the short trip out to Three Bears Valley. They exchanged casual conversation that helped her relax. The occasional steamy glance kept a nice little buzz running through her blood.

At his first look at the valley, Jax gave an appreciative whistle. "Now that's something right out of a tourist brochure."

"That was my first thought, too. I'm so excited to have the opportunity to live here for a little while. Wait until you see the inside. Shannon Garrett created these fabulous mosaics in the kitchen and bath and on the fire-place facade."

"Shannon from Murphy's Pub?"

"Yes."

"That baby of hers is a beauty. How old is she? Six months?"

"Five, I think. Brianna is a doll and Daniel—Shannon's husband—is so cute with her. Have you heard how he ended up in Eternity Springs?"

Jax shook his head. "I don't believe I've met him."

"He's a great guy and what happened to him is horribly sad." She gave him a brief rundown of the tragedies Daniel Garrett had suffered and his role in Hope Romano's happy ending. "He's a real hero to the Romano family. Everyone is thrilled that his heart finally mended, and he's found his second chance at love."

"You know, Claire," Jax observed. "For a woman who isn't looking for a relationship, you sure sound like a romantic."

"Oh, I'm a believer in relationships, and I love romance. Romance novels are my secret vice. It's just that relationships and forever-after are just not for me."

They drove the next two miles in silence until Jax observed, "The lawyer really did a number on you, didn't he?"

She reached for nonchalance and studied the damage moving boxes had done to her manicure. "The contemptible Lying Lizard Louse? Yes."

Jax took his gaze away from the road long enough to shoot her a steamy look. "His loss is my gain. If I ever meet him, I'll shake his hand." He waited a few beats and added, "After I've knocked him on his ass."

"My hero," Claire said with a smile. Jax Lancaster was good for her psyche.

After they moved her boxes into Baby Bear and Jax

toted the majority of her books up to the cabin's attic, God bless him, they returned to Forever Christmas where he insisted on helping tote the boxes that she needed upstairs up to her former apartment.

He trapped her twice beneath the mistletoe and kissed her senseless. Claire was happily anticipating a third time when he got a cell phone call and his first official job as Eternity Springs's new handyman.

"Gotta go," he told her, catching her hand in his. "Larry has hooked me up with somebody who needs a faucet installed."

"I can't thank you enough for your help, Jax."

"I enjoyed it." He skimmed his finger down her nose. "I discovered my newest favorite plant."

"Mistletoe can kill its host, you know."

"Yeah, but what a way to go."

He gave her a thorough good-bye kiss and grabbed his flannel shirt and headed for the front door. Once she recovered enough to think again, she hurried after him. "Jax? Let me thank you for your help today. How about I cook dinner for you and Nicholas?"

"We would never turn down a home-cooked meal. When?"

She considered the question. "Give me today and tomorrow to get settled. Friday?"

"It's a date," he said. Then with amusement glimmering in his eyes he added, "Although, that was a poor choice of words. This meal won't be a date, either, since I'll have Nicholas with me. And, you invited me rather than vice versa."

"I can invite you on a date," she protested.

"Absolutely. And I hope you will. Just not for our first date. I'd have to turn in my man card."

"Now that's being chauvinistic, Jax Lancaster."

"I'm a traditionalist about some things, Miss Christmas.

Fair warning." He gave a wave, and then the door chime sounded as he exited the shop.

Claire returned to her boxes and floated along in a happy daze for hours. If a soft little voice whispered in her ear to be careful, that she wasn't cut out for mistletoe flings and she was setting herself up for heartache, well, she did her best to ignore it. By mid-afternoon, she had three-fourths of the apartment converted to showroom, and she decided she'd shift her attention to settling into Baby Bear.

She set up her kitchen, made up her bed, and unboxed about half of her books before declaring that she'd done enough work for the day. Then she poured herself a glass of wine and took Tinsel out to play.

For supper, she decided to grill a steak. "I want to test out the gas grill before we have our first dinner guests," she told Tinsel. "Although I might actually cook something. Maybe Tuscan chicken. Nothing smells better than rosemary and garlic sautéing in olive oil."

And she wouldn't need to worry about garlic breath and . . . mistletoe . . . since Nicholas would be there.

Happy with her decision, her dinner, her life, Claire switched on the gas fireplace, chose a book from her to-be-read stack, cuddled Tinsel in her lap, and settled down to lose herself in a swashbuckling pirate historical romance. She hadn't enjoyed a day so much in a very long time.

It established a pattern for the next week. Claire had fun rearranging Forever Christmas, and she fell more in love daily with Tinsel. Chewing proved to be a bit of a problem, but house training was going better than she'd expected, so all was good.

After much debate, she stuck with steaks the night Jax and Nicholas came to dinner. Good thing, too, since Jax didn't let the lack of mistletoe stop him from taking advantage of his son's rapt attention on the puppy to steal a kiss.

That Saturday, despite the fact that for a rare weekend, Angel's Rest wasn't hosting a conference or wedding or other event that brought tourists to town, Forever Christmas had its biggest sales day ever. Maybe her buying craze at the summer market wouldn't turn out to have been such a disaster after all.

The excitement didn't stop there. On Wednesday, she was on a ladder in her Angel Room dusting the ornaments in preparation for the day when someone pounded on the front door of her shop. "What in the world?" She glanced at her Christmas cuckoo clock. Nine-fifty. She didn't open until ten.

Knock. Knock. Knock.

"Just a moment," she called, more than a little annoyed as she descended the ladder. Who was in such a hurry today?

Walking toward the front of the shop, she spied a familiar figure through the glass. She stepped up her pace, threw the lock, and opened the door. Brick Callahan looked tired and disheveled, and he had a red stain on the front of his shirt. "Oh, Brick. What happened? Sit down, let me get the first-aid kit."

"I don't need first aid."

"But you're bleeding!"

"Bleeding?" he repeated, frowning in confusion. When she gestured toward his shirt, he glanced down. "Oh. No. That's not blood. Strawberry Kool-Aid. I've been babysitting the monsters while Nic and Gabe were busy bringing another one into the world."

Relief washed over her. "Oh! Nic had her baby?"

Though his eyes remained tired, his smile flashed bright as lightning. "Yep. John Gabriel Callahan, Jr., arrived safe and sound twenty minutes ago, weighing in at a hefty eight pounds, twelve ounces." He picked Claire up, spun her around, and kissed her hard on the mouth. "We have another Callahan man to unleash upon the world!"

Her friend's joy was infectious, and Claire laughed and returned his hug. It wasn't until he set her back on her feet that she saw someone had been watching the exchange.

With arms folded. And wearing a scowl.

She wiggled her fingers. "Hi, Jax."

Jax knew he had no right to be so pissed at the sight of Claire with her mouth on another man. Nevertheless, he wanted to march forward and demand that the cowboy get his hands off Jax's mistletoe. Instead, he drawled, "Am I interrupting?"

Callahan turned toward him with a wide smile and not a glimmer of guilt. "Lancaster! Here, I have something for you."

He reached into his pocket and pulled out a cigar and handed it to Jax. "I have a new cousin to celebrate. I know that handing out cigars is usually the father's job, but Gabe asked me to help spread the word, and my grandfather sent about a million of the things to pass out. You want one, Claire? I know some women are into cigars these days."

"Not me. No, thank you."

The baby news mollified Jax. He wouldn't begrudge a friend a celebratory kiss—even if it was a shade too . . . enthusiastic. "Congratulations, Callahan."

Claire asked, "Speaking of your grandfather, I thought Gabe and Nic were going to name the baby after him?"

"They originally intended to do that, but once Branch got word of it, he put the kibosh on the idea. Said it felt like a memorial, and he wasn't on the wrong side of the grass yet."

Claire laughed and explained to Jax. "Branch Callahan

is a rancher and oilman from Texas, and the best example of a lovable old curmudgeon I've ever met."

"That reminds me," Brick said. "Word around town is that you might be interested in doing some finish work we need done out at the North Forty, Lancaster. If you've got time in the next few days, I'd like to get your bid."

Another job. *Yes.* With that he felt a little more generous toward the man. "The North Forty?"

"It's the family's summer retreat out at Hummingbird Lake. My uncles work together to build something every summer. This year's project was a dance hall, and as usual, the scope of the thing grew while they were building it. They didn't get it finished. I have my hands full with Stardance, so I don't have time to mess with it."

"I'd be happy to take a look at it. How about tomorrow morning after I drop my son off at school?"

"That'd be great." As Callahan gave him directions to the property, he spied someone else with whom he wanted to share news about the baby. He handed Jax a second cigar and moved on.

Jax arched an eyebrow toward Claire. "So, Miss Christmas. You share your mistletoe often?"

She scolded him with a look. "Actually, at least once a day. Mr. Pritchett stops by for his kiss every afternoon."

The look in her eyes challenged him to ask, so he obliged her by guessing, "How old is Mr. Pritchett?"

She wrinkled her nose, obviously unhappy that he'd guessed her ploy. "Ninety-two this month."

"You vixen, you."

Now she rolled her eyes and headed back inside, calling over her shoulder, "What brings you by this crisp autumn morning, Mr. Lancaster?"

"Two things." He caught up with her, snagged her hand, then pulled her beneath the nearest doorway. "This." He kissed her thoroughly, and his tone was husky as he added, "And this. Nicholas has been invited to a birthday party on Friday the fourteenth. I won't have to pick him up until ten. So, Claire, would you like to go to dinner with me that evening?"

"A date."

"Yeah. A real, honest-to-goodness, official date. Our first. I know it's still a couple weeks away, but I worried your social calendar might fill up."

Her smile bloomed like a daffodil in spring. "I'm free on the fourteenth, and I'd love to go to dinner with you then."

"Excellent." He kissed her once more, then said, "I've gotta run. I have a job at Vistas Art Gallery today, and if I'm not mistaken, you have an angel waiting at your door."

Claire twisted her head around to see Celeste with her hands cupped against the glass, peering inside Forever Christmas. She rapped firmly on the door.

"Now I'm embarrassed," she said. "She'll tease me mercilessly, you know."

"Maybe I'll stick around and watch for a minute." Jax stuck his hands in his pockets. "I do love to see you blush."

She made a strangled sound, then opened the door. "Good morning, Celeste. Sorry I'm a few minutes late opening but—"

"Claire, dear. I have troubling news. I was having coffee with Savannah and Zach this morning when Zach got a call. Do you have Tinsel with you today?"

"No. Why?"

"Oh, dear. I hate to be the bearer of bad news, but there's a fire out at the Three Bears."

Chapter Ten

I never realized that positive thoughts could offer a lifeline.
—CLAIRE

"Wildfire season is over!" Claire exclaimed, certain there had to be a mistake. Before the sentence left her mouth, Jax was out the door.

Celeste said, "I know. I'm not sure it's a wildfire. Honey, could you have left something on in Baby Bear that might have malfunctioned? The gas fireplace?"

"No." Claire hurried toward her checkout counter where she kept her purse and keys. "I haven't used it in days. I didn't even make coffee this morning. I have to get out there. I have to get to Tinsel."

"Yes, but first we should stop by the sheriff's office and tell the dispatcher to radio Zach and let him know that Tinsel is inside Baby Bear."

"Do you know his number? I'll call him."

"Better to use the radio," Celeste advised, her bright blue eyes dimmed with concern. "His phone is sure to be tied up. With a volunteer fire department, that tends to happen—no matter how much training our people receive."

Claire was startled to hear the wail of a fire engine as she hurried out to her parking spot in the back of the building. The sheriff's office was only a short walk away, but she'd take her car so that she could head up to the valley right after delivering her news.

She was scared to death for her puppy. Fires were horrible things. She'd never forget the time a house burned across the street from the home where she'd grown up in a north Dallas neighborhood. It had happened fast, the result of a lightning strike during a springtime thunderstorm. No one had died in the fire, thank God. The owner's dog had alerted the family to smoke that had begun to pour from the second-story attic while they ate their supper down in the first-floor kitchen. Everyone made it safely out of the house—though with seconds to spare.

Claire and her parents and her younger sister, Michelle, had stood on their front lawn and watched flames envelop the house as firefighters fought a losing battle to save it.

Within half an hour, it was over. Claire would never forget the devastation on the neighbors' faces as they viewed the smoldering ruins.

It was a twenty-minute drive to Three Bears. What would she find upon her arrival? Fear wrapped a noose around her throat. *I never should have left Tinsel crated. I don't care what the experts say. I'm not doing it again. I'll keep a crate at the shop.*

Celeste followed on her heels and climbed into the passenger seat of Claire's SUV. They delivered the message to the dispatcher in less than five minutes.

Five minutes seemed to take five hours when a fire was burning. The twenty minutes up to Three Bears took a lifetime.

"Who discovered the fire?" she asked Celeste as they took the first hairpin turn on the road to Three Bears.

"Cole Hoelscher's wife gave him a drone for their anniversary, and he was taking it up to Lover's Leap to fly. He spotted smoke, checked it out, and called it in."

"Was he sure that it was Baby Bear that's on fire?"

"No. He said the big house, so I'm assuming it's Papa Bear. Hopefully, that's all that is involved."

"Okay. Good. That's good." Claire found that bit of news reassuring. "I'll bet Tinsel is scared to death."

Celeste didn't speak, but reached over and gave Claire's leg a comforting pat.

Claire's car was one of a line of vehicles heading up to Three Bears Valley as members of the volunteer fire department responded to the call. She was glad to see them, but she really wished that she were in the front of the pack instead of the middle. She'd have driven a lot faster if she were leading the way.

She held her breath as they finally approached the curve in the road that provided the first look down into the valley. *Please, God. Let Tinsel be okay.*

The car rounded the curve. Claire's gaze went straight to Baby Bear. "Oh, dear God. No."

The roof was on fire.

"It's arson," Jax said to Sheriff Zach Turner. He'd arrived at the scene moments after the sheriff and before the fire truck.

"Yep. Has to be. All three places are on fire."

"How far out is the pump engine?"

"Four minutes, they say."

Jax looked at the flames climbing across the roof of Baby Bear. "Claire's dog is in the small one. I don't think we can wait on gear."

The blanket Nicholas had used to cuddle beneath on their trip from Washington was still in the backseat of Jax's truck. He grabbed it and a hammer and headed for the creek.

"Wait a minute, Lancaster," Zach called. "I'll go. I've had training."

Running toward Baby Bear with a soaked blanket in his arms, Jax called, "Me, too! I lived on a nuclear submarine. We had fire training all the damned time!"

That rescuing a puppy from a burning building hadn't been part of that training wasn't something he wanted to dwell on at the moment.

He hoped like hell that whoever had built these cabins had used fire-retardant shingles. Smoke figured to be the biggest problem at this stage of the game. He also hoped like hell that she hadn't moved the spot where she kept Tinsel's crate since his previous visit. Jax needed to get in and get out without any delays.

"At least the place is small," he muttered to himself as he covered the last few yards to Baby Bear, dread slithering through him at the possibility of what he'd find. He prayed he wouldn't be forced to make a terrible choice, but as Nicholas's only living parent, he couldn't be reckless.

A glance through the window reassured him. A little hazy, but no visible flames. Draping the wet blanket around him, Jax decided to try the door before he broke the window. He gave it two sharp kicks and sprung the lock.

He heard Tinsel's whimpers the moment he stepped inside, and he breathed an inward sigh of relief. He wouldn't have wanted to face either Claire or Nicholas if the pup had suffocated in her crate.

Keeping low, he made his way to the crate and in less than a minute and without incident emerged safely from Baby Bear with a shaking puppy in his arms.

"Damn, man," Zach Turner said. "That scared the crap out of me. I hate fire."

"Me, too." Jax's response was heartfelt. But even as he stood in the safe morning sunshine scratching Tinsel behind her ears, his gaze strayed back to the cabin where flames continued to spread across the roof.

Zach said, "We're gonna work this from the least engaged property to the most. Tackle Mama Bear first, then come here."

Jax thought of all those boxes of books he'd hauled up to the attic. She hadn't brought much else. The books must be a treasure of hers. *She's going to lose them.*

Well, better books than her puppy.

He remembered the one box marked "Favorites" that she'd asked him to carry to her bedroom. Dare he try?

Make up your mind. Every second counts.

He shoved the dog toward the sheriff. "Hold her a moment, please."

As he headed back toward Baby Bear, he heard Zach exclaim, "What the hell!"

Jax scooped up the wet blanket on his way and darted back inside the cabin. The smoke was heavier, but still not too bad. He'd give himself no more than a minute and a half. Entering her bedroom, he surveyed the area and cursed. It had been too much to hope that she'd have been slow to unpack the box.

She'd brought in a five-shelf bookcase. He scanned the titles. Mostly children's books. Christmas-themed children's books. *Grooge, my ass.* Tattered and taped spines suggested oft-read stories. He glanced around, spied her laundry basket—it contained only a pair of red thong panties.

Miss Christmas!

Making an instant decision on what to save, Jax went to work. He emptied three and a half shelves, and when the basket was full and instinct told him to get the hell out, only paperbacks remained. He picked up the basket and dashed for the door.

Outside, Zach identified what he carried and slowly shook his head. "You are one crazy guy. If you even think about going back in there again, I'm going to arrest you."

"I'm done. What can I do to help?"

The sheriff pointed toward the fire truck. "See the guy

on the radio at the front of the ladder engine? He's our chief. Go ask him."

By now cars and trucks and SUVs were spilling into the small valley, and soon what appeared to be the majority of the residents in town pitched in to help. With the fire at Mama Bear out and a full crew working at Baby Bear, Jax went to work battling the blaze at Papa Bear.

What had everyone nervous was the not insubstantial risk that the increasing breeze would kick up the flames and spread the fire. Locals told Jax that although it was late in the season for wildfires, the beetle kill had been especially bad just over the hill from Three Bears Valley, so there was plenty of dead wood to burn.

When the fire chief finally declared the fire out, the collective population heaved a sigh of relief. Then talk turned to the cause and the probability of arson raised the threat level all over again.

"Jax?"

He turned away from his discussion with Lucca Romano and Cicero to see Claire standing with Tinsel clutched against her chest. Her gaze was round, her gorgeous brown eyes luminous with the remnant of tears. "Hey."

"Can I speak with you a moment?"

"Sure." He excused himself from the conversation and placed his hand on the small of her back, guiding her away from the crowd. When they'd walked far enough to have some privacy, Claire turned to him. "They told me what you did. Jax . . . I don't know what to say. That's the most stupidly heroic thing anyone has ever done for me, and I feel like I should scold you for taking such a risk, but I can't. I'm so grateful."

"I couldn't let Tinsel get hurt. She's a sweetheart, and besides, Nicholas would have killed me."

"He'd have killed you if you'd died in that fire!"

"Now, that's silly. He can't kill me if I'm already dead."

"You obviously don't watch zombie TV." She poked his chest with her finger. "Enough of that sort of talk. Jax, going in after Tinsel was above and beyond the call. Going back after my books . . ." She shook her head. "What in the world were you thinking?"

"They are your treasures. I didn't want you to lose them."

"They *are* treasures, and I'm glad they didn't burn up but they are only things, and no *thing* is worth risking your life!" Frustration flashed in her eyes as she added, "You are Nicholas's only parent!"

I even like the way she scolds. Jax reached out and scratched Tinsel behind the ears, then smiled down into Claire's reproachful gaze. "Believe me, I considered that. If I had judged it to be too risky, I wouldn't have gone into Baby Bear at all."

"Okay. Good." She nodded decisively. "That's good. It makes me feel better."

He gave Tinsel another good scratch. "My judgment is pretty good, Claire. You can trust me."

Her lips twisted and he heard a bitter note in her voice when she spoke again. "Trust isn't my strong suit."

"Oh, honey." Jax shook his head, then gave in to his desire to touch her and trailed the pad of his thumb down her cheek. "I've decided it's going to be a goal of mine to make you forget all about that lawyer. What's his name?"

"Landon. Landon the Lying Lizard Louse."

Pursing his lips didn't keep them from twitching. "Quadruple L."

She smiled, shrugged, and when her eyes filled with tears, dipped her head and rested it against his chest. Softly, she said, "I was so scared."

"I know. I know you were. But it's over. Nothing has been destroyed that can't be fixed or replaced. Smoke is your biggest problem. You might have some trouble getting it out of your bedding and clothes."

"That's not a big deal. Clothes and bedding are easy to replace."

Expensive, too, Jax thought. Those silk shirts she liked to wear to work couldn't be cheap. He thought back to his married days. If Lara had lost her entire wardrobe, not only would the world have come to an end, but she would have bankrupted him replacing what she'd lost.

"They say it's arson," she said, her gaze sweeping over the valley's three cabins, one of which had burned to the ground. "Who would do such a thing? Why?"

"I don't know. Some people are just crazy. Whoever it was, I have a feeling that your sheriff won't stop until he finds the guy. Zach Turner strikes me as a badass, and he's seriously pissed."

As he said it, Jax turned his head to look at Turner and realized that at some point during the past few minutes, he and Claire had become the center of attention for a number of people in the crowd. Mostly the women. Females must be born with some sort of romance radar, he thought. And Celeste . . . well . . . that woman was simply scary.

The puppy began to squirm. Claire stepped away from Jax and set Tinsel down on the ground as Jax heard Lori Murphy call his name. She and Chase Timberlake walked toward them. "I need to give you a hug," Lori said to Jax. "You are this veterinarian's hero of the day! That puppy wouldn't have tolerated much smoke."

"Look, it wasn't a big deal. I got in and out before the smoke got bad."

"You're wasting your breath, Navy," Chase said. "This is a dog-loving town. You went into a burning building to save a puppy. You're a bona fide hero from here on out."

"He's right," Lori agreed. "You might as well—"

She broke off abruptly at the sound of a gunning engine and screeching tires. They all looked around to see the sheriff's truck race toward the road.

Within moments, news of the reason why Zach had sped off filtered through the crowd, and the worried expressions that had dissipated with the extinguishing of the fire returned.

Brick Callahan was the one who clued them in. "Looks like we have a motive for arson at Three Bears Valley. Someone wanted to get people out of town so he could rob the bank."

Chapter Eleven

*It feels good to do something for someone
you care about.*
—JAX

"Rob the bank? You're kidding," Claire said in a disbelieving tone. "People don't rob banks in this day and age. Not in Eternity Springs."

"Apparently they do," Brick responded.

"What about the school?" Jax demanded, his lips flattening into a grim line. "Do I need to worry?"

"It's on lockdown. The sheriff's department is telling everyone to stay inside and keep their doors locked."

"Good."

Lori shook her head. "I can't believe this. I don't know that our school has ever been on lockdown before. Our bank hasn't been robbed since the 1880s, and if we've ever had a case of arson, it didn't make the history book. I would have remembered studying that in school."

"Today has certainly been a day for the history books," Chase observed. "A new Callahan, a fire, a bank robbery. And it's not even noon. I'm almost afraid to see what's going to happen after lunch."

"I probably should get back to town," Lori observed. "I want to check my clinic, make sure we haven't had a vermin invasion."

"You're not going anywhere without me. Not until Zach catches this jackwagon."

The news of the bank robbery cleared out Three Bears Valley quickly as people rushed back to town to protect their property. Indecision kept Claire rooted to her spot. She didn't know whether to remain here and get to work assessing the damage to her things, or return to town to make sure that Forever Christmas didn't have any bank robbers hiding in the Angel Room or stockroom.

"What do you want to do?" Jax asked her.

"I don't know. It's a bit overwhelming."

"I think you should stay here and go through Baby Bear. For one thing, traffic back to town is going to be nasty for the next little while. Give it a chance to clear out and you'll save yourself the headache of a traffic jam."

"An Eternity Springs traffic jam," she mused. "Now that is a rare animal. Happens only a few times a year, I understand. Mostly when we pack the town for one of our tourist festivals. You make a good point, Jax. I think I'll stay."

"*We* will stay," he corrected. "I'm not leaving you out here by yourself. Not until the arsonist is caught, anyway."

She wasn't going to argue with him. She'd probably be more than a little creeped out if she were out here by herself today. Except . . . "What about Nicholas?"

"The school sent a text saying they'll give parents a thirty-minute warning once the decision is made to release the kids. That's plenty of time to—" He broke off abruptly when Celeste approached at a brisk walk.

"Claire, honey. I'm going to ride back into town with Lori and Chase. Before I leave I wanted to let you know that I've spoken with Bob Hamilton. He said to tell you to make a list of everything you own that's been damaged in any way, and he'll see that it's replaced. He has excellent insurance. You won't be out a dime. Also, he suggested you move into Mama Bear until whatever necessary repairs are done to Baby Bear. He'll ask the contractor he hires to begin work there."

"That's good," Jax said. "Sounds like you've lucked out with your landlord, Claire."

"He's a wonderful man," Celeste commented. "Jax, you might be interested to know that his father was a navy man during World War II. A submariner."

"Really," Jax said. "Now those men had it tough. Today's boats are like a luxury yacht compared to what they put to sea in during the Second World War."

"Yes, I imagine so. Bob had a message for you, too, Jax. I told him about your new business, and he wants to know if you'd like the contract to restore the buildings. I can assure you he pays top wages, and as soon as Baby Bear is livable again and Claire can return to it, Mama Bear will be available for you and Nicholas. Rent free, of course. It will be good, steady work for months."

Jax's chin dropped. "Seriously? Why would he do that? He doesn't know me."

"I vouched for you. The work you did for me was excellent."

"Celeste, I fixed a loose step on your back porch!"

"And you did a fine job of it. You showed up when you said you would, you did the work, and you charged me a fair price. You also have the authority to work with some of our more . . . independent, shall I say . . . subs."

"Independent?" Claire said. "What they are is impossible. We have one electrician in town and one plumber. You can't count on either one of them to do what they say."

"And Jax was a naval officer. I have no doubt he'll manage them. So, dear, shall I give you Bob's number so you can call and discuss the particulars?"

"Absolutely. I'll call him this afternoon."

Celeste gave one of those brilliant grins that seemed to light up the entire sky. "Wonderful. Now, Lori and Chase are waiting, so I'd best hurry along. I want to be there when Zach captures that horrible person who's responsible for today's trauma. I'm quite unhappy that he chose today of all days to cause his mischief. Although no one will ever forget John Gabriel's birthday."

"True," Claire agreed. "I'm thankful this didn't happen on Lori's wedding day."

"Oh, Claire." Celeste covered her mouth with her hand. "Perish the thought."

Both women took a moment to imagine the turmoil that would have caused and shuddered. Celeste took her leave and Claire turned her attention back to Jax. He appeared stunned. "I hate to feel grateful for your misfortune, Claire, but this job is a godsend. I'll be able to get Nicholas out of that awful motel we're in!"

The smile he aimed her way rivaled Celeste's in brightness and proved just as infectious. Claire laughed aloud as he picked her up and twirled her around, then kissed her hard.

"I do like exuberant men," she observed when he set her down. "But you cheated."

"Cheated?"

She pointed toward the sky above. "No mistletoe."

Now his smile slid into a sexy grin that she felt clear to her toes. He made a show of looking up. "You're wrong, Miss Christmas. Look at those clouds. If that's not a ball of mistletoe above us, then I'm Frosty the Snowman. Believe me when I tell you, I'm not the least bit cold."

"Yeah, well, neither will the gossip be once the subject of babies, arson, and bank robberies dies down," Claire pointed out. "Residents will return their attention to the usual fare of who's romancing who, who is no longer romancing who, and what in the world is so-and-so thinking by going out with that you-know-what? After that display you just put on, you and I will be hot topic number one."

Jax shrugged those broad shoulders of his. "I don't care. Actually, I'm glad to make my claim public if it'll help discourage other guys from making a run at you."

"Your claim?" she repeated, arching a challenging brow. "Did you really say that? Your *claim*? Not very PC, are you, Lancaster?"

"Nah. I'm a Neanderthal. Fair warning." Proving his words, he slapped her butt. "Ready to tackle Baby Bear? I'd like to get a sense of how long it'll take to get it livable again. I suspect Nicholas's grandparents are going to swoop in for a surprise visit any day now, and it would be better for everyone if we're not still residents of the Elkhorn Lodge."

Claire took a minute to consider her next words. He had no way of knowing it, but his lack of concern about gossip warmed a place in her heart that had been cold for over a year. The Lying Lizard Louse always had been careful to keep their relationship low-key. At the time, it had hurt her feelings. When she'd finally discovered the reason why he'd placed so much emphasis on privacy, she'd felt totally stupid for having missed the clues.

Jax wasn't a liar. He wasn't a louse or a lizard, either. He was a hardworking, honest, straightforward man who was trying hard to be a great father. In other words, he wasn't anything like Landon.

And he'd gone into a burning building to save her puppy.

"You don't have to wait, Jax," she said. "Mama Bear has three bedrooms. As far as I'm concerned, you're welcome to move in today."

He jerked his gaze around to stare at her. "Seriously?"

"Sure. Why not?"

"Aren't you worried about what people will think?"

"No. I find I don't really care."

He repeated the pick-her-up, swing-her-around,

plant-a-hot-kiss-on-her move. She was still reeling from it when he said, "Am I good or what? Sleeping together even before our first date!"

She elbowed him in the side, then walked on toward Baby Bear, a smile on her face.

Jax did a walk-through of each of the cabins and compiled a list of the extent of the damage. Mama Bear's roof needed only a bit of patching. Baby Bear needed a whole new roof, new attic insulation, some wiring repair, and a complete interior paint job. Unfortunately, after viewing the extent of the damage at Papa Bear, he concluded the best solution there would be to clear it to the slab and start over.

He made the call to the property owner, and in the forty-minute conversation that followed, secured the job that offered a stress-relieving salary and arrived at a rebuilding plan. Bob Hamilton wanted Papa Bear restored exactly as the original but for the minor change of a different style of front door. Luckily, he'd kept a detailed file of everything Jax needed to know to complete the job.

"I'll overnight it to you, Jax," he said. "The only real concern I have is that Shannon won't be willing to recreate the mosaics. Since little Brianna was born, she's cut way back on her work schedule. We might have to sweet-talk her into doing it."

Jax had met Shannon Garrett in July, and he was pretty sure he'd won the exhausted new parent's eternal gratitude when he'd passed along a trick that had worked when Nicholas was teething. "I don't think it'll be a problem, Bob. I have a marker with her I can call in if necessary."

"Excellent."

Before ending the call, Jax thanked him again for both the opportunity and the housing. "Don't thank me. Thank Celeste. She gave you a glowing recommendation, and I've learned I can rely on her judgment."

"I won't let either of you down," Jax replied, his promise solemn. "You have my word on it."

As Jax thumbed the red circle on his phone to end the call, a wry smile lifted his lips. He wondered if Celeste ever did anything that wasn't "glowing." That seemed to be her modus operandi.

Returning to Baby Bear to check on Claire, he found her in her kitchen unloading the contents of a refrigerator into a cooler. Seeing him, she asked, "How did it go?"

"Great. He seems like he'll be easy to work with."

"I'm so glad."

"Any word from town?"

"I talked to Lori a few minutes ago. She said tensions are high. Zach doubts that the guy hung around Eternity Springs, but until he picks up a trail, no one can be certain. She also said you need not worry about Nicholas. In addition to the school being on lockdown, Zach has stationed a couple of deputies on the grounds as added precaution.

"Good."

Claire shut the refrigerator door and lowered the lid on the cooler. When she went to pick it up, Jax said, "Let me carry that."

"It's not heavy, Jax. I can get it."

He ignored her and headed for the door and short walk to Mama Bear. He didn't miss her muttered, "Neanderthal," and he grinned in response.

It didn't take long for them to get Claire settled into Mama Bear. He attempted to insist that she take the master suite, but she flat-out refused to do it, showing a stubborn side of her personality Jax hadn't seen before.

It only attracted him more.

At two P.M., they received word of an official announcement from the sheriff's department that an arrest had been made. The man in custody had a Denver address and a trunk full of money and empty cans of gasoline. The townspeople breathed a collective sigh of relief and life returned to normal, with the dismissal of schoolchildren to occur at the usual time.

Jax followed Claire back to town, then honked good-bye when she turned toward Forever Christmas while he drove on to the school. He worried how his son might take the news of evil having touched Eternity Springs, but his concerns disappeared when Nicholas climbed into their truck bubbling with excitement.

"Did you hear what happened, Dad? We had a bank robber! They locked up all the doors and wouldn't let us go out to recess. We got to play dodge ball in the gym!"

They still played dodge ball in the school here? It had been forbidden at the boy's last school. Labeled too dangerous. "I know about the bank robber, yes. Did you hear about the fire at Miss Claire's house?"

Nicholas's eyes went wide and round. "No! Is Tinsel all right?"

"Yes, Tinsel is fine. But don't you think you should have asked about Claire first?"

Nicholas's gaze grew stricken. "Is *she* hurt?"

Jax inwardly cursed. *Ham-handed there, Lancaster.* "No. She's okay."

Quickly, he told his son the news that he figured would distract him. "Distracted" wasn't close to being the right word for Nicholas's response at the news that he'd be sharing a house with Tinsel for a little while. He bubbled, he giggled, he clapped his hands and asked about a million questions. Why did the house have such a superstupid name? Where would the puppy sleep? Could he feed her? Take her on walks? Maybe she'd be lonely during the day. Wouldn't she be lonely? They didn't want her to be lonely. "We should get a dog, Daddy."

We should get a dog, Daddy. Jax recalled the little boy who'd screamed in terror when unexpectedly coming upon some woman's leashed purse pet at a sidewalk café during Jax's last visit home prior to his discharge. Nicholas had been scared clear to the marrow by a Maltipoo. A Maltipoo!

"What kind of dog?"

"A golden retriever like Captain."

Captain was Chase Timberlake's dog, that magical mutt who, with the help of the Rocking L summer camp and Chase and Lori in particular, had healed the part of Nicholas's damaged psyche that had sent him into tremors at even near proximity to a seven-pound dog.

Now, the boy was asking for a dog of his own. Damned if Jax's eyes didn't tear up at the thought. "Tell you what, hot rod. Let's see how we like living with a dog, and if everything's cool, we'll talk to Dr. Lori."

"Really? I can have a puppy of my own? Really?"

"We might want to get one who's out of the puppy stage. They're a lot easier to care for."

"That's okay. I'd like any dog. He doesn't have to be a golden or a collie. I'd rather have a boy dog, but a girl would be okay, too."

"If we decide to get a dog, I'm sure we can find a boy dog."

"I've decided, Daddy."

"And I said we are going to wait and see. Now, enough about a dog. Since we've been a bachelor household, we haven't worried too much about niceties. That's gonna change. We'll be living with a lady for a few weeks, and they're particular about such things. So, there's gonna be a few rules. I expect you to follow them, matey, or I'll make you walk the plank."

"Aye, aye, Captain."

They discussed important matters like hanging up towels, raising and lowering the toilet seat, putting dirty dishes in the dishwasher, and managing a belch and fart in polite company.

"James didn't put the toilet seat down," Nicholas confided. "I remember Mom yelling at him about it."

Jax glanced at his son. He rarely spoke about his mother
or his stepfather. The fact he did today in such a matter-of-
fact manner served to bolster Jax's confidence that bringing the boy to Eternity Springs had been a good decision.

"It was one of her pet peeves. Most women feel the
same way. Do yourself a favor and get in the habit now
and save yourself a world of grief when you grow up."

They returned to the Elkhorn Lodge and packed up
their gear, then made a quick stop at the lumberyard to
pick up a few supplies for their new digs. "Wow!" Nicholas exclaimed upon catching his first look at Three Bears
Valley. "That house is all burned up!"

"Yep."

"That robber was a bad man."

"Yes, he certainly was."

Flatly, Nicholas announced, "He didn't belong in Eternity Springs."

"You are exactly right about that, son."

Jax pulled his truck to a stop in front of Mama Bear
and Nicholas scrambled out of his seat and was halfway
up the front porch steps before Jax managed to follow.
The boy burst inside calling, "Miss Claire? Miss Claire?
Can I play with Tinsel?"

Upon entering the house, Jax followed his nose and
a delicious aroma to the kitchen. Claire had chocolate
chip cookies still warm from the oven and glasses of milk
waiting for them. Cookies and milk. *I'll be damned.*

Jax decided he liked playing Santa Claus to her Miss
Christmas.

As the days passed, they settled into a routine. Claire
drove Nicholas to school in the mornings on her way to
Forever Christmas. Jax worked at Three Bears Valley

until mid-afternoon when he went to town to do errands before picking Nicholas up at the end of the school day. He stopped in at Forever Christmas most days to lure her beneath the mistletoe for a few minutes, since he seldom found the opportunity to do so at Mama Bear—despite the fact that he'd tacked up numerous sprigs of the stuff at appropriate spaces around the house. He and Claire traded nights cooking dinner and cleaning up afterward, then for Jax it was homework supervision, bath, and bedtime. Some nights stretched out longer than others because he was reading the last book of the Harry Potter series to Nicholas, and he often got caught up in the story and read longer than he'd intended.

Only twice during that first week did they find time at the end of the day to share a glass of wine, a little conversation, and some mistletoe time. To his surprise, Jax discovered that he enjoyed the slow pace of the seduction.

Because that's what it had been. A slow, sensual seduction the likes of which he hadn't enjoyed in a very long time.

Then on Wednesday of their second week at Three Bears, an excited Nicholas climbed into the truck after school and presented Jax with an interesting opportunity. "Guess what, Dad? Galen invited me for a sleepover at his house after the birthday party on Friday. Can I go? Please?"

A sleepover at the Cicero house on date night! Yes! "That might be doable. I need to speak with Dr. Rose or Cicero first and make sure it's okay."

"Can you call them right now, please?"

"When we get home."

Home. For the first time since leaving the navy, he felt like he actually had one. Complete with waiting woman. Emphasis on the waiting.

Friday night. If Nicholas wasn't teasing him, if the

stars finally aligned and nobody got a stomach bug or had a Christmas crisis or accidentally cut off his leg while using a Skilsaw, Friday night just might see the end of his drought and the dance that up to this point had been his mistletoe fling.

Back at the Three Bears, he'd just hung up the phone from speaking to Rose Cicero when a Jeep entered the valley and drove toward the cabins. Outside playing with Tinsel, Nicholas turned toward the sound. "It's Mr. Chase. Look, Dad, it's Mr. Chase! I wonder if he has Captain with him? Maybe Captain and Tinsel would like to play. What do you think, Dad? Would that be all right? Would Miss Claire let Tinsel play with Captain?"

"I imagine it's fine as long as the puppy doesn't appear to be afraid of Captain."

"She won't be. I know it. She's a great dog."

When Chase opened his door and a golden retriever hopped out, Nicholas cheered in delight. "Captain! Look, Dad. It's Captain. He likes her. See? Mr. Chase, is it okay if Tinsel plays with Captain?"

"Sure." Chase strode over to where Nicholas wrestled with the two dogs. He ruffled Nicholas's hair and said, "Howya doin', Tadpole?"

"Great! Tinsel is staying at my new house until my dad gets Baby Bear fixed and I get to play with her every day. I'll get to play with her even when Miss Claire goes back to Baby Bear. Isn't that awesome?"

"Totally awesome." He hunkered down beside Nicholas and petted the puppy. "So, this is the famous Tinsel. She is cute, isn't she?"

"She's famous?" Nicholas asked, his eyes going round with wonder.

"In Eternity Springs, she is. After all, your dad went into a—" Chase caught sight of the slicing motion Jax made across his throat and finished. "Long story about how cute she is when I saw him at the lumberyard the other day. Dr. Lori sent some puppy treats with me for her. They're in the backseat of my Jeep. Want to go get them?"

"Sure."

Chase rose and sauntered on toward Jax, who checked his watch. Ten to five. Close enough. "Want a beer, Timberlake?"

"With every fiber of my being, thank you."

Jax made a quick trip inside to the refrigerator, then rejoined Chase, who said, "Today was final tuxedo-fitting day and Cam and Devin had an issue with theirs. I thought my veterinarian bride might take a gun and shoot a dog."

"Let me guess. The infamous Mortimer was up to his old tricks? What'd he do? Eat a bow tie?"

"No. Cummerbund. I am grateful for the wonderful women I have in my life, but I have to tell you, weddings are not for the faint of heart."

Neither were divorces. Under the circumstances, with Chase's wedding a little over a week away, Jax kept that reality to himself. He tossed a beer toward Chase. "Truer words. So, what brings you out our way?"

Chase caught the can, popped the top, and took a long sip before answering Jax's question. "My blushing bride and I were talking about Tadpole today, and she made a suggestion." He glanced over to make certain that Nicholas couldn't hear him when he said, "No pressure here, because we have other arrangements made already, but Lori thought that if you and Claire were amenable, we'd ask Nicholas if he'd like to dog-sit for us while we're on our honeymoon."

Jax glanced toward his son, who stood throwing a stick for Captain to fetch. Nicholas's expression was lit up like a tree in Forever Christmas. "I'll have to speak with Claire—"

"Lori already did. She thinks it's a great idea."

"In that case, I think it's a great idea, too. He'll be thrilled." Plus, it would give Jax a chance to evaluate how the boy would manage the responsibility of having a dog were Jax to decide to give the go-ahead to get one for the boy. Since Claire acted as caretaker for Tinsel, Nicholas had all the fun without the responsibility. With a dog of his own, that would need to change. "Why don't you go ask him?"

Jax sat on the front porch steps and sipped his beer as he watched Chase Timberlake's long-legged saunter toward his son. While the two played together with the two dogs for a few minutes, Jax reflected on the blessing the former jet-setter had been in the Lancasters' lives. Last summer when Nicholas arrived at the Rocking L summer camp, he'd been a fearful shell of the boy he was today. Much of that transformation was due to the man playing with the boy now. Chase had not only taught the boy to swim, he'd accomplished the first breakthrough in Nicholas's recovery from the traumatic events of his mother's death.

I owe him more than I'll ever be able to repay.

Jax's gaze slid down his son's figure and focused on his ankle where vicious scars served as evidence of his son's horror.

Nicholas's excited cheer diverted Jax from the dark direction of his thoughts, and he watched with a glad heart as the boy's joy exploded like a skyrocket on the Fourth of July. If the Hardcastles could see him now, they couldn't deny that Jax's decision to bring his son to Eternity Springs had been the right one.

"Dad! Dad! Guess what? You gotta say yes, Dad. Please say yes!"

He gave his lecture about responsibility and care and then said yes. Much happiness abounded in Three Bears Valley.

He relayed the details of the moment with Claire later that evening when they shared a glass of excellent wine after he put Nicholas to bed. "Chase and Lori are good people. I didn't know everything Chase had been through when I met him last summer, but I heard the story from Shannon when I grabbed a burger for lunch at Murphy's one day last week. It's no wonder Nicholas bonded with him. They both lived through a really horrific experience."

Claire swirled the wine in her glass. "I know that Nicholas survived a car accident that killed his mother. Yesterday when he stripped off his soccer cleats and socks after showing me his new peewee uniform, I noticed the scars on his legs. Is that from the accident? Or did something else happen to him?"

Jax rubbed the back of his neck. He rarely spoke of the event that had caused such grief for so many people, and even when he did, he only relayed the basic facts. Facts couldn't convey the horror, and he'd never told anyone the entire story.

To his surprise, he found he wanted to tell Claire.

He swallowed hard, licked his lips, and began. "For me, it all started on Christmas Eve. According to our custody agreement, I had Nicholas every other Christmas. My ex had him for Christmas the first year following our divorce. It was my turn."

Excitement hummed through Jax's blood as he pulled his car to a stop at the curb in front of Lara's home in Seattle on the twenty-third of December. He'd been on a boat for the past ten months, and as a result, hadn't seen his son since Valentine's Day. Ten months was a significant chunk of the life of a six-year-old, especially when the boy's mother didn't send the pictures and updates Jax had requested. His need to see his son was a living, breathing being inside him.

He bounded up the front steps and rang the doorbell precisely at ten A.M., the time he'd told Lara to expect him in the e-mail they'd exchanged a week ago about the arrangements. He was prepared for Lara to be difficult about this. She hadn't responded to any of the e-mails he'd sent over the past two days that asked questions about supplies he would need during the eight days Nicholas would be with him. More than likely, he'd be winging this visit, but that was okay. He was a submariner. He'd been trained to handle a nuclear accident on a sub. He could deal with any surprises a six-year-old boy threw his way.

Then Nicholas's stepfather opened his front door and threw out a surprise that Jax never anticipated.

"What do you mean, they're not here?" Jax demanded.

"I thought you were Mr. Brilliant," James Karston sneered. "What's so difficult to understand? They're gone. Outta here. Vamoosed. Lara took the kid and left me. She left me three effing days before Christmas!"

She's trying to keep Nicholas from me, he thought. Fury ignited in Jax's gut. Grimly, he asked, "Is she with her parents?"

"Hell if I know. She probably did go home to Daddy. She could have climbed on a rocket ship to the moon. The woman is batshit crazy."

The first wave of unease rippled through Jax. "Why do you say that?"

"Because she is! She's been this way ever since she lost the baby in August."

She'd lost a child? Jax hadn't known that. The fact gave his heart a little twist. Before their marriage fell apart, he'd wanted more children. She'd refused to consider it.

Karston started to slam the door in Jax's face, but Jax

stuck his foot inside to prevent it. "Have you called her parents' house?"

"Hell, no. Let her run to Mommy and Daddy. I don't care anymore."

The Hardcastle home would be Jax's first stop. He fully expected to find her and Nicholas there, but just in case . . . "What's she driving?"

"If I tell you, will you go the hell away and leave me alone?"

"I'll leave." Though he might come back if she wasn't at her parents' and he needed more information—like access to her credit cards—in order to track her.

"She's in a sweet little BMW hybrid. I gave it to her for our anniversary. How stupid am I?"

"Tags?"

Jax committed the license tag number to memory and turned away as the door slammed. Back in his car, he took a few minutes to rein in his temper before he began the fifteen-minute drive to the Hardcastles'. He wasted those few minutes because by the time he arrived at his former in-laws' home, he was loaded for bear.

No one answered the doorbell. He walked around the house peeking in the windows and saw no signs of life.

Nor did he see a Christmas tree.

The sound of a shotgun being racked behind him was unmistakable.

"What in sam blazes do you think you're doing, young fellow?"

Jax pinpointed the voice. The neighbor. The widowed rancher from Montana who'd moved in with his daughter's family after his wife died. He raised his hands away from his body and slowly turned to face him. "Mr. Waggoner? I'm Nicholas's father."

"Navy man. Submariner."

"Yessir."

The Montanan lowered the shotgun. "What you doin' snoopin' around the Hardcastle place, son?"

"I'm looking for Lara. I was supposed to pick up Nicholas from her house this morning, and they're not there. Have you seen them?"

"Miss Lara? No. No. Not for quite some time. She and her folks have had a falling-out. Brian and Linda are heartbroken about it. They haven't seen the boy since Halloween. They've gone to Hawaii for Christmas to get away. Left yesterday afternoon."

That bit of news left Jax speechless. "Perhaps they reconciled. Maybe Lara went with them to Hawaii."

"Well, if she did, her mother didn't know anything about it when she came over yesterday and had a cup of coffee with my Cecilia. She was right upset about not seeing her girl on Christmas."

What the hell, Lara? Was this the same woman who had refused to meet him in Tahiti—Tahiti!—for his R & R because it meant she'd miss Christmas with her parents?

Jax needed to get in touch with Brian Hardcastle, but the only number he had for the man was their landline. "Did they leave an emergency number with you, by any chance?"

"I don't know. Come on inside and ask Cecilia."

Ten minutes later he left the Hardcastles' neighbor's house with Brian Hardcastle's cell number, a sackful of homemade chocolate chip cookies, and a heightened sense of anxiety.

He climbed into his car, took a moment to compose his question, then placed the call.

He awakened Lara's father from a sound sleep. "Lancaster. How the hell did you get my number?" Before Jax could respond, Brian added, "Oh, no. Is it Nicholas? Did something bad happen to Nicholas?"

"No." Jax damn sure hoped the answer was no. "That's not why I'm calling. I'm trying to locate Lara."

"Why? You sure nothing's wrong with Nicholas?"

"I haven't seen Nicholas," Jax snapped. In crisp, concise sentences, he relayed the events of the morning, ending with, "I expected they would be with you."

"No." Brian's tone was clipped. "She left James? This is worse than we realized."

Jax's unease spiked at the admission.

"We invited Lara and James to join us in Hawaii, but she didn't want to come with us."

There was no love lost between Jax and Brian Hardcastle, but the worry Jax heard in Brian's voice convinced him that his former father-in-law was telling the truth. Jax verbalized his one hope. "Maybe she plans to surprise you."

"I don't see how. We never told her where we are staying."

Jax dragged a hand down his face. *What the hell have you done, Lara?*

It was a question he repeated often over the next twenty-four hours. Then, forty-eight. Then, seventy-two. Christmas came and went without any sign, anywhere, of his ex-wife and son.

Now two years later, he still asked the same question. Sharing the story with Claire, his voice went rough as he relived the torment of those dark days.

"We reported her missing to the police, but that was mostly a waste of time. She was an adult who'd left her spouse. Besides, it was Christmas. Everyone was too busy spiking their eggnog to worry about a woman who'd had a fight with her husband."

"I can't imagine how horrible that must have been for you, Jax. I hate when policies prevent people from listening. There was a child involved!"

"I tried to play the kidnapping card, but it went no-where. I hired a private investigator and the Hardcastles flew home from Hawaii. Brian had social ties with the police chief, so he was able to light a fire under the authorities and get the search taken seriously. They were the longest four and a half days of my life."

"How were they found?" Claire asked.

"By the grace of God. Honestly, Claire. I had begun to despair. She wasn't using her credit cards. We got no response when we pinged her phone. It was as if they'd disappeared off the face of the map. Then at nine-seventeen on the morning of the twenty-seventh, a call came in from Idaho."

His throat tightened up, and he paused a moment until he figured he could speak without his voice wobbling. "Snowmobilers had discovered the wreck. She'd gone off a mountain road. The car slid thirty feet down the side of a mountain and slammed into a tree. She died of blunt force trauma. The doctors told us that she probably didn't live through the crash."

Claire placed a comforting hand on his knee. "Nicholas?"

"He must have been in his booster seat. Physically, he suffered a few scrapes and bruises—mostly from when the rear side airbags deployed."

"The airbags caused those scars on his ankle?"

Jax closed his eyes and sucked in a deep breath. He recalled his first glimpse of the damage done to his son's ankle and leg when a nurse changed his bandages following his surgery. "No. The snowmobilers saw animal tracks in the snow. They couldn't identify them, and by the time the rescue crew got finished, the tracks had been obliterated. Best we could figure was that at some point, Nicholas got out of the car and was attacked. Wolves or wild dogs."

Claire covered her mouth with her hands. "Oh, Jax. My heart just breaks for him. For you both."

"An analysis of the time and distance they traveled and, frankly, the decomposition of Lara's corpse, proved that he'd been trapped in that car with his mother's body for days. He didn't utter a word for weeks afterward."

Jax rose and paced the room, lost in the memory of that horrific time. The Hardcastles' collapse. The funeral. Nicholas's pallor and his pain and silent suffering.

Jax's own despair after opening that first hospital bill.

His fury when the navy deemed him mission critical and refused his request for early discharge.

"I could have used your positive-thoughts journal during those months, Claire."

She made a little whimper, drawing his glance. A pair of tears trailed slowly down her cheeks.

Jax's heart warmed. He couldn't resist a woman who would cry over his little boy's pain. Not that he wanted to resist her.

I want to win her. Keep her. Marry her.

The truth of the thought rocked him. What the hell? Marriage! What in the world was he thinking? This was a fling, not a relationship. That had been clear from the very beginning. They hadn't even been on a date yet. He hadn't slept with her. How could his mind possibly go to marriage?

Because your mind follows your heart, Lancaster. It always has. Always will.

Damn, he was in trouble.

"I can't imagine. I think I would have melted into a messy blubbering puddle. How afraid you must have been."

"Terrified."

That part hadn't really changed.

The breakup with Lara had nearly destroyed him, both

financially and emotionally. He didn't have it in him to go down that road again, not even with someone who did it for him as much as Claire Branham did.

Oh, get your head out, Lancaster. Talk about borrowing trouble. He had them married and divorced before their first date!

Jax was almost glad when Claire asked another question. "It's obvious why Nicholas developed a fear of dogs. I guess he associates the accident with Christmas?"

"Yes. After he got out of the hospital in Idaho, he went to live with his grandparents in Seattle." Jax told her a little about his futile battle to secure an early discharge and the panicked phone call he'd received the day after his sub arrived in port in Hawaii. Speaking of the events catapulted him into the past.

"What do you mean he's catatonic?" Jax demanded of Brian Hardcastle.

"Linda took him to a charity event this afternoon and when they walked into the building, he froze and went stiff and . . . away. He just checked out, Lancaster. No reason. No warning."

Jax rubbed his temples between his thumb and forefingers and tried to make sense of what he was hearing. "What sort of building was it? What type of charity event?"

"It's an exhibit hall in the convention center. Nothing special about it. The event was her sorority's Christmas in August Craft Fair."

"Christmas," Jax repeated. Sonofabitch! What the hell had Linda been thinking? "He must have had a flashback."

"Whatever is going on, it's lasted six hours."

And I'm just NOW getting a phone call? "What's the prognosis?"

"The damned doctors can't tell us a blessed thing. I'm headed back up to the hospital now. Came home to

change clothes and found your message on the landline. Thought I should call since you're on land. I'll e-mail you updates as we get them."

Jax went straight to his commanding officer and begged leave. Six hours later, he went wheels up on a military transport headed to Southern California. From there he caught a commercial flight to Seattle and arrived at the hospital just in time for evening rounds the following day.

Nicholas had opened his eyes, but he had yet to interact with anyone. The doctors had concluded he should be transferred to a psychiatric hospital, and Brian jumped in and began making arrangements. Jax let him. He took a seat beside Nicholas's bed and held his hand. Throughout an interminable night, he didn't let go.

At 4:22, Nicholas made his first sound, a little soulful moan. Jax rose from his chair and stepped toward the bed. "Hey, buddy."

"Daddy?"

"I'm here, buddy."

"No. No. No. No. No." Nicholas kept his eyes scrunched closed, grabbed the blanket, and pulled it over his head. "You're not real. You're one of the monsters. My daddy's far, far away."

"I am *real*, little guy, and I'm right here." Jax rested his hand on the lump that was Nicholas's shoulder. "I heard you were sick and I came home."

A full twenty seconds passed before his little hands tentatively lowered the covers. "Daddy?"

"Hello, Nicholas."

"Are we in heaven?"

"No. We're at a hospital in Seattle. Your grandparents brought you here after . . . well . . . I'm not really sure what happened. The doctors are going to find out, though."

"I just want to go home, Daddy. Can we go home?"

"Not right now, but soon, I hope. We need to find out what happened so we can make sure it doesn't happen again."

The little boy's big blue eyes flooded with tears. "I know what happened. I heard the music again. I don't like that music. It scares me. I got scared, Daddy."

Christmas carols. Bet they'd been playing Christmas carols at the charity fair. Bet Lara had been playing Christmas carols when she wrecked the car.

Nicholas's next words confirmed the suspicion.

"I was so cold and Mommy wouldn't answer and the songs played and played and played and I couldn't make them stop but then they stopped and the animals howled and I was so scared, Daddy. I was so scared!"

Jax sat on the side of his son's bed, took the boy in his arms, and rocked him while he cried.

As he remembered that exchange, Jax's heart broke all over again. He cleared his throat and responded to Claire's question. "The car was packed full of wrapped Christmas gifts. Lots of red and green and ribbon and bows. And we're pretty sure that the radio continued to play long after the accident. He hasn't opened a Christmas present since."

Claire pushed to her feet and crossed the room to grab a tissue from the box on a table. "I think this might be the saddest story I've heard in a very long time," she said, wiping her eyes. "Now I better understand what a victory it was for him to conquer his fear of dogs."

"It was huge. Chase and Lori and Eternity Springs worked a miracle with my son."

"Well . . . here's what I think." Claire picked up the wine bottle and topped off their glasses. "I think Eternity Springs needs to go for a two-fer."

"You're talking about working on his fear of Christmas?"

"I am."

"I appreciate the thought, Claire. Truly, I do. I'm just not sure that either Nicholas or I is ready to tackle that beast. He's getting along so well right now, and after the hypnosis debacle, I'm hesitant to upset the applecart."

"Isn't healing his Christmas phobia a big part of the reason why you moved here?"

"Yes, but—"

"You have to think positive, Jax. You have to believe. Don't forget, this is Eternity Springs."

"I know. The longer I'm here, the easier it is for me to believe in its mojo. My fear is doing something that back-fires. I don't want another situation like the one we went through in September. Nicholas's grandparents had good intentions and look what happened."

"Well, we're not his grandparents, and this isn't Se-attle. Chase and Lori found the right combination to deal with his fear of dogs. I'll bet we can come up with a plan to tackle his issues with Christmas in a nonthreatening way. Let me put a little thought into it, Jax. They don't call me Miss Christmas for nothing."

Hearing that bit of positive thinking and seeing the confident determination on Claire Branham's face, Jax Lancaster took a tumble toward love.

Chapter Twelve

*Winston Churchill said we make a life by
what we give. Smart man.*
—CLAIRE

The following morning as she got dressed for work,
Claire's mind buzzed with ideas for her newest project.
After Jax gave her his blessing to launch a well-considered
Christmas campaign on Nicholas's behalf, she'd focused
her thoughts on creating a plan that incorporated the successful exposure-therapy strategy Chase had employed in
order to overcome the boy's fear of dogs. She had an idea
she thought might work, but only if Nicholas would buy
into it.

Claire and Jax agreed that springing something unexpected on Nicholas would be the worst thing they could
do. But if Nicholas was ready and willing to dip his toe in
the holiday pool, so to speak, then she was ready to assist.
How terrible for this to happen to a child, to lose Christmas. She knew from personal experience. However, as
complex as her own Christmas-related issues were, they
paled in comparison to Nicholas's.

Maybe helping Nicholas would do something for her,
too. That's how the volunteer work she used to do had
worked. She'd always felt best about herself when she
brought a little joy into the lives of others. Maybe this
project would help them both.

The boy who skipped downstairs that morning and

chattered nonstop about Captain and Tinsel through breakfast showed no sign of emotional stress. If the right moment presented itself during their drive to school, she planned to broach her idea. From her perspective, they had little time to waste. Eternity Springs might start the official Christmas season later than other towns in America these days, but Thanksgiving and Deck the Halls Friday were right around the corner.

Claire knew that helping Nicholas find his Christmas spirit would be rewarding. This undertaking might well be exactly what she needed to finally kick her own Grinch to the curb.

The boy's excited chatter continued during the drive to school. They were halfway to town when he let out a joyful sigh and said how happy Chase's request had made him. Claire concluded that she wouldn't get a better opportunity.

"So, Dr. Lori told me about how Chase worked with you during summer camp to conquer your fear of dogs. She said you were one brave little boy."

His smile didn't dim. "Dr. Lori helped, too. We worked on it a little bit each day."

"Your father said you thought if you came to Eternity Springs you might be able to do the same thing where Christmas is concerned."

At that he went still for a long moment, then sent a cautious gaze her way. "Yeah."

"You know, Nicholas, I wouldn't mind helping you with the project. Sort of like Chase and Dr. Lori did. I think I'd be good at it. I am Miss Christmas, after all."

"I don't know . . ."

"That's okay, Nicholas. No pressure. You just think about it and let me know."

He remained silent the rest of the way into town. If Claire felt just a little bit of disappointment, well, she knew she had to temper her expectations. If Nicholas's troubles were easily solved, his father wouldn't have moved him from Washington to Colorado.

Approaching the intersection where one of the town's two stoplights switched to yellow and then red, she braked to a stop. She told herself she shouldn't be discouraged. Considering everything the boy had been through, they all should probably look at this journey as a marathon rather than a sprint. And every long-distance runner began by taking baby steps, right?

Can you mutilate a metaphor any more, Branham?

Probably. Nicholas tickled her imagination. Didn't he remind her of another bedraggled angel with a broken wing? If she hadn't sworn off creating any more adventures for Gardenia, she could easily see her making a new friend.

He'd have blue eyes and wear big glasses that wouldn't stay up on his nose. He'd wear a T-shirt with paw prints all over it and . . . No, wait. He'd be a dog. A talking dog. His T-shirt would say DOGS ARE PEOPLE, TOO.

Gardenia sits on her mantel blowing dust off her wings. The new cleaning service people are afraid to dust her at night and Holly Sugarplum hasn't looked twice at Gardenia in weeks.

"So what else is new?" Gardenia said, rustling her wings, sweeping dust off her shelf to settle on the beautiful china doll angel with golden hair and a satin gown.

Achoo. Achoo. Achoo. Achoo. Gardenia's eyes rounded at the unexpected sound.

She peered over the edge of the shelf. A white dog with honey-brown spots and droopy ears stood on his hind legs, his front paws folded over his chest. He wore round black glasses and growled up at her. "Stop that. It's rude to blow your dust around. Some of us are allergic to dust, you know."

"You are talking to me?"

"Yes. You're the one blowing dust, aren't you?"

"Nobody but Holly Sugarplum ever talks to me."

"Why? Are you mean?"

Gardenia shook her head. *"I'm a good angel."*

"No you're not. Good angels blow golden angel dust. Your dust is gray and makes me sneeze."

"You're a mean dog! Why are you in the Angel Room?"

"I'm not mean. I'm lost. My name is Nicholas, and I'm looking for the Christmas Key."

"Miss Claire? Miss Claire?"

She turned her head toward the voice, expecting to see a droopy-eared dog wearing black-rimmed glasses. Nicholas Lancaster said, "The light is green, Miss Claire."

"Oh. Oh!" Embarrassed, she felt her cheeks flush with heat as she flicked her gaze up to the rearview mirror before pressing the gas pedal. Three cars were lined up behind her. She stuck her arm out the window and gave a little "I'm sorry" wave as she drove on through the intersection.

"I'll hear about that later," she murmured. "I've been caught daydreaming too many times lately. People like to tease."

"I get teased, too, Miss Claire. Dad says when it happens, to put on your cool look."

"My cool look? What's a cool look?"

"Well, it works better when you're standing up. You have to put your hands in your pockets and get all loosey-goosey. Loosey-goosey. Isn't that a stupid word? Anyway, you roll back on your heels and bounce a little. That doesn't matter. But you gotta keep your shoulders squared and your chin up. That's important."

"I see."

"That's not all, though. This next part is *really* important. You smile at 'em and say, 'Thank you for sharing that with me.'"

Claire gave him a sidelong look. "Oh, yeah?"

"Yeah. Dad says it really works. I was going to try it with the bullies in Seattle, but we moved to Eternity Springs instead."

"Awesome. I'll be sure to remember to try it. Maybe I'll practice my loosey-goosey to get ready." Claire pulled her SUV into the circular drive in front of the school and said, "Thank you for the tip, Nicholas."

"You're welcome." The boy unfastened his seat belt, but rather than hop out like he usually did, he remained seated, staring straight ahead. "How would you do it? The . . . um . . . other thing."

Claire's pulse picked up. "You mean Christmas?"

Still not looking at her, he nodded.

Yes! Claire managed—just barely—not to pump her fist. She strove for a casual tone. "I'm certainly open to suggestions, Nicholas, but I thought that a good place to start might be books. Your dad told me y'all are about to finish reading Harry Potter. What would you think about me reading a little bit to you at night from my collection of Christmas stories? For the most part, they are very short."

He pursed his lips. "One of them has ghosts. I don't want any ghosts."

"That's Dickens's *A Christmas Carol.* We'll mark that off the list. Actually, I thought we'd start with the story where it all began—the Gospel of Luke from the Bible. That seems appropriate, don't you think? We can give it a try and if it's a problem for you in any way, then we'll just forget it."

Nicholas sat for another fifteen seconds, staring straight ahead. Then he licked his lips and opened the car door. "I'll think about it, Miss Claire."

"Fair enough. You have a good day at school today, Nicholas."

"I will. Bye."

He slammed the door and ran off toward the school's front door.

"Yes!" she exclaimed, giving in to the fist-pump urge. Claire grinned all the way to Forever Christmas.

She spent every free moment during her workday in her book section choosing stories to share with Nicholas. By the time she closed her shop and headed home, she had three tote bags stuffed with books.

Over supper that evening, she asked Jax how many nights of Harry Potter they had left. "Three chapters. One tonight. I figure we'll do two tomorrow night and finish it up."

"Saturday night is movie night. We don't read on Saturdays. Want to watch movies with us, Miss Claire?"

"Well . . ." She glanced at Jax for a signal, and he nodded enthusiastically. "I like movies—as long as they're not tearjerkers. What are you watching on Saturday night?"

"Submarine movies," Nicholas said. "It's fun because Dad talks all the way through them, and he gets grumpy when they get things wrong, and they always get things wrong. You should watch with us."

"Submarine movies, hmm? Okay. Thanks for the invitation, Nicholas. It's a date. I'll bring the popcorn and hot chocolate."

"Cool! Then maybe Sunday night you could read to me."

In the midst of spooning a second helping of green beans onto her plate, Claire froze. Her eyes widened and she darted a look at Jax before she responded. "If it's okay with your dad, I'd like that very much, Nicholas."

"Good." The boy shoveled another bite of spaghetti into his mouth, sucked in an errant strand, then added, "Dad, Miss Claire is going to read to me about Christmas. From the Bible."

"And Dr. Seuss. Clement C. Moore. O. Henry," Claire added as clarification.

"She said they're short. Is it okay with you, Dad? You'll still read Percy Jackson to me, right?"

"Absolutely." Jax stabbed a meatball off his son's plate and brought it toward his own mouth. "Sounds like an excellent idea to me."

"Hey, Dad! I was saving that!"

"Snooze you lose, boyo." Jax's eyes twinkled with pleasure as he looked at his son, and when he shifted his gaze toward Claire, they softened with a combination of gratitude and hope and approval that warmed her to her toes. "Miss Christmas's meatballs are spectacular."

Claire schooled her expression into one of disapproval. "Don't worry, Nicholas. I believe there are two meatballs left in the sauce on the stove. You may have them both."

"Score!" Nicholas chortled.

The rest of the evening passed in an easy, upbeat atmosphere that reminded Claire of the happy family of her childhood before Michelle got sick. When Jax went upstairs to read a chapter of *Harry Potter and the Deathly Hallows,* Claire knew a yearning that all but took her breath away.

She wanted this. She wanted a family.

She wanted to be part of *this* family.

Whoa. Whoa. Whoa. Hold your jingle bells right there, Miss Christmas.

Family wasn't on the table. They'd made that clear from the beginning. She'd been the one to take relationship *off* the table! Tables weren't even involved here. Just a bed. This was a mistletoe fling.

Although, come to think of it, there was no reason a table couldn't be involved. Jax seemed like the type who, once he'd begun flinging, wouldn't care too much just where the mistletoe lay. So to speak.

Needing a distraction from her thoughts, Claire

considered skipping the nightcap with Jax that had quickly become their habit and going up to bed herself. But that struck her as cowardly, so instead she fell back on another crutch. She took a box of brownie mix from the pantry and set about mixing them up.

She'd just slid the pan in the preheated oven when Jax entered the kitchen. "Brownies? You're making brownies? Better be careful, Claire. I'll sabotage the repairs to Baby Bear to keep you here."

Because words that were totally unacceptable hovered on her tongue, Claire diverted by asking, "How are the repairs coming along?"

"I'm afraid we've ground to a halt until the electrician manages to find his way out to Three Bears. Every day I call and every day he gives me another excuse for why he can't make it out. I've done all I can do without a license. It's frustrating."

"It's hunting season," Claire explained. "Unfortunately, our plumber and our electrician are serious hunters, and as a result, jobs back up."

"Oh . . . that explains a lot." Jax lifted the bottle of Chianti they'd opened to have with their dinner and topped off Claire's glass and then his own. "I should have picked up on it. I'll work at Papa Bear in the meantime, but if Nicholas and I are wearing out our welcome . . ."

"Not at all," she hastened to say. "I enjoy the company."

It was true. She hadn't realized just how lonely she'd been until now.

He handed her the wine. "Claire . . . about the Christmas bedtime stories . . ."

"If you don't think we should—"

He interrupted. "No. It's brilliant. Especially beginning with the Bible story."

"He's the reason for the Season."

"And your plan is nonthreatening, and most important of all, it's something Nicholas wants to try. But if it doesn't work . . . if he's not ready . . . I don't want you to be disappointed."

She sipped her wine and smiled. "Like I told Nicholas, no pressure."

She had to repeat those words to herself Sunday evening as she waited for Nicholas to get ready for bed. She was surprisingly nervous. She wanted to help him so badly. And, she very badly didn't want to frighten him or cause him any grief.

When the mantel clock chimed eight P.M., Jax set down the thriller he'd been reading since Nicholas went up to take his bath half an hour ago and stood. "That's our cue. Are you ready, Miss Christmas?"

No! "I am."

She picked up her Bible—her mother's worn and tattered one—and took the hand that Jax extended to her. Her mouth was dry as straw in a manger.

"I'm nervous," Jax told her.

"I'm not," she fibbed. "No pressure."

Nicholas wore Seattle Seahawks pajamas, and he held the first volume of the Percy Jackson series in his lap. His blond hair was damp from his shower. He'd obviously neglected to comb it after toweling it dry since it stuck up all over his head. He sat a little stiffly in his bed, and behind the thick lenses of his glasses, his blue eyes were round and big as an owl's.

"Did you brush your teeth?" Jax asked.

"Yep."

"Prove it."

Nicholas opened his mouth, stuck out his tongue, and made an "ah" sound.

Jax nodded, then sauntered over to the dresser, where

he picked up a small black comb and tossed it to his son. "Use it. Claire, you want to sit in the rocking chair?"

"Okay."

As she took a seat in the chair at the foot of the bed, Jax nonchalantly slid onto the mattress beside his son and slung his arm around the boy's shoulder. "I'm ready. You ready, Hot Rod?"

The boy's knuckles went white as he tightened his grip on the book. "I'm ready."

Claire cleared her throat and said, "Dr. Lori shared something Celeste shared with Mr. Chase not long ago. She said that courage is a muscle that is strengthened by use. You're getting to be a very strong young man, Nicholas."

Then she opened her mother's Bible to the second chapter of Luke and read. "'And it came to pass in those days there went out a decree from Caesar Augustus that all the world should be taxed.'"

When she closed the book a few minutes later, she was almost afraid to look at the troubled eight-year-old. Then he asked, "I thought there were camels in the story?"

Relief rolled over Claire in a wave. "That's Epiphany. It's in the Gospel of Matthew." She hesitated a beat, then added, "We can read it tomorrow if you'd like."

"Okay." Nicholas handed the Percy Jackson book to his dad. "Your turn."

Jax's smile was Star of Bethlehem bright.

Chapter Thirteen

It's nice to work in the sunshine.
—JAX

A week of good weather, available subcontractors, supply orders that arrived in a timely manner, and three not insignificant checks for progress on projects he'd been hired to complete had put a spring in Jax's steps on Friday morning. The fact that Claire and Nicholas had plowed through *How the Grinch Stole Christmas!, The Polar Express,* "'Twas the Night Before Christmas," and "The Gift of the Magi" so far this week didn't hurt his mood any.

Neither did the fact that he had a date tonight.

While varnish dried on the wood floor at Baby Bear and the framing crew tackled Papa Bear, Jax drove over to the Callahan compound on Hummingbird Lake. He went to work installing reclaimed wood on the walls of the dance hall to the notes of Texas country music loaded into the portable sound system that sat on what would be the stage once the building was finished. The physical work was just what he needed, and he was whistling along to Pat Green's "Carry On" when the music abruptly switched off. "Buy you a beer, Lancaster?"

Jax turned toward the speaker. Brick Callahan looked like hell. "You okay, man?"

"Yeah."

His expression said otherwise. Jax arched a brow and waited.

Brick scowled at him and said, "Okay, actually, my day has sucked. Seriously sucked. It's Friday afternoon. You're not on any hard deadline here. Clock out early. Come have a beer with me."

Jax checked his watch. "I have an hour and ten minutes before I need to pick up Nicholas from school. You want to go to Murphy's?"

"Nah. I'll raid my dad's refrigerator. Meet me down at the pier."

"Okay."

Jax pulled the tools from his tool belt, returned them to his toolbox, and stowed it in the bed of his truck. Then he strolled down to the pier that stretched out into Hummingbird Lake. He heard the bang of a screen door, and he glanced behind him to see Brick Callahan carrying a small cooler on a strap over one shoulder and a tackle box. In his opposite hand, he carried two fishing poles.

He didn't say anything when he joined Jax at the end of the pier, simply handed him one of the poles, then set down the cooler and fished out a couple of microbrews.

Jax understood the peace that could be found in silence, so he didn't press the issue. The men fished and drank their beer for a good ten minutes before Brick said, "Women."

Aha. So that's what this is about.

"I hear you, brother."

"Scuttlebutt in town says you got divorced before your boy's mother died. Is that true?"

"Yep."

"Wasn't it hard to do that with your kid?"

"It wasn't my preference." Jax grimaced as he recalled those soul-crushing days and his despair when he realized his efforts to retain shared custody were sunk. "Not my choice."

"Funny how often it's not our choice, isn't it?" The bitterness in Brick's voice said as much as his words did.

Jax rarely discussed his marriage, but something told him Brick needed to know he wasn't alone. "She left me for another guy."

"Well, that sucks rocks."

"My ego certainly took a hit." He waited a beat, then asked, "You have a kid, Callahan?"

"Me? No." He shook his head. "My ex does."

"You're divorced, too?"

"Nah. I was engaged, but we never made it to the altar. Money got in the way."

"Now, that's something I understand."

"Oh, yeah?"

Jax nodded. "Money caused a lot of our problems. My wife's family was loaded. I didn't realize going into the marriage how much I would resent her going to her daddy for everything she wanted." For her part, Lara hadn't realized how much she'd hate being a navy wife.

"See . . . what is it about women and money? My ex wanted me to take anything and everything my grandfather offered. The man's favorite pastime is giving stuff to his grandkids. But I didn't grow up wealthy. I was adopted as a baby, and my mom and pop are salt-of-the-earth, middle-class folks. Hell, I didn't meet my dad until I was ready to go off to college. He and my uncles are all hardworking men who've built their businesses and earned everything they have with their own two hands. That's what I wanted. She couldn't see it. We had a big fight about it and she decided the grass—not to mention the cash—was greener with a banker. Damned if she didn't marry him. Have a baby with him."

"You still love her." Despite the fact that the woman sounded like a gold digger.

Brick finished his beer and tossed the empty into the cooler. "Want another?"

"I'm good."

He reached for another beer, twisted off the cap, then took a long sip. Then he set down his beer and picked his fishing pole back up. Reeling in the line, he said, "I loved her for a long time. Maybe a part of me does still love her, but I don't like her very much. She calls me. Called me again just this morning. She says she's leaving her husband. The old 'marry in haste, repent at leisure' thing. She wants me to take her back."

This time Jax was the one who took a long sip of his beer, more to fill his mouth with something other than advice than because he was thirsty. The man hadn't asked. He wouldn't offer. Guys didn't do that. "What did you tell her?"

"No, I told her no." Brick gave his fishing pole a hard yank, and cranked the reel with excess enthusiasm. "It just about killed me, but I told her no."

Good.

Brick changed his bait and cast his line once again. "Sure would like to catch some fish. My mouth has a hankering for trout tonight for dinner."

"It does sound good," Jax agreed.

After a few moments of silent fishing, Brick declared, "I'm not going to be her crutch. I'm not going to be her excuse. Even if her marriage really is over and it has nothing to do with me, the things that got in our way are still there. Some things can't be fixed. Some things don't change. My attitude toward money hasn't changed. Did yours? Did the breakup with your ex change how you felt about money?"

"No. Not at all. If anything, I think it solidified my position. I don't care how gorgeous she is, I'm not ever getting involved with a wealthy woman again. Money makes life easier, but it doesn't necessarily make life happier. My boy is happier now than he ever was in Seattle. I screwed up when I didn't listen to my instincts. I'm not doing that again."

"You're telling me I should listen to my instincts."

"I'm not offering any advice here, Callahan. You asked a question and I answered it."

"Yeah . . . yeah . . . yeah. The thing is . . . I know that telling her no was the right thing to do. I haven't changed. My grandfather is my business partner. We're in it fifty-fifty. He provided the stake, but I'm building sweat equity. I'm not going back to the Bank of Branch anytime things get a little tight. I'm scraping by with Stardance right now, but that's okay. I'm pouring almost everything I make back into the business. I think it will succeed. I think I'm building something I'll be proud of someday. Hell, I'm already proud of it. You're a guy. You can understand that, right?"

"You don't have to be a guy to understand that, Callahan. The right woman will understand."

Claire understands why I've strapped on a tool belt rather than send out my resume to corporations who have a use for nuclear engineers.

"The right woman," Brick repeated. "I'm afraid that in order to make room for her, I gotta get the wrong woman out of my head first. My ex has really messed with my mind."

"Looks to me that by telling her no, you've taken the first step towards fixing that."

"Yeah. Well. I guess." Brick gave his head a shake, shrugged his shoulders, and then a sly look come over his face. "Maybe you're right. Maybe I do have room now, and I should start looking for her. Maybe I should start with a certain shopkeeper with an affinity for red and green."

Jax knew that Callahan said it as a friendly dig. Nevertheless, that didn't stop his hackles from rising. He snapped, "Claire is taken."

Callahan smirked. "Is she now?"

"Yes." Honesty made Jax add, "I think so. I hope so. We have a date tonight."

"Oh, yeah? Where are you taking her?"

"The Yellow Kitchen."

"Points for that." Brick's pole bent and he yanked and set the hook. Reeling in his catch, he added, "Best place in town."

"So I understand. I haven't been there yet."

"How did you get a table for tonight? Town is bursting at the seams with all the visitors for the big event tomorrow."

"I guess I'm living right."

"I guess you are. Treat her good, Lancaster. Miss Christmas is special."

"I will. I know. She's . . . right."

Brick pulled his catch out of the water. Not a trout, but somebody's lost sneaker. "Story of my life, Lancaster," Brick lamented, staring at the dirty, dripping shoe. "Story of my life."

Friday at five after three, Claire rang up a sale for an Advent calendar purchased by a former crew member of Chase's TV show who was in town for the wedding. She slipped the calendar into a bag, thanked him for his business, and told him not to miss the Italian cream cake at the wedding reception the following day. Once the customer left, she flipped her OPEN sign to CLOSED.

Yes, she was closing two hours early. Yes, she'd likely

miss some sales because the streets were busy with visitors, but that's okay. She had bigger fish to fry today.

She needed to go back to Mama Bear and prepare for her date.

Her date.

She couldn't believe she had a date tonight. A first date.

The last first date she'd gone on had been with Landon. She'd worn a little black dress and stiletto heels and carried the Jimmy Choo evening clutch bag she'd bought at a resale shop for the occasion. He'd taken her to a five-star restaurant and ordered five-star wine and entertained her with tales of the sports stars his firm's entertainment division worked with.

"Need a new train of thought," she scolded herself. She refused to spoil the excitement of her mistletoe fling by dwelling on the past.

She *was* excited. Jax had a dinner reservation at the Yellow Kitchen. She'd been surprised by that bit of news when Jax shared it this morning, since she'd assumed the restaurant would be closed for Chase and Lori's rehearsal dinner. According to Jax, the Timberlakes were hosting that event in their home at Heartache Falls. With so many people in town for the wedding, they wanted the restaurant available to accommodate the visitors.

"Ali took my reservation when I called," he'd told Claire. "When I told her I was taking you out on our first date, she said she'd give us her best table."

"That was nice of her."

"That's what I told her. She said she's always happy to further the cause of romance."

Claire had almost challenged him on the word "romance." After all, a fling did not a romance make. The opportunity passed when Nicholas came running downstairs in a panic because he'd forgotten to study his spelling words and the test was that morning. Jax had calmed him down and quizzed him, and Nicholas had sailed through the list, stumbling only on one of the words. "Remember, '*i* before *e*, except after *c*,' big guy."

Nicholas had hit his head with the palm of his hand and said, "D'oh!"

Then the pair traded lines from *The Simpsons* TV show until Claire and Nicholas left for school.

She smiled at the memory of the exchange throughout the day. The more time she spent with Jax, the more she liked him. He was such a good dad, and his doubts about that only made him more endearing. He was smart and witty and hardworking. Sexy. My oh my, the man was sexy.

Which was why after her shower, she spent a ridiculous amount of time choosing which body lotion to smooth onto her skin.

She had plenty from which to choose. Claire liked fragrances. Luxurious body lotions were one of her personal indulgences. Ordinarily, she chose her scents by what mood she was in. Tonight, she had Jax on her mind as she surveyed her selection. Would he like spicy? Floral? Exotic? Something heavy? Light? Which would make her feel good? Pretty? Sexy?

For her mistletoe fling.

Her teeth nibbled at her lower lip. Was she really going to do this? She'd never had a fling before, never gone to bed with a man unless they were in a committed relationship.

As far as you knew at the time, anyway.

Yeah, well, she wasn't going to think about the Lying Lizard Louse tonight now, was she?

She chose a fragrance that made her think of summer nights in Hong Kong and slathered her skin with lotion and pulled on a robe before facing her closet. Deciding what to wear proved to be a significant challenge. Only a couple pieces of the limited wardrobe she'd brought with her to Eternity Springs had survived smoke damage in the fire, and when she'd sat down and ordered an entire new wardrobe from her favorite retailer, she'd gone a little overboard with "date night" clothes. This was Eternity Springs, after all. With winter just around the corner. She didn't have much use for little black dresses and four-inch heels when there were four inches of snow on the ground.

So why did she have three of them hanging in her closet?

"Too much mistletoe," she murmured as she debated between an off-the-shoulder gold blouse that brought out the streaks of summer sunshine in her hair or a green V-neck with an after-five plunge. She finally settled on the green blouse and her black silk bolero pants and chose filmy, emerald-green silk lingerie to wear beneath them.

She finished dressing, touched up her lipstick, then turned toward Tinsel. "Well, sweetheart. How do I look?"

Tinsel's ears perked up and she abandoned her chew toy to come stand at Claire's feet. "I'll take that as a positive response."

Claire took the puppy outside for one more potty break, then tucked her into her crate with a rubber chew toy stuffed with peanut butter and settled down to wait for Jax. She'd heard him leave with Nicholas half an hour ago. He should be back soon.

The ringing of the doorbell a few minutes later initially surprised her, but then she smiled. *He's treating this like we aren't living together.* The gesture made her feel special.

Excitement hummed through her as she took one last glance in the mirror. She wiped her suddenly damp palms on her slacks, reminded herself that flings were meant to be enjoyed, and opened the door saying, "Good evening . . . oh."

Two strangers stood on the front porch of Mama Bear. Both were in their sixties, she'd guess. Both were handsome people, both expensively dressed. The expression on their faces was as confused as hers. "Can I help you?"

The man spoke first. "I'm afraid we've taken a wrong turn. We were looking for Three Bears Valley?"

"This is Three Bears."

"Oh. Well." They shared an unreadable look, then the man said, "We were told our grandson is living here?"

"You're Nicholas's grandparents?"

"Yes. I'm Brian Hardcastle. This is my wife, Linda."

"I'm Claire Branham." She stepped back, opening the door wide. "Please, come in."

They stepped inside Mama Bear and both made a quick scan of the room. Linda's voice held a note of censure in her tone as she asked, "Our grandson is living with you?"

"Yes, he is." Claire recognized that the optics here weren't good, but she didn't figure it was her place to explain it. So she said, "Jax will be here in a few minutes. May I take your coats?"

"Thank you," Brian said.

He helped his wife off with hers, and when he handed both coats over to Claire, she added, "May I get you something to drink? Something to warm you up, perhaps? It's chilly out this evening."

"No, thank you," Linda said.

At the same time, Brian said, "I'd love a cup of coffee."

Claire could have kissed him, so grateful was she for his having provided an excuse to flee the room. Thank goodness Mama Bear's floor plan wasn't "open" with the kitchen part of the great room like Papa Bear's and Baby Bear's. "Please make yourselves at home, and I'll be right back with your coffee."

She hung up their coats and retreated to the kitchen

where she instantly regretted not detouring by the mantel where she'd left her phone. Jax should have a heads-up that he had company.

It was obviously a surprise visit. A surprise visit with impeccably poor timing from her point of view. Nothing like having former in-laws pop in for a first date.

She delayed her return to the living room as long as she could manage by putting together a plate of cookies. She placed it, along with Brian Hardcastle's coffee and paper napkins, on a serving tray and carried it into her guests.

She almost dropped it when Brian demanded, "So, what's going on here? You're shacked up with our grandson's father? That's a damned poor example for the boy. How long has this been going on? Did he bring you with him from Seattle?"

Claire was saved from answering because halfway through the man's diatribe, the door opened and Jax stepped into the room. Claire had never been so happy to see someone in her life.

He wore a dress coat and a suit, and he looked so handsome that under other circumstances, he'd have set her heart aflutter. The thunderous scowl on his face distracted her from everything else, even the bright bouquet of flowers he set down on the entry table.

"That's enough, Brian," he snapped, his voice as cold as a snowdrift. "You've stepped way over the line."

"Oh, have I? Have I really? Nice flowers, Lancaster. Where's my grandson?"

His arms at his sides, Jax fisted his hands. "Claire," he began.

"Excuse me," Claire said. "I hear my dog crying. I should run up to my room and check on her."

"A dog?" Linda asked, aghast. "You've forced Nicholas to live with a dog?"

Oh, for heaven's sake.

Claire heard the echo of her mother's voice. *If you can't say something nice, don't say anything at all.* She continued upstairs without responding to Nicholas's grandmother.

There, she sat on the edge of her bed and waited. She heard raised voices downstairs, but she didn't try to eavesdrop. She was too busy brooding. She was so disappointed. She'd been looking forward to their date so much, and now it was ruined. The fact that she was thinking about herself right now made her feel small and petty and mean.

This was one night. Her date. Her fling. It was Jax and Nicholas's life.

"Pity parties are so unattractive," she muttered aloud.

Finally, she heard the front door open and close, and moments later, car doors slammed and an engine started. She waited a few minutes before opening her bedroom door in case Jax needed time to settle himself.

She was surprised to find the great room empty. *He's probably in the kitchen raiding the above-the-refrigerator liquor cabinet and pouring himself an extra-tall bourbon on the rocks.*

She'd taken two steps toward the kitchen when the doorbell rang for the second time that night. "What now?" she murmured. Had the Hardcastles forgotten their coats?

She considered darting back upstairs to hide, but sympathy for Jax stopped her. She noticed that the flowers were missing just as she reached for the doorknob.

Jax stood on porch, the flowers in his hand, an easy smile on his face and a determined glint in his eyes. "Hello, gorgeous. Sorry I'm a little late. I was temporarily held up by a little unimportant family business."

So he thought to pretend that she hadn't been party to the drama of the past twenty minutes? "I appreciate the effort, but that didn't sound like unimportant family business to me, Jax."

"I have a first date with a fascinating woman tonight. I'm not going to let uninvited visitors spoil it. Tomorrow is soon enough for that drama."

He sounded so certain that Claire's heart soared. He wasn't going to allow their date to be ruined. *Works for me.*

Playing along, she said, "Not a problem. I was running a little late myself. Would you like to come in and have a drink before we go?"

"Absolutely."

He stepped inside and handed her the bouquet. "For you."

"Thank you. They're beautiful. I love peonies. Would you like to fix the drinks while I put these in a vase?"

"Happy to. What's your preference?"

"Whatever you're having is fine."

She all but floated into the kitchen. When she returned a few minutes later with a vase filled with flowers, he was pouring drinks into a pair of crystal martini glasses. "How many olives?"

Might as well go wild. "Three, please."

He handed her a vodka martini with three olives and lifted his in a toast. "To mistletoe."

Her pulse went thud-a-thump and her mouth went dry.

He held her gaze over the top of his glass as they sipped their drinks. "Mmmm . . ." Claire said. "I haven't had one of these in a long time. I'd forgotten how delicious they are."

She licked her lips, and he abruptly set down his drink. "Okay, that's all I can take. I tried, Claire. I really tried."

Then he dragged her beneath the mistletoe and kissed her senseless.

Jax had intended to treat this evening like a real first date, which to him meant holding off for a good-night kiss.

He'd been prepared to resist the pull of her beauty, but that sensuous slide of her tongue across her full, moist lips defeated resolutions already weakened by his confrontation with Brian.

Right this moment, he needed something positive to offset the negative looming tomorrow and, as usual, Claire Branham supplied it. In spades.

"I feel so lucky to have met you," he told her when the kiss finally ended.

"That's an incredibly nice thing to say, Jax."

"You make me feel pretty incredible." He released her and took a step backward. "Shall we go to dinner?"

He left the words "while we still can" unspoken.

"Sure."

They chatted about inconsequential things during the drive into town. Upon their arrival at the restaurant, they visited a few minutes with Brick, who introduced Jax to his father, Mark Callahan, and Mark's wife, Annabelle, before being seated at their table.

After their waiter took their orders, conversation turned to tomorrow's big event—Chase and Lori's wedding. "I'm looking forward to it," Jax said. "I've been hearing about this special wedding cake ever since we moved to town."

"Maggie Romano's Italian cream cake. It's become quite a tradition for weddings, not to mention the adult-only cakewalk that's part of the school fund-raising festival. I think this year they're talking about selling tickets to watch the competition. It's become quite the brawl."

Jax smiled. "This is the first time I've lived in a small town. I wonder, are all these traditions common in small towns everywhere or is Eternity Springs special?"

Claire sipped her wine. "Eternity Springs is definitely

special, but I don't know about other small towns. This is my first, too."

Over their entrées, they talked about places where they'd lived and then places they'd visited. He'd grown up in Arizona, gone to college in California, and traveled the world in the navy. She'd been born and raised in Dallas, attended college in Austin, and her foreign travel was limited to one European trip during high school. It was an appropriate get-to-know-you-better first-date conversation that gave Jax new insight into Miss Christmas. "Dallas, hmm? How did a city girl come to choose Eternity Springs for her new home and business?"

Claire hesitated. She lifted her napkin and wiped her mouth and Jax thought she might deflect the question. She surprised him.

"After I discovered the truth about a certain Lying Lizard Louse, I basically ran away from home. I ended up in this little town about two hours west of Fort Worth, and I needed a potty break and gas for my car. In the bathroom at the minimart, I had a bit of a meltdown." She paused and searched and found a smile. "It was my good luck that a biker gang had pulled in right behind me."

Jax did a double take. "A biker gang?"

She nodded, and a sparkle entered her eyes. "I was sobbing my heart out in the ladies' room, and one of the riders walked inside and took me in her arms and rocked me like a baby."

"Wait a minute." Jax held up his index finger, making a point. "I think I know where this is going. Did this particular biker woman dress in white and gold leathers and drive a Honda Gold Wing?"

"Got it in one. Celeste was riding with a group of friends she'd made while visiting the Callahan ranch in Brazos Bend. She asked me what was wrong, and I started blabbering—surprise, surprise. Seems to be a habit of mine. I still don't know how she managed to get me to tag along to lunch with the group, but before I knew it I was sitting in a little country diner having chicken-fried steak."

"Cream gravy? Fried okra and mashed potatoes, too?"

"Yes."

"Wait a minute, Claire. We should have a moment of reverential silence."

"Seriously, Lancaster? You just plowed away enough pasta to feed a high school cross-country team."

"Yes, and it was delicious. The Yellow Kitchen has more than lived up to its reputation. However, I haven't had chicken-fried steak and cream gravy since I was in college. It was a religious experience."

Claire gave a little laugh. "Well, my meal at Mary's Café was delicious, but I'd classify it as therapeutic rather than religious. Celeste somehow managed to pry the low points of my woebegone love life from me, and show me a path forward if I were brave enough to take it. That woman has an uncanny way of saying just what you need to hear when you need to hear it."

"She convinced you to move to Eternity Springs?"

"Nothing that direct. She talked up the town, though. She mentioned that she thought a Christmas shop would do well here, and that planted the seed. She said something else that resonated in me."

"Oh, yeah? What was that?"

"It sounds a little woo-woo, but remember, we're talking about Celeste. She told me that the way out of the darkness was to discover my own inner light and let it shine. I took that to heart. It took me a little while to get my light lit, and frankly, it still flickers from time to time, but I'm making progress."

"Well, if it's any consolation, from my perspective your light is high-voltage."

"That's a lovely thing to say, Jax," Claire said, beaming.

"It's true." He wanted to ask her for more details about her relationship with old quadruple L and the "truth" that had sent her running away from home, but he reminded himself that this was a first date, and the conversation had taken a serious turn. Better to lighten it back up.

So he asked her what kind of music she liked, then after their server brought dessert—chocolate cake to share—she asked him what exotic foods he'd sampled during his travels. That conversation lasted until the plates had been cleared, and as they sipped one final cup of decaf, talk turned to Forever Christmas and her plans for her upcoming reception unveiling the Twelve Dogs of Christmas ornaments. "By the way, Nicholas made his final layaway payment for his Captain ornament last week."

"He told me. He says you're holding it for him until we put up a Christmas tree."

She lifted the coffee cup in toast. "Thinking positive."

So was Jax. He was positively rethinking his decision about his approach to the end of this first date.

On the drive back to Three Bears Valley, she asked him about life aboard a submarine, and he shared a couple of the more amusing stories. Her laughter was a welcome sound that Jax couldn't help but compare to the tight-lipped, angry response that any mention of the navy invariably elicited from Lara.

When he pulled the car to a stop in front of Mama Bear, the easy mood evaporated. Tension hummed between them. Claire reached for her door release and Jax said, "Wait. Let me come around."

She grinned up at him when he extended his hand to help her out of the car. "Opening the door for a lady, Jax? A little old-fashioned, aren't you?"

"I'm Navy."

"An officer and a gentleman?"

"I'm trying, Claire," he told her honestly. He didn't release her hand. "You make it difficult."

That shut her up. They didn't speak as they climbed the steps toward the front door.

The porch light cast a soft yellow glow across the portal. Claire's shoulders lifted as she sucked in an audible breath, then exhaled a little giggle. "Okay, this is a little weird. I'm not sure of the rules here. Do I ask you in, even though you live here? This is my first mistletoe fling."

Her obvious nervousness was just the push he'd needed. "Don't be nervous, Miss Christmas." He drew her into his arms. "The nice thing about having a mistletoe fling is that we get to make up the rules as we go along. As much as I'd like to dive into Christmas morning, I think it's only fair to us both to have a bit of an Advent, don't you?"

She blinked. "You don't want . . . ?"

"Oh, I want, Claire. I want very, very much. But this was our first date. As much as it pains me to say this, I think first dates should end with a kiss. Don't you?"

Her smile dawned slowly, but its brilliance lit up the night. "I do."

Jax set about to give her a first-date kiss to remember. He figured he must have succeeded because when he finally lifted his head, she stood stupefied until he reached past her and opened the door. "Good night, Claire."

"Oh. Um, good night, Jax. I had a lovely time."

"I did, too."

"Okay, well. I guess I'll . . . um . . . see you in the morning?"

"Yes. I'll see you in the morning, though I expect I'll dream of you tonight."

It was as good an exit line as he'd managed in a very long time, so he turned and left. He was halfway to his destination when she called out. "Jax? Where are you going?"

"To jump in the ice-cold creek."

Her laughter rang out upon the night like a song.

Chapter Fourteen

Mistletoe, mistletoe, and more mistletoe.
—CLAIRE

Saturday morning dawned clear and crisp and gorgeous. As Jax drove into town to pick up Nicholas after his sleepover, he noticed the heavier-than-normal bustling of both vehicle and pedestrian traffic. Lots of visitors in town for the big wedding, he guessed. Wonder if Brian and Linda had had trouble finding a place to stay.

The argument yesterday had been intense. Jax had seen red when he'd heard Brian attacking Claire, and for a few minutes there, he'd come close to throwing a punch. He might have done it, too, if not for dinner reservations for the date. He'd wanted the Hardcastles out of the way fast, and he'd known that decking Brian wasn't the way to accomplish that. Making an appointment to meet them first thing Saturday morning with Nicholas was, so that's what he'd done.

He rang the doorbell at the Cicero home and visited with Rose and her husband for a few moments before hustling Nicholas toward the car. Ordinarily, coaxing his son away from his friends would have taken effort, but Nicholas knew they'd be picking up Captain for his visit to Three Bears, so he was ready to go.

"Did you call Mr. Chase, Dad?" the boy asked as he

climbed into Jax's truck and fastened his seat belt. "Does he know we are on our way?"

"I talked to him. We've had a bit of a change of plans. Instead of you and me driving up to the Timberlakes' house to get him, Chase's dad is bringing Captain to us in town. I have another surprise for you. Guess who has come to visit you?"

"Who?"

"Your grandparents."

"Really?"

"Really. We're meeting them for breakfast at Angel's Rest."

"Cool. Except I already ate breakfast. Miss Rose made us pancakes."

"Your grandfather said something about cinnamon rolls."

"I can always eat cinnamon rolls."

"That's what I figured."

They arrived at Angel's Rest five minutes early for their eight-thirty appointment, and as Jax parked his truck, he spied the Hardcastles already waiting on the front porch of the resort's main structure, Cavanaugh House.

"There they are," Nicholas said. He scrambled down from the truck and took off running toward his grandparents.

Jax watched the reunion with mixed emotions. Obviously, Lara's parents loved his son, and Nicholas returned that emotion. It was in the boy's best interests for Jax and the Hardcastles to reach some sort of peace between them.

Upon spying Nicholas, the Hardcastles rose from their seats and descended the porch steps.

Nicholas ran into his grandparents' arms. "Mimi! Pops! I didn't know you were coming."

"We wanted it to be a surprise," Linda said to the boy.

Brian extended his hand toward Jax. "Good morning, Lancaster."

"Brian."

"Thanks for coming," Brian added as the two men exchanged a handshake.

"I said I'd be here."

"Guess what?" Nicholas broke in. "I'm taking care of Captain while Mr. Chase is on his wedding vacation. Remember Captain? He's Mr. Chase's dog who I made friends with during camp. I get him today because Mr. Chase and Dr. Lori are getting married later. Dad and I are going to the wedding. I got new clothes to wear because I've outgrown my other dress-up clothes. Captain isn't going to be at the wedding. He's going to stay at Three Bears with Tinsel. Tinsel is Miss Claire's dog. She let me pick out her name. I help take care of her, but I'm not in charge of Tinsel. I'm gonna be in charge of Captain. I have to feed him and make sure he has water. Dad says he can sleep in my room, but he's not allowed to sleep in my bed."

When the boy finally stopped to catch a breath, his grandmother laughed. Brian said, "Sounds like you're happy here, Nicholas."

"I love it here. I have three new best friends and a bunch of regular friends. Guess what? I scored a goal at soccer practice yesterday! Can I have a cinnamon roll now? Daddy said we're having cinnamon rolls."

"I'm sorry, Nicholas, but the bakery is closed today, and I wasn't able to get any cinnamon rolls. However, Ms. Blessing has coffee cake for us. I sneaked a bite. It's very good."

"Cake for breakfast? Cool!"

Brian met Jax's gaze. "The dining room is full, but we have a table reserved on the upper verandah, if that's all right with you."

"That's fine."

"Is Mr. Timberlake on his way with Captain now, Dad? I don't think Miss Celeste allows dogs upstairs."

"You have time to eat coffee cake with your grandparents before Captain arrives. You'll be able to watch for him from the verandah."

Linda and Nicholas led the way, and when Jax started to follow, Brian stopped him with a hand on his arm. "If I could have a minute, Lancaster?"

Expecting another attack, Jax braced himself. "Sure."

"I owe you an apology."

If he'd declared he was a Martian, Jax wouldn't have been more surprised. In his experience, Brian Hardcastle didn't apologize for anything.

"I was out of line last night. I'm sorry I gave Ms. Branham a hard time."

"You owe her the apology."

"I know," Brian said with a wince. "I intend to see to that before we leave town."

"Good."

Brian stuck his hands into his pants pockets and rocked back on his heels, his expression earnest. "I want this to be a good visit, Jax. Can we start over?"

Brian Hardcastle was treating Jax with a deference he'd never shown before, and Jax didn't quite know what to make of it. "Sure. We'd better catch up with Nicholas and Linda or the kid will eat our share of coffee cake. He's been a bottomless pit lately."

Up on the verandah, Nicholas chattered on like a magpie while downing two and a half pieces of coffee cake. Jax didn't miss the fact that the Hardcastles asked probing questions of the boy, but he honestly didn't mind. If they'd traveled to Colorado thinking they'd find their grandson unhappy and more emotionally troubled than before, the best way to prove them wrong was to let Nicholas ramble.

Nicholas was telling them about the haunted house Brick Callahan was putting together out at Hummingbird Lake for Halloween. "It's gonna be a haunted pirate ship. My friends Meg and Cari say it's going to be really, really cool. I can't wait."

"A haunted house?" Linda repeated. To Jax, she asked, "Do you think that's something he should be doing?"

Annoyance rolled through Jax's gut. "I think I'm going to take my cues from Nicholas."

"But—"

"There's Captain!" Nicholas said, his voice filled with gleeful excitement. "I've gotta go."

He waited long enough to shovel one last bite of coffee cake into his mouth, then he scrambled from his chair and darted toward the staircase.

"Don't run in the house," Jax called after him.

"Well," Linda said, a bittersweet smile on her face. "He certainly seems to have settled in well here. It also appears he's conquered his cynophobia."

"I think we can pretty much call him cured in that respect," Jax agreed. "He's trying to convince me that he should have a dog of his own."

"That's amazing," Brian said.

Jax met his gaze directly and said, "Eternity Springs is amazing. He's made some progress with regard to Christmas, too."

"Is it the psychologist he's seeing? The one from the camp?"

"Dr. McDermott. Actually, Nicholas hasn't been able to meet with him yet because Dr. McDermott has been on an extended vacation with his wife. He's due back around Thanksgiving. Nicholas has an appointment then."

"So who is he seeing in the meantime?" Brian asked.

"No one," Jax responded, his chin lifted and a defiant gleam in his eyes.

Brian and Linda shared a look, but to Jax's surprise, they didn't attack. So he told them about Claire's reading program and Nicholas's positive response to it. "She owns a Christmas shop in town, and she's having a big event there next week. Nicholas wants to go."

Linda brought her hand to her chest. "To a Christmas shop? Is that advisable, Jax?"

"Nicholas is the one steering the boat here. I take all my cues from him. So far, it seems to be working."

"The change is amazing," Brian said. "And after all the things we tried to do to improve the situation in Seattle. To think that all it took was a small town."

"It took *this* small town," Jax corrected. "And these people."

"Hey, Mimi and Pops!" Nicholas called from below. "Look. This is Captain! Come down and meet him."

Brian signed the tab and the adults went down to join Nicholas. Outside, Jax spied Mac Timberlake speaking to Celeste, and he veered toward them while the Hardcastles joined his son.

"I loaded Captain's bed and some food in the back of your truck, Lancaster."

"Thanks. How's everything going at your place?"

"So far, so good. Chase is Mr. Cool today."

"Good for him."

Jax heard Nicholas call his name. "We're going for a walk, Dad. I'm gonna show Mimi and Pops my school and the park where I play soccer. Want to come?"

"Sure."

Nicholas answered his grandmother's questions about his teacher and his classmates as they strolled toward the footbridge that crossed Angel Creek. They continued down Sixth Street to the school and then on to Davenport Park. After that, Nicholas wanted to show his grandparents the library and Galen's dad's glass studio. "It's really cool, Pops. Mr. Cicero has these ovens and they're super-hot and the glass is all melted and he puts it on a stick and shapes it. He's working on a big project right now, but when he's finished he's going to let me and Galen make something."

"I've heard of Cicero," Linda said. "He's a very talented artist."

"He has long hair like a girl. But I like him. I like Galen's mom, Dr. Rose, too. She made really good pancakes."

Jax tagged along, not really offering much of anything to the conversation, giving Nicholas free rein to wander where he liked. It was a perfect day for a stroll. Eternity Springs buzzed with energy, the streets and shops bustling with visitors in town for the wedding. "Based on the notices in the shop windows, this place is shutting down at noon," Brian observed.

"The wedding is at two," Jax said. "I think they've invited every local resident."

"Miss Claire is closing at noon." Nicholas looked at his father. "I think we should go there now. Mimi and Pops need to meet Miss Claire."

Jax couldn't hide his surprise. "You want to take your grandparents to Forever Christmas?"

Nicholas nodded. "Captain and I can wait outside."

Jax placed his hand on his son's shoulder. "Hot Rod, you might not know this because we never go down that block of Cottonwood. Miss Claire has Christmas trees in pots outside on the sidewalk."

Nicholas sucked in a breath, and for the first time that morning, his tone sounded subdued as he said, "Oh. I didn't know that."

"We can visit your Miss Claire another time," Linda suggested.

"No." Nicholas lifted his chin and he courageously met Jax's gaze. "I can walk down the street."

Jax had a flashback of the last time he'd seen the boy lying in a hospital bed, and he had to bite back a ferocious "No!"

Instead, he reminded himself to take his cues from his son. "All right. We can give it a try. If you change your mind, no harm, no foul."

Brian Hardcastle opened his mouth, but at a sharp look from Jax, shut it without comment. Linda didn't take the hint. "Jax, I don't think—"

"Linda!" Brian interrupted. "Remember . . ."

She listened to her husband, zipped her lips, and followed Nicholas.

The closer they drew to the intersection of Third and Cottonwood, the slower Nicholas walked and the quieter he became. When he fell back to walk beside his father, Jax rested his hand on the boy's shoulder.

The big pots with lighted evergreens that sat on either side of Forever Christmas's front door came into view on the opposite side of the street. Nicholas saw them and stopped. Linda Hardcastle reached for her husband's hand. Jax gave Nicholas's shoulder a reassuring squeeze. "No harm, no foul, buddy."

Nicholas shoved his glasses up on the bridge of his nose, took a deep breath, and said, "It's okay, Dad. I can do this. They are just trees. I can do it."

And darned if he didn't do exactly that.

Nicholas and Captain walked right up to the street lamp across from the Christmas shop, and while Captain sniffed around the base of it, Nicholas's gaze darted toward the big glass display windows where lights twinkled and angels flew and a snowman bowed his top hat. The kid didn't flinch. "Take Mimi and Pops inside, Dad. Captain and I will hang here. I doubt Miss Claire would want Captain running around her shop. He's pretty big."

Grinning, Jax nodded. "I think you're right. Want me to tell Miss Claire you said hi?"

"That'd be good."

"Stay out of the street." Jax motioned toward the Hardcastles. "Shall we?"

As the three adults crossed the street, Brian said, "He's a different boy."

Jax held the door for Linda and as the chimes rang "Jingle Bells," he said, "He's healing. He's getting back to being the boy he used to be."

Claire's welcoming smile upon seeing Jax faded somewhat when she spied who arrived with him. Brian kept his word by rolling out an apology that sounded sincere, and graciously, Claire accepted it before excusing herself to answer another shopper's question. While Jax positioned himself in the book section near a window where he could keep an eye on Nicholas, Linda said, "If we have a few more minutes, I think I'll look around a bit. It truly is a fabulous store."

Brian nodded. "Go ahead. I'll take this opportunity to speak with Jax."

What now? Jax wondered as Brian perused the shelves. "This is quite an excellent selection of books. I'm impressed. Looks like she needs to restock *The Christmas Angel Waiting Room,* though."

Jax shook his head. "Do me a favor and don't bring that up. What is it you want to talk to me about, Brian?"

The older man sighed and rubbed the back of his neck. "Well, first thing I'll say is that it's obvious that this trip to Colorado has been good for the boy. In all honesty, it's not what we expected. You were right and I was wrong."

"Wow," Jax drawled. "I feel like we need a plaque or something to mark this moment."

"I deserve that." Brian exhaled loudly, then added, "I might as well eat the whole crow. Linda and I were wrong to try to take the parenting decisions out of your hands."

At that, Jax's suspicions went on high alert. "What's your game, here, Brian? What do you want from me?"

Hardcastle's gaze shifted toward the window, and Jax watched him watch Nicholas. The older man cleared his throat and said, "We miss him. We came out here hoping to convince you to come home to Seattle."

"Seattle is not my home."

"It can be. I come bearing a job offer."

As Brian reached into the inner pocket of his jacket, Jax shook his head. "I'm not a bookseller, in any way, shape, or form."

"It's not from Hardcastle Books."

He handed over a sealed envelope. Jax recognized the logo in the upper left-hand corner. Boeing.

His breath whooshed from his lungs. He pulled out his pocketknife and slit the envelope open. Removing the three-page offer, he scanned the contents and his heart began to thud. A dream job—in his field. A dream salary. Hell. It was three steps higher than the job he'd originally applied for.

"How did you manage this?"

"I play golf with the CEO."

Jax's mind spun. His pride would prefer that he got a job as a result of his own efforts, but there was truth in the old saying that it wasn't what you knew, but who you knew. The man couldn't have pulled this particular string back in July? Nevertheless, it didn't matter. "I promised Nicholas we would stay here through the end of the school year. I'm not going back on my word."

"Fair enough. It's obvious he's happy here. Believe it or not, Linda and I wouldn't want to do anything to change that. Coming here . . . seeing him . . . seeing the progress he's made . . . we don't want to upset that apple-cart. Check the offer dates, Jax. You have some time."

He scanned the letter once again and located the date on the third page. "July Fourth? It's good to July Fourth?"

"My golf buddy is a patriot. He supports the military. Supports veterans. And, he knew Lara when she was a little girl. He cares about her son."

Wow. As Jax rubbed his hand across his stubbled jaw, his gaze sought and found Claire. Beautiful, sexy, and sweet Miss Christmas.

Miss Eternity Springs.

Damn. He couldn't be a handyman the rest of his life. "I don't know what to say, Brian."

"You don't have to say anything. It's something to have in your back pocket."

"And in return?"

"Nothing. No strings attached. Linda and I recognize that we could have . . . we should have . . . handled the situation better. Like I said, we miss Nicholas. We hope you'll allow us to be part of our grandson's life."

"It's not my intention to keep him from you. I think—"

He broke off when Claire and Linda approached. "Mrs. Hardcastle said you have a surprise for me?"

"I do. Actually, though, it's Nicholas who has the surprise. Take a look." Jax motioned toward the window and Claire's face lit up. Seeing that Nicholas was looking their way, she waved. The boy waved back. "He wanted his grandparents to meet you."

"He's looking into the shop, Jax."

"I know. Isn't it great? I think I've figured out what this is about. He's working up to attend the big event next week. I'll bet you money."

"The Dog Room," Claire said. "That does make sense. He's asked a lot of questions about it."

At Linda's quizzical look, Claire explained about the

Twelve Dogs of Christmas ornaments and described the special display of all things pet-and-Christmas-related that she planned to unveil during a reception the following week. "I want to go out and say hi to him. Jax, would you watch the shop for a few minutes for me?"

"Sure."

The Hardcastles accompanied Claire, and Jax watched through the window as his son began speaking animatedly to his grandparents and Claire. Idly, he reached out and ran his finger along the wing made of feathers on an angel ornament hanging on the Christmas tree decorating the window. He recognized that he needed to readjust his thinking where his former in-laws were concerned.

They'd done him a solid when they stepped up and cared for Nicholas when Jax couldn't get free of his contract to the navy. He didn't often think about it from their point of view. It couldn't have been easy for them. Healthy six-year-olds were a lot of work. A child like Nicholas who suffered nightmares and panic attacks and instances of inconsolable crying had been exponentially more work. But Brian and Linda never hesitated. They'd stepped up and given him a home and loved him—even in the depths of their grief over the loss of their beloved only daughter.

Nicholas was all they had left of Lara. Since Jax's parents were deceased, the Hardcastles were the only grandparents his son had. They didn't threaten the boy's health or safety or security. They no longer threatened Jax's relationship with his son. He needed to let go of the anger that he'd nursed since the hypnosis debacle and welcome them back into his son's life.

Claire returned to the shop with her eyes sparkling. "Your son is spectacular."

"I know. I'm so proud of him."

"Looks like he's soothed the grandparent waters, too.

The last thing I expected was for Mr. Hardcastle to walk in here and apologize."

Jax smirked. "Must be that Eternity Springs mojo at work."

"Must be."

"So, you're closing at noon? We'll see you at home shortly afterward?"

"That's my plan, but if you need to spend more time with Nicholas's grandparents, I'll certainly understand. I can find my way to the church by myself."

"Nope. We're not missing the wedding. I suffered through the trauma of buying the boy new dress clothes, new shoes, and getting him a haircut in preparation for Chase and Dr. Lori's wedding. We're not missing it." He leaned down and kissed her cheek. "I'll see you in a couple of hours."

Jax rejoined Nicholas and the Hardcastles, and they continued their walking tour of Eternity Springs, ending back at Angel's Rest. There, Nicholas grabbed a tennis ball from Captain's box of toys, removed the retriever from his leash, and he and his grandfather began taking turns throwing the ball.

Linda took a seat on a park bench to watch the action. Jax sat atop a four-foot rock wall that divided Celeste's contemplation garden from the open area where the boy and dog played. The silence between them was comfortable enough, so when Linda finally spoke, he wasn't expecting an attack. "You and Lara never suited."

Jax almost groaned out loud. It was always one step forward, two steps back with the Hardcastles.

"Her father always put her up on a pedestal, and right or wrong, she needed the same from the man in her life. You expected more from her, and she couldn't make that jump."

Jax couldn't argue with that, so he kept his mouth shut.

"I think she could have been happy with James," Linda continued, "but the miscarriage damaged her. I don't know if it was hormonal or emotional or a combination of the two, but she wasn't thinking right. I told her to seek help, but I blame myself for not following through, not making sure it happened. As a result, I overcompensated where Nicholas is concerned."

"It's not your fault, Linda. Or Brian's. In the end, it wasn't even Lara's fault. In her right mind, she never would have done anything to put Nicholas at risk."

"She was a good mother."

"She was a fabulous mother. I remember how great she was with Nicholas when he was a colicky infant. I would be tired and frustrated and at my wit's end, and she always stayed calm and collected. That is the Lara I'm going to try to remember from now on. That's the Lara I plan to share with Nicholas as he grows up."

"You are a good man, Jax. I know that Brian apologized, but I need to do so, too. I'm so sorry, Jax. You and Lara might not have been right for each other long-term, but I think you must have been meant-to-be for a time in order to give this world Nicholas. You and my daughter created a fabulous, special child. Seeing him today so happy and engaged has been so reassuring. You're a good father, Jax."

"Thank you, Linda. I appreciate your saying that." He focused on the rush and bubble of Angel Creek and thought of his ex-wife without resentment for the first time in a very long time. "Nicholas is lucky to have you and Brian. I've been lucky that Nicholas has you. Claire told me recently that Eternity Springs is a great place for making fresh starts. What do you say we give it a try?"

"I think that's a fabulous idea."

"In that case, do you and Brian have plans for Thanksgiving? Claire and I have already made plans to cook for a few friends. If you and Brian would like to join us, we'd love to have you."

Tears flooded her eyes and she gave him a tremulous smile. "We'd like that very much. Your Claire wouldn't mind?"

He didn't correct her "your" reference. He certainly thought of Claire as his at this point. "I'll check with her, but I'm sure she'd want Nicholas to share the holiday with his grandparents."

"She's a lovely woman, Jax. I can tell that she cares about both you and Nicholas."

"She is. She does. We like her very much."

"I'm glad, Jax. I want you both to be happy."

"We're getting there." His gaze shifted in the general direction of Forever Christmas. If Nicholas managed to conquer his fear to the point where he could enter the store, Jax would change that from "getting" to "almost" there.

"One other thing I might mention," Linda said. "Brian and I recognize how difficult it is to be a single parent. If you ever want a break, if you ever need a babysitter, I hope you'll consider us. We'd be happy to fly in for a long weekend, or even bring Nicholas out to Seattle, if you think that would be good for him. I promise we'd be careful with him, and we'd follow all your wishes."

Jax considered her. At this point, he wouldn't have any reservations about allowing Nicholas to spend some time with his grandparents and without him. Fresh starts, and all. "That's quite an offer, Linda. Quite a timely offer. Nicholas has a Friday and Monday off from school the first week in November. Teacher in-service days. Shall we ask him if he'd like to visit Seattle?"

"Nothing would make me happier."

The prospect of four days alone with Claire made Jax pretty darn happy, too.

Chapter Fifteen

*Whoever invented teacher in-service
days needs a raise.*
—JAX

Claire attended Lori and Chase's wedding and reception with Jax and Nicholas. The ceremony was lovely, the party fun.

Before the father-daughter dance, Cam Murphy made a speech about love and the power of perseverance that brought everyone to tears. Chase gave a public tribute to his mother that made every woman in the room a little wistful. Later in the evening, Claire discovered that Jax was quite the dancer, and following a discussion about Texas red dirt music with Brick and Devin Murphy, Jax had joined in with Daniel Garrett to sing a few old Willie Nelson tunes. She discovered he had quite a voice, too. Celebration, laughter, and joy proved to be quite the mood lifter, and by the time the bride and groom departed Angel's Rest to begin their honeymoon in Tibet, she had a whole chapter's worth of positive thoughts to record in her journal.

The Hardcastles departed Eternity Springs for their return trip to Seattle following a Sunday-afternoon picnic at Hummingbird Lake. That night, after Nicholas's bedtime stories, Claire and Jax shared their first time alone since their Friday-night date.

He caught her beneath a sprig of mistletoe that hadn't

been hanging from the kitchen doorway threshold when she'd gone upstairs to read "'Twas the Night Before Christmas."

After kissing her senseless, Jax said, "Claire, have you ever been to Silver Eden Resort?"

"No, I haven't. I've heard it's fabulous, though."

"I happen to have a voucher for a two-night stay at Silver Eden, part of a swag bag that was given to parents of Rocking L campers. Nicholas is going to Seattle for a long weekend the first weekend in November. It's a perfect opportunity to put the fling in our mistletoe. How about it, Claire? Would you go away with me for the weekend? I thought I'd make a reservation in the name of Stamina Sven."

Claire's heart began to thud. A long weekend at a romantic resort? Heck yes! "I'd love that, Jax."

"You can get someone to cover for you at the shop?"

"I'll just close it for the weekend." She could do that. She was the boss. "I'll look forward to the trip, Sven. Thanks for the invite."

They exchanged another long kiss beneath the mistletoe, and she had a difficult time going to sleep that night. Luckily, prep work for the Chamber of Commerce event scheduled the following week kept her busy during the days, so she didn't waste too much time in daydreams. The evenings were a long, slow sexual-tension build, held in check by the presence of a third-grade chaperone.

Each evening, she continued to read to Nicholas, and with every day that passed, he seemed a little more comfortable with the subject matter. He walked by the shop on two separate occasions. A third time, he actually crossed the street and walked right past her Christmas tree pots just as a customer opened the door to exit the shop.

He went a little pale at the sound of the jingle-bell chimes, but he didn't run away. Claire was so proud of him.

On Thursday night, he asked about the upcoming chamber event. "Are you really going to have a whole room in your shop for dog stuff, Miss Claire? A room like your Angel Room?"

"Yes. I'm calling it the Christmas Doghouse."

Nicholas giggled. "That's funny. Isn't that funny, Dad?"

"I think I've been there before," Jax drawled, a teasing glint in his eyes. "So which of the rooms are you using for your Doghouse?"

"One of the ones upstairs. I've noticed that some of my customers hesitate to go up there, and I think the Doghouse will draw them up."

"Good thinking. You have a knack for retail, Claire. Which room are you using? The living room?"

"No." She hesitated a moment before confessing, "My bedroom."

Jax grinned. "Is there some symbolism in that choice, Miss Christmas?"

"Only square-footage concerns, Mr. Lancaster," she replied. "It's the largest room upstairs, and I have lots of merchandise to display."

"Is it all set up already?" Nicholas asked.

"It's about half done. I hope to finish up on Sunday afternoon while the shop is closed."

"I sure would like to see it," Nicholas said, a wistful look on his face.

Claire patted his hand. "When I get it all set up, I'll take pictures. I'll show them to you if you'd like."

"Maybe." He picked up one of the Christmas books she'd left lying on the foot of his bed and flipped through it. "All the kids at school are going to the party. Galen says Mrs. Murphy is baking cookies for you shaped like dog paws."

"Yes, she is." Claire shared a quick look with Jax. "You know, Nicholas, you're welcome to visit the shop any time you'd like, but things are going to be pretty crazy around there Tuesday night. I could give you a sneak peek once it's all set up if you want to try it."

He shrugged. "Is there really going to be a dog parade? Galen said so. He said all the dogs who are on ornaments are going to be in a parade wearing costumes. I said I don't think that's true because I'm in charge of Captain and Captain's on an ornament and I haven't heard anything about a parade. And what about Mortimer? I don't think it's a good idea to let him go inside Forever Christmas."

"Twelve dogs in Forever Christmas? The very idea makes me shudder. No, Nicholas. Galen is mistaken about that. We're not having a parade. The dogs will be there in ornaments, only. Well, except for Tinsel, of course."

"Is *she* going to wear a costume?"

Claire tilted her head and considered the answer. "I don't know. I've considered it, but honestly, I have too many too cute costumes to pick from." Casually, she said, "Would you like to help me choose? I could bring the possibilities home tomorrow night."

"Sure. We could try that."

Later when Jax came downstairs after his part of storytime, Claire handed him his glass of wine and lifted hers in toast. "Here's to progress."

They clinked glasses. "He wants it. That's a big part of the battle, I think."

"I have a large selection of Tinsel-sized dog costumes from which to choose. They run the gamut from innocuous to five-alarm Christmas. What do you think I should bring?"

"Bring 'em all. I have a sneaking feeling that he's going to show up at your reception on Tuesday night."

"From your mouth to an angel's ears," Claire said.

After closing the shop the following day, Claire filled a bag with a variety of costumes for Tinsel. Had she really purchased twelve different costumes for dogs ten pounds and below? "Ridiculous, Branham."

Although she'd bet that Sage Rafferty would buy seven or eight of them for her Snowdrop.

She arrived back at Three Bears Valley to find Jax on a ladder at Baby Bear, adjusting the downspout of a gutter. She took a moment to appreciate the view of worn jeans stretched tight across a firm butt. "Tinsel, the first week in November can't get here soon enough."

As she and Tinsel exited the car, Captain rounded the corner of Mama Bear, a big rawhide bone in his mouth. Jax waved and descended the ladder. He met her with a toe-curling kiss. "You're home early."

"I wanted to get home before Nicholas. He's still at soccer practice, isn't he?"

Jax checked his watch. "It ends about now. Cicero is driving him home."

"Good. I'd like you to look at these costumes. Weed any out that you think might be too much for him."

"Okay."

He asked her about her day as he and both dogs followed her up the steps into Mama Bear and on into the kitchen. While he washed his hands, she spread the costumes out on the kitchen table. Jax dried his hands on a dishtowel and surveyed the stack. He checked the Forever Christmas price tag on the reindeer costume at the top of pile and shook his head. "Seventeen dollars? Seriously? People will pay that for a dog costume?"

"It's cute. It has matching reindeer antlers."

"People have more money than sense, I swear."

"How do you think Nicholas will react to them?"

Jax flipped through the stack. "Honestly, I don't have a clue. I don't know what to expect from him at this point. The only thing that gives me pause is the jingle bell necklace."

"I know." Claire bit at her bottom lip. "I debated even bringing that one home."

"Still, I hate to underestimate him. The door chimes didn't faze him. I say keep the bells in there and see how it goes. The 'take our cues from Nicholas' approach seems to be working all right."

"Okay."

She returned the costumes to the bag and then suddenly found herself backed up against the kitchen cabinets. His hands on her hips, Jax stared down into her face, a now-familiar wicked glint in his eyes. "Fifteen days, Miss Christmas."

She smoothed her hands across his chest, the soft, well-worn flannel of his shirt a sharp contrast to the hard, unyielding muscles of his chest. She wanted to purr. "I know."

"It seems like forever."

"I know. I looked at their Web site today during lunch. They have a spa that makes the one at Angel's Rest look spartan."

"Oh, yeah?" He was staring at her mouth. "We'll have to check it out."

"The massages looked interesting."

He arched a brow. "I think you're already booked for massages with Sven."

"Oh? He does massage, too?"

"Honey, Sven will massage anything you want, for however long you want. As many times as you want."

She blinked. Twice. And blushed red as Santa's suit.

Jax laughed then closed his mouth over hers in a

steamy kiss that ended only when the bark of the dogs alerted them to an approaching vehicle. "The anticipation may be the death of me."

"I know . . ." Claire moaned. "You know, Jax, I do close the shop for lunch breaks. While the children are in school."

"Miss Christmas, I'm shocked, I say. Are you proposing a nooner?"

"I . . . uh . . . that's not the term I'd use."

"Oh? Do tell."

"Well . . . how about . . ." She licked her lips slowly. "Rendezvous?"

"French. Brings to mind French maids. Claire, you have all those costumes . . . what do you have in adult sizes?"

She trailed a finger down the center of his chest. He sucked in his gut reflexively when she reached his navel. "I do have a closet you might want to peruse sometime during the next two weeks. It's in the second bedroom of the old apartment. I keep it locked. You can ask for the key."

As Nicholas's footsteps pounded on the porch, Jax grabbed her finger and nipped it. "You play to win, Miss Christmas."

"Always," she said lightly, though it took effort to maintain the tone. As much as she enjoyed this long seduction, it was killing her, too.

Especially since this fling had taken on the sense of being something more serious.

Jax released Claire's hand and took a step backward as Nicholas burst into the kitchen. "I'm home. I'm starving! Do we have cake? I want cake."

"I want to win the lottery, too," Jax replied. "Guess we will both have to settle for fruit."

"Fruit! Ah, Dad. We ran laps today. I should get something better than fruit."

"It's pizza night. You know the rules."

"Pizza!" Without further argument, Nicholas ran to the fruit bowl and grabbed a banana and an apple. He sat in his usual chair and eyed the bag sitting in the middle of the kitchen table. "What's that?"

Mindful of his previous reaction to her red-and-green logo bags, she'd used an unmarked trash bag for her booty. "I brought home costumes for Tinsel."

"Oh." He contemplated the bag as he ate his banana.

"Want to talk about school, Hot Rod? How did you do on your math test?"

"Good. I'm sure I aced it. I suck at soccer, though."

"Language, boyo," his father cautioned.

"Sorry. I don't like bouncing the ball off my head and I keep forgetting I'm not supposed to use my hands. I'll be glad when soccer is over. I want to do basketball."

"Didn't you score a goal recently?" Claire asked, "I think you're probably better than you give yourself credit for."

Nicholas shrugged. "I'm still ready for basketball to start."

"It won't be long now," Jax said.

"November tenth. Right when I come back from visiting Mimi and Pops. I saw Coach Lucca at school and he told me." He shot them a wicked grin and added, "I caught him smooching on Mrs. Lucca when I delivered a note for the principal to the kindergarten room."

"Oops," Claire said.

"Mrs. Lucca had a message for you, Dad. She said that Holly would finish her CPR class this weekend, so she'll be ready to start babysitting. What's CPR, Daddy?"

"It's an emergency first-aid technique."

"Oh. Are you going to let Holly Montgomery babysit me? I like her. She's good at basketball."

"We might give that a try," Jax said, with a glance toward Claire.

Nicholas polished off his banana, licked his fingers, and said, "In the picture Miss Celeste showed me of Three Bears before the fire, Papa Bear had a basketball goal. Are you going to build it back, Dad?"

"I am."

"You should do it next."

"That could probably be arranged."

"Awesome. Miss Claire? Would you show the costumes to me?"

"I will. How should we do it? One at a time or should I lay them out for you to see all together?"

"All together, I think. So what sort of costumes do you have?"

She ticked them off on her fingers. "I have three or four different Santa suits, a reindeer, a snowman, one that's made to look like a gift box. An elf. An angel. A Christmas tree. Hmm . . . what else?"

"Those all sound sorta lame. Of course, Tinsel is a girl so she can wear something embarrassing. Captain wouldn't wear a costume."

"I'm not sure, but I think I should be annoyed about that," Claire teased. "I'll set them out on the sofa in the family room, and you come out when you're ready."

Nicholas bit into his apple as Claire exited the kitchen. Her nerves were strung tight. She sent up a quick little prayer that they were doing the right thing, then she set out the dog costumes. Nicholas and Jax exited the kitchen a few minutes later, both looking tense.

Nicholas took small steps toward her. His gaze zipped over the items she'd left out on the sofa, right to left. He looked a second time, and then relaxed.

He stepped forward, studied the costumes one by one, and slowly shook his head. He picked up a Santa beard and held it out toward her. "Miss Claire. Do you really want to embarrass Tinsel this way?"

"Too much, you think?"

"Yeah."

She motioned toward an elastic band covered in green velvet and sporting a dozen jingle bells. "What about the necklace?"

Claire held her breath as Nicholas picked it up. Bells jingled. Tinsel tilted her head toward the sound.

Nicholas went down on his knees and snapped his fingers for Tinsel. Both she and Captain moved toward him. He slipped the jingle bells around Tinsel's neck. The collie shook. Bells pealed. Claire gripped her hands so hard that her knuckles turned white.

Nicholas shrugged. "I guess that's okay. Just don't put a hat on her. Hats on dogs are just embarrassing."

Then he looked up at his father. "Can we go out and play, Dad?"

"How much homework do you have?"

"None!"

Jax hooked a thumb over his shoulder. "Hit the grass, Jack."

Claire grabbed the jingle bells off Tinsel right before she darted outdoors after the boy and the other dog. Laughing, she turned a triumphant gaze toward Jax. "How about that!"

He picked her up, spun her around, and said, "You are a miracle, Claire Branham. I want you to know one thing. Hats . . . you know, those little French-maid lace blob things? Hats are okay with me."

At noon on the day of the Chamber of Commerce fundraiser, Jax sauntered into Fresh bakery and waved a hello to Sarah Murphy, who was speaking on the phone. She held up a finger signaling just a minute. Jax made himself at home by pouring a cup of the complimentary coffee Sarah kept available for customers whenever the bakery was open. He sat sipping the strong brew and waited for Sarah to finish her conversation with her son Devin. After his sister's wedding, the young man had returned to the Caribbean, where he ran a charter fishing service out of Bella Vita Isle.

Sarah had tears in her eyes when she hung up the phone. "Everything okay?" Jax asked.

"Yes. I'm just missing my kids. I've decided I don't like having an ocean or two between us."

"Any word from the honeymooners?"

"We heard from them yesterday. They're having a blast. Chase is over the moon with excitement over the rafting trip Lori arranged as a surprise. He asked about Captain. I told him that Nicholas brought him by to visit over the weekend. Your son is just so darned cute about being the dog-sitter for Lori and Chase."

"He's taking his responsibilities very seriously," Jax said.

"He seems to be doing well. Eternity Springs agrees with him?"

"It does. He says he's going to Claire's reception tonight."

"Oh, that would be fabulous, Jax."

"I'm hopeful. And I'm here to pick up dog paw cookies for Claire."

Sarah laughed. "They're ready. I'll bet she's a busy little beaver today. Our chamber meetings aren't always well attended, but I haven't heard of anyone who is planning to skip tonight's reception." Slyly, she added, "So, you're an insider. Have you seen what she's doing with this Christmas Doghouse?"

"Not yet. She's putting the finishing touches on it today. That's why she's closed this afternoon."

"She's such a clever girl. People around here do love their pets. I'll be curious to see just how much money she raises for the chamber with the ornaments. Celeste is president of the organization this year, and she has big plans for the money."

"Claire mentioned to me that the chamber has earmarked the funds the ornament sales raise for new Christmas decorations for the town."

"The stuff we have now is tired and tattered and a mishmash of styles. I know Celeste has been poring over catalogues for months and she has a wish list a mile long. The past couple of years we've had a decent bump in the winter tourist season, and we need to put a good foot forward year round." She reached beneath her counter for a stack of cookie boxes marked "Claire" and added, "Besides, the whole dog ornament thing is just fun. Sage and Claire kept the drawings secret, so we don't quite know what to expect—especially when it comes to Mortimer. Have you seen them?"

"Nope. One thing I'm learning about Claire, when she wants to keep a secret, she keeps a secret."

He didn't mention that she'd offered to give him and Nicholas a sneak peek. Claire thought the boy might do better facing his demons in a setting that wasn't filled with other people, but Nicholas had disagreed, telling them he was tired of being "special." He wanted to be a normal kid and go to the party just like everyone else.

"I can do it," he'd said this morning at breakfast. "I'm not afraid anymore."

Jax prayed the boy was right. He'd have preferred Claire's approach, but since he'd committed to taking his cues from Nicholas, he couldn't argue with his son.

He finished his coffee, loaded the cookies into his truck, and called Claire to tell her that he was on his way.

"The back door is unlocked," she told him. "Will you come in that way, please? Leave the cookies in the storeroom."

"Is there anything else you need me to bring?"

"Not right now. The champagne's being delivered, and Ali won't have the hors d'oeuvres ready to pick up until four."

Jax parked next to Claire's car in the alley behind the store, and he carried the boxes of cookies inside. Deciding his efforts had earned him a treat, he stole a cookie and headed for the stairs. The life-sized display of Sage Rafferty's Snowdrop dressed in an elf suit complete with ears brought him up short.

A similar display starring Mortimer in a Scrooge hat made Jax laugh out loud. Claire's voice greeted him from the second-floor landing. "Cute, aren't they?"

He lifted his gaze, and his heart grew like the Grinch's. "You sparkle, Miss Christmas."

"I'm excited. I'm so pleased with how this whole project has turned out. Eternity Springs has given me so much since I moved here. It's a great feeling to give something back in return."

"Do I get a tour?"

"I should make you wait, but I could use your long arms. Come on up."

He took advantage of the mistletoe hanging in the doorway to what had been her apartment before the upstairs remodel.

"Ten days," he murmured when they ended the kiss. "You gonna let me have a peek at the costume closet while I'm here?"

She rolled her eyes. "I swear, Lancaster, the dog room is a perfect fit for you."

Then she took his hand and led him into the "Dog-house."

An artificial tree stood in the center of the room, and it showcased the Twelve Dogs of Christmas ornaments. The glass balls had a white background and the sketches of the dogs were done in red, green, gold, and silver. He recognized Gabe Callahan's Clarence, Zach Turner's Ace, and the Cicero family's wheaten terrier. He didn't know who the little terrier belonged to, and a couple of the dogs depicted didn't fit any breed he recognized. Mutts, he imagined.

In addition to the ornaments, Claire had trimmed the tree with dog-themed ribbon, garland shaped like dog bones, twinkling lights and bubbling lights shaped like doghouses. "So what do you think?" she asked.

"If it starts barking, I'm outta here." Then he shot her a grin. "You've hung Captain front and center. Nicholas will love this. It's all wonderful, Claire. The ornaments are great."

"I think so, too. They turned out even nicer than I envisioned."

"To be honest, I expected something cutesy and cheesy. More along the lines of the dog costumes. These ornaments are traditional and classic—they'll fit into a lot of different décors. I'm impressed."

"Thank you. Sage deserves most of the credit. She did a fabulous job with the drawings. They're individual enough that those of us who know the dogs will recognize them, but she kept enough of the different breeds' particular qualities to appeal to owners of a variety of dogs."

"I don't know, Claire. I can't imagine there being another Mortimer in the world."

She laughed. "He is unique. Sage drew a more generic Boston terrier for me. I've had them produced, but I'm not featuring them tonight. Could I get you to put the topper on the tree for me? Do you want the ladder?"

Jax shook his head and gestured toward the stepstool that leaned against a wall. "That'll be fine."

She handed him a theme-appropriate angel for the top of the tree. Jax took in the floppy-eared, plush dog with a goofy grin, wings made of feathers, and a gold halo that was tilted at an angle that suggested the dog wasn't always angelic.

With the tree trimming finished, Jax took a few minutes to study the other merchandise displayed in the room. In addition to the costumes, she had holiday sweaters, Christmas-themed treat jars, food bowls, and chew toys. Collars, leads, stockings, photo frames, wrapping paper, and more. He picked up a bag of bacon-flavored treats shaped like little elves and asked, "What more could a dog want?"

"Tinsel loves them," Claire said. "Captain does, too."

"I'm sure." An old memory flashed through his mind and, without thinking about it, he shared it with her. "Lara had a dog when we got married. A little terrier. She kept treats for her in a cookie jar in the kitchen. We had a party one weekend, and some of my navy buddies came to it. One guy drank too much and bunked on our sofa. Raided the cookie jar in the middle of the night. The next morning, he asked Lara for the recipe for the cookies. Said he'd never had bacon-flavored cookies before, but he loved them."

Claire smiled and waited a couple of beats before observing, "That's the first time I've heard you mention your ex-wife with a smile on your face."

Jax tossed the dog treats back into their basket. "I think it's Eternity Springs. My boy wasn't the only Lancaster who needed healing. So, what else can I do to help you?"

He thought of that moment later that evening as he showered before returning to town for the reception. It was nice to be able to think of Lara without all the rage and pain. Someday, Nicholas would want to talk about his mother. Jax needed to be able to remember and share memories of the good times in his marriage.

Knock, knock, knock. "Hurry up, Dad. We don't want to be late!"

"Hold your horses," Jax called out as he towel-dried his hair. His phone lay beside his razor on the countertop beside the bathroom sink and he checked the time. "The doors don't open for forty minutes yet."

"But we have to find a place to park. That might be hard. Everyone is going to Forever Christmas tonight. Hurry up, Dad."

Jax switched on his electric razor and grinned at his reflection in the mirror. Nicholas wouldn't be this excited if he was still afraid. *Everything is going to be okay.*

With a towel wrapped around his hips, he exited the master bath and walked into his bedroom. Nicholas sat in the middle of his bed with Captain in his lap. "On my bed? Really?"

"Sorry." Nicholas pushed the dog off the bed. "Guess what, Dad? Miss Claire left a present in my closet. It wasn't in a box or a gift bag. It was just hanging there. See?"

He scrambled to his feet, standing in the middle of the mattress. "It's a new shirt. Look what's on the pocket. It's a paw print and it says 'The Twelve Dogs of Christmas.' She pinned a note to it and said I didn't have to wear it, but I wanted to. It's soft. And, it's red and green and I'm wearing it. I'm wearing it! And guess what? I looked in your closet and she left one for you, too. Will you wear it? It's not the same color so we won't match and be lame."

"We wouldn't want to be lame."

"Hurry up, Dad. Cari Callahan says that Mr. Chase's mom is sending meatballs, and they're really good. And Coach Lucca's mom is sending cake. We don't want them to all be gone before we get there."

Jax pulled on jeans and then the brown flannel shirt with the dog logo embroidered in tan thread on the pocket. "All right. All right. Take Captain out to pee and then we'll go."

"Hurray!" Nicholas scrambled off the bed calling, "Come on, Captain. Gotta go do your business."

He chattered all the way to town, and his excitement was infectious. Jax's mood was upbeat as he parked his truck on Third Street, a block and a half away. Nicholas ran ahead of him, and Jax had to lengthen his stride to keep up. Maybe it was the power of positive thinking at work, but he honestly believed that Nicholas had his issue beat as they made their way toward Forever Christmas.

So it was especially crushing when the boy came to an abrupt halt ten feet from Claire's front door.

Jax detected the aroma of mulled cider in the air at the same moment he saw color drain from Nicholas's complexion. The boy weaved on his feet and brought his hands up to cover his ears. He let out a scream.

The shrill sound drowned out the sweet voices of Meg and Cari Callahan, approaching the shop from the opposite direction and singing the chorus of "Angels We Have Heard on High."

Chapter Sixteen

Positive thoughts are difficult to come by some days.
—CLAIRE

When Jax heard his son scream, his heart dropped to his feet. He sprinted toward Nicholas and scooped him up into his arms even before the boy drew another breath.

"It's okay, buddy. It's okay. I'm here. Daddy's here."

Heedless of the attention they'd received from others on the street, Jax turned around and started walking, not sure where he was going to take the boy, just knowing they needed to get away from Forever Christmas.

Nicholas buried his head against Jax's chest and sobbed. "I'm so scared, Daddy. I don't want to be scared."

Jax's heart broke right along with his son's. "I'm here, Nicholas. I've got you. It's okay."

They were one block away from the health center. He should go there. Nicholas might need a doctor. Hell, Jax needed a doctor. He needed somebody who knew what the hell they were doing. He damned sure didn't know what to do. He sucked at this. At parenting. What had he been thinking? Whatever made him think that reading a few books and wearing a shirt meant the boy had overcome a traumatic experience almost beyond imagining?

The idea that a place can heal a damaged psyche? What a crock.

In his arms, Nicholas cried his heart out. "Daddy. Daddy. I hate that music. I hate it. It scared me so bad . . ."

"I'm here, buddy. I know. I'm sorry."

"She was singing, Daddy. Mommy was singing that song and playing the music loud."

Jax's steps slowed. Was he talking about the accident? Nicholas never talked about the accident. *Oh, hell. What do I do?*

"She was singing and she was crying and then she started laughing. I was so scared."

Six years old. He'd been six years old. Could he remember details like this about what had happened? Were these real memories or his nightmares? And did that even matter? This was what was in his mind.

And he's talking about it. He's talking about his mother. He never talks. Never.

Talking was good, wasn't it? Keeping everything inside was poison. He needed to talk. Hadn't the psychologists told Jax that?

Yes. Back before you stopped taking him to psychologists.

I suck at this.

Jax needed to keep him talking. He needed to vomit out the poison like when you drank too much. Vomiting kept you from getting alcohol poisoning. Jax wished he had alcohol right now.

Ahead of them half a block, Jax spied a couple of boys on Nicholas's soccer team. Crap. Not what they needed now. Not at all.

Thinking fast, Jax crossed the street to where the gate to the prayer garden beside St. Luke's Episcopal church stood open and welcoming. He entered and carried his son toward a wrought-iron bench that sat across from a concrete birdbath and a metal plaque inscribed with a

Bible verse that read: "*Your word is a lamp to my feet and a light for my path.* Psalms 119:105."

Nicholas continued to cry, though his sobs had quieted somewhat. Gently, Jax rocked his son back and forth, murmuring soothing sounds, whispering calming words.

Nicholas shuddered. "I put my fingers in my ears because I didn't want to hear her sing anymore. Then the car was going sideways and there was a big boom and we crashed. I bumped my head and it hurt. I cried for Mommy but she didn't answer. She didn't talk to me at all. I said, 'Mommy, Mommy, Mommy,' and she wouldn't answer."

"I'm so sorry." Jax was horrified. Poor Nicholas. Poor Lara. Knowing that she'd broken her neck in the accident had been bad enough, but hearing this account of the event from his son . . . dear Lord. His heart squeezed in pain. No child should see something like this. Ever.

"It's awful. She died. She wrecked the car and she died and I was all alone. I even yelled 'Help!' but nobody came. Nobody."

"It was a terrible thing, Nicholas. It was a horrible, terrible thing that happened to you. But you aren't alone anymore."

"Why am I still scared? I don't want to be scared anymore. I'm a baby. The kids at my old school said that, and now everyone here will say it, too, because I couldn't go into Miss Claire's shop."

"No. You're the bravest boy I've ever met."

"No I'm not, Daddy. I'm not brave at all. I'm not better. I thought I was better."

"You *are* better, Nicholas. It's true. I'm not a doctor, and I could be wrong about this, but I think you have some really scary memories hiding in your brain. Something happened a few minutes ago, something touched those memories and they came out of hiding."

The song the Callahan girls had been singing, he'd bet.

"I smelled it," Nicholas said.

He smelled it? "What did you smell? Christmas trees?"

"No. Not that." Nicholas shrugged. "I don't know what it is."

What had the boy smelled a moment ago? The cider? Could Lara have had a thermos of cider with her? Jax tried to recall what had been found in the car with Nicholas, but beyond the wrapped Christmas gifts, he came up empty.

He brushed Nicholas's bangs off his forehead. "Smells are a powerful memory trigger, son."

"How do I make it stop?"

"That's something we can ask Dr. McDermott when you see him in a few weeks. In the meantime, I'm not a doctor, but I'll tell you what my gut tells me. I think maybe that something like what happened today needs to happen. I think those memories need to come out."

Nicholas stirred and sat up. He gave Jax an incredulous look.

Jax attempted to explain. "Remember when we were moving that lumber at Papa Bear last week, and you got a splinter in your hand?"

"Yeah."

"You tried to ignore it. Tried to pretend it wasn't there. But it didn't go away, did it? Every time you bumped it, it hurt."

"It hurt when you dug in my finger with a needle."

"Yep. But I opened a path to the splinter and got hold of it with the tweezers and pulled it out. It hurt coming out, but once it was out, the hurting stopped."

"You're saying my memories of what happened with Mommy are splinters?"

"Big sharp thorny ones. But I'm thinking that maybe talking about them works like a needle and tweezers."

"Huh." Nicholas considered the idea, then his eyes filled with fresh tears. "I don't think you're right. If the splinter was gone, I could go look at the Christmas Doghouse, but I don't want to. I mean . . . I *want* to . . . but I can't."

"Here's the thing about splinters, big guy. Sometimes you can't get hold of them and pull 'em out whole. Sometimes you've got to make a couple runs at getting them. Sometimes they break and little pieces get left behind. But if you've opened a path to them, lots of times they'll work themselves up toward the surface so that you can get 'em."

"I don't remember Mommy very good," Nicholas said in a small, hesitant voice. "Except for the bad time. I remember that. She made me sad and scared. Mimi says Mommy loved me a whole lot."

"She did."

"I want to remember good things about Mommy."

"You will, buddy. I'll help you."

"You will?" Nicholas swiped the back of his hand across eyes now filled with hope, then wiped his nose on his sleeve.

"Absolutely, I will." Jax shifted his son out of his lap and onto the bench beside him. He fished his handkerchief from his pocket and handed it to his son. "Blow."

Nicholas did, then handed it back. Jax continued, "It'll do me good to remember the good times with your mother. Let's start right now, shall we?"

"Okay."

Jax pursed his lips and made a show of thinking hard. "Hmm . . . let me see."

He snapped his fingers. "Here you go. I remember that your mommy liked the color purple a lot. And she loved for the three of us to play the game Twister together. Remember that?"

"Maybe . . ."

"She also loved to make peanut butter cookies and put a big Hershey's Kiss in the middle of them."

Nicholas's eyes rounded. "I remember that! I used to help her take the foil off the Kisses."

"That you did." Hoping that this was a good direction to take, Jax ventured, "What else did Mommy like?"

Nicholas thought for a moment, playing with an imaginary spot on Jax's sleeve. Then he smiled. "She liked to go to the zoo! We'd take a cooler that rolled and go to the zoo and have a picnic. I'd eat pimento-cheese sandwiches."

Jax nodded, recalling the photos of the zoo trips that she'd e-mail to him when he was at sea. "Did she have a favorite animal?"

"Giraffes. Mommy liked giraffes."

"Good job, Nicholas. Those were some really good memories."

The boy exhaled a heavy breath. "I wasn't so scared. Usually, I'm too scared to remember because instead of good things I always remember that bad time."

"Whenever you try to think of Mommy and get scared, come and find me and we'll talk about her just like we did now. Anytime you want to talk about Mommy or about being scared or about anything at all, you just let me know. Okay?"

"Okay."

"All right, then. You ready to go home, buddy?"

"Yeah. What about Miss Claire? She'll worry when we don't show up."

"I'll send her a text."

"Meg and Cari saw me cry. Everyone is going to know I'm a scaredy-cat. They'll make fun of me at school."

"I don't think so. This is Eternity Springs. Everyone I know is rooting for you, Nicholas."

"Maybe. Galen said his mom died, too. In a hospital,

though. She was sick for a long time, he said. I told him I was sorry. People say that to me sometimes."

"I didn't know that about Galen. I'm glad you guys are friends. Did you tell him about Mommy?"

"No. He already knew she died so I didn't have to talk about it."

"See? People are different here in Eternity Springs."

"Yeah, I like it here, Daddy."

Jax stood and extended his hand to his son. The boy took it, and they walked back to Jax's truck in silence, both of them lost in their own thoughts. On the drive back to Three Bears, Jax replayed the incident in his mind. Had he handled it okay? Should he have taken the boy to the clinic, after all? Should he call Rose and ask her advice? Maybe she'd advise him not to wait for Dr. Mc-Dermott's return from vacation.

Maybe she'd tell him not to send Nicholas to Seattle.

Well, hell. He needed to consider that possibility. Maybe sending his son away for a long weekend would be the absolute worst thing he could do.

When it comes to parenting, I am so in over my head.

"Dad?"

"Hmmm?"

"Would you think Miss Claire has pictures of the Doghouse on her phone?"

Jax shot Nicholas a sidelong look. "Actually, I know she does. I watched her take a few when I dropped off cookies."

"Maybe I'll ask her to show them to me. Maybe."

"If you want to see what it looks like, I think that's a fine plan."

Since they'd planned to make a meal on Yellow Kitchen appetizers, Jax had to scrounge for his and Nicholas's supper upon their arrival back at Mama Bear. He decided to keep it easy and do breakfast for supper, and he'd just pulled bacon out of the refrigerator when he heard a car approach.

Sitting on the kitchen floor wrestling with Captain, Nicholas scrambled to his feet and ran to the window. "It's Miss Claire. Why is Miss Claire home so early? The party isn't over yet."

"I don't know."

Moments later, she hurried inside carrying two bags with the Yellow Kitchen logo on the side, Tinsel trailing at her feet. Jax saw the worry on her face as she studied Nicholas. Nevertheless, she kept her voice casual as she said, "Hey, guys."

"Why are you home early, Miss Claire? Did something bad happen at the party?"

"No. Everything is going fine. Since Celeste is president of the Chamber of Commerce, I turned the evening over to her." Claire set the bags on the kitchen table. "I brought food."

"Good. I'm hungry." Nicholas pulled a kitchen chair away from the table, climbed up on his knees, and peered into the bag. "What's in the box?"

Claire reached into the bag and pulled out a large square gift box adorned with red glitter hearts against a silver background. She set it on the table. "Well, I visited Shannon Garrett at Heartsong Cottage the other day, and her house put me in the mood for Valentine's Day. I'll tell you a secret, Nicholas, if you promise not to tell anybody else."

Interest lit the boy's eyes. "I promise."

"My favorite holiday isn't Christmas. It's Valentine's Day."

Nicholas gave her a "you're crazy" look. Claire laughed.

"It's true. I've been known to put up a Valentine's Day tree and decorate it. So, I thought I'd better bring home a few Valentine's tree ornaments before they were all gone."

Nicholas narrowed his eyes. "I'm not dumb, Miss Claire. I know what's in that box. You brought home the Twelve Dogs of Christmas. You brought them so I can see them."

"Okay. You caught me. I know how badly you wanted to see the ornaments and I thought this might be a way to do it. You keep this box and open it when you're ready. And it's not too much of a stretch to think of them as Valentine's-themed things. After all, what's the main message of Christmas?"

"Presents?"

She ruffled his hair, then leaned over and kissed the top of his head. "Love, Nicholas. The key to Christmas is love."

Three days later, Claire's thoughts were on the Lancasters as she restocked the shelves in Forever Christmas shortly before closing time. Despite Nicholas's setback the evening of the reception, Claire was encouraged by his progress. He'd asked to see pictures of the Christmas Doghouse. He'd requested she continue to read to him each night. Last night, he'd opened her Valentine's box.

And Jax was at the boy's side offering support every step of the way.

He was such a good father. She wished he could see that. Ever since Nicholas's setback, Jax had second-guessed each of his parenting decisions. He'd had a conference with Nicholas's doctor and his teacher. He'd called the Hardcastles and updated them about their grandson's situation, and they'd gone back and forth about whether or not to go forward with Nicholas's trip to Seattle. The fact that the boy wanted badly to go had weighed heavily in the decision not to change their plans.

Selfishly, Claire had wanted to cheer.

She also believed that Jax was doing everything right

with Nicholas. True, she wasn't a health-care professional, but she lived with the boy. She witnessed the progress he made on a daily basis. Jax was too hard on himself.

Her door chimes sounded, and she exited her stockroom to see the man himself rush in with a panicked look on his face. "Help!"

"Jax, what's wrong?"

"I need your ideas. I'm not asking you to do it. I want to be clear about that. But I'm coming up with a great big goose egg, and I need some fresh ideas."

"About what?"

"Halloween. Tomorrow is Halloween. I didn't know it was such a big deal. Have you seen the costumes kids do these days? Talk about elaborate. The kid showed me some on the Internet. Whatever happened to throwing a sheet over your head and cutting out eyes and going as a ghost? And Nicholas tells me parents dress up now, too! I'm not dressing up to take my eight-year-old trick-or-treating. That's crazy."

The affronted expression on his face made her laugh. "What does Nicholas want to be for Halloween?"

"He doesn't know, but it has to be cool. What the heck am I supposed to do with that? Why do I have to come up with an idea, anyway? It's not like he's five and needs help. Shouldn't he be doing this himself?"

"I think Halloween has changed in recent years, Jax. It's not just for kids anymore. Adults are really into it. Parents do dress up."

"Yeah. Well. Not me. I'm drawing the line there. He said the Ciceros have been working on their costumes for weeks. We have a little more than twenty-four hours to come up with something for Nicholas. And never mind that I'm trying to fit four days of work into two out at Papa Bear because I actually have a firm commitment from the electrician for next week, and I can't miss that window.

I'm not dragging out the sewing machine that's in the storage closet in Mama Bear, so if Nicholas and I can't put a costume together with safety pins, Super Glue, or staples, it's not happening."

"You can use a sewing machine? I'm impressed."

That distracted him from his rant. He shot her a quick grin and said, "I'm extraordinarily talented with my hands. I'm looking forward to showing you. In fact . . ."—he gave her a slow once-over—"if you haven't had any luck finding that French maid outfit, I could be persuaded to fire up the sewing machine."

Claire's cheeks heated. "You are such a flirt."

The teasing glint in his eyes changed to something hotter and more intense. "One week, Miss Christmas. Seven days."

She wanted to fan her face. Instead, she decided to give him a taste of his own medicine. She slowly skimmed her gaze down his body, licked her lips, and dragged her gaze back up to his face. "One hundred sixty-eight hours."

He fell back a step. Thumped his hand over his heart.

Claire couldn't stifle a grin. "First, though, we have Halloween to deal with."

Jax grimaced. "From the sublime to the ridiculous. Any suggestions for me?"

"Let me think about it. We'll come up with something Nicholas will like."

"Thanks, darlin'." He picked her up, whirled her around, and kissed her hard. "I knew I could count on you."

She mulled over possibilities as she finished stocking her shelves. Something "cool" that didn't involve needle-work and could be thrown together in one evening. That was the stumbling block. Internet shopping made life in Eternity Springs easier, but experience had taught her that you couldn't count on overnight delivery. The last thing they needed was to be waiting for UPS to show when the sun went down on Halloween.

She had a pretty good idea of the clothes they had to work with currently in Nicholas's wardrobe. Bet she could scrounge up other supplies by calling around to friends. They needed a theme.

"Hmm . . ." she murmured aloud. She took a look around her Angel Room, but nothing there gave her any ideas. Though she did wonder how many Starlinas she'd see tomorrow night. "Now there's a thought guaranteed to put me in a witchy mood."

At least Nicholas won't want to dress up as that commercialized fake.

She shook her head, chased away the annoying thoughts, and finished prepping the shop for closing, cleaning the restrooms, adjusting the heat, turning on some lights, turning others off. Upstairs in the Christmas Doghouse, she hesitated. An idea flitted through her mind.

She had an entire line of items embroidered or embossed or printed with "Believe." She thought of Jax every time she sold one of those items, every time she stocked one. *Wonder if he ever used his journal?* She'd never had the nerve to ask him. Probably not. He probably considered the whole thing silly, and if that were the case, she didn't want to know it. She wanted to keep that particular fantasy alive.

Fantasy. Jax Lancaster was a living, breathing fantasy. Was he just teasing her about the whole French-maid thing, or did he really want to go into role-playing during their first . . . fling? Wasn't that a little bit much for the first time out? This whole situation was simply beyond her experience. She was living with the man, but not sleeping with him. Playing house. Playing mother to his son.

And my, oh my, was she having the time of her life.

Seven days. Seven days of waiting, then three days of wicked. She'd bought the little costume complete with fishnet hose and the little blob of a cap. She'd probably pack it. If she'd be brave enough to wear it . . . well . . . who knows?

"And first you have another costume to concern you," she murmured.

The more she thought about it, the more she could see it. She could be wrong, but she thought her idea might appeal to Nicholas. And, it could be managed with scissors, staples, and Super Glue—though a needle and thread would make it nicer.

Claire gathered up the supplies they'd need if the boy liked her idea, locked up her shop, and went home to Three Bears Valley.

Chapter Seventeen

Best. Halloween. Ever.
—JAX

"I can't believe you got me to dress up for Halloween," Jax groused as he parked his truck at the Callahan compound on Hummingbird Lake.

Claire rolled her eyes. "You are wearing your suit, Jax."

"And an armband."

Claire shared a look of disapproval with Nicholas, who sat between them in the front seat of the truck. "You should bite him, King Komondor."

Nicholas rolled his head around and the long strands of coiled cotton glued to his old baseball cap went flying. Then he bared his teeth and growled.

Jax narrowed his eyes. "Careful there, you'll lose your Best in Show ribbon."

The boy panted and pawed at Jax's suit jacket. "Mutt," he declared, but belied his gruff tone by reaching into his pocket and producing a vanilla wafer "treat." Nicholas freed himself from the seat belt, nipped the cookie from Jax's hand, then went up on his knees and kissed his father's cheek.

Jax grinned. The kid was really getting into this.

Frankly, so was he.

Exiting the truck, they joined the crowd of Eternity

Springs trick-or-treaters making their way toward the bank of Hummingbird Lake, where Brick Callahan had docked his haunted pirate ship, which on other days was his uncle Luke's houseboat, the *Miss Behavin' VI*.

Halloween in Eternity Springs was one big party for both children and adults. They'd been blessed with good weather, so the door-to-door part of the evening had been a convivial stroll through the residential streets. Word quickly passed among the crowd of kids about not-to-be-missed houses. The Murphys were giving away Sarah's cookies. The Rafferty house had caramel apples. Maggie Romano at Aspenglow B and B was giving popcorn balls.

"Dr. Davis is handing out toothbrushes and toothpaste again," a boy on Nicholas's soccer team had warned.

"We have to go there," Galen had told an alarmed Nicholas. "It'll hurt his feelings if everyone skips. Besides, the Davis home is next door to the Turners'. Sheriff Turner usually gives full-sized candy bars to make up for the toothbrushes."

Overhearing the exchange, Jax had made sure they didn't miss the town dentist's home.

With the trick-or-treating part of the evening over, the revelers had moved on to the climax of the evening— Brick's pirate ship. According to Claire, a number of the Callahan family members had gathered in Colorado for the event. They met Brick's aunt Maddie at the spot where the line formed. The redhead introduced herself then turned her attention to Nicholas.

"Now whoever designed your costume was thinking," she said in a slow, sexy voice full of the South. "I can recall plenty of Halloweens where my life would have been easier if I'd had a leash on my kids. I take it you're a show dog?"

"Dad and I are going as the Westminster Dog Show. I'm a komondor and I'm Best in Show."

"You certainly are." She grinned at Jax and Claire, then handed Nicholas a child-sized life jacket. "And now, me matey, in order to set sail aboard the *Black Shadow* with Captain Callahan, you'll need to don your pirate's vest. Jax, if you and Claire want to wait for him at the dance hall, we have a selection of grog from which to choose."

"Thank you," Claire said. "That sounds—"

Maniacal laughter boomed across the night, and Claire turned toward the sound. Brick Callahan stood decked out in full pirate regalia—tall boots, skintight black pants, a low-cut flowing white shirt, a pirate's eye patch, and a tricorn hat. He held a sword up in the air as he threatened to make Cari Callahan walk the plank.

In line behind them, Rose Cicero observed, "Now that's a sight to make a damsel's heart go pit-a-pat."

Her tone nonchalant, Claire said, "I certainly enjoy a good costume as well as the next damsel."

Jax twisted his head and stared at her. Claire arched a saucy brow. *"Oui, Monsieur Lancaster?"*

Keeping his voice low and for her ears only, he said, "You're trying to kill me, aren't you?"

She laughed and led him toward the dance hall, where Gabe Callahan introduced Jax to more members of the Callahan clan. Claire glanced around the crowded hall. "Celeste mentioned that your father made the trip this time. I'd like to say hi to him."

"Branch is working the boat with Brick," Mark Callahan said. "Playing a curmudgeonly old pirate is right up his alley."

Nic Callahan scolded her brother-in-law with a look. "Your father is a sweetheart. Have you seen how wonderful he is with the baby?"

"He's great with all his grandchildren," Mark's wife, Annabelle, observed.

Gabe Callahan laughed. "Have you talked to Brick lately? I suspect he'd weigh in on our side of the argument. Branch has decided your son needs a woman."

Mark winced. Luke and Matt laughed out loud. Luke clapped Mark on the back. "Might as well start planning the wedding now."

"What do you want to bet he has another . . ."—Mark made quote signs with his fingers—"heart attack?"

Gabe shook his head. "Nobody's dumb enough to take that bet. So, who needs another beer?"

About half an hour after they'd left Nicholas to board the *Black Shadow* with his friends, a gaggle of boisterous children invaded the dance hall looking for their parents. "He made us touch eyeballs in a bowl, Mom," said one girl.

"And brains, too!" called another.

They chattered about ghosts and sea monsters and chain saws. "Chain saws?" Clair asked. "On a pirate ship?"

Jax spied his son, his face alight with happy excitement, and he waved Claire's protest away. "Creative license. Hey, you can't have a decent haunted house without a chain-saw massacre."

Nicholas obviously agreed. Ten minutes later, loaded back into the truck and headed toward town, he talked nonstop about his "perilous journey."

". . . and some parts were really stupid. Everyone knows that the eyeballs were peeled grapes and the brains were spaghetti. But the girls screamed and Mr. Brick's grandpa was kinda scary. I don't know what he meant by 'Davy Jones' locker' but it didn't sound good."

"I'm glad you had fun, son," Jax said.

"I didn't get scared at all. And some of it was pretty scary. Mr. Brick's aunt Maddie can really sound like a witch."

The boy fell silent then, and Jax thought he might

have finally run out of steam. But after a few minutes of quiet, Nicholas surprised him. "I'm not a wussy. I'm very brave."

"Yes, you are."

"You are the bravest boy I've ever met," Claire added.

"I knew those things weren't real. I let myself get scared, because I knew they weren't real, and they couldn't hurt me." He turned his head and looked at Claire. "Nothing in your shop can hurt me. It's just a store. The things inside it aren't eyeballs."

Jax met Claire's startled gaze. She was looking to him for guidance, but he had none to give.

"That's true enough. I don't have any peeled grapes, either."

They drove another mile in silence, then Nicholas said. "I want to go there. Now. I went through the *Black Shadow,* and I didn't scream once. I can go inside Forever Christmas. Will you take me, please, Dad? Now?"

Jax gripped his steering wheel hard. Hell. What should he do? Today had been a great day. He didn't want to ruin it by exposing Nicholas to his terrors. And yet, wasn't the plan to take his cues from Nicholas? If he turned the boy down, what sort of signal was that sending? It might make matters worse.

He glanced down at his son and noticed the leash and dog collar that had been part of his costume tonight. Believe.

Well, hell. What else could he do?

"If that's what you want, Nicholas. Of course, I'll take you to the shop. As long as it's okay with you, Miss Christmas?"

"Of course."

A few minutes later, Jax parked his truck on the deserted street in front of the store. Claire suggested, "Why don't you let me go in first and turn on a few lights. I expect you want to see the Christmas Doghouse?"

"Yes."

"Okay. I'll wave to you from the door when I'm ready."

Claire slipped out of the truck. Jax watched her remove her keys from her purse and unlock the door. Moments later, lights switched on inside. Not twinkling tree lights, but overhead lights. *Smart girl.*

"You sure about this, Nicholas?" Jax asked as the second floor lit up.

Nicholas unbuckled his seat belt. "Yeah."

"If you have any second thoughts, just say the word."

"Okay."

Claire appeared in the doorway and gave them both a little wave. Nicholas said, "Nothing in that store is going to hurt me. Let's go, Dad."

Jax sent up a quick, silent prayer and took his son's hand. Together, they approached Forever Christmas to face Nicholas's demons on Halloween night. The irony of the moment wasn't lost on Jax.

Nicholas kept a tight grip on Jax as he paused at the front of the shop and drew a deep breath. Claire offered an encouraging smile. "Welcome to Forever Christmas, Nicholas. The Doghouse is upstairs."

After that moment's hesitation, the boy forged right ahead.

The lights Claire had turned on cast a soft glow throughout the shop, chasing away the shadows but not highlighting any of the displays. Nicholas darted glances right and left, but he didn't dawdle as he followed Claire toward the staircase.

"Doing all right, buddy?" Jax asked, bringing up the rear as he climbed the staircase. Tension gripped him.

Nicholas responded with a nod.

Claire glanced back at them and began to patter. "I ordered twice as many of the Twelve Dogs of Christmas ornaments as I thought I'd need. Based on the first few days of sales, I should have ordered four times more. The chamber has sold enough to get everything on Celeste's wish list. I hope we have plenty of volunteers for Deck the Halls Friday because we're going to need them. Time is flying. It'll be here sooner than we know it."

"Maybe we can volunteer to help, Dad."

Jax briefly closed his eyes. "That would be great."

Claire led the way to her Doghouse. There, she'd turned on a few more lights—including those on the room's centerpiece Christmas tree. Jax held his breath and waited for his son's reaction. To his shock, the boy did something completely unexpected.

Nicholas laughed out loud. "Are those real dog biscuits on the tree? How do you keep Tinsel away from them?"

Jax took his first easy breath since Nicholas expressed the desire to visit Claire's shop.

Nicholas took his time exploring the Christmas Doghouse. He picked things up. Turned them on and off. He shook the snow globes and jingled the bells. When he twisted the key on a music box, Jax opened his mouth to caution him, but Claire stilled him with a slight shake of her head. The music box played the theme song from *Paw Patrol*.

Throughout it all, Nicholas chattered excitedly. The only reason they heard the sound of something crashing downstairs was because it happened while he was taking a breath. Jax looked at Claire. "What was that?"

"I don't know," she said, starting toward the stairs. "It sounds like something fell off one of the shelves."

Jax frowned. They hadn't locked the door behind them. Crime wasn't a problem in Eternity Springs as a rule, but . . . "Hold on, Claire. Let me go check."

She dismissed him with a wave. "No, you wouldn't know what to look for."

Jax listened to the sound of her footsteps as she descended the staircase. He heard a few clicks as she switched on more lights. Then . . . nothing. He didn't like this one bit. "Wait here, Nicholas."

Jax followed Claire downstairs, his gaze scanning the area for signs of an intruder. The front door remained shut, the store felt empty. He found Claire standing in her books section, a perplexed look on her face. He asked, "Everything okay?"

"Yes. Everything's fine. I found four books on the floor. Someone must have looked at one of them today and didn't shelve it properly. Law of physics at work."

Jax figured she probably was right, but it wouldn't hurt to take one quick turn through the shop. He proceeded to do that and had just exited the stockroom, where he'd double-checked that the back door was locked, when he heard Nicholas say, "Wow, Miss Claire. That's really pretty."

The boy stood at the threshold of Claire's Angel Room. Shocked to see his calm and collected son downstairs in the middle of Christmas central, Jax pulled up short.

Nicholas said, "Look, Miss Claire. Something has fallen."

The boy disappeared into the room, followed by Claire. Jax hurried to join them and arrived in time to see Nicholas pick up a tattered angel off the floor, the same angel that had set Claire off the day he'd compared it to the children's book character. Nicholas handed the angel to Claire.

"Gardenia," she said softly. "How did she wind up on the floor?"

"Maybe she fell from the sky," Nicholas said. "Look. Her wing got broke."

"Her wing has been broken for a very long time," Claire said. She brushed off the angel's bedraggled skirt and gently straightened its halo. "Of all the angels in the Angel Room, she is my favorite. She didn't fall from the sky, Nicholas. My mother and my sister and I made her for our family's Christmas tree. She was born out of the love in our hearts."

"You must have used her for a long time for her to be so beat up."

"Actually . . . no. Gardenia never made it to the top of our tree. My sister got sick, and we didn't have Christmas anymore."

"Did she die like my mom?"

"Yes. Yes, she did."

"So she's an angel, too. I'm sorry, Miss Claire."

"Thank you, Nicholas. Me, too."

"Why didn't you have Christmas?"

Claire set the angel on a shelf half hidden by new and sparkly angels. As he watched her, a hazy thought drifted at the edge of Jax's mind, but before he could grasp hold of it, Claire distracted him with the answer to Nicholas's question.

"My sister was sick a long time. She was in the hospital the first year we didn't have Christmas. And the second. After she died, my mom just didn't have the heart to celebrate the holiday."

"What about your dad?"

"I'm afraid his heart really broke. He passed away not long after my sister did."

"That's terrible, Miss Claire. I'm really sorry."

A lump formed in Jax's throat as he watched his son wrap his arms around Claire's waist and give her a hug. "You and I are alike. You lost Christmas, too."

"Yes, Nicholas. You're right. For a long time, I did lose Christmas."

"But you got it back. You have Christmas every day now, don't you?"

"Forever Christmas," Claire said, returning his son's hug.

Nicholas stepped away and gazed up at her solemnly. "You know what, Miss Christmas?"

She pulled one of the cotton strands hanging on the hat he still wore. "What, Mr. Best in Show?"

"After tonight, I'm pretty sure that I got Christmas back, too."

It was all Jax could do not to break out into the chorus of "Joy to the World."

After she read Nicholas his Christmas story, Claire considered going straight to bed rather than wait downstairs for Jax for their customary shared nightcap. Talking about Michelle tonight had left her emotions raw. At the same time, she wanted to celebrate Nicholas's big step forward with Jax. It didn't seem right to bail on him just because his son's questions had stirred up old hurts.

Nicholas. What a tough little trouper he was. She was so proud of him and, frankly, pleased that she'd played even a small part in his recovery. Because it was a recovery. Yes, he might well have more setbacks. Yes, he would likely fight this particular fight for years to come. But tonight, on this special Halloween, he'd won.

"Forget the wine," she murmured to herself. She reached into the refrigerator for the bottle of champagne she kept on hand. If any occasion called for champagne, this did.

She was up on her tiptoes reaching for the champagne glasses on the top shelf of the wet bar cabinet when Jax joined her. "Wait. Let me help."

"I thought champagne was in order," she said, as he snagged the glasses.

Emotion hitched in Jax's chest. None of this would

have happened had he not come to Eternity Springs and met Claire Branham. In a voice husky with feeling, he said, "I wholeheartedly agree. I like the way you think, Miss Christmas."

He popped the cork, poured the champagne, then lifted his glass in toast. "To you, Claire."

"Not me. To Nicholas."

"To you and Nicholas, then." He clinked his glass against hers, then sipped his champagne. "He might have eventually taken this step on his own, but you made it happen a whole helluva lot faster. I can't thank you enough for all you've done."

"I'm glad I could help."

He leaned in and took her lips in a long, steamy kiss that left her weak in the knees. "I'm not ready for this evening to end. How about I make a fire? Will you sit with me, Claire? Talk with me? Make plans with me?"

"What sort of plans?"

"We haven't discussed your wishes for our trip. Silver Eden has all sorts of amenities we can choose from. I don't know if you're the tennis type or if you'd want to go horseback riding. You should take a look at the spa brochure on the Web site because we should probably book that before we go."

She put the champagne bottle in an ice bucket and carried it and their glasses to the coffee table near the fireplace. While he started the fire, they discussed the upcoming trip and decided they both preferred a visit to the resort without a set agenda. With logs crackling and flames flickering in the hearth, he took her hand and led her over to the sofa, where he pulled her down to sit beside him, keeping his fingers threaded with hers. He dropped his head back against the cushion and released a heartfelt sigh. "What a day. An exhausting day, but a great day."

"I'll second that."

"Something tells me that the kid is going to keep me on my toes for the next ten years."

"Ten?" Claire laughed. "Try twenty. Maybe thirty."

"True, that. However, I'm going to remember this day for a long time. A very long time." He brought her hand up to his mouth and kissed it. "I'm happy that you shared it with us."

"I am, too," she said softly.

They sat in comfortable silence for a few moments, watching the fire. The scent of burning pine swirled through the room. Claire sipped her champagne, relaxing and reflecting on the evening's events at Forever Christmas.

Jax's thoughts must have gone that in direction, too, because he said, "I feel like a heel. I've been so focused on Nicholas and our problems that I never asked you about your family. Tell me about your sister, Claire. Was she your only sibling?"

"Yes." The image of a pale young body wasted away by illness flashed in her memory. "Her name was Kelley Michelle, and she was my baby sister. She was two years younger than me. She fought leukemia for four years."

"That's tough. Hard on your whole family."

"Yes, it was a horrible time. A roller coaster of hope and despair. My parents tried to stay positive, but I could tell they were scared to death. Michelle was so frightened, so sick. Some of the treatments were worse than the disease. I was . . ." Her voice trailed off.

"You were what? Frightened? Sad? Confused?"

"All of the above." She stared into the fire, remembering. She never talked about Michelle or her parents. Never talked about that life-changing time.

She knew so much about Jax. He'd shared his struggles, his failures, and now, this great success. She'd told him very little about herself, and after tonight, that didn't seem right. Jax shared so much, but she'd kept all her secrets.

Maybe it's time you opened up. Not about everything. But about some of it.

"I had a great family, a great childhood. I was ten, not much older than Nicholas, when my sister got sick and my whole life changed. My parents did their best, but they focused all their energy and attention on the child who was ill. I was scared and I felt . . ."

"Neglected," Jax suggested.

"Yes. I felt neglected and angry and oh, so guilty because I felt neglected and angry. I mean, my sister was dying. What sort of evil person was I because I was upset that we skipped Christmas a few times?"

"How long did she fight it?"

"Four years. We lost her the year I turned fourteen. At Christmas."

"Oh, Claire." Jax brought her hand up to his mouth and kissed it. "And then you lost your father. That's devastating. What of your mother? Is she . . . ?"

"She's gone now, too. She lived fourteen years after we lost Dad and Michelle, though I would say it was more existing than living. Her light died with them. Three years ago, she caught the flu and developed pneumonia. I don't think she had the heart to fight."

"Nicholas got it right, didn't he? You lost Christmas, too. It's no wonder you relate to him so well."

"He's a special little boy, Jax. He's lucky to have you as his father."

"Not always," he said. "I can't go back and change the past, but I am determined to be a good father from this day forward." He trailed his thumb gently down her cheek and studied her intently. "To that end, tell me something, Miss Christmas. What made you so strong?"

That startled her. "Strong?"

"Like Nicholas, you had Christmas stolen from you. How did a girl with every reason to be Ms. Grinch find her way to becoming Miss Christmas?"

"Oh, believe me," Claire replied with an uneasy laugh. "I can still get my Grinch on. I think I learned . . . I am learning . . . just what is truly important in life."

"Christmas?"

"What Christmas represents. It's personal and it's different for everyone. For some people who come into my shop, Christmas is all about family. For others, it's about tradition. I'm encouraged that the religious nature of the holiday remains strong and important to the majority of people with whom I deal, despite claims to the contrary. Of course, there are some who don't look beyond the gifts stacked at the bottom of the tree, but they definitely are not the majority."

"What does Christmas represent to you?"

She stared into the fire. "It's a mountain I'm trying to climb. I'm making progress, but I still have a ways to go to reach the summit."

Admiration gleamed in his eyes. "You and my son make quite a pair."

"He inspires me."

"You fascinate me."

His voice was a caress and made her shiver. He kissed her as the hall clock began to chime, his lips gentle and sweet and almost worshipful. Jax Lancaster had kissed Claire many times, in many ways, but never quite like this before.

This kiss paid her tribute and for some strange reason made her want to cry.

The clock chimes had long faded by the time he lifted his head. "Claire . . . I . . ."

Suddenly nervous, she stood and stepped away. "Oh, wow. Eleven o'clock. I have a breakfast meeting at

six A.M. I'd better go upstairs before I turn into a pump-
kin." She made a general wave toward the hearth. "Will
you . . . ?"

"Yes. I'll tend the fire and lock up. Good night, Claire."

"Good night."

He waited until she was halfway up the stairs to say,
"Claire, you are farther up the mountain trail than you
think. I want you to know that I'm damn glad to walk
beside you."

Chapter Eighteen

I've always liked the name Sven.
—CLAIRE

Five.

"Hello. I want to book the spa romance package, please, on Saturday afternoon. Yes. For two. It's under Lancaster." *Aka Stamina Sven.* "Yes. Yes. On my credit card. Excuse me? You said it's how much, again?" *Sheesh.* "Yes. That's fine."

Four.

"Did I hear you cough, Nicholas? Are you getting sick? C'mere. Let me check your temperature. You're not getting sick, are you? If you feel the least bit sick I want you to tell me so we can get you to the doctor and on some medicine. It'd break your grandparents' hearts if you couldn't go to Seattle this weekend."

Three.

"Hello. Jax Lancaster here. Wondering if I could stop by and pick up a check for that work I did two weeks ago? Yes, I invoiced you. Sure. I'd be glad to make another copy." *Deadbeat.*

Two.

"We don't have a dry cleaners? How can a town not have dry cleaners? I have Racer Rafferty's caramel apple handprints on my suit coat, and I need to wear it Saturday night."

The resort restaurant had a dress code. Why hadn't he thought to check that before today? He'd have to get his suit cleaned at the hotel. Guess he could switch around their reservations, and they could do the casual restaurant the first night instead of the fancy one.

Or maybe room service. Room service would be good.

One.

"Hello. Jax Lancaster again. Yes, tomorrow. For the dinner in the suite tomorrow night, go ahead and change it to the premium menu selection, please."

This weekend was going to cost him a fortune. Not that he cared. He didn't. Claire was worth every penny. It's just that he got sticker shock every time he contacted the hotel.

Besides, deadbeats aside, he was doing just fine, wasn't he? He was turning away work. Barring some unforeseen disaster, he wouldn't have any trouble paying his bills, not even this weekend's already humongous tab at Silver Eden.

This weekend. Tomorrow.

Today!

"Mistletoe!"

Five.

"This is Claire Branham. I'm sorry to bother you again, but I'm hoping you can add a few more things to my order? The off-the-shoulder two-piece swimsuit that's on page four of the current catalogue. Style number seven seven five. In red, please. In fact, why don't you go ahead and send me everything the model is wearing on that page. Yes, the cover-up, shoes, and jewelry, too. The sunglasses? Hmm . . . yes, why not? Overnight, please."

Four.

"This is Claire Branham. Yes, it arrived, thank you. I love it. That shade of red is spectacular. I think I've changed my mind about the dress. Why don't you go ahead and send the one on page ten. Everything. Suitable lingerie, too."

Three.

"Hello, Susie. Yes, it's me. I know, I know. How did I ever manage without a personal shopper? The dress is fabulous, but I'm not certain about the evening bag. And I love, love, love the silk teddy! The emerald green is spectacular."

Two.

"Luggage! I can't believe I never thought about luggage!"

One.

"Forever Christmas. How may I assist you today? Oh, hello, Susie. Yes, I'm all packed. Thank you so much. You've been a godsend."

Today!

"Fling!"

Silver Eden Resort took luxury to a new level. Perched halfway up the side of a mountain, the resort blended into its surroundings with clean, modern lines and plenty of glass. "Look at that infinity pool," Claire said as they approached the hotel's entrance. "Is it indoors or outdoors? I can't quite tell."

"Both," Jax said. "It has a retractable roof."

"Cool."

Their personal concierge greeted them upon arrival. Amy Gilbert was an attractive, efficient woman in her mid-forties who vowed to see to their every need. Based upon his interaction with her during their numerous phone conversations, Jax could attest to her attentiveness.

She took them on a tour of the facilities before showing them to a two-bedroom, three-bath suite with three fireplaces, and a private outdoor hot tub. Because he hadn't wanted to appear presumptuous—despite his presumptions—Jax had requested that his and Claire's bags be placed in separate bedrooms. When Amy left them alone in the suite, he spent a moment arguing with himself. He wanted to pick Claire up and carry her straight to bed. Instead, recognizing her nervousness by the way she kept playing with the shoulder strap on her purse, he asked if she'd like a little time to herself in order to freshen up after the drive.

"Thank you," she said with evident relief. "That would be perfect."

She turned toward her room, but he reached for her hand and stopped her. "Hold on a minute, honey. I'd be remiss if I ignored this."

"Ignored what?"

He pulled her into his arms and nipped at her earlobe. "Look up."

She looked up at the light fixture above them and laughed. Laughter that Jax cut off abruptly when he captured her mouth in a hot erotic kiss—beneath the mistletoe.

When the kiss finally ended, Jax pointed Claire toward her bedroom and gave her fanny a gentle swat. "Go on while you still can."

She floated into her room, and once the sensual haze created by his kiss dissipated, she went into her bathroom, stripped off her clothes, and took a quick shower. When she reached for a towel to dry herself, she noted the trembling in her hands.

She was nervous. She wanted . . . she *needed* . . . to get this first time behind her. When she realized she'd squeezed antibacterial ointment onto her toothbrush instead of toothpaste, she'd admitted that this fling needed to be flung before she lost what little sense she had left.

She didn't know exactly why her nerves were strung tighter than a fiddle string. Yes, she hadn't been with a man in a long time, but she wasn't a rookie. She was a modern, experienced woman who knew what she was doing in the bedroom. One thing she'd say about Landon, he'd taught her to be adventurous. So what if that adventurousness had gone rusty?

Or had it? Heaven knows, a fling was adventuresome. At least, it felt that way to her.

She rifled through the basket of toiletries the hotel provided and found a new toothbrush. As she brushed her teeth, she concluded that her problem was the fling aspect of the fling. She was a rookie in the fling department. Every other time she'd gone to bed with a man she'd been in a committed relationship.

Correction. She'd *thought* she was in a committed relationship at the time.

This was the first time she'd ever planned to have sex for the sake of sex alone. Casual sex. A fling.

It doesn't feel like a fling.

It felt more serious than that. It felt important. It felt like commitment.

It feels like love.

"Whoa. Hold it. Wait one blessed minute." Watching herself in the mirror, Claire saw the color drain from her face.

No. She wasn't in love with Jax. No. No. No. No. No. This was sex. Just sex. Casual sex. They'd agreed to that from the beginning. Fun and games and mistletoe flings.

Yeah, but . . . this guy seems different.

"No!" Claire took a deep breath. *Eyes wide open, woman. Can't go there. Can't get hurt like that again. Can't. Won't. Ever.*

"You'd better remember that," she told her reflection. "You'd better make darn sure you don't forget it. This weekend is a short-term adventure, not a lasting relationship. Treat it that way."

Determined to heed her own warnings, Claire decided to act. She plucked another item from the basket and announced, "Let the flinging commence."

After kissing Claire senseless, Jax went into his room and called to check on Nicholas. His son had arrived in Seattle safe and sound and seemed happy as a clam. After the call, he took a shower. A cold shower, since it appeared that this ongoing seduction would continue at least a little while longer.

They'd left Three Bears Valley at nine o'clock that morning, arriving at the Gunnison airport half an hour before the charter carrying Brian and Linda arrived from Seattle to pick up Nicholas. Jax had felt a little guilty about being so happy to see him off, and he'd confessed as much to Claire during the four-hour drive to Silver Eden.

"That's understandable, but silly, considering how excited he was about seeing his grandparents," she'd replied.

"True. He was one happy little boy, especially after he learned that the Hardcastles invited his friend from camp to join them for the weekend. Brian and Linda may live to regret that. Trevor is a live wire."

The trip had passed quickly. They'd argued about sitcoms from the nineties, discussed their favorite curries, and talked about novels they'd read so far this year. Claire had seemed comfortable with him right up until their arrival at Silver Eden. "Nerves," he said to his reflection in the mirror as he towel-dried his hair.

She hadn't even seen his bedroom yet.

Jax had requested the room be staged for romance, and wow, had the folks at Silver Eden gotten it right. Candles, flowers, soft music, sapphire satin sheets on a bed the size of a lake, the duvet turned back and waiting. A champagne bucket and chocolate-covered strawberries sat on the bedside table. A fire flickered in the hearth and French doors opened onto a private patio complete with a steaming hot tub and a million-dollar view of the sunset over the Rockies waiting to be enjoyed.

Though Jax figured that by the time he got Claire into his bed, the only sunset he'd care to view was the one that glistened in her luscious auburn hair.

If pressed, he would admit to a little nervousness himself. It had been a long time for him. Years, in fact, since he'd made love with a woman who mattered to him as much as Claire.

If anyone had ever mattered as much to him as she did. Maybe Lara, although he didn't remember having feelings this strong for her in the beginning of their relationship.

Relationship.

The word stopped him as he dragged the towel across his body. Is that the point where he and Claire were now? If so, when had their mistletoe fling become more than a simple fling? Especially since they hadn't actually started flinging?

It worried him. He didn't know how they'd make a relationship work. She'd put down roots in town. He couldn't ask her to leave her shop, but he couldn't work in Eternity Springs forever. Not in the profession in which he'd been trained, anyway. How could he provide for Nicholas, give him what he needed, working as a handyman? That Boeing job offer weighed heavily on Jax's mind. There was an option for them in Seattle. A good one.

And they wouldn't be able to live with free rent forever. Their life at Mama Bear was really just a fairy tale. Living like a family—well, except for the separate-bedroom thing—who were they kidding, other than themselves?

"Stop it," he muttered to his reflection in the mirror. No sense worrying about that now. Besides, he might be totally off base. He didn't know how Claire felt. The R-word might not be anywhere on her radar.

He was here for a fling, so a fling he'd have. With romance, mistletoe, and lots of sex. That's a fling.

Because if he thought about it in any other terms, it got downright scary.

He wrapped his towel around his waist and dug his razor from his shaving kit. He shaved, brushed his teeth, and combed his hair. Then he exited the bathroom and headed for the closet.

He stopped dead in his tracks. Lust hit him like a freight train.

Claire was in his bed.

Seeing him, she sat up. The blue satin sheet slid down her chest and pooled at her waist.

Claire was in his bed *naked*.

His gaze swept over her. Her glorious hair hung loose and long and fell like a sunset over her creamy shoulders. Taut rose-colored nipples crowned her full breasts. One shapely leg stretched out from beneath the covers. She wore scarlet polish on the toes she'd curled around and tucked beside her hip. She offered him a wobbly smile.

Claire was in his bed *completely naked*.

"Hi."

"Hi."

Jax's mouth went dry and his dick went hard as a submarine. Without conscious thought, he yanked off the towel wrapped around his waist. Fully aroused and drawn like a moth to a flame, he moved toward her.

He'd had all sorts of plans for their first time. All sorts of fantasies. After all, he'd been thinking about it since July. He'd intended to continue this seduction in the manner in which it began. Slow and steady and steamy.

Dinner in their room, then dancing beneath the mistletoe to a playlist of songs from singers she'd told him she loved—Frank Sinatra, Michael Bublé, some Righteous Brothers. He'd hold her close and nuzzle her ear. Breathe in the scent of her. Kiss her temple, her throat, her lips. Jax loved kissing, and the past weeks had shown him that Claire did, too. Slow, sizzling seduction.

When they reached the point where, up until now, they broke it off and went upstairs to their separate bedrooms, he'd planned to take her by the hand and invite her to his bedroom. Slow, scorching seduction.

He'd fantasized undressing her. Piece by piece. Down to her glorious lingerie. He couldn't know which color she'd wear, but he expected it to be a jewel tone. He lived with her. He'd seen the lacy, front-clasp bras and tiny thongs she preferred in the laundry room once or twice. Slow, scorching seduction.

When he had her naked, he would breathe her name in a whisper, like a prayer, and press her down against the mattress. He'd take his sweet time exploring her luscious body. He'd lose himself in the scent of her, the taste of her, the wonder of her. He'd stroke her all over. He'd knead and massage and discover how she liked to be touched. He'd use his mouth on her. Tasting the hollow at the base of her throat. Suckling her full breasts. Licking his way down her flat stomach to . . . heaven.

Slow, scalding seduction.

He'd make her come. He'd make her scream. He'd make her sob his name before he slipped inside her tight, moist heat. He'd ride her then, going deep, going slow, making it last. Making her come again before he finally . . . finally . . . let go.

Claire was naked in his bed waiting for him.

Who needs plans?

Thank God she pressed a condom into his hand before

he touched her. He managed . . . just barely . . . to put it on before he entered her. Hard and fast.

Too fast.

It was over in about a minute.

He collapsed against her, breathing hard. "I can do better than that. I can *so* do better than that."

He lifted his head and frowned down at her. "You ambushed me."

Her eyes sparkled and her mouth lifted in a self-satisfied smile. "I made you lose control."

"Well . . . yeah. It's been hanging by a thread since we moved into Mama Bear. To find you gorgeous and naked and waiting . . . damn, woman. Talk about a surprise. It's a wonder I didn't have a heart attack."

"I was nervous," she admitted a bit bashfully. "It's been a long time for me, and I wanted to get our first time over with."

"Well, you got it half right."

"What do you mean?"

"I had *my* first, but unless I'm misreading the signs, you're still waiting."

"Waiting?"

"I have plans for you, Claire Branham." Jax rose up on his knees. His gaze burned a path up and down her gorgeous nakedness. "Slow, steamy, sizzling, screaming plans."

Jax leaned over and licked the tip of her breast. And then proceeded to show her his plans. In detail.

Slowly.

Chapter Nineteen

Something positive? Men are positively idiots!
—CLAIRE

Claire lost track of how many times they made love. In bed and on the sofa, on the floor, in the shower, in the hot tub. They didn't leave their room until after lunch the following day, and by then she was sore enough to really need the massage he'd booked at the spa.

She'd enjoyed startling a laugh out of him when they arrived for their appointments and she innocently told the clerk that their reservation was under the name S. Sven.

"Stamina Sven," he murmured into her ear while they waited for their masseuses to lead them to their room. "I'm glad to know that I've redeemed myself."

"Any more 'redeeming' and I wouldn't have had the energy to walk to the spa."

Following the spa appointment, pampered and relaxed, they returned to their room for a decadent nap. She awoke three hours later to find Jax propped up on his elbow, his head resting in his hand as he watched her.

"What? Was I snoring?"

"No. I was just enjoying the scenery."

Her gaze stole to the wall of windows and she smiled. "It snowed while we were sleeping!"

"Yes. The forecast called for four inches. Looks closer to six to me."

"It's beautiful."

"Not as beautiful as you are, Claire. Flat-out, drop-dead beautiful. Inside and out."

The look in his eyes, the admiration in his tone, made her melt, and her response almost made them late for their dinner reservation.

The following morning, she awoke before he did, and leaving him a note, she went down to the pool for a swim. It was her favorite form of exercise and one of the things she missed most about living in Eternity Springs. Swimming freestyle. Maybe if she ever decided to spend the money that was accumulating and build a house in Eternity Springs, she could build a pool like this one. The indoor/outdoor aspect was pretty darn nice.

Maybe Jax could be her contractor. Nicholas would love to have a pool to swim in year round. Nicholas would love to live in Eternity Springs year round.

But what about Jax? He'd promised Nicholas that they'd stay until summer. He believed he had to move in order to financially provide for his son. What if . . .

Stop it, she scolded herself as she made a racing turn. That was dangerous thinking. Despite the sweet things he'd said and done, despite the fabulous sex, Jax Lancaster had given her no indication that he wanted anything beyond his mistletoe fling.

Of course, she hadn't given him any such indication either, had she?

What if . . .

She could so easily imagine a life with Jax, being a mother to Nicholas and maybe another baby or two. It wouldn't even have to be in Eternity Springs. She loved Eternity Springs and the life, the friendships she was building there, but she could leave it. There was no reason why she couldn't open a Christmas store somewhere else, if that's what she decided she wanted to do. Maybe she'd be happy being a stay-at-home mom.

Jax was building a life and friendships in Eternity Springs. Maybe if she told him about the health of her bank account, he'd decide to make a life in Eternity Springs, too.

Right, Branham. Nothing like having a man want you for your money, is there?

She was gun-shy. She wanted to be wanted for herself. But she also believed that Jax wasn't anything like Landon.

She heard a splash and lifted her head to see who had joined her. Jax.

They raced for two laps, and she thought she just might beat him until he pulled away with a quarter lap to go. Waiting when she reached the end of the pool, he grabbed her around the waist.

"To the victor go the spoils," he said, and then he kissed her.

When his hand began to wander underwater, she laughed and pushed away from him. "The swimming pool is public, Mr. Lancaster."

"Yeah, that's a shame. Maybe I'll win the lottery and buy Three Bears from Bob Hamilton and build one of these. Nicholas would love it. And on those nights when he's at a sleepover . . . how do you feel about skinny-dipping, Ms. Branham?"

The intensity of the yearning that filled her at the idea of living permanently with the Lancasters at Three Bears shocked her. The feeling stayed with her as they went horseback riding and while they showered together afterward, then packed to leave.

When her bags were ready, she stood at the window gazing out at the incredible view. She heard Jax exit the other bedroom and set his suitcase beside hers near the suite's doorway. Without turning around, she said, "This is a breathtaking spot. Thank you for bringing me here."

"My pleasure." He walked up behind her and wrapped his arms around her, holding her against him. They stood without speaking for a bit, then Jax said, "This weekend has been one of the best weekends of my life."

She smiled. "Same for me, Jax."

"So where do we go from here?"

Outwardly, she went still, but her pulse began to thunder. "What do you mean?"

"This no-strings fling of ours hasn't turned out quite like I'd imagined." He turned her around and stared down into her eyes. "I have feelings for you, Claire. Strong feelings. I know that wasn't our deal, and I should probably keep my mouth shut about it, but I want to be honest."

Honest. A lump formed in her throat, and she swallowed hard.

"You matter to me, Claire."

"You matter to me, too, Jax."

He exhaled a heavy breath. "Okay, then. That takes us back to my question. Where do we go from here? I'm teetering right at the edge of the deep end of the pool here. I can probably still take a step back if I need to do that. The fact is, we have a couple of obstacles that stand in the way of a relationship. We'd be stupid to ignore that."

Obstacles. "You're talking about Nicholas?"

"Actually, I don't see my son as a problem. A consideration, definitely. I think we need to be careful that we don't dangle a dream in front of him and then snatch it away."

"A dream?"

"A mother. We've been careful so far not to let him see that we're anything more than friends. Before we change that particular status quo, I need to know where we stand obstaclewise."

"And those obstacles are?"

"My career and your business. I can't be a handyman all my life. I still need to provide for my son, so I still need to leave Eternity Springs after school is out. Here's the million-dollar question. How settled are you in Eternity Springs, Claire?"

Million-dollar question? How about twenty million? She bit back a little hysterical giggle.

Nervous now, she pulled out of his arms and began to pace. What did she say to him? How much truth did she tell?

How much do you want a life with him?

A lot. She wanted a life with Jax and Nicholas as badly as she'd ever wanted anything.

You have to tell him. You can't keep your secret any longer. You have to trust him. He's not Landon.

He's not Landon.

She drew a deep, bracing breath. "Jax, I love Eternity Springs, but I don't have to stay there. For the right reason, I would be willing to leave."

"Am I the right reason?"

"You could be."

A fierce, bright look entered his eyes. He grinned and took a step toward her, but Claire held up her hand, signaling him to stop. "I have more to say."

"Okay."

"Like I said, I'd be willing to move, but you should know that if you and I worked out, it wouldn't be necessary."

"What do you mean?"

She took a deep, bracing breath, then said, "Jax, I'm wealthy."

His smile froze. "Wealthy."

"Yes."

He slipped his hands into his pockets, the light in his

eyes dimmed. "Okay. Well. 'Wealthy' means different things to different people. Maybe you could define it a little better for me?"

She wasn't exactly sure why, but Claire felt insulted. "I could probably buy this resort. With cash."

"Holy shit." He literally took a step back, and when he finally spoke again, his entire demeanor had changed. He accused, "You never told me."

"I'm telling you now." Claire felt tears sting at the back of her eyes.

Jax took another step backward. He turned and looked out the window and remained pensively silent for an eternity. When he finally spoke, it was to spit a curse worthy of the sailor he'd once been.

That put Claire's back up. "Excuse me?"

"It puts a whole new spin on things," he said, his eyes blazing with sudden anger. "I've been down this road before and, frankly, I didn't like the view."

"What do you mean by that?"

"The imbalance in our individual financial situations is what doomed my marriage."

"So?"

"It's a bitch of a thing to deal with."

She wasn't Lara Hardcastle. She got that his wife was a spoiled brat, but Claire had never acted that way around him. Hadn't she proven herself? He was being irrational and a jerk for no reason.

"I wish you'd told me before this, Claire."

I wish you weren't such a jackass.

She folded her arms and pasted a fake smile onto her face. "It really wasn't any of your business before now, was it? We weren't in a relationship. We were having a fling. A no-strings, mistletoe fling."

He scowled and rubbed the back of his neck.

Claire continued, "Only when we started to discuss changing the parameters of our relationship did it become relevant. And now you know, and so do I. It's been fun, Jax, but me being wealthy . . . well, it's obvious that the obstacle is insurmountable. I'm glad we had this talk. So, shall I call for a bellman now?"

He ignored the question and said, "Wait a minute. Wait just a minute. That sounds like . . . what . . . are you ending this?"

"Our fling?" Claire was proud of her nonchalant shrug. "I can go either way on that. I enjoyed the sex. Now that we've cleared the air about any potential emotional entanglements, I don't see why we couldn't continue as we have been."

It was a lie, but she'd figure a way to get out of it if he called her bluff. "Of course, our chaperone will be back from Seattle, so opportunities will be limited. Since I'll be moving back to Baby Bear—"

"What?" he demanded.

"The work there is finished, isn't it?"

"Well, yes. It's been finished for two weeks."

"I was tied up with the Twelve Dogs of Christmas reception, but I have time to move now, a little gap between now and the start of the Christmas season."

A muscle worked in Jax's jaw. "You're just pissed because I'm pissed that you weren't honest with me. Now you're trying to rile me up even more by saying you're going to move out."

No. She was trying to hold her tears at bay. "Honestly, Jax, I'm looking out for Nicholas. Your comment about a mother struck home. I think we've been playing house a little too realistically, and it's better for all of us, Nicholas in particular, that we redefine our boundaries. Now, about the bellman?"

"I'll carry the damned bags down," he groused, marching toward the door. He wrenched it open, gathered up the bags, and banged his way out of the room.

With great gentleness, Claire shut the door behind him. Then she leaned her back against it and allowed the tears to fall.

Jax needed time to rein in his temper. The woman had totally blindsided him. He had known she wasn't destitute. She had a lot of green tied up in inventory at her shop. But lots of times small-business owners had all their assets wrapped up in their business. If Eternity Springs had been Aspen or Vail, he might have wondered. But it wasn't. It was tiny little almost-off-the-map Eternity Springs. And she'd never acted like a society princess. She'd never acted like someone who could buy him and sell him a dozen times over.

Wealthy. Claire Branham was wealthy with a capital *W*. He'd fallen for another wealthy woman.

Frustration rolled through him like a big black wave. Wouldn't it be easier to stick a knife in his heart now and get it over with?

Been there, done that. Lost the custody fight because of it.

Because he needed to blow off steam, a full half hour passed before he returned to their suite, ready to calmly discuss the situation. Claire was nowhere in sight. His name was on the outside of a note lying on the coffee table. He picked it up, read it, and about a million pounds of torque flooded into his jaw.

The damned woman had bailed on him.

Under the circumstances, she'd written, she thought that a four-hour drive would be uncomfortable for them both. She'd find her own way back home.

"Probably phoned in an order for a Rolls-Royce and is having it delivered," he muttered, quitting the suite.

He unloaded her bags from his truck and left them with the bellman. He'd kept a heavy foot on the gas pedal and made the four-hour trip to Eternity Springs in three hours and twenty-seven minutes.

He picked up Captain from the Cicero house, thanked them graciously for watching him, and drove home to Three Bears Valley, leaving Tinsel with the Raffertys for Claire to retrieve. Captain proved to be a good listener, but Jax's temper hadn't subsided much by the time he reached Mama Bear. So the first thing he did upon arriving was to take down every last piece of mistletoe and throw it in the garbage.

Then he packed up all her stuff and hauled it over to Baby Bear. "Just being helpful, after all," he murmured to Captain as he left the key to the cabin on the kitchen table. "Gotta define those boundaries."

Back home, he grabbed his toolbox and headed for Papa Bear. An hour of swinging a hammer helped, but after he showered and went scrounging in the empty refrigerator for something to eat, he muttered, "Screw it."

He drove back into town to grab a burger and a beer at Murphy's Pub and ended up playing pool with Brick Callahan until close.

A light was on at Baby Bear when he came home. He glanced around the clearing for a Rolls. Nothing. Not a Jag or a Maserati, either.

"A chauffeured limousine, then," he'd said to Captain. Or else she'd sent the Rolls back for a different color.

He found her key to Mama Bear on his kitchen table. He kicked the plastic trash can across the kitchen and went to bed. Alone. Lonely.

Damn woman.

After a fitful night's sleep, he awakened in a foul mood and spent the two-hour drive to the airport trying to talk himself out of it before Nicholas arrived. If he were being totally honest with himself, he would admit that he could understand her keeping quiet about her money. But the way she'd turned up her nose and used that snippy little tone when she calmly announced she was leaving him and moving back to Baby Bear rubbed in his craw. Then, to run off and hide rather than ride home with him—that really took the cake.

Jax was pissed, and underneath the anger, he was sad.

Dammit, he'd been falling in love with her.

And she was rich.

Really rich.

Son of a bitch.

A part of Jax recognized that he'd overreacted to her news. But she'd darned sure overreacted to his reaction, too. If she hadn't decamped from their room while he'd been busy blowing off his first head of steam, then maybe they wouldn't have reached the key-trading stage.

The whine of a jet engine drew his notice, and he lifted his gaze to the sky to see the private Cessna that was ferrying his son home approaching from the west. "Let it go, Lancaster."

His boy was coming home. He was coming home and he deserved to have a father who wasn't as grouchy as the Grinch. He would have questions about Claire and Jax needed to be ready for them.

What answer would he give about why Claire wasn't here to meet him? Because Nicholas would expect that. Claire had been right about the whole playing-house thing.

He'd tell the truth. Claire had to work today. Except, did she ever really have to work? He wasn't sure why, but something about the way she'd snotty'd all up made him think that her money might put Lara's family's to shame.

If that's the case, then why did she work so hard at Forever Christmas? Retail wasn't for the faint of heart, and from everything he'd seen, Claire did work at it harder than most.

The plane landed and taxied to a stop. It took a good ten minutes for the ground crew to get stairs in place and the hatch to open, but when it did, Nicholas was first off the plane.

Jax's heart swelled. He'd missed the squirt. The boy started talking long before Jax could hear him.

". . . took me to the market and watched 'em throw the fish. Then we went to the Space Needle. I'm taller than Trevor now. And Mimi made chocolate chip cookies. Pops took us to a Seahawks game! They won!"

"That's awesome," Jax said, giving his son a fierce hug. "I'm sorry you had such a terrible time."

"I didn't have a terrible . . . oh. You're teasing me."

"Yeah." Jax ruffled the boy's hair, then shook Brian Hardcastle's hand. The two men visited for a few moments and finalized their plans for the Hardcastles' visit for Thanksgiving. Then Nicholas hugged his grandfather good-bye and asked Jax if they could stay and watch the Cessna take off. Jax agreed and they grabbed a sandwich in the terminal and found a spot where they could watch the planes.

After Brian's plane was airborne, Jax and Nicholas headed for his truck. Nicholas asked the question that Jax had anticipated. "Where's Miss Claire? I thought she'd be here to meet me, too."

"She had to work, Nicholas."

Actually, that wasn't precisely true, was it? The woman *chose* to work.

He couldn't argue that she didn't dedicate herself to the activity, either. He wondered why. What would make her work so hard at her business when she didn't have to do it? He wondered if he'd ever have the opportunity to find out.

The boy continued to rattle on about his trip. His grandparents had certainly packed a lot into the visit. Nicholas finally wound down an hour into the trip home and fell asleep. Jax appreciated the peace and quiet, and yet, without his son's chatter he returned to his brooding.

He'd probably screwed up big-time. Claire was the best thing that had happened to him in years. She wasn't Lara. She wasn't anything like Lara. Why had he reacted to her news as if she were?

Because you're a too-proud SOB, that's why.

In the front passenger seat, Nicholas stirred and rubbed his eyes. Jax was glad for the distraction from his troublesome thoughts.

"Where are we?" the boy asked.

"About ten minutes out of town."

"Can we stop by and see Miss Claire? I want to tell her about my new Christmas book. I thought she had every Christmas book there is but Mimi gave me one Miss Claire doesn't have. I want her to read it to me tonight."

Well, crap. "About that, Nicholas. I'll be the one reading Christmas stories from now on. Miss Claire moved back to Baby Bear."

"What?" The boy's brows knitted. "Why?"

"It's her place, and I finished all the repairs."

"But . . . I like having her with us. Does that mean she won't fix me breakfast anymore? And dinner? And take me to school?"

"Probably not, Nicholas."

"That stinks. So, she's not your girlfriend anymore?"

Jax whipped his head around to stare at his son. "What makes you think she was my girlfriend?"

"I'm not stupid, Dad." Nicholas folded his arms. "I saw you kissing her."

Busted.

"I like her. A lot. I was hoping that . . . well . . ." He shrugged and added, "Miss Claire would be a really good mom. Did you make her mad?"

Just plunge the knife into my heart, why don't you?

Better nip this in the bud right now. "Nicholas, remember our deal when I agreed to bring you to Eternity Springs? It hasn't changed. We still have to move when school is out."

His son turned his head away from Jax and sat staring out the side window. They rode in silence for a few minutes, then Nicholas asked in a timid voice, "Couldn't she come with us?"

Jax sighed. "Nicholas, here's the deal. Just because grown-ups kiss doesn't mean that they're ready to get married and leave their friends and business and move across the country. I'll be honest with you. I may never want to get married again. The first time I did it, it didn't work out so great."

"Did you hate my mom?"

"Oh, buddy, no. I loved your mother. I truly did."

"So why did you break up with her?"

She dumped me for another man was his immediate response. But Jax couldn't say that to his son about his son's mother. Besides, honesty made him admit that it wasn't as straightforward as that, either. "That is a simple question with a complicated answer. I think your mother and I were too young and too selfish to love unconditionally, and that's what it takes to make a marriage work."

"And you don't love Miss Claire that way, either," Nicholas said in a mournful tone.

Apparently not.

The black mood that his son's return had dispelled returned. Nicholas remained quiet after that insightful remark, so Jax didn't have a distraction from his brooding. He hated this. Maybe he was too proud and stubborn and gun-shy to love Claire the way a man should love a woman, but dammit, he'd needed . . . they'd needed . . . more time. He'd no sooner begun to start thinking long-term when she went and threw a grenade into the works. Hell, if she'd told him she had five ex-husbands it wouldn't have thrown him as bad as learning that he'd gotten tangled up with another wealthy woman.

Jax didn't realize he'd exhaled a heavy sigh until Nicholas reached across the seat and patted his knee. "It'll be okay, Dad. It's like what Miss Celeste says. You just have to think positive and believe that good things will happen, and they will."

Jax's mouth twisted in a crooked smile. Eternity Springs was definitely rubbing off on the kid.

Nicholas launched into a story about his friend Trevor that lasted until they approached the outskirts of Eternity Springs. At that point, the boy said, "Could we go by Forever Christmas before we go home, Dad?"

"Nicholas, did you hear anything I said about Miss Claire?"

"I'm still her friend, aren't I? Besides, I want to get Mimi a present and mail it right away. I want to get her something from Miss Claire's Angel Room. I have my allowance money. Pops and Mimi didn't let me pay for a thing."

Of course they hadn't.

Jax considered his son's request. The kid had just given him the perfect excuse to see Claire. He realized he wanted to see her. They had some unfinished business between them.

Not that they could finish said business in front of Nicholas, but a visit to her shop could be a good ice-breaker. Besides, think of what a huge step his son had just taken! Nicholas nonchalantly asked to go to a Christmas store. How could Jax possibly say no?

"On one condition. Don't say anything to her about the girlfriend stuff. Let me work on fixing this in my own way, on my own time. Okay?"

"Okay."

Jax found a parking place right outside of Forever Christmas. The moment he switched off the engine, Nicholas grabbed up his backpack from the floorboard and scrambled out of the truck. He didn't hesitate a second, but ran right past the planters with their lighted Christmas trees, pushed open the door, and ran into the shop. Where . . . oh, hell . . . Claire had Christmas carols playing.

Jax bolted for Forever Christmas, fearful he'd find his son in the midst of a panic attack. But when he rushed inside, he heard his son's animated voice saying, ". . . Trevor's dad will bring him skiing over the Christmas holidays. And my Mimi and Pops want to come, too, but they don't want to intrude so we have to wait to see if Dad invites them after they come for Thanksgiving."

Well, what do you know. Jax breathed a sigh of relief. "What Child Is This" wasn't bothering him one bit.

Claire shifted her gaze away from Nicholas long enough to send him a look he couldn't interpret. He said, "Hello, Claire."

She might have nodded imperceptibly before turning her attention back to his son, but he couldn't be sure.

Nicholas unzipped his backpack and pulled a couple items from inside as he continued to talk. "I want to show you what my Mimi gave me to keep as a special treasure to remember my mom."

Jax's throat went tight. He recognized the music box that his son removed from his backpack. He'd given it to Lara, the first gift he'd ever given her.

Nicholas twisted the key, and the music box began to play "Lara's Theme" from *Doctor Zhivago*. Jax closed his eyes as the memory of his wife . . . a good memory, for a change . . . washed over him.

"The song has the same name as my mom. It was one of her favorite things. Mimi said my dad gave it to her as a present. So whenever I get to missing her, I can play her song, and it's like she is with me."

"That's a lovely idea, Nicholas."

"I like it. So, I told Mimi about your sister and we got a present for you." He pulled a box from the backpack, one covered in Valentine's hearts like the one she'd given to Nicholas with his ornaments.

"Oh, Nicholas." Claire's expression went a little weepy.

"Open it."

She set the box on her checkout counter, but before she managed to remove the lid, the boy spilled the beans. "It's a music box, too, only it's a snow globe and the song it plays is called 'Michelle.' Mimi said you'd know it."

"By the Beatles. Yes. I do." Claire pulled back white tissue paper and lifted a snow globe from the box. Jax saw a model of the Eiffel Tower before she turned it over, wound the key, then set it on the counter. As the haunting notes of "Michelle" rose on the cinnamon-scented air, Claire traced the sphere of glass with her index finger.

"Do you like it?" Nicholas asked.

"Oh, Nicholas." Claire went down on her knees and took him into her arms. "I love it. I just love it. It's the nicest present anyone has ever given me. Thank you so much."

"I thought you'd like it. Now we have to find something for my Mimi. I need a present for her, Miss Claire. An angel present for the bedroom. It used to be my mom's room, but Mimi is redecorating, and she let me pick the paint color so I picked blue because heaven is blue. That's why I want to send her an angel present because my mom is an angel and when Mimi looks at it, she will think of Mommy. Will you help me find the perfect present, Miss Claire?"

"I'll be proud to help, Nicholas. Let's go see what we can find."

Neither Claire nor Nicholas paid any attention to Jax as they went into the Angel Room. He hung back, his gaze on the music box, memories of Lara drifting through his mind. They'd been happy for a time. Young and in love and blind to the differences that would prove too significant to overcome. Jax had been exactly right when he told Nicholas that they'd been selfish. They'd been selfish, both of them. Both unwilling to compromise.

But he'd loved her. Once upon a time, oh, how he'd loved her. He'd asked her to marry him during a romantic, after-dinner walk on the beach in Cabo. She'd worn a filmy white linen dress, carried her sandals in her hand, and she'd gazed up at him with such love in her eyes it made him feel ten feet tall. And the morning when he came home from his run to find her standing in their bathroom, her expression filled with surprise and awe and happiness, her hand holding the positive pregnancy test, he'd never known such joy.

Jax reached out and flipped open the music box. *Somewhere my love.*

When she'd left him, it had ripped his heart out.

That's what he couldn't forget or forgive. The soul-wrenching pain. The hollow sense of loss. The transformation of love into something dark and ugly that sucked the soul from a man.

Jax closed the music box and followed the sound of Claire's voice to the Angel Room. His gaze was drawn to the angel in his son's hands. The hand-painted face on a round wooden ball was simple and sweet, her dress made of something shimmery blue beneath a tan muslin over-skirt. Her wings, six white feathers, three on either side.

Not the fanciest angel in the room, for certain. Not the angel he'd have chosen with Lara in mind.

As Nicholas handed his choice to Claire and she care-fully wrapped it in white tissue paper and placed it in a gift box, Jax's throat closed on a lump of emotion and his eyes grew misty.

His son had come into Claire's carol-blaring Christ-mas shop today. He'd talked about his mother. In memory of her, he'd bought an angel to send to the grandmother who'd finally redecorated her late daughter's bedroom.

Nicholas had defeated his demons. His heart had healed.

Why hasn't mine?

Suddenly, Jax needed to be out of that shop, away from Claire, far away from her Angel Room. "Nicholas, I'll wait for you at the truck."

Taking two long strides, he reached Forever Christ-mas's front door, yanked it open, and barreled out onto the street. He shoved his hands into his pockets. He gritted his teeth. He was breathing hard, and he didn't know why.

He almost ran right over Celeste Blessing, who had her arms overfilled with bags from the Trading Post grocery store.

"Sorry," he said as she lurched out of the way and her bags went swinging. He dove for the bags, catching one of them just before it hit the ground. "So sorry, Celeste. I wasn't looking where I was going. Here, let me help you." He scooped the other three bags from her arms. "Are you heading home?"

"Thank you, Jax. I'm on my way to Lori's house to stock her refrigerator. Since you're keeping Captain, I'm sure you know that she and Chase are due back from their honeymoon late tonight? I'm afraid I bought more than I'd intended. I'm happy to have the help."

Lori's house was two blocks away. Jax smiled at Celeste and said, "After you."

She and Jax made small talk as they walked, and he was glad for the distraction from his thoughts. By the time he followed Celeste up onto the newlyweds' front porch, he'd begun to relax.

So he had absolutely no explanation for what he did next.

He set the grocery bags on Lori's kitchen counter then met his companion's gentle, blue-eyed gaze. The question came out of nowhere. "Celeste, how do people earn their wings?"

Her smile beamed right into that dark part of his mood. "You are referring to the official Angel's Rest blazon awarded to those who have embraced love's healing grace?"

"Yeah." He'd noticed a handful of people around town wearing them, and he'd asked what they were.

"The path is different for everyone, dear, but in order to walk it, you must find your way onto it to begin with. You can do that by listening to your inner angel."

Angels, again. He couldn't get away from them. They were everywhere he turned and, frankly, it was getting a little creepy.

"Unfortunately as we grow older, we often have trouble tuning in to them. Luckily for you, you have an angel hearing aid."

"Excuse me?"

"A child. Angels don't use an inside voice to speak to children, so they hear the message better. Learn from your Nicholas, Jax. Soak up his truth and you will find your path. Then . . ."—she reached up and patted his cheek— "walk it and be a raindrop."

"Be a raindrop?"

"Moisten the parched heart of someone around you with your love and watch her flower before you. Together you will walk in beauty, light, and love."

"Celeste, I suspect you just said something important, but I don't have a clue what it could be."

She laughed and reached into one of her bags and pulled out a box from Fresh bakery. She handed it to him saying, "Here. This is a new product we're going to be selling in the gift shop at Angel's Rest. I want you to have the first box."

Jax read the label aloud. "'Angel's Rest Fortune Cookies'?"

"Sarah's recipe, my fortunes." She slipped her arm through his and ushered him toward the door. "Now, thank you for the help, but you should run along back to your truck. You don't want to keep your son waiting. Thanks again for the help."

"No problem. Thanks, Celeste."

He was halfway down the street when he heard her call, "Oh, Jax?"

"Yes, ma'am."

"Be sure to listen closely. You'll hear your angel cheering you on."

As Jax approached his truck, Nicholas exited Forever Christmas carrying a box wrapped for mailing. "It's all ready, Dad. Miss Claire let me call Mimi and I got her address."

They stopped at the post office. Jax waited in the truck while his son mailed his package, and his gaze stole toward the box of fortune cookies. "What the heck."

He opened the box, took a cookie, and cracked it open.

He removed the little white paper from inside and un-rolled it. Aloud, he read, "'Forgiveness is fresh air for the soul.'"

Forgiveness? Who was he supposed to forgive? For what?

Or maybe he was the one who needed to be forgiven.

"Huh."

Nicholas returned to the truck, and as they continued the drive to Three Bears Valley, Jax subtly questioned the boy about the time he'd spent with Claire. He listened very closely to Nicholas's answers.

The kid said a lot. He didn't shut up the whole way home. Nevertheless, Jax didn't hear one damned thing he would label as a "truth."

Nicholas played with Captain while Jax worked at Papa Bear that afternoon. He fixed hamburgers for supper, and when bedtime rolled around, read more Percy Jackson to Nicholas along with his new Christmas book—*The Christmas Angel Waiting Room.*

When Jax went to bed that night, an oppressive silence seemed to hang over Mama Bear. He couldn't fall asleep and couldn't get comfortable, tossing and turning and punching his feather pillow into shape.

So far, his angel wasn't talking.

So much for help from Celeste and his "hearing aid."

Deciding a late-night snack was in order, Jax went downstairs to raid the pantry. Pickings were slim.

Then he remembered the cookies.

He chose three cookies, set them on a paper plate, and poured a glass of milk. He cracked open all three cook-ies and ate them without bothering to read the fortunes inside. The cookies were good. Full of flavor. Cinnamon and ginger and something else he couldn't quite place. Almond, perhaps?

He drank his milk. Stared at the fortunes. Listened

for those cheers Celeste had promised. Sighing heavily, he unrolled the three papers and read them one after the other.

Don't give up. Let go.

Take a leap of faith and fly.

Believe.

Jax drained his glass of milk. He picked up the slips of paper and took them upstairs to his bedroom. There, he dug the fortune he'd opened earlier from the pocket of his jeans and added it to the stack.

He picked up his journal and a pen and wrote, "I think I might have heard my angel today."

When he closed the book, he traced the embossed word upon the cover with his finger and thought of Claire. *Believe.*

Then he tucked the four angel-cookie fortunes in the journal and turned off his light. That night, Jax slept like a baby and dreamed of a red-haired angel atop a Christmas tree.

Chapter Twenty

You've done dumber things in your life.
It's just been a while.
—JAX

"Hand me the knife," Claire said, extending her palm like a surgeon in the operating room.

Brick Callahan's wary voice drawled, "You're not going to stab me with it, are you?"

Kneeling on the floor of an old silver-mine-turned-storage-facility on the grounds of Angel's Rest, she looked up sharply at her friend. "What?"

"I'm not exactly sure why, although I do have my suspicions, but I'm already bleeding from a thousand cuts from that tongue of yours. Are you ready to put me out of your misery?"

"I . . . oh." Awareness washed over her and she winced. "I'm sorry, Brick. I'm terrible."

"You're in a terrible mood." He handed her the box cutter. "Have been for a week or so."

Claire couldn't argue with the observation, so rather than respond, she busied herself by slicing through cardboard and packing tape with the blade and yanking the box open. Inside she spied the lighted green wreaths with red all-weather bows that would be mounted around the streetlights in town.

Under other circumstances, the sight would make Claire smile. Celeste had lobbied the chamber for this style because, she'd confessed to Claire, they reminded her of halos. Count on Celeste to get her angel on whenever possible.

Only, Claire didn't have any smiles inside her. She was not a happy woman.

"Want to tell Dr. Brick why you are such a grouch?" When she didn't immediately answer, he added, "I suspect it has something to do with a certain hammer-swinging sailor. He's been almost as pleasant to be around as you of late."

Her attention perked up at that, and the recognition of her reaction only served to stoke her temper. "Men are so stupid."

"Because . . . what . . . we forget to put the toilet seat down?"

"Because . . . just because." She handed him the box cutter and said, "Would you please open up the other boxes for me? I've learned the hard way how important it is to inspect each box. I'd hate to wait until next Friday to discover that something was shipped wrong or is damaged."

Brick chastised her with a look, but thankfully refrained from commenting.

Claire knew she was acting crabby, but honestly, she was tired of being nice. Tired of pasting a smile on her face and acting like holly-jolly Miss Christmas when she was feeling Halloween witchy. Black hats and black cats and a high-pitched cackle—that suited her much better than the Twelve Dogs of Christmas these days.

Men *were* stupid. But *she* was an idiot.

She'd let her guard down. Again. It had bit her in the broomstick. Again. One would think that after the debacle that was Landon the Lying Lizard Lawyer, she would have known better. But oh, no. The first low-slung tool belt who struts by makes her forget everything she'd learned. She'd let her glands do her thinking for her, and she'd let Mr. Mistletoe into her heart. She'd fallen head over heels for his son, and she'd allowed herself to dream of love and marriage and family.

Again.

Stupid. Stupid. Stupid.

Her temper hadn't cooled in the two weeks since she'd returned from Silver Eden. If anything, the constant reminders of her foolishness served to stoke its fire. It didn't help that she couldn't seem to get away from the man. Every time she turned around, something was there to bring Jax Lancaster to mind.

Go to brush her teeth and there was the bathroom sink that leaked before Jax fixed it. A stop at the market to pick up produce and she automatically reached for bananas. She didn't eat bananas. Jax and Nicholas had one every morning with their breakfast. And then there was the blasted mistletoe. Every time she turned around someone was buying something mistletoe related. It didn't help that over the past six weeks she'd ordered a ridiculous amount of mistletoe-themed items. Nor was she happy that the Chamber of Commerce had elected to store their new Christmas decorations in the space Celeste had designated as Mistletoe Mine.

Maybe she should close the shop and go on a vacation. One that lasted until June.

"Okay, sugarplum," Brick said. "All the boxes are open. Are you sure Eternity Springs has enough public space to display all of this stuff?"

"Oh, yes. The committee was quite deliberate about what they ordered. Thanks for the help, Brick."

"I'm always ready to help a friend." Following a deliberate pause, he added, "That includes listening. Why don't you tell me what Lancaster did that has put a burr beneath your saddle?"

"I don't want to talk about him." She rose to her feet and braced her hands on her hips. "Or his idiotic pride. Or his exceedingly stupid prejudice."

"Okay."

"I had a fling. No strings. No big deal. It happened. It's over."

"Sure it is."

Now she folded her arms and glared at him. "Wait a minute. What do you mean by that?"

"If it's over, then why the attitude? You should be happy as a pig in mud right now, checking in the fruits of your not insignificant labor." He waved his arm expansively toward the row of open boxes. "You worked hard to make this happen. You should be enjoying it."

"I am enjoying it," she snapped.

He rolled his tongue around his cheek. "Uh-huh."

"I am. I'm proud of my contribution to this project. I can't wait to decorate next Friday."

It was such a lie. The Christmas Comfort-and-Joy Season bore down upon her like a big black tornado. Which reminded her. All the lights and ornaments and, yes, the angel tree topper that she'd taken out of inventory and set aside for the tree she'd hoped to put up at Mama Bear next week needed to go back into stock. What Landon had begun, Jax had finished.

"I talked to him yesterday. He's no happier than you are."

Claire went still. She should tell Brick she didn't want to hear anything about Jax Lancaster.

"He said he's tried to talk to you, but that you refuse to let it happen."

"He has no business spreading my personal business around town."

"Wasn't exactly around town. He was finishing up the work on the dance hall at the North Forty, and he was swinging his hammer so hard I thought he might hit right through the wall. Not all that different from the way you handled that box cutter a few minutes ago. I asked him what the heck was wrong, and he said the two of you had a misunderstanding."

A misunderstanding? A misunderstanding! "Grrr . . ."

Brick looked at her and shook his head. "Honey, as someone with up-close-and-personal experience with living with a broken heart, I think—"

"He did not break my heart," she snapped. "I don't want to talk about Jax Lancaster, Brick."

He held up his hands in surrender. "Okay. Okay. I'll change the subject. What do you need me to do next here?"

She put him to work testing strings of lights, and by the time they completed their job and departed Mistletoe Mine, she had a short list of items that needed to be exchanged and a longer packing list of items she needed for the ski trip to Aspen she'd just decided to take. She would close the shop, load up Tinsel, and spend Thanksgiving on the slopes.

Happy with her plan, she returned to Forever Christmas and made reservations at a pet-friendly lodge in Aspen. Then she chose a piece of holiday-themed printer paper and wrote out a CLOSED notice for her front door that included the day of her return—Black Friday.

"Wait." She crumpled up the paper, tossed it into the trash, and got another sheet. "Just because your outlook has changed . . ."

She changed the return date on the second notice to "Deck the Halls Friday."

She'd have some disgruntled customers from now until then, but she didn't really care. People could delay their shopping until Deck the Halls Friday. She was the boss. She could close the shop whenever she wanted, and what's the use in being rich as Midas if she never spent anything? She wanted away from Eternity Springs. Away from Three Bears Valley.

Away from Jax Lancaster.

Maybe she'd go to Aspen and find a boy toy to use for the weekend. She could have another fling. An Aspen fling. Mistletoe didn't grow in aspen trees, did it?

She should have known better than to go down that mistletoe path from the start. After all, mistletoe was a parasite. She should have picked up on the message of that.

Except, Jax was the farthest thing from a parasite there was. Unlike Landon. Landon was . . . is . . . a parasite.

As she carried her notice and Scotch tape toward the front door, it opened and a whirlwind blew inside, calling, "Miss Claire! Miss Claire! Guess what?"

Nicholas came to a halt in front of her and pushed his black-framed glasses up on his nose. "You'll never guess what happened at school today!"

Excitement lit the boy up like the Christmas tree behind him, and Claire couldn't help but smile in the face of his joy. "Hmm . . . whatever happened is obviously very exciting. Did somebody throw up their lunch or break their arm at recess?"

"No! I got a part in our Christmas pageant. I get to be an angel and I get to say something. I was hoping I'd get to be a camel because they get to wear a hump, but it's okay that Galen got that part. I get to talk. Will you help me make my costume, Miss Claire? I need wings. And a halo."

Oh, Nicholas. You already have them.

"You will come watch me in the pageant, won't you?"

"Of course I'll be there. I'll go early and do my best to get a seat in the front row."

"And the costume? You'll help me with the costume? I think we are gonna have to sew something this time, and you know Dad."

Yes, she knew his dad. If only she could figure out a way to forget him.

As Nicholas continued to rattle on about his costume, Claire's attention remained divided between his actions and his words. Nicholas explored while he talked. He picked up snow globes and shook them. He pushed buttons and switched on switches. He flipped through the pages of books.

Claire's heart gave a little bittersweet twist. Look at him. He'd told her and Jax back before the Twelve Dogs of Christmas reception how badly he wanted to be like everyone else—a normal kid. As he turned and watched the miniature electric train chug through her Christmas village display, it was clear that Nicholas had defeated his demons.

She wished she knew his secret.

Jax loaded the last of the Thanksgiving dishes into the dishwasher, then filled the sink to tackle the pots and pans.

"Where are the dishtowels?" Brian Hardcastle asked.

"Underneath the coffeepot. Third drawer down."

Since Linda had prepared their Thanksgiving feast, she was taking a well-earned after-dinner nap. Nicholas was sitting in the living room perusing the pet finder Web site and dreaming of getting his heart's desire.

Jax gazed out the window toward dark and empty Baby Bear. *One of us might as well get our heart's desire.*

Standing beside him with a white flour-sack dishtowel in hand, Brian noted the path of Jax's gaze. "Nicholas expects her to come home sometime today."

"Yeah. She left a sign on the door to her shop saying she'd be open tomorrow."

"So what did you do to screw things up with her?"

Jax gave Brian a sidelong look. "Nicholas must have been saying a lot."

"No. I have keen powers of observation. Following our first visit to Eternity Springs, I predicted that you'd be engaged to marry her by the end of the year."

"Yeah, well, I'm going to have to dig myself out of a pretty deep hole to prove you right."

Brian went still for a minute, then he nodded. "So she is what you want. I thought so. It's difficult for me to think of another woman filling Lara's role of mother, but he needs someone. I liked her. She seems like a lovely young woman."

"She's wonderful." Jax realized that Brian Hardcastle had just given him his blessing. He also realized that receiving it meant more to him than he ever would have imagined. "I just hope I'll get the chance to make things right with her."

"I have faith in you. You're a hardheaded SOB, Lancaster. You'll get the job done."

Throughout the rest of the afternoon, Jax kept a close watch on Baby Bear. He had a lot he wanted to say to Claire Branham, and he didn't care what it took, she was going to listen to him.

Jax would be the first to admit that he'd acted like an ass when she'd shared her news at Silver Eden. Under the circumstances, he could understand why she hadn't wanted to make the return trip to Eternity Springs with him. Sometimes a person needed time to work off their mad. Heaven knows he'd needed time to process the information she'd thrown at him. A little time apart can be an effective tool to be used to repair a relationship.

But enough was enough. She'd dodged him long enough.

He needed to talk to Claire. He had apologies to make, explanations to share, and questions to ask. He had a game plan to put into motion.

If only he could get the woman to sit still long enough to listen.

Events of the past few weeks had proved one thing. Claire was definitely a runner. It shouldn't have come as a surprise. Hadn't she told him she'd been running away from home when she met Celeste at that little town in Texas? She'd run from him at Silver Eden. She'd run from him by leaving Mama Bear. She'd run on this mystery Thanksgiving trip.

Jax recognized that instincts were difficult to ignore, so his intention, his challenge, was to convince her to change direction, to run toward him, toward love, rather than away from it.

If he ever managed to pin her down long enough to talk to him again, that is. The woman was as slippery as an eel.

He watched for her arrival all afternoon and into the evening. When her car finally drove past Mama Bear shortly before ten P.M., he breathed a sigh of relief. *She's back.*

He briefly considered marching over there now, but better sense prevailed. Who knew how long she'd been traveling today? She might be exhausted. The confrontation could wait one more day.

Besides, it made sense strategically to wait until tomorrow to approach her. After all, Deck the Halls Friday was right up Miss Christmas's alley. She'd be in a good mood tomorrow, full of Christmas cheer. The timing was actually working out quite nice.

Jax went to bed with a lighter heart than he'd had in days.

Claire awoke to her cell phone sounding Jax's ring tone of "You're a Mean One, Mr. Grinch." She glared at her phone, then pulled the covers over her head and told herself to go back to sleep. This was not how she wanted to start her day.

She didn't want to talk to Jax. She didn't want to see him. She didn't want to think about him.

She lay in bed, hiding beneath the covers. He called twice more during the next ten minutes. She didn't answer. When her phone rang for the fourth time that morning, it took her a moment to recognize the different ringtone—"I Hate Everything About You" by Three Days Grace. Her day went from bad to worse before it even started.

Not Jax this time. Landon.

She let that call go to voicemail, too. She *might* work up her courage to listen to it later, but probably not. She wasn't up to dealing with Landon today.

Today was Deck the Halls Friday. She had to put on her big-girl panties and go to town and be nice. Be happy. Be Miss Christmas.

"Bah, humbug."

She threw off her covers and rolled out of bed, groaning a little due to muscles sore from three days of skiing. She took a long, hot shower and decided to call the Angel's Rest spa and book a massage.

An hour later, wearing a red ski jacket, a green wool scarf, and a knit cap with antler ears to complete her ensemble, she pasted on a smile that apparently passed as real and accepted the townspeople's kudos for her efforts toward making their new decorations possible. As president of the Chamber of Commerce, Celeste heaped such praise upon Claire that under other circumstances, she'd have basked in the glory.

However, Jax's constant presence and steady stare had her anxious as Frosty on a summer afternoon.

She'd tangibly felt his gaze during the entire Deck the Halls kickoff gathering in Davenport Park. She'd tried her best to pretend he wasn't there, but the man was impossible to ignore. She felt as if she were under siege. When the mayor assigned volunteers into decorating teams of three, she'd closed her eyes and prayed she wouldn't be paired with him.

Fate had been kind to her. She ended up on Chase and Lori Timberlake's team and got to hear about their travels in Tibet on their rafting-trip honeymoon. Claire had been so relieved to escape Jax Lancaster's undivided attention that she actually enjoyed herself while hanging lights and garlands and red all-weather bows along Cottonwood.

Her tension returned when Three Days Grace sounded from her cell phone again. What was so freaking important that Landon wouldn't leave her alone?

"If you'd listen to one of the twelve voice mails he's already left, you probably would discover the answer," she muttered as she slipped her key into the lock at Forever Christmas and opened the door for what she expected to be her biggest sales day ever.

She traded her jacket and cap for her usual Forever Christmas apron. In the twenty minutes she had to herself before opening the shop, she added mulling spices to apple cider in an electric beverage urn, which she switched on to heat. Soon the aromas of apples, cinnamon, and clove drifted through the shop.

She should probably restock her cider supply, she decided as she removed the day's cash from her bank envelope and added it to her register drawer. When Liz came in for her shift, Claire would send her over to the Trading Post for some. Liz Bernhardt was one of two part-time workers Claire had hired to help her from now until Christmas. Both of her new employees were high school seniors saving for college, and they'd impressed her with their enthusiasm. She hoped they'd be as dependable as their resumes led her to expect.

Claire restocked the ornaments on her depleted Dog-house tree and carried the empty boxes out to the trash dumpster in the alley behind the shop. She turned on the music and moved about the shop, switching on light fixtures, Christmas tree lights, and the Christmas village display. She added more peppermints to her giveaway bowl and decided everything was ready for the opening. Everything but her, that is.

She checked her watch. Ten minutes. She had ten minutes of freedom to scowl and be cranky and fight back tears. She wished she'd never come to Eternity Springs. She wished she'd never gone to the hot springs to soak her sore shoulder that night in July. She totally wished she hadn't moved to Three Bears Valley and fallen in love with the cabins, the man, and his son.

She had to talk to him. She realized that. Eternity Springs was too small to avoid him much longer. Besides, despite his ridiculous overreaction upon learning the news . . . she missed him.

Maybe she should listen to one of Jax's voice mails. Maybe just one. The last one?

Her finger shook just a little as she hit the voice-mail icon on her phone. "Hey, Claire. I miss you. Can we talk?"

Oh, Jax.

A rap on her front door interrupted her musings and demanded her attention. Liz had arrived for work. Claire worked up a smile and let her in. "Before you take your coat off, I need you to run to the Trading Post for me."

"Okay," the teenager said.

Claire gave her a list and money from petty cash. "When you return, come in the back door—it's open. Leave the groceries in the storeroom, and you'll see a couple aprons hanging on hooks. Wear one of them, and you can hang your jacket there."

"Yes, ma'am. I'll be right back." Liz beamed a smile and added, "I can't tell you how excited I am about having this job. It's like I get to have Christmas every day."

Claire smiled and sent Liz on her way. Alone in the shop once more, she repeated, "Bah, humbug."

When the Rudolph cuckoo clock sounded the hour, Claire flipped her sign from CLOSED to OPEN and prepared to get Christmasy. Three shoppers arrived immediately. She sold ornaments and lights, two Christmas village collectibles, and an angel tree topper in the first five minutes.

Claire had anticipated a busy day.

Catastrophic caught her by surprise.

She never expected Landon Perryman to slither into Forever Christmas with Jax Lancaster right behind him.

Chapter Twenty-one

You've done dumber things in your life.
It's just been a while.
—CLAIRE

Jax didn't want to confront Claire while she was at work. If she'd answer his calls or one of his knocks, he wouldn't have to do it. But she wouldn't, so he would. This nonsense had gone on long enough.

He headed toward Forever Christmas armed with a sincere, ready-to-grovel apology and a heartfelt declaration of love. While he hoped he'd arrive to find a lull between customers, he was prepared to state his case in public. He wouldn't risk her running again before he had a chance to talk to her.

He sighed inwardly when he realized that the tourist in front of him was headed for the shop, too. *Oh, well, an audience it is.*

Bells jingled on the door as Jax followed the man into the shop. He scanned the room for Claire, and immediately realized something was terribly wrong.

She spared Jax barely a glance, her focus fixed on the tourist. She'd gone as pale as the snow on the ground of her Christmas village.

"Hello, Claire," said the stranger.

"What are you doing here?" she demanded. "I don't want you here. Go away."

"If you'd answered my phone calls, this visit wouldn't have been necessary. You didn't, so it is."

"Landon, you need to leave right now."

Landon. The lawyer. The Lying Lizard guy. Quadruple L. Jax's gaze skimmed the store looking for other shoppers as he stepped forward to join Claire, setting his mouth into a grim line. Thankfully, Forever Christmas appeared to be empty of shoppers at the moment. Claire wouldn't want observers for this exchange.

"I'm not leaving until you hear me out, Claire. This is something you can't refuse or ignore. You've been invited to read at a White House holiday party! It's December nineteenth, and they need our answer by this afternoon."

"No."

"Claire, the party is for sick children. The invitation is from the First Lady herself! You can't say no to this!"

"Yes I can. I am."

"I already told them yes!"

Claire twisted her head to look at Jax. Her eyes had gone wild and round like a reindeer caught in the headlights. "Make him leave, Jax. Please?"

Jax stepped forward, planted his feet wide apart, and folded his arms. "The lady has asked you to go."

"And I will. As soon as she tells me she'll make the appearance." He reached into his jacket pocket and pulled out an airline ticket folder. "It's the White House, Claire. All the arrangements have been made. You fly out of Denver on the eighteenth and return on the twentieth."

"Okay," Claire snapped. "Okay. Just go. You have to go now."

The lawyer nodded once, then turned to go. He was halfway to the door when, her voice filled with despair, Claire asked, "Why?"

"Because Starlina is every little girl's fantasy and you are her creator."

As Landon exited the shop, a group of seven women entered. Jax recognized the members of the Eternity Springs Garden Club and knew them as the biggest gossips in town. Thank goodness they arrived after Landon's big announcement or the news would be all over town in minutes.

Jax stood at an angle that allowed him to see into the storeroom. As the garden club entered through the front door, he saw Liz step inside through the back. She set down a grocery sack and swapped her jacket for a Forever Christmas apron.

"Hello, Claire, dear." Janice Peterson, the grande dame of the gossips, swept forward. "I want to be one of the first to tell you how lovely all the decorations look. You are a treasure for our town. Just a treasure. I predict that merchants this year will double their usual sales. Walking around town has surely put me into the Christmas spirit like never before. I'm just . . ."—she clicked her fingers—"spending, spending, spending.

"Which brings me to the reason for my visit. My dear sweet granddaughter just had her visit with Santa Claus in Davenport Park. She asked Santa for that Christmas angel doll, Starlina, from *The Christmas Angel Waiting Room*. I heard on the news that it's going to be one of the year's hottest toys, so I thought we'd best get one while we still can. Will I find it in your Angel Room, dear, or somewhere else in the shop?"

Claire whipped her head around. Her eyes went round and wide and wild. In a high, shrill voice more befitting the Wicked Witch of the West than Miss Christmas, she said, "I don't carry that doll. I will never carry that doll. It's ugly. It's a bastardized commercialization. It's everything that's wrong with Christmas. You just said it, Mrs. Petersen! You're spending, spending, spending!

That's not what Christmas is supposed to be about! Who cares about gifts? It's supposed to be about love, family, and charity. But one look at that bug-eyed Starlina and everyone forgets that part. She is the worst of all. You know why? Because she's a fake. A lie! The message of that story is bullshit. I hate that doll! I hate that story! And I! Hate! Christmas!"

The women in the shop gasped as one.

"Well, I never!" Janice huffed. "Who do you think you are, talking to me like that?"

Claire burst into tears and ran into the storeroom. A moment later, the back door banged open and slammed shut.

Jax headed after her, pausing only long enough to instruct Liz. "Call the other worker in. Do the best you can. If it gets to be too much for you, close up shop."

"Okay. I will. What just happened, Mr. Lancaster?"

"I'm afraid Miss Christmas just got outted."

Claire fled Eternity Springs. She might not have stopped at Baby Bear had she not left Tinsel snuggled in her bed this morning. Claire might be willing to walk away from the responsibilities of her shop, but she couldn't abandon her dog.

She sniffed back tears all the way to the valley, but when Tinsel met her at the door of the little cabin, tail wagging and jumping happily, Claire broke. She sank onto the floor, cradled her dog against her, and sobbed. She cried for herself, for her sister, for her parents. She cried for all of the losses in her life. She cried for the self-destruction she'd just visited upon herself with her outburst in Forever Christmas.

Tinsel mewled and licked the salty tears from her cheeks. But then, like everyone else, she abandoned Claire, trotting away toward the kitchen where a moment later, lapping sounds arose from the water bowl.

Lonely. I'm so blasted lonely.

Lonely and alone.

Lost in misery, she wasn't aware of being lifted from the floor or carried to her bed. She didn't make a conscious decision to lay her head against the broad chest and sob, but that's what she did. Claire clung to the silent offer of compassion, the comforting stroke of a gentle hand, and cried until her tears ran dry.

Only then did Jax speak. "Want to tell me about it, sweetheart?"

No. It was a humiliating story. She didn't want him to know. She didn't want anyone to know. So why she opened her mouth and started babbling, she absolutely couldn't say.

"I volunteered at a local hospital. I held storytime. I read to the kids who were like me, the siblings who sat in hospital waiting rooms while their parents dealt with their sick child. I wrote the story for them, and when a few of them asked for a copy of it, I self-published it so I had copies to give away."

She closed her eyes and recalled the moment she'd first noticed the handsome man who had taken a seat near her story circle. "He was there one day. Landon. He listened and afterward told me how much he loved the story."

She'd been so flattered. So . . . easy. "He invited me to dinner and after that—it was a whirlwind romance. I slept with him. I fell in love with him. I believed him when he told me he loved me. We got engaged, but never quite managed to set a wedding date."

Jax murmured a soothing sound and pressed a kiss against her hair.

"He was so slick. I was so trusting, stupid, and naïve. I have terrible instincts. I signed the partnership agreement without getting independent advice."

She'd signed it without even reading it, that's how stupid she'd been.

"You're business partners with him?"

She nodded. "He's an entertainment lawyer. He got the movie deal, and I was so excited. I thought all my dreams had come true. I didn't like that they changed her name. She's Gardenia, not Starlina. He convinced me to listen to the marketing gurus. I resent that so much. He convinced me about everything. The only good piece of advice he gave me was to use a pseudonym. I used my sister's first name."

"M. C. Kelley," Jax murmured.

"We both went by our middle names. I'm Mary Claire. Stupid Mary Claire because I never suspected Landon. That's what is so hard to take. He told me he traveled a lot, and I took him at his word. I didn't suspect a thing—until I met his wife."

"Ouch," Jax said. "The men in your life have certainly let you down, haven't they?"

"I have terrible instincts. I'm stupid."

"What you are is stubborn. You have to let me apologize, Claire. I was an ass. I'm sorry. Money was a hot button in my marriage, and I let that experience color my relationship with you. Please forgive me."

She pulled out of his arms, a wave of despair washing over her. She couldn't do this. "It doesn't matter."

He reached for her hand and held it. "Yes it does. You deserved better than that from me. Hear me out. I was gun-shy. And I let my past and my pride get the best of what is usually my good sense. I shouldn't have reacted the way I did. I should have listened."

"Jax . . ."

"Hush, now. Listen. You were right. You don't owe me an explanation about your finances. Hell, you don't owe me one even now. It was stupid to make you think I was comparing you to Lara, because you're not remotely like her. And you know what? I'm not the guy I was back then, either. I've changed, too. For the better. I don't care if I'm a handyman for the rest of my life. Nicholas is happy here. I'm happy here. We can stay here, but I can be happy anywhere—as long as you are part of the picture. I want you, Claire. I don't care if you're a billionaire. I want to be with you. You make me happy. You make me believe."

"No. Truly. It doesn't matter." Agitation propelled her from the bed. She stalked nervously around the room. "It was a fling. We said it from the first. That's all it was. All it can be."

Jax rose and faced her. "I want more than a fling, Claire. I want you. I want a future with you. I am in love with you."

Claire held up her hands, palms out. "Don't say that. Don't you say that to me! Not today. Not ever!"

"Honey . . ." He took a step toward her. "It's going to be okay."

"No! It's not going to be okay!" Hysteria added a shrill note to her voice. "I just humiliated myself in front of all of Whoville. News of my meltdown has probably made it to Gunnison by now! There is no coming back from this. I can't show my face around here anymore. So I won't. I'll leave town. I'll close up Forever Christmas and just go."

"Claire, you can't do that."

"Yes, I can! This is America. I'm free and I'm the boss."

"Honey, it's time you stopped running away. Run to me. To us. We need you."

"No. I can't stay in this town. I can't be Miss Christmas. I tried. I tried to take it back, but I can't do it. I failed. I have to leave."

Jax slowly shook his head. "That first instinct of yours is a killer to overcome. Okay, Claire, if you're determined to go, then we will go with you."

"What?"

"Nicholas and I will go with you. We aren't anchored

to Eternity Springs. Where do you want to go? We will go with you."

"What? Why you say that? You can't say that."

He braced his hands on his hips. "Yes I can. I love you."

I love you. Oh, God. She was too raw. It was too risky. "You promised Nicholas you'd stay until school is out. You can't go back on your word. Nicholas is happy here. You can't uproot him."

"Okay, that's a problem. However, I'll bet on my son. I'll bet if given the choice, he'll choose you."

"No. You can't bring him into my crazy world. He found Christmas. You can't take it away from him."

"You're being irrational, Claire. No one has taken Christmas from you! You can get it back. Don't let that bastard ruin this for you. So you had a public meltdown. I'm sure it's not the first one that's happened here in Eternity Springs. And you don't have to go read your book at the White House. You're right. This is still America. You have the freedom of choice. I get it that it's a big deal and it's sick children, but if that lying loser is going to be there, too, then the hell with that. You don't have to go. None of that matters, anyway."

Her heart was breaking. Crumbling into pieces. It was too much. She couldn't think. "Please go, Jax. I need to be alone." *I'm always alone.* "Please, just leave me be."

"Irrational and overwrought," he murmured. "All right, honey. I'll give you time alone this afternoon—as long as you give me your word that you won't pick up and run on me. Promise me you won't disappear."

"I have to leave Eternity Springs, Jax."

"Not today. You don't have to go today. Promise me."

"Jax, I—"

"Your word, Miss Christmas."

She closed her eyes. "Okay. Okay. I won't leave today."

He walked toward Baby Bear's front door, pausing at her side long enough to give her a kiss on the cheek. "I'll stop by the shop and check on things, make sure your girls are handling it okay."

Guilt fluttered in Claire's stomach. Poor Liz. What a horrible way to begin a new job. "Thank you. Please tell her I'm going to give her two weeks'—no, a month's—pay as a bonus."

"Will do." At the door, Jax paused and glanced over his shoulder. "You can trust me, Claire. I am a man of my word."

When the door shut behind him, she buried her face in her hands. She wanted to believe him. She wanted to believe *in* him. Would she never learn?

Claire spent the rest of the day huddled in Baby Bear, curled up with a historical romance novel. Nothing like a good old Viking love-story fantasy to make her forget all about the realities of her own existence. Her phone rang off and on all afternoon, but she didn't bother to check the numbers. When a knock sounded at her door just before dark, she tried to pretend that she didn't hear it.

Tinsel put the kibosh on that by perking her ears and thumping her tail. *"Woof. Woof. Woof."*

That particular three-bark hello invariably announced that Nicholas had come to call. No matter how badly Claire wanted to ignore the knock, she couldn't refuse to respond to Nicholas. She opened the door.

The boy beamed up at her. "Hi, Miss Claire."

"Hello, Nicholas."

"Can I come in?" Without waiting for her to respond, he strode inside. "Dad told me your secret! He said you wrote *The Christmas Angel Waiting Room,* and that you have the original version, that it's different from the one Mimi read to me. Daddy said it's about Gardenia from your Angel Room instead of Starlina, and that he saw the book when he saved it from the fire. I want to see it, Miss Claire. That's the coolest thing ever! Will you show it to me? Will you read it to me?"

"Oh, Nicholas." The maelstrom of emotion that she'd quieted with Viking tales came roaring back. "Nicholas."

"Were you maybe saving it for sometime special? Today is a pretty special day. It's Deck the Halls Friday, and I helped decorate the town just like any other kid."

"Nicholas." *You're breaking my heart.*

"Please, Miss Claire? Read to me about Gardenia. Read to me about how she learned to have faith. To believe."

Believe.

Claire closed her eyes and surrendered to the power of a child.

Jax stood in front of his bedroom window staring down at Baby Bear's front door. It had just about killed him to send his son alone into battle, but strategically, he believed it the best approach. He didn't think Claire had it in her to refuse Nicholas's request. Based on the fact that seventeen minutes had passed since the boy disappeared into her cabin, Jax had guessed right.

Thirty-seven minutes after he'd knocked on Claire's front door, Nicholas stepped outside and headed toward Mama Bear. The boy's furrowed brow and worried frown gave his father pause. That didn't look good.

Jax hurried downstairs and met his son at the door. "Well?"

"She showed me the book. I couldn't get her to read it to me, though. She tried, but she would read a couple of sentences and then she'd get choked up, and finally, I took it and read it for her. I don't think it worked, though, Dad. She told me she has to leave town."

Jax swallowed a curse.

"She said that tomorrow she was going to close down

Forever Christmas and leave Eternity Springs." Lip quiv-
ering, he added, "She told me good-bye, Dad."

"Damn," Jax said, unable to hold that one back. "Was
that before or after you read her book?" The book whose
theme about believing was so wonderful and strong that it
had struck a chord in the hearts of millions.

"After."

"Stubborn, stubborn woman." He rubbed the back of
his neck.

"She's just scared like me, Daddy."

From the mouths of babes, Jax thought. "Okay, well.
Did you bring up the Christmas pageant? Remind her of
her promise?"

"Yes. She promised she'd come back for it."

"Good. If she said she would, then she will."

"So you'll give her the present?"

"Yeah."

"Okay." Nicholas nodded decisively. "That's good. I
think the present will work. I'm going to believe it."

Jax slung his arm around his son's shoulder. "Me, too,
son. Me, too. We just have to believe."

The Lancaster males worked late into the night on the
next phase of their battle plan. A labor of love, it turned
out better than Jax had imagined. As he wrapped it in
plain brown paper and tied it with a bow made of twine,
he sent up a little prayer that their message would get
through the hard head of the woman he loved.

She'd promised not to leave today, but he didn't trust
her not to run at first light, so before he went to bed that
night, he carried the package over to Baby Bear and
leaned it against the door.

In the morning when he looked, the package was gone.
So was she.

Chapter Twenty-two

My faith is bigger than my fear.
—JAX

Claire almost didn't pick the package up because she expected it would be something that would tug her heartstrings. However, she didn't have the strength to resist it. People didn't give her presents very often. She didn't have the heart to leave it behind. He'd used duct tape and a cut-up paper grocery sack to wrap it. She found that so endearing.

Yet, she feared if she opened it, whatever was inside might sap the strength she'd gathered to leave. She couldn't afford that. Staying required even more, and her bank of strength was overdrawn.

She compromised by taking the package with her, but placing it in the backseat of her car.

She drove into town and before even the early birds stirred, she slipped into her shop, wrote checks to her two employees, paying them full-time wages for the weeks that she'd committed to employing them, and finally drew a FOR SALE sign by hand. She taped the sign to her front window, locked the door, and returned to her car, where she tried to tell herself that the wetness in her eyes and on her cheeks was the result of the cold winter air, that's all.

She didn't have a destination in mind when she left

Eternity Springs. She had a couple weeks to kill before the Christmas pageant. Then another week until the White House event. She guessed she would go to it. It seemed easier to attend than to beg off. And she would sleep better knowing she hadn't let the White House down.

Where would she go after that?

What would she do with herself after that?

"What do you think, Tinsel? Shall we shoot for something totally different? Somewhere warm? South Beach? The South Pacific?"

Tinsel rested her snout on Claire's leg and went to sleep. Claire drove mindlessly, lost in thought and trying not to think. She didn't consciously make the decision to drive to Silver Eden, but when she found herself at the entrance to the resort shortly after snow began to fall, she was glad to be there.

Luckily they had a room for her and were willing to accommodate Tinsel. After hours in the car, Claire and Tinsel both needed exercise, so they played in the snow for a while before going up to their room. She took a long, hot shower, ordered room service for dinner, then sat cross-legged in the middle of the plush bed, staring at Jax's box.

Why her heart thundered, she couldn't say. Why fresh tears threatened was more obvious. His words echoed through her mind. *I want you. I want a future with you. I am in love with you.*

I love you.

It scared her so badly.

She pulled the box toward her and tugged on the bow of twine. She tore off the paper, licked her suddenly dry lips, and slowly removed the lid from the box.

Two handwritten notes lay atop the tissue paper. She picked up Nicholas's carefully printed page and read:

Dear Miss Claire,

   I love you.

   It's okay to be scared. Remember what Gardenia says. The trick to learning to fly is to wear a helmet.

   Thank you for being my friend. Please come home. Daddy and I miss you. We want you to be our family.

   Love,

   Nicholas

Claire closed her eyes and clutched the letter to her heart. That sweet, courageous, darling boy. If only she could be as brave as he.

The thought fluttered through her mind like an angel's whisper. *Maybe you can.*

Claire sucked in a shuddering breath and picked up Jax's note.

Dear Claire,

   I love you

   I love you for a million different reasons, but for the moment, allow me to focus on one of those reasons in particular.

   The night we met, you changed my life. You taught me to Believe.

   Let me return the favor.

   When I was growing up, one of my favorite family traditions of the Christmas season was opening the door on the Advent calendar. Using that as a framework, I invite you to . . .

   Believe.

   Find your faith, Claire. In me, in us, in what we can become. Change directions. Run to us. Run to me.

   I love you,

   Jax

Claire's hands trembled as she pulled back the tissue paper and revealed the contents of the box. Surprise washed through her. It was a journal like the one she'd given him.

She picked it up, traced the word "Believe" with her fingertip, and noted the worn corners. She flipped through the pages and caught her breath. She recognized the handwriting. Pages and pages of it. Six months' worth of it.

This *was* the journal she'd given Jax. He'd been using it.

And now he had given it to her? Why?

For the answer to her question, she looked at the other item in the package. It was a box made of wood, a rectangle about twelve inches wide and twenty-four inches long. A script *B* had been burned into the wood, its lines broken intermittently by little square doors. Upon each door was a number.

Claire opened the door marked "1" and saw a date beneath it. October 12.

She couldn't recall anything special about the date. What did he want her to . . . "Oh."

She picked up the journal, flipped to the entry marked October 12 and began to read Jax's bold handwriting.

"Today, Claire proved once again that she is a force of positive energy and light in my life."

The entry went on for a page and a half. Claire read it through the blur of tears.

Jax strode into Forever Christmas on Saturday, December 12, with his arms full of boxes. Meeting the gaze of the clerk behind the counter, he said, "I think those angels you've been waiting on came in."

"Excellent!" Celeste beamed a smile his way. "When Liz arrives for her shift, I'll ask her to call our customers on the wait list."

Jax carried the boxes to the storeroom and set about unpacking them and marking them into inventory. Luckily, Claire ran a straightforward system, and he'd been able to easily pick up on what needed doing in order to keep the business open. He'd made the decision to do that the morning Claire left town.

It was a case of putting his money where his mouth was, so to speak. He had to have faith in Claire. He had to believe that she would be back to stay. Keeping the shop open expressed that viewpoint loud and clear to the people of Eternity Springs, to Nicholas, and to himself.

When he'd put out a call for help, the response had been gratifying. In addition to Celeste, his temporary workers included members of the Eternity Springs Garden Club, led by none other than Janice Petersen. Miss Christmas was in for quite a surprise when she came home.

Jax was elbow deep in Styrofoam packing peanuts when Nicholas ran into the store calling his name. "The show starts in an hour and a half. Daddy, has anyone seen Miss Claire? Is she back?"

"No, son. We haven't had a Miss Christmas sighting yet."

"Oh." Nicholas's two front teeth bit his lower lip. "You're not worried, though. Right? She promised she'd come."

"She promised and I'm not worried." Much, anyway.

"What if she goes to Baby Bear before coming to town? What if our surprise gets ruined?"

"She doesn't have the new key yet. And I pulled the window curtains closed. The only way into Baby Bear is down the chimney, and she's Miss Christmas, not Santa Claus."

Nicholas laughed. "She's way too skinny to be Santa. I can't wait to see her, Dad. I hope she likes everything we've done. I've said so many prayers that our plan works and she says yes to marrying us."

"That's good, Nicholas. I believe in the power of prayer. And, I believe in Claire. We've got to keep thinking positive." Jax held out his fist. "We've got this."

Nicholas fist-bumped his dad and repeated, "We've got this."

Jax continued to tell himself that as the afternoon waned and the clock ticked toward the start of the Christmas pageant. As usual, it was the hottest ticket in town, and the school auditorium was packed to the rafters.

Rather than sit in the front row with Brian and Linda, who'd come to town for Nicholas's big performance, Jax stood at the base of the stage in the spot that allowed the best view of the entrances.

A chime sounded from the school's loudspeaker, and then the principal asked visitors to take their seats. "Our pageant begins in five minutes."

Jax's stomach made an uneasy roll. Softly, he whispered, "Where are you, Miss Christmas?"

Claire skulked in the science lab among the taxidermy collection of small animals native to the Colorado Rockies, muttering to the glassy-eyed beaver. "I don't think I'll be this nervous when I meet the president."

The beaver offered neither comfort nor advice.

She had arrived in Eternity Springs half an hour earlier, having timed her departure from Silver Eden carefully. Her plan was to slip into the back of the auditorium just as the curtain rose. With any luck, she could watch the pageant and escape at its finish without having to speak to a soul.

"There you are, Claire," came a cheery voice from the door at the back of the room. "I've been watching for you, but I almost didn't recognize you in that puff coat, knit cap, and sunglasses. It's a good thing I recognized your walk. Come along, now. Nicholas said you promised to sit in the front row, so I've saved you a seat beside me."

Claire dropped her chin onto her chest. She should have anticipated Celeste.

"Chop-chop, dear." Celeste snapped her fingers.

Claire surrendered, cast her friend the beaver a rueful look, and joined Celeste. At least there wouldn't be time for more than a few seconds of chitchat before the lights went down.

They entered at the auditorium's side door and Celeste led Claire toward one of three empty seats in the first row, center. As the lights began to dim, Celeste rose from her seat and walked up onto the stage as someone took the seat beside Claire. Jax leaned over and gave her a quick kiss on the mouth. "Merry Christmas, Claire."

A floodlight illuminated Celeste, who sparkled in a floor-length gown of cream-colored silk trimmed in dazzling gold. When the applause died, she smiled widely and said, "Good evening, everyone. Merry Christmas."

"Merry Christmas," the audience responded.

"I know we are all excited to see tonight's show, but before we get started, I have a special presentation to make. Nicholas Lancaster, would you join me, please?"

The audience applauded. Jax sat up a little straighter as Nicholas walked out onto the stage. Claire's heart melted at the sight of the boy dressed in jeans, a white shirt, a black bow tie, and wearing the feathered angel wings Claire had helped him make. "What's this?" she asked. "And where are his glasses?"

"He got contacts last week. I don't know what Celeste is up to."

Celeste's voice rang out over the auditorium like church bells. "Dear friends. As you know, we live in a special place that has a unique energy. Eternity Springs is where broken hearts come to heal. Because I believe that such accomplishments should be recognized, a few years ago I commissioned the design of the official Angel's Rest blazon that I award to those who have found love's healing grace. Tonight, I want to award our young angel here a pair of wings that are a little easier to wear than the feathers he has on right now."

Laughter rose from the audience. Celeste motioned Nicholas to come closer, and she slipped a silver necklace and angel wing pendant over his head. "Nicholas, you are an inspiration to us all."

"Thank you, Mrs. Blessing."

The crowd erupted in cheers. Jax and Claire and everyone else rose to give Nicholas a standing ovation. The boy shot Jax a bashful grin, but when he noticed Claire standing beside his father, a smile as bright as the spotlight burst across his face.

When the cheering finally died down, Celeste motioned the boy backstage. "I don't know about you all, but I'm ready to see the show."

Gracefully, she seemed to float off the stage and return to her seat. Jax met her, kissed her cheek, and said, "Thank you, Celeste. I know Nicholas will treasure his wings forever."

The houselights dimmed once again and the crowd quieted. A trumpet fanfare sounded out and the curtain slowly rose. Once the set was revealed, the smile that had graced Claire's face since Celeste's presentation froze. Her mouth went dry.

Nicholas stood to one side of the stage at a microphone. He thumped it with his finger, then said, "Welcome to the sixteenth annual Eternity Springs Christmas pageant. I am the master of ceremonies, Nicholas Lancaster. This year, in honor of our very own beloved Miss Christmas, we present to you our production of *The Christmas Angel Waiting Room*. Ladies and gentlemen, we hope you are ready to Believe. Please welcome our narrator tonight, the one and only . . . Gardenia!"

Claire clapped her hands over her mouth. "Not Starlina," she murmured.

"Of course not," Jax responded. "This is Christmas in Eternity Springs. We don't do the commercial version here."

On the stage, twelve-year-old Holly Montgomery spoke the opening words now made famous in storybook, song, movie, video games, and more. "'When nighttime falls in the tiny Christmas shop, the angels come out to play.'"

And so began the most magical hour of Claire Branham's life.

Jax had attended dress rehearsal earlier in the day, so rather than watch the play, he seldom took his gaze off Claire. She cried through the whole thing, but he *thought* they were the good kind of tears. He hoped so, anyway.

When the pageant ended and the children on stage took their bows, Jax and Claire rose with the rest of the crowd to give them a standing ovation. Then when the pageant director released the kiddos, they dispersed to find their parents. Nicholas shrugged out of his wings and ran toward Jax and Claire.

"Miss Claire! Miss Claire! You came. Dad and I knew you would. We believed, just like Gardenia and the other angels in your book do. Did you like our play?"

"I loved it," Claire said. "It was wonderful. You did a fabulous job."

"My wings kept drooping. But at least they didn't fall off." Nicholas focused his attention on his father. "Has Miss Claire been to Baby Bear?"

"I don't know." Jax gave Claire a sidelong look. "I haven't had the chance to ask her."

When Nicholas turned his questioning gaze her way,

Claire shook her head. "No, I was late getting back into town, and I didn't want to miss any of the pageant, so I didn't get out to the valley."

"Okay. Good. Dad said you are Miss Christmas and not Santa Claus, but I was worried. Let's go home, Miss Claire." He tugged her hand toward the door. "We have a surprise for you. Dad and I worked really hard on it."

"I . . . um . . ."

Further conversation was interrupted by a swarm of people surrounding them. Nic Callahan told Claire how much she loved her story. Sage Rafferty complimented her on keeping the facts about her fame quiet. Hope Romano thanked Claire for the positive message her book passed along to grade-schoolers, and Janice Petersen patted Claire's hand and said, "Don't you worry about that little meltdown you had at the shop, dear. Jax explained where you were coming from. Perfectly understandable. Why, if I were in your shoes, I'd have totally blown a gasket."

"I . . . um . . ."

Janice continued, "Now that you're back, I want to get my dibs in first. I had such fun working at Forever Christmas. You know, Christmas has been a challenge for me ever since my Harry died and with the children living so far away. Working in your shop has allowed me to find my joy in the holiday once again. If you find that you need a pair of helping hands, I hope you'll consider me. I work very cheap."

Claire's eyes had gone round with shock. Jax figured he'd best step in before she committed herself to anything involving the shop. "You've been a lifesaver, Janice," he said. "I'll be sure to put in a good word for you with the boss. But now, if you all will excuse us, Nicholas and I are anxious to get Miss Christmas alone."

Even as he spoke, Jax began easing Claire toward the

side door. He managed to get her into his truck without resistance, and then Nicholas filled all the empty spaces with chatter and questions. "I knew you'd keep your promise. I wasn't really worried. Well, maybe a little worried. Did you like our pageant, Miss Claire? I'll bet you were surprised."

The boy twisted around in his seat, trying to see out the back window. "Are Mimi and Pops behind us? Think they can find their way to Papa Bear in the dark?"

"Yes, son."

"Good. They're staying at Papa Bear tonight. It's done but for the punch list." He let out a giggle and added, "That's not when you hit somebody, don't worry. It's a funny name. It means the last things you do before the project is completely finished."

When Nicholas finally paused to take a breath, Claire spoke to Jax directly for the first time since her return. "What just happened? Why is everyone being so nice?"

"Honey, why would you expect anything different? This is Christmas in Eternity Springs."

She fell silent then and stared straight ahead. Nicholas was off and running again, catching Claire up on events in Eternity Springs over the past three weeks. Jax let him ramble. He was busy trying to project a calm and collected attitude, when inside he was a bundle of nerves.

What if his Believe calendar hadn't done the trick? What if she'd missed the point of the kids' pageant production? What if the surprise they had waiting at Baby Bear missed its mark?

You'll keep trying, that's what. You'll keep believing in Claire, believing in yourself, believing in you as a couple. You'll keep trying until you convince her to believe, too.

"Okay, then," he murmured beneath his breath. She'd taught him to think positive. From here on out, he'd be the most positive-thinking man in Colorado.

They arrived at the turnoff to Three Bears Valley, and when they rounded a curve, light from the full moon reflected off the light of six inches of new-fallen snow and illuminated the three cabins, lights glowing golden and warm and welcoming within. "It's so beautiful," Claire said.

"It's home," he said simply.

Despite all his positive thinking, nervousness continued to rumble in Jax's gut as he drove the truck toward Baby Bear. Even Nicholas seemed to feel it, because his chatter had subsided. When Jax shifted the truck into park and twisted the ignition key to kill the engine, a pregnant silence settled over the occupants.

Jax cleared his throat. "Claire, if you'll give us a couple minutes' head start, Nicholas and I need to add a few final touches inside. Okay?"

"Okay."

Jax glanced over his shoulder. "Nicholas? You have the package?"

"Yep."

The boy opened the back door of the extended-cab pickup and jumped down into the snow. Immediately, he reached for Claire's door, opened it, and stepped up onto the running board. He held a box the size for a bracelet and wrapped in red foil in his hand. "This is for you, Miss Claire. I love you."

He threw his arms around her neck and hugged her hard. Then he scrambled down from the truck and darted around toward Baby Bear's back door.

Jax opened his door and followed his son, pausing only long enough to meet Claire's gaze. "Believe, Claire."

Claire's hands trembled as she tore the paper off the box. She didn't know what to expect from the Lancaster men. She didn't know what to think of anything that had happened tonight.

She drew a deep, bracing breath, then lifted the lid from the gift box. Against a layer of white cotton lay an old-fashioned, ornate gold key. String attached a tag the size of a business card to the loop at the top of the key. The tag read "The Christmas Key."

"Okay," she murmured. She glanced up toward Baby Bear. The light visible between the cracks in the window curtains appeared brighter. She had the sense that something spectacular waited inside for her.

If she only dared to believe.

The porch light flashed on and she took that as her signal. Heart pounding, she exited the truck and approached Baby Bear's front door. That's when she spied the new lock on the door.

A simple latch had been added at shoulder height to Claire. The lock that secured it was shaped like a heart. Her lips fluttered up in a little smile when she slipped the Christmas Key into the lock and turned it. *Snick.* The lock released.

She took a deep breath, then opened the door.

To . . . Valentine's Day.

Jax and Nicholas each held a large, heart-shaped box and stood on either side of a Christmas tree that stretched to the rafters. White lights and red lights trimmed the tree along with ornaments shaped like hearts and garlands made of hearts. Hearts adorned the ribbon that encircled the tree. Hearts, hearts, and more hearts. Hearts were everywhere.

Claire blinked back sudden tears that threatened. She tore her gaze away from the tree and spied other additions they'd made to the room. Three red and white stockings at the chimney. More hearts. Heart-shaped throw pillows on the sofa. A heart-shaped rug in front of the hearth.

Even a plate of heart-shaped sugar cookies on the coffee table.

She cleared her throat and asked, "Am I having a Rip Van Winkle moment? Did I sleep through December and January and it's now February 14?"

"I know the Rip Van Winkle story," Nicholas said. "That's not it, Miss Claire. You know what this is. You are the one who told me. Remember when I was afraid, and you brought the Twelve Dogs of Christmas to me? You told me Valentine's is your favorite. Then you told me what the key to Christmas is."

"Love," she murmured.

Nicholas nodded. "Yep. You don't have to be scared, Miss Claire. You have the key."

He crossed the room to her and solemnly offered the candy box. "This is for you from me, Miss Claire. I hope you like it. We took the candy out, but don't worry. We saved it. We got the idea from the Angel's Rest fortune cookies."

Claire opened the box. Inside were dozens of scraps of paper, all marked with Nicholas's carefully printed handwriting. She picked up one and read aloud. "I love that you make pancakes in different shapes."

A second paper read: "I love that you love dogs as much as I do."

A third: "I love how you make my daddy smile again."

"Oh, Nicholas. I don't know what to say. This is wonderful. Just wonderful. You put a lot of work into this."

"There's a hundred of them. I was kinda running out of things to say at the end, so some of them aren't real good."

Claire dropped down onto her knees and wrapped the boy in her embrace. "I will treasure every single one of them. Thank you so much. This is one of the most special gifts I've ever received."

"I love you, Miss Claire. Please say yes to Daddy."

Claire lifted her gaze to Jax. He smiled tenderly, and said, "Nicholas, I heard your grandparents drive up a few minutes ago. I imagine by now they have the video they took of the pageant loaded up and ready to watch on the TV."

"Cool. Okay. I gotta go, Miss Claire. I'll see you in the morning. Right?"

"Right." She could give him no other answer.

Seconds later, the door slammed behind him and Claire and Jax were alone. Still on her knees, she went to rise and accepted the hand he offered to help her.

He didn't let go. "So did you read my journal?"

"I read the days you marked with your calendar."

"One each day?"

"Yes. The Advent calendar was a tradition in my family, too. I had forgotten how much I enjoyed it."

"What else did you learn from my gift?"

"I learned . . ." Her voice trailed off when he raised her hand to his mouth and kissed it.

"I missed you, Claire. Have you forgiven me yet?"

She closed her eyes. "For what?"

"For being an ass. For being stupid. For being prideful."

"Have you forgiven me for being rich?"

"Again, let me be clear. That was totally stupid of me." He cupped her cheek in the palm of his hand. "Thank God you are such a forgiving, understanding woman."

Her lips quirked. "I don't know that I understand anything, Jax. I wasn't truthful with my friends and the people of Eternity Springs. I expected to come back to scorn and ridicule. Instead, Janice Petersen has been playing salesclerk and wants a job?"

"You should hire her. The woman is a selling fool."

"Why did you do that, Jax? Why did you keep the store open?"

"Because one warm summer night, a redheaded water sprite challenged me to believe, and it changed my life.

You see, I believe in the magic of Eternity Springs, in the goodness of its people, and the capacity of their hearts. I believe in the power of positive thinking."

He set down the candy box he held and grabbed her free hand. His stare never left her face as he brought both her hands up to his mouth and kissed them. Sincerity and something else, something warm and wonderful, gleamed in his eyes as he said, "Most of all, Miss Christmas, I believe in you. I believe in us. I believe in the family that we can create with Nicholas and, God willing, a brother or sister or two for him. I believe that you love me as much as I love you."

"I do love you. I'm just afraid."

"I know, baby. We are all afraid. You need to forget all the reasons why it won't work, and believe in the one reason why it will. Love. I love you. You can trust me. You can believe in me. Believe in me, Claire."

Yearning filled her. She wanted to say yes. She wanted to believe. It was so close. He was here. He loved her.

Yet her lips couldn't form the word her heart was screaming.

Jax sighed. "Okay, then. Guess I'll have to bring on the big guns."

He released her hands and picked up the heart-shaped candy box. His look chastising, he handed it to her.

"More fortunes?" she asked.

"Open it."

She lifted the lid. Nestled inside among Valentine's-red tissue paper was Gardenia. Claire lifted her gently from the box. Tears stung her eyes. "You fixed her wing."

"Believing fixed her wing, Miss Christmas. Here's the problem. You neglected to turn the page. There's an epilogue."

"There is?"

"Absolutely. In the epilogue, Gardenia meets a new, woefully tarnished angel with a broken heart and his little boy who had not one but two broken wings. Gardenia befriends them. She challenges them to believe. As so often happens in nature, the boy learns quicker than his dad and, lo and behold, the boy's broken wings are made whole again. He learns to fly."

"Lo and behold," Claire repeated, not lifting her gaze from the angel.

"But the tarnished old guy isn't so dull that he completely blows the lesson. It's close, but he pulls it out. Gardenia has taught him that the way to mend a broken heart is to give it again. Once that tarnished angel's heart is mended, he's ready to fly again. There's just one problem."

"What's that?"

Jax put his finger beneath her chin and tilted her head up toward him. He stared down into her eyes. "He doesn't want to fly alone. He has to convince Gardenia to stop running and fly beside him, instead. He has to convince Gardenia that her broken wing has mended, too."

Claire swallowed hard. She darted a glance toward Gardenia with the mended wing, then returned her gaze to Jax's. "How does he do it?"

"Love, of course. Love is the glue that can mend everything. You just have to believe, Claire. Will you believe? In me? In us? Will you fly with me, beside me, wherever life takes us? I give you my word, my solemn promise, that I will never let you fall."

Tears welled in her eyes. She lifted her hand and cupped his cheek. "I believe you. Oh, Jax. I love you. I believe you. I believe."

He sealed the promise with a long, heartfelt kiss that wordlessly conveyed his devotion, his commitment, his love. When the kiss finally ended, he continued to hold her, staring down at her with such tenderness that it brought new tears to Claire's eyes.

In an effort to lighten the mood, she quipped, "So, that's the epilogue, hmm? I guess that means that this is the end?

"Oh, no, Miss Christmas. Not at all." With a roguish grin and wicked twinkle in his eyes, he added, "This is just the beginning."

Epilogue

Don't be afraid to turn the next page.
—JAX AND CLAIRE

WASHINGTON, D.C.

"That's a big Christmas tree, Daddy."

"Yep, Nicholas, it sure is."

"It's not as good as ours, though. They don't have any bubble lights or tinsel or dog ornaments. What good is a Christmas tree without the Twelve Dogs of Christmas hanging on it?"

"Shush, now, son. Here comes Claire."

Claire, along with the First Family of the United States, entered the room to an enthusiastic round of applause.

"Look, Daddy. There are the president's dogs. I've seen pictures of them. They're pretty cute. Maybe Santa Claus will bring me a puppy like those dogs."

"Maybe, but I think Santa leans more toward mutts."

"I love mutts, too."

The First Lady stepped up to a podium and welcomed the visitors to the People's House. She gave a quick summary of the scheduled events for the afternoon, spoke of her love of reading, then introduced M. C. Kelley.

Wild applause erupted. Claire smiled her thanks, returned the little wave of a girl in a wheelchair, and when the room finally went silent, she opened a copy of *The Christmas Angel Waiting Room*.

"'When nighttime falls in the tiny Christmas shop, the angels come out to play. With pretty porcelain faces and brilliant wings unfurled, they shimmer and sail and sing, 'Glory . . . Glory . . . Gloria!'

"'One wears a gown of glittering gold and turns cartwheels through the air. Another floats, serene in green, with her hands folded in prayer.'"

Jax watched the rapt faces of children and adults alike as Claire brought her characters to life. It was a gift, he thought. Her gift.

She'd certainly brought life back to the Lancasters.

Life. Love. Believing.

If they were ever blessed with a daughter, they'd decided to name her Faith.

As Claire turned to the last page of her book, she lifted her head and their gazes met and held. She recited the last line by memory.

"'And Starlina said, "We all will live happily ever after."'"

The Christmas Wishing Tree

For Blake and JD.

*May your Christmas wishes
always come true.*

Part One

Chapter One

Christmas carols played softly in the background. The scent of spiced cider perfumed the air. Shoppers munched happily on gingerbread cookies and perused the bookshelves for that perfect gift.

Dr. Jenna Stockton imagined ripping the halo off the angel's head and choking her with it. Instead, she reached deep within herself for patience and managed to find a smile for the costumed character behind the bookstore counter. "If I could speak with your manager, please?"

"She's awfully busy."

Jenna thought of the ridiculous length of her own to-do list as she fought to keep her smile from turning into a sneer. "Yes, well, it's that time of year, isn't it? Your manager?"

The little angel gave a haughty sniff, and then said, "If you'll step out of line, please?"

Without missing a beat, the angel turned a bright smile toward the woman waiting behind Jenna. "I'm *so* sorry for this unfortunate delay, ma'am. I'll be as quick as I possibly can."

Jenna didn't snarl like a rabid dog. She didn't. She smiled at the woman behind her in line. Sweetly. Without canines.

The woman and the four people behind her each gave Jenna an annoyed glower. She gave them all a smile too, then reached for the nearest book, which she pretended to read until the clerk returned, accompanied by a fiftysomething woman dressed like an elf. The angel gestured toward Jenna and said, "This is the one, Ms. Thomas."

The elf spoke in a harried tone. "May I help you?"

"I hope so." *Especially considering that I went out of my way to support a local business rather than ordering online.* Jenna set down the paperback. "I placed a special order two weeks ago and someone from this store called me last week to tell me it was in. However, your . . . angel . . . can't find it in your computer system, so she insists I'm mistaken."

"Do you have your receipt?"

"Not with me, no."

"Well, if you'll come back—"

"I don't have time to come back. I ordered the books for an event that begins"—Jenna checked her watch—"in three hours. I'd like you to check your stockroom. My name is Jenna Stockton."

"Ms. Stockton, I can't—"

"I ordered thirty copies of *New Adventures in the Christmas Angel Waiting Room.*"

"Oh." The manager pursed her lips. "Oh. I recall that order."

"Good."

Then the manager winced. *Uh-oh. Maybe not so good.* Jenna drew a deep, calming breath, then asked, "If you will get it for me, please?"

"Oh dear."

Jenna closed her eyes.

"I'm afraid we had some internal miscommunication. We sold out of our stock of that particular title and an employee unfortunately failed to notice the hold notice on your order. She put them on the shelf."

"How many are left?"

"It's a popular title," the manager hedged.

Jenna leaned forward. "The books are for pediatric cancer patients at Children's Hospital. The Christmas party is at four o'clock."

"Oh dear," the manager repeated. "Four o'clock, you say?"

Jenna nodded curtly.

"I'll call our distributor. If you can stop back by—"

"You'll need to deliver them directly to the hospital. To the attention of Dr. Jenna Stockton." She removed a card from her purse and handed it to the manager. "Here's the address. Take them to the information desk in the lobby. I'll tell the volunteers working there to expect them."

"But we don't have a delivery—"

Jenna folded her arms and gave the manager her best take-no-prisoners look.

"I'll do my best to have them there by four, Dr. Stockton. I apologize for the inconvenience. Now, is there anything else I can help you with? I saw you looking at the new Liza Holcomb thriller." She picked up the book and handed it to Jenna. "It's a fabulous book. Scariest stalker story I've read in years."

Jenna quickly returned the book to the display table. *A stalker story?* That was all she needed. "No, thank you. All I need today is what I ordered. Thank you for the help. You have my phone number. I trust if there is any further problem, you will give me an immediate call?"

"Yes. Of course."

"Perfect. Merry Christmas, Ms. Thomas."

"Merry Christmas to you too, Dr. Stockton." The manager gave her a bright smile that didn't quite hide the worry in her eyes.

Jenna headed for the door, glancing over her shoulder before pushing it open. The elf was on the phone, the angel had been replaced at the register by a reindeer, and Frosty the Snowman was on hands and knees beside the urn of mulled cider wiping up a spill. She sighed. Angels with attitude aside, she liked this little store. She really hoped they didn't let her and the children down.

Outside, the jangle from the Salvation Army bell ringer mingled with the shrieks and laughter of children embroiled in a snowball fight in the park across the street. Jenna tugged leather gloves from her coat pocket and pulled them on as she walked to the street corner and waited for the light to change. Her gaze drifted back to the snowball warriors. It did her heart good to see healthy, happy children playing, especially after a morning like this one.

When the walk signal flashed on, she crossed the street and cut through the park headed for her car, which she'd left in a lot a block away. Her thoughts returned to her to-do list. She could save a few minutes if she bought cookies at the grocery store instead of making the extra stop at the bakery before picking up Reilly from daycare. But she'd promised Reilly a gingerbread man from—

Whack.

Something cold and wet stung her cheek. *What in the world?* Reflexively, Jenna lifted her hand to her face and the remnants of . . . a snowball. She'd been hit with a snowball. Had the battlefield moved without her noticing and she'd been struck by an errant shot? Or had the attack been deliberate? If that was the case, one of these heathens was about to get a piece of her mind.

But when she turned to identify the culprit seconds after the snowball landed, her gaze skidded over a group of youngsters to an adult standing nearby. The pockets of a black wool coat concealed the man's hands. A black knit cap pulled low on his brow and the matching scarf looped around his face shielded everything but his eyes.

Eyes that watched her.

A shiver of fear skidded down Jenna's spine. She whirled around and picked up her pace. By the time she reached her car, she was all but running. She thumbed the key fob and unlocked the door as she approached, then locked it again the moment she was inside. She sat behind the steering wheel breathing hard, her heart pounding. Her gaze locked on the path through the park.

Nobody had followed her. Chased her. She'd let her imagination run wild.

"You didn't imagine the face full of snow," she muttered.

She should call the cops. File a report.

Sure. Be one of "those people." Tie up a law enforcement officer's time over a child's prank. Because surely, that's all it had been. One of those kids probably threw the snowball, and the guy dressed in black probably saw it as it flew by. He'd watched her to see if she'd pitch a fit about it.

She slipped her key into the ignition, started the car, and did her best to dismiss the incident. Forty minutes later—after stops at the dry cleaners, grocery, bakery, and party store—she made it back to the office in time for her one-thirty appointment with five minutes to spare. If she'd checked her rearview mirror more often than usual and paid close attention to those around her as she completed her errands, well, she was simply being responsible.

Whenever she had a few free minutes during the rest of the afternoon, her thoughts drifted back to the troubling events of recent months. The harassment had begun in October, although for the first few weeks, she hadn't recognized the threat. Everyone got hang-up calls. She explained away the texts as wrong numbers. But once on-line orders she hadn't placed began showing up on her doorstep, she realized she had a problem.

She'd thought she'd been a victim of identity theft. She'd spent an entire weekend canceling cards and changing accounts. Then last week when a particularly difficult case kept her at the hospital until early morning hours, she came out to the physician's section of the parking garage and found the air had been released from each of her tires.

Random vandalism, the police said. Teenage pranks. Jenna wasn't so certain, but she didn't know who would be doing this to her or why.

As she exited Exam Room 4, her receptionist met her with the news that her three o'clock was a no-show, which meant she was done for the day. Jenna tucked away her dark worries and turned her thoughts to the light and bright. Now she'd have time to pick up Reilly from school rather than have his after-school caregiver drop him off at the hospital.

Luck was with her for a change because a parking place became available just as she pulled up. As she got out of her car, a bell rang, and the door to the kindergarten classroom opened. Reilly was the third youngster out.

"Mom!" exclaimed her six-year-old son. "You're here! It's time for the Christmas party, isn't it? Is it time for the party? Is Santa going to be there? I have my list all ready."

"Hello, little man. Yes, it's time for the Christmas party and yes, Santa has promised to make an appearance."

"I'm *so* excited!"

"Me too, Reilly. Me too."

She'd been trying to make the Santa visit happen for two weeks now. Because kids grew up so fast these days, she knew that this might be the last year that Reilly believed in Santa Claus. Jenna had wanted to make it a special event for them both.

For the initial effort, she had planned an all-day Saturday holiday adventure beginning with breakfast at a pancake house, followed by shopping for gifts for Reilly's friends, then a matinee performance of *Rudolph* at the children's theater, and culminating with a visit to Santa's Wonderland and a conversation with the big man himself. They'd had a great time eating and shopping and watching the play, but as they left the theater, her pager had gone off. She'd tried again the following Saturday with a different itinerary, but with similar Santa results. She and Reilly both were counting on "The third time is the charm" axiom working today.

Arriving at the hospital, she took advantage of valet parking due to the amount of party supplies she had to tote inside. She loaded up a collapsible wheeled cart with gifts and decorations and bakery boxes, then Reilly helped her tug it inside, where she approached the information desk with trepidation. "I'm Dr. Stockton. Do I have a package waiting, I hope?"

"Books," the volunteer said. "Yes, they're here."

Yes!

She reached beneath the counter then pulled out a box. Jenna spied twice as many gift-wrapped items as she'd expected. The folded note taped to the front of the box read, "*Your complete order is enclosed. In addition, please accept these thirty copies of the first book in the Christmas Angel Waiting Room series as a gift to the children from the staff here at Hawthorne Books.*"

"Well, isn't that nice?" Jenna murmured.

"Isn't *what* nice, Mom?"

"The Christmas spirit."

He nodded in all seriousness. "I love the Christmas spirit. I wish it could last all year long."

"You and me both, little man. You and me both."

The Christmas party that followed was a bittersweet success. Local and a few national celebrities showed up to shower attention and gifts and good cheer on the patients of Children's Hospital and their families. It was always nice to see the smiles, but invariably, tears were shed too. The what-ifs and if-onlys were unavoidable. Hospital events always caused Jenna to hug Reilly a little tighter and spend a little more time on her nightly prayers.

The books Jenna gifted were well received by parents and patients alike. Reilly finally had his visit with Santa, and Jenna shed a tear or two of her own while she snapped photos of the moment with her phone.

In the car ride on their way home, Reilly bubbled about the party—the food, the games, the gifts. "There were a lot of dads there," he observed. "Did you see, Mom? There were a whole bunch of dads."

"Yes." Then, in an effort to alter the direction of the conversation, she said, "I was surprised to see how many football players attended. How many autographs did you get?"

"I don't know," Reilly answered with a shrug before proving that he was not to be distracted. "I thought Dr. David would be there. Why didn't Dr. David come?"

Oh, Reilly. Dr. David Henderson was Reilly's pediatrician, a widowed father whom she'd dated briefly last summer. "I told you he moved back to Minnesota to be closer to Bella and Jessie's grandparents. Dr. Larimer is your new doctor."

Reilly gave a long sigh. "I pretended I forgot. I thought he would make a really good daddy for us, Mom."

"Oh, Reilly."

"We really do need a daddy."

"Reilly," Jenna said, warning in her tone. "Please. It's been a long day. Let's not get started on that subject again."

"But, Mommy . . ."

She silenced him with a stern glance. Her son could be a terrier when he got an idea in his head, and lately, every time she turned around, he'd been yipping and yapping about needing a daddy.

How about I just order one online? Everything else was showing up at the house. She'd certainly have more use for a daddy for Reilly than a yodeling pickle electronic noisemaker.

She switched on the radio, which was tuned to the Christmas music station. Listening to Alvin and the Chipmunks hope that Christmas wouldn't be late wasn't much better than the yodeling pickle. However, the music did manage to distract Reilly, who sang along the rest of the way home, so she wasn't about to complain.

Her son helped her unload the car, and then he dashed about the house turning on the lights of all of their Christmas decorations while Jenna sorted through the mail. One envelope in particular caught her notice. Whitewater Adventure Rafting on the Snake River? Her stomach took a sick little flip.

Dread filled her as she stared down at the envelope addressed to JENNA M. STOCKTON, MD.

This was coincidence, surely. Just bad timing of an advertisement that probably went to everyone in her zip code.

She slid the letter opener blade beneath the envelope flap and removed the folded paper.

A reservation for one. Paid in full. January 23rd at 10:00 a.m.

She dropped the paper as if it were on fire. Her hands trembled. Her heart pounded.

Her always-adventuring parents had drowned in a whitewater rafting accident seven years earlier . . . on January 23.

"Mom, can we read a story?"

Jenna saw her son standing in the doorway with his stuffed Rudolph beneath his arm. His request was a life preserver tossed to a drowning person. "Absolutely. I have a new book for us."

Because she wasn't on call tonight and she had no patients she suspected of being in imminent need of her services, she poured herself a glass of wine, traded her shoes for slippers, and settled into the overstuffed easy chair in the family room with the copy of *The New Adventures in the Christmas Angel Waiting Room* that she'd reserved for her own family. "In my lap, little man."

He bounded over to her, his face alight with joy.

Story time was special for them both. She'd finished the first book and allowed herself to be talked into reading a second and a third. They were negotiating a fourth when she answered the doorbell to a pizza delivery she had not ordered.

By nine thirty, her doorbell had chimed eleven more times with deliveries of eleven more cheese and mushroom pizzas. Jenna was allergic to mushrooms.

At nine forty-five she called the police.

Chapter Two

Devin Murphy dreamt about home, about the warmth of the sun on his shoulders and the taste of salt in the air as he sailed his boat on a sapphire Coral Sea. A handful of puffy white clouds dotted a true-blue Australian sky. The breeze was stiff, a steady fifteen knots, as he turned into it. He was on a busman's holiday, free of tourists to guide in a dive of the Great Barrier Reef or fishermen on the hunt for something huge, but he wasn't alone.

In Devin's dream, a woman waited for him in his bed. She lay naked and needy and just beyond his sight, but he knew she was there. Knew she waited for him. A redhead, which was unusual because he'd never dated a redhead. Her scent drifted through his senses like a song. Exotic, like the beaches of Tahiti, and as sweet as a mango fresh off the tree. He wanted to lick that sweetness off her lips, to—*whoomp!*

Something heavy pounced on his back. "Wake up, Dev! It's Christmas Eve!"

The dream evaporated, Devin dragged his head off his pillow and aimed a hairy eyeball at his five-year-old brother. His voice gruff with sleep, he said, "Get off me and out of my room or die."

"You can't kill me on Christmas Eve. You can't kill

me ever. Mom would be mad. She told me to come wake you up. You promised to do a favor for Celeste today and Mom said daylight is wasting."

"Go. Now." He dropped his head back onto his pillow. "Or I'll slit your gullet from stem to stern and feed your entrails to the sharks."

"Oooh. I'm scared." Michael Cameron Murphy grabbed the ends of the pillow, yanked it free, then hit his big brother with it once before giggling his way out of the room.

Devin grinned. One of his favorite parts of the visits to see his family in Eternity Springs was horsing around with Michael. Devin had little use for kids as a rule. He certainly didn't want any of his own, but this kid hero-worshipped him. It was good for a man's ego. He figured that being a big brother must be sort of like being a granddad. Play with the curtain-climbers when you want, then give 'em back to Mom and Dad.

Though he probably shouldn't mention that theory to his parents, Cam and Sarah Murphy.

With a groan, he tossed back the comforter and shivered in the morning cold as he climbed from his toasty warm bed. Downstairs, his mother bustled around the kitchen and his father was locked in his study wrapping gifts. Devin ate a quick breakfast of oatmeal, kissed his mom on the cheek, twisted his brother's ear, then bundled up and headed over to Angel's Rest Healing Center and Spa to do a favor for a friend.

It was a picture-perfect December day—windless, with temperatures in the twenties and a blue sky dotted with puffy white clouds. At the resort's main building, Cavanaugh House, Devin hoisted a long, skinny box over one shoulder and carried it out onto the porch. There he paused a moment to appreciate the beauty of the winter scene. "It's like living in a Christmas card," he murmured.

Three inches of new snow had fallen overnight, frosting rooftops and tree limbs and shrubbery and giving Angel's Rest and Eternity Springs beyond the perfect Victorian snow-village look. This was a whole different world from Christmas where he'd come of age. Cairns, Australia, was hot and rainy as a rule on the twenty-fourth of December. So too was Bella Vita, the island in the Caribbean where he'd lived for the past few years.

Devin climbed down the porch steps and made his way to the stone walk that led toward Angel Creek. Groundskeepers had been through here already this morning and the pathway was clear and lined with candy canes tied with sparkling gold bows. Angel's Rest's owner, Celeste Blessing, did like to get her sparkle on, didn't she?

And yet, candy canes—even ones with sparkling gold bows—invariably made him think of his dad. How many times had he seen Cam Murphy at the wheel of the *Bliss,* his face into the wind and the hooked end of a candy cane hanging from his mouth? More times than Devin could count. Originally, his dad had used peppermint sticks to help him give up cigars, but one habit had replaced the other. Now, Devin kept a supply of canes on his own boat, *The Office,* in honor of Cam.

Or at least, he had kept them there until Danielle, the vicious Category 4 bitch, had sent *The Office* along with the *Lark* and the *Sunny Luck,* Devin's other two fishing boats, to the bottom of the harbor on Bella Vita Isle.

Devin looked out over the sea of white covering the grounds of Angel's Rest and imagined an ocean of blue with a rainbow of colors below. The Coral Sea and the Great Barrier Reef. He yearned for them. The Caribbean was a beautiful place and he'd been happy living there, just like he'd been happy living in Eternity Springs for a stretch of time prior to that. But Australia was home, the place where he'd been born and raised and never thought he'd leave—until the day an American tourist and her daughter booked a tour on his dad's boat and turned his world upside down.

At the sound of jingling bells, Devin twisted his head to see Celeste headed his way dressed in a fluffy gold jacket with matching boots and a knit hat with a rolled brim worn with a cocky tilt over her silver-gray hair. Gold bells trimmed the scarf draped around her neck. He grinned. People liked to say that she was Eternity Springs' very own angel.

He wouldn't argue the fact. Without Celeste, Cam and Sarah might have never found their way back to each other, and he wouldn't have the family he treasured, or this Victorian Christmas village complete with a white Christmas. And candy canes. And angel cookies. *And our very own angel.*

Devin truly did love Eternity Springs at the holidays. He would be happy to come back for Christmas at least every other year. And that's what he planned to tell his mother when he broke her heart after Christmas and finally confessed his intention to move back to Cairns.

"I brought box cutters," Celeste said as she approached.

"Thanks." He carried the box across the footbridge, and then set it onto the ground atop a large, flat, snow-dusted rock. He took the tool from Celeste and moments later removed sections of aluminum tubing along with a half-dozen smaller unlabeled boxes. Inside those he found strings of twinkle lights, LED lights, battery packs, rolled vinyl, glitter tape, and zip ties. He didn't have a clue where to start. "What exactly is this supposed to be, Celeste?"

"I don't really know." She clapped her hands, her blue eyes sparkling with delight. "It's a gift from one of my repeat guests. Isn't this a wonderful surprise?"

"It's something." He hunkered down and sifted through the contents, looking for a set of instructions. Just as he spied a folded piece of paper tucked inside the roll of vinyl, his cell phone rang. He fished it from his pocket and checked the screen. His mother. He thumbed the green button and lifted the phone to his ear. "Hey, Mom."

"Devin, are you still at Angel's Rest?"

"Yes." He shook the paper open, revealing a child's drawing done in colored pencils instead of the instructions he was hoping for.

"Good. I called Celeste, but she isn't answering her phone. Will you track her down for me? I'm about to leave Fresh with these cookies, but I neglected to ask her if she wants the extra pinwheels I baked this morning too."

Fresh was the bakery his mother owned and operated, and her mention of his favorite cookies was enough to distract him from his search for the package instructions. "Um . . . Mom . . . you do remember that your strawberry pinwheels are my favorite, right?"

"Oh really?" Sarah observed in a dry tone. "I'm sure I didn't notice that you've plowed through more than a dozen since you came home the day before yesterday. Don't worry. I restocked our pinwheel tin."

"I love you, Mom. And Celeste is here with me. I'm helping her with a new decoration for the Angel Creek footbridge. How about I just hand her the phone?"

The older woman glanced up from the pile of supplies she'd sorted into a semblance of order and took the phone from him. "Yes? Hello, Sarah. Merry Christmas!"

Devin paid scant attention to the phone conversation as he turned his attention to assembling Celeste's newest holiday decoration using the drawing for guidance. It was to be a lighted, decorated arch placed on the town side of the bridge. The rolled vinyl was a welcome sign. He decided that Celeste should do the official unfurling, so he went to work piecing together the poles.

Celeste's conversation with Sarah proved to be more

involved than answering a simple pinwheel-cookie question. Devin had the arch's aluminum framework completely assembled when he realized that Celeste was standing at the center of the footbridge, leaning over and peering down into the frozen stream as she talked to his mother.

Unease snaked through Devin at the sight. He felt the urge to call out and tell her to be careful, but he stilled his tongue. Celeste wasn't Michael's age. She was an adult.

Tuning into the conversation, he heard her say, "Yes, I know. It's been a while, but I do remember. Hot flashes are simply not any fun."

Quickly, Devin tuned right out again. TMI. He focused his attention on the box, and that was why less than a minute later he didn't see what happened. He only heard it.

The bump. The screech. The crack and the splash. Devin glanced up in horror to see that Celeste Blessing had fallen facedown into the icy water of Angel Creek.

"Celeste?" Devin tossed aside the Christmas decoration and scrambled to the bank and down its icy slope. His heart raced. His mouth had gone dry. A fall of ten feet onto a rocky creek bed could be disastrous for anyone of any age. For an older woman like Celeste . . . *Please, God* . . . three feet of water wasn't much to break a fall.

She moved. Devin exhaled in relief.

"Talk to me, Celeste," he demanded as he stepped into the creek, his boots breaking through honeycombs of ice into the freezing water. She rose up onto all fours. *Okay, good. That's good.* "Celeste? You okay? Where are you hurt?"

"I'm all right," she replied in a voice that was reassuringly firm. "I'm not hurt. But . . . ooh . . . this water is cold."

"Careful . . ." Devin took quick, but cautious, steps on slick stones through the icy water toward the woman who was trying to find her feet. "Hold what you have, Celeste. Let me help you up. We don't want you falling again."

"True. I've given my poor guardian angel enough of a workout as it is." Celeste gave Devin a shaky smile as he reached her side and steadied her as she climbed to her feet. "Thank you, Devin. I don't know what happened. I'm not ordinarily so uncoordinated."

"We're lucky you didn't break something." *Like your neck.* "What matters now is getting you to dry land without taking any more spills. I think the going might be just a little easier if you head upstream just a tad. I'll let you find your footing and you can use me for balance. Okay?"

"Yes. Thank you, dear. I just—oh—look."

Devin was prepared for Celeste to lose her balance again. He didn't anticipate that she'd halt mid-step, bend over, and scoop something out of Angel Creek. His phone, he realized. He'd forgotten she'd been talking to his mother on his cell phone when she took her dive.

Handing it to him, she said, "I spotted it because your phone case is so cute and colorful."

Devin's Scooby-Doo phone case had been a birthday gift from Michael. Watching the classic on the Cartoon Network together was a favorite brother-bonding activity. Too bad the case wasn't waterproof. "I'm glad you rescued it, but please, Celeste. Let's get out of this creek while we can still feel our feet. Watch your step, now."

He firmed his hold on her elbow. It took another couple of minutes and a pair of precarious slips, but Devin finally managed to lead Celeste to dry land. She was visibly shivering as he tugged her up the slick, sloping bank of the creek, and the wail of an approaching siren was a most welcome sound. "Either someone saw you take a tumble or Mom called in the cavalry."

"Oh dear. That wasn't necessary, but Sarah wouldn't

have known that, would she? I do have such wonderful friends."

"It won't hurt to let the doctor look you over."

"I suppose you're right."

The ambulance pulled to a stop and two EMTs exited the vehicle. Celeste waved at them and called, "All is well. Merry Christmas!"

The medical personnel's expressions relaxed at Celeste's greeting. Devin called, "She fell from the bridge into the creek. She needs to get warm and dry, and to see the doctor."

As one EMT opened the back of the ambulance, the other approached, saying, "Miss Celeste, are we glad to see you up and walking. Sarah's phone call gave us all a fright."

The second EMT approached, carrying a silver emergency blanket, which she wrapped around Celeste. "Let's get you into the ambulance."

"Devin, you need to get out of those wet things too," Celeste observed. To the EMTs, she added, "He should ride along and we can drop him by his parents' house on our way to the clinic."

As the two shared a look meant to obviously frame a protest, Devin jumped in. "No, Celeste. You go on. Mom or Dad is sure to be right behind the ambulance. In fact"—Devin gestured toward the pickup that had just made the turn from Fifth Street onto Cottonwood—"here comes Dad's truck."

"Excellent." Celeste gave a satisfied nod. "In that case, I'll toddle along to the clinic. I am terribly cold."

She was halfway to the ambulance when she turned and said, "One thing, dear. About your phone . . . I'm aware of a method . . . it's possible I can save it and return it to working condition, if you'll allow me the opportunity to try?"

Probably the old rice-in-a-bag trick, Devin thought.

He didn't have a lot of hope for its success, but then, she *was* Celeste Blessing. "Sure." He crossed the distance between them, handed her the phone, and bent down to kiss her cheek. "Thanks, Celeste. But I don't want you to worry about it. Take care of yourself first."

"I will."

The EMTs helped her into the ambulance as Cam Murphy braked to a stop behind it. He jumped out of his truck's cab, and just before the ambulance door closed, he heard Celeste call out, "Merry Christmas, Cam."

After waving at Celeste, Devin's dad gave him a quick once-over. "Don't *you* look like a drowned wallaby. What happened here? Your mother is scared to death."

Devin gave his father a quick summary of events, and then repeated the story to his worried mother upon reaching home. He took a long, hot shower, then dressed and went downstairs to find a bowl of hot tomato soup and a grilled cheese sandwich waiting. Comfort food. "You are the best, Mom."

Sarah smiled. "You're today's hero. Thank God you were there to help. That's as frightened as I've been in a while. Celeste had mentioned that she was standing on the bridge, and we were talking about tonight's open house. She said something about seeing a reflection in the water, and the next thing I know, she yelps and the phone goes dead."

"We're lucky the phone is the only thing that died," Cam observed as he entered the kitchen carrying gift tags and in search of a pen. "May it rest in peace. Though I'm compelled to wonder how the young women of the world will survive the loss."

"Very funny, Dad."

"You'd better go buy another phone before the stores all close for Christmas," Michael said as he intently watched his father write a name on a tag.

Devin's lips twisted. This was Eternity Springs. The stores all closed for Christmas yesterday.

"It might be nice for Devin to have a break from tending to his harem," Sarah observed.

"What's a harem?" Michael asked.

"Not a topic for Christmas Eve," Devin declared before smoothly changing the subject. "So, have you had an update on Celeste? Everything check out okay?"

"Yes, she's on her way back to Angel's Rest with dry clothes and a clean bill of health. She told me she's ready to dive back into party preparations."

"As long as that's the only diving she does," Cam said. "What do we put on the tags for the senior center angel tree gifts?"

Sarah responded. "Put 'To a woman' or 'To a man' and add 'from the Murphys.'"

"Got it."

Displaying wisdom beyond his age, Michael observed, "It would ruin Eternity Springs' Christmas if Miss Celeste got hurt."

The adults nodded their agreement, and then Devin asked his mother what was on the agenda for the afternoon. Sarah summarized the day's itinerary—a happy blend of traditional activities and new events that reflected the changes to their growing family.

Cam spoke to Devin. "I need to deliver our senior center gifts. Want me to drop you by Angel's Rest on my way so you can retrieve your truck?

"Thanks. While I'm there, I might as well finish setting up that decoration Celeste had me working on when she took her tumble. Shouldn't take more than a few minutes."

"Celeste will appreciate that," Sarah said. "You know how she is about her holiday trimmings."

"She's the decoratingest person I've ever known," Cam observed.

Devin finished his soup and sandwich, then borrowed dry outerwear from his dad and hitched a ride back to Angel's Rest. He finished assembling and installing the welcome arch, tested the lighting, and shook his head in amusement at the twinkling, flying angels. "The decoratingest person," he repeated to himself. His father had that right.

With the task finished, Devin gathered up the trash. He had just tossed the cardboard box into the bed of his truck when he heard Celeste call his name. He turned to see her rushing toward him. He started forward, praying he'd intercept her before she slipped and fell and, to quote Michael, "ruined Eternity Springs' Christmas." Devin yelled, "Slow down, Celeste!"

"It's Christmas Eve! There's no time for slow."

Devin swept her with a studious gaze. "You're feeling well?"

"Fit as a cherub's fiddle. I saw the welcome sign. Thank you so much, Devin. You truly are my hero today."

"Glad I could help."

"I have a little something for you."

When she reached into her pocket, Devin took a step back. "I don't need—"

"Yes, you do need this." She handed him a prepaid phone. "I keep a few of these for emergencies. I'm afraid it doesn't have text messaging or the Internet, but it will keep you connected until we know whether my efforts with your phone will prove successful."

Devin grinned down at the gift. "A burner phone? You keep burner phones around the house?"

"I always try to be prepared."

"Celeste, you are amazing." As he tucked the phone

into his pocket, she gave him a smile so brilliant and bright that it warmed him from the inside out.

"I've a special Christmas message for you this year." She took his hands, her blue eyes gleaming with a mesmerizing intensity that had Devin holding his breath as she said, "Christmas is a promise. Christmas is a gift. Don't be a prisoner of the past. If at first you don't succeed, don't be afraid to make another run at the dream. Open your eyes and heart and imaginings to the possibilities that await. You must believe. Wishes can and do come true. And when the Christmas bells ring, Devin Murphy, don't you fail to answer."

He responded the only way he knew how. "Yes, ma'am."

Later that afternoon as he searched through his mother's craft room for the tape he needed to finish his gift wrapping and "Carol of the Bells" began to chime from his pocket, he recalled her words.

Part of him didn't want to answer. He'd been around Eternity Springs and Celeste Blessing long enough to know that when she started talking, weird, weird things tended to happen.

He touched the green button to connect the call and brought the phone to his ear. "Hello?"

A small voice asked, "Is this Santa Claus?"

Devin's gaze locked on a roll of wrapping paper—red with white Santa silhouettes. *Okay, genius, how do you handle this?*

He cleared his throat. "Who is asking?"

"I'm Reilly from Nashville. Remember? I gave you my Christmas list at the hospital last week. At the party for sick kids?"

A party for sick kids. Devin sat down abruptly. "Hello, Reilly from Nashville."

"So you remember me?"

"Santa has a great memory."

"Okay. Good. I'm sorry if that sounded mean. I didn't mean to be mean. I'm scared to be calling you."

"No need to be scared, buddy. Talk to me like I'm a normal dude."

"Okay. Sure. I can do that."

Devin waited, but Reilly didn't appear to be in much of a hurry to continue. After a pause of more than half a minute, Devin prodded. "I expect you had a reason for calling Santa Claus?"

The boy spoke on a heavy sigh. "I do. We were supposed to go to see *Charlie Brown's Christmas* at the hotel and throw snowballs and ride the slide. We had tickets and everything. But Mom got called to work—she *always* gets called to work—and we're not going to have time. So that's why I thought maybe . . . well, I wanted to ask you . . . is it too late to add to my list, Santa?"

Well, crap. "It *is* Christmas Eve."

"I know. It's too late, isn't it?"

The boy sounded so dejected that Devin found himself wanting to fix the problem. He gave the lazy Susan on his mother's craft table a spin as he formulated his response. "It's complicated, what with the sleigh already loaded and everything. Let me ask you a few questions, and I'll see what I can do. First, how did you get this phone number?"

"An angel gave it to me."

Devin stopped the lazy Susan mid-spin. *Why does this not surprise me?*

"Not a real angel," Reilly clarified. "There's this store at the mall where little kids can buy presents, and the lady who wrapped the perfume I picked out for my mom was dressed like an angel. She's the one who told me your phone number is North-Pole-One."

An angel. *Christmas is a promise. Christmas is a gift. . . . Open your eyes and heart and imaginings to the possibilities.*

Except this angel worked at a store in Nashville. Devin wondered if Celeste had a sister. Or maybe a cousin. She *was* from the South, wasn't she? "Are you calling from your own phone, Reilly?"

"No. I don't have my own phone. Mom won't let me have one until I'm at least eight, and that's two whole years away. This is Mom's phone. She lets me play games on it when I'm waiting for her at work."

Okay, that was good. That meant Devin had the mother's phone number. He could call her later and let her know about this conversation. "All righty, then. Now, back to your Christmas list. I need you to understand that I can't make any promises. My sleigh is all loaded up and most of my elves have already clocked out and are taking off for vacation."

"It's not really a list, Santa. It's a wish."

"I think fairy godmothers are the ones in charge of wishes."

"Not Christmas wishes. This is a Christmas wish."

A Christmas wish, huh? For a kid who visited Santa at a hospital party for sick kids. *Murphy, you are so in over your head.* Devin cleared his throat, closed his eyes, and braced himself. "So, Reilly. What is your Christmas wish?"

"A daddy. I want a daddy of my own."

Devin let out a long breath. While he searched for the right words to respond, the boy continued. "If Mom and I had a daddy, everything would be so much better. She wouldn't have to work so much, and I wouldn't have to stay with Mrs. White so often."

"Mrs. White?"

"My sitter. And if I had a dad, he'd throw a football with me and take me fishing and we could go on vacation and camp in the national parks. And when we had tickets to the ice show and Mom got called in to work, my dad could take me."

"Have you talked to your mother about this wish of yours?"

Glumly, the boy replied, "Yes. She told me that daddies don't grow on trees—not even Christmas trees."

Smart mom.

"So what do you think, Santa? Can you make my Christmas wish come true?"

Noise outside in the backyard caught Devin's attention, and he glanced out the window to see his little brother chucking snowballs and taunts at their dad. *Reilly from Nashville doesn't have a Cam Murphy in his life.*

But he did have ties to a hospital.

Devin rubbed the back of his neck. "Well, I'll tell you what. This is a tough one. Even if this wasn't Christmas Eve and my sleigh was already packed up, I couldn't very well wrap up a dad and leave him beneath your Christmas tree, could I?"

"I guess not. Unless you put him in one of those big bags like bicycles come in."

"He couldn't breathe if I did that," Devin pointed out. "By the way, never put a bag over your head, buddy. That's dangerous."

"Yessir."

"Now back to this wish. Someone reminded me today that Christmas is a gift. It's a promise. There's the answer to your Christmas wish question right there."

"I don't understand."

"You gotta believe in the promise, Reilly. You gotta hold onto your hope, even when what you wished for isn't under your tree on December twenty-fifth. Because Christmas isn't just a day. It's not just a season. It's the love that's in your heart."

Following a moment of silence, Reilly said, "I still don't understand."

Devin closed his eyes. *That's because I'm not making sense. I've been hanging with Celeste way too much.* "It's a good wish. You hold onto it. Keep wishing it. Believe it will come true."

"And then it *will* come true?" Reilly asked, his question full of hope.

"You believed enough to call Santa on Christmas Eve. What do you think?"

"I think I'm gonna believe!"

"There you go. And now, I have an elf giving me the stink eye. It's time for Rudolph and his pals to do their thing. Goodbye, Reilly from Nashville. Merry Christmas!"

"Merry Christmas, Santa Claus."

Devin disconnected the call and let out a low, slow whistle of relief as out on the back lawn, his little brother gave a delightfully terrified squeal. Devin glanced out to see that Cam had the boy in an armlock and was washing his face with snow.

In that moment, Devin remembered Celeste's advice. *Don't be a prisoner of the past. If at first you don't succeed, don't be afraid to make another run at the dream. Open your eyes and heart and imaginings to the possibilities that await. You must believe. Wishes can and do come true.*

"It's a nice idea, Celeste," he murmured. But like the saying went, *If wishes were horses beggars would ride.* And little boys wouldn't be going to hospital Christmas parties.

And somewhere in another part of the world, another little boy built sandcastles on a beach with his daddy. The daddy who wasn't Devin after all.

Chapter Three

"One more," Jenna murmured as she measured the box against the roll of wrapping paper to gauge where to make the cut. Every year when she found herself wrapping packages on Christmas Eve, she promised herself that next year she'd do better. Of course, the Christmas Eve wrapping problem wouldn't be so bad if she'd do something about her Christmas Eve buying problem.

It was a bad habit. Invariably as the final hours ticked by toward Christmas, no matter how many packages sat beneath their tree, panic kicked in. Jenna worried she hadn't bought enough or purchased the right thing. Guilt had gotten the better of her again this year because she'd had to drag Reilly to the clinic when she got called in to cover for another doctor. On the way home, she'd stopped by the bookstore and covertly purchased three more books.

"It's always okay to buy books," she justified as she skimmed the scissors along the paper with precision. That's what her mom had always said, anyway. At the thought, a wave of grief rolled through her. She missed her parents every day of her life, but holidays always sharpened the sense of loss. The ugly gift in last week's mail had made the pain unusually acute. If Mom were here today, she would tell Jenna not to fret over her last-minute purchases, but she'd also add, "Next time, get them gift wrapped."

Jenna was tying a bow of green yarn around a wrapped book when she heard the muffled ringtone of a cell phone coming from her handbag. She shot a worried look toward it. This couldn't be good. Who would be calling her at four o'clock on Christmas Eve? Only a handful of people had this number, and they'd all be busy with family this afternoon. A call on that phone at a time like this might well mean somebody she cared about was ill or hurt.

She dug her phone out of her bag and checked the number. She didn't recognize it. She didn't recognize the area code.

Her stomach did a sick flip.

She'd changed her phone number after the harassment started in the fall. This number was unlisted. Anyone who had this number knew to phone her work line in an emergency. If the caller was a friend with a problem, her pager would go off any second now. Her friends all knew what to say to have the answering service put their call through.

This caller wasn't a friend.

Maybe it was simply a wrong number. It could be that simple. Everything didn't have to be part of the prankster's assault on her.

Whoever the jerk was, surely he had better things to do on Christmas Eve than to prank call her. "Even sociopaths have families," she muttered before tossing the phone back into her bag. She wasn't going to answer it. She had presents to put beneath the tree and a six-year-old boy to get to the children's service at church.

She didn't hear the phone ring a second time ten minutes later because she was on her hands and knees looking beneath Reilly's bed for a missing shoe. The next time it rang, Jenna had it silenced for the church service, and since she neglected to switch it back, she didn't hear the fourth or fifth calls either.

It wasn't until the evening of Christmas Day that she pulled her phone out of her purse and checked the display. Five missed calls from that same number. She froze as tension washed through her.

In the den, Reilly cheered and called excitedly, "I did it, Mom! I put the train track together all by myself. It works!"

"Awesome. I'll be right there, Reilly."

Jenna tossed the phone back into her purse. She wasn't going to let these phone calls bother her. She and Reilly had enjoyed a perfectly lovely holiday, and she wasn't going to spoil the mood by fretting over something that was probably nothing more than a wrong number, somebody wanting to wish Merry Christmas to someone he or she obviously seldom called. Since she'd never set up voice mail for her new number, he wouldn't know he had the number wrong. If the phone calls continued into next week, well, she could worry about it then.

She went into the den and played trains with her son.

The following day, she never heard her phone ring. With Reilly out of school, Jenna had cleared as much of her work schedule as possible. She stayed so busy with her son that she forgot all about the unsettling calls—until a friend phoned three days after Christmas and she took a good look at her call history.

In the days following Christmas, it turned out that Reilly from Nashville had a lot to say to Santa. Devin didn't quite know what to do about it.

He'd tried to get hold of the boy's mother on Christmas Eve to tell her about the dad request, but she never answered the phone. Once Christmas was over, Devin figured his responsibility to inform her of Reilly's call was over too.

But then the day after Christmas when Devin was up at the Rocking L summer camp helping his brother-in-law repair damage done to one of the cabins by some mischievous raccoons, the boy called again. "Hi, Santa. This is Reilly from Nashville. Thank you for all the nice presents. I really love everything, especially the book about Yellowstone National Park. That was a really great surprise. I want to go there some day. I want to visit all the national parks. There are fifty-nine of them. Did you know that?"

"I did not know that," Devin replied. He propped a hip on a sawhorse and set his hammer down.

"You should read the book you gave me. I learned it there. Did you have a good Christmas, Santa?"

"I had an excellent Christmas."

"That's good. I'll bet you were tired. Were you tired?"

"I *was* tired."

"Because you went all over the world delivering presents. You have to go to lots and lots of places. What's your favorite place in the world to visit? Is it Orlando? Because of the Magic Kingdom?"

"No." Devin's lips twisted. Personally, he wasn't a fan of theme parks. Give him real parks anytime. "My favorite place to visit is a little town in Colorado called Eternity Springs. For me, it's the most magical place in the world."

"Because it has magicians and wizards and superheroes?"

Devin thought of Celeste and he grinned. "Not exactly. Eternity Springs has family magic. People who come to Eternity Springs think it's very special."

As the conversation continued, Devin tried to subtly

pump Reilly for information in an attempt to ascertain the state of the boy's health. *Was* he a cancer patient? And if so, how sick was he? Devin desperately wanted to know.

But nothing Reilly said answered the question, and when he mentioned his mother, Devin cut to the chase. "That reminds me. I'd like to speak with your mother. Would you put her on the phone, please?"

Following a moment's silence, Reilly said, "You're not going to tell her I've been bad, are you?"

"No, that's not why I want to talk to her." Devin waited a beat and asked, "Have you been bad, Reilly?"

This time the silence lasted longer. Finally, the boy said, "No, I haven't been bad. But Santa, she can't come to the phone. She's talking on her work phone so she can't talk to you. She's supposed to not be working this week because I'm out of school, but that never works out. She works all the time. That's why I need a dad. I gotta go now, Santa. And don't worry, I'm still believing! Bye!"

The call disconnected. Devin stood staring at his phone when Chase Timberlake walked into the cabin toting a two-by-four. He gave Devin a quick once-over, then asked, "Something wrong?"

"No. Not really." Devin considered explaining the call, but before he decided what to say, his phone rang again. The call was from his own number. "Hello?"

"Good news, Devin," Celeste Blessing said. "I fixed your phone."

"Wow. I'm impressed. You have a magic touch, Celeste."

"Like I said, I had a little trick. The bad news is that it's ringing off the wall. You're missing a lot of calls."

Devin realized he didn't really mind. It had been nice not to be tethered to his screen these past few days, though it might have given his social life a hit or two.

Wonder if his New Year's Eve date with the ski instructor at Wolf Creek was still on?

He shrugged, not really caring one way or the other. *Message there, much?* "That's okay. They've waited this long, they can wait a little longer. I'm up at the Rocking L helping Chase with a project. I'll pick my phone up on my way home."

"That sounds great. I'll leave it at the front desk." With amusement in her voice, she added, "On silent."

As he drove to Angel's Rest later that afternoon, Devin considered the problem of the burner phone. He couldn't very well return it to Celeste. What if Reilly called again? He couldn't have Santa going MIA. But neither could this Santa Claus hotline go on forever. Well, unless the boy was sick. He'd talk to him every single day if that was the case and talking to Santa helped him.

He really needed to get in touch with the little guy's mom. When he parked his truck, he dialed Reilly's number hoping his mother would pick up. After twelve unanswered rings, he gave up. Maybe tonight he'd get on the Internet and see what sort of luck he'd have tracking her down. If worst came to worst, he'd ask Daniel Garrett to help him. The former police detective could probably track her down in minutes.

Celeste did indeed have his phone working like new, and he spent the rest of the evening returning calls and soothing ruffled feathers. The New Year's Eve date was off but he didn't mind. Ringing in the New Year with family and friends at Murphy's Pub had more appeal than hitting the slopes, so to speak.

The following morning he tried Reilly's number again before meeting his sister and brother-in-law for a couple hours of cross-country skiing. Again, nobody answered. That afternoon, he offered to do errands for his mom. He had just tossed a twenty-pound sack of dog food into his basket at the Trading Post grocery store when the burner phone rang. "Hello, Reilly."

"How did you know it was me? Magic?"

Or caller ID. "Something like that. Why are you calling today, buddy?"

"I wanted to tell you about a show. It's on TV and you need to watch it, Santa. I watched it last night even though it was after my bedtime because Stephanie lets me stay up later than Mrs. White."

"Who is Stephanie?"

"The Stephanie who lives next door. She stays with me sometimes when Mom has to go to work. She's in high school and she talks on the phone to her boyfriend a lot. My mom had to go to work again last night even though she wasn't supposed to. Anyway, the show is so cool. It's all about Yellowstone. Did you know that underneath Yellowstone is a volcano? You probably know that because you gave me the book, but Mom just reads me one chapter a night so we haven't gotten to that part yet. So I learned it from the show. It's on the National Geographic Channel. You should watch it, Santa."

They talked about volcanoes while Devin finished grocery shopping and checked out. When he loaded his Jeep, the conversation moved to camping. He'd just pulled to a stop in his parents' driveway when the topic of Reilly's new bike came up.

"Mom is going to take me and my friend Dustin to the church parking lot so we can ride our bikes where it's safe. I'm almost ready to take off the training wheels, Santa."

"That's great."

"And after we ride bikes, Mom is going to make us chocolate chip cookies!"

"She is?" Devin seized the moment. "You know, my elves have a secret ingredient that makes chocolate chip cookies taste magical. Would you like your mom to add it to her cookies?"

"That'd be great, Santa!"

"Okay. Put her on the phone, and I'll tell her what the ingredient is."

On the other end of the line, Reilly went silent. After a long pause, he said, "If I do that, she'll make me stop calling you."

"Your mom doesn't know about these calls?"

"No."

Devin grimaced. He'd been afraid of that. "That's not good, buddy. You can't hide things from your mom."

"I know." Reilly's voice held a world of misery. "Because of the bad guy."

Devin's brow furrowed. Had he heard wrong? "Did you say 'bad guy'?"

The boy's voice went small. "I'm not supposed to know, but I do. She got a whole new phone because of him. He's playing mean jokes that scare her, but the policemen can't find him. They don't know who he is."

With that, Devin knew that the phone calls to Santa had to change. "Reilly, I like talking to you, but we can't—"

"I gotta go, Santa. It's time to ride my bike. Goodbye! I'm still believing!"

Devin stared down at the phone. Crap. What the hell had he gotten mixed up in? He didn't regret playing Santa for Reilly and he didn't want to spoil the boy's fantasy, but this had taken a strange turn. It couldn't continue.

A bad man who played mean jokes?

Devin needed to get ahold of Reilly's mother. She wouldn't answer his calls, but maybe she'd respond to a text. He considered the problem as he unloaded the groceries. What to say without writing a novel? 'Lady, your kid is in trouble. Call me.' He didn't want to scare her, but if that's what it took. . . . Devin placed the last grocery sack on the kitchen counter and said, "Mom, if you don't need me for anything else, I think I'll walk over to the store. Dad said he has a new line of fishing tackle he wants me to check out."

"I'm done with you, thanks," Sarah replied. "Remind Cam that there's a high school basketball game this afternoon. He's promised to take Michael."

"Will do."

The scent of wood smoke drifted on the air along with the sound of laughter from children taking advantage of the sunny afternoon to play touch football in Davenport Park. As Devin walked up Spruce Street, he found himself wondering what the weather was like in Nashville. Probably pretty good since Reilly said he was going bike riding.

Reilly. This whole situation plagued Devin. As much as he hated the idea of letting the boy down, he really couldn't answer Reilly's calls again until he'd talked to the boy's mother. With that decision made and a short, but hopefully compelling, text message composed, he reached into his jacket for his phone. When he pulled out the burner phone instead, he hit redial one more time. He almost dropped the phone when on the second ring a female voice demanded, "Who is this!"

Devin opened his mouth to give his name, but the woman didn't give him a chance to speak. "Who are you? Why are you doing these things? What have I ever done to you? I swear, if I find out you're a pervert who's been preying on my child in any way, I will hunt you down and carve you up like a coroner."

"Whoa," Devin muttered.

"I don't know what your motive is, mister, but when you decided to drag my son into this twisted little game of yours you went too far."

"Hold on, lady," Devin fired back. He crossed the street and aimed for the relative privacy of a park bench, temper revealing his Aussie roots as he continued, "If you'll quit your whinging for just one minute I'll tell you what you need to know."

"Quit my what?"

"Whinging! Bitching. For a woman who can't take time to be a proper mother to her kid, you sure are quick to throw around accusations."

The woman on the other end of the call gasped in outrage.

Devin was full of outrage himself. "I assume you're Reilly's mother. Well, if you will hold your tongue for one bloody minute, I will tell you about my motive. Your boy called me. On Christmas Eve. He believed he was phoning Santa Claus and he had something he wanted to add to his Christmas list."

"And you talked to him?"

"It was Christmas Eve! He told me he's six! I wasn't going to ruin his Christmas by telling him he had the wrong number. So yes, I played along and I let him think I was Santa. And the minute we were done, I did what any responsible person would do. I tried to call you! Only you were too busy flossing your teeth to answer the damn phone!"

"Excuse me?"

"Yeah, well, I've been doing that for days and now I'm done with excuses. Why don't you answer your phone, lady? Do you know how lonely your little boy is? Care to guess what his Christmas wish was? A daddy. The boy wished for a dad."

The sudden silence on the other end of the line indicated that Devin might have gotten through to her. He was tempted to keep talking, to roll out some of the truths he'd been chewing on for days, but he forced himself to wait for her response.

Finally, she cleared her throat. "Mr., um . . ."

After her threats, Devin wasn't all that anxious to give her his name. "Why don't we stick to Claus?"

When she spoke again, her voice was tight. "It appears I am missing some important information. I would very much appreciate it if you would explain from the beginning."

"I'll be happy to do so." If his voice had a note of moral superiority to it, well, she had it coming.

Devin started with the Christmas Eve phone call and detailed the conversation as best as he could remember. Reilly's mother let out a little groan of misery when he repeated Reilly's daddy wish. She murmured a pained moan when Devin brought up the boy's complaints about her work hours. He told her that he'd asked Reilly to put her on the phone. "He wouldn't do it. He said you'd make him stop calling me."

"Well, of course I'd make him stop calling," she fired back. "This is just unacceptable. Sneaking my phone out of my purse, calling strangers, and lying about it—I can't believe he'd do this."

"Well, technically, I'm not a stranger. I'm Santa. And you are . . . ?"

"What?"

"Your name. Reilly only calls you Mom. I imagine I could track you down, but I haven't gone snooping. I'd like to know your name."

There was a long pause. "I don't know what to do about this. You could be the guy."

"The one who the police can't find?"

She gasped. "It *is* you. Who are you? Why are you doing this to us? How did you get this number?"

Devin's eyes rounded upon hearing the fear in her voice. "Whoa. Hold on. Wait a minute. I don't know what game you're talking about. All I've done is answer the phone when your kid calls and try to get hold of you to tell you about it. I'm not the bad guy here. Reilly told me some lady dressed like an angel in a department store gave him this number. It's North-Pole-One."

"How do you know about the pranks?"

"I don't. Not really." He told her about Reilly's mention of the bad man. "That's when I knew I had to keep trying until I connected with you. I don't know what sort of trouble you are in, but I'm invested in Reilly at this point. I don't want to rip the Santa rug out from under him. However, I need some guidance. I need information. First of all"—Devin closed his eyes, braced himself—"is he sick?"

"Six. He's six years old."

"That's not . . . I said 'sick.' Is he sick? He told me he saw Santa at a hospital party for sick kids."

"Oh." Reilly's Mom sighed heavily into the phone. "No. No. He's fine. I'm a . . . volunteer."

"Thank God." Devin's breath fogged on the winter air as he lifted his face to the sky and blew a heavy sigh of relief. "I'm so glad to hear that."

For a long moment, neither of them spoke. Motion in the fir tree above him caught Devin's notice and he watched a pair of squirrels scamper from limb to limb. In a quiet voice, Reilly's mother said, "Your number really is North-Pole-One, isn't it?"

"I wasn't lying."

"Do you get a lot of these types of calls?"

"Actually, Reilly is the only one. It's a new number for me."

"Ah. I see. Me too. A new number, I mean. I had to change mine. I'm being harassed, and it started with phone calls. That's why I didn't answer on Christmas Eve. I didn't recognize the number. And a couple of weeks ago someone sent more than a dozen pizzas to our house."

"Oh. I see." Devin did see. *Asshat.*

"The police call it doxxing. It was a new word for me—the modern word for pranks—and I don't think this guy is necessarily dangerous, but his pranks could be. He slashed my tires and that has a sinister feel."

"That's more than harassment. That's criminal behavior."

"And in the midst of all this I'm standing here talking on the phone to a total stranger."

"I repeat. I'm not a stranger. I'm Santa."

"Well, Santa," she said with a laugh that had a hint of despair in it. "What am I going to do about this hotline of yours?"

"We need a game plan. I'm happy to keep talking to the little guy, but I'm afraid we have a bit of a ticking clock to deal with. I'm scheduled to leave the country next week. I won't be able to talk to him after New Year's Day."

"Oh. Well . . . I need to put a little thought into this. And . . . oh dear . . . Reilly just fell and skinned his knee. Can I call you back later? After Reilly goes to bed?"

Devin had plans to watch tonight's college football bowl game with some friends from high school. He wasn't really interested in the matchup. "Sure."

"It'll probably be around nine. We're central time. Goodbye." Before the call disconnected, he heard her say, "Oh, honey."

Oh, honey. She'd sounded just like Mom when Michael hurt himself. Lots of love in those two words.

A mother's love. He closed his eyes as an old pain wrenched his heart.

Breast cancer had taken his biological mother when

he wasn't much older than Michael. If not for Cam
Murphy . . .

Then Devin gave his head a shake, drummed his fingers against the park bench, and brought his thoughts
back to the phone call. This situation had taken an unexpected turn. The tire-slasher thing worried him. He'd
have to quiz her about it when she called tonight. Sounds
like Reilly's Mom wasn't the neglectful mother after all,
but a woman with a lot on her plate.

He hoped she actually called. He liked the sound of
her voice.

Bet she's a redhead.

Chapter Four

"Hey, Santa."

"Good afternoon, Reilly, my man."

"Guess what? I told Mom about calling you, and she wasn't too mad. I'm only in a little trouble."

"That's good."

"You were right. I needed to believe. So guess what we're going to do tomorrow? We are going to a big cave! It's huge and we get to go inside it. It's a national park like Yellowstone only there's no volcanoes. It's called Mammoth Cave National Park. Did you know that there used to be big elephants called mammoths, but they all died? I don't know if they lived in the cave or not. Mom says we'll learn about it on our tour."

"You'll enjoy that."

"Hi, Santa."

"How's my spelunker?"

"I know what that is! I learned it today at Mammoth Cave National Park. It's the funniest word."

"So tell me all about your visit."

"You're not too busy? It will take me a long time."

"I'm not too busy for you, little man. So tell me, why is it called Mammoth Cave National Park?"

* * *

"Hi, Santa. Guess what? I told my mom what you said about the Great Barrier Reef, and we went to the bookstore today and got two books about it!"

"You're going to love those books."

"And you know what else? I'm going to have a big brother! Not a real big brother who you have to share a bedroom with like my friend Jason. This big brother will take me places and do guy things."

"Guy things are the best."

"I don't think having a big brother will be as good as having a dad, though. I'm still going to keep wishing for that. I told Mom."

"You keep talking to your mom, Reilly. You have a really great mom and it's important that she knows what you're thinking."

"I will. I wish I could keep talking to you too, though. I hate that we only have one more call. Mom says it's not a real vacation if you have to take your phone with you. But Santa, I'm worried about something. What will you do if you have a 'mergency and you can't call nine-one-one?"

"Oh, you don't need to worry about that, Reilly. My elves take excellent care of me."

"Like my mom does me."

"Like your mom does you."

"I'll talk to you tomorrow, Santa. Happy New Year."

"Happy New Year, Reilly from Nashville."

At twenty minutes after eight on New Year's Eve, Jenna finished reading a chapter about Big Bend National Park and kissed Reilly good night. When she checked on him fifteen minutes later, he was sound asleep. She went downstairs, brushed her hair, and rummaged through her makeup drawer for her lipstick.

"You're an idiot," she murmured at her reflection in the mirror. This wasn't a FaceTime call. He couldn't see her. She could call him with her hair in a rat's nest and with mascara running down her face and spinach stuck between her teeth and he wouldn't know. Nevertheless, she reapplied her lipstick before walking into her kitchen and pouring herself a glass of wine. At quarter to nine, she dialed North-Pole-One for the fourth time.

He answered on the second ring and she could hear the grin in his voice when he said, "Happy New Year, Reilly's Mom."

"Happy New Year, Santa."

By an unspoken agreement, they'd never breeched the anonymity of their contact by exchanging names. When Jenna phoned him that first night, she'd been filled with suspicion and skepticism as he repeated his explanation of events. Her focus had been on Reilly and his safety, and she'd shared nothing about herself.

In the end, she'd believed "Santa's" story. They'd developed and agreed upon a strategy for going forward. Only after they'd ended the call had she realized that he had never shared his real identity. During the subsequent calls, she'd learned that he was visiting family in the Colorado Rockies for the holidays, that he was single and in his late twenties, and that he loved *Star Trek* and *Lord of the Rings* and *Game of Thrones*. He'd never shared his name, where he made his home, or what he did for a living.

He did have the most delicious accent, and she'd spent a ridiculous amount of time analyzing it, finally setting on a Hugh Jackman Aussie sprinkled with an occasional Bob Marley Caribbean flare. If he occupied a lot of real estate in her imagination at the moment, well, that was understandable, wasn't it? He was a mystery who, unlike the doxxer, wasn't threatening or frightening. He'd inserted a little sparkle into her holidays, and she'd decided to enjoy the experience.

"So what are you and the little caveman doing tonight?" he asked.

"We have an exciting night planned. Reilly is already asleep. I'm going to binge watch *The Carol Burnett Show* and maybe splurge and have two glasses of wine."

"You wild woman, you."

"Carol makes me laugh. I've decided I don't have enough laughter in my life, and that's something I'm going to work on during the coming year."

"So that's your New Year's resolution? To laugh more?"

"I don't do resolutions, but lately, I have been taking stock. This doxxing business has me rethinking a lot of things."

"Did you call that private investigator?"

"Not yet." Jenna propped her legs on an ottoman and stretched them toward the fire. "Santa" had a detective friend who'd recommended someone based in Nashville whom she could enlist for help in tracking down the jerk. "I thought I'd wait until next week. Things have been quiet this week. I think this guy must have taken the holidays off. Honestly, I needed the break from worrying about all that, but I will make the call early next week."

"Promise."

"I promise."

She decided to change the subject. "So, how about you? What is Santa Claus doing on New Year's Eve?"

"My night is a little more exciting, but not much. I'm meeting my sister and brother-in-law at a local pub. I'm told the proprietor is breaking out a new microbrew in honor of the holiday."

"That sounds lovely," Jenna said, her tone wistful. "Are you close to your sister?"

"Lori and I are friends, which based on our beginnings

says a lot. We fought like angry cassowaries when we first met. We were teenagers."

"Cassowaries? What's that?"

"Huge bird. Think ostrich, only bigger. They have razor claws and spikes on their wings. Nasty fighters when provoked."

"Tell me about your sister. I take it yours is a blended family?"

"Not in the traditional sense. Both my sister and brother are my parents' biological children. My dad adopted me after I was orphaned as a tyke. Mom officially adopted me after she and Dad married, but I was all but grown by then. Lori and I had some serious sibling rivalry to work through before we became friends."

"It's no wonder you and Reilly hit it off. You have a lot in common."

"He has an evil sister?"

Jenna laughed. "No. It's just the two of us. I adopted him after his mother died."

Following a moment of silence, he spoke in a quiet but warm tone. "Tell me about it."

Unexpectedly, tears sprang to Jenna's eyes. "His mom was a troubled young woman. Too young. A runaway. I met her through some volunteer work I did. She was . . . lost."

Jenna's throat closed up. She rarely spoke of Marsha Rocheleau. The events that brought Reilly into her life still left her emotions raw.

"And Reilly's father?"

"He was the reason she was a runaway." Jenna sighed heavily. "It's an ugly story, but the bottom line is Reilly's mother gave him to me, the monster who fathered him signed away his parental rights, and I'm blessed to be Reilly's mom."

"Sounds like he's a pretty lucky little boy too."

"That's my goal. I want Reilly to grow up believing he's the luckiest boy in the world. I may not pull it off, but I'm going to try."

"It's a worthy goal. So, let me ask you a question. Hold on a minute, if you don't mind."

Jenna heard what sounded like footsteps on a staircase. Next she heard a door open and a screen door creak. They both banged shut.

"Whoa, it's cold outside tonight, but I needed to move. So, back to my question. Say you hit a home run in the parenting department. Reilly grows up happy and healthy, and he has a great life. That security you've given him has made him strong and independent. He decides to move half a world away, so your visits will be cut in half at best. You'll probably be crushed, won't you?"

"Probably, yes."

"How do you deal with it? What could Reilly do to make it easier for you?"

Jenna's heart did a little dip. "This trip you're going on tomorrow. It's more than a vacation, isn't it? You're moving."

"Yeah. I'm going home."

"To Australia?" she guessed.

"How did you know? I'm told my accent has softened a lot and most people peg me as Irish."

"Your vocabulary is a hint, but mainly it's the way you shared the Great Barrier Reef with Reilly. It's obvious you've spent a considerable amount of time there."

"Ah. Yes, I have. I grew up diving the reef." He told her about his role in his father's tour boat business. "We came to the States when I was sixteen. I loved the mountains, but I missed the sea. The Caribbean was my compromise. It's a long flight, but it's manageable for visits with the family. Then Danielle blew into my life and changed everything."

Frowning, Jenna put the clues together. "The hurricane."

"Sank my boats. Damaged my home. It's the second storm in three years. I'm done with it. I'm not rebuilding in the Caribbean again. I'm going home, and it's going to break my mother's heart, make my brother and sister cry, and give my dad a tick. Any suggestions on how to soften the blow?"

Jenna sipped her wine, and then gave him her best advice. "Be honest with them, but let them be honest with you in return. Acknowledge and respect their emotions."

"In other words, be a man and stand there and take it."

"Maybe bring some cotton to protect your eardrums."

He sighed. "Too bad I'm not really Santa. I could live where I want, then hop onto my sleigh and have Rudolph and friends zoom me to Eternity Springs for dinner once a week."

"Eternity Springs? You mentioned that to Reilly. That's your little mountain town?"

"Yes. It's pretty much in the middle of nowhere, home to less than two thousand people—and that's after a growth spurt the past few years. It's a beautiful place and I do love to visit. Eternity Springs is a safe harbor, but I need a rolling deck beneath my feet."

Jenna rose and walked to the bedroom that served as Reilly's playroom, where the lighted globe she'd given him for his birthday last spring sat on top of a bookshelf. She sent it spinning with her index finger, watching the blue oceans and colorful continents roll by. She stopped it on Australia.

"Something tells me your parents won't be as surprised as you fear."

He sighed again, then said, "You know what? That's a worry for tomorrow. It occurs to me that I've neglected my Santa Claus duty this evening. Want to hear what Reilly and I discussed this afternoon?"

"Of course."

"Well, he's planning a birthday present campaign."

"What?" Jenna sent the globe spinning once more. "He's hardly played with all of his Christmas presents yet. And his birthday isn't until March."

"Apparently he's going to need every minute to convince you to approve his request."

Jenna couldn't imagine what . . . oh. Of course. "That boy," she groaned. "Let me guess. He wants a puppy."

"Got it in one."

"We can't have a dog. Never mind that he's too young to be responsible for a dog or that my plate is already overflowing as it is. His babysitter doesn't like dogs, so that's the end of the argument right there."

"He thinks he can change Mrs. White's mind. He's *believing*."

Jenna closed her eyes and groaned again. "I swear, I've heard that word more since Christmas than in the entire previous year. Thanks, Santa."

He chuckled. "You're welcome."

She hesitated a moment, then added, "Actually, I do want to tell you again how much I appreciate all that you've done for my son in the past week. I don't know that you understand what an impact you've had on our lives."

"I'm glad I could help, but as far as I'm concerned, it's been a two-way street. Who knew I had so much to learn about caves?" As Jenna laughed softly, he added, "This has been the best holiday I've had in years. I'm going to miss talking to Reilly and to you too, Reilly's Mom."

She traced the outline of Australia with her finger. "You still want him to call you tomorrow at noon?"

"I do. He's going to love my special goodbye message."

"Just promise me you won't make him any promises that include a dog."

"Santa's honor. I . . . oh, wow. I just saw a shooting star."

"I'm jealous. I've never seen a shooting star. Eternity Springs sounds like a really cool place."

"Cold. Bitter cold this time of year, but the homes are warm and welcoming, as are the people who live here."

Jenna's eyes filled with tears. "That sounds so lovely. If it were my home, I doubt I'd ever leave. Well, speaking of leaving, I'd better let you go so that you get some of that microbrew before it's all gone. One last time . . . thank you for your kindness to my son. May you have fair winds and following seas in this New Year, Santa. Goodbye."

"Good—wait. One more thing. Can I ask you a personal question?"

My name. He's finally going to ask my name. Should I tell him? "Okay."

"What color is your hair?"

"My hair!" Surprised, she blurted out. "Auburn. I'm a redhead."

"I knew it," he replied, satisfaction in his tone. "Goodbye, Reilly's Mom. I wish you and your boy nothing but peace, joy, and happiness in the New Year. And, no pizza."

The line disconnected.

Jenna sent the globe spinning once again, the writing on its surface blurred by both motion and the tears flooding her eyes. It was ridiculous, really, for her heart to tug with such loss. She'd spoken to the man four whole times!

But he'd been kind. He'd been funny and entertaining and . . . that accent. He'd been a fantasy. An escape.

After the past four months, she'd needed an escape.

And Reilly . . . he'd been so sweet to Reilly.

Jenna gave the globe one final spin, and then retraced her steps to the family room. She topped off her glass of wine, searched through her DVD collection for Carol Burnett, and then settled in to work on that New Year's non-resolution of hers.

She was laughing at Tim Conway playing a dentist when Reilly came downstairs. "Mom?"

"Reilly, what are you doing out of bed?"

"I'm hungry. Can I have a banana?"

Bananas were the boy's favorite middle-of-the-night snack. "Sure, buddy. Help yourself."

"Thanks, Mom."

She heard his Thomas the Train slippers scuff against the kitchen floor and the fruit bowl slide across the granite counter top. A moment later, he spoke with a mouth full of fruit. "Mom, can I watch TV with you?"

She opened her mouth to repeat her ordinary "No," but reconsidered. It *was* a holiday, after all, and not too long until the ball dropped in Times Square. Except, she hadn't watched it in years. Was the broadcast family friendly? Guess he could watch Carol Burnett with her. She could pay attention to the clock and switch it over a few minutes before eleven their time.

"Yes, you can. This one time since it's a holiday. C'mere, little man."

He was halfway across the room when the noise began. Loud hammering. Alarmed, Jenna set down her wine and started to rise.

The next few seconds were a firestorm of fear and confusion. *Bang. Wham.* Light flashes. Sound booms. For a moment, Jenna was stunned into inaction.

Men shouted, "We're in, we're in. Clear!"

Reilly screamed, "Mommy!"

Men with guns poured into the room and ran right over Reilly. Jenna lunged for her son.

"Halt! Halt! On the ground! On the ground! Now!"

A little boy's scream of pain reverberated across the air and terror gripped Jenna.

"Now! On the ground! Show your hands!"

"Get the boy. Get the boy."

"Mom-my!" Reilly wailed. "Mommy! Mommy! Mommy!"

"Reilly!"

Footsteps thundered down the hall, up the stairs. Sirens approached. Jenna's heart pounded.

"Separate your feet. Hands on your back."

"Clear! Clear!"

"Reilly!" *Oh God, oh God, oh God.*

"Be quiet. Don't move."

"Don't shoot! Please, don't shoot. My son . . ."

Whop. whop. whop. whop. Bwee bip bip bwee!

"Who else is here?"

A knee pressed at her back. Her arms jerked. Cold metal slid against her wrists. Handcuffs snapped.

"Got one in custody. Who else is here?"

Jenna trembled, her teeth clattered. Fear was a copper taste in her mouth. "No one. No one. It's just me. Me and my son." *Oh God.* "Reilly. Where's my boy?"

"Any weapons in here?"

"No."

"What's your name, lady?"

"Jenna." Her heart pounded. "Jenna Stockton. Doctor Jenna Stockton."

"We're clear upstairs."

"Clear downstairs."

Faintly, she heard Reilly crying and his panicked voice call, "Mommy! Mommy! Mommy!"

Rage welled up inside Jenna. Reilly! She wanted to yell and scream and pull a Wonder Woman and burst out of the handcuffs. Common sense made her remain still and silent until the activity around her calmed down.

The crystal ball had long since dropped in Times Square before the situation was finally sorted out. The 911 operator had received a call from a child who claimed his mother had just shot and killed his father and sister. He said she was searching the house for him and he was hiding.

"It's called swatting, Dr. Stockton," the team leader explained once all had been sorted out. "Prank calls on steroids. That said, it is seldom done as a random act like the prank calls I used to make when I was in elementary school. 'Hey, lady, is your refrigerator running? Better go catch it.' These calls take a level of sophistication in that often, the callers know how to shield the origin of the call. Bottom line is someone has something against you."

No, Jenna told herself as she thought about the SWAT team leader's comment while she waited in the emergency room for her son's broken arm to be set. The fact that someone had something against her was not the bottom line.

Reilly was.

The scum-sucking rat bastard had gone too far this time. Police had pointed guns at Reilly. Six-year-old Reilly. They'd pointed guns at him and knocked him over and broken his arm.

Six years old and he'd had eight police officers pointing a gun at him because he was near the front door. Six years old and frightened so badly that he wet himself when the stun grenade went off and he thought he was being kidnapped.

Six years old and trampled and broken and carried screaming away from her.

He clung to her like a toddler on their way home. *This could scar him for life.*

The crazy excuse for a human who had targeted her for some unknown reason had gone too far tonight.

Reilly had been traumatized. Reilly could have *died.*

That was the bottom line.

So Jenna intended to make sure something like what happened tonight would never, ever happen again.

Devin hadn't been this nervous since his first skydiving jump, but all in all, telling his parents about his move had gone about as well as could be expected. His mother had teared up, but she never allowed the tears to fall. His sister had bubbled and smoked like a volcano threatening to blow, but his brother-in-law managed to calm her down. His dad hadn't been surprised, which had surprised Devin.

Michael . . . ah, hell . . . Michael had broken his heart.

Michael cried every time Devin left following a visit. He cried every time the family came to visit Devin. The little boy's tears always broke Devin's heart, so this wasn't really anything new. Michael was too young to understand how much farther Cairns was from Bella Vita Isle, but he was bright enough to realize that the reactions of his family meant he wasn't going to like it.

Michael's tears stabbed Devin's heart like nothing else.

So after the morning family meeting and with three hours remaining before he needed to leave for the airport, Devin took his brother sledding. They had a great time, and as a result, Devin failed to watch the time closely.

At the end of one particularly laughter-filled run, he glanced at his watch. Eleven minutes past eleven? *Oh, crap.* Had he missed hearing Reilly's call? That would be so uncool for this, their final exchange.

Devin fished in his pocket for the burner phone and

checked the display. No, no calls yet, thank goodness. "Hey, squirt," he called to his brother. "It's time for a hot chocolate break."

"Hurrah!" Hot chocolate was one of Michael's favorite things.

Their mother had packed a thermos of hot chocolate, plastic cups, marshmallows, and Devin's favorite brand of trail mix. They sat on a picnic bench out of the wind and dug in. Michael chattered away about his scheduled return to preschool at Gingerbread House the following day and the gifts that his friends had received for Christmas. Devin was happy that sledding had managed to distract the boy from his sadness. Oh, he'd blubber up again when Devin left, but at that point, Devin wouldn't be around to watch.

Devin checked the burner phone once again. Eleven twenty-seven. Scowling, he double-checked the reception. Four bars . . . plenty of connectivity. The ringer was on. No missed calls.

Maybe he'd misunderstood. Maybe Reilly's Mom had meant noon Mountain Time.

That had to be it. He should have listened closer. That's what he got for spending his time fantasizing instead of paying attention. "You about finished with your snack, squirt? We have time for one more run."

"I think two more, Dev."

"All right. Two more fast ones. No dillydallying at the top." In the end, they had time for three more runs.

Noon Mountain Time came and went without a phone call. Devin told himself to be patient while he showered, dressed, and finished packing. He kept the burner phone close during lunch, but saying goodbye to his family distracted him for a time after that.

"Sure you don't want me to drive you to the airport?" Cam asked as Devin tossed his duffle into the backseat of his Jeep. His blurry-eyed mother and whimpering little brother watched from the front window.

"I have to return the rental car, Dad."

"Mom and I can do it. It'll give us an excuse to drive to Gunnison for Mexican food."

"Thanks for the offer, but you know Michael would want to tag along. I don't know that I have the energy for another round of goodbyes."

"You're right. Well . . . you be careful, son. We'll see you in June." Cam extended his hand for a handshake, then wrapped his arms around his son in a hard hug. "Fair winds and following seas."

"Thanks, Dad," Devin managed without choking up. Barely.

Fair winds and following seas. It was Cam's traditional farewell. But as Devin took the highway north out of Eternity Springs, his thoughts returned to the other person who recently had offered him the sailor's wish. Why hadn't they phoned?

On another day, he'd have already placed a call to Reilly, but Devin had put a lot of thought into this final contact between them. It was well choreographed to ensure that Reilly's Santa calls ended on the right note. Devin didn't want to screw that up. So he waited. And fretted, especially during that forty-five minute stretch of road with no cell connection.

But when he emerged into civilization once again, his phone showed no missed calls, no voice mails. No nothing. He drummed his fingers against the steering wheel. "What the hell, Reilly's Mom?"

At the airport, he kept the phone in his jacket pocket when he turned in his rental car. He held it in his hand as he checked his luggage and stood in the security line. At the restaurant near his gate, he set the phone on the bar as he ordered and drank a beer. Time ticked by.

Ten minutes before he was due to board, he threw in the towel and hit redial. It rang twice, but when the call connected, the voice on the other end wasn't Reilly or his mother. The canned recording said, "The number you have reached is no longer in service."

He called again, this time dialing the number himself. Same result. Next he called the phone company, fought his way through to a human being, and checked for a service outage. *Nada.*

They made the boarding announcement for his flight as he waited in line to inquire about a flight to Nashville. He dialed her number again. "The number you have reached is no longer in service."

Dammit. Temper churned inside him. Why? If she didn't want Reilly to talk to him again, the least she could have done was call him and explain!

But that didn't make sense. Reilly knew his number. Reilly could call him from any phone. Why would she disconnect—

The stalker. *Oh holy hell.*

"Final call for flight three forty-seven to LAX."

Devin stared at his boarding pass and rubbed the back of his neck. What the heck did he think he could do? He didn't know her name. He didn't know what she did for a living beyond work long hours. He'd talked to her four times. Spoken with Reilly only a few times more than that. It was nonsense to think she needed his help.

"Sir?" The gate attendant gave him a chiding look. "Your boarding pass?"

"Yeah. Okay." Devin handed the slip of paper to the attendant. He didn't need to decide this very moment. He had a layover in LA.

He made his way onto the plane and took his seat. He was feeling around for the seat belt when the burner phone rang. He didn't recognize the number, but he didn't hesitate to answer. "Hello?"

Reilly's Mom's voice sounded rushed and harried as she said, "You've been kind. It seemed only right to let you know. Reilly won't be calling today. His arm was broken and he's . . . sedated. So, goodbye. Good luck in Australia. Thanks for the fantasy, Santa."

The connection went dead.

Chapter Five

ONE YEAR LATER

At the summit of Sinner's Prayer Pass, Jenna pulled into the observation point parking lot and said, "I need a little break before I tackle the descent. Let's get out and explore a few minutes, shall we?"

"Okay." Reilly unbuckled his seat belt and scrambled out of the truck. Immediately, he bent and scooped up a handful of snow, made a snowball, and threw it at the nearest target—the wood sign declaring the pass's elevation.

"Get your gloves if you're going to play in the snow."

"Mo-om," the boy protested.

She lowered her sunglasses and gave him a warning stare. He returned to the pickup and dug around for his gloves as Jenna walked to the edge of the scenic overlook. The town lay nestled at the center of the narrow valley, snuggled up against a meandering creek that flowed into a frozen lake to the south. She counted four main avenues and a dozen or so cross streets. Garlands of greenery bedecked with twinkling white lights and big red bows stretched across the intersections. Instead of one central business district, commercial structures appeared to be interspersed with residences. All over town, wood smoke rose from redbrick chimneys.

From this vantage point Eternity Springs appeared to be the quaint Christmas village in a department store display window. The only thing missing was the train.

Reilly threw a snowball over the guardrail and stood beside her to watch it fall into nothingness. After it disappeared, he stared down at the little town. "Is that it? The place where we're spending Christmas?"

"Yes, it is. Eternity Springs." Jenna waited, holding her breath for his reaction.

He had none. Jenna's sigh fogged in the cold mountain air. She had high hopes that this Christmastime visit to Colorado would revive her son's excitement over the holiday. It was just wrong for a seven-year-old boy to be so ambivalent about the holiday season.

Not that she blamed him. Even she had trouble disassociating the trappings of Christmas with assault rifles and masculine shouts. It had been a bitch of a year.

After the New Year's Eve SWAT raid, she'd transferred to a new OD/GYN group in Memphis and hired a private nanny for Reilly and a private investigator to find the jerk who was terrorizing them. But after identifying three likely suspects—all men with professional ties to Jenna—the PI had cleared them each of any wrongdoing.

For seven months, they'd led a peaceful life. Reilly's arm healed, and he stopped waking from nightmares in the middle of the night. Jenna settled into the new practice and found a new church for her little family to attend. Then in July, she received shipments from a fruit-of-the-month club, a jelly-of-the-month club, a razor club, a coffee club, a salsa club, and a jerky club—none of which she requested. In August, she began receiving text notifications from social media accounts she'd never created. She reengaged the private investigator, but when eighteen pizzas arrived at their front door on September the third and Reilly's nightmares resumed, she packed up their belongings and moved to Tallahassee.

While waiting for her Florida license to be processed, she worked screening phone calls for a physician practicing concierge medicine. In October, she and Reilly had accepted an invitation to attend a Florida State football game with the divorced CPA who lived in the apartment next door. They'd had a fabulous time and that date led to numerous others. Jenna had grown fond of Joel Mercer, especially because Reilly had thrived under the man's attention. After she'd cooked Thanksgiving dinner for the three of them, he'd invited Jenna and Reilly to join him and his children on a Disney cruise over Christmas.

Then last week, Joel had rescinded the invitation after his children pitched a fit about sharing the cruise with their dad's girlfriend and her son. Reilly had been crushed. Jenna was steamed. Boy, had she misjudged Joel's character. When had—

Reilly tugged on her sleeve. "Mom, look! Is that a bear?"

Alarmed, Jenna whirled around. "Where!"

"Nowhere. Scared you!" Reilly giggled, his eyes sparkling with happiness she hadn't seen in days.

"Reilly James Stockton!" she scolded, her hands on her hips, her expression schooled into a fake scowl. His laughter was music to her soul. "You shouldn't scare your poor mother like that."

"You shouldn't have been fooled. Bears are hibernating now. It would be very unusual for us to see one. Didn't you pay attention to what the park ranger told us yesterday?"

"Obviously, I didn't pay close enough attention."

This morning they'd visited the Great Sand Dunes National Park and Reilly had peppered the ranger with questions. His enthusiasm had reassured Jenna that the decision to come to Colorado for Christmas had been a good one. After the Joel disappointment, she'd wanted to do something totally different from Disney. She'd considered taking Reilly to New York City, but decided the crowds wouldn't suit. They lived near the beach, so that wasn't a solution.

Then she'd recalled the praise Reilly's Santa had given his parents' mountain hometown. She'd recalled the wonder and yearning in her son's voice when he told her about Santa's favorite place to deliver toys. *Santa's favorite place is Eternity Springs, Colorado, Mom. Because it's magical. It has family magic.*

Since Jenna's little family could use some magic, she'd picked up the phone and booked a Christmas trip to a place called Angel's Rest Healing Center and Spa. *So, here we are, Eternity Springs. I hope you're ready to do your thing.*

"It's starting to snow, Mom. Isn't it cool?"

"Frigid." For the next few minutes she watched her boy catch big fat snowflakes on his tongue, and hope filled her heart. Maybe this would be a good Christmas, after all.

"Better load up now, Riley. We're running out of daylight. Plus, we need to get down off this mountain pass before it starts snowing any harder."

Half an hour later, they were introduced to Celeste Blessing, the Angel's Rest innkeeper. She wore her gray hair in a stylish bob. Gold filigree angel wings dangled from her ears and friendliness sparkled in her light blue eyes. Jenna liked her immediately.

"We had a last-minute cancellation so we've upgraded you to our best two-bedroom cottage at the same charge as your regular room. It has plenty of space for a lovely, large Christmas tree. I hope that's all right with you?"

"That's fabulous. Thank you."

Celeste chattered on about holiday events in Eternity

Springs as she ferried Jenna and Reilly and their luggage in a golf cart to a cottage sporting a plaque beside the door that read BLITZEN.

"We absolutely love Christmas here at Angel's Rest," Celeste explained as she led them into the cottage. "All our cottages get a special holiday name. I trust you'll be comfortable here. Don't hesitate to ask for anything you need."

Jenna looked around and her spirits took flight. She saw a fireplace with a mantle built for stockings, a spot in front of a picture window made for a tree, and a bar separating the kitchen from the living area that cried out for a plate of cookies and a glass of milk for Santa.

"This is fabulous. Just fabulous."

Celeste reached into the pocket of her gold ski jacket and removed a Christmas-green ticket. "As part of your rental, you are allowed to harvest one Christmas tree from the Angel's Rest property. If you wish to take advantage of this offer, you need to make an appointment with our Christmas tree elf. I'm sure he'll have time to take you tomorrow. Just pick up the house phone and dial X-M-A-S."

Jenna glanced at her son. He'd gone quiet in the face of all the Christmas talk, shoved his hands into his pants pockets, and started scuffing his boots against the cabin's wooden floor. *We'll get through this, buddy. I'm going to make this such a good holiday that you'll forget all about last year.* "I love that idea. We'll do that."

"Let me recommend our local Christmas shop, Forever Christmas, for trimmings. You'll find a tub with tree-trimming basics in the downstairs closet, but I'm sure you'll want to buy a few things to make the tree your own. At Forever Christmas you'll find everything you need to trim the tree and deck the Blitzen halls—lights, garland, ribbons and bows, ornaments, and of course, the

Twelve Dogs of Christmas. Mention you're guests at Angel's Rest and receive a ten percent discount."

"Dogs?" Reilly repeated.

"Yes. Forever Christmas has an entire room dedicated to dogs. It's called the Dog Haus. If you like dogs, you need to pay it a visit, and be sure to check out the special collection of ornaments that features the dogs of Eternity Springs. They can be purchased individually or as a set."

"I love dogs," Reilly said.

Celeste gave him a warm, gentle smile. "You're going to love Eternity Springs, Reilly. I can just tell." Glancing up at Jenna, she added, "It's where broken hearts come to heal."

The statement resonated through Jenna's mind as Celeste finished the tour of the cottage and departed. It stayed with her as she fixed supper, negotiated a bedtime with Reilly, then built a fire in the fireplace and read aloud two chapters of *Harry Potter* before overseeing bath time and tucking the boy into bed.

She checked on him twenty minutes later and found him still rosy cheeked from his hot bath and sleeping peacefully.

Peacefully. *Where broken hearts come to heal.*

Jenna went to bed with a smile on her face.

The following morning, she and Reilly had breakfast in the dining room at Angel's Rest and registered for a slot to choose and cut their own Christmas tree. They arrived at Forever Christmas shortly after it opened for the day. In short order, *finally*, Reilly got his Christmas on.

It was the Dog Haus that did it. Everywhere you looked, you found something related in some way to dogs. Gifts for pets, apparel for dog moms and dads. Ugly-Christmas-sweater dog costumes and chew toys and bubbling dog-bone tree lights and ornaments celebrating dozens of different breeds. Reilly was in heaven, and it quickly became apparent they'd have a dog-themed Christmas tree.

Reilly had been lobbying for a dog almost since he learned to talk, but a pet was one too many responsibilities for single mother Jenna. So far, she'd managed to withstand his numerous requests. But now as she watched him load up his shopping basket with dog-themed trimmings, she wondered if the time had come to relent. Maybe a puppy from Santa was just the medicine her son needed to bring joy back to the holiday.

"Isn't that little dachshund ornament cute?" asked the woman behind the checkout counter. She'd introduced herself as Claire Lancaster, the store's owner. "It's one of my daughter's favorites. She loves her some wiener dogs. One of our local residents owns a dachshund whose hind end is paralyzed and the dog gets around in a wheelchair. She's the sweetest little thing. Her name is Penny."

"What happened to her?"

"I believe the story is that she jumped down off some lawn furniture and landed wrong. Broke her back."

"That's sad."

"Yes, but it honestly doesn't appear to bother her. She's a happy dog."

"Do you have an ornament that has a wheelchair?" Reilly asked.

"Not this year. I'm having one made for next year, though." To Jenna, she said, "If you'd like to join my mailing list, you'll be notified when they become available."

As a rule, Jenna didn't join mailing lists, but she couldn't resist Reilly's reawakened enthusiasm for Christmas. This was the most animated he'd been about the holiday since his last phone conversation with Santa. "Yes, I'll sign up."

While Jenna recorded an email address in a notebook

Claire kept beside her register, Reilly said, "We're going to cut down our own Christmas tree this afternoon."

"You'll enjoy that. Do you have one of the national park permits?"

"I honestly don't know," Jenna answered. "It's something arranged through the place where we're staying."

"You must be at Angel's Rest."

"Yes." Jenna snapped her fingers. "The innkeeper told me to mention that."

"You get a ten percent discount," Claire said with a cheery smile. "The forest where you'll choose your tree is acreage that Celeste recently purchased from a rancher that expands the Angel's Rest resort. You are going to love your trip into the forest. It's a gorgeous section of land and you have perfect weather for it. Sunshine and crisp, but not bitter, temperatures. Two inches of new snow to make everything pretty. My friend Cam Murphy handles the tour for Celeste. He takes you in a horse-drawn sleigh and it's a beautiful ride."

"That sounds great. Don't you think so, Reilly?"

"I guess," he said with a shrug, but Jenna didn't miss the note of interest in his eyes.

On the way out of Forever Christmas, Jenna noted that Reilly slowed as they passed a Santa-themed room. When he stopped and stared, she held her breath. Was he about to make a breakthrough?

He had not asked to visit Santa this year. He had never mentioned last year's Santa calls. He certainly had never mentioned the final phone call that never happened because the Nashville SWAT team had burst through their front door, screaming and sweeping the house at gunpoint. The break in her son's arm had healed just fine, but mentally, he still had a ways to go. He'd gone from being fearless and friendly before the SWAT team raid to fearful, suspicious, and shy—especially around men. It had taken him weeks to warm up to Joel—and then that had turned out to be another kick in the teeth.

Jenna wanted her son to find the right balance between caring and carelessness. She wanted him to find his sense of security. She wanted him to rediscover the innocence and magic of being a child. She prayed these ten days in Eternity Springs would help in that regard. If they could just have a normal Christmas, it would do Reilly a world of good.

To that end, she walked past him into the Santa room. She picked up a red and green plate with the words COOKIES FOR SANTA written at its center. "I think we need this. Don't you?"

He stood there for a long moment before he shrugged. "You haven't made cookies in a long time. I bet Santa likes chocolate chip cookies."

"I'll bet you're right. Let's do it!" Jenna carried the plate back to the register and paid for it.

She exited Forever Christmas with a spring in her step and hope in her heart.

"We sure wish you were coming home for Christmas, son," Cam Murphy said, watching Devin's image on the computer. Devin had called to pick his father's brain about a recurring engine problem he'd been having on the *Out-n-Back*, and the two had talked shop for almost half an hour before the conversation turned to more personal matters.

"I know. I'll miss you guys." Because Devin had taken time away from work to come home for Brick Callahan's wedding in October, returning two months later simply wasn't doable. "If our foolish friends ever wise up and stop getting married, maybe we can stick to that visit schedule we planned when I decided to move home."

"Foolish friend, my ass. Brick Callahan is so happily married, his smile can power a generator."

"Hey. I smile plenty myself and I don't have a ball and chain to haul around."

Cam shook his head. Devin was the very definition of a rolling stone who never hid his lack of interest in marriage. Cam figured he'd really enjoy it the day his boy met his match. *Hard heads fall harder.*

"You're still planning to come over in June, aren't you?" Devin asked.

"We are," Cam said. "I'd like to make a trip before then, but with your brother in kindergarten now that puts a hitch in our git-along. He'd never forgive us if we went to Australia without him."

Devin laughed. "When Mikey's not happy, nobody's happy."

"Tell me about it," Cam said. "He and your mother are locked in a battle royal right now."

"Oh yeah? Over what?"

"Cell phones. He thinks he needs one. Sarah isn't having any of that."

"I should hope not. The kid lives in Eternity Springs. If he needs to get hold of you or Mom all he has to do is raise his voice."

"Well, he's not getting what he wants, though he's made the end-around play and asked Santa to bring him one."

Devin burst out laughing. "Why does this not surprise me?"

"Well, I'm afraid the surprise is going to be on him. Santa might bring him a cell phone, but it won't be a smart phone. No camera. Mrs. Claus is adamant about that."

"Good for her. By the way, this reminds me. Remember

that phone I gave you when I was back in the States for Brick's wedding?"

"Celeste's burner phone. Yeah."

"Don't forget to turn it on."

"I already have." Cam had been touched by the story Devin told him about playing along with a little boy's Christmas Eve wrong number. "I charged it up and turned it on four days ago. Not a peep so far."

"I don't expect it to ring," Devin said. "The mom knows I moved, so I imagine she'll have run interference. But, just in case . . ."

"I'll take care of it."

"Thanks, Dad."

They spoke a few more minutes, and then Sarah entered the room and shouldered Cam out of the way. Mother and son were still talking ten minutes later when Cam went upstairs to change his boots prior to departing for Angel's Rest and his two o'clock tree-cutting trip. Sitting in the easy chair in front of the bedroom suite's fireplace, he bent over to tie his laces. Michael burst into the room and made a running leap onto the bed. "Hey, Daddy. You going somewhere?"

"I have an appointment at Angel's Rest."

"Can I go?"

"Nope."

"Aw, Daddy." Michael went up on his knees. "Please? I'm so bored."

"Then go do your homework."

"I don't have homework. We're on Christmas break. Let me go with you, Dad."

"Nope. This is work."

The boy bounced on the mattress.

"You'd better hope your mom doesn't catch you jumping on the bed. She'll tan your hide."

"She's downstairs talking to Devin. Dad, after you finish your work, will you take me to Forever Christmas?"

Cam sensed a trap, but dang it, he couldn't see what it was. "Why?"

"It's the Saturday before Christmas."

"Yep. What does that have to do with anything?"

"Ms. Claire is going to have gingerbread cookies and hot apple cider, and Santa is going to be there!"

Bingo.

"You've already visited Santa."

"Yes, but I need to tell him something else."

"Nope, doesn't work that way. You get one shot at Santa, boyo."

"But—"

"Zip it. Tell you what. I'm taking a lady and her son to cut their Christmas tree. I think the boy is around your age. If you promise to behave and do exactly what I tell you to do when I tell you to do it, I'll bring you along."

Michael's eyes lit up. "I'll behave! I promise."

"If you don't, I'll ask Mom to make liver and onions for supper."

"Ick. I'll be good, Daddy."

"Go get your gear on and meet me downstairs." The boy was off the bed like a rocket and almost ran down his mother, who had come to stand in the master bedroom doorway. Cam looked at Sarah and let out a weary sigh. "I'm too old to be raising a little kid."

"That sentiment is going on seven years too late."

"Just think. We still have the teen years to go through. Devin almost did me in and I swear, for boys who aren't blood related, those two couldn't be more alike."

"Well, if Michael grows up and moves to Australia, I'll be the one who goes Down Under."

"Excuse me?"

"You'll be burying me in a shallow grave. I won't survive losing another son to Oz." She gazed at Cam with watery violet eyes. "I miss Devin so much!"

Cam opened his arms and Sarah walked into his embrace. His wife undid him. Devin had been a seventeen-year-old with an extra load of teenage baggage when he came into Sarah's life. Sarah couldn't love him any more if she'd given birth to him herself.

Cam hugged her tight, then put his fingers beneath her chin and tilted her head up to meet his gaze. "No shallow grave for you, my love. I'll dig you one nice and deep."

"You're so good to me, Cam Murphy."

"Aren't I though?"

She snorted, and he playfully slapped her butt. "Actually, something tells me if we manage to survive Michael's teenage years, we'll be ready for our heavenly reward."

"Teens? I might not survive grade school."

"Like I said at the beginning of this conversation, I'm too old to be raising kids."

"It's the school holidays that make it so hard. The 'I'm bored' complaint is getting old. Seriously, I don't know what I'm going to do with him next summer."

"That's easy." Cam shot her a wicked grin. "We ship him off to Devin."

Sarah laughed. "Mr. No-Kids-for-Me? It would serve him right. I don't know why he's so adamant about not having children, anyway. He's great with Michael."

"I don't know why you're worrying about that. Boy needs a wife first and from what I can tell, he likes having a harem too much to settle down."

"Men." Sarah said it like a curse.

"Hey, don't paint me with that brush. I married my high school sweetheart."

"Eventually."

"Hey, better late than never. Am I right?" He swooped down and captured her mouth in a lusty kiss.

From downstairs came the sound of their son's impatient voice. "Daddy, let's go!"

Cam met Sarah's gaze. "Military school is always an option."

He headed downstairs and was in the truck watching Michael buckle his seat belt when a rap sounded on the driver's side window. He glanced up to see Sarah holding the Santa phone. Cam winced. That's the second time he'd forgotten Devin's phone.

"What's that, Daddy? Is that a phone? You already have a phone. Why do you have two phones? I don't have any, and I need one!"

Cam gave his son a sidelong look. "It's the Santa hotline. I'm bringing it along in case you don't behave and I need to report."

Michael's eyes went round. He zipped his lips. Cam whistled "Santa Claus Is Coming to Town" all the way to Angel's Rest.

"Here it comes," Reilly called down from the cottage's loft bedroom. "I see the sleigh, Mom."

"Well, come on downstairs and get your hat and gloves."

"I'm gonna go pee first!"

"Good idea." Jenna took one last sip of hot tea, then decided to follow her son's example and made a quick trip to the downstairs restroom.

She was kneeling to help Reilly zip his coat when a rap sounded on their door. "Come in!" Reilly called loudly before Jenna could manage a word.

The door opened, and Celeste Blessing was there carrying two ceramic mugs sporting the Angel's Rest logo. "Merry Christmas!"

"Merry Christmas, Celeste," Jenna said.

"Are you ready to go?"

"We are."

"I hope you don't mind if I tag along with you. I have an errand to do in that part of the forest, and as much as I enjoy taking a snowmobile out for a spin, nothing beats a horse-drawn sleigh."

"We're happy to have you join us."

"Wonderful." Celeste smiled down at Reilly. "I'm thinking I might harvest one more tree for the main house if we find the perfect specimen. There's a spot on the second-floor landing that cries out for a tree. Reilly, do you like marshmallows in your hot chocolate?"

"Yes, ma'am."

"Good. I had a feeling you might. I put a couple extra in yours."

Outside, Celeste introduced them to their driver, a handsome man with friendly, forest green eyes, and his young son Michael, who pinned a blue-eyed gaze on Reilly. "There's a Reilly in my school. She's a girl."

"Don't be rude, Mike," his father said. "Don't forget I have the phone."

The boy appeared honestly insulted. "What's rude about that? She *is* a girl!"

Jenna quickly changed the subject by asking, "How old are you, Michael?"

"I'm almost seven."

"I'm almost eight," Reilly informed them in a superior tone.

"Scoreboard," Cam said to his son.

Michael shrugged that off. He turned back to Reilly. "Do you have a cell phone?"

"No. My mom won't let me have one."

"Me either!"

With that, the boys bonded.

The sleigh was something right out of a Dickens novel,

red with gold accents, seating for nine plus the driver, runners that curved on the front end, and jingling bells on the harnesses of the two sorrel horses hitched to it.

Reilly accepted Cam's invitation to sit up front with him and his son. Celeste topped off everyone's hot chocolate from a thermos, then Cam took up the reins and, to the jingle of bells, the sleigh glided smoothly across the snow.

Celeste pointed out valley landmarks as they crossed the main area of the resort. When they entered the forest and the winding trail began a gradual climb in elevation, she fell silent. Even the chattering boys spoke more softly. Snow frosted the branches of evergreens and sunshine dappled the ground. The fragrance of fir . . . of Christmas . . . drifted on the air. Jenna sipped her hot chocolate and enjoyed the peace of the snow-dusted afternoon.

"It's beautiful here," she murmured.

Celeste beamed at her. "We call it a little piece of heaven in the Colorado Rockies."

"I can see why. In some ways this forest reminds me of a cathedral."

"That's a keen observation, Jenna. Many people find that communing with nature enables them to tap into spirituality. I like to say that while God is everywhere, in some places He's a little more obvious."

Just then the sleigh rounded a bend to reveal a scene right out of a postcard. Majestic snowcapped mountains stood against a brilliant blue sky. Jenna was suddenly so glad they weren't on a Disney cruise. "It's breathtaking."

Gently, Cam pulled up on the reins, slowing the horses. He gestured to the left. "Look, boys. Through the trees, just beyond that big boulder. See him?"

"Him?" Instinctively, Reilly went stiff.

Michael asked, "See who, Dad . . . oh. I see." He tugged the sleeve of Reilly's jacket. "Look, Reilly."

Jenna saw the animal at the same time Reilly did. The boy sat forward on his seat. "Wow. Is that a reindeer?"

"He's an elk," Cam answered. "Majestic, isn't he?"

"Those are really big antlers."

"They're called a rack," Michael informed Reilly. "My brother Devin says guys really like big racks."

Jenna made a strangled noise in her throat. Michael continued, "I've seen lots of elk and deer and mountain goats. Once I saw a bear. I was spending the night with Mr. and Mrs. Callahan at Stardance Ranch and one of the campers didn't put the lid on the trash can the right way and the bear got into it. He was licking a can of barbecue beans. He almost got his nose stuck in it. Have you ever seen a bear?"

"No. I'd really like to see one."

"I want to see a shark. One time, my brother caught a great white shark. He lives in Australia."

Jenna pulled her attention away from the elk and focused on the boy. "Australia? That's a long way from Eternity Springs."

Michael nodded. "I know. It makes me sad that he wants to live there. It's so far away that I don't ever get to see him. And you know what? It's summer there now! On Christmas, he's going to church on a beach and he'll wear flip-flops."

"Wow." Reilly's brow furrowed in thought. "I don't know if I'd like that. Seems like Christmas should have snow."

As Cam gave the reins a slap, the horses moved and the sleigh slid forward. Jenna watched the passing scenery, though her thoughts were turned inward. Could the world be that small? What were the chances that two men with younger brothers from Eternity Springs lived in Australia?

Slim, she imagined. Very, very slim.

She gave Cam Murphy a studied look. So, he was Reilly's Santa Claus's father. Michael was his brother.

Reilly's Santa Claus's name was Devin Murphy.

Celeste leaned toward her, saying, "The Murphys are close. This will be the first Christmas holiday that Devin isn't spending with his parents and siblings. They're planning a nice long visit to Australia in late June, but that seems a lifetime away to Michael."

"Holidays make the absence of family members all the more acute," Jenna said, her thoughts drifting back to the reason for Reilly's original North Pole call. He'd wanted Santa to bring him a dad for Christmas.

I tried, buddy. Joel had been a great father—for his own kids.

"That's true. Luckily, the Murphys have a large support system—the entire town." Celeste patted Jenna's leg. "One thing you'll like about Eternity Springs is that we are family fluid."

"Family fluid?"

"What defines a family but the family itself? Eternity Springs is welcoming and generous. You and Reilly are spending your holiday with us so this season, you are part of our family. Now, see this bridge up ahead? Once we cross it, we're less than five minutes to the part of the forest where you can choose your tree. Do you know what kind you want? A Douglas fir? A lodgepole pine? A Colorado blue spruce?"

Jenna was glad to change the subject to Christmas. "I don't know. What do you think, Reilly?"

"I want one that's really tall!"

"We can do tall," Cam said. Less than ten minutes later, he pulled back on the reins and the sleigh slid to a stop. The boys scrambled down to the ground.

"We have a tall tree," Michael told Reilly. "You wanna come over and see it? Maybe you can come spend the night with me. Dad, can my new friend Reilly spend the night with me?"

Reilly went still and his eyes went round. He looked from Jenna, to Cam, and back to Jenna. Cam shrugged. "It's okay by me. We'll have to check with Mom, but I imagine she'll green light the idea. She won't be home tonight."

"It's Bunco night," Celeste explained to Jenna.

"Will you call her, Dad? Please?"

Cam looked at Jenna, his brow arched in silent question. Jenna's heart melted at the hope in her little boy's eyes. She nodded. Moments later, Michael's mom had given her blessing and the tree hunt began in earnest.

Jenna thought cutting a Christmas tree might be anticlimactic.

Celeste chose a five-foot spruce shortly after they stopped. While Cam removed a chain saw from a compartment beneath the driver's seat, the boys ran like banshees through the forest. Jenna gave up her attempts to chase them down when Cam told her not to worry. "As long as we can hear them, they're fine. That said, I didn't mean for my boy to crash your family moment. I'll make him sit—"

"No," Jenna was quick to say. "No. This is wonderful. It's just what we needed. What Reilly needed."

"Good." Cam braced his hands on his hips and slowly shook his head. "It's what I needed too, to be honest. Did you ever watch Bugs Bunny?" After she nodded he continued. "Remember the Tasmanian Devil? That's our Mike. And this time of year with all the excitement of Christmas . . . it's even worse. If your Reilly can drain some of his battery, I'll be a grateful man."

Jenna followed the path of his gaze and saw the boys playing tag. Wistfulness overcame her. Once upon a time, her son had run at life in a similar manner. Once upon a time—before a New Year's Eve SWAT raid.

The boys ended their game, and Reilly ran back to her. "Let's pick a tree, Mom. We need to get it back and decorated before it's time to go to Michael's house."

"Hey, I've been the one waiting on *you*."

Cam saw to harvesting the tree for Celeste while Jenna, Reilly, and Michael searched for the Stockton family's perfect tree. They narrowed it down to two trees, both fir, and Michael was running back and forth between them trying to make a final decision when he said, "What is Miss Celeste doing? Maybe she found a better tree for us."

He took off running toward the spot where Jenna could just see a speck of color that was Celeste's gold coat. With a sigh, Jenna trekked after them. What she discovered when she drew closer put a smile of wonder on her face.

It was a perfectly shaped noble fir that stood probably ten feet tall. In the middle of a forest in the middle of nowhere, it was trimmed like a Christmas tree, but with items made from natural elements. A garland of bright red berries encircled the tree. Carved wooden ornaments hung from the branches. Jenna spied twigs formed into stars and snowflakes, and acorn tops shaped into hearts. And at its top stood a most magnificent angel with a face carved from stone, a halo of silver, a gown of golden fur, and graceful wings of snow white feathers.

"What is this?" Michael asked, awe in his voice.

"It's my Christmas wishing tree," Celeste replied.

Reilly said, "I've never heard of that."

The smile that Celeste showed him was warm enough to melt the snow. "The Christmas wishing tree is a generations-old tradition in my family."

"How does it work?" Michael asked. "Do you ask for presents like with Santa Claus?"

"Well, not precisely. The Christmas wishing tree definitely has more of a spiritual aspect to it."

"Like ghosts?" Reilly asked.

"No, dear. While the term 'spiritual' means different things to different people depending on their worldview, in this case it refers to the sacred, that which is beyond ourselves, that existence that speaks to the soul."

Michel frowned. "I don't understand."

Reilly raised his hand like a schoolboy. "Sacred is Baby Jesus in the manger. That's what's Christmas is supposed to be about, we just forget about it because of all the commercials."

"Not commercials," Jenna corrected. "Commercialism."

Celeste laughed. "Commercials have something to do with it too. Let me try to explain it this way. Earlier when we entered the forest and you boys went still and quiet, do you know why you reacted that way?"

The boys looked at each other and shook their heads.

"Jenna, do you recall what you said to me?"

"I said it was like entering a cathedral."

"What's a cathedral?" Michael asked.

"A great big church," Cam told him.

"Why did the forest make you think of entering a cathedral, Jenna?"

The boys turned to Jenna expectantly. She took a moment to frame her response in a simple way the boys would understand. "Because when I go into a cathedral, it's so huge and beautiful and peaceful that it touches my heart deep down inside. Sometimes it makes me cry good tears."

"My mom does that a lot," Michael offered.

Jenna smiled at him and completed her explanation. "Walking into a cathedral reminds me that I'm a tiny human being and the universe is huge and created by a power that is bigger than my mind can comprehend."

"That's an excellent description, Jenna. The Christmas wishing tree tradition came about because while we might not always have a cathedral handy, we can usually find a tree growing in the woods somewhere."

Reilly asked, "What about somebody's front yard? Would that count?"

"Why, yes. Yes it would. Although I will admit that a forest is beneficial to get the full effect."

He pressed. "What about fake Christmas trees, the kind you buy in a store?"

"Actually, I've never considered that question before, Reilly, but I believe that probably crosses the line. It needs to be a living, growing tree."

"So do you decorate the exact same wishing tree every year?"

"No. Each year it's a different tree. That's one of the things that are so wonderful about a Christmas wishing tree. It doesn't matter where I'm living or visiting, I can designate any tree to be my Christmas wishing tree.

"How does it work?"

"Reilly, that's what she's trying to tell us." Jenna made a zipping motion over her mouth. "Let her talk."

Celeste winked at Reilly, then continued. "Each year when I decorate my wishing tree, I make one special ornament that represents a particular challenge or circumstance I overcame during the past year and my biggest wish for the one upcoming. When I hang it on a tree, in the cathedral of a forest, I reflect on those two events. That's when the magic happens."

"Magic?" Cam asked, his green eyes watching Celeste closely.

"My wishes have a way of coming true."

"Because of magic?" Michael asked.

"Because I choose to live my vision, not my circumstance."

She focused her gaze on Jenna and continued, "All of us have circumstances. For some it's health related. For others, it's financial struggles. The choice each of us has is whether we allow circumstances to rule our lives, or whether we live according to our vision, how we want our lives to be. If I were the one who'd named my family tradition, I'd have called it the Christmas vision tree. Circumstances are temporary; vision lasts forever."

The words resonated inside of Jenna like a song. She had the sense that something important had just taken place, and she was still trying to think it through when Reilly asked, "Has your wish come true? The one you made when you hung your special ornament this year?"

"Actually, yes. Yes it has. My wish came true yesterday, in fact." Then the older woman clapped her hands and added, "Now, we'd better see to finding your Christmas tree, young man, before the afternoon gets away from us. I remember seeing a tall, full, beautiful spruce over this way." She gestured toward the northeast. "Would you like me to show you?"

"Yes!" Reilly bounded after her with Michael close on their heels.

Jenna stood staring at the decorated tree, her gaze focused on a carved wooden angel ornament. Sensing Cam's gaze upon her, she said, "I get the feeling that something important just happened, though I can't really say what it was."

"That's our Celeste," he told her. "All I can say is ignore her at your own peril. She has an uncanny ability to offer up advice that a person needs to hear at exactly the time they need to hear it. I've seen it happen time and time again."

I choose to live my vision, not my circumstance.

My wishes tend to come true.

"Mom? Hey, Mom! We found it! C'mere, Mom! It's the perfect Christmas tree!"

Cam pulled the work gloves out of the back pocket of his jeans and said, "Sounds like it's time for me to get to work."

"Mom! Hurry!"

Jenna laughed and said, "Me too."

She followed her son's footsteps through the snow to where Reilly, his new friend, and a woman who seemed to have an inner glow about her admired a perfectly shaped Colorado blue spruce.

Two hours later it stood in front of Blitzen's main window sporting blinking lights, glass balls, dog bones, ribbon garland, Eternity Springs' Twelve Dogs of Christmas, and an angel tree topper that had the face of an Irish setter. The tree was so big it needed some fill-in decor, but all in all, Jenna decided it was the most beautiful Christmas tree ever due to the joy she saw in her son's face when he looked at it.

"'Where broken hearts come to heal'," she quoted softly. Eternity Springs was doing its thing.

The sleepover at the Murphys' house was a huge success. On Christmas Eve they attended church services and watched Michael shine in his role as a Christmas pageant shepherd. On Christmas Day Reilly did *not* find a puppy beneath the tree because Jenna judged he didn't need one. Neither did she. The reasons against having one had not changed. Instead, Santa brought him a remote control car as a surprise, and he was thrilled with the gift.

Between Christmas and New Year's Eve, they filled their days with activities. They went snowmobiling and sledding and horseback riding. During a day trip to Wolf Creek, Reilly learned to snowboard and made a good effort at learning to ski. They attended story time at the library and participated in the official Eternity Springs Boxing Day Snowball Fight. Michael spent the night with Reilly once at Blitzen, and Reilly returned to the Murphys' home for another sleepover the night before New Year's Eve.

Jenna changed her mind half a dozen times about how they should spend New Year's Eve. They'd been included in invitations for an adult party at Angel's Rest and a corresponding children's slumber party at a daycare center called Gingerbread House. Reilly desperately wanted to attend, but the thought of being separated on the swatting anniversary gave her cold sweats.

It was foolish, she knew. She had no reason to think that the stalker had traced them again. Nothing since their move to Tallahassee in September had given her cause for concern. She should allow Reilly to attend the party, go to one herself, and end their holiday trip on a positive note.

What finally made up her mind was finding Reilly sitting at the table in the cottage's kitchen with a pile of pinecones, stones, sunflower seeds, and a bottle of glue. "Whatcha doin' there, hot rod?"

"I'm making an ornament."

"To take home as a souvenir?"

"No. It's for my Christmas wishing tree. You can choose a wishing tree and decorate it anytime you want. I asked Ms. Celeste."

Jenna's heart did a little flip. "You did?"

"Yep. When we come back to Eternity Springs next year for Christmas I can add more decorations."

Choose to live your vision, not your circumstance.

Peace rolled through Jenna like an ocean wave. "That sounds like a plan. Looks like you have plenty of supplies there. Mind if I join you and make an ornament too?"

"Sure, Mom. You can come with me when I hang it. Just don't ask me what my wish is. Ms. Celeste said it works better if you keep it in your heart."

"Ah. Okay, then."

When Jenna hung her ornament on a tree in the cathedral of the Angel's Rest forest an hour later, she didn't try to keep the tears from her eyes. "Good tears," she assured Reilly.

They walked hand in hand back to Blitzen and got ready for their respective parties. Reilly left her at Gingerbread House without a backward glance, and Jenna enjoyed herself so much at Celeste's party that she stayed past midnight and even shared a friendly midnight kiss with a handsome lawyer named Boone McBride.

On New Year's Day with real regret for the end of their vacation and after Michael and Reilly secured promises from their mothers that phone calls between them would be allowed and encouraged, Reilly and Jenna headed home to Tallahassee.

As they passed the Eternity Springs city limits marker, Jenna promised them both. "We'll be back."

Cairns, Australia

At five a.m. on the second of January, Devin filled his travel mug with piping hot coffee and prepared to head down to the marina. He had a busy day ahead. The dive boat tour was three-quarters full this morning and both fishing boats were fully booked. The three pharmaceutical executives from Boston going out with him on the *Out-n-Back* were repeat customers, and since fishing had been excellent the past three days, he had high hopes that he'd put them on to something big.

He'd just picked up his keys when his phone rang. He checked the number. "Hey, Dad. I'm just heading to work. Running a little late, in fact."

"I won't keep you. I just wanted to tell you about a phone call I had during the New Year's Eve party last night."

Cairns was seventeen hours ahead of Eternity Springs, so his dad was calling from New Year's Day afternoon. Devin wanted to ask about the college football games, but he didn't have time.

"Guess who phoned me a little before midnight? Your Reilly from Nashville."

In the process of reaching for his coffee, Devin froze. His lips stretched in a smile. "Oh yeah?"

"It was a short call and I'm afraid I couldn't hear him very well. Lots of noise on my end and on his. But what I did hear was him thanking Santa for his presents—I couldn't tell what—and he said something about believing."

Believing. Well, how about that? "Awesome. That's great. I'm glad you heard from him. Thanks for filling in for me."

"Glad to do it. I just hope that next year, you're here to serve this duty yourself. Your mother missed you terribly."

Just Mom? Devin rolled his eyes. "I missed being there too. But don't worry, I won't miss it. Christmas in Eternity Springs—I can't think of anything that sounds nicer."

TALLAHASSEE, FLORIDA

Reilly stood in the card shop with his hands clasped beneath his chin as he stared at the packaged valentines on the shelf. "I can't decide, Mom. I just can't decide! Do I get Minions or Paw Patrol?"

Jenna shook her head at her son's genuine distress over the momentous decision he faced. She was tempted to buy both, but she knew that would only complicate the issue when he went to choose which card to give to which friend at tomorrow's Valentine's Day party at his Sunday school. "I'm sure either one would be just fine, Reilly. Better make up your mind. We still have a lot to do this afternoon."

"Like cookies to decorate! Do you think they've cooled off enough, yet?"

"I expect so, yes." She and Reilly had spent the morning making two-dozen heart-shaped sugar cookies for tomorrow's party.

"Then we'd better hurry, Mom! We still have to go to the grocery store for sprinkles."

"I know," Jenna replied. "We need red food coloring too."

Thus motivated, Reilly made his choice, and as they walked toward the checkout counter, he said, "You know what I think, Mom?"

"What do you think, Reilly?"

"I think we should send a valentine to Santa at the North Pole. He was really nice to me and people shouldn't forget about Santa just because it isn't Christmas."

Jenna smiled down at her son. "I think that's an excellent idea, son."

Pride at Reilly's thoughtfulness warmed her heart, and during their stop at the grocery store, her thoughts drifted to a certain Santa. Too bad that a valentine sent to the North Pole wouldn't find its way to Australia.

They returned home with sprinkles and food coloring and a box of Paw Patrol valentines. Reilly donned his child-sized apron and chef's hat to help his mother whip up a batch of royal icing. After tinting one bowl of icing red and another pink, they sat at the kitchen table with cookies, icing, spatulas, and pastry bags before them. Reilly chatted like a magpie as he spread icing over golden brown hearts. Contentment rolled through Jenna like a tropical sea wave.

She was piping a red outline around a sugar cookie heart when the peace exploded. Light flashed, sound boomed, and men shouted, "We're in, we're in. Clear!"

Reilly screamed, "Mommy!"

Not again! Jenna lunged for her son and wrapped protective arms around him, bumping the table hard in the process. Cookies hit the floor.

Hearts broke.

Part Two

Chapter Six

Traveling from Cairns, Australia, to Eternity Springs, Colorado, was no easy jaunt under the best of circumstances. This journey back to the States had been a nightmare of missed connections, crying babies, and mechanical problems that included a malfunctioning toilet on the Brisbane to Honolulu leg of the trip. By the time his plane from Denver landed in Gunnison and he exited security to see his mom, dad, and little brother waiting for him, Devin felt like wallaby roadkill.

"Devin!" Michael ran toward him, arms outstretched.

Devin dropped his backpack and stooped to scoop up his brother. "Hey, squirt. You've grown a foot since last October."

"Nope. I still only have two of them."

Sarah followed a few steps behind Michael. She wore her dark hair short in a style that framed her unusual violet eyes, eyes that gleamed with happiness and love as she wrapped Devin in her arms. "Finally. You're finally here. Oh, Devin."

He buried his face in her hair and inhaled the fragrance of . . . home. "Mom."

She looked up at him with tear-flooded eyes. "We've missed you so much."

Michael began to wiggle and Devin set the boy down as his gaze fell upon Cam. Tall and lean and broad of shoulders, his father had gone a little grayer at the temples, the laugh lines along his eyes carved a little deeper and stretched a little longer. His eyes hadn't changed. Mountain eyes, Sarah called them, because of their myriad shades of green. Neither had his grin, the devil-may-care pirate's smile that Devin had so admired and mimicked as a boy until he'd perfected it.

Devin extended his hand. "Hello, old man."

"Boy." Cam took Devin's hand in a punishing grip. "You look like you went ten rounds with a 'roo on a walk-about."

"Feels like fifteen."

"C'mere, son." Cam wrapped him into a bear hug and when they finally broke apart, Devin couldn't miss the sheen of tears in his father's eyes. "This has been too long a stretch. We have to do better."

"I won't argue with you."

After a late-season blizzard grounded his family in Eternity Springs at Easter, they'd attempted to reschedule their trip. Trying to coordinate schedules proved too difficult, however, and eventually they'd decided the best solution was for Devin to make a summertime trip home. Now, though, Devin was home for a three-week visit planned around the Callahan family's big Fourth of July celebration and an engagement party for Lori's sister-in-law, Caitlin Timberlake.

Sarah shoved her husband out of the way and swooped in for another hug. "Lori said to tell you she's sorry she isn't here. She wasn't feeling well this morning—she's had the stomach bug that's been going around town and she wasn't up to a car ride—but she and Chase are planning to come to dinner tonight as long as she's feeling better and Chase remains healthy."

"Are you killing the fatted calf?" Devin asked.

Cam shook his head. "She's killed the Crisco. You're mother's been baking for days."

Devin gave him a droll look. "She bakes every day. It's her job."

Sarah sniffed. "I'll have you know I made two extra batches of strawberry pinwheels and they're in the kitchen cookie jar. Of course, I could always take them back to Fresh."

"I love you, Mom."

"We're having Tex-Mex. Enchiladas, refried beans, Mexican rice, and chips with homemade salsa. Torie Callahan's recipe. It's your brother's new favorite food."

"Guacamole, too?" At his mother's nod, Devin stopped and put his hand over his heart. "That's almost enough to make me forget the horrors of the flights."

He shared the joys of the trip while they waited for his bag. Once they'd loaded into his dad's SUV for the two-hour drive to Eternity Springs, he asked for the local gossip update. That kept the conversation going for an hour. Then, as usual, his mother began grilling him on the status of his love life.

"I'm not dating anyone in particular, Mom."

"What about that schoolteacher you said you were seeing this spring?"

"That didn't work out." Lisa had been a nice woman, but the spark just hadn't been there in the bedroom.

"Oh. I'm sorry."

Devin shrugged. He'd been sorry too. Although he wasn't ready for a steady relationship yet, the dating scene was starting to grow tiresome. What had been fun when he was younger had become . . . well . . . work. Not that he wanted to settle down. He didn't. His flirtation with that idea two years ago had cured him of ever reaching for anything permanent. But he wouldn't mind having someone in his life who mattered for longer than a weekend or two—if he could find someone looking for a similar level of commitment.

Better not tell his mother that, though. She hounded him enough as it was. If she thought he might actually be ready for something serious, she'd dial it up to "incessantly."

He went for distraction. "So, Dad, let me tell you about the engine trouble I had last week on the *Out-n-Back*."

That got them all the way to Eternity Springs. At home, he took a long hot shower then surrendered to jet lag and fell into bed. He slept until his mother sent Michael to drag him down for dinner. The lively conversation with his family revived him, but he over-indulged on the delicious Mexican food and returned to bed when supper ended.

When he finally rolled out of bed mid-morning the following day, he took another long hot shower, and almost felt human again. Except the enchiladas lay in his gut like adobe bricks, and he knew he'd better get some exercise. He tugged on running shorts, an ancient Rockies baseball T-shirt, and his sneakers. Downstairs, he filled a water bottle and waved off breakfast.

He took off running down Aspen Street and decided he'd make the loop around Hummingbird Lake. The brisk morning temperatures moderated as the summer sun climbed over the mountains on the eastern side of the valley. Soon, Devin was sweating. By the time he'd completed the first half of the four-mile path around the lake, he'd taken off his shirt and draped it around his shoulders to use as a rag to wipe the sweat off his face. Too much beer last night. Too many carbs. Too much altitude. He felt like an out-of-shape runner twice his age.

So he had slowed to a walk as he approached the pier where the movements of a pair of fishermen caught his notice. They were a woman and a boy who appeared to be a year or two older than Michael. They kid wore his hair in a bleach-blond mohawk with blue tips. She wore jeans, a blue plaid flannel shirt with the cuffs rolled up over a V-neck white shirt, and hiking boots. A thick black pony tail was pulled through the back of her baseball cap and danced back and forth as she moved. A legal-size trout dangled from the end of the boy's line, which unfortunately appeared to be tangled with that of his mother's.

As a professional fishing guide, Devin had seen entangled equipment more often than he could count. While he watched, she grasped the fish—left hand, ringless—and the boy dropped his pole. She grabbed for the boy's pole—right hand, pretty sterling silver ring—and in doing so, dropped the fish.

This did not look promising.

Devin turned onto the fishing pier and sauntered toward them. "Looks like you have a rat's nest on your hands. Want some help?"

The woman stiffened and turned suspicious brown eyes in his direction. "No, thank you. We're okay."

Maybe so, but the fish wasn't. They were going to kill that rainbow trout if they weren't careful. "Are you guys planning to eat that 'bow?"

"No." Now, those big brown eyes flashed with annoyance. She lifted her chin. "We catch and release when we fish."

"In that case, you'd better let me help."

"Mister, we don't need—"

Devin cut her off. "The quicker we act to free him and get him back in the water, the more likely he is to survive." He reached for the tangled fishing lines. "Do you have a knife in your tackle box?"

At the question, the boy finally spoke in a voice barely above a whisper. "Are you going to kill him?"

"I'm going to save him," Devin replied as he wrapped his fist around the fish. A glance at its mouth revealed it had two hooks in it. The one attached to the boy's line and another rusting barbed hook. "Or try to, anyway. This isn't this guy's first rodeo."

Moving quickly, he opened the tackle box and by-passed the knife for the needle-nose pliers he spied. At least Ms. Snippy had a well-stocked tackle box.

"Don't get me wrong," Devin said as he labored to free the trout. "I don't have anything against fishing. The opposite, in fact. Among other things, I make my living as a professional fishing guide. But fish are a precious resource and we need to be responsible fishermen."

"We weren't trying to be otherwise," the woman replied defensively.

"It's my fault," the boy mumbled, his voice barely above a whisper. He'd moved so close to the mother that he stood almost on top of her. "I got excited and didn't pay attention."

The woman frowned at the boy. "You did nothing wrong, RJ."

Having freed both hooks, Devin leaned off the pier and lowered the trout into the icy mountain lake. He gently opened his hand and was glad when the fish darted off.

Her tone as cool as the lake, the woman said, "Thank you for your assistance. We will handle it from here."

It was just the sort of challenge that appealed to Devin. He rolled back on his heels and shot his very best sexy-but-boyish grin up at her. "I don't mind helping. I love to help folks catch fish. I'm truly an excellent guide."

"I'm sure you are."

"I'm happy to give you a few pointers. No charge."

"How kind of you," she drawled, her smile one hundred percent fake. "However, my son hooked a fish within five minutes of getting his line wet. I don't believe we need any guidance."

"Five minutes, huh? Excellent work . . . RJ, was it?" Devin kept his gaze on the boy while continuing to take note of the mother's stick-up-her-ass expression. "So, I see you're fishing with salmon eggs. Ever try a fly?"

The boy stubbed the toe of his hiking boot and shrugged.

"It's tricky to learn, I'll give you that. I'm not nearly a pro, myself."

"What kind of a guide are you?" Mom murmured sotto voce.

Devin wanted to laugh, but he continued to talk to the boy. "I've been fishing all my life, but I was seventeen before I tried fly-fishing. See, I'm not from Colorado. I'm not even American. I'm an Aussie—Australian. Saltwater is my specialty, and it's a whole different kettle of fish."

The hint of interest in the boy's darting glance encouraged Devin to continue. "It wasn't until I visited Eternity Springs for the first time that my dad brought me to this very lake to teach me to cast a fly. You should have seen me. We were right over there." Devin pointed toward the shoreline about two hundred yards from where they stood. "I drew back my rod and let loose. Hooked a bird's nest in an aspen tree behind me. Yanked it right out of the tree and it flew through the air and whacked my dad's head."

The boy laughed softly and Devin thought he'd won a prize. He glanced at the mother and found her staring at him in shock. He arched a challenging brow. "What? You think I'm kidding? My dad was not a happy man with a head full of straw, I'm telling you."

"No. I . . ." Her voice trailed off and she stared at him, the look in her eyes unreadable. "You live in Australia?"

"Yes."

Following a long moment, her lips twitched. Her eyes softened like a mountain vista at sunset. "I . . . believe. You. I believe you."

Then her smile warmed and widened, and the act took her from attractive to downright stunning. Whoa. Talk about a difference. Icy Mom to Hot Mom in seconds.

Devin reacted like he always did in similar situations. He turned on the flirt, adding a twinkle to his eyes and flashing his famous grin. "I've learned a lot since the flying bird's nest. To be a good fly-fisherman, one needs a soft touch and a great clinch."

She scolded him with a look.

"A clinch knot." He held up his hands palms out. "It's a knot. You need a clinch knot and a surgeon's knot."

The boy piped up. "Mom knows those. Mom can tie *any* knot."

"Oh really?" Devin gave her a measuring look. "Girl Scout?"

She nodded. "Among other things."

"Interesting." She *was* interesting. Wonder why she'd gone from frosty to friendly in a heartbeat? The bird's nest story wasn't *that* great.

Devin knew he probably should wish this mother and son well and go on about his business. He did have items on his docket. His mom would expect him to drop by the bakery. Odds were she had something special in the oven meant for him. He'd promised Michael that he'd play catch with him this morning, and Lori had guilted him into working a volunteer shift at the local pet shelter.

But he didn't want to continue his walk. He wanted to stand here and flirt with Hot Mom. So he extended his hand and said, "My name is Devin, by the way. Devin Murphy."

The boy made a strangled noise. His mother put her

hand on his shoulder and gave it a squeeze. "Call me Jenna," she replied, accepting his handshake.

Devin waited a beat, but when she didn't offer a surname or introduce her son, he inquired, "Are you visiting Eternity Springs, Jenna, or are you residents?"

"We're visitors."

"Well, welcome to Eternity Springs. I'd love to show you my skills. Fly-fishing skills, of course."

"Of course," she repeated, her tone dry, but her smile still in place. "I'm sure that my son would love to learn to fly-fish, wouldn't you?"

At his mother's question, the boy's mouth gaped. He stared up at her in shock.

Gently, she said, "It's true, isn't it?"

Hesitantly, he said, "Yes."

Jenna smiled regretfully at Devin and gestured toward the gear lying on the pier. "Unfortunately we don't have the right equipment."

Devin bit back a suggestive remark about carrying a rod around with him and rose to his feet. "See, we're in luck there. My dad owns the local outfitters shop and he'll let me borrow what we need. What does your day look like? I have time this afternoon for a lesson. Say, around two?"

"Two would be just fine. Do we meet back here?"

"Here will be good. Once your boy gets the hang of things, we can give creek casting a try. Now, I'd better finish my run and get home before my little brother calls the sheriff on me. I promised him a game of catch." Devin gave the boy a wink, tipped an imaginary hat to the pretty lady, and then took off running up the fishing pier. As he turned onto the lakeside trail, he turned back toward Jenna and called, "See you at two!"

She smiled and waved.

The boy looked up at his mother as though she'd lost her mind. *Huh. Wonder what that's about?*

It's him! I can't believe it's him!

And Santa Claus had an excellent ass.

Jenna stifled a semi-hysterica giggle as she watched Devin Murphy jog away in gym shorts, which were appropriately red. What were the odds? The first extended conversation she had in two months with a man who was younger than forty, and he turned out to be Reilly's Santa.

When she'd decided to bring her traumatized son back to Eternity Springs this summer, she'd known that they took a chance of crossing paths with someone they'd met during their Christmas visit. But she'd thought the potential benefit of basking in what Celeste called Eternity Springs healing magic would outweigh that risk. It had worked last Christmas, hadn't it?

She had hoped that by arriving at the height of tourist season when visitors crowded the streets and at a time when she knew that the Murphys were scheduled to be in Australia, she and Reilly could avoid being recognized. With their hairstyles significantly different and Jenna's colored contacts hiding the unique blue of her eyes, the plan had worked too. They'd made two trips into town in complete anonymity since their arrival yesterday.

She never expected to run into Santa Claus himself. And to meet him on their very first full day in town, no less. To have him approach them in a place where retreat literally was impossible and for him to be so darned friendly that her well-practiced cold shoulder didn't frighten him away before he provided enough clues to identify him . . . it was all simply incredible. Unbelievable.

Believe. Devin Murphy aka Santa Claus is the King of Believing. Wonder if—

"Mom!" Reilly interrupted her thoughts.

"Hmm?" Her gaze remained locked on Murphy's retreating form. His shoulders were broad and thickly muscled, fitting for a man who often battled big fish. He ran with a long-legged fluid stride. Bet he—

"Mom! You're not listening to me!"

"I'm sorry." She gave her son a distracted smile. "What is it?"

"What are you doing? That is Michael's brother! We can't go fishing with him. What if he recognizes us? That would be terrible."

Bless your heart, Reilly. You see danger everywhere you go now. "How would he recognize us?" Jenna asked in an effort to reassure her son. "We never met him."

"Maybe Michael told him about us."

"He probably did." When Reilly's eyes went round with worry, she put her hand on her son's shoulder and added, "And why would he connect a woman with black hair and brown eyes and a boy with a blue-tipped mohawk to the Stockton family who spent a few days here last Christmas?"

"You told him your name was Jenna. Not Jane or even J.C.!"

"I did?"

"Yes!"

"Oh dear." Jenna tried not to wince. For the past two months she'd gone by the name Jane Tarver, having used her most excellent Photoshop skills and a 3D printer to create a fake ID good enough to fool anyone but law enforcement. Since she studiously observed every rule of the road, she planned to never need to use her real ID.

But she'd forgotten all about Jane once she'd realized just who was tickling the trout. Her gaze shifted back to the running figure now on the verge of disappearing from view. "I guess I had a brain freeze."

Or a hormone flare.

"That's not good, Mom. And something else. If Michael's brother isn't in Australia today, then I bet Michael isn't there, either. He's probably in Eternity Springs too. Oh, Mom. What if Michael sees us? What if Devin brings Michael fishing with us? That would be a disaster. We have to go back to the camper right now and pack things up and leave right away! Something bad could happen to Michael!"

Oh, Reilly, you break my heart.

Plus, he did have a point. As much as she hated the thought of moving on from Eternity Springs, knowing that Cam and Sarah and Michael were around town changed things. She and Reilly had spent too much time with the Murphy family at Christmas.

"Why did you talk to him, anyway?" Reilly continued. "Devin Murphy was a stranger. Mom, that's so dangerous! You're not serious about meeting him later, right? You were just trying to get rid of him?"

Jenna used the act of picking up their fishing poles to buy time as she formulated a response. She walked a narrow line between seeing to her son's safety and feeding his fears. If not for Reilly, she'd go home to Nashville and challenge the stalker to come after her, goading him in every manner she could imagine. She'd buy ads on radio. Talk her way onto TV. She'd post on every Internet message board and social media site in existence, and she'd have an entire army of investigators ready to track his digital footprints back to his physical feet.

Then she'd show him what it was like to be baking cookies one minute and battling a SWAT team the next.

Except she *did* have her son to consider, and the boy's fears *were* justified. While she didn't worry that being recognized by the Murphy family or Celeste Blessing or even her New Year's Eve midnight smoocher, Boone

McBride, would lead the stalker to their fifth wheel door, Reilly did. And who knew? He might be right.

Jenna had believed they were safe in Tallahassee and look how that turned out.

At the memory of that horrible afternoon, a shiver skittered up her spine. Better safe than sorry. As much as she would have liked spending time with Santa, it wasn't meant to be.

"Okay. Okay, honey. We will leave Eternity Springs."

Visible relief rolled over the boy, and Jenna knew she'd made the right decision. Thinking aloud, she added, "I'm a little concerned about where we'll go, though. It's tough to find a campsite vacancy this time of year."

That was a legitimate concern too. They'd lucked into the slot at Stardance Ranch. Jenna had called seeking a reservation minutes after the RV resort received a cancellation. "Let's head back to camp. I'll get online and see what I can find."

"You'll find something, Mom. I know you will."

They carried their equipment back toward the truck, which Jenna had left parked in a lot conveniently positioned between the fishing pier and the Hummingbird Lake Hike and Bike Trail. As they approached the trailhead, a group of five young Scouts scrambled out of a Jeep and into backpacks, laughing and poking fun at one another. Jenna didn't miss the yearning that flashed across her son's face. For what must be the three hundred millionth time since she'd put the clues together and realized she had a stalker, she silently cursed the bastard.

Reilly should be a member of a Scout troop, she thought as she stowed the fishing gear in the bed of the truck and climbed behind the wheel. He should have friends his own age with whom he roughhoused and made fart jokes and played Little League baseball.

All he has is me.

Jenna sighed as she waited for her son to buckle up, then turned the key, put the truck in gear, and pulled out onto the two-lane road that circled Hummingbird Lake. The situation wasn't ideal, but she was doing her best. Frankly, her best was pretty darn excellent. If life on the road was a little light on friends . . . well . . . that wasn't the end of the world. First things first. Safety and security first. Eventually, the rest would come. One day they'd no longer jump at loud noises. Strangers wouldn't make them nervous. Someday this permanent crick she had in her neck from constantly looking over her shoulder would completely disappear.

In the meantime, she'd make her living without using her medical license, and she'd pay for everything with cash. They would continue to conceal their real names and place of origin. Every day put more time and distance between them and the stalker.

Whenever she got down, Jenna reminded herself that the nomadic lifestyle suited them. She and Reilly had spent the last four months touring parks. National parks. State parks. Even local parks. What began as flight had evolved to an enjoyable way of life. The solitude soothed them. The anonymity reassured them. For the first time in a very long time, Jenna didn't schedule her life down to five-minute blocks. She provided for Reilly's basic needs—shelter, sustenance, and safety. Living out of a trailer tended to whittle away the fluff.

She'd homeschooled her son and educationally he was thriving. He'd mastered the third-grade curriculum and would begin fourth-grade work in September following their summer break. While she was pleased with his academic progress, she recognized that this lifestyle put obstructions in the path of his social development. Reilly could use a Scout troop. He needed friends. His social life was as barren as the moon.

So is yours.

True. Maybe that's why a shirtless Devin Murphy sent her heart thumping in a completely different way from what had become her new normal.

Maybe? Hah! Don't lie to yourself, Jenna. He's been your fantasy man for the past year and a half.

Reilly interrupted her brooding by asking, "Can I unbuckle for just a minute?"

"No," she responded automatically. A moment later, she asked, "Why do you want to unbuckle?"

"I have fish gunk on my hands and the wet wipes rolled under the seat. Can we have spaghetti for lunch, Mom?"

"Next time put the wipes back in the glove box where they belong. We'll be at the campsite in a few minutes. You can put up with fish gunk a little longer. Besides, why are you thinking about lunch? It's not even ten o'clock yet."

"I got scared. Being scared always makes me hungry."

Oh, Reilly. "I'd be happy to fix spaghetti for lunch, but I need to check the pantry. I'm not one hundred percent certain we have pasta. I'd intended to shop for groceries this afternoon at the Trading Post."

"Oh," her son replied, disappointment heavy in his tone. "You should keep more spaghetti in the trailer, Mom. Sauce, too."

Jenna's reply was a noncommittal "Hmm." Reilly would eat spaghetti every day if she'd allow it. However, she had learned early on during this odyssey of theirs to shop carefully with space limitations in mind.

During their first week on the run, she'd bought a pickup with a pop-up trailer off Craigslist in South Carolina. During their second month on the road, once they'd decided the lifestyle suited them, she'd upsized to a twenty-one-foot travel trailer—another Craigslist score, in Indiana. The truck had been dependable, and both campers had been clean and serviceable, but small. Then two weeks ago the wealthy retired couple parked next to them at a campsite in Wyoming had decided on a whim that they'd tired of the vagabond life. They'd made her a deal on the King Ranch pickup and a thirty-two-foot fifth wheel that she couldn't pass up. This rig was a mansion compared to the others, but Jenna still tried to shop smartly.

She flicked her turn signal as she approached the entrance to Stardance Ranch RV Resort and bit back a sigh. She'd been looking forward to their stay in Eternity Springs. As much as she enjoyed life on the road and the fancy new rig, she could use her own summer break from towing a trailer.

Jenna drove slowly through the campground toward their slot, braking when a pretty golden retriever wandered into the road and stopped. Jenna rolled down her window and leaned her head out. "Move along, girl."

The dog didn't budge.

Jenna heard a loud whistle, and then the resort owner's annoyed voice call, "Sugar! Move your tail!"

Jenna gave Brick Callahan a friendly wave as his dog leisurely vacated the road.

"Sorry about that," Brick called. Sauntering toward the truck with a gas-powered weed-eater in hand, he added, "Sugar minds about as well as my wife does."

Having exited the laundry room moments ago with a stack of folded towels in her arms, Lili Callahan gave an exaggerated roll of her eyes. Brick's green eyes twinkled and his grin was unrepentant as he asked Jenna, "So, are you all settling in all right, Ms. Tarver? Everything to your liking here at Stardance Ranch?"

"It's very nice. We're settling in just fine, thank you." Jenna felt the weight of Reilly's questioning gaze, but these were not the circumstances to share their change in plans. Besides, she wanted to be sure she had a place to go before she gave up this campsite.

"Good. That's good. If you need anything be sure to let us know."

"I'll do that."

"And don't forget to check the bulletin board for changes to the weekly schedule. We posted an important one a little while ago. I'm afraid we've had to cancel pizza night this week."

"Pizza night?" Jenna asked.

He nodded. "It's our most popular event. You'll want to get in line plenty early, believe me." Ducking his head, he looked past Jenna to Reilly. "Saw you loading up your fishing gear earlier. Any luck?"

Reilly met his gaze quickly, and then nodded. "I caught one."

"Excellent. You did better than I did, in that case. I fished this morning and got skunked."

Reilly's eyes widened with alarm and he reared back away from the open window. Jenna deduced the direction of his thoughts. "He wasn't sprayed, RJ. That's slang that means he didn't catch anything."

"Oh."

She explained to their host. "When we were camping in Texas last month, the two dogs at the site next to ours had an unfortunate incident with a skunk. It made quite the impression."

"Ah. Sorry for the confusion." He winked at Reilly and added, "I had a similar situation with a dog of mine in the past. It's not fun, is it?"

"No. Not at all," Reilly agreed.

Since Brick had brought up fishing, Jenna took advantage of the opening. "RJ caught his fish on salmon eggs, but one of your neighbors has offered to give him a fly-fishing lesson this afternoon. Devin Murphy. Do you know him?"

"Devin? I do. He's a good guy. Lives in Australia now. I knew he was coming home this summer for a visit, but I didn't know he'd already arrived. He'll do a good job with the lesson. He's a professional fishing guide. Earlier this year he helped a guy catch a five-hundred pound marlin."

Reilly's gaze flicked toward his mother, then back to Brick. "There aren't fish that big in Hummingbird Lake, are there?"

"Oh no. Freshwater fish don't grow that big. But trout are good fighters and a lot of fun to catch. The welcome packet you received when you checked into Stardance Ranch has a copy of my favorite fishing holes map. Once you get the hang of using a fly rod, you should give some of them a try."

"We'll do that," Jenna replied. "Thanks for the tip."

She pulled into the parking spot beside their trailer. They exited the truck, and when Reilly started to run toward the camper, she said, "Slow down, hot rod. I need you to help me . . ."

Her voice trailed off as a motorcycle pulled to a stop at the foot of their lane. The driver wore silver and gold leathers and a sparkling gold helmet. Jenna thought, *Uh-oh*.

Reilly said, "Uh-oh."

The motorcycle rider removed the helmet to reveal a bob of gray hair. She waved at Brick Callahan and he waved back. Then the Angel's Rest innkeeper turned her attention toward Jenna and Reilly.

"What do we do, Mom?" Reilly asked, panic in his voice.

Jenna eyed the motorcycle and muttered, "Wing it."

"What?"

Jenna rested a reassuring hand on her son's shoulder

as the newcomer approached carrying a package she'd removed from her saddlebags. "Hello," she called, a wide smile wreathing her face. "Ms. Tarver? My name is Celeste Blessing and I'm the Welcome Gold Wing."

"The what?" Reilly asked softly.

"That's the name of her motorcycle," Jenna murmured. "It's a Honda Gold Wing."

Her blue eyes gleaming with friendly earnestness, Celeste continued, "Lili Callahan shared the news that you are new seasonal residents of Eternity Springs."

Jenna hesitated, waiting for the expected moment of recognition. It didn't immediately come. *Okay, then.* "Well, we rented the space for a month. I don't know that it makes us residents."

"Absolutely! Anyone who remains with us longer than two weeks counts. The city council made a proclamation. Anyway, I am here to officially welcome you and your boy and give you a little goody box from some of our local merchants. You'll find discount coupons from shops in town including Whimsies and Heavenscents and Forever Christmas. The Yellow Kitchen restaurant has an offer for a free dessert with the purchase of an entree. Tarkington Automotive will balance and rotate your truck tires for free. Trust me, you won't go wrong taking advantage of the specials at Angels' Rest Spa. There's a coupon for a free fishing lure from our outdoors shop, Refresh, and one for two free cinnamon rolls from Fresh bakery."

Jenna watched Celeste closely, but saw only friendliness in her blue-eyed gaze. "We've heard the bakery is fabulous."

"You've heard correctly. You must try the cinnamon rolls. They are divine. Now, do you have any questions about Eternity Springs or the area? I am a veritable font of information. For example, do you enjoy hiking?"

"We do."

"Has anyone mentioned the Double-Dog Dare Trail up on Murphy Mountain?"

"No. I'm sure I'd have remembered that name."

"It's a public trail that recently opened."

Their visitor went on to talk at length about the trail that came about as a result from a football bet between Michael's dad, Cam, and another local landowner, Jack Davenport. It was an amusing story and Celeste told it with flair. Soon even Reilly was laughing.

The sound was more rare than Jenna liked and always music to her ears. She wanted to reach over and hug the twinkling-eyed innkeeper for the gift. That, and the fact that she showed no sign of recognition. None whatsoever. Jenna and Reilly had spent almost as much time with Celeste at Christmas as they had with the Murphys. *Maybe* . . .

Her welcome complete, Celeste told them goodbye and returned to her motorcycle. As she donned her helmet and fastened her chinstrap, Reilly spoke with wonder. "She didn't realize it's us."

"It appears not."

"Huh."

They both stood watching as she started the motor. Once she pulled away, Reilly said, "Ms. Celeste is really smart. I guess that means we have really good disguises."

"I guess so." As the sound of the motorcycle faded, Jenna looked at her son. "Reilly, we spent of lot of time with Ms. Celeste last Christmas, didn't we?"

"Yes. A bunch."

"If we fooled her, I'll bet we can fool most anyone."

Her son, however, wasn't easily fooled. He narrowed his eyes suspiciously. "Not Michael."

Jenna shrugged nonchalantly. "No, probably not Michael. But what if we did a little investigating? What if we met Devin Murphy for his fishing lesson and subtly pumped him for information about his brother's schedule? If we can find out where Michael is spending his time this summer, we can avoid those places. If we're careful to stay away from Michael, we should be able to remain at Stardance Ranch. This resort is a perfect home base for us as we explore Mesa Verde, Black Canyon of the Gunnison, and the Florissant Fossil Beds. When you think about it, we won't be in Eternity Springs itself all that often. Since Celeste didn't recognize us, I think it's safe to assume that nobody else will either. Except for maybe Michael."

Reilly shoved his fish-gunk smelling hands into the back pocket of his jeans. "What if Devin brings Michael with him to the lesson?"

"Well, we could stay in our truck until he arrives. If Devin is alone we go meet him and if he's not, we don't. Maybe we could use that opportunity to go into town and see about getting that certain late birthday present I promised you."

Michel's entire face lit up. "A dog? Mom, you're finally going to let me get my dog?"

"I told you we'd get one when we settled. If we stay here for a month, that's as settled as we'll be for the foreseeable future."

"That sounds like a bribe, Mom. You're making me choose between a dog and Michael being safe?"

"Nope." Jenna shook her head. "Not at all. I wouldn't put Michael Murphy at risk any more than you would. This is the same deal we've had since your birthday in March. I want you to have your puppy, but training is vital in order to have a well-behaved dog that will protect us both. Constantly changing campsites is not conducive to establishing an effective training schedule. However, if we decide to leave Eternity Springs, I intend to find somewhere else where we are able to camp for a month. I want to get you that dog, plus I need a break from windshield time with a trailer in tow. It's stressful now that the roads are crowded with tourists."

Reilly rolled back and forth on his heels. "I don't know, Mom."

"Well, we still have time to decide. Let's go inside and you can wash up and I'll inventory the pantry. If the cupboard is bare, I believe I saw a grocery section in the office. They might have spaghetti supplies."

"I hope so."

She unlocked the camper's door and as was her habit, verified that their home had remained undisturbed in their absence. "All clear," she called.

Reilly dashed inside and disappeared into the bathroom.

Jenna checked her pantry cabinet, confirmed the paucity of foodstuffs, and then broke the news to a disappointed Reilly. "Here." She pulled a ten-dollar bill from her purse. "Run over to the office and buy something I can fix for lunch."

"Can I buy anything they have?"

Jenna was smarter than that. "You can buy anything that is something that is ordinarily on our lunch menu. So no sugary cereal."

"Okay." Reilly darted off to the Stardance Ranch RV Resort office, and Jenna grabbed her laptop and a notepad and pen. She took a seat at the table, booted up her computer, and logged into a VPN service, which allowed her to surf the Internet anonymously.

In the days following the Tallahassee SWAT raid, Jenna had spent her time studying up on how to go off the grid. Within a week she'd had bitcoins in the bank, a serious stash of cash, and a part-time job doing technical writing for a former colleague who'd left medicine for the nonprofit world and agreed to pay her in Visa gift cards. They'd hit the road and done their best to disappear.

She didn't fool herself that she was all the way off the grid, but she had moved significantly off center. Opening her browser, she searched for campgrounds within a hundred-mile radius of Eternity Springs, made a list in order of preference, and then began placing calls. Soon she'd expanded her search to two hundred miles and then to five hundred.

By the time Reilly returned with hotdogs, buns, and a can of beans, she had two less-than-ideal options to present to him. She did so when they sat down to their early lunch. "I don't guess the desert would be too terrible," he said as he squirted ketchup on his third hotdog. "It was hot in Florida."

"It was warm and humid in Florida. This will be hot and dry." Jenna shook her head in wonder as her son polished off the hotdog and spooned another serving of beans onto his plate. The kid's growth spurt was beginning to look like a growth geyser.

"Do dogs like the desert?" he asked.

"Dogs are adaptable. Giving them a loving home is the most important thing. That said, some breeds do better in extreme heat than others and vice versa."

"So we probably wouldn't want a great big hairy dog if we're going to camp in the desert?"

I don't want a great big hairy dog at all. "We'll have to see what dogs are available at the shelter and make the best choice possible for our particular circumstances."

Reilly licked ketchup from his fingers. "The mountains sound a lot better."

Jenna sipped her water and gave him a little more time to think before asking, "So, do you want to meet Devin Murphy for the fishing lesson and see what we can find out about Michael's summer plans? It's up to you."

"Can I have a cookie?"

"May I."

"May I have a cookie?"

"Yes."

In seconds, Reilly had his hand in the cookie jar. "I think we can meet Michael's brother, Mom. As long as we can hide first and make certain he comes by himself."

"We absolutely can do that."

With his mouth full of chocolate chip cookie, the boy added, "I hope we're able to stay in Eternity Springs."

"From your mouth to God's ears."

Reilly's expression brimmed with eight-year-old disgust. "I don't know that He would like having ears full of cookie crumbs."

Chapter Seven

Devin eyed the strawberry pinwheels in the bakery case and debated whether or not he should swipe one more. He *had* gone on a run this morning—but he'd reloaded what he had exercised off in the first half hour behind the counter at Fresh. If he had known then that he'd be filling in for his mom in Temptation Central, he would have run a second lap around the lake.

The jangle of the doorbell provided a distraction, and he gave a wink and a wolf whistle when two of Eternity Springs's downtown merchants walked into the bakery. Shannon Garrett owned and operated Murphy's Pub. Glass artist Gabi Brogan's Whimsies gift shop sold her art along with other handmade items. Both women smiled with delight upon seeing him.

"Well . . . well . . . well," Gabi said. "And here I thought Sarah's cinnamon rolls were the prettiest thing in Fresh. Boy was I wrong."

"Pretty!" Devin protested. "I don't think that's the proper term, do you?"

"He's right." Shannon flipped her sunglasses onto the top of her head. "Sarah's cinnamon rolls are downright beautiful."

The two women shared a look, and then laughed. Gabi

said, "Come around from behind that counter, handsome, and give us a hug."

He did exactly that, picking up each woman in turn and giving them a twirl. Shannon said, "Welcome home, Devin. I'll bet your folks are over the moon to have you back. I know your mom has been counting the minutes ever since their Easter trip got cancelled."

"Counting the minutes and baking all your favorites," Gabi added. She leaned left and peered through the doorway leading into the kitchen. "Is she in there whipping up some more strawberry pinwheels?"

"Actually, Mom is upstairs in bed. When I got home from my morning run she'd gone as green as guacamole. That's why I'm filling in here. Apparently Michael had a stomach bug last week, and she thinks he passed it on to her."

Shannon winced. "Poor Sarah."

"That virus has been making the rounds," Gabi said. "The Cicero kids have all had it. So have the Lancasters. I think your sister had it, too."

Devin nodded toward a plastic bottle beside the cash register. "I bought the last four bottles of hand sanitizer at the Trading Post before I rang up my first sale here today. Speaking of sales . . . what can I get you lovely ladies? I assume you came in for something more than a hug?"

"Absolutely. We're both here for our Saturday morning cinnamon rolls and milk. I don't know if you've heard the news yet, but Shannon and I are both eating for two." Gabi patted her stomach proudly.

"Babies?" A smile stretched across Devin's face as he gazed from one woman to the other. "That's awesome. No wonder the two of you are glowing. Congratulations. I take it everyone is thrilled?"

Gabi nodded. "Flynn is already knee-deep in baby-related inventions. We're not due until December."

"Daniel is thrilled," Shannon confirmed. "Brianna . . . well . . . let's just say she's reserving judgment."

"She's . . . what . . . two and a half?"

"She just turned three and we're having to work on the concept of sharing. It doesn't come naturally to her, I'm afraid."

"I could make an observation about women and sharing in general, but I think that instead, I should probably get you ladies your rolls."

"Good thinking," Gabi said, her tone dry. "We'll sit over by . . . oh look, Shannon. Sarah has done some redecorating since last week."

"She has! Isn't it cute?"

Devin served the rolls, then glanced around the shop, trying to decide what was different. Were the yellow gingham curtains new? He couldn't remember. The soda-shop tables were the same, and Mom had always decorated them with fresh flowers in clear glass vases. "The dry-erase board is new, isn't it?"

"Yes," Gabi said.

"'When life gives you lemons, decide yellow is your favorite color,'" Devin read aloud. "That sounds like something Celeste would say."

"It's a quote from her book *Advice for Aspiring Angels*. I think—" Shannon broke off when the doorbell jangled again and three more customers entered the bakery. Zach Turner, town sheriff and Gabi's older brother, led the way followed by Gabe Callahan, who was one of Devin's father's closest friends. A third man, someone closer to his own age that Devin vaguely recognized, brought up the rear.

"Well, look what the great white dragged in," Gabe said as Devin approached with his hand outstretched. "When did you get home, Dev?"

"Last night."

"Your mom already put you to work?"

"Yeah. It's like I never left. Never grew up."

"You grew up?" jibed Zach as he shook Devin's hand in turn. "Seems like just yesterday I arrested you."

Devin scratched his cheek with the middle finger of his hand extended. "Hardy har har, Sheriff Turner. So, how's that beautiful daughter of yours doing? Old enough to date yet?"

"Only if you want to die," Sheriff Turner fired back. He walked over to the women and kissed first his sister's cheek and then Shannon's. Then he grinned. "Welcome home, Devin. How long are you staying this visit?"

"Three weeks."

Gabe gave a satisfied nod. "So you'll be here for both of the big parties—the Callahan Fourth of July festivities and Caitlin Timberlake's engagement party."

"Yep." Devin nodded. "Wouldn't miss either one of them. Caitlin was like a sister to me even before her brother married my sister. Josh Tarkington is getting a princess."

"That's what her daddy believes," Sheriff Turner observed, his lips twisted in an amused smirk. "He's been grumpy about his little girl tying the knot."

The third man nodded. "That's because Caitlin and Ali are hip deep in wedding planning and the bills are beginning to hit."

Devin suddenly placed the newcomer—the lawyer who joined Mac Timberlake's legal practice. Devin extended his hand. "I know we've met before. You're another Callahan, aren't you?"

"A cousin. My name's McBride. Boone McBride."

"How are you liking life in Eternity Springs, Boone? You're from Texas, right?"

"Dallas–Fort Worth. It's been an adjustment, I'll admit, but for the most part, I'm loving small-town life."

The men placed their to-go orders, and visited with

Shannon and Gabi while Devin filled up white bakery bags. Talk returned to babies, and Devin learned that the sheriff and his wife, Savannah, could be counted among the expectant Eternity Springs families too. "Wow," Devin said with a knowing smirk. "That must have been some winter. Two grandbabies for your mother. Maggie must be in heaven."

Zach gave a rueful nod. "She's knitting like a mad-woman."

Another group of customers entered Fresh—tourists this time—and Devin returned to work. Business remained steady all morning until he flipped the OPEN sign to CLOSED and started on clean up. His mother came into the bakery as he loaded the last utensil into the commercial dishwasher and turned it on. "Look at you, Devin. What a lifesaver you are. This is not the welcome home for you that I had imagined."

"Hey, no big deal. I'm glad I was here to help. Especially since Dad is tied up with tours this morning. Are you feeling better?"

"I am. The nap helped."

"Is there anything I need to do to get things ready for tomorrow?"

"Yes. I called the Trading Post, and they'll sell our day-olds if you'll bag them up and run them over there. I'm going to stay closed tomorrow. Eileen gets back from vacation tomorrow night and can handle things here on Monday if I'm not over this bug."

"Sounds like a plan. Anything else I can do? Do you need help with Michael? I have plans to go fishing, but I'm happy to take him along."

"Thanks, but he's staying up at the Rocking L with Chase all day. I didn't want to saddle you with too much on your first full day back when jet lag can be such a killer. I felt terrible asking for your help here as it was."

"I feel fine, Mom. Don't worry. You, however, still don't look too good."

"Gee thanks," Sarah grumbled.

"You know what I mean. Why don't you go on back upstairs? I've got this."

To Devin's distress, tears welled in his mother's eyes. "I just hate that I'm sick when you're home."

"Hey, as long as you don't give the crud to me, we're cool." He shooed her away. "Don't worry about me, Mom. I'm here for three weeks."

"That's hardly any time at all! What if I'm sick for more than a day or two?"

"Then I can tack a few days onto the end of the trip. I have some flexibility. That's one of the good things about being the boss."

Sarah sniffed. "That's not a good solution. It wouldn't make sense for you to return to Eternity Springs after we all go to the Caribbean for Mitch's wedding. Besides, being the boss means you work all the time. You know that."

His mother must really be feeling bad. Sarah Murphy didn't often play hostess of her own pity parties.

He shooed her away again and this time she left. By the time he finished at the bakery, he had a little over an hour to kill before meeting the ravishing redhead and her son.

He spent half of it at his father's outdoors store gathering up gear appropriate for the fishing lesson. He arrived at Hummingbird Lake ten minutes early, and it took him five to unload the truck. Really, he'd gone way overboard with the snacks. When Jenna and RJ had yet to arrive by ten after, he began to think his efforts might be for naught. The extent of his disappointment surprised him. It wasn't like he'd been stood up for a date. This had been a casual invitation to strangers. That's all. Nevertheless, when the pair emerged from the trailhead adjacent to the parking area, he found himself grinning.

"So sorry we are late!" Jenna called as they walked out onto the fishing pier. "We got here early and decided to take a hike and got distracted when we spied an elk."

"No problem. Being waylaid by wildlife is always a valid delay."

Devin got down to business and spent the next half hour on technique. RJ proved to be an attentive student who willingly followed directions and picked up things quickly. As Devin had expected, the boy did enjoy the act of throwing a fly much more than drowning salmon eggs. He wasn't all that interested in catching fish, either, which made it easy for Devin to flirt with lovely Jenna, who flirted right back. Subtly. After all, there was a kid within hearing distance.

He learned that she and RJ were from the South— she didn't say exactly where—and they were touring the western states in a fifth wheel currently parked at Stardance Ranch. She worked remotely for a health care–related nonprofit and she planned to homeschool RJ in the fall. However, the conversation revolved more around his life in Australia, the Caribbean, and Eternity Springs than it did on her world. Apparently Jenna was one of those women who preferred asking questions to talking about herself, and she appeared genuinely interested in his answers. Devin talked more about himself, his work, and especially his family than he had on a first date in . . . well . . . forever.

Not that this was a first date. He was working his way around to that. It's really too bad Mom sent his little brother up the mountain with Chase today. He had a feeling Michael and RJ would hit it off, which would free up the lovely Jenna for more adult activities.

And yet, why he was even considering spending his

time pursuing the delectable Ms. Tarver was a puzzle. He had three whole weeks at home. Why was he spending his time with strangers instead of friends and family? His father often said that Devin had never met a pretty woman he didn't hit on, but that wasn't true. Devin's social life had been awfully dry of late. He couldn't recall the last time he'd been this interested in someone so quickly.

For all the good it would do him. Again, three whole weeks.

Maybe that was the appeal. For the past year and a half, he'd been working his butt off building the business. For the next three weeks, he had nothing to do but rest and relax. What was more restful and relaxing than sweaty, vigorous sex?

She sure had a kissable mouth.

He watched it closely as she shared a story about Celeste's Welcome Wing. He wondered what she'd do if he leaned over and covered those lips with his. Suddenly, he rather desperately wanted to find out.

He tore his gaze away from Jenna and tried to focus on what she'd said, not the way she'd said it. "Celeste is the most pure-hearted person I've ever met, and she is a fabulous ambassador for Eternity Springs. My mother says the town wouldn't have survived without her contributions."

"RJ says her smile warms him from the inside out."

Devin smiled at the picture and watched the boy work the rod and line. "He's gotten the hang of that quickly. How about we load up our gear and go up to the Devin Murphy super-secret fishing hole? It's about a ten-minute drive and then a five-minute hike. It's a beautiful spot and I took the precaution of packing a basket of snacks in case."

RJ's head whipped around. "Snacks?"

Jenna threw back her head and laughed. "He's a bottomless pit these days."

Captivated by the beauty of her joy, Devin drew in a sharp breath and hesitated a moment too long to say, "Growing boys."

"What sort of snacks?" RJ asked.

"For your mom I have cheese, crackers, fruit, and fresh-baked bread. For you I brought potato chips, corn chips, bean dip, beef jerky, and because I am a generous soul, one dozen of the best cookies ever to come out of an oven—my mother's strawberry pinwheel cookies. Oh, and soda pop."

Reilly turned a beseeching gaze toward his mother, and Devin knew he had won before she said, "We'll follow you."

"Awesome." Devin began gathering up the gear and RJ and his mother pitched in to help. A few minutes later, he led them away from Hummingbird Lake and back toward town, then took the turn onto Cemetery Road. The climb from that point was steep and the turn off he desired easily missed, marked only by a sign that read PRIVATE ROAD.

She fell behind him a bit at that point, and Devin thought maybe he ought to have warned her about his fishing hole's remote location. He hoped she wasn't afraid he was a serial killer leading her toward her doom. He should have told her that the fishing hole was on private land—his father's land, to be precise—and part of a parcel of property the ownership of which went back to the founders of Eternity Springs. Upon occasion, his dad brought a tour up here to fish, but for the most part, the trout in this section of the stream didn't have to deal with anglers. In addition to being some of the best fishing in Colorado, the scenery was exceptional.

He parked his truck on the shoulder of the road at the usual parking spot, and when Jenna pulled in behind him a few moments later, he figured she must have ruled out the serial killer possibility. RJ scrambled out of the truck and ran toward Devin. Jenna stepped down from the truck and then made a slow three-sixty turn, a look of awe on her face.

"Gorgeous," she said.

Devin knew she referred to the craggy, snowcapped peaks set against a brilliant blue sky, the hillsides painted with summertime in a dozen different shades of green, and the alpine meadow blanketed in a rainbow of wild-flowers that stretched out before them. However, he never took his gaze off her as he replied, "Absolutely."

The glance she darted his way acknowledged the awareness humming between them and revealed that the attraction wasn't one-sided.

"This looks like a place where we could see a bear," RJ observed. "What if we see a bear? He'll be a black bear, not a grizzly. They don't have grizzlies in Colorado. When we go to Yellowstone we might see a grizzly. We're going to Yellowstone in September after the crowds have died down. I can't wait. When Mom and I visited Rocky Mountain National Park we took a class about bear safety. The ranger told us to carry pepper spray. Do you have pepper spray?"

"I do."

"Mom does too. Are there berry bushes around here? Bears eat berries. We might see a bear if he's looking for food. If a black bear attacks you, you're not supposed to play dead. Have you ever been attacked by a bear?"

"No, I haven't, I'm happy to say. I've only seen a bear three times and two of those were in town when folks didn't practice proper food disposal."

"What about the third time? Was it at your fishing hole?"

"Nope, I've never seen a bear up here. I don't think there are berry bushes on this part of the mountain."

"Oh." RJ appeared disappointed. "I guess that's good."

Devin hated letting the boy down, so he offered, "I did see a mountain lion one time."

"A mountain lion!" RJ's eyes went round. "We haven't taken a safety class for mountain lions. What are you supposed to do when you see a mountain lion? Is there mountain lion spray?"

Devin glanced at Jenna, wondering if he'd made a misstep here. He hadn't wanted to frighten the boy. "Um . . . I don't think there is mountain lion spray. They don't tangle with humans nearly as often as bears do. I only saw one because I happened to spy him with my field glasses as I was looking up at the rocks. He wasn't here in the meadow."

"Oh."

Jenna asked, "You said we have a bit of a hike? What can we carry for you?"

"A short hike. You can't see it from here, but we'll go up over that ridge"—he pointed toward the north—"and down the other side. The creek pools at the base." Devin divided up the supplies and they started off. Within five minutes of making their first cast, both Jenna and RJ landed trout.

They fished for half an hour before Devin broke out the snacks for RJ, and another half hour before he spread the quilt he'd brought atop the boulder that had served as the Murphy family picnic table in this spot for years and set out the grown-up snacks. He pulled the cork on a nice Sauvignon blanc and offered a glass to Jenna along with a toast. "Here's to new friends."

"To new friends," she repeated.

They clinked glasses and he casually asked, "So, Jenna. It hasn't escaped my notice that beyond telling me that you're single, you've managed to dodge my questions about RJ's dad. Are you divorced? Widowed? A single mom from the git-go?"

She delayed her answer by taking a sip of her wine, watching him over the top of her glass. The light in her brown eyes reflected an inner debate he found intriguing. What was so hard about the question? Did she expect him to be judgmental?

She licked her lips, then said, "RJ's biological mother was a single mom. I adopted him after she died. I've never been married."

Chapter Eight

As the words left her mouth, inwardly Jenna winced. *Why don't you just hand him a pencil to connect the dots?*

Just why she'd felt compelled to repeat a fact she had already shared with him during the Santa calls and thus play unusual-personal-facts roulette, she couldn't say. Except, Devin Murphy had proved himself to be a really great guy. She didn't like lying to him. She didn't like lying to anybody in Eternity Springs. She didn't like lying, period.

"Wow," Devin said. "That's a coincidence. My own situation is similar." He told her about his biological mother's death and Cam stepping up afterward. "He was a single parent for over ten years. It's not an easy job."

Jenna breathed a little easier. Devin's mind hadn't gone to Reilly from Nashville. She hadn't given them away. "No, it's definitely not easy, but it is rewarding."

Their conversation was interrupted when Reilly's cast went awry and his line got tangled in a bush. Devin hopped up to help and Jenna watched the summertime Santa assist her son. A pang of yearning twisted her heart. Would she and Reilly ever be able to have a normal life? Would she ever be free to have another romance or give Reilly that father he craved?

Her thoughts returned to that first Santa phone call. *Do you know how lonely your little boy is? Care to guess what his Christmas wish was? A daddy. The boy wished for a dad.*

Here it was a year and a half later, and she was no closer to making his wish come true than she had been that Christmas Eve.

Devin "Santa Claus" Murphy wouldn't approve. He'd been impatient with her reaction to being doxxed. What would he say if she told him that they'd been swatted two separate times? He'd probably be on the phone to his private investigator friend before she got the whole story out.

For all the good *that* would do. *Been there, done that, have the invoices and no fresh leads to prove it.*

After freeing the tangled line, Devin returned to the picnic quilt. "You know, despite my gypsy ways, I've always had a permanent address. Have you always been a camping aficionado?"

"My parents were campers," she replied, happy to be able to tell the truth about that. "We tent camped mostly, but when I was ten they bought their first pop-up. We spent at least one weekend a month and every vacation camping. It was heaven. I fell in love with the outdoors during those years and it's an interest I wanted to pass along to my son. Since I can work from anywhere that has an Internet connection and RJ was game for the adventure, we thought we'd give the camping lifestyle a try. Fifth-wheel living in RV parks isn't tent camping in a place like this, but it's a nice compromise."

Devin grabbed a grape and popped it into his mouth. "I like the way you think, Ms. Tarver."

The sound of her fake name on his lips dimmed her smile, but since his gaze had shifted to Reilly, he didn't notice.

"Although, I do have a question. If you grew up camping

in the great outdoors, how come you made such an amateur mistake taking the trout off RJ's hook this morning?"

Jenna's mouth twisted in a rueful smile. "That's what men are for."

Devin gaped at her. "Seriously? Did you seriously just say that? What sort of modern-day self-sufficient outdoors woman are you if you can't take your own fish off the hook?"

"I can. I just don't like to. I don't like scales. That goes for snakes and lizards too."

"Snakes have skin, Mom," Reilly called, proving the truth about little pitchers having big ears.

Devin then proceeded to prove his maleness by launching into an in-depth explanation of snake "skin" and the protective properties of scales on reptiles. He had Reilly hanging on his every word. When he mentioned the six-foot long rattlesnake skin from the family ranch in Texas that Brick Callahan kept in his office at Stardance Ranch, it quickly became obvious that her son's interest in fishing was done for the day. Next stop for this outing of theirs was the RV resort office.

She started packing up the picnic supplies while Devin enlisted Reilly's help with the fishing gear, taking care to teach the boy best practices in the process. Soon they began the climb back up the trail with Jenna leading the way, her son in the middle, and Devin bringing up the rear, cooler in hand. She was a dozen steps from the top when she heard the sound that struck terror in her heart. Jenna halted abruptly. Behind her, Reilly gasped aloud.

Not a bear. Not a mountain lion.

"Hurry up, Dad," came a little boy's familiar voice. "Dev is gonna catch all the fish."

Jenna saw a flash of red as the figure topped the hill and raced downward. She had no chance to move out of the way before Michael Murphy barreled into her. He knocked her backward, and her foot came down wrong on something—a root, a rock, she didn't know what. Pain exploded in her ankle. She fell and began to tumble down the hill.

"Mom!" Reilly cried.

"Jenna!" Devin tossed aside the cooler and lunged for her, but right before he reached her, she slammed into the trunk of a tree and lost her breath.

"I'm sorry!" Michael exclaimed. "I didn't see . . . Reilly? What are you doing here? What did you do to your hair?"

Reilly emitted a low moan.

Cam Murphy topped the hill and took in the scene. "Geeze, Mike. Jenna, are you all right?"

She closed her eyes against the pain in her ankle and struggled for breath. Devin knelt beside her, saying, "Obviously, there's a story here, but first things first. Got the breath knocked out of you, did you? Take your time. Let us know what hurts when you're able."

She used the seconds while she fought for breath to process what had just happened. Not a total disaster. The cat was only halfway out of the bag. What happened to Michael spending the day at summer camp with his sister's husband?

Oh, well. What's done is done. Deal with it.

"Mom!" Reilly was down on his knees beside her, worry wreathing his face. "Are you okay, Mom?"

"I'm fine. I'm fine. Everything is okay, buddy. Go pick up the things you dropped." She started to stand, but when she went to put weight on her right foot, pain arrowed through her. She sank back down. "Yikes."

"Your ankle?" Devin asked.

"Yeah."

"Broken?"

"I don't think so."

"You have ice in that cooler, Devin?" Cam asked.

"Yeah." Devin shrugged off the flannel shirt he wore over a plain white tee and tossed it to his dad. Cam used it to create a makeshift ice pack that he tied around Jenna's swelling ankle.

Michael watched the proceedings with narrowed blue eyes. "How come you and Reilly are at our fishing hole, Ms. Stockton? And why did you stop letting him do FaceTime with me?"

"Stockton?" Devin repeated.

Reilly groaned. Jenna grimaced. Cam said, "Michael Cameron Murphy, zip your lips. You've done enough for now."

"But Dad!"

Cam gave his younger son the father's hairy eyeball stare and, when the boy shut his mouth, continued. "Jenna, I think this will work best if Devin and I get on either side of you. At least until we get you up over the hill. Okay?"

"Yes. Thank you."

"Boys, pick up your gear. You go up first. Wait for us at the edge of the meadow." To Jenna and Devin, he muttered, "I want Michael out of the way. The last thing we need to happen is for him to get in a hurry and knock you down again."

Devin helped her to stand, and then the two Murphy men all but carried her up the hill. Nobody talked, a detail for which Jenna was grateful, and when they topped the hill and reached level ground, Devin said, "I'll carry her from here. Will you get the cooler, Dad? No sense baiting the bears."

He swept her off her feet and strode toward the spot where she saw Michael and Reilly sniping at each other. "Enough," Devin snapped as he walked past them.

As the boys fell in behind them, Jenna closed her eyes and tried to think. Under other circumstances she would have enjoyed being swept off her feet by Devin Murphy. Actually, she had entertained a similar fantasy or two involving Sexy Santa in the past. But since she figured she had only a handful of minutes before the questions would begin, she needed to drag her mind away from the hard body cradling hers and come up with some answers.

When Cam caught up with them, Devin asked, "Did I miss the memo about you and the squirt coming fishing this afternoon?"

"My afternoon tour got cancelled. It's your first day home. We thought we'd surprise you."

"Mission accomplished."

"Yep." Cam gave Jenna a sidelong look and added, "Lots of surprises going around."

Okay, so she didn't even have a handful of minutes. *Too bad I didn't bang my head.*

Jenna knew what she had to do. She'd known almost since the moment she identified Michael's voice. Shoot, if she was being honest with herself, maybe she'd intended for the truth to come out all along. Why else come to Eternity Springs?

She needed help.

She lifted her mouth toward Devin's ear and spoke in a tone only he could hear. "Please don't react. Please don't ask questions. It's a long story and I need to explain . . . I will explain . . . when Reilly isn't around. Devin, do you remember the North Pole wrong number? He's Reilly from Nashville. I'm Reilly's Mom."

Santa Claus almost dropped her.

Devin's mind spun like the winds of Hurricane Danielle, which had taken out his boats in the Bella Vita Isle harbor. RJ was Reilly. Jenna was Reilly's Mom. Somehow, they knew his family. For some reason, they'd lied about their names. Changed their appearance—blue tips and black hair when she'd told him she was a redhead. Why? What sort of trouble was she in? Something bigger than tangling with an asshat who'd doxxed her with pizzas eighteen months ago, obviously.

"You can't drive with that ankle. I'll take you into town and to the clinic to have it looked at. I'll drive your truck if you'd like." He halfway expected her to protest, but she simply nodded. "Dad can take Reilly home with him. We can come back for the extra truck tomorrow."

"No!" her son said, an edge of terror in his tone. "No, Mom. I'm going with you. You can't leave me!"

"I'm not going to leave you."

"I'm taking her to the clinic on Cottonwood Street to get that ankle treated. The clinic is only a block away from my dad's house. I'll bring her there as soon as she's finished. I promise."

"Mom!"

The plea in the boy's gaze convinced Devin that the boy would be coming with them. No way anyone could say no to those puppy dog eyes.

"Go with Mr. Murphy, sweetheart. It'll be okay."

"But, Mom. It's not safe."

Michael scowled with insult. "We won't hurt you, Reilly!"

Reilly rounded on Michael. "I'm not worried that you'll hurt me! I'm worried they'll hurt you. I got my arm broked the first time, and the second time Mom got a black eye. They have guns! Next time they could shoot somebody!"

As he burst into tears, Jenna said, "Put me down, please, Devin. Let me hold him. I need to hold him."

Guns? What the hell happened to them? Devin's jaw hardened. "We're almost to the truck. Dad, would you get the tailgate?"

"Sure." As Cam deposited the cooler into the bed of

the truck Devin was using and lowered the tailgate, he looked as grim as Devin felt.

In a dozen long strides, Devin delivered Jenna to the truck. He set her down gently and then lifted Reilly up beside her. The boy buried his head against her breast and began to sob.

"Shush, honey," she said. "It's okay. It's gonna be okay."

"No, it's not. That's what you always say and it never is okay."

She stroked his bleached hair. "Well, this time might be different. I have a good feeling about it. I have a good feeling about this place and these people. I'm not giving up and I don't want you to give up either."

"But if he finds us—"

"He won't," Jenna was quick to deny. "Nothing has really changed, Reilly."

"They know!"

"The Murphys know. Nobody else. And Michael's dad and brother won't talk about us on the Internet, not after I tell them what happened. They're good people. They'll keep our secret."

"But I'm scared!"

"I know. I'm sorry about that, Reilly. I'm going to do everything in my power to make sure you're never scared again." She tilted his chin and directly met his gaze. "I promise."

She used the pad of her thumb to wipe away his tears and said, "Will you go with Michael? Please? You can tell him about our visit to the Great Smoky Mountains National Park, and Hot Springs National Park."

The boy hesitated.

Devin offered, "I'll bet my dad would take you to Stardance Ranch to see Brick's snakeskin."

That caught Reilly's interest. He darted a glance over

toward Cam, who said, "We can do that. It is an awesome snakeskin. Six feet long."

"I would like to see it."

"Now is the perfect opportunity. After you see the snakeskin, if you want, I'll bet I could get us access to the special mountain animal exhibit room at our community school."

"Oh yeah!" Michael nodded enthusiastically. "It's super cool. There's a real bear and a mountain lion and mountain goat. Beavers and a hawk and a ton of cool things. They're stuffed and have glass eyes like the ones hanging on the wall at the Mocha Moose. Remember those?"

Reilly nodded.

Cam explained. "Our local taxidermist donated his collection to the school when he moved away."

Michael tugged Reilly's hand until he climbed down from the tailgate. "You'll like it, Reilly. C'mon. Let's get in Dad's truck. Bet we can talk him into getting us a snow cone too. Have you been to the snow cone stand? I like the blue ones best. They're coconut. Have you ever eaten a coconut? Devin says he had a coconut tree in his yard on Bella Vita Isle, but I don't remember it. That's where my brother used to live before he moved to Australia."

Reilly gave Jenna one more conflicted look. Gently, she urged him, "Go on, buddy. Have fun. I'm fine. Devin and I will find you once the doctor has examined my ankle."

The boy had one last concern. "Make him promise about the Internet."

Jenna gave Cam an apologetic smile. "Reilly and I appreciate all of your help, Cam. Do you mind reassuring him that you won't put our names on the Internet in any way this afternoon?"

"Of course I won't." Cam hunkered down in front of Reilly. "You have my word. Believe me?"

Reilly reluctantly nodded.

"Let's go!" Michael shouted, running toward his father's truck. "Wait until you see Mr. Brick's snake. It's awesome."

Cam rose and offered Reilly his hand. Devin spied Jenna's sigh of relief as he took it and they followed Michael to his father's truck. Devin waited until Cam had started the engine, made a U-turn on the road, and headed back toward town. Then he met Jenna's gaze. "Well, this trip certainly took an unexpected turn. How bad is your pain? I can't tell you how anxious I am to hear your story, but I'm willing to wait until after you've seen a doctor."

"I don't mind answering your questions." She tugged her keys from the pocket of her jeans and handed them to him. Devin opened the passenger door, gently lifted her off the tailgate, and settled her into the truck's front seat. By the time he climbed behind the wheel, she'd found her purse and dug a small bottle of ibuprofen from its depths. Devin spied the six-pack of bottled water in the back seat, reached for one, and handed it to her. "Thank you," she said and took two of the painkillers.

Devin adjusted the seat and mirrors and started the engine. But before he shifted into gear, he turned his head to look at her. "You're Reilly's Mom."

Her mouth twisted wryly. "Yep."

"Okay, then. Before we get everything else, there's one thing I need to get out of the way." He leaned toward her, cupped his hand on the back of her head, and without jostling her leg, gently pulled her face toward his.

Then he captured her lips with his for the kiss he'd been fantasizing about for the past eighteen months.

Chapter Nine

Jenna's head spun. Her body flushed with heat. Either someone had slipped something illegal into her bottle of ibuprofen or Devin Murphy's kiss packed a serious punch. *Sexy, sexy Santa.*

He took his time with it, his mouth gentle and firm, curious and exploring stirring up a cloud of lust like an easy summer breeze through a mountain meadow. When he finally released her, he backed away slowly, his eyes closed, his lips pursed as if to savor the final trace of taste for the longest possible amount of time.

"Mmm . . . ," he murmured. "Thank you, Reilly's Mom. You don't know how many times I've thought about doing that."

"I . . . um . . ." No way would she clue him in that she'd entertained similar thoughts herself. "That was nice."

"Very nice." Shifting the truck into gear, he turned around and headed back the way they'd came. "So nice that I hate to put a damper on things, but I don't know how long this story you need to share takes to tell. We're twenty minutes from the clinic. Maybe you should get started."

And poof. There goes the mood.

Jenna leaned back against the headrest, shut her eyes,

and attempted to gather her thoughts while ignoring the pain in her ankle. She'd rolled it and hit hard when she'd landed. She suspected an exam would rule out a fracture, and predicted a Grade 2 sprain. Possibly Grade 3. The bottom line was that the sprain was bad enough that it impaired her ability to drive safely, especially while pulling a trailer and with Reilly in the car. For the next week or so, anyway, their wings were well and truly clipped.

"Do you remember the last phone call we made to Santa? The one on New Year's Eve when I spoke to you and told you that Reilly had a broken arm?"

"I do."

She then told him about the New Year's Eve SWAT raid, their move to Memphis, the private investigator's lack of success, and the seven months of relative peace followed by a flurry of assaults that precipitated their flight to Tallahassee. She glossed over the reasons why they decided to spend last Christmas in Eternity Springs, but she went into some detail about SWAT raid number two.

With every fact she shared, Devin grew progressively more quiet and intense. His grip on the steering wheel tightened until the veins in his hands protruded and his knuckles went white.

"Reilly was traumatized and I was at the end of my rope. We had detectives assigned to our case who legitimately tried to help, but they couldn't promise me it wouldn't happen again. I knew what we had to do."

"Run," Devin said, firing the word like a bullet.

"Depend on ourselves. Only on ourselves. That's what we've done since February. We've done okay. Honestly, it's been a grand adventure, and in many ways, Reilly and I are better off because of it."

Devin cut to the heart of the matter. "Then why show up in Eternity Springs, where people know you?"

Jenna massaged her temples with her fingertips. A dozen different reasons and excuses and justifications rolled through her mind, but in the end, she too cut to the heart of it. As the truck descended Cemetery Road and turned onto Aspen Street, she said, "Because Celeste Blessing assured me that Eternity Springs is where broken hearts come to heal."

They didn't speak any more after that. He carried her into the clinic and then into the examination room. He told her he'd wait for her outside and to ask someone to get him when she was ready to leave.

Jenna sat on the exam table with her leg outstretched and elevated as a nurse took her vitals and asked a series of general questions. Upon learning that her examining physician would be Dr. Rose Cicero, Jenna tried to recall if she'd met the woman during last winter's visit. She didn't recall the name.

Neither did she remember the face when Dr. Cicero introduced herself. Jenna chose not to mention her own medical degree during the initial workup or while the physician performed her subsequent exam. She didn't want to field the questions that bit of news would certainly elicit.

However, she liked Rose Cicero's competent, friendly manner, and had their positions been reversed, she'd have ordered the same diagnostic radiography and soft tissue ultrasound. Jenna agreed with Rose's diagnosis of a Grade 2 ankle sprain and the recommended treatment protocol that included crutches and a brace.

"We see a lot of ankle injuries around here," the nurse told Jenna as she fitted her with the brace and crutches. "Primarily hikers who get distracted by beautiful views and don't watch where they put their feet on our rocky mountain trails. Do you have experience using crutches, Ms. Stockton?"

"No, actually, I don't. This is my first ankle sprain."

"In that case we'll want you to take a couple of practice spins around the room to get comfortable before we turn you loose."

Jenna was halfway through her second circuit when Dr. Cicero exited the exam room across the hall and smiled at her. "Looking good. Walk on it as soon as you're able to tolerate it. You'll want to start physical therapy by the weekend. Lisa, did you give her the list of exercises?"

"Yes, Dr. Cicero."

"Good. I'd wait until Sunday to take advantage of the hot springs we have here in town, but then you'll find them a lovely treat. Now, do you have any questions for me?"

"No. I think I'm clear on everything."

"Great. Feel free to call if you need us."

"Thank you."

The doctor disappeared into another examination room and Jenna made her way toward the clinic's registration desk and fished for the debit card she habitually carried in her back pocket. The clerk said, "Mr. Murphy took care of your charges, ma'am. He's out back. I told him I'd give him a ring when you were ready."

"Don't bother," Jenna said. She slid the card back into her jeans. "I'll find him."

The rubber tips on the aluminum crutches squeaked against the tile floor as she hobbled toward the building's automatic doors. They *whooshed* outward at her approach, and she stepped into the warm afternoon sunshine. With her attention focused on the ground and the placement of her crutches, she didn't immediately notice the group waiting for her.

"Here she comes," she heard Cam say.

"Jenna!" Devin scolded. "They were supposed to call me when you were finished so I could help you."

She turned toward the voices—and darned near dropped a crutch. Men. A whole gang of them. A mountain range of tall, dark, and handsomes. Devin and his father and three or four more who seemed vaguely familiar. And another three or four who were total strangers. To a man, they turned to look at her. She saw irritation and indignation and concern. Devin looked angry enough to spit nails.

"I . . . uh . . ." Were she not on crutches, she'd have turned around and fled.

Devin met her gaze, smiled, and made a valiant attempt to gentle his expression. "So, no cast?"

"No break."

"Good. That's good."

Jenna's gaze slid past him, to Cam, and then back to Devin again. "Reilly?"

"He's with Michael at my sister's. She's a vet. Doing rounds at the local shelter and taking the boys with her."

Lori. Yes. Jenna had met her last year over their Christmas visit. "Reilly will like that."

"Jenna, I want to introduce you to some friends of mine. I'll start with the Callahans. You're staying at Stardance Ranch. Before the . . . um . . . accident, remember how we were headed there to see Brick Callahan's snakeskin? Well, this is Brick's family. His father Mark"—Devin gestured toward one of the men—"and Brick's uncles Matt, Luke, and Gabe. One of the Callahan family's primary businesses is security. And this is Eternity Springs' sheriff, Zach Turner. Daniel Garrett here is the private investigator who put us in touch with the investigator you hired in Nashville."

"Sorry that didn't turn out so well for you, ma'am," Daniel Garrett said, his expression serious, but his tone kind.

"And finally," Devin continued, gesturing toward the man who had yet to be introduced, "this is Jack Davenport. Jack is . . . well . . . Jack is a spook."

Davenport showed her a predator's smile. "Former spook. I'm retired."

Spook? As in . . . spy? Jenna pasted on a smile and tried to pretend that she was at a garden party instead of a . . . wait . . . what exactly was this? The back parking lot of a small-town health clinic? "Okay. Well. Nice to meet you all."

Devin said, "There's a park bench over here where you can sit down. Will you please join us, Jenna?"

"You told them," she accused.

"I gave them a broad overview, enough to convey the severity of your situation. No one has taken his phone from his pocket, much less typed your name into a search engine. It's a happy circumstance that among the citizens of Eternity Springs we have a small army of brilliant, experienced professionals willing to offer their expertise and advice. We'd be fools not to listen to what they have to say."

We? So he considered himself to be part of this now?

Good. That's what you wanted, isn't it? You were hoping he'd magically make your troubles disappear.

Well, he is Santa Claus, after all.

"Where's this park bench?"

The mountain of masculinity parted to reveal a park and playground area with benches, picnic tables, a swing set, a jungle gym, and a wooden climbing fort. On another day, she'd have headed for the swings. Today, she went for the bench. The men gathered in a semicircle around her, leaning against trees, seated at or atop the picnic table bench. Cam took a seat in one of the swings. Devin helped Jenna get seated, her leg propped up, and her crutches stored out of the way but within reach.

He hunkered down in front of her and met her gaze. "If anyone can help, it's this group of guys. Share your story, Jenna, and let's get this monster off your back and behind bars once and for all."

Now that the moment was upon her, she hesitated. Maybe they should just keep running. They'd been doing all right. Why take the risk?

Because you can't run forever and you can't fix this alone. You know that. Trust your instincts, Jenna. They brought you here to Eternity Springs, didn't they?

She closed her eyes, said a brief prayer that she was making the right choice, and started at the beginning. They let her get all the way through the telling of it before the questions started. Different men seemed to naturally home in on different aspects of the story. Daniel Garrett's questions focused on the actions of the investigator in Nashville. Zach Turner asked pointed queries about the actions of the police. The Callahan brothers zeroed in on her digital footprints. Jack Davenport never said a word, but Jenna didn't doubt that he absorbed every detail.

The questioning went on for more than half an hour, until it finally appeared as though they'd run out of things to ask. The men discussed different aspects of the situation amongst themselves, but nobody offered a solution or even a path forward. Jenna was beginning to wonder if this had all been a waste of time when by some unspoken signal, everyone looked toward Jack Davenport.

"Should be easy enough to set a trap."

Devin straightened and his brow furrowed with a scowl. "What's the bait?"

"Who, not what," Jenna said, not taking her gaze off of Jack. "Me. I'm the bait, right?"

Davenport nodded.

"I won't have Reilly involved in any way," she warned. "The boy can attend the next camp session at the

Rocking L. Timing is perfect. It begins right after the Fourth of July."

Jenna knew that the Rocking L Summer Camp had been established to serve children who had suffered a significant loss. In addition to traditional camp activities, the Rocking L had special programs designed to help children learn to cope with and conquer their individual difficulties. She'd heard about the camp during their Christmas visit to Eternity Springs, and she'd gone through the application process upon their return to Florida. "That would be awesome. I know Reilly would love it. Unfortunately, I tried to get him a slot earlier this year and we were turned down."

Davenport flashed a grin, and his entire expression changed. Gone was the cool, intimidating predator and in his place stood a rogue with a gleam in his eyes. "Reilly will be welcome. I have particular influence with the head of the selection committee. I sleep with her."

Devin rolled his eyes and explained to Jenna. "He's married to her."

Ahh.

Cam asked, "What sort of trap are you talking about, Jack? I assume she'll stay here in Eternity Springs where we can keep her safe?"

Jack nodded, and the sheriff added, "Where swatting is limited to flies at the Fourth of July picnic."

Davenport spoke to the Callahans. "You'll submit a technology plan by the end of the day?"

The brothers shared a look, and then Matt nodded. "Can do, boss."

Davenport addressed Daniel Garrett. "I'd like you to touch base with the investigator she hired. We'll herd the stalker from that end too."

Garrett met Jenna's gaze. "I'll need you to sign some paperwork that I can fax him and get access to your information. If you'll come to my office when we're through here?"

"All right."

"What's our job in this, Jack?" Cam asked.

"You're the designated bodyguards. How long do you plan to be in town, Devin?"

"I planned to head home after Mitch's wedding. I can rearrange things if necessary. I *will* rearrange them." He met Jenna's gaze, daring her to protest as he added, "I won't leave until we've caught this asshat."

Jenna wasn't stupid. She wouldn't argue with Devin. Whether she'd recognized it or not at the time, this was why she'd come to Eternity Springs. She'd decided to put her trust in the Murphys and there was no going back now. The man would know how much time he could afford to be away from his life in Australia.

Davenport shook his head. "I can't imagine this taking longer than three weeks. I expect you'll make your flight without any trouble."

"Good deal." Devin nodded and folded his arms in satisfaction.

Jack Davenport said, "May I suggest we get about our business and reconvene Sunday afternoon at Eagle's Way? We'll cook out. Bring the wives and kids. We'll swim. Make it a holiday pre-party. Does that suit everyone's schedules?"

"Maybe you should check with Cat first?" Cam suggested.

"His wife," Devin explained as Jack winced and nodded. He excused himself and stepped away, reaching into his pocket for his phone. Devin used the opportunity to move around from behind the bench and hunker down in front of Jenna. "You good with all of this?"

"Honestly, I don't know. My head is spinning."

"I could talk for hours about some of the challenges

these men have overcome. To a man, they've walked some rocky paths. But the main thing you need to know . . . the bottom line for everything . . . is that you can trust them, Jenna. You can trust all of us. We won't let you down."

He gently stroked her cheek with the pad of his thumb and promised, "*I* won't let you down. You have my word on it."

Tears flooded Jenna's eyes and she blinked them back. The earnestness in his gaze, the offer of a burden shared after so many months of going it alone, spoke to the very center of her soul. Her emotions were too big, so she deflected with humor. "Your word or Santa's?"

"Both. All you have to do is believe."

Chapter Ten

Devin fitted his hands at Jenna's waist and lifted her into the truck. He stored her crutches in the cab's back seat and shut the passenger door. He didn't speak to her until he exited the medical clinic parking lot and turned the opposite direction from Stardance Ranch. "How's the ankle?"

"Grade 2 sprain. Partial ligament tear. Four- to eight-week recovery."

"Michael is such a hoon—a hooligan. He never looks where he's going. I can't tell you how many times I've seen him run into a wall because he's looking over his shoulder flapping his jaw about something instead of paying attention to what's in front of him."

"He was excited about spending time with you. When we were here last winter, he never stopped talking about his big brother."

Devin's mouth twisted with a rueful smile. "He's growing up so fast. That's the hardest part about living so far away. When we're apart, I can convince myself that I'm watching it happen through video calls, but when I'm with him"—he shrugged—"sometimes I want to kill him. I'm sorry he hurt you, Jenna."

"I'll heal. Where are we going, Devin?"

He drew in a bracing breath. "We are covering all the bases. We don't want you living alone until we've taken care of this pizza jackass once and for all. The crutches are a limiting factor, but we found a good solution. It's actually the house where my dad grew up, where he and I stayed when he came home to Eternity Springs to win back my mother's heart. Celeste Blessing owns it now. It's a rental property, furnished and currently unoccupied."

"Wait a minute. What's wrong with my camper?"

"Quarters are a little close considering that we've yet to have our first official date, don't you think?"

He watched her work her way through it.

"You're planning to stay with me?"

"I wouldn't be much of a bodyguard if I didn't, would I? You're not going to argue with me about it, are you?"

Jenna opened her mouth, and then shut it. She closed her eyes. "This day has taken more turns than the switchbacks up Sinner's Prayer Pass. Was it only this morning when I seriously considered picking up Reilly and running when you approached us on the fishing pier? Now we're shipping my kid off to summer camp and moving in together?"

"Separate bedrooms," he was quick to say. "Reilly will love the Rocking L. Michael's gonna be pea green with envy. He loves his visits and gets to go as a camper for a week at the end of August with the other local kids, but he'd live up there all summer if he could."

"I do believe that it's a fabulous opportunity for Reilly, but I'm not one hundred percent certain I'll be able to convince him to go. His little world has been rocked time and again. It's left him insecure and angry and, in many instances, afraid of his own shadow. I don't think you realize what a big deal it was for him to leave the fishing hole with your father. This is the longest Reilly and I have been apart since before the last raid."

Devin darted a look at her. "Seriously?"

Jenna nodded. "I'm feeling a little like a new mother leaving her baby with a sitter for the first time."

"He got to see Brick's snakeskin. And now he's playing with puppies!"

"He's wanted a dog for a very long time. I'd decided to let him get one. If he's going to camp, we'll have to put that off."

"Not necessarily." Devin stopped the truck in front of the house where he'd lived when he and Cam first arrived in Eternity Springs. "Animals have held a prominent role in Rocking L therapies for some time now. My brother-in-law will be the first to tell you that working with his pup at the Rocking L helped save his sanity. Reilly wouldn't be the first camper who brought his dog with him."

"Really?" When Devin nodded, she added, "That might be the perfect solution."

"Let me show you the house. If it suits, we'll make a plan for going forward."

He opened the electronic lock using the code Celeste had texted. A second bathroom added during a recent remodel of the cozy, two-bedroom cottage along with new appliances and restoration of the three original fireplaces had turned the cottage into a showplace.

Jenna didn't try to hide her delight. "It's darling, and I won't pretend that I won't look forward to having a little elbow room, but I hate the idea that I'll be taking you away from your family. Your time with them is limited enough as it is."

"We'll see plenty of my family. I just won't be sleeping there. It's not a hardship, believe me." Devin gave her a droll look. "Michael likes to jump on me to wake me up."

"I won't do that," she said with a laugh.

It was a hanging curve ball Devin could have hit out of the park, but he refrained from taking a swing. Instead, he pulled a chair away from the kitchen table and gestured for her to sit. "Want to help me make a list of things we'll need?"

"Sure."

He grabbed a note pad and pen from the table beside the front door and placed it before her, then opened the fridge. "Milk. Whole milk. None of that sissy skim stuff. Butter. Real butter. Cheese. Eggs. Red meat."

"Not one to worry about cholesterol, hmm?"

Devin shrugged. "If you're one of those granola and tofu girls, more power to you. Just don't expect me to exist eating twigs."

Her lips twitched. "What about fruit?"

"I'm a fan of fruit. Berries and bananas are my favorites. But I'll warn you, we probably won't do much cooking here. My mother will insist on us joining them for supper, and on nights that she's not cooking, we'll be invited elsewhere. We should stock up on breakfast food and stuff for sandwiches, but beyond that, we'll be good."

Jenna glanced around the kitchen, her expression a little wistful. "When we lived in Nashville, I had an awesome kitchen. I make an excellent roast and a fabulous chicken parm, but I never had the time to invest in learning to cook the way I wanted. Maybe once I'm off the crutches, I can invite—"

Devin's phone rang, interrupting her thought. He pulled it from his pocket and checked the number. "Hey, Lori."

"Devin, Chase phoned and he needs me to run a couple of puppies up to the Rocking L. Reilly and Michael would like to ride up with me and hold the dogs. Is that all right with Reilly's mother?"

He relayed the question to Jenna, who signaled her permission and asked to speak to her son. Devin grinned to hear her speak the usual mother-cautions like "Behave" and "Mind your manners." When she handed the phone back to Devin, he arranged for Lori to drop Reilly off at the Stocktons' camper at Stardance Ranch upon their return to town.

Devin studied Jenna as he wrapped up the call, noting the weary lines around her eyes and between her brows. "How about we wrap up here and I take you back to Stardance? You should have time to get in a nap before Lori brings Reilly back."

"That sounds fabulous."

Devin made one final inventory circuit around the cottage and added "paper goods" and "coffee" to the shopping list. Then they exited the house and together picked a key code they would both remember. He helped her negotiate the three steps that led down from the porch. "If you're by yourself, there's a ramp to access the back porch so you won't have to worry about steps with the crutches."

"I suspect I'll be able to discard the crutches within a few days."

Jenna grew quiet during the drive through town that took longer than usual due to streets crowded with tourists. Devin noticed her pensive look and said, "Dollar for your thoughts."

"What happened to a penny?"

"Inflation."

Her lips twisted in a crooked grin. "I think I'm a little shell-shocked. This all happened so fast and I'm having a hard time processing it."

"You're accustomed to playing your cards close to the vest. I can understand why laying them down could be disconcerting."

"'Disconcerting' is a mild word for it. It's terrifying. I made a little small snowball of a decision to bring Reilly back to Eternity Springs for a summer visit, only the snowball started rolling downhill getting bigger and bigger, and now it's big enough to be the base of a snowman built by a giant. After months of going to great lengths to hide and remain hidden, I not only shared our entire story with a group of virtual strangers, I handed over control of our lives to them. This morning I wouldn't take Reilly into town to buy a cinnamon roll at the bakery. By suppertime, I'm sending him off to summer camp and moving in with Santa Claus? This isn't me, Devin. At least, not the 'me' who I've become since the first batch of pizzas arrived at my door."

Because he wasn't stupid, Devin bit back a suggestive comment about Santa's lap. Instead, he gently chided. "No one is trying to control you, Jenna. We're trying to help you."

"I know. And I appreciate it. I do. Don't get me wrong. But my actions today are completely out of character, and I'm wondering why I—oh."

She broke off abruptly and shifted her gaze away from him. She sat still and silent, and Devin could all but see the wheels turning in her mind. They'd traveled half a city block and were approaching the intersection of Spruce and First streets when she repeated a pained, "Oh."

"Jenna? Everything okay? Is the ankle bothering you?"

She glanced around as though trying to get her bearings. "Where are we? Are we near Angel's Rest?"

He hooked his thumb over his shoulder. "That way."

"I think . . . can I go back? Please? Would you take me to Angel's Rest?"

Along with not being stupid, Devin had enough experience with women to know the best course of action to take at times such as this. Without protest, he made a left at the corner onto Spruce, headed north, and waited for further explanation.

And waited.

And waited.

"Oh," she said a third time as they approached the entrance to the resort.

Devin spared her a quick glance and saw that her focus was directed inward. *Patience, Murphy.* He gave a friendly wave to guests fishing from the bridge over Angel Creek and slowed the truck to a crawl as they approached a fork in the road. "We're here, Jenna. Is there a particular part of the resort you want to visit?"

"Yes, please. Take me to Blitzen."

At his clueless stare, she grimaced. "Sorry. The cottages at the back. Celeste said she renamed them for the holidays. We stayed in Blitzen. If you'll drive around to the cottages, that would be perfect."

He did as she asked and stopped in front of the cottage she indicated. "Looks like someone is staying there, Jenna. Angel's Rest cottages stay booked all summer long as a rule."

"I don't need to go in." She opened her door and started to reach for a crutch.

"Hold your horses!" Devin said. "I'll help. Let me help." He scrambled from the truck and hurried around to assist her. Moments later, she was hobbling across the resort grounds, going exactly where he hadn't a clue.

She was acting peculiar. Had they given her something stronger than Tylenol at the doctor's office?

When she entered the forest, he fell in behind her. Twice he started to ask her what she was up to and twice he thought better of it, silently repeating his new mantra. *Patience.*

Then she veered off the trail and his concern grew. "Jenna . . ."

"Almost there."

"Okay," he murmured, half beneath his breath.

She finally stopped . . . somewhere. In the middle of

the forest. She was staring at a tree. One of millions of trees.

Devin shoved his hands into his pockets, rocked back on his heels, and glanced around. *Okay, she officially has me baffled.* Then she started mumbling and his bewilderment only grew.

". . . can't believe . . . *mumble mumble* . . . clueless . . . *mumble mumble* . . . ostrich . . . *mumble mumble mumble*. Seriously, I actually believe this . . . this . . . what, am I a seven-year-old?"

Devin cleared his throat. "Um, Jenna, this is getting a little strange. Want to tell me what we're doing here?"

The look she gave him was faintly accusing. "I'm a scientist."

"You are?"

"A physician. I'm a doctor."

"Cool." Devin nodded thoughtfully. "Although, I've always considered doctors to be part artist."

"I believe in what I see before my face. Not . . ." She waved her hand around in little circles.

Devin had no clue what the hand circles meant.

"The stress must have taken its toll."

"That's understandable."

"I've been delusional."

"Did Dr. Cicero give you something for pain? You're seeing things? Maybe you're having a reaction."

"Oh, I'm having a reaction, all right," she said, a note of hysteria hovering at the edge of her voice. "My brain freeze finally thawed."

"I don't mean to be dense, but I'm lost. I don't have a clue about what you're trying to tell me."

"I'm telling you that I am a fool. I got the wool pulled over my eyes. Conned by a flimflam artist."

Devin frowned. Did she think someone from Eternity had screwed her around?

"I suppose you think that today's events occurred by chance, that our meeting you at Hummingbird Lake was spur-of-the-moment happenstance? Nothing more than coincidence?"

He rolled his tongue around his mouth. Did she really want him to answer or was this simply a rant?

Well, it was one thing to go along to get along, but that scornful note in her tone rubbed him wrong. "I don't see how it could have been anything but chance. When I went out for my run, I almost took the route that goes up Cemetery Road, not around the lake. I wouldn't have seen you two fishing. I wouldn't have taken you up to our fishing hole. Michael wouldn't have run like a heathen and knocked you down. What is that if not happenstance?"

"See, that's what's sneaky about it. I tried to tell myself too. It's safe to go to Eternity Springs. The Murphys will be visiting Michael's brother in Australia. We won't run into them. They won't be around to recognize us. No one else knows us well enough to see past colored contacts and purple tips."

Distracted, he asked, "Reilly wears colored contacts?"

"No. I do. And I don't like them. I don't need them to see and my eyes are dry all the time. I won't be sad to ditch them, I'll tell you that. They were a lie. Another lie. Here's the deal, Devin. What happened today wasn't coincidence. It wasn't happenstance."

"It wasn't?"

"No! What we have here is the power of suggestion at work. That sweet but ditzy woman's power of suggestion and I—a scientist—fell for it."

That woman? When anybody in town said "that woman" in that tone of voice, they invariably referred to one person—Celeste Blessing. Suddenly, Jenna's nonsensical ramblings began to make a little sense. Celeste had her fingers in this. Exactly how, he didn't know, but something told him he was about to find out.

"I can't believe I was so dishonest with myself," Jenna continued. "I'm deliberate in my decisions and calculated in my actions. I don't lie to Reilly and I never *ever* lie to myself. But I've been lying to myself for the past four months. This morning if you had asked me when I made the decision to come to Eternity Springs this summer, I'd have said a week ago last Thursday. That's when I called Stardance Ranch searching for a campsite. But that's not the truth. I see that now. Do you know when I really decided to come here, Devin? When I heard Reilly's screams and saw broken hearts lying on my kitchen floor, that's when."

"Oh, Jenna."

"You see, above all else, I must protect my child. I had done my best. I had used logic and reason and followed the rules, and I failed him. I failed him miserably. He was terrorized while decorating cookies in his own kitchen."

"It wasn't your fault, Jenna."

"Wasn't it? I did something, sometime, to cause a crazy person to fixate on me. Who knows what? Maybe it's something as random as I cut him off in traffic. So, in a very real way, what happened to us was my fault. My fault, and my sweet boy went from decorating cookies to non-medical shock. I knew how to diagnose and treat that, but I didn't know how to neutralize the threat."

"I'll bet you were so frightened."

"Yes. But on top of being scared, I was angry. Furious. In the aftermath, Reilly was exhausted and fell asleep. I put him to bed, but he was restless and I didn't want to leave him. I paced his bedroom like a caged tiger, and I didn't know what to do or where to turn. When I get nervous or angry or scared, I clean. I needed to clean the kitchen and deal with the cookie mess, but I needed to be with Reilly more so I started cleaning his room.

Tears pooled in her eyes she turned toward Devin. "I straightened his bookshelf. You want to know what book I found? *The Christmas Angel Waiting Room*."

He recognized the title, of course. *The Christmas Angel Waiting Room* was a children's book written by Eternity Spring's own Claire Lancaster. Hollywood had made a movie out of the story that had become an instant Christmas classic. "I'm not surprised. Claire has sold a bazillion books."

Jenna nodded. "I didn't put it together. Not until ten minutes ago. I stood in Reilly's bedroom that evening and swore I was done asking anyone else for help. From then on, we would take care of ourselves, by ourselves. We couldn't . . . we wouldn't . . . depend on anyone else. It was Reilly and me against the world. Self-sufficient. Self-dependent."

"That's completely understandable."

"I planned how we would disappear, and we hit the road. We made no reservations. Followed no set itinerary. Going where the wind blew us. I was so . . . smug. So stupid. What I did was drive halfway across the country with my head buried in the sand. I was lying to myself and to Reilly, and that's inexcusable."

"Lying about what, Jenna?"

"I bought it. Hook, line, and sinker. I picked up *The Christmas Angel Waiting Room* and I bought"—she waved her hand toward him in a flourish—"Santa! And I bought Celeste and her"—she hooked her thumb over her shoulder pointing toward a fir tree she stood before—"Christmas wishing tree!"

"What's the Christmas wishing tree?"

"A myth. A fairy tale. It's a fairy tale just like Santa

and safety and a CIA agent who runs a children's camp! Oh, no." She closed her eyes. "What have I done?"

Had a meltdown, that's what. The woman still wasn't making sense, but Devin recognized when someone needed a hug. Careful of her crutches, he put his arms around her and guided her head onto his shoulder. "You've done an amazing job, that's what you've done."

"Because I bought into the myth? Because this small town is somehow going to make everything right again?"

"Because your son is safe, Jenna. He has food on his table and shoes on his feet and a roof over his head— even if it does roll. Now, I'm not sure what this wishing tree business is, but I take my Santa duties seriously. You need to believe it when I tell you that you made the right choice today. You've put your faith in a group of men who are worthy of your trust. We will keep you and Reilly safe while we locate your tormentor and eliminate the threat he poses."

Jenna remained silent for a long moment. Finally, in a small voice she asked, "Why? Why would you do that for us? We're nobody to you."

"Ah, now that's where you are wrong." Devin tilted up her chin and stared down into her eyes. "You are Reilly's Mom. You've been important to me for a year and a half. Now that I know your story, I can understand why trust might be a scarce commodity. But how or why it happened aside, you are in Eternity Springs now. You're not alone anymore."

He sealed the promise with a kiss.

Chapter Eleven

After Devin helped her climb the steps of her camper and said goodbye, Jenna removed the blasted contact lenses, dug the hair color remover shampoo from the back of her cabinet, and took a long hot shower. She pulled on her favorite yoga pants and a Hot Springs National Park T-shirt, dried her hair, and crawled into bed for a nap. Exhausted, she fell right to sleep and didn't wake up until . . .

Something licked her cheek.

She let out a screech and her heart pounded and her eyes flew open. She stared into the blue eyes of a little black and white bundle of fur and heard her son's delighted giggles. The sound was so welcome, such music to her ears, that she smiled instead of scolded.

"What do we have here?" she asked, sitting up.

"Isn't he cute? I wanted to show you because he has eyes like yours. I've never seen a dog with blue eyes before. He's one of the puppies Dr. Lori took up to the summer camp. She did show-and-tell on how to give dogs a bath. It was fun."

"Oh yeah?" She scratched the pup behind his ears. "Is this a puppy from the animal shelter?"

"No. They don't have any puppies in the shelter right now. He belongs to one of Dr. Lori's customers. She borrowed him for today. He's a borador, which is a mix of a border collie and a Labrador. We're taking him home now, but I wanted to show you first. Isn't he cute?"

"He's a doll. What's his name?"

"Sinatra. It's a weird name, but so is Mortimer. That's Michael's dog. Do you remember him, Mom?"

"I do." Mortimer, bless his heart, had to be the ugliest Boston terrier ever born. "Frank Sinatra was a singer whose nickname was 'Old Blue Eyes.' Maybe that's why his owner picked it."

"Maybe. Whatever. But he's cute, isn't he? Mom, when I get back from taking Sinatra home, can we talk about my birthday present?"

"Sure, buddy. We'll do that."

"And can I make my hair normal again too?"

"Absolutely."

"Great." His eyes bright with happiness, Reilly scooped the puppy into his arms and headed for the door. "I'll be back soon."

"Hold on a minute, buddy. I'd like to talk to Dr. Lori before she leaves."

Jenna managed to make it out of the camper with her crutches without hurting herself, and followed her son toward the van sporting an Eternity Springs Animal Clinic logo on the side. With her attention on Reilly, she was slow to notice that the van didn't appear to be occupied. Michael lay on his belly in a swing on the swing set, twisting the chains so he'd spin like a top when he lifted his legs. Lori Timberlake was on the Stardance Ranch office porch, bent over and vigorously rubbing the Callahans' dog's golden coat as she spoke with Devin, Brick and Lili Callahan, and Boone McBride—Jenna's New Year's Eve midnight kiss.

"Well," Jenna murmured. "This could be awkward.

Would Boone remember her? Recognize her? Lori had

been informed about the day's developments, but what about the Callahans? Had Brick's father or uncles given them the lowdown?

Devin noticed her first and his eyes went wide. He made a thumping motion over his heart and said, "Wow, Reilly's Mom. You were gorgeous as a brunette with brown eyes, but now . . . whoa. I'm speechless. Did you get to rest? Feel better?"

"Thank you, I did," she said with a hesitant smile. "I do."

Lori straightened and gave her a curious once-over, wincing as her gaze lingered on her ankle. "Ouch. Bet you thought the only wild animals you needed to worry about were bears and bobcats. Someone should have warned you about baby brothers."

"I'm not a baby!" Michael called from the playground, where he'd slid off the swing and knelt beside Reilly, who was playing tug-of-war with the puppy and a stick.

"Your hair is gorgeous, Jenna," Liliana said. Her eyes twinkled as she added, "Pretty name, too."

Okay, that answers one question. "I'm sorry for the deceptions."

Brick waved the apology away. "Hey, forget about it. I'm impressed as hell that you managed so well in the face of all of your challenges."

Boone glanced from Jenna, to Devin, to Brick, then back to Jenna again. "It's obvious I'm out of the loop about something here. I'll be curious to learn what I've missed. In the meantime, though . . ." He stepped forward, leaned down, and gave Jenna's cheek a friendly kiss. "Jenna, welcome back. I've thought of you often since New Year's Eve."

"Hello, Boone," she replied, ignoring Devin's sharp look. "I hope the new year has treated you well."

"It's been downhill since midnight, New Year's Eve, I'm afraid."

"I take it y'all met last Christmas," Devin said.

"No," Boone replied, not taking his gaze off Jenna. "On a memorable New Year's Eve."

Devin's eyes narrowed.

Jenna decided a change of subject was advisable so she focused on Lori. "I'm sorry to interrupt your conversation, but I wanted to say hello and thank you for your help with Reilly today."

"I was glad to have him along. Having Reilly around makes dealing with Michael half as much work."

Devin sidled up beside Jenna and placed a proprietary hand at her back. "Why don't you come sit down? You probably need to keep your ankle elevated, don't you?"

Boone smirked, but took a step back as if surrendering the field. Yet Jenna didn't miss the quick little wink he gave her.

"Actually, I'd like to speak with your sister alone for a moment. Could you guys distract the boys for a few minutes? Is there another super-cool snakeskin you could show Reilly?"

"No. I wish there was."

"I made chocolate chip cookies earlier," Lili said. "I have some in the office that are still warm from the oven. Think that would work?"

"Works for me," Boone said. Then he glanced at Brick. "You have a super-cool snakeskin?"

"I do. Something I found on the ranch. Want to see it?"

"Cookies first."

Brick called. "Boys, y'all come with us. Lili is going to give us some homemade cookies and then I'm gonna get my snakeskin out to show my cousin."

"Cookies!" Michael exclaimed, hopping to his feet. "I love cookies and Mom hardly ever lets me have any."

"It's true," Devin said to Jenna. "We're limited to two a day."

Lori snorted. "Two plus all the ones you sneak. And don't think Michael isn't following in his big brother's footsteps."

"I'm afraid Sarah's cookies put mine to shame," Lili said with a note of regret. "But sometimes a girl just needs a bite of chocolate chip cookie dough. You know?"

"Amen, sister," Lori replied before turning to Jenna. "You might not need to sit down, but I do. How about we adjourn to that picnic bench by the playground?"

Jenna nodded, and as Lili and the men headed for the office, the boys rose to join them. Lori called, "Reilly, why don't you let us hold Sinatra."

"Okay, Dr. Lori."

Jenna added, "And wash your hands before you eat."

"But Mom, a dog's mouth has fewer germs than a human's."

"You've been playing in the dirt."

He rolled his eyes and handed the puppy to Lori, then scampered after the others.

Lori watched them go and smiled. "I like the hair."

"I think he and I are both ready to be done with dyes." She blew out a breath, then asked, "How much of Reilly's and my story has your father or brother shared with you?"

"Dad hit the highlights. Or lowlights, to be more exact. I'm so sorry this has happened to you, Jenna. And poor Reilly."

"It's been terribly hard for him. Children should grow up feeling safe and secure, and that's been stolen from him. My goal is to give that back. We had a shaky start today, and I didn't know if sending him off with your father was the right thing to do. He and I have been together twenty-four seven since Valentine's Day. But in these last few minutes, I see my old Reilly. He's forgetting to be afraid. What was he like when he was with you this afternoon?"

Lori tilted her head and considered the question. "I see what you're saying. I did notice a moment or two when he seemed to withdraw. That was when we were at the shelter and someone came in with a stray they'd found on the Gunnison highway. He opened up again once we were alone."

"How did he act up at the camp?"

"Reilly was too busy playing with the puppies to be nervous. Plus, Chase met us when we arrived, and Reilly remembered him from your visit last Christmas. He did act a little shy at first around the other children, but it was nothing out of the ordinary. I will say that he impressed me with his kindness toward our two wheelchair-bound campers."

Jenna's heart warmed. "Thank you for sharing that. He's always been a tenderhearted boy, and I'm glad for the reminder that there is value to that trait. I'm afraid I lost sight of that during the past four months as I've concentrated on trying to toughen him up."

"He's a good kid, Jenna. He's a good influence on my little brother, which is something I know my parents appreciate. Michael can be a little monster—but then, that's no news to you since he put you on crutches. As a veterinarian I probably shouldn't admit to this, but I believe it's Mortimer's fault."

"Michael's dog?"

"He's actually my father's dog, and a troublemaker like none other. When Michael was born, Mortimer became his shadow. I think he knew he was getting old and slowing down, so he transferred his devilry to the baby."

Jenna looked for a teasing light in the other woman's eyes, but Lori appeared to be serious. *Okay. Well. Hmm.* "Speaking of dogs, that's something else I wanted to discuss with you."

She told Lori about her plans to finally get Reilly the

dog he'd wanted. "Devin mentioned it might be possible for Reilly to take a dog with him to camp?"

Lori nodded. "We've done it at other sessions. Pets are excellent therapy. I will confirm with Chase, but I'm ninety-nine percent certain that Reilly could attend camp with a dog."

"In that case, I'd like to move forward with this. Considering our situation and with the possibility that we may be living in our camper for some time to come, do you know of any available dogs that might be a good fit for us?"

"Depends. How much exercise could you commit to for your dog?"

"Honestly, more now than when we lived in an apartment. Neither Reilly nor I tolerate being cooped up very well. My son might not be quite as active as Michael, but he's not far behind."

"In that case, then why not this little guy?" Lori gave Sinatra a good scratch.

Jenna's brows arched in surprise. "Reilly said he's not a shelter pup."

"No, but he is up for adoption. The dam's owner wanted her to have one litter of puppies so that the owner's children could have the experience. I know both the dam and the sire. They're good dogs. I expect that Sinatra will be smart and friendly and an excellent companion for Reilly—as long as he gets plenty of exercise. He'll be ready to leave his mama next week."

"The same time Reilly will leave me to go to camp. The timing couldn't be any more perfect. Oh, I hope this works out."

Lori held up a finger, pulled her cell phone from her pocket, and called her husband, then Sinatra's owner. By the time the boys spilled out of the office with milk mustaches and giggling like fools, arrangements had all been made.

Later that evening after Jenna trimmed the blue from Reilly's hair, he brought up the subject of his birthday present.

"Yes, we need to talk about that," Jenna replied.

He slumped onto his seat at the table and buried his head in his arms. "You're gonna tell me no. It's because of what happened today, right? Did Michael's dad and brother break their promise and put us on the Internet? The bad man is on our trail and you're going to hook up the trailer and sneak out of town after dark. It's not safe, after all, is it? I'll never see Michael again."

"Oh, Reilly, no. Slow down." Jenna sat opposite him, reached out and placed her hand on his shoulder. "That's not it at all. No one broke his or her promises. I actually have a pretty spectacularly wonderful surprise for you."

Now the boy lifted his head. Hope filled his expression. "The police found the bad guy?"

"No. No. I'm afraid not. If that was my news I wouldn't wait until after your shower to tell you. Honey, I told Devin and Mr. Murphy about what happened to us and then we talked to some of their friends who are investigators. They have promised to help us."

"But we've had an investigator."

"True. But instead of one investigator looking or a handful of policemen working our case and dozens of other cases, we have ten people ready to help us."

"Ten?"

Jenna nodded. "Yes. From what the Murphys tell me, these men are really sharp and they're experienced and they have the tools it will take to track the bad guy down. I don't know about you, but I'm tired of always looking over my shoulder. Wouldn't it be nice to put this behind us and have a normal life?"

"But I like living in the camper. We still have lots of national parks to visit."

"Hey, you and I have a deal. We are going to visit every single national park whether we're living in this camper or a penthouse condo in New York City."

"I don't want to live in a condo."

Jenna licked her lips and asked, "What about a log cabin?"

Reilly's brow knitted as he narrowed his eyes in suspicion. "What log cabin?"

"One at the Rocking L camp. You liked what you saw up there today, didn't you?"

"Well . . . yeah. It was cool, I guess. Mr. Chase is nice and he has a really awesome dog. His name is Captain."

"Reilly, you've been offered a slot there in the session that begins next week. I'd like you to go."

Reilly's eyes got round and worried, so Jenna was quick to press on. "It will be so much fun. They have horseback riding and rock climbing and swimming and hiking."

"Where are you going?"

"Nowhere. I'll be right here in Eternity Springs. I promise."

"All by yourself?"

"Actually, I won't be by myself. I'm going to have my own personal bodyguards—Devin and Mr. Murphy. And the sheriff is on our team too. He's not going to fall for any bad tricks."

"It scares me, Mom. I don't think I like this. I think we should stay together. I think we probably *should* leave Eternity Springs."

Jenna smoothed Reilly's still-damp bangs away from his brow. "Honey, I don't expect there to be any trouble. Things are different now. This is a small town where people know us. It's like living in our own little castle and we have knights standing at the ready to protect us. You'll be up in the parapets at camp and if you get too lonely for me, I can climb up to see you or you can come down to see me."

He gave her a droll, *Really, Mom?* look and she decided it was time to roll out the big guns. "However, you'll be so busy taking care of the puppy that I don't think you'll have time to be lonely."

He sat up. "What puppy?"

"There's a puppy who will be sleeping apart from his mother for the first time. He'll need a lot of love and care and company. I thought that would be a good job for you—if you're interested."

"Like, to babysit?"

"Like, for that birthday present I promised."

"Mine! A puppy? Not an older dog?"

"A puppy. And yes, he can be yours if you want him. This little guy will be ready to leave his mama next week, and Mr. Chase said you can bring him with you to camp—if you're prepared for the responsibility."

"I am! Oh, I am!" He clasped his hands prayerfully, but the frown lines between his brows showed he wasn't ready to believe. "But Mom, Dr. Lori said they don't have any puppies at the shelter. We didn't see any when we visited."

"Sinatra needs a home."

Reilly's mouth dropped open. His eyes went round as saucers. "Sinatra? Really, Mom? For me?"

"It's a little bit of a bribe. I need you to go to camp, Reilly. Will you do that?"

"And take Sinatra with me?"

"And take Sinatra with you."

"Yes!" He launched himself out of his seat and into her arms. "I'll do it. I can do it. I'll be super responsible. I promise. I'll be the best ever."

Jenna's heart swelled with happiness as she hugged her son and absorbed his joy. Through the camper's window, she saw the evening shadows fade to full night. What a wild ride this day had been.

Riley pulled away from her. "We have to get him a bed and food bowls and a collar and a leash. And treats. Lots of treats. What day do I get him, Mom? Can I go visit before then? And we need to get him a tag for his collar that has his name. Can we go get one tomorrow?"

"Maybe. It'll depend on if we can catch a ride to town. I won't be able to drive for a few days yet because of my ankle."

"I'll bet Devin will drive us. He's your bodyguard, right? In the movies, bodyguards drive people around."

"Well, we'll see. We took up a lot of his time today, and he's here to visit family. We don't want to intrude more than we already have." Looking for a distraction, she added, "About Sinatra. You do know that it's okay if you want to change his name? He'll be your dog and you get to name him."

"Oh. I'll have to think about that."

"You do that. Now . . ." Jenna rose and ruffled his hair. "Get your book and get into bed. Quiet time officially begins in"—she checked her watch—"seven minutes. Lights out in thirty-seven."

For once, he gave her no argument. Jenna got ready for bed and settled down with her own current read, a cozy mystery by one of her favorite British authors. They read for their usual half hour, though she noticed that Reilly did more staring out the window than page turning. At nine thirty, she said, "Lights out. Good night, buddy. I love you."

"G'night, Mom. Love you too."

From outside, she heard the faint sounds of laughter and farewells as the campsite settled down for the night. Worn out from the day, she drifted easily toward sleep.

From out of the darkness, she heard her son murmur, "This was the best day in forever."

"Amen." For the first time in longer than she could recall, Jenna fell off to sleep with a smile on her lips.

Devin fixed bacon and eggs for the Murphy men for breakfast. Sarah didn't come downstairs due to the slow bounce back from her bug. Afterward, he spent some quality time with Michael shooting baskets in the driveway, then met his dad for lunch at the Mocha Moose coffee and sandwich shop. Finally, a little after two o'clock he ran out of reasons not to wander out to Stardance Ranch. He turned into the RV resort entrance just in time to see the local florist van stop in front of Jenna's trailer.

Like many camping enthusiasts do, Jenna had set up a patio that looked homey and inviting beside her fifth wheel. With an outdoor rug and chair cushions in earth-tone stripes, she'd accented the space with splashes of yellow. Wearing khaki shorts, a pepper orange V-neck T-shirt and a floppy brimmed hat, she sat in a rocker with her foot propped up on a matching ottoman. A tall glass of what looked like iced tea sat on a table beside her. She was reading a paperback book.

When the driver removed a huge bouquet of sunflowers from the back of the delivery van and carried them toward her, she set the book aside. The smile that bloomed across her face was almost as bright as the sunflowers.

"Boone McBride," Devin muttered beneath his breath, knowing in his gut who'd sent them. "That sonofanoilman."

I should have thought to send flowers.

Devin parked his truck and sat stewing for a moment, drumming his fingers on the steering wheel. He should probably think this through. He'd just met the woman yesterday. Flirtatious phone calls a year and a half ago did not a relationship make. Not that he was in the market for a relationship, because he wasn't. Especially not with a woman who lived . . . well . . . not in Australia.

So what was he doing getting so . . . territorial?

It was the Santa thing. They'd formed a bond during those phone calls, he and Reilly's Mom. He'd bonded with Reilly too. Shoot, he'd remember that first phone call until the day he died.

"So, Reilly. What is your Christmas wish?"

"A daddy. I want a daddy of my own."

Devin's eyes closed and he heard the echo of his own words. *"It's a good wish. You hold onto it. Keep wishing it. Believe it will come true."*

Believe. Devin wondered if Reilly remembered that conversation. He wondered if the "believing" had been crushed out of Reilly's little soul by the events that followed their week of Santa calls. He'd wished for a daddy of his own. Had it ever come close to happening? Jenna hadn't mentioned leaving anyone behind when she gave her summary of events. Had she found anyone special, someone she regretted leaving behind when she had to leave Nashville or Memphis or Tallahassee?

Or Eternity Springs.

Devin's gaze drifted toward the Stocktons' fifth wheel. *"A daddy. I want a daddy of my own."*

In the echo of his memory, he heard Celeste's voice as clear as a Christmas bell. *"Open your eyes and heart and imaginings to the possibilities that await. You must believe. Wishes can and do come true. And when the Christmas bells ring, Devin Murphy, don't you fail to answer."*

What the heck was the thought nibbling at the edges of his brain?

Santa Claus.

"I want a daddy of my own."

*Whoa. Whoa. Whoa. Whoa. Back this truck up. That
way there be dragons.*

Devin let out a nervous little laugh. Must be delayed
jet lag. He'd met Reilly and his mother yesterday. Yesterday! What the heck was wrong with him? He should
probably turn his truck around and head back into town.
Go home and take a nap. Shoot, maybe he was coming
down with whatever was plaguing his mother.

The unexpected peal of a bell startled him. He turned
toward the sound and saw a little girl decked out from
helmet to sneakers in red and green teetering on a bike
with training wheels while she flicked the bell mounted
on the handlebars. *Brring brring. Brring brring.*

*"When the Christmas bells ring, Devin Murphy, don't
you fail to answer."*

"Oh, man. No. Celeste! Don't tell me I'm having a Celeste Blessing moment."

"Is this Santa Claus? I want a daddy of my own."

Devin's gaze returned to Jenna's camper, the same
camper where moments ago, the local florist had delivered a big honking bouquet of flowers.

Boone McBride.

Wait a minute. This was June, not December. It was a
bicycle bell, not a Christmas bell. He didn't have snowy
white hair and a belly that shook like a bowl full of jelly.
*You soon will if you don't stop eating so many straw-
berry pinwheels.*

Maybe so, but he wasn't there yet. He didn't leave
presents under a tree, and he didn't grant little boys their
Christmas wishes. He wasn't effing Santa Claus.

He'd come home to Eternity Springs for three short
weeks to visit his family. Period.

"I want a daddy of my own. Are you Santa Claus?"

Slowly, Devin reached up to the dashboard and twisted
his key, cutting the engine. He blew out a heavy breath.

What the heck was he thinking? He'd let Celeste Blessing get in his head, that's what. Did he truly believe some cosmic force was at work here? Did he believe?

Well, he'd definitely had a front-row seat to many of the Eternity Springs' more woo-woo moments. And what he didn't witness himself, he'd heard about firsthand. Everything from Gabe Callahan's now-ancient boxer, Clarence, just happening to show up in time to save Gabe's life to Hope Romano finding her lost child to the reunion of long lost lovers—his own parents—after Sarah won a vacation to Australia that brought her face-to-face with Cam. They all had one thing—one person—in common. Celeste Blessing.

And how had Jenna and Reilly found their way to Eternity Springs?

Through a cell phone of Celeste's.

"There's your sign, dumbass." The clues were right there in front of him, clear as a Christmas bell. Only an idiot—or someone who didn't believe in Eternity Springs woo-woo—would fail to connect the dots. Reilly called Santa and asked for a dad. Devin said enough to attract them to Eternity Springs for Christmas vacation and then, unless he was totally off on the clues he picked up yesterday, Jenna ended up at a local's party on New Year's Eve and locked lips with the lawyer at midnight.

Then she comes back to town with trouble on her tail at the exact same time that Devin happened to be here—after a freak snowstorm changes the family's plans. "Can Celeste control the freaking weather?"

Devin wouldn't put anything past her.

So now here he was about to move into close quarters with Hot Mom for whom he definitely had a thing and the sorry Christmas bells ring. Goodbye hot tub daydreams. So long vacation-fling fantasies. Arrivederci any idea of taking advantage of Jenna while Riley was away at camp.

Because Devin wasn't The Guy. Devin didn't dream about finding The One. His MO was The Many. He liked having a harem, to use his father's term. He was a love 'em and leave 'em kind of guy, and the ladies knew that from the beginning. He was always up front when he started dating. He didn't lie about his intentions—or lack thereof. He didn't lead anyone on. Because . . . he would leave. He always left. That's what he did.

The one time he'd considered doing it differently had bitten him in the ass. He'd learned a hard, bitter lesson, one that he'd never forget.

And now that he'd heard the Christmas bells, he knew what was what. He wasn't meant for Jenna. He certainly wasn't meant to be Reilly's dad. He was home for three weeks and then he'd be history. He would be her bodyguard. He would be part of the team to solve the stalker problem. But he wasn't the answer to Reilly's Christmas wish. Reilly and Jenna needed something different. Some*one* different.

The clues were too many, the Christmas bells too loud to ignore. The Eternity Springs woo-woo was at work with Jenna and Reilly Stockton, and Devin couldn't help but believe. He had to do his part.

He was Santa Claus.

Santa's job was to play Cupid. For Jenna and Boone McBride.

Well, if that's not a kick in the balls, I don't know what is. Maybe he'd better stop by his dad's shop and get a bow and some arrows.

He'd take aim at Boone McBride first.

Chapter Twelve

The handwritten card read, *Keep your face to the sunshine and feel better soon! Boone*

Jenna had always been a sucker for flowers, and bright cheerful sunflowers invariably brought a smile to her face. They couldn't have come at a better time either, since she'd been sitting on her patio and pretending to read, while in reality she'd been staring at the pages, brooding and second-guessing her decision to send Reilly to camp.

While part of her was positively giddy at the thought of having a month to herself, another part feared she'd spend the entire time missing Reilly and fretting about how he was managing without her. Intellectually, Jenna recognized that living in each other's pockets these past four months had changed the dynamics of their relationship in a way that wasn't good for either of them. But since the February SWAT team invasion, in matters that involved her son, emotions ruled the day more often than not.

Now she had a big, bright, beautiful bunch of flowers to distract her from her doldrums. "Keep my face to the sunshine," she murmured, smiling. "Don't you know that gives a girl wrinkles?"

Nevertheless, she took off her hat and tilted her face toward the sun. As sunshine warmed her skin, she tried to recall the last time a man had sent her flowers. It had been a long time, that's for certain. Joel Mercer brought her a red rose when he picked her up for a date one night, but he never had a florist deliver to her. If she tried to name a flower-sending man who she hadn't been sleeping with at the time . . . whoa. That took her all the way back to high school.

And honestly, she wasn't certain she would call her sweet, shy, nerdy boyfriend a man. He'd been a boy learning to be a man.

There was nothing left of the boy in Boone McBride.

What did she think about this overture? Was it an advance or just a gesture of friendship? Or, maybe these flowers had more to do with Devin than with her. She hadn't missed the posturing between the two men yesterday. The feminist in Jenna had been annoyed. The woman in her had been secretly thrilled.

"Hey, pretty lady."

Startled, Jenna opened her eyes to see the figure dressed in Hawaiian board shorts and a Refresh Outfitters T-shirt standing just beyond her patio. "Devin."

"You look relaxed. Enjoying the weather?"

"I am. It's a gorgeous afternoon."

He gestured toward an empty chair. "Mind if I join you?"

"Please, be my guest. Would you like something to drink?"

"If that's iced tea in your glass, I wouldn't turn it down—as long as you'll let me fix it myself."

Jenna gestured toward the camper. "Make yourself at home."

Moments later, she heard the sound of ice hitting a glass from inside the camper. When he rejoined her, she saw that he'd chosen Reilly's Scooby-Doo glass. "Okay, now *that* amuses me. Care to guess where we got that particular glass?"

Devin gave the tumbler a closer look, then grinned. "Mikey. He is a Scooby fiend."

"He gave it to Reilly when they got to be friends over Christmas."

Devin lifted the glass in toast. "To friendship."

After they clinked glasses, Devin sat and stretched his long legs out in front of him, crossing them at the ankles. Ray-Ban sunglasses hung from a cord around his neck. On his feet, he wore flip-flops. She couldn't quite read the look that came into his hazel eyes as he studied her.

He took a long sip of tea, then asked, "How is your ankle today?"

"A little better. I expect that by tomorrow I'll be down to using one crutch. I'll be much more mobile at that point."

"Good. I'm glad to hear that." Devin made a broad gesture toward the surrounding campground. "So where's the squirt?"

"In town visiting the puppy. Liliana had a few errands to run in town, so she offered to take him along."

"I heard through the pinecone telegraph that he's whittled his list of possible names down to seventeen."

Jenna laughed. "The pinecone telegraph?"

"Your son to my brother to our sister to her husband to his sister to her fiancé to my father to me."

"Well, you can add another link in your chain. I happen to know that as of twenty minutes ago, the list was down to eleven."

"You have a prediction on the winner?"

"I do. I think he'll decide against changing the puppy's name. Reilly was never comfortable with changing his name by using his initials. I think he'll take Sinatra up to camp with him."

"It's a good name." Devin lifted his sunglasses and slipped them on. "Pretty flowers you have there. Got a secret admirer?"

"A get-well message from a friend."

The nosy man reached over and plucked the card off the bouquet and read it. "I figured as much. So I gather you and McBride have a past?"

Jenna rolled her eyes. "Yes, it was quite scandalous. We met at Celeste's New Year's Eve party and made small talk. He handed me a glass of champagne and kissed me at midnight."

The words Devin spoke next were at odds with the slight thinning of his lips. "McBride is a relative newcomer to town and I don't know him well personally, but he has an excellent reputation. Have you met Mac Timberlake, my sister's father-in-law?"

Jenna nodded.

"Mac is a former federal judge and he's an excellent judge of character. He convinced McBride to move here from Fort Worth and take over his law practice. Scuttlebutt is that he tried to set McBride up with his daughter Caitlin. That's about as good a recommendation as you can get around here."

And you are telling me this why? "It was nice of him to send flowers."

"He's related to the Callahan clan too. A distant cousin or something. I'm not exactly sure how. I met him at Brick and Lili's wedding."

Jenna had other things on her mind than Boone McBride, so she changed the subject. "How is your mother feeling today? Better, I hope?"

"I think so. She has more color in her cheeks than she did yesterday."

"Good." Jenna made a mental note to call in her own order of get-well-soon flowers. Sarah Murphy had been nothing but kind to her and Reilly, and Jenna would like to brighten her day with some sunflowers. "I hope she's not upset about the change in your sleeping arrangements during your visit home."

"No, not at all. She did bring up family dinners, though, so I was right to warn you about that. She said Lori will join us more often than not too, since Chase stays up at the Rocking L when camp is in session."

"Please let her know that I'm happy to help with the cooking. Reilly doesn't exactly have a sophisticated palate. It'll be a joy for me to make something other than spaghetti."

"I'll do that. So, any idea when Lili and Reilly will be back?"

Jenna glanced at her watch. 2:38. "Any time now, I imagine. Lili said she needed to be back by three. She and Brick have an appointment."

Devin gave a satisfied nod. "I'll wait then, if you don't mind. I have a little something to give him. A birthday gift."

"That's sweet of you, but his birthday is in March."

"I remember. But I also understand that Sinatra is a birthday gift."

"How do you know . . . oh. The pinecone telegraph?"

"Nothing in Eternity Springs stays secret for long."

They both turned to look when three quick beeps of a horn announced Liliana Callahan's return. Devin set down his drink and then rose and said, "I'll be right back."

Jenna watched as her son exited the Jeep sporting the Stardance Ranch logo and started running toward their campsite. Upon spying Devin, her son veered in his direction. "Hi, Devin. Guess what?"

"You've whittled your list of puppy names down to ten?"

"You know about my dog?"

"Everyone in Colorado knows about your dog. Come with me. I need help carrying some things."

"Yessir."

Devin reached into the bed of his pickup and lifted out a shopping bag and then another and another and another. He handed two of the bags to Reilly, and then reached back for two more and a box.

Jenna murmured, "What have you done, Devin Murphy?"

Reilly bobbed from side to side as he carried the obviously heavy bags. Although she couldn't hear what he was saying, his mouth never stopped moving. Devin grinned down at him and said something that caused Reilly to giggle in such a carefree manner that it took her breath away and brought tears to her eyes. What a difference a couple of days—and a dog—could make.

"Set the bags down by your mother," Devin said as the pair drew near.

Reilly did as instructed then pulled a phone out of his pocket. "Look what I have, Mom. Don't worry. Ms. Lili gave it to me. It's an old phone she had in her car but it's not connected to the Internet or anything and the camera works. I took a whole bunch of pictures of Sinatra."

"Oh yeah?"

"Let me see 'em," Devin said as he deposited his packages on the patio beside the two that Reilly had dumped. He sat in the chair he'd vacated earlier and motioned Reilly to hand over the phone. He flipped through the photos. "Those are some blue eyes on that pup. Maybe you should call him Sky. Sky is a good name for a dog."

Reilly's lips pursed. "Sky. I hadn't thought of that."

Devin then rattled off another dozen names that had Reilly finally clapping his hands on his head and wailing. "I can't decide!"

Devin's chortle had a smidgen of evil in it. "Or you could just call him Sinatra and be done with it. While you're thinking about it, why don't you open your birthday presents?"

Reilly blinked. "My what?"

"I know. I know. Your birthday is in March and this is June, but I didn't know you this past March and next March is too far away and besides, you need this stuff now."

"You're giving me a birthday present?" Reilly repeated, awe in his tone. "Why?"

A private smile played on Devin's lips as he replied, "I like to give presents to good boys and girls."

"I try to be good."

"So your mom tells me. I heard she was giving you a belated birthday gift so I thought I'd get something to go along with it."

"Thank you so much! I'm so excited! Which bag is the present?"

"All of them."

Reilly's jaw dropped.

Devin folded his arms. "Now, I don't want any whining because they're not wrapped. They're in bags and boxes, and you can't tell what they are until you open them. I seriously don't understand why a person needs to take something out of one bag and plunk it into another. Oh . . . wait. Before you dig in I have one thing . . ."

He reached into one of the shopping bags that sported the Forever Christmas logo and removed a small white bakery bag. "I thought about getting you a cake or a cupcake, but believe me, this is better. You turned eight on your birthday, right?"

"Yessir."

"Inside this bag are eight pieces of heaven—my mother's strawberry pinwheel cookies. I'll have you know I took them from my private stash. Want us to sing to you?" Without waiting for a response, Devin launched into song in a pleasing tenor. "Happy birthday to you, you belong in a zoo. You look like a monkey, and you smell like one too."

Reilly giggled happily as Devin finished by saying, "Happy birthday, Reilly. Now, share your cookies."

"Okay. Thank you. Thank you so much." He took three cookies from the bakery bag and passed them out.

Devin popped one into his mouth. "Mmm. I could eat my weight in these. Have at it, kid. Tear into those bags."

In that Devin was doomed to disappointment, Jenna knew. Reilly had never been one to "tear in." He opened gifts reverently. He wanted to make the moment last as long as possible. He picked at tape and tugged gently at ribbons. Even with these bags, he'd find a way to go slowly. The boy reached tentatively for the nearest bag. "All of them? They're all for me?"

"Yes."

Reilly filled his cheeks with air then blew out a slow breath. Jenna recognized that he was overwhelmed by the moment. When was the last time that anyone had treated him with such kindness and generosity? Not since their original trip to Eternity Springs. *He's never going to want to leave here.*

That's something she probably should spend a little time thinking about.

Devin snagged a second cookie from the bag. "Hurry up, boy. You're slower than Christmas."

Reilly looked up at Devin and grinned. "If these were Christmas presents instead of birthday presents, that would make you Santa Claus, wouldn't it?"

In the process of reaching for his iced tea, Devin jerked and came close to knocking Scooby-Doo over. He met Jenna's gaze and his lips twisted in a rueful smirk. Reilly didn't notice because he'd finally pulled something from the bag. A Scooby-Doo dog leash. It took him ten more minutes to unwrap the rest of the gifts—a Scooby snack treat jar and Scooby-themed dog bowls, collar, tag, toys, and, finally, a deluxe dog bed. When the boy threw himself into Devin's arms and declared his undying thanks, Jenna blinked back tears. Needing to lighten the moment, she cleared her throat and said, "Now I understand. Michael isn't the only Murphy who likes Scooby-Doo."

Now Devin's grin turned sheepish. "What can I say? I'm a fan."

Jenna watched her son hug his Santa Claus and murmured, "Me too."

Everyone in Eternity Springs knew that Jack Davenport was a descendant of one of three partners who had discovered the Silver Miracle mother lode in the 1880s. Townspeople knew that he and his wife Cat ran a charitable foundation named after their deceased daughter Lauren, and one of its numerous projects was the Rocking L summer camp, which had been built on Davenport family land. The grand estate Jack had built in a picturesque valley on Murphy Mountain was more of a mystery. Rumor had it that Eagle's Way had a level of security that rivaled Camp David's, and the handful of people in town in position to know the veracity of that rumor didn't talk about it.

They did, however, gather at Eagle's Way on Sunday afternoon with potluck offerings, swimsuits, and pieces of a plan to rid the Stocktons of the threat under which they'd been living. Because they came with a whole gaggle of children in tow, the decision had been made to party first, thus giving the little ones a chance to wear themselves out.

Eagle's Way boasted an outdoor living space and swimming pool worthy of a five-star resort, with floating step pads, chaise lounges on a tanning ledge, a spillway spa and rain curtain, and a bar table inside the pool. Every time he visited, Devin wondered why the Davenports only spent about half their time in Colorado.

If he owned Eagle's Way, it would take a bulldozer to get him out of this valley. That was saying a lot, considering how far away this place was from an ocean.

In keeping with his bodyguard role, Devin had volunteered for lifeguard duty. The boy in him chortled with glee when Jack produced a whistle and a red throw float to assist in the effort. "Cool. Thanks, Jack. Though I'd have brought zinc oxide for my nose if I knew I'd be in uniform."

With more than a dozen young people in the pool, Devin did pay close attention. He blew his whistle judiciously and used his stern voice to demand obedience, but the only time he got seriously sidetracked was when Jenna emerged from the pool house in a one-piece swimsuit. His mouth went dry and he'd have licked his lips except that he felt the weight of his mother's interested gaze. Due to his beachfront lifestyle, Devin was accustomed to seeing women in scraps that barely covered anything. How was it that a conservative one-piece in a gray-blue that matched Jenna's eyes and complimented her creamy skin distracted him so thoroughly?

"You feeling a little hot?" his father asked, his tone brimming with innocence. "Want me to take over as lifeguard so you can cool off?"

"Gee thanks, Dad." Devin shoved the float at his father and started to walk away.

"Hey! What about the whistle?"

Devin rolled his eyes, tugged the whistle chain over his head, and tossed it to his dad. Then he strolled toward the end of the pool where the women had congregated, tugged off his T-shirt, and kicked his flip-flops beneath a chair.

Then a splash from one of the Callahan girls caught him by surprise, and he had no choice but to cannonball in beside them. He played with the kids until his father blew the whistle loud and called everyone out of the water to eat. After dinner, Cat Davenport took the children inside to the theater room, and Jack asked the adults to gather around. He called the meeting to order by asking Jenna if she had anything she wished to say before individual team members began their presentations.

Jenna glanced at Devin, who gave her a reassuring nod. She blew out a breath, then said, "I'm even more overwhelmed by your kindness and generosity today than I was last week."

Jack's answering smile to her was gentle. "We're happy to help you, Jenna. Those of us here have benefitted from the efforts of friends in the past. It's good to be able to give back in some small way. Now, why don't we start with your report, Daniel? I trust you were able to speak with your colleague about Jenna's case?"

"I was." Proving that old police detective habits die hard, Daniel removed a small notebook from his pocket. "He faxed me your file, Jenna. After studying it and making a few follow-up inquiries, I don't see any glaring mistakes. He identified three suspects."

Daniel looked toward his wife and nodded. Shannon Garrett drew a handful of manila folders from a briefcase and passed them out to team members. Daniel continued. "First, we have Nashville attorney Jeremy Tomlinson, whose wife was an obstetrical patient of Dr. Stockton's."

"Wait. Excuse me." The sheriff's wife, Savannah Turner, stepped forward. "You're a doctor? An obstetrician? I missed this piece of news." She turned a scolding gaze toward her husband. "Zach, you didn't tell me that."

The sheriff gave his wife an apologetic smile. Savannah waved dismissively, then said, "I'm sorry, Daniel. I'll be quiet."

He gave her a blue-eyed wink. "Jeremy Tomlinson accosted Jenna in her office building parking lot and struck her with a slap to the face following his wife's first-trimester miscarriage. Another physician witnessed the altercation and called the police. Dr. Stockton refused to press charges."

Everyone looked at Jenna, who shrugged. "He was grieving. I didn't take it seriously. Besides, he apologized."

"Tomlinson's firm learned about the incident and he lost his job."

"Serves him right," Luke Callahan muttered.

"I've never believed he was my stalker."

Devin imagined his own expression mirrored the skeptical looks he spied on the faces of the people around him.

Daniel continued. "Our second person of interest is Dr. Alan Snelling. Jenna reported the surgeon for sexual harassment to hospital administration. He denied it and started a campaign of innuendo against her. But after seven more women came forward with similar charges, he lost his hospital privileges. At that point, word of the scandal made it onto social media, and that apparently was the last straw for his wife of"—Daniel checked his notes—"thirty-four years. She filed for divorce. Jenna, anything to add?"

"I know that surgeons often have the reputation for being egotistical jerks, but in my experience, that's seldom true. Dr. Snelling, however, is a different animal. He's an egotistical pig. While I could easily picture him hiring someone to torment us, I still don't see him doing it himself."

"Which brings us to the third suspect identified by Jenna's investigator, Adam Zapel," Daniel said. "Mr. Zapel is a singer-songwriter whom Jenna dated briefly three months before the first harassment incident. He was unhappy when she told him she didn't want to see him anymore. He contacted her three subsequent times in an effort to change her mind. And"—Daniel glanced her way—"he wrote a song about her."

"Jenna!" Sarah said. "A song? This was in Nashville. So, a country music song? Did he record it? I want to hear it."

"No. Please, no." Color stained Jenna's cheeks. "It's so embarrassing."

"He's cute," Savannah said, peering over her husband's shoulder at the file.

Devin flipped through his own file folder to a picture of Zapel. Huh. He didn't look like a country and western singer. More of a used-car salesman, to Devin's way of thinking. Of course, he could be prejudiced.

"He's also married now with a baby on the way," Daniel continued.

"So does that take him off the list?" Maddie Callahan asked.

Daniel shook his head. "Actually, it makes me want to dig even deeper. Here's what I propose to do."

He outlined a plan of investigation that revisited these three characters, doing a deeper dive with the technological assets the Callahan family was able to bring to the table. During a pause in the discussion, Jenna asked the question that had occurred to Devin. "Is what you're suggesting legal? That seems awfully intrusive."

"We're fighting fire with fire, Jenna," Mark Callahan explained. "The law hasn't caught up with technology, I'm afraid. However, you can be assured that law enforcement will be able to use any information we give them to aid in the prosecution of the man—or woman—who has caused you such grief."

"Woman?" Savannah repeated. "You think this person could be a woman?"

"We'd be foolish to ignore the possibility," Daniel observed.

Mark nodded. "We won't do anything that jeopardizes the end goal, which is putting this jackwagon in jail for a very long time."

"I appreciate that, but—"

Seated beside her, Devin placed a hand on Jenna's knee and spoke one word. "Reilly."

She closed her mouth.

After Daniel wrapped up his presentation, Zach outlined his security plans. "The music festival presents a unique challenge. On one hand, we'll have all the extra security the Callahan family has arranged, and they'll obviously be brought up to date on this situation. On the other hand, our town will be busting at the seams, and my guys will have their hands full. You and Cam will need to be on your toes, Devin."

"With any luck, this will all be over by then," Jack said. "It's quite possible that our prey will reveal himself shortly after we start the clock ticking."

"All we need is a nibble," Mark Callahan said. "We'll be on him like ducks on a June bug."

Jack asked, "Do you foresee any problems having your monitoring in place by the fifth?"

Luke Callahan stretched out his legs and laced his fingers over a belly still admirably flat for a man in his fifties. "None at all. We have a few last things to tie up tonight, but we'll be ready when the clock starts ticking on Thursday."

"That's one thing I'm not clear about," Jenna said. "How exactly do we kick things off?"

Daniel responded. "We have an eight-point list to return you to the grid, Dr. Stockton. First on the list, and most important, is for you to apply to practice medicine in Colorado."

"Awesome," Shannon Garrett said. "Do you know how badly Eternity Springs needs our own obstetrician?"

Chapter Thirteen

Retail businesses in Eternity Springs counted the Fourth of July as one of their busiest and most profitable days of the year because they benefited from the crowds who collected to watch the parade travel the length of town on Spruce Street. Members of the public were invited to join the parade, the sole requirement being that the entry be decked out in red, white, and blue. As a result, led by the Eternity Springs Community School band, it was a patriotic conglomeration of motorized vehicles, pedestrians, and pets.

"If we're here next Fourth of July, I'm going to put Sinatra in the parade," Reilly declared.

"It's fun," Michael said. "Last year we dressed up dogs from the shelter and took them."

With her ankle much improved and numerous offers for a ride to and from the day's events, Jenna had invited Michael to attend the parade with her and Reilly, thus freeing Devin to help his father at Refresh and Lori to spend time alone with her husband before the second summer session at the Rocking L began the following day.

Jenna was glad to have the distraction. She was nervous about sending Reilly off to camp and borderline paranoid about launching the effort to find the stalker.

Not that she doubted the talents of the people on their team, because she didn't. Especially not after witnessing them in action. However, reliving the stalker-related events during a three-hour interview with Daniel yesterday had stirred up the memories of all those fear-filled moments and left her with a lingering sense of discontent. Dare she hope that Jack Davenport was correct in his assessment that this nightmare might possibly end within a week?

On the way back to town last night, Devin had told her to believe. *Well, he is Santa Claus, after all.*

Reilly tugged on her arm. "The parade is over. Is it time to go to the party yet?"

She checked her watch. "Not yet. Another hour and forty-five minutes."

"Oh."

Jenna smirked at his obvious disappointment. Reilly would just as soon skip the picnic and fireworks. He was counting the minutes until morning when he picked up Sinatra on their way to the Rocking L. He'd lobbied hard to get the puppy today, and Jenna finally put the matter to bed by asking Lori to explain to Reilly about the trouble dogs have with fireworks. Of course, after that he'd tried to convince Jenna to pick up Sinatra and head up into the mountains away from the noise. She'd finally used her Mean Mom stare, and the boy got the message.

"What are we going to do for an hour and forty-five whole minutes?" Reilly asked.

"We're not far from the park. We could go to the playground."

"That's a great idea," Michael said.

Ten minutes later Jenna sat on a park bench watching the boys as they climbed on a wooden jungle gym. The park was crowded, the children loud. She didn't notice the man approach until an ice cream cone appeared in front of her face. "Ice cream solves everything."

She smiled up at Devin. "Hello."

"For you. It's strawberry and vanilla with blueberries."

"Thank you." She took a lick and said, "Mmm. Delicious *and* patriotic."

"It's the theme of the day. I like the sock."

Jenna lifted her leg, showing off the toeless, flag-themed sock she'd slipped over her brace. "Thank you. It was Reilly's idea."

"You're still on one crutch, I see. So all the activity yesterday didn't adversely affect you?"

"No. I'm fine as long as I'm careful. Steps give me a challenge, and I certainly won't be dancing anytime soon, which is a shame because I hear the band tonight is supposed to be fabulous and I love to dance." She paused to savor another lick from her ice cream cone, then asked, "I thought you were helping your dad?"

He was staring at her mouth. "Huh? Oh. Yeah. I am. I had time to tie a few flies that a customer ordered before we opened this morning. I was going to deliver them to him before the picnic, but when I saw you and the boys, I called and asked him to meet me here."

From the playground Michael yelled, "Devin, what are you doing here?"

"I'm looking for a brother to spank."

Michael stuck out his butt, daring Devin, then when another child called his name, promptly ignored the adults. Devin gave his ice cream cone a lick and wryly observed, "He might as well just say 'Go on back to Oz.' So, did you enjoy the parade?"

"I did. I especially liked the Krazy Kazoo Bicycle Band."

"Aren't they awesome? Mom usually rides with them,

but she decided to skip the parade this year." A frown knit his brow as he added, "I'm getting a little worried about her. She's just not acting like herself."

"She said she was feeling great yesterday. She certainly held her own in pool volleyball."

"Yeah." He considered a moment and shrugged. "You're right. I think that flu bug really knocked her back. Maybe once she . . . oh . . . here comes my customer."

Hearing the odd note in his tone, Jenna followed the path of his gaze to see Boone McBride strolling toward them.

She hadn't seen Boone since he sent her the flowers, so she needed to thank him. But wow, this again would be a little awkward. Why did she only see the man when she was with Devin?

"Red, white, and blue ice cream. I like it," Boone said when he drew near.

"It's delicious." She lifted her cone up to him. "Want some?"

"Thank you." He took a testing bite. "Okay, that tastes a lot better than it looks. Where did you get it?"

She dipped her head toward Devin. Boone drawled, "What . . . none for me?"

"The lady gets ice cream. You get flies."

"Story of my life," the lawyer said with an exaggerated sigh.

He really was a fine-looking man, Jenna observed. "I want to thank you for the flowers, Boone. It was a lovely surprise, and the sunflowers make me smile every time I look at them. That was so sweet of you."

"You are welcome." He gave her a flirtatious wink and added, "I'm sweet as ice cream."

The sexual innuendo was obvious, and judging by the gleam in Boone's eye, another place, another time, he might have offered to let her lick him. Devin must have noticed too, because he warned, "Gotta be careful with ice cream. Listeria can be a problem. Wasn't there a Texas ice cream maker that shut down due to listeria?"

Boone ignored that and extended his hand. "Let's see my flies. I'm hoping to do a little fishing during the picnic. There's a great little spot on a creek that runs through the North Forty."

Devin handed him the bag containing the flies. Boone opened it, and while he studied the contents with interest, Devin nonchalantly asked. "So you are going to the Callahan picnic?"

"Wouldn't miss it."

"I hear Branch Callahan made it up to Colorado again this year."

"He did. I'm pretty sure Branch will outlive us all."

Devin spoke to Jenna. "You should have seen how Branch threw every single woman in attendance at this cowboy last year. Between Branch and Mac Timberlake's shenanigans, it's a wonder he didn't end up married to Caitlin Timberlake before the fireworks ended."

Boone smirked. "It was an interesting event, to say the least."

"So, are you bringing a date today in self-protection?"

"No, I'm going stag. Probably a mistake on my part, though."

Devin took a deliberate bite of his ice cream, and then pursed his lips as though it tasted sour. He cleared his throat and suggested, "In that case, you should take Jenna as your date."

Jenna almost dropped her ice cream cone. Did he just say what she thought he'd said? This from the man who'd kissed her socks off more than once? The man with whom she was moving in with tomorrow?

Yep.

Hurt rolled through her and it took every bit of acting

talent to keep it out of her expression. Now she saw why Cam joked about Devin's harem. He bargained away women like rugs at a bazaar.

Boone was obviously caught off guard by the suggestion too, but the interest on his face proved a soothing balm to Jenna's raw feelings. "Now there's a fabulous idea. My bad for not thinking of it myself. Jenna, would you and Reilly do me the honor . . . and solid . . . of attending the Callahans' Fourthfest with me?"

Jenna didn't bother to spare Devin a glance. "I'd love to, Boone. Thank you. Although I've promised to take Michael also. His parents aren't planning to arrive until later in the day."

Boone's smile beamed like a camera flash. "That's one Murphy I don't mind tagging along on our date." Giving Devin a pointed look, he added, "I trust you have other plans?"

He shoved his hands into the pockets of his jeans. "Yeah. I'm going with my parents. My time here in Eternity Springs is limited, and I want to spend as much time with them as possible."

Well. That only made it worse. Jenna gave Boone her brightest smile. "What time are you planning to go to the Callahans'?"

"Actually, I was on my way now. Branch requested I come early to visit. Personally, I think he wants to grill me. Do you mind going this soon?"

"Not at all. The boys are anxious to head that way."

"Cool. Do they like to fish?"

Jenna recalled Michael's excitement the day of the accident. "Definitely."

"Excellent." Boone clapped Devin on the back. "You just made my holiday, Murphy."

"Oh joy," Devin muttered.

"Shall we go?"

As Jenna started to stand, both Boone and Devin reached to help her. When she had her crutch securely beneath one arm—and her churning emotions locked away—she gave Devin a cool smile. "Thank you for the ice cream."

"Sure. You're welcome." He hesitated a moment, then said, "Jenna, I . . ."

She waited, but it quickly became obvious that the thought was to remain unfinished. Abruptly, he turned away. "I need to say goodbye to my brother."

Watching his long-legged strides eat up the distance between the bench and the playground, Jenna stewed. Devin Murphy ran more hot and cold than the shower room at Stardance Ranch at the end of square-dance night. He called Michael's name, and while he spoke to the boy, Jenna mentally focused on dismissing him. *Forget Devin Murphy. I'll go have a wonderful time with Boone and . . . and and set off some fireworks.*

She looked away from Devin to find Boone watching her with a knowing look in his eyes. "It's the Aussie accent, isn't it?"

Jenna winced. "I'm that obvious?"

"I'm an extremely observant guy."

She tossed what was left of her ice cream cone into a nearby trash can. "It's not the Aussie accent. It's a long story and I'll have to tell you when the boys aren't around. Let's just say I'm having Santa Claus issues."

"On the Fourth of July?"

"Pitiful, isn't it?"

Leaning against the white bark of an aspen tree at the edge of a grove off away from the picnic goers, Devin watched his father approach with two bottles of a local microbrew in his hands. "So what put the bee in your Uncle Sam hat?" Cam asked as he handed Devin a beer.

"I'm fine." Devin took a pull on the bottle. Though he didn't know why the heck his mother had chosen to lay out their picnic within spitting distance of the Callahan clan. Their spot was crowded to begin with because the Timberlake and Murphy families blended at all events ever since Chase married Lori. Today, in addition to his parents, his brother, and his sister and brother-in-law, their picnic spot included Mac and Ali Timberlake, their oldest son Stephen and his wife and three kids, and Caitlin Timberlake and her fiancé Josh Tarkington. And of course the Callahans had about a million people as part of their group.

A million and one, because they had Jenna. She sparkled like a firecracker in a sleeveless, flag blue summer sundress, and she really lit Devin's wick. He cleared his throat and added, "I'm accustomed to an ocean of water rather than an ocean of people. I just needed a little space."

"Uh-huh." Cam gave Devin a look that said he didn't believe a word of it.

"Everything is great. The weather is beautiful, the food excellent, the beer cold. I'm enjoying the holiday with family and friends. What do I have to be pissed about?"

"That's my question."

"I'm *fine*."

Cam sipped his beer and chose not to argue.

A full minute passed before Devin said, "Maybe it sticks in my craw a little bit to see everybody worshiping at the feet of that lawyer. He's a nice enough guy, but he's not the star of the Second Coming."

"Everybody? Or one body?"

Devin took another long sip of his beer. "I'm going home in two weeks."

Now it was Cam's turn to scowl. "I wish this place was home to you."

"It is. When I'm there. When I'm here, home is there."

"That's not the way it should be, Devin. That tells me that your life is missing something vital."

Devin shrugged. He couldn't argue with his father about that. He agreed with it. He simply hadn't figured out the way to fix it . . . yet. "That's a problem for another time."

"Bull. Are you forgetting every lesson I ever taught you? Life is short, Dev. Only a fool ignores that."

"I have a good life," Devin defended. "My business is growing. I love what I do. I'm a damn good captain."

"I know. Been there, done that. I had a good life in Australia. I had a thriving business that I loved. I had a family—you. It was a good life and I thought I was happy. But it was half a life."

"Gee, thanks."

"Stuff it. You know I'm not talking about you. If Sarah and Lori hadn't won that vacation to Australia and booked a snorkeling trip on my boat, you and I would probably have had a decent life. We might have even thought we were happy. But I will tell you this, son. My life would have been missing the biggest and best part of it."

Devin shrugged. "Not everybody has a high school sweetheart who they were in love with for most of their lives."

"If you like Jenna Stockton, you should explore the possibilities, not shuffle her off to—" Cam broke off as his daughter caught his attention with a wave.

"Dad? Devin?" Lori called to the Murphy men. "Would you please join us?"

"A Texan lawyer," Cam finished. "I'll share one last thought, son. The biggest mistakes I made in my life were the decisions I rushed. Take your time and be sure to keep your eyes open. Life presents more possibilities than are readily apparent. Now, it looks like we're being summoned."

Devin trailed his father back toward his family. Cam took a seat in the empty lawn chair next to Sarah, who sat beside Ali. Mac Timberlake sat next to his wife. Lori and Chase stood and faced their parents.

Chase said, "Lori and I had a conversation the other day about how lucky we are with regard to our families. We realized that whenever we refer to you all, we use the singular, not the plural. We really have become one big happy family, and that makes life even sweeter for Lori and me. Since the entire family is with us here today, we decided to take this opportunity to acknowledge and recognize what a great job our parents have done."

He gestured for Lori to continue. She smiled at the Timberlakes and then at Cam and Sarah. "You guys are the greatest. You've done an awesome job as parents. In fact, you've done such great jobs, that we think you should be promoted."

She reached into the picnic hamper at her feet and pulled out two small boxes wrapped in Old Glory paper and tied with red, white, and blue ribbon. She handed boxes to the mothers.

Sarah and Ali shared a curious look, and then began tugging the bows. Ali got hers open first. She removed a smaller box wrapped in Christmas paper and ribbon. "What's this?" Sarah asked when she revealed a similar box.

"Open them," Chase suggested.

Ribbon slid. Paper tore. Sarah and Ali each opened her box.

Sarah gasped aloud. Ali laughed.

"What is it?" Michael demanded. "Let me see."

Chase and Lori clasped hands as their mothers pulled Christmas tree ornaments out of their boxes. Written across Sarah's ornament was the word NANA. Ali's read MIMI.

Tears spilled down Sarah's face and she launched

herself at Lori. Grinning like an idiot, Chase said, "There are ones for you too, Dad and Cam. Or should I say, Grampy and Puppy."

"Well, Merry Christmas to us," Mac said, his smile wide.

"I don't understand," Michael wailed.

Devin slung an arm around his little brother. "You're gonna be an uncle, Mikey. Lori's going to have a baby."

Lines of worry carved across Michael's brow. He stared hard at Lori. "But I'm not old. How can I be an uncle?"

"I'm not old either, buddy," Cam said. Having had his turn hugging his daughter and shaking Chase's hand, he stepped back and rested his hand on his youngest child's shoulder. "How can I be a grandfather?"

"You are too old, Dad. You have some gray hairs."

"And you gave me every last one of them," Cam fired back.

Once the 'rents backed off, Devin added his congratulations to his sister and her husband. The festive atmosphere kicked up a notch and banished Devin's foul mood. When talk turned to the due date—December, thus the Christmas wrapping—and morning sickness and swollen ankles and heartburn, he bailed and joined a game of Frisbee being played by a group of teens and other young adults. After that, he joined a horseshoes tournament and got his butt whipped by an eighty-seven-year-old.

An hour before sunset, Branch Callahan and his sons congregated on the outdoor stage and officially welcomed everyone to the celebration. Mark Callahan said, "We're about to fire up the band, but before the dancing kicks off, my son has requested a moment of our time. Brick, the floor is yours."

Brick sauntered onto the stage and took the microphone

from his father. "Thanks, Dad. Howdy, everyone. Hope you're all enjoying yourselves."

The crowd responded with cheers and whistles.

"I'm going to try to keep this short, so I hope you'll bear with me. Most of you probably know that I am the chairman of the Chamber of Commerce fundraising committee to benefit the Eternity Springs Community School. The Fall Festival remains our primary fundraiser, and I know y'all are looking forward to the third weekend in October. In the past few years the town's and, subsequently, the school's growth rate has skyrocketed. The Chamber has accepted the challenge to fund the addition of a new wing onto our school without raising taxes."

"Good luck with that," someone called.

Brick gave a dismissive wave. "Today, I'm announcing a new fundraiser to help us achieve that goal. I want to ask a few fellow citizens to join me here on the stage. Daniel Garrett, Sheriff Zach Turner, Flynn Brogan, and Chase Timberlake—y'all come on up here."

The men must have been tipped off to the request, because they all joined Brick onstage. Brick waved his hand in a gesture that encompassed all of them. "So . . . the five of us here . . . anybody know what we have in common?" Without giving the crowd time to respond, he answered his own question. "We're all fans of blizzards."

Zach got it first. He folded his arms and grinned at Brick. "You and Lili are expecting, too?"

"We are."

The crowd erupted in cheers and catcalls with a few risqué comments thrown in. Off to the side of the stage, Brick's father and uncles grinned. "So, there are five families with babies due in December. Unless . . . is there anyone else who's part of this club whose news I've missed?"

No one joined them, so Brick continued. "So, back to

the fundraiser. Because I always think events are more fun when wagers are involved, we are going to hold a contest. I have two words for you: permutations and combinations. Entrants have dozens of opportunities to win. We're picking genders and weights and lengths. Birth dates and times. Chamber members are donating lots of prizes, including a brand new ATV—let's all hear it for Poppy Murphy!"

Cam waved. Devin saw his mother twist around to look at her husband. "Did you already know about Lori's baby?"

Cam turned his wave into a gesture of innocence, holding his palms out toward Sarah. "No . . . no . . . that was a complete surprise. I knew about Brick and Lili's baby and the others were already public news."

"Of course, the biggest prize we will award is bragging rights. Those are important here in Eternity Springs. Don't you agree?"

The crowd cheered.

Brick continued, "We have five babies on the way, all due about the same time. Pick up your baby parlay entry form and make a predication and a donation before you leave here today. They'll also be available from any Chamber member beginning tomorrow. Again, all proceeds benefit the Eternity Springs Community School expansion project. Now, I'm gonna get off the stage so the band can get going. Y'all come on and dance. Fireworks will begin in about an hour. Happy birthday, America!"

As soon as Callahan vacated the stage, the band kicked off with an up-tempo medley of patriotic songs. Following that, they segued into dance tunes and the dance floor began to fill up.

Devin's gaze drifted back toward the Callahan group, where Boone McBride knelt on one knee talking to Gabe and Nic Callahan's twin daughters. He appeared to be folding paper into origami figurines and delighting the girls. Was there anything Mr. Perfect couldn't do?

For once, Jenna wasn't glued to his side. She sat in a lawn chair with her ankle propped on top of a cooler, talking with Cat Davenport and three of the Callahan wives. Devin didn't consciously make a decision to approach her, but all of a sudden, there he was, standing in front of her.

When she noticed him, the light in those gorgeous blue eyes went a bit frosty. She lowered her foot to the ground and stood. "Devin, I've been hoping I'd have a chance to speak with you. Please excuse me for a few minutes, ladies."

With her crutch beneath her arm, Jenna walked toward the aspen grove where Devin had sought refuge a little earlier. She held her back ramrod straight. Devin had enough experience with women to recognize when one was about to chew his ass. He shoved his hands into his pockets and braced himself for the onslaught.

When they walked far enough away that their conversation wouldn't be overheard, she faced him and surprised him. She didn't snap at him for embarrassing her or being a clod or serving her up to McBride like a steak. No, she tried to weasel out on him.

"I feel terrible, Devin. I appreciate the sacrifice you were willing to make on my behalf, but I can't in good conscience take you away from your family. We need to call off this move tomorrow. I'll stay where I am. I've managed just fine so far without a live-in bodyguard. That's really overkill."

"And that's a really poor choice of words," he fired back. "For one thing, living with you will be no sacrifice. An exercise in willpower, maybe . . . definitely . . . but in no way a sacrifice."

She pursed her pretty little lips. "Willpower?"

Devin's gut churned. He glanced toward the crowd and saw that they were the object of his mother's and sister's attention. He muttered a curse and said, "Let's dance."

"I can't dance."

"Sure you can."

He took her crutch and leaned it against a tree, and then he swept her up into his arms and headed for the dance floor.

"Devin!" Jenna protested. She tugged at her skirt and tucked it close.

Having Jenna Stockton in his arms and away from Boone McBride lightened Devin's heart in a dangerous way. As they reached the dance floor, the band began a country waltz. He stepped into the song, turning and twirling in time with the beat.

She followed his lead gracefully and he pulled her close. They didn't speak. Devin was vaguely aware that the other dancers moved aside to accommodate them, but his attention remained on the woman in his arms.

He recognized the fragrance she wore—a lightly floral, old-fashioned scent with a French name. L'Air-something, it had been called. He'd always liked it and had gifted it to women he'd dated in the past. On Jenna, it smelled heavenly.

At some point during the afternoon she'd taken her hair out of its customary ponytail, and now it brushed against the skin of his arm like a silken waterfall. She was soft in all the right places, but hardly any heavier than Michael. Devin couldn't remember the last time he'd enjoyed a dance so much. The song ended way too soon.

When the opening bars of the next number sounded, he swallowed a sigh and moved toward the edge of the dance floor. Navigating the choreographed moves of a line dance with Jenna in his arms was more than he figured he could manage. But he didn't want to put her down. So, he didn't.

He was on shaky ground here. He should cart her pretty little ass back to McBride and deposit her in the pretty-lawyer-boy's waiting arms. Devin needed for those two to become a couple. Devin had many faults, but he wasn't a poacher. Once Jenna Stockton was officially some other guy's lady, the buzz zipping through his veins would surely fade. He just needed to let things play out.

But dammit, he'd delivered the gift this morning. He shouldn't have to hang around and watch it being opened this evening. How much responsibility did Santa have? McBride could take it from here.

And Santa should get his cookies and milk.

The shadows deepened as twilight descended on the forest. The music and sound of partygoers faded. When it became obvious that this wasn't simply a shortcut back to her date, Jenna slightly stiffened. "Now where are we going?"

"Too many people. I need some space."

"Space for what?"

"Being."

He took half a dozen more steps before she said, "What does that mean?"

"Have you ever been out on the ocean and surrounded entirely by the water?"

"No."

"There's nothing like it, especially if you are the only person on the boat and drifting on the current. It'll make you feel like the smallest, most insignificant creature in the universe. At the same time, it's empowering because it makes you one with the universe. I never feel alone when I'm on the ocean. Sometimes when I'm in a crowd, I need the ocean."

She thought about that a moment, and then asked with a knife edge of insult, "You felt alone when you were dancing with me?"

"No, not at all. I wanted to *be* alone when I was dancing with you. Alone with you."

"Oh."

He carried her into the woods away from the music and the people. They'd hiked three or four minutes before she spoke again, this time with wariness instead of slight. "I don't know about this, Devin. It's getting dark. I shouldn't leave Reilly, and Boone will be looking for me."

"We're almost there. Technically, Reilly left you because he went out on the houseboat to watch the fireworks from the water with Michael and the Callahan kids. As far as your date goes, McBride can take a flying leap off the fishing pier for all I care."

"You were the one who suggested the idea. You—"

"Yeah. Yeah. Yeah," Devin interrupted. "Can we not talk about him please? At least for the time being?"

"Fine." She gave a snooty little sniff.

"Don't worry. We won't miss the fireworks." The postage-stamp-sized meadow he headed toward had an excellent angle on the pertinent part of the sky.

"I'm more worried about missing the bears."

"Honey, a bear isn't the animal you need to worry about tonight," he muttered beneath his breath.

Since his mouth was inches from her, she most likely heard him—and that shut her up. Moments later, he reached his destination and was pleased to discover that none of the other Fourthfest guests had beaten him to it.

"We're here."

"Where's here? Other than the middle of nowhere?"

"It's a hot springs pool like the ones at Angel's Rest. You can soak your ankle."

"Oh."

The purr of delight that replaced the wariness in her voice sent a shudder of lust racing through him. Devin knew he was in trouble. *Don't do this. Don't be stupid.*

I won't be too stupid. This can't go too far. We might be isolated, but it's still a public place. Just a little nibble, a little sip. I'm just so damn hungry.

Gently, he lowered her to a grassy spot on the ground beside the pool. He knelt beside her and slipped off the red flat she wore on her uninjured ankle, then carefully untied the ribbon from her brace and pulled the Velcro tabs.

"You make me feel like Cinderella," Jenna said, her voice soft and husky.

"I'm no Prince Charming." He set the brace aside. "There . . . I have you naked. Dip your toes and see how you like it."

Jenna sank her ankle into the hot springs pool and released a sensual groan. "That's fabulous. It makes me want to go all the way."

"Jenna, please! You're killing me here."

She laughed like a wicked, teasing siren as he sat beside her and took off his boots and rolled up the legs of his jeans. In a soft, Eve-in-the-Garden voice, she said, "Devin?"

"Hmm?"

"Come here." She cupped her hand at the back of his neck and pulled his mouth down to hers.

Chapter Fourteen

What better time to play with fire than the Fourth of July?

Jenna knew she shouldn't bait the bear—or whatever animal Devin purported to be—but the man sent more mixed messages than a drunk-texting coed. She was tired of it. Her nerves were shot. She was on edge. Tomorrow was a big day, what with sending Reilly off to camp and launching their offensive operation against her stalker, and she needed a distraction.

She was lonely and he'd held her close and with tenderness. And she did love the way he kissed. Hungry and hot and wild as a mountain thunderstorm. His hand plunged into her hair and anchored her. His lips crushed hers, devouring her, as if the taste of her drove him into a frenzy.

The taste of him certainly fired her hormones. Lust snapped through her like a whip. She wanted to crawl on top of him, she wanted contact and friction and the glorious heat of combustion. She moaned with desperate pleasure when his teeth nipped and scrapped at the sensitive skin at the base of her neck.

She melted back onto her elbows when he murmured her name and his kisses trailed lower toward the scooped neckline of her dress. Thrill zinged along her nerves as his hand swept up the length of her thigh. Need became an aching, clawing animal inside her, and she arched her back and . . . gasped in pain when she banged her ankle on a rock.

Devin muttered a curse and pulled away from her. "Jenna. I'm sorry. Are you okay? I'm so sorry."

"No. Not your fault." She closed her eyes and grimaced as she absorbed the waves of pain. "Mine. I started it and then I forgot about . . . everything."

"I know. Me too. Is there anything I can do to help? I don't guess I can kiss it make it better?"

She groaned a laugh. "I think you'd best keep your kisses to yourself."

"Yeah. This spot feels isolated, but we're just a stone's throw away from a hundred people. We were playing with fire."

The first skyrocket of the night shot into the air and burst in a shower of red, white, and blue sparks in the sky above them. She let out a shaky sigh. "I know. But it *is* the Fourth of July. It's a night for it, don't you think?"

"Fourth. Fifth. Fifteenth." Devin released a long sigh. "I don't think the date is going to matter. I tried. I am trying. But we have lots of hours of darkness ahead of us to make it through. Alone together. You and me. I don't know about you, Jenna, but after tonight, I don't think I have that much willpower."

Jenna's heart began to thunder anew as a scandalous notion took hold. She liked this man so much. It had been so long.

He lives in Australia.

So what?

Without giving herself any more time to consider, she asked, "I don't know that you need it."

He went still. With a whiz, whistle, and bang another skyrocket exploded overhead. Sparks of purple and green lit the night, and Devin cleared his throat. "Are you suggesting we . . .

Jenna wasn't quite brazen enough to proposition him outright, so she looked up into the sky and gave a whistle of admiration. "Wow, look at that one. Those gold chrysanthemums are my favorite."

He waited for a full minute before picking up a stone and chucked it into the hot springs. "Jenna, you know that I'm leaving the country in two weeks, right? My work . . . my life . . . is in Australia. I have to go back. I *want* to go back. Don't lose track of that detail, because I'm giving you fair warning. I'm not a forever guy."

"If I may point out that except for that kiss a moment ago, I haven't asked you for *anything*, much less forever?"

"I'm not saying you did. Although I think we should observe a moment of silence in honor of that kiss because it truly was in my top five all-time favorite kisses. Okay, top two. And you can't hold it against me that it's competing for number one with the kiss I got from Angelina Jolie when I was nineteen, and she chartered Dad's boat for a day. That was a kiss on the cheek, so it's an entirely different category, but I'm trying to be honest here."

"You're crazy."

"You don't know the half of it. I did something today that went against every instinct I possess. I failed pretty spectacularly at it, but I did try."

"What did you do?"

"Put my foot in it," he grumbled.

She folded her arms and glared at him. Dark though it was, she felt certain he sensed it. "Well?"

"Let's enjoy the fireworks."

"Oh, I'm about to show you fireworks. This has something to do with Boone, doesn't it? Is that why you manipulated him into bringing me to this party?"

"You know, if you ever get the chance to watch New Year's fireworks over Sydney Harbor, you should do it. It's just spectacular."

"That's a pitiful attempt to change the subject and an insulting action you are attempting to cover up. Just because I asked for assistance finding a stalker doesn't mean I need help finding someone to date!"

"Look. That makes it sound worse than it was. Besides, it's not you. It's me."

"Oh, brother."

"Okay, fine. You know what I did? I'll tell you what I did. I set you down in front of McBride like a fly in front of a trout."

"Excuse me?"

"No, excuse *me*." Above them a rapid series of explosions lit the sky. Devin raked his fingers through his hair. "Dammit, it's true. I won't deny it. But I have my reasons and they're good reasons, but I don't want to tell you because you'll think I've lost my ever-loving mind."

"Try me."

Two more rockets burst up in the sky before he acquiesced and launched into a convoluted tale about cell phones and Eternity Springs and Christmas bells and wishes. When he finally wound down, Jenna attempted to summarize. "Let me bottom line this. You think some sort of Eternity Springs mojo means you're supposed to find a father for Reilly? And you decided that father needs to be Boone McBride?"

"The McBride part isn't set in stone."

"Okay, I agree. You have lost your mind."

"Call me Santa Cupid," he grumbled unhappily.

Jenna laughed and they both looked skyward as a starburst set off an extended number of crackles and pops. When the sounds finally faded, Devin continued. "I know it sounds unbelievable, but that's part of it too. In my very first conversation with your son, I talked about believing."

"I remember him telling me that."

"I don't know where the words came from, Jenna.

They just appeared on my tongue out of the blue. Kind of like his call appeared on my phone—the brand-new phone given to me by none other than Celeste Blessing. Maybe you're too new to Eternity Springs to recognize when woo-woo knocks on your door, but believe me, it happens. This town has a long history of strange experiences and coincidences, especially when Celeste is involved. I don't bet against them."

Loud booms accompanied a rapid series of fireworks. Devin raised his voice to be heard above the noise.

"And think about it. You didn't, either. You chose to come to Eternity Springs as a result of one of those coincidences, didn't you?"

She couldn't argue with that. However . . . "I'm not interested in Boone and he's not interested in me."

"Bull."

"It's true. We discussed it. You weren't exactly subtle with the hot up this morning."

"He sent you flowers."

"As a friendly gesture."

"Yeah. Right. Are you always this naive?"

She wasn't going to argue the point with him, but Jenna knew she was right. Boone didn't hesitate to flirt, but he didn't mean it. A woman could tell these things. After spending a bit of time with him, she sensed that there was much more to Boone McBride than he let on. He carried some serious baggage.

Devin continued, "Even if neither of you are interested right now, that could change. Or maybe somebody new will come to town tomorrow. Who knows? One thing I do want to stress, though. I don't want you to worry that I'm so far off my rocker that I won't protect you like I promised. I vow that I will guard you with my life until the stalker is caught."

Jenna couldn't resist commenting, "Or for the next two weeks, anyway."

"If this takes longer than Jack expects—something I can't imagine because Jack and the Callahans managed to track down Chase outside of a remote mountain village in Chizickstan—I'll stay longer. I'm not going to abandon you. Although, do you have a passport?"

"A passport!"

"Yeah, a passport. Do you have one?"

"Yes, why?"

"My friend Mitch is getting married on Bella Vita Isle. I planned my trip home around the wedding. You can be my plus one if worst comes to worst. A bunch of us are going." He paused as if a new thought had just occurred to him. "Lori and Chase are going. Wonder if the baby news changes their plans. Is there a reason she couldn't travel?"

"I'm a doctor, but I'm not your sister's doctor. However, unless she's had a problem with her pregnancy that she hasn't shared, I know of nothing that would prevent her traveling."

"Cool. I'm excited about the baby. Lori is gonna be a great mom. You've seen how fabulous she is with animals. Imagine how she'll be with her own little one. And Mom and Dad as grandparents? That'll be a hoot to watch." He hesitated a moment then added, "From afar. Good thing the world has Skype. I can have a front-row seat even from the other side of the world. Although, this news will change the family travel plans again. Guess I'll be hauling myself back to Eternity Springs again for the holidays, after all."

"Can we go back to this passport and wedding issue, please? I could not go out of the country and leave Reilly behind at camp."

"Why not? He'll be doing whatever he's doing whether you are in the mountains or at the beach."

"But . . ."

"It's the Caribbean, Jenna. Not the South Pacific. The flight isn't bad at all. I've made it plenty of times. But we are getting ahead of ourselves worrying about that. Although, consider yourself officially invited to join me. Bella Vita is an awesome place. I'll take you out in a boat and show you what I meant about being one with the universe."

"I'm not going to crash a wedding.

"You wouldn't be crashing. My invitation includes a guest, and I accepted for two figuring I'd invite somebody when I'm there. I hate going to weddings alone, don't you?"

"Yes, but . . ."

"Mitch is good friend of mine and the woman he's marrying is super nice. You'll like them both. Mitch lived in Eternity Springs for a while when he apprenticed with our resident glass artist. Have you met Cicero?"

"I met him tonight. His son Galen is a couple years older than Reilly."

"His wife is one of Eternity Spring's doctors."

"Rose Cicero. She treated my ankle. I liked her."

"They're great people. Have four children. They're adopted, too. Reilly has that in common with the Cicero kids. Anyway, my friend Mitch was Cicero's apprentice. When I ran boats out of Bella Vita, he and I spent a lot of time together." Devin threaded his fingers through hers and brought her hand to his mouth for a kiss. "Say yes. Say you will come whether we've found the stalker or not. It's a beautiful place. Tropical breezes, sugar sand beaches, umbrella drinks. We'll take moonlit walks on the beach."

"I do not understand you, Devin Murphy. One minute you're telling me you're playing Yente trying to marry me off and the next you're inviting me on a Caribbean getaway?"

"Yente?"

Fiddler on the Roof. The matchmaker."

"Oh. Okay. I like 'Santa Cupid' better, but whatever works. What can I say? I can multi-task. Come with me to Bella Vita Isle, Sugar Cookie."

"Sugar Cookie? Really?"

"Yep. C'mon. Let Santa have a nibble." He laid her back against the grass, and when the grand finale burst across the sky a few minutes later neither of them noticed.

Sitting in his truck in the parking lot at Eternity Springs Community School, Devin reached across the console and awkwardly patted Jenna's knee. Tears had been rolling down her cheeks ever since Reilly had climbed into the Rocking L bus for the trip up to the summer camp ten minutes earlier. Devin hadn't felt this helpless since a tour last year when a little girl's teddy bear blew out of her arms and into the Coral Sea during a trip out to the Great Barrier Reef. "Reilly will be fine, Sugar.

"I know."

"He wasn't upset."

"I know! That's what was so bad. He's not going to miss me at all."

"That's a bad thing?"

"No. Not at all. I'm happy!" She covered her face with her hands and released a little sob.

Devin sighed and twisted the key, starting the ignition. "I can tell."

"I'm being silly. I know. And I never cry. It's just that Reilly and I haven't been apart in months and months. It's a good thing that he's gone to camp. I just wish he could have acted the tiniest bit sad to leave me."

"I'm sure that inside he's sobbing his little heart out. But he's a guy. He has to show a stiff upper lip."

"That's true, isn't it? I tend to forget just how silly males are no matter what their age. Thank you."

"You're welcome."

"He was awfully cute with Sinatra, wasn't he?"

Devin nodded. "He and that dog are going to be great

friends. Now, Daniel will be expecting us, so we need to get going. Are you ready?"

"Yes. Let's go."

He put his truck into gear and exited the parking lot. The plan was to meet at Daniel Garrett's office, where Jenna would file the paperwork that would launch the team's effort to track down the stalker. By the time they made the short trip to the office building, Jenna had herself under control.

The Garrett Investigations office was located in the three-story building on Pinion and Fourth that also housed Timberlake and McBride law offices, Rafferty Engineering, and a few other professional concerns. As they climbed the narrow wooden staircase to the second floor, Jenna observed, "What a neat old building."

"It started out as a saloon and whorehouse. Every mining town needed one or two. Various remodels over the years have made it a hodgepodge, but it's hodgepodge with character." Devin rapped on the frosted glass panel of Daniel's door before opening it. Daniel was on a phone call, but he waved them inside and gestured for Jenna to take the chair behind his desk.

"Thanks, Bob," Daniel said into the phone. "I appreciate that. You've been a tremendous help." He listened a moment, then replied. "She's doing well. We're very excited. Yes. Eternity Springs has been very good to me."

Daniel pointed toward a single-serve coffee maker on a credenza, and Devin made two cups while Daniel completed his call. Once he'd disconnected, he offered them a welcoming smile. "Good morning. So how did the bus drop-off go?"

"As well as could be expected," Jenna told him. "Reilly barely spared me a look back. I managed to hold off the tears until I made it to Devin's truck."

"Never mind that he told her she was the best mother

in the whole universe ten minutes before that when we picked up his new puppy. I've never seen a kid so happy."

Reilly had thrown himself and his arms full of puppy into Jenna's. He'd said the whole universe line and added, "This is my number-two biggest wish in the whole world."

Jenna and Devin had shared a silent look that acknowledged they both knew which wish was the boy's number one.

To Daniel, he added, "I don't know whose tail wagged more, Reilly's or Sinatra's."

Daniel grinned. "I hope he's ready for all the mewling that pup will do for the next few nights as he adjusts to being away from his mom. You're lucky to be missing that, Jenna."

"True," she replied. "I'm definitely counting my blessings today, and you are on my list. I can't thank you enough for helping us, Daniel."

"I'm happy to be of service. Are you ready to get down to it?"

"I am."

She spent the next hour and a half filling out online forms and hard copy paperwork for Daniel to file. She made a series of phone calls from a list he had created. If her hand trembled a time or two while affixing her signature to documents, well, Devin didn't point it out. Before the job was done, she'd applied for a Colorado driver's license, subscribed to three professional journals and four general magazines, signed up for a credit card, and submitted her credentials in order to become licensed to practice medicine in Colorado.

The last one shifted the steadiness needle from "tremble" toward "shaking." She murmured, "I guess it's too late for second thoughts now. Anything else?"

"I think that takes care of it," Daniel replied. He checked his watch and added, "Right on time, too. I need to beg your indulgence, Dr. Stockton. My wife arranged a little reception in the wake of this morning's events. I hope you won't mind joining her and her friends."

"Of course I won't mind," Jenna replied.

"Devin, if you'll wait here, there's a few things I'd like to go over with you. We can join the ladies in a bit. Jenna, if you'll follow me?"

While he waited for Daniel's return, Devin checked his cell and was pleased to see the text from his brother-in-law. Camp Director Chase had sent a trio of photos of Reilly's arrival at the Rocking L. So far, so good. The kid was all grins and giggles. He'd show Jenna the photos when they finished up here.

When Daniel reentered the office, he asked, "Do we have a problem? Are these things you need to go over bodyguard-duty related?"

"No. No problem. Actually, what I have to go over isn't all that important. This was mainly an excuse to send Jenna into the lion's den alone."

"Uh . . . lion's den?"

Daniel took his seat behind his desk. "Remember how your mom and her friends held what they called interventions when they thought one of their lives needed interference from people who cared?"

"Oh, yeah. They were big on that."

"Shannon decided your Jenna needs one. At the picnic yesterday, she told the Callahan wives that she has no intention of staying in Eternity Springs and practicing medicine. Well, the wives want an OB/GYN in town and they have no intention of letting her get away. Shannon has gathered the prego parade to work on changing Dr. Stockton's mind."

Devin let out a long, slow whistle. "Jenna doesn't stand a chance."

And maybe Boone McBride will get a second one.

Chapter Fifteen

Jenna loved her profession. She loved working with women and being their sounding board and their source of information during one of the most important events of their lives—pregnancy and childbirth. Few experiences in life equaled that moment when a child slid from his mother's body into her waiting hands.

But as she left Daniel Garrett's office building, she seriously needed a break from pregnant women. "Can we go do something physical?"

Devin stumbled and she realized that she had too. "Not *that* kind of physical. I want to go running or hiking. I need to move!"

"You have a sprained ankle. You're in a brace."

Yeah, yeah, yeah. She could pretend otherwise, couldn't she? "There has to be something I can do."

He opened his mouth.

"Other than that. What about rowing? I could do that, couldn't I? Does somebody rent rowboats on Hummingbird Lake?"

Devin suddenly understood her agitation. He rolled his tongue around his mouth and asked, "So which was more difficult? Spitting in your stalker's face or telling my sister and her cohorts that you don't want to be their doctor?"

Jenna shook her head. "They're an amazing group of women. Intimidating when they're all together."

"Did they change your mind?"

She sighed. "I promised to think about it. So, about that rowboat?"

"I got a better idea. How about we go four-wheeling? Daniel told me about a new trail that's opened up since the last time I've been back. Dad has raved about it too. Riding an ATV isn't as physical as rowing, but it's not like sitting on a sofa knitting an afghan, either. You should be able to manage it just fine with your ankle braced. I can promise it will clear the cobwebs from your head."

"I've never ridden an ATV."

"Well then, Sugar, you are in for a treat."

"We have time? Remember, we promised to have dinner with your parents."

"I haven't forgotten that. Mom is making lasagna using Ali Timberlake's recipe. Her lasagna is the best you can eat this side of Rome. No way I'll be late for dinner tonight."

"In that case, let's go."

The outing sounded like just what she needed. Her head was full of, if not cobwebs, then of arguments and ideas and decisions waiting to be made. On top of that, her heart had problems of its own. She didn't know why sending Reilly off to camp had reawakened all the fears and insecurities she'd experienced when he was wounded, but it had. Add in the incessant pull of her attraction to Devin and the possibility—no, probability—that she was about to embark upon a short-term affair with him, and she was definitely a basket case.

Devin drove to his father's shop and pulled around to the back lot where the Murphys stored their personal outdoor toys, which included ATVs, a fishing boat, and a pop-up camper. He sent Jenna to the sandwich shop across the street with instructions to "buy lunch and lots of it" while he hooked up the trailer and got directions from his dad.

She placed an order, and then took a seat at a table to wait for it. She was scanning a copy of the *Eternity Times* when she heard her name and looked up with a smile. "Hello, Celeste."

"Hello, dear. I was so pleased when I spied you crossing the street a few minutes ago. I was looking for you at the school this morning, but I apparently just missed you. I have a little something for you—a gift I stumbled upon in Claire's shop that made me think of you. Since you were sending Reilly off to camp this morning, I thought you might need a little pick-me-up." She sat at the table and pulled a box sporting the Forever Christmas logo from a sparkling gold tote bag and handed it to Jenna.

"Aww," Jenna said. "How sweet. That's so thoughtful of you, Celeste." With the box in her hand, Jenna hesitated. "Before I open this, I want to say something. About your Welcome Wing visit to us at Stardance Ranch . . . I feel terrible about misleading you . . ."

Celeste interrupted her with a touch on her arm. "Now, honey. Don't give that a second thought. I knew you had your reasons, and it wasn't my place to interfere."

"So you recognized us?"

Celeste chided her with a look. "Open your gift, dear."

Jenna opened the box and pulled back red tissue paper to reveal the thick round glass of a snow globe. She lifted it from the box and saw that the scene inside showed a Christmas tree in a forest. "It's beautiful."

"It's a Christmas wishing tree. One that's portable."

"I love it." She gave it a shake and watched the snowflakes float. "Thank you, Celeste."

"You are very welcome. I was so pleased to learn that

Reilly wanted to adopt the tradition after I shared it with you. I hope you will continue it in years to come."

"We definitely will. It's a lovely idea and it really struck a chord for us." As she reached across the table to give Celeste a hug, the young woman behind the sandwich shop's counter called her name.

"That's a large sack of sandwiches," Celeste observed.

"Devin told me to buy a lot. He's taking me four-wheeling. I've never ridden an ATV before."

"Oh, you'll love it." Celeste rose and kissed Jenna's cheek. "Go have fun. I hope you'll stop by Angel's Rest one day soon for a cup of tea."

"I'll do that."

Jenna tucked the snow globe into her purse, paid for her sandwiches, exited the shop, and crossed the street to find Devin tucking water bottles into the storage compartment of an ATV. "Hey, beautiful. Are you ready?"

"Let's do it."

During the drive up to the trailhead, they talked about music and movies and monotonous highway drives. Upon reaching their destination, Devin pulled his truck and trailer onto the shoulder of the road. A few moments later, he fired up the ATV and backed it off the trailer. Then he handed Jenna a helmet and told her to climb aboard and wrap her arms around his waist. "Or, you can use the hand-holds, but I'd really enjoy it a lot more if you held onto me."

For the next forty minutes she bounced, swayed, squealed, and giggled her way up a mountain trail with her arms wrapped tight around Devin's waist.

He stopped at what felt like the top of the world, the vista beyond a patchwork of color from craggy snow-capped peaks to forests in varying shades of green to wildflower-dotted meadows. "Now, isn't this pretty," Devin said as he took off his helmet. "I think we've found our picnic spot, don't you?"

"It's fabulous." Jenna set her helmet beside his atop a boulder.

"Did you enjoy the ride?"

"I did. Much more than I expected to, to be honest. Riding a four-wheeler is a lot more fun than it looks."

"I know *I* enjoyed it. Feel free to hang onto me anytime, Sugar Cookie." He opened the ATV's storage compartment and removed their sack lunch and a thin tarp.

She snorted a laugh. "That's the silliest nickname."

"Hey, I like it. And it's totally appropriate." He spread out the tarp and gestured for her to sit down.

She passed out sandwiches and chips while he pulled bottled water from the storage space. They ate in silence, enjoying the peace of the place. When she finished her sandwich, she pulled the dessert she'd purchased from the bag—iced sugar cookies in the shape of a hammock. Devin laughed and polished off a third of the cookie in a single bite.

She stretched out her legs and leaned back with her weight resting on her elbows. "This has to be one of the most beautiful places I've ever been."

"Have you not done much traveling?"

"Until this road trip, no. I attended a symposium in London when I was in medical school, but since I adopted Reilly, trips have been limited."

"Wait until you see Bella Vita."

Jenna took a bite of her own cookie. She had not told him she'd make the trip. "Is it something in the water?"

"Excuse me?"

"You're not a lot different from those ladies who spent an hour pressuring me to become their doctor."

"Hey. Wait a minute. I'm not pregnant and I'm not asking you to be my doctor. I'm not opposed to playing doctor, mind you, but . . ."

A grin on her face, Jenna dropped her head back and

lifted her face toward the sun. "I'm not going to be pressured. I have enjoyed life on the road. It's really nice to work the hours I want to work. I don't make much money, but we don't need much money. I don't know that I'm ready to give this up."

"That's understandable." He took another bite of his cookie. "It's nice to check out from the hassles from time to time. I've done it myself."

"We have reservations at a campground in Wyoming beginning the week after Labor Day. I've never planned to stay here permanently."

"You went to school a long time to become not just a doctor, but a specialist."

In a warning tone, she said, "Don't try to education-shame me."

He made a zipping motion over his lips.

"How can I say no when this town is doing so much for me? How selfish is that? What kind of person does that make me? Those women have every right to lobby for their interests. And, the salary they threw out—whoa. I'm shocked they don't have obstetricians streaming over Sinner's Prayer Pass in hope of securing the job."

"May I ask a question that has nothing to do with shaming of any sort?"

"Okay."

"Why not stay? It's a great little town. You've already made friends here. Reilly has already made friends here. You can't remain on the road forever."

"I know." Jenna shoved to her feet. "But I don't make snap decisions. Even deciding to go on the road four months ago took me three days to decide. I think things through. I'm deliberate." She paced back and forth. "Everything has happened so fast. I've been dealing with this stalker for a year and a half. A year and a half! I can't

make a life-altering decision over tea and crumpets with
a room full of hormonal women."

"Okay. Okay, that's fair enough," Devin said.

"I have time to think about it. Even if I loved the idea
of establishing a practice in Eternity Springs, I couldn't
do anything about it yet. There's the little detail about my
license. Until I'm licensed to practice medicine in Colorado, I won't so much as tell anyone to take a Tylenol."

"You're right. You do have time to think about it. I just
wonder . . ."

When his voice trailed off, Jenna waited for him to finish his thought. He didn't, so she prodded, "You wonder
what?"

"It's nothing. How did you like your sandwich? Ham
and cheese, wasn't it? Are you a mustard and mayo girl,
or mustard only?"

She narrowed her eyes and repeated, "You wonder
what?"

He scooped up a rock from beyond the tarp, and threw
it out into the nothingness. "I wonder why your reaction
to the notion of staying in Eternity Springs is so intense.
Could it be that it has more to do with what you don't
want to do than what you do want?"

"I don't follow you."

"All indications suggest that the obsessive loon we're
chasing intersected your life in some way through your
work. I'm no psychologist, but it's understandable that
you'd be gun shy about hanging out your shingle once
again."

"You think I'm afraid to return to medicine?"

He shrugged. "In your shoes, that's probably how I'd
feel."

Jenna frowned. "That would be letting my enemy win."

"I don't think it's that black and white, but perhaps
something to consider as you think about what you want

to do when this is over. Now, how about we change the subject to something more pleasant? Do you know how beautiful you look with that gorgeous hair of yours on fire with sunshine and roses in your cheeks from the ride? One thing's missing, though. Your lips need a little puff and shine to them."

He leaned over and took her mouth in a slow, sweet kiss that scrambled her pulse and heated her blood. Her arms lifted and wrapped around his neck, and he pulled her onto his lap. She was lost, drowning in him, when suddenly, he set her aside with a curse. "This is insane. We have to stop doing this in public.

Even as the protest formed on her lips, she heard the chug of approaching engines. A moment later, five ATVs, each carrying two people, rounded a curve in the trail. The lead vehicle pulled to a stop behind Devin's four wheeler and as the riders disembarked, Devin asked Jenna, "Ready to go?"

"Yes."

Devin helped her to her feet and they exchanged greetings with the newcomers—tourists from Texas riding ATVs rented from Refresh—while packing up their picnic supplies. Jenna pulled on her helmet, fixed the chinstrap, and then wrapped her arms around Devin's waist for the trip down the mountain. The ride down was as exhilarating as the trip up. Nevertheless, Jenna was unable to lose herself in the activity like she had on the ascent.

Had Devin hit the proverbial nail on the head? Was she afraid? Was that why she was so conflicted by the notion of making Eternity Springs her home?

Perhaps. Something certainly had her hesitant to buy into the idea, despite the fact that the town had so much to offer. Really, in many ways it was a perfect solution. She and Reilly couldn't be road rats forever. They liked it here. The outdoors lifestyle it offered suited them. They both already had friends here. Once the stalker threat was eliminated, why wouldn't they settle down?

Reilly could go to school. He could join a Scout troop. He could play baseball and basketball and soccer.

And you? What will you do if you put down roots in Eternity Springs? Sit around and wait for Devin Murphy to pay a visit home from Australia?

Ding Ding Ding Ding. The ATV hit a dip hard and her stomach followed suit.

Jenna closed her eyes. That's what this was all about. She was already halfway in love with him.

Which was crazy. She didn't believe in love at first sight. True love didn't happen in a week. She couldn't be in love with him. In lust, sure. Definitely in lust. She had a serious case of the hots for him. She would have had sex with him last night had they been somewhere private.

They had tonight. They had the next two weeks.

She'd been planning to have an affair with him. A nice short two-week fantasy, then he'd be off to Oz and she'd roll on down the road. But if she had an affair with Devin, she couldn't stay in Eternity Springs. It was one thing to love 'em and leave 'em and something else entirely to love 'em and run into his mother in the grocery store.

This was his world, even if he only occupied it for a short time on rare occasions. Eternity Springs was his mother. His father. His sister and brother. She knew her own heart well enough. If she had an affair with Devin, feeling like she did about him already, she'd be setting herself up for real heartbreak.

She couldn't sleep with Devin Murphy and make a home in Eternity Springs. So until she made her deliberate, well-considered decision, she couldn't sleep with Devin Murphy at all.

Her heart twisted. Her eyes filled with moisture. While she couldn't remember the exact moment, she had a sneaking suspicion that this was how she'd felt when she learned that Santa Claus wasn't real.

Devin stepped into his parents' house that evening a happy man. He had an excellent bottle of Chianti in one arm, a beautiful, smart, sexy woman on the other, and the promise of homemade lasagna on the menu. Sarah would serve tiramisu for dessert and Devin planned to eat his share, but he intended to have his real dessert upon returning to the rental house. Hopefully it would be an early evening.

He had clean sheets on his bed and a bottle of champagne chilling in the fridge.

"Hello, 'rents," he called as he walked through the living room. "We're here."

He strode into the kitchen expecting to see his mother at the stove or the island or even in the depths of the large walk-in pantry. She wasn't there. "Mom?"

Jenna touched his arm and nodded toward the floor, where the sight of a broken wine glass and a puddle of red wine spilled across on the floor brought him up short. He took a step toward the glass. "Mom? Dad?"

Michael burst through the door, his expression wreathed in fear, and started babbling. "Devin. Mom fell down. For no reason. She just dropped. Boom! Now Mom and Dad are fighting because Dad wants to call the ambulance, and Mom says no, that she's fine. But Dad doesn't believe her."

"Where are they?"

"He carried her to their bedroom. She said if he called an ambulance she'd never forgive him."

Devin was walking toward the stairs before his brother finished talking. He was halfway up the stairs when Cam exited the master suite. He stopped Devin by holding his palm out. His gaze went directly to Jenna. "Will you come talk to her, please?"

"Of course." Jenna started for the stairs.

Cam continued. "Just convince her to let me take her to the clinic. This has gone on way too long. I think she's scared because our friend Mac Timberlake had a serious health scare last year, and it's made us aware of our mortality."

"Let me see what's going on."

"Can I get you something?" Devin asked as she climbed past him up the stairs. "Your black bag?"

"I'm not her doctor, Devin."

"It won't hurt you to have it, though, right?" Cam asked.

Devin nodded. "It's an emergency. Is your bag at the trailer or did you bring it to the house?"

"Fine. It's in my bedroom closet at the house. A blue nylon messenger bag."

"I'll be back in five."

Devin flew from the house. His hand trembled as he twisted the key in his truck's ignition, and his tires spun as he gunned the gas pulling away from the house. *Mom. Mom. Mom.* He said her name like a litany. She couldn't be sick. She couldn't! This couldn't happen again. Michael was just a kid. He still needed her. *I'm* still a kid. *Her* kid. God wouldn't be that cruel as to take a second mother from him, would He?

"Don't go there," he muttered. "Do not go there. That's bad juju."

Fear rolled through his belly like an ocean wave. A stomach bug. What sort of stomach bug lasts this long? And comes and goes? She'd been sick ever since he came home, and what had he worried about the most? Not catching it. *Selfish bastard.*

Mom. Mom. Mom. Mom. She can't leave us. She can't. She can't. Please, God. Don't take her. Not again.

At the house, he ran to Jenna's bedroom and threw open the closet door. The bag was on a shelf at eye level.

He grabbed it and ran, and was back at his parents' house within minutes.

"I'll take it up," Cam said, meeting him at the door. He took the stairs two at a time climbing to the master suite.

With his task accomplished, Devin suddenly felt adrift and alone and . . . hell . . . abandoned. Then Michael slipped his hand into Devin's. Devin forced a smile as he gazed down at his little brother, and in the boy's terrified blue eyes, he saw himself. *You've got me, Mikey. You'll always have me.*

"I'm scared, Dev."

"It'll be okay, Michael. I believe that. I really do."

The master bedroom door opened and closed. A grim-faced Cam came down the stairs. "How is she?" Devin asked.

"I don't know. She was in the bathroom. Your doc lady wouldn't tell me a damn thing and I can't read her face, but I don't think she's calling an ambulance. She said they'd be down in a few minutes, and your mother asked us to set the table and toss the salad."

"Toss the salad!" Devin exclaimed.

Michael scampered toward the kitchen. "I'll set the table."

Cam dragged a hand down his jawline. He looked like he'd aged five years in the past five minutes. "Thanks, buddy. Devin, would you clean up that mess on the kitchen floor, please?"

"Sure, Dad. I'll do anything you need."

"In that case, maybe pour me a bourbon too."

Upstairs, Sarah Murphy stepped out of her bathroom in a zombie-like daze, her complexion as pale as the Murphy Mountain snowcap. "You were right," she croaked.

"Yes," Jenna replied. "I know."

"This can't be!" Sarah whined. "I'm old! I'm going to be a grandmother! I had hot flashes. Mood swings. Weight gain. I thought it was menopause. It's supposed to be menopause!"

"Perimenopause, and you'd be surprised at how many surprise pregnancies we see in women over forty. People get lax with birth control."

"Not me! Not since I was a teenager. Been there, done that, and had a bouncing baby girl as a result of it. I learned my lesson. Cam and I always . . . well . . . except . . ."

"It only takes once." Jenna's mouth twisted wryly. "That was some snowstorm. At Easter, wasn't it?"

"Yes. An Easter blizzard. An Easter miracle. Oh my. I have to sit down." Sarah sank onto the edge of her bed. "Oh my. A baby. Another baby. *And* a grandchild." She looked up at Jenna with a wild look in her eyes. "If Cam dyes his hair and starts wearing turtlenecks, I'll lose my mind. I need to throw away the sleeping pills right now!"

"Sarah, what are you talking about?"

"It's *Father of the Bride Part II*. The movie. I'm married to Steve Martin."

"Ah. Yes."

"You know, sometimes he even sort of looks like Steve Martin. Well, Steve Martin when the movie was made. Young Steve Martin. Except, Cam is old. Like me. We're in our forties! That's too old to be having another baby."

"Mother Nature didn't think so, obviously."

"Oh my." Sarah waved her hand in front of her face. "Oh my. What am I going to tell Cam?"

"Not to shop for turtlenecks?" Jenna suggested, trying to stifle a grin.

Sarah's eyes widened, then she burst out in a laugh. The tinge of hysteria didn't worry Jenna. Neither did the tears pooling in Sarah's eyes. Many women cried upon learning of impending motherhood—sometimes in joy, sometimes in despair. Hormones running amok combined with the realization of a major life event tended to bring emotions close to the surface.

But regarding emotions . . . "Your family is worried. Shall I ask Cam to come up so you can share your news?"

"Yes, thanks. No, wait. Maybe I'll go down. Tell them all at once. Which should I do?"

"It's totally up to you."

"He'll have questions. I'll be a high-risk pregnancy because of my age, won't I? When Nic Callahan was pregnant with the twins, she was high risk and she had to go to Denver to be near doctors and a state-of-the-art medical facility. But that was before the new clinic was built. And you're here now. You'll have your license back. You'll stay, Jenna, won't you? You'll stay in Eternity Springs?"

Jenna's heart gave a little wrench. She thought about Devin and the cozy rental house and clean sheets on her bed. She thought about two weeks without Reilly under foot.

She thought about Gabi Brogan and Savannah Turner and Lili Callahan and Shannon Garrett. She thought of Devin's sister Lori.

"You will be my obstetrician, won't you, Jenna?" Sarah asked.

Sarah, Devin's mother. His beloved mother, who had been so kind to Jenna and Reilly. This whole town had been a gift to her. A gift. In her mind's eye, she saw herself pulling back red tissue paper to reveal Celeste's Christmas wishing tree snow globe.

She made her deliberate, well-considered decision with only a twinge of regret. "Of course I will, Sarah. I'll be honored to be your doctor."

Sarah filled her cheeks with air then blew it out in a puff. "Okay, then. Let's do this. Let's go downstairs and give my husband something different to worry about. You know, he thinks I have a tumor. That's his default whenever something is wrong." With a snicker, she added, "I guess, in a way, he's right this time."

"I probably wouldn't use that terminology tonight," Jenna suggested.

"Probably not."

Sarah paused in front of the bedroom mirror to fuss with her hair. In the past few minutes, color had returned to her cheeks, and Jenna thought she was as pretty an expectant mother as she'd ever seen.

Cam paced at the foot of the stairs, and his head jerked up when he heard them coming. His forest green eyes lasered onto Sarah as he murmured, "Honey?"

"I'm fine," she said as descended the staircase. "I'm not sick, Cam."

"There's no tumor?"

"No." Sarah snorted and glanced over her shoulder toward Jenna. "See, I told you so."

"Then what's wrong? I still think you need to go to the clinic. They have night hours, you know. Why have you been so sick? This isn't normal."

Devin exited the kitchen and looked at his mother with an assessing gaze, then focused on Jenna. Sarah reached the bottom of the stairs. "Actually, it is. It's totally normal and I should have realized it. After all, I've done this twice before."

The furrows in Cam's brow deepened. "Done what?"

Sarah rested her hand on his chest and smiled up at him, an impish light in her violet eyes. Their gazes locked. She waited.

The color drained from Cam's face. The crystal highball glass he held slipped from his hand and shattered on the wood floor. He croaked, "You're kidding."

"What?" Devin asked.

"Tell me you're kidding," Cam added.

Sarah shook her head. "Nope. I'm not kidding."

"Are you okay, Mommy?" Michael asked.

"I'm fine, Michael. Watch your feet. Don't step on the glass."

"What are you talking about?!" Devin demanded.

Cam reached out and swiped the glass out of Devin's hand. He chugged back the contents and said, "She's not kidding."

"About what? She hasn't said a damn thing!"

"Don't curse, Devin. I'm pregnant! We're having another baby."

"A baby!" Michael exclaimed. "Cool."

Devin's jaw dropped. "But . . . but . . . you're too old."

It was just the observation Cam needed to hear to bring his world back into focus. He pulled his gaze away from his wife long enough to shoot his son a smirk.

"Apparently not." Then he pulled Sarah into his arms and kissed her thoroughly before adding, "This grandpa still has game."

Chapter Sixteen

Five days after his mother's big surprise, Devin still had trouble accepting that his parents' sex life was playing so much havoc with his own. The mood hadn't been right for him to make a move on Jenna that night, so they'd said their good nights and retired to their respective rooms. The following morning, she'd cooked him breakfast and proceeded to ruin his appetite by explaining that barring any unforeseen problems, she intended to keep the promise she'd made to his mother and remain in Eternity Springs, at least through Christmas and possibly for good.

Because of that, she didn't think it was advisable to start an affair.

"It would be awkward, Devin. If I'm trying to make a life here for Reilly and me, if these people are going to be my friends and neighbors, I don't want to open myself up to slut-shaming. If we don't sleep together, I can hold my head up and speak with truthfulness and authority when I deny that you and I have something more than friendship here."

He'd wanted to protest, but he understood her argument. One of the drawbacks to small-town living was that everybody knew everybody's business. That said, just because he sympathized with her point didn't mean he had to like it. Just because he tried to ignore the whole Santa bell-ringing revelation about finding a father for Reilly didn't mean it didn't slither and shake its rattles in his mind. He'd whined a little and made an attempt to change her mind, but his heart wasn't in it. He knew she was right. So every night they retired to their respective rooms and he yearned—and cussed the very thought of blizzards.

On this Tuesday morning at his mother's and sister's urging, they were on their way to participate in a mid-morning yoga class. Devin might have preferred a hard run or, let's face it, a bout of athletic sex—but he had nothing against yoga. He needed physical activity and it was better than nothing. Though he'd made a mistake lining up behind Jenna. There wasn't anything downward about his dog when she stuck that sweet little butt in the air right in front of him. He was damn glad that he'd worn a long T-shirt over loose-fitting gym shorts or he'd have embarrassed himself in front of his mom and sister.

When class ended, the prego parade congregated around Jenna. She prefaced her answers to their questions with her standard line, "I am a doctor, but I'm not *your* doctor and I'm not licensed to practice in Colorado." That didn't stop anyone from trying to pin her down. When the hen party finally broke up and they left the studio, Jenna bubbled with happiness. Devin gave a crooked smile and said, "You are such a fake."

"What?"

"You tried to say you were happy doing your online job. I eavesdropped on you this morning as you were taking your calls and I listened to you just now. Sugar, you are meant to work with patients. You're a natural."

They walked half a block before she responded. "I've missed it. I didn't realize how much until today."

They had exited the studio with Lori and his mother

and walked north on Aspen. Their plan was to spend an hour or two doing yard work at his mom's. Or, as Jenna happily called it, playing in the flowerbeds. He had discovered the previous day that she had a thing for digging in the dirt, and he knew his parents would be happy to indulge her. Mom could never have enough posies.

They stopped at the local lumberyard, which kept a nursery and a landscaping section stocked during the spring and summer. Jenna picked out garden gloves and shoes and tools, and then debated over flowerpots and annuals as a gift for his parents' patio. "Do you think Sarah would like this rustic-wood look, or is the clay pot better?"

"Which do you like best?"

"I like the clay, but—"

"Get it. From what I've seen, you and my mom have similar tastes."

It was true. Jenna shared a lot of common interests with his mother. She didn't bake, the only mark against her that Devin could see, but the two of them could go on for hours about the pros and cons of youth sports and decorating trends and movie soundtracks and technology rules for their boys.

Sarah and Lori were as close as a mother and daughter could be, but there were some parts of their relationship he'd never understood. They could make each other bristle with nothing more than a look. War had started over a single word.

For them both to be pregnant at the same time . . . whoa. *Dad might want to move back to Australia with me.*

And yet, a part of Devin regretted that he wouldn't be around to watch. How would his parents be with their first grandchild? What sort of relationship would Lori develop with her youngest sibling?

What will mine be like with the new kid? Will I know him at all?

The ringing of his cell phone jerked Devin from thoughts that had turned brooding. He checked the number. The Yellow Kitchen? Who was calling him from the restaurant?

"We didn't have a lunch date I forgot about, did we?" he asked Jenna as he thumbed the green dot and brought the phone up to his ear. "Hello?"

"Devin, it's Ali. It looks like we just had a bite on your plan. I assume Jenna didn't actually place an order for thirty-four pizzas to be delivered to the medical clinic?"

Devin halted mid-stride. "Hot damn. Phone order or online?"

"Online."

"Even better. Thanks for the heads-up, Ali. I'll call the team."

Ending the call, he met Jenna's gaze. "It's on."

"What happened?" She covered her mouth with a hand as he explained. "Thirty-four? Why thirty-four? Why any of this? Oh." She waved her hand in front of her face. "I need to sit down. This is actually happening. Oh, wow. I think I'm going to faint."

"Don't do that!" Devin turned a large flowerpot upside down just in time to provide the seat she needed. "Around here, people will think you're pregnant. Put your head between your knees, Jenna." He patted her back. "It's okay."

"Make sure that Chase gets the news. I know Reilly is safe and happy and having fun at camp, but please, make sure everyone at the Rocking L knows what's happened."

"I will. I'll start making calls right now if you promise you won't topple off your flower pot and crack your head on the floor."

"I promise." She breathed deeply and exhaled loudly once, twice, three times. "Why thirty-four?"

"It's a curious number. Think about it, Sugar. Maybe there's a clue there."

Jack Davenport made the same suggestion later that day when the team gathered at Daniel's office to discuss the development. "If you think of anything at all, even the slightest possibility of a connection, reach out to me or Daniel. You never know what seemingly obscure bit of information will be key."

"I will," Jenna vowed.

Jack turned to the Callahans and said, "I trust that with today's contact, your worker bees are already hard at work?"

"Absolutely," Mark said. "Our best hackers . . . I mean . . . professionals are on the case."

"Good. Daniel, you want to summarize where we stand with our guys on the ground?"

"Sure. We've had our three persons of interest under surveillance since the fifth. I've let our guys know that we've had movement on our end, though I expect since we're dealing with online contact, your hackers will be the ones who hit pay dirt."

"Professionals," Mark repeated, giving Jenna a wink.

Daniel continued, "I'll admit that a part of me figured you'd never hear another word out of this guy. The fact that he's continued his pursuit this long suggests that this guy's mind is seriously disturbed. I still feel confident in your safety, Jenna, and I have absolutely no doubts about Reilly's, but it's not the time to get lax. Don't go anywhere in public without Devin or Cam or one of the rest of us."

"She won't," Devin declared. "I'll make sure of it."

The rest of that day and all the next they waited for something to happen. The phone didn't ring. Pizzas didn't arrive. The deliveryman didn't show up with dozens of packages. By the third day, Jenna's nerves stretched tight as a guitar string. Devin's nerves weren't exactly loosey-goosey either. His time in Eternity Springs was quickly drawing to a close. He wanted this stalker situation settled so he could leave in good conscience, but at the same time, he didn't want his time with Jenna to end.

He *really* didn't want his time with Jenna to end.

Five days after the pizza order, Jack called another team meeting and this time they met up at Eagle's Way, where Jack had electronics that allowed the Callahans to illustrate the points they were trying to make.

Mark Callahan led off the meeting with disturbing news. "We got bubkes. I do not believe it, because our guys are seriously good at what they do, but this guy is obviously no amateur. We will track him down eventually. Of that I have no doubt. But it's going to take some time or another event for us to find him. Unless you have something new for us, Daniel?"

"What I have is bubkes part two." He met Jenna's gaze with an apologetic smile. "We've basically confirmed your original investigator's conclusions. Based on a thorough examination of their records combined with both electronic and physical surveillance, we eliminated the lawyer and the songwriter as suspects almost immediately. I wanted to finger the surgeon, believe me. The guy is a total prick. Two more women have accused him of sexual harassment since you left Nashville, Jenna. However, we can't find anything that suggests he's our guy. So we're back to square one."

Jenna closed her eyes. Devin muttered a curse beneath his breath before saying, "This totally sucks."

"I won't argue the point," Jack observed. "That said, we knew that might be the case. Daniel and I talked it over before you all arrived, and we want to come at this from another direction. Perhaps this isn't about Jenna, after all, but about Reilly."

"Reilly!" Cam exclaimed. "I get that kids grow up fast these days and cyberbullying is a thing, but at this age? Seriously?"

"My questions are about his biological father. We only brushed on him during our initial conversation, Jenna. What can you tell us about . . . ?" He checked his notes. "Steven Caldwell?"

"Oh. Well . . ." Jenna took a moment to gather her thoughts. "I guess it's possible. At this point, anything is possible, isn't it? I only met him once. Actually, we didn't officially meet. I saw him once when I testified against him in court. Reilly's mother was a patient of mine. Early on in her pregnancy she confessed to me that the father didn't want the baby. He wanted her to end the pregnancy, but she refused to do it. She was eight months pregnant when he started beating her. She went into labor and delivered three weeks early."

"Did he kill her?" Mark Callahan asked, his expression carved in granite.

"No. She called a lawyer and filed for divorce before leaving the hospital. Reilly's father was charged and convicted of assault and a few other crimes . . . I don't recall exactly what. He went to jail. I honestly don't recall what his actual sentence was, but I remember the lawyer warned her that he'd probably be out before Reilly's first birthday. He signed away parental rights and as far as I know, he never once came to see Reilly."

"What about child support?" Daniel asked.

"She came from money and didn't need it. We stayed friends. She was happy. Loved motherhood. She was diagnosed with pancreatic cancer when Reilly was eighteen months old. Shortly thereafter, she asked me to be his guardian."

"Grandparents?" Daniel asked.

"None on either side. No extended family on her side. I honestly don't know about his."

Daniel looked pointedly at Mark Callahan, who opened his computer and started typing.

They quizzed Jenna at length, and by the time the meeting broke up, Jenna was obviously exhausted. Devin wasn't feeling all that chipper himself. When they climbed into his truck for the trip back to town and Jenna reminded him of the stop he'd intended to make, he considered calling it off.

"Maybe we should skip it."

Jenna gave him a hard look. "You're not going to tell Reilly goodbye before you leave?"

He tightened his grip on the steering wheel. "Maybe I won't leave."

"What are you talking about? Of course you'll leave."

"Well, I'll go to Mitch's wedding, but maybe instead of going on to Cairns, I'll come back here."

"For heaven's sake, why?"

"I'm not comfortable leaving before your stalker is caught."

"Devin, you have a business to run. You can't put your life on hold like that."

"The business can manage without me a little longer, and I don't look at it as putting my life on hold. Just because I like to wander the world doesn't mean I don't keep my word. I promised to protect you and that's what I'll do. I don't bail. That's not who I am."

Jenna folded her arms. "Welcome to the nineteen-fifties where the little lady really needs a big strong man to protect her."

"Now, Jenna."

"No! Stop it. You know, I wish this bastard would come after me. I'm not afraid of that. I took self-defense classes after Alan Snelling started harassing me. I'll put him down and make it hurt."

"Good. I hope you do. But what will you do if an FBI agent shows up to arrest you for money-laundering or child porn?"

"What?" she screeched.

"Can you definitely claim that someone who thinks doxxing and swatting are good ideas wouldn't take it a step further? What if he created a digital trail that ties you into a real crime? Or some dark web scenario that gets some real bad actors after you? I can imagine you being handcuffed and swept off to a secret room full of rubber hoses and an interrogator named Hans Gruber."

She blinked once. "A *Die Hard* reference? You're bringing up *Die Hard*?"

He shrugged. "It's my favorite Christmas show."

She burst out with a laugh, though it was filled with tension rather than joy. "What kind of man are you that you'll change your life plans so drastically for a woman you barely know, a woman who isn't even sleeping with you?"

"Yeah, that last part is dodgy, I'll admit. But the rest of it . . ." He shrugged. "I can't do anything different. I don't want to do anything different. I'm trusting my instincts on this one."

"But what if they still don't find him?"

"I'm trusting Daniel and Jack and the Callahans on that."

"Okay, so what if they find the stalker while you're at your friend's wedding?"

"While *we* are at the wedding. You're coming with me."

"I can't. I won't. Look, all along I've assumed that the stalker focused on me, but the idea that Reilly's biological father might be involved changes everything. I still believe Reilly is safe at camp, but I can't travel thousands of miles away if there's any possibility that he's the stalker's target."

"Fair enough. However, you shouldn't underestimate the team. If Steven Caldwell isn't involved, they'll eliminate him fast. That question could well be solved before it's time to leave for the island."

Jenna shrugged. "Nevertheless, that's not the issue at hand. If the team solves my problem while you're in the Caribbean, you won't come back here, which brings me back to my original question. Are you going to leave town without telling my son goodbye?"

He drummed his fingers on the console between them. No, he couldn't do that. But dang it, he didn't want to see the boy right now. "Here's the truth, Jenna. The story you told about his prick of a father has my stomach churning. How could anyone with a heart act that way?"

"I don't consider Steven Caldwell to be Reilly's father. He's a sperm donor. That's all. Reilly doesn't have a father."

"Which is why he asked me to bring him one for Christmas," Devin said glumly. "Look, I'm afraid if I go see him right now, I'll take one look at him and start bawling like a baby. That's not how I want Reilly to remember me. I'm a tough guy."

She gave him a tender smile. "You're Santa Claus."

"Hey, he doesn't know that. I have to keep up my rep."

Jenna reached across the console and gave his forearm a squeeze. "You'll manage, Murphy. I know you will. I believe."

He gave her a sidelong glance and a doubtful smirk.

"We told Chase to expect the visit and he might well have told Reilly."

"Okay. Okay. We'll go up to the Rocking L. But if I start to blubber, I expect you to cover for me. I think—"

He broke off when his cell phone rang, and a glance at

the screen revealed Jack Davenport's number. Devin accepted the call. "Hey, Jack."

"Devin, is Jenna with you?"

"Sitting right beside me. You're on speaker."

"Good. I thought she'd want to know what we've learned ASAP. Steven Caldwell isn't our guy."

Devin shot Jenna a quick *I told you so* look. "Oh, yeah?"

"He's dead."

Jenna's eyes rounded and she covered her mouth with her hands. Devin pulled off the road and parked. "What happened?"

He expected to hear that the bastard had been knifed in prison or OD'd on crack. Jack surprised him. "He settled in a small town in California following his release from jail. Worked in a hardware store and joined the volunteer fire department. He was killed fighting a wildfire the summer before last. He's credited with saving three lives."

"You're certain you have the right Steven Caldwell?" Jenna asked.

"We're positive," Jack replied, his tone gentle. He provided further details about what the team had learned about Reilly's biological father and, when Jenna had no further questions, ended the call after giving his reassurance that the search would continue.

Devin did not immediately resume their drive. Instead, he studied Jenna closely. Tears had pooled in her eyes. "Sugar, you okay?"

"Yes. I just . . . whew." She exhaled a heavy breath then wiped the corners of her eyes with the pads of her fingers. "It's so sad. He's lost both parents."

"*Biological* parents. He has you, the lucky little boy."

A smile flickered across her lips. "It's just a lot to absorb. I've worried about this in the past. I know he'll ask about his parents someday, and I worried about what I would say about Steven Caldwell. Now I'll have something good to say, won't I? He saved three lives. That's a good thing."

"Yes, that's a very good thing." Devin leaned over and kissed her lightly on the cheek. "And you are a very good person, Jenna Stockton."

"Thank you."

Devin checked the traffic, then pulled out onto the road. They made the rest of the drive in comfortable silence, and it was only when the log structures of the summer camp came into view that Devin posed the question burning in his brain. "So, are you going to tell Reilly that you'll be away for a few days? You'll come to Bella Vita with me?"

She waited until he'd parked in a visitor space and switched off the engine to respond. "Yes. Yes, I'll go to Bella Vita with you. As long as we can find room in your sleigh, that is. How booked are flights to Bella Vita Isle as a rule? You said quite a few people from Eternity Springs are attending this wedding?"

Devin pursed his lips and considered the question. Because it was still tourist season in Eternity Springs, which made it hard for his parents to get away for long, they'd decided to go down just for the weekend. He'd planned to fly commercial with them, and he didn't worry about there being an open seat for Jenna. But Flynn Brogan was flying down tomorrow in his Gulfstream.

"I have an idea." He reached for his phone, scrolled through the contacts, and made a call. "Hey, Flynn, Devin here. Are you guys still heading to BV tomorrow?"

"We are."

"You're flying your Gulfstream, I assume?

"Yep. Sure am. Do you need a ride?"

"We do. Plans have changed, and Jenna Stockton and

I would like to get to the island a couple days ahead. Do you have room for a couple of tagalongs?"

"Sure, we'd be happy to have you join us. Gabi's clan is flying down with us, so fair warning, my wife and Savannah may well talk the doctor's ear off with pregnancy questions."

"I'm sure she won't mind."

"Will Jenna want a ride back on Sunday?"

"Actually, we both need a ride back on Sunday. I'm extending my stay in Eternity Springs for a bit."

Devin glanced at Jenna, who was gaping at him in surprise. "When and where do we meet you?"

They made plans, and then Devin ended the call. He grinned at her. "We're all set."

"Flying in a private jet. Tomorrow. Not Friday. That's a long weekend, Devin."

"Yeah, doesn't it sound great? I am ready to be back on the water. Which reminds me. I don't have a boat there anymore. Cursed hurricane." He called a friend on Bella Vita who owed him a big favor and made arrangements for a boat, which banished the last vestiges of the black mood that had started sucking on him as he listened to Jenna speak of Reilly's father.

Devin whistled cheerily as they exited the truck and went in search of Chase. They found him on the phone speaking to the parent of a camper who'd changed his mind about wanting to participate in a hike into the national forest for overnight tent camping. The camp needed a signed permission slip before the boy would be allowed to go.

When the call ended, Chase greeted Devin with a handshake and Jenna with a hug. "Any word on your license? When you'll be official? Lori likes her doctor in Gunnison well enough, but we're all anxious to have a local specialist."

"Jack told me he's been pulling some strings and maybe by next week I'll be good to go."

"If anyone can pull strings, it's Jack Davenport."

"So, is Reilly behaving himself? How is he doing with Sinatra?"

"He's doing great. The puppy has been so helpful. He uses Sinatra's needs to verbalize his own insecurities, so his counselor is making real progress with him. The fear we saw in him those first couple of days hardly makes an appearance now."

"That's so good. I'm so relieved." Jenna exhaled a heavy sigh. "I believed camp would be good for him, but you always have a niggling worry."

"I'll give you one warning. If you've come up here expecting him to want to spend much time with you, you are headed for disappointment. Reilly is a busy boy."

"Nothing could make me happier than to have him snub me," Jenna responded.

Chase checked his watch and then his clipboard. "He's due at the stables in fifteen minutes. Why don't you meet him at the bonfire site? You know where it is, Devin. I'll message his counselor to send him on. Does he know you were planning to visit?"

"No. Not unless you said something about it."

"I did not. I'll send for him now and I'll make sure he knows there's no emergency."

Five minutes later, Jenna sat on one of the logs set in an octagon around the fire pit. Devin had picked up a stick and was drawing in the dirt when Reilly came running up. He wore jeans and the red Rocking L uniform T-shirt and ball cap. He gave her a hug and then asked, "Mom, why are you here? Is something wrong?"

"No, everything's fine."

"Did they find the bad man?"

"Not yet, but they're looking hard for him."

"Okay. That's good. Look, I don't have much time. I have to go to the stables so we can go horseback riding."

"Okay, we won't keep you. I just wanted see how you were doing and tell you that I'm going to go with the Murphys and some of our other Eternity Springs friends to an out-of-town wedding this weekend. We'll leave to-morrow, and I'll be back on Sunday."

"Okay. That's cool. On Friday we're going to go hike up in the mountains and go camp in a tent for two nights. Sinatra is going to stay here. Not all the kids want to go, so Miss Cheryl will be here and Sinatra is going to stay with her while I'm gone. I think he'll be fine, don't you, Mom?"

"I think he'll be absolutely fine."

"All right. Well, I better go." He started edging away. "Today I get to ride Bubba. That's the horse's name. Bubba."

"Whoa there, cowboy," Devin said past the lump of emotion that had formed in his throat. "Don't go yet. I gotta say . . . I need to . . ."

Reilly peered up at him, expectant and impatient. "What?"

Damn. Devin dragged his hand across his mouth. "Say goodbye. See, once we find the bad guy, I'm going to have to go back to work. So it's possible, by the time you come home from camp I'll be gone.

"Oh." The boy's expression fell. "That makes me sad, Devin."

"Yeah, I know. It makes me sad too. But you know, we can always talk on the phone. You can call me whenever you want."

"We can FaceTime."

"Yep. We sure can. I can tell you this right now. I'm going to want to hear all about this tent-camping trip you're about to take. I'll bet that's a real adventure."

"Yep. We have bear spray to carry."

"Always be prepared." Devin went down on one knee and held out his arms. "C'mere and give me a hug, Reilly."

The boy ran into the man's embrace. "I'll give you a bear hug!"

Devin closed his eyes and gritted his teeth against the emotion rolling through him. Then he growled like a bear and squeezed Reilly tight. When the boy giggled and wiggled, Devin released him and stood. "Take care of yourself, Reilly James Stockton."

"I will. I gotta go now. Bye, Devin. Bye, Mom."

"Wait!" Jenna called. "I need a hug."

Like any healthy, happy eight-year-old boy, Reilly rolled his eyes in disgust. "Mo-om."

Reilly gave her a fast hug, then pulled away and headed toward the stables in a run. Just before the path took him out of sight, he stopped, turned around and waved. "I love you!"

"Love you too, buddy!" Jenna called.

Devin swallowed hard. His eyes stung. His heart twisted. Softly, he said, "I love you, Reilly."

Damned if he didn't mean it.

Chapter Seventeen

Bella Vita Isle was a feast for the eyes, an emerald island awash in tropical flowers and surrounded by a turquoise sea. Colorful birds flittered from tree to tree, bloom to bloom, and as Jenna sat on a porch swing watching one bird the size of a robin sporting a bright blue breast, shocking yellow neckband, and fire-engine red crest perched on the weathervane atop the house next door, she felt a little like Cinderella at the ball. Flying on a private jet, vacationing at a beachfront cottage, and now motoring about the Caribbean on a private boat? "Dr. Stockton, you're not in a trailer park anymore."

They were staying in the house that had been Devin's home. The darling three-bedroom, two-bath structure had sustained only minor damage during Danielle, and rather than sell it when he moved to Australia, he'd chosen to repair it and market it as a vacation rental.

Jenna found it easy to picture Devin living here. Although he'd removed all personal items from the property, the house was decorated in a nautical theme that included photos of the vessels he'd lost to Hurricane Danielle—*The Office*, the *Lark,* and the *Sunny Luck*. Moored at the marina on the opposite end of the island, the boats had taken a direct hit from the dirty side of the storm.

The wistful look on his face when he talked about them made her want to give him a comforting hug. She didn't do it. Jenna was being extra careful not to touch him too familiarly.

They hadn't kissed since she'd made the decision to stay in Eternity Springs. They rarely touched. However, sexual awareness remained a constant hum in the background whenever they were together, and as a result, her nerves remained strung tight. More than once she'd caught him watching her with that heavy-lidded gaze that spoke more loudly than words ever could. More than once, he'd caught her at it too.

They didn't acknowledge the tension by either word or deed, but it was always there. She had thought that getting away from town and the stress of the stalker hunt along with being in a new setting might ease the edginess. Yeah, right. And tomorrow she'd be able to play a Beethoven concerto on the piano when she could barely manage "Chopsticks" today. *Stupid. Stupid. Stupid.*

It didn't help the situation that during the two days they'd spent here on Bella Vita, she'd seen Devin in a new and even more intriguing light. He was in his element in the tropics. He was at home on a boat. Yesterday, they'd joined one of his friend's fishing tour operations for a half-day trip. Despite being a paying customer, he'd taken on the role of a crewmember, assisting and advising the person in the fighting chair, rigging the outriggers, and baiting the hooks. Jenna had caught two fish—a wahoo and a yellowfin—and while she'd enjoyed the experience, she thought he'd had more fun than she.

Last night, they'd met a large group of his friends at a local restaurant for dinner. She'd met the bride-to-be and the groom, Mitch, who'd told her stories about Devin that had her helpless with laughter. Toward the end of the evening, when she'd stepped outside to get a breath of air, Mitch had followed her out. "Ya like our mon Oz, don'tcha now?" he'd observed, his voice heavy with the lilt of the Caribbean. "Ya really like him."

"Devin has been very kind to me and my son."

"Kind, eh? He's a good man. He told me about being your boy's Santa Claus. Him, he loves the little ones. 'Tis not right what that evil witch Anya"—he paused and spat on the ground—"did to him."

"Anya?"

Mitch tilted his head in a considering manner. "Not my story to tell. Ask him, pretty lady. You should understand why he will not toss an anchor."

Jenna had been digesting that remark moments later when Devin came outside looking for her, and the conversation turned to the couple's upcoming honeymoon in Paris.

"Evil witch Anya," Jenna murmured, wondering for the dozenth time since last night just who Anya was and what she'd done to Devin.

The thought evaporated when the bird spread his wings and flew away at the same time the sound of an approaching car engine reached her ears. Devin was back.

Jenna had returned from a shopping trip to the local market with Gabi Brogan, Savannah Turner, Hope Romano, and Maggie Romano to find a note from Devin saying he'd gone down to the marina to ready things for their excursion and would return shortly. She'd relished the time alone, but seeing him climb out of the Jeep he'd rented for the duration of their stay nevertheless sent her heart going pit-a-pat.

"Hey there, Sugar. Did you and the girls have fun shopping?"

"We did. I bought way too much, but I blame it all on Gabi because she assured me that I don't have a luggage limit since I'm flying back to Eternity Springs with the Brogans."

"Bet I can guess one of your purchases. A mandolin."

"How did you know?"

"Last week at dinner I heard you tell Mom that you wanted Reilly to learn to play a musical instrument. I knew that if you saw them at the market they would catch your eye. They're fabulous, aren't they? The man who makes them is a real artist."

Jenna nodded. "I'm going to save it and give it to Reilly for Christmas."

"He'll love it."

"I hope I can find someone who can teach him to play."

"Get him a good beginner book and once he learns the G, C, and D chords, he'll be playing simple songs on Christmas Day. I picked it up quickly."

"You can play the mandolin?"

Devin nodded. "My dad has one. I gave it to him a couple years ago. If I'm still in town when Reilly comes home from camp, I'll give him a lesson or two if you don't think it would spoil the surprise."

Reilly doesn't come home until Labor Day. I can't live with Devin for another six weeks. She'd be so far gone by then there'd be no coming back.

Jenna hesitated so long with her response that he said, "But if you'd rather I didn't . . ."

"No. No. That'd be great." Jenna smiled brightly and changed the subject. "So, before I forget. Do I need to bring anything special for the boat ride this afternoon? Towels? Sunscreen? Snacks and drinks?"

"The *Windsong* is fully outfitted. All you need to bring is your swimsuit." His eyes took on a devilish glint as he teased, "Though if you want to leave it off, you'll get no complaints from me."

Jenna rolled her eyes.

Devin continued, "Are you ready to go?"

"I am. I just need to grab my tote. I bought a new one at the market today."

"Let's do it."

During the twenty-minute drive to the marina, Devin quizzed her about her opinions of the various vendors in the market, their wares, and if she thought a demand for any of it might exist in Eternity Springs. They were enthusiastically discussing the possibilities of importing the mandolins when she caught sight of dozens and dozens of boats moored at the marina. "Wow. For a small island, that's a lot of boats."

"Danielle thinned 'em out, but the marina is coming back. I'm glad to see it. Of course, this time of day, this time of year, fishing boats and tour boats are all out. They'll be back tonight and even some pleasure craft will have wandered in when we return this evening."

He pulled the Jeep into a parking spot and switched off the motor.

"Which boat are we using?" Jenna asked.

"The *Windsong* is there. The blue and white one. She's pretty, isn't she?"

"Wow. You said we were taking out a boat. You didn't say a yacht."

"In my world, yachts are sailboats. She is a big boat, I'll give you that, at sixty-five feet. Let's go aboard, Sugar, and we'll have us a cruise."

They cast off the lines with the assistance of dockhands and Jenna took a seat beside him in the lower helm. "We'll move up to the flybridge once we're out on open sea." He explained the workings of the instrumentation as he guided the *Windsong* out of the harbor. "I thought we'd take a leisurely three-sixty around Bella Vita first and then head out to sea. Does that work for you?"

"Sure." Jenna was back to her Cinderella-at-the-ball

moment. This boat was utter luxury with teak decking, a wet bar and barbecue, a dining area, and a convertible sundeck on the flybridge. The main deck had three cabins with a chef's dream of a galley, a living/dining area, a full-standing head, and a full-beam stateroom.

Devin captained the boat with familiar ease. Jenna asked, "Tell me about your boats."

"My boats aren't anything this fancy-schmancy, that's for sure," he told her. "This is a pleasure boat. Mine are workboats. I make my living with them. That's the most basic difference."

"But what type of boats are yours? Sailboats? Catamarans? Fishing boats like what we were on yesterday?"

"We've had each of those at different times. When I was growing up, Dad ran snorkel and dive tours out to the Reef off of catamarans and sailboats, but I learned early on that I preferred fishing charters."

"The three that you have hanging on the wall were like the one we took out yesterday."

"Basic sport fishing boats. Workhorses. Two of the three I have now are the same thing." A satisfied smile stretched across his face. "The *Out-n-Back* is different."

"Tell me about it."

"Her. She's a fine, fine boat that began as another man's pleasure boat. For me, she's a workboat—a dream of a boat—but she's still a fishing boat, a Boston Whaler. Her original owner had her less than a year when he ran into some financial problems and needed out fast. I'd just received my insurance check from Danielle so I was able to manage the down. I have earned a reputation as a guide, and between that and the accommodations, I can charge a pretty penny for charters. But the nut is steep. As long as I can keep the little boats going out, I'm okay but—" He broke off abruptly.

Jenna realized he'd said more than he'd intended to

say and she gave him a knowing look. "It *will* hurt you financially to stay longer in Eternity Springs than you'd originally planned."

"I'll be fine. The little boats are doing great. Now look, we're on the windward side of the island. Look up at about ten o'clock and you'll see the restaurant where we had dinner last night."

Jenna decided to allow the change of subject—for now. She couldn't in good conscience allow him to be hurt financially by assuming responsibility for her problems out of some sense of Santa psychology. If the problem wasn't solved by Sunday, he needed to go home to Australia just like he'd originally planned. She'd have to do whatever was necessary to make it happen.

But Sunday was still three days away. She wasn't going to worry about it. She was going to enjoy her Cinderella Thursday aboard the *Windsong*.

They moved up to the helm on the flybridge, where Devin could captain the boat with the wind in his face. Jenna sat beside him, her gaze shifting between the beauty of the island and that of the man who was so in his element here on the water. And she was so out of her own.

When they rounded the southern tip of the island and started up the leeward side, he said, "The Brogans' place is on this side of the island. See that stretch of beach there? The red clay roof behind the hedge?"

"I see it."

"They got hit pretty hard from the hurricane, but Flynn wanted to redesign the place anyway, so he was glad to have the excuse."

"Gabi said he's always designing something."

"True, that." When they'd puttered halfway up the island, he asked, "So, you want to take a turn at the wheel?"

Jenna instinctively drew back. "Oh, I couldn't. I've never driven a boat."

"No worries. We're in eighty feet of water here."

"How do you know that?"

"Here." He released the wheel and stepped back.

Panicked, Jenna grabbed the wheel. He chuckled and began teaching her to read the electronics and gauges. Accustomed to reading machines in the operating room, she caught on quickly. As they neared the southern tip of the island, she asked, "How many miles per hour is five knots?"

"About five and three quarters."

"It feels like we're going faster than that."

"Because your face is in the wind. Go below and it won't seem so fast."

"We went a little slower when we were trolling yesterday."

"Yes. About three knots."

"And when we were going faster? Out toward the spot where we started trolling?"

Devin pursed his lips and considered it. "Eight to ten."

"It was fun." Jenna waited a few moments, then confessed, "Yesterday was the first time I'd been on a boat."

He glanced over at her and his chin dropped. "Seriously?"

"Not even a rowboat on the lake."

"Now, that's just wrong. Why didn't you say anything?"

"I don't know. I just didn't want to admit it. I was too busy worrying that I'd get seasick."

"Seas were a little rougher yesterday than they are today. Boat a lot smaller. You didn't mention feeling queasy. Did you?"

"No, not at all."

"Then hold on, Sugar." He stood behind her, covered her left hand with his, and rested his right hand on the throttle. "I'm going to open her up."

He applied pressure, the engines accelerated, and the

Windsong shot forward like a thoroughbred at the starting gate. Soon they were flying across the sea, the wind whistling a song as it rushed past her ears. Devin's eyes gleamed and he gave her a pirate's smile.

What a rush this was! She could get used to this—with Devin and being free upon the sea. Jenna had the wayward thought that this might be what having sex with Devin Murphy was like. Maybe she should throw caution to this whistling wind and really enjoy herself.

After a while, he slowed the boat to cruising speed, set a waypoint on the autopilot and declared it was time for lunch. They went down to the galley on the lower deck, where Devin set out fruit, cheeses, and sandwich fixings from a well-stocked fridge and pantry. Jenna took her ham sandwich and grapes to the dining table, where she tried to listen to Devin's conversation about the engines powering the boat. However, she truly didn't care about motors of any sort as long as they started and ran when she wanted them to run. Also, she kept popping up from the table to look out of the window.

Devin asked, "What in the world is wrong with you?"

"It's the autopilot. It sort of freaks me out. What if there's another boat coming?"

"This is the most sophisticated system on the market." He began ticking items off on his fingers. "We have radar, sonar, radio, stereo, DVDs, MP3s, telegraph, duotronic transporter . . ."

"A *Star Trek* reference? You are so funny. Laugh at me all you want, but wasn't the U.S. Navy involved in a collision or two in recent years?"

"Fine. I'm not laughing. Your concerns are valid and understandable. I should have demonstrated the system when we were around traffic and you'd have been more comfortable with it. Tell you what." He nodded toward her sandwich. "How about after lunch, we turn off the autopilot, stop the boat, and go for a swim."

"Is it safe? I won't be fish bait?"

"We're in good swimming waters. That's why I took us this direction.

A swim sounded fantastic. Between the heat of the afternoon and the never-ending strum of sexual tension, she could use a cool dip and some exercise. She polished off her lunch and went into the stateroom where she'd left her bag upon their arrival to change into her swimsuit. There, she hesitated over her choice. She'd brought the modest one-piece she usually wore, but she also had the bikini she'd purchased yesterday at the market under peer pressure from Gabi and Maggie because they said it was made for her.

"It matches your eyes," Maggie had said.

"You have the body for it too," Gabi added. "I'm so jealous of your curves. Your hips are made for the match-ing sarong."

In the end, Jenna had bought the bikini and the sarong and a wide-brimmed hat with a matching scarf. Now as she pulled the items from her tote, she wondered if she'd be playing with fire to wear them.

Maybe. Probably. She'd wear the one-piece. She kicked off her deck shoes, pulled off her T-shirt and bra, and slipped out of her shorts and panties. But somehow when she left the stateroom, she wore her new bikini.

The sound of steel guitars and reggae music drifted from hidden speakers. Devin stood on the swim deck deploying the second of two coral-colored foam floats behind the boat. Attached to the *Windsong* by ten feet or so of line, they bobbed up and down on the turquoise waves. Shirtless and shoeless and wearing board shorts that hung low on his hips, he looked tanned and toned and so sexy that she felt itchy and needy inside. She almost moaned aloud. Instead, because she was both physician and mother, she asked, "Did you put on sunscreen?"

He turned around and, upon seeing her, froze. Then he lowered his sunglasses and gave her a long, smoldering look. "Sugar Cookie," he said, drawing it out to about twelve syllables. "Don't you look fine?"

"Thank you. So . . . my question. . . . Sunscreen?"

He tilted his head, still considering, and took a long time to answer. "Will you get my back?"

That's when she realized she'd made a mistake. Talk about playing with fire. As she stepped down onto the swim deck, he opened a compartment at the back of the boat and removed a bottle of sunscreen. Solemnly and without saying another word, he handed it to her and presented his back.

Devin was tall, his shoulders broad and roped with muscle. Yesterday she'd witnessed firsthand just how those cords had come to be. Devin was no gym rat who jerked a barbell. He jerked around thirty-pound groupers and mahi-mahi.

Jenna's mouth went dry and, as she squirted white, coconut-scented lotion into the palm of her hand, she suddenly thought of high school English and Coleridge's "Rime of the Ancient Mariner." "Water, water everywhere, nor any drop to drink."

"Hmm? You're thirsty? There's a cooler right behind you. The center cushion. There's water, juice, soft drinks. Beer if you want it. I'm serving mojitos at cocktail hour."

"Thanks." Jenna wouldn't mind a bottle of water, but the Coleridge quote had referred to a totally different type of thirst. Bracing herself, she slid her hand across his back. His skin was warm and taut, neither smooth nor rough, just normal. Lovely. Scarred here below his left shoulder. *Wonder what happened here?* An old scar, long healed. She lingeringly traced it with her index finger. Six inches long. It had been stitched.

"About done?" Devin asked, his voice sounding strained.

"Oh, sorry. Let me just . . ." With quick, clinical motions, she smoothed lotion over the places she'd missed, and then stepped back.

"Thanks." Devin cleared his throat and held out his hand and wiggled his fingers. "My turn."

Oh. Well. Oh. She gave him the sunscreen and whirled around, happy not to have to face him as heat flushed her cheeks. "Just . . . um . . . right above my . . . um . . . strap. I could . . . um . . . reach everywhere else."

Her bikini top didn't have a strap. It had a string. A thin, tiny string she'd secured with a bow. A bow he could easily untie if he pulled on one of the knotted ends. She closed her eyes. She heard the squish sound of lotion leaving the bottle. For a long moment, nothing happened.

She shivered in anticipation. Goose bumps rose upon her flesh. She felt his index finger grasp one of the knots on her bow. His voice low and gravelly, he asked, "You don't want to get burned, do you, Jenna?"

Her voice escaped in a squeak. "No, but—"

He tugged once, quick and hard. The bow slipped. Instinctively, her arms lifted to clasp the triangles of her top against her breasts.

The lotion was cool. His fingers were hot. They stroked across her skin slowly, back and forth. Back and forth. Jenna held back a moan.

When finally he spoke, it was in a low, throaty tone from right beside her ear. "Seems to me we have a choice here, Jenna. Do we go swimming?" His lips brushed across the sensitive skin of her neck. "Or . . . not?"

She wanted him. Oh, how she wanted him.

His finger trailed down the base of her spine and the edge of the sarong. Moisture pooled between Jenna's legs.

He tugged at the knot at her hip and the sarong drifted to the *Windsong*'s deck.

Jenna turned around. Devin's gaze made a slow, hot crawl up and down her body, desire turning his eyes dark and dangerous.

Swim? Or sink? That was the question here, wasn't it? She tried to recall all the reasons why this would be a mistake. Only one hovered like a half-formed protest in her mind—Eternity Springs.

Well, Dorothy, you're not in Kansas right now, are you? Much less Colorado. And he's not in Oz. Not yet.

And, oh, she had the feeling that he likely was a wizard.

She was Cinderella on a genuine-freaking-yacht and if she wanted to mix her metaphors and movies and fairy tales, well then she had until midnight before Jaws ate her glass slipper and she had to put on her red glitter shoes.

She wanted Devin's mouth on her. Every inch of her.

"You told me being on the ocean is empowering because it makes you part of the universe. You said you never feel alone. When you asked me to come with you to Bella Vita Isle, you said you'd show me. I'm tired of being powerless, Devin. I'm tired of being alone. I want to swim . . . later. Now, just for today, while we're here on the ocean aboard the *Windsong,* make me part of your universe."

He put his hands on her waist. "Just so I'm positively certain, you're saying yes?"

"Yes, I'm saying yes."

His lips twisted in that slow pirate's smile. His fingers tightened and he lifted her off her feet. He crushed his mouth to hers and turned in a slow circle once, twice, three times.

Jenna felt him lift her and she expected to find herself seated on the sundeck, where he'd lay her back and have his wicked way with her. She nearly laughed aloud.

So to find herself sailing through the air caught her

completely by surprise. Screeching, she caught her breath just before her head sank beneath the surface of the cool Caribbean.

She surfaced sputtering to find Devin treading water beside her, laughing maniacally. "What in the world did you do that for?"

"Look around us. See all the steam rising from the water? Sugar, you and I have been on slow burn for weeks. Without a bit of a cool down I'd have gone off like a rocket."

"So you throw me in the ocean?"

"Yeah." He continued to laugh. "You should have seen your face."

"Why . . . you . . . you"—she drew back her hands and splashed him—"pirate!"

"Well, this *is* the Caribbean." He grabbed her hand and pulled her close. "C'mere, me pretty. Give us a kiss. Later I'll let you walk my plank."

"Oh, for heaven's sake." Her mouth curved against his as he kissed her and they sank beneath the waves.

When they came up for air, he stared deeply into her eyes and said, "Welcome to my world, Jenna Stockton. Let's play, shall we?"

Chapter Eighteen

Devin opened his eyes. The moon was a tiny sliver of a fingernail in a midnight blue sky awash with stars. Underway at four knots with a following sea, the *Windsong* rocked gently on the waves, making her way slowly along the course he had plotted after dinner—a large circle around Bella Vita Isle. He lay stretched out on the lounge on the flybridge with Jenna tucked up against him.

What a great day.

Great weather. Great boat. Great sex. Really great sex. Really great woman.

He had just enough energy left to turn his head and nuzzle her behind the ear. "Not again . . . ," she groaned. "I have to sleep."

Bravely, Devin worked up enough strength to smile. "I just don't want you to miss the Milky Way, Sugar. It's at its best this time of year."

She angled up on her elbows and dropped her head back to gaze upon the filmy cloud of stars arching across the sky. "Oh, wow. How fabulous is that? Do you know the constellations, Devin?"

"I'm a mariner. Of course I know the stars. If all the electronics on the *Windsong* were to fail, I could get us home with a compass and a sextant."

"Point some of them out to me?"

They spent the next twenty minutes stargazing, and she shared with him a childhood memory of her father. "We lived in a small town in Mississippi. I was about Reilly's age. It was summer and our air conditioner was broken. It was so hot that we gave up attempting to sleep in our beds and moved to the lawn furniture in the backyard. My dad tried to help me see the constellations, but I just couldn't mentally draw the pictures. I did see the Milky Way, though." After a moment's pause, she added, "Thank you for the nice memory of my father, Devin."

"My experience wasn't all that different from yours, except Cam and I were on a boat. I was around the same age, maybe a little younger. I could see the Southern Cross, but beyond that, forget it."

"Seeing the Southern Cross is on my bucket list. Crosby, Stills, and Nash, you know."

"Great song." Devin pressed a gentle kiss against her hair. "Maybe you should plan a visit to Cairns. I'll show you the Southern Cross."

She stiffened ever so slightly, and even before she spoke, Devin knew that the magic of the night had been broken. She rolled away from him and reached for one of the white terrycloth bathrobes they'd donned at the end of their late-night swim and then discarded during lovemaking.

She slipped it on, belted it, and faced him. It was too dark to see her expression, but he thought he could hear tears in her voice. "I can't, Devin. This has been a fairy tale of a day, but Cinderella has to leave the ball. I need you to keep to your original plans and return to Australia on Sunday."

"But the stalker—"

"Isn't as big a danger to me right now as you are."

"Excuse me?"

"I am on the verge of losing my heart to you, Devin. I

have to put a stop to it. There's no future in it and I need a future. I need to give Reilly a future. I need to give Reilly a father."

Well, if she'd wanted to shut him up, she'd chosen the best possible way to do it. He didn't have a comeback for that.

"I am going to return to Eternity Springs with the Brogans, and I'll take Jack Davenport up on his offer to stay at Eagle's Way until my stalker is identified. From the beginning, everyone said that was the safest thing for me to do. You won't need to worry about me and you can return to Australia and get back to business making payments on the *Out-n-Back*. I'll get my Colorado medical license and set about giving your mother and sister and friends the best possible prenatal care."

"And get married," he grumbled, unable to help himself. He grabbed up the second robe, shoved his arms into the sleeves, yanked the belt around his waist, and tied it.

After a significant pause, she asked, "Who is Anya?"

The name came right out of left field to sucker punch his gut. While he was still recovering from the blow, she continued, "Last night at dinner, Mitch said I should ask you about the 'evil witch Anya' so that I would understand why your boat has no anchor."

"Now? You have to ask now?" He exhaled sharply, angry at his friend and at himself. "Anya is nobody. Someone I used to know is all."

"Someone from Bella Vita?"

"Dammit, Jenna." He yanked open the wet bar's fridge and pulled out a beer. "She doesn't matter. She never mattered. The baby was all that mattered."

At her audible gasp, he literally bit his tongue. *I'm gonna kick Mitch's ass next time I see him.*

"You have a child?"

He had enough experience with women to recognize

the futility of attempting to avoid spilling the beans at this point. He might as well open the can and start pouring.

"I started seeing a woman here on the island. She got pregnant and I'm old-fashioned about such things, so I offered to marry her. She moved in, but she wanted to wait until after the baby was born to get married. Said she wanted the wedding gown and photos, and I bought her story. Turns out I was her backup plan. I wasn't the baby's father. He'd left her, left the island. After the hurricane hit he had a change of heart, returned, and they rode off together into the sunset. End of story."

"Oh, Devin. That's despicable. I'd use a much stronger word than 'witch' to describe her."

He shrugged. "I dealt. It was okay. I didn't love her. It's not like losing her broke my heart."

Losing the baby, now . . . He'd been a boy. Devin had believed he'd had a son on the way. He gave his head a shake, took another pull on his beer, and then said, "It was for the best. I'm a rolling stone, or, to keep it nautical, a spinning prop. So, that's the story—but why did you pick now to ask about it?"

She'd sure as hell managed to spoil the mood.

"It was the tone of your voice when you said the word 'marriage.' It reminded me of Mitch's cryptic comment."

Jenna reached up and framed his face in her hands. "Devin, thank you for this fairy-tale day. Thank you for caring for me and for my son and for being our champion. Being our hero. Being our Santa Claus. You've taught me to believe again."

She pulled his mouth down to hers and gave him a kiss so sweet, so honest, so full of an emotion that he dared not name that it staggered him. When it ended, he drew her unsteadily away. "Jenna . . ."

"Take me back to port, sailor. I'm afraid Cinderella's clock is starting to chime.

* * *

By mid-morning the following day, what seemed like half of Eternity Springs arrived for the wedding. It didn't happen a moment too soon as far as Jenna was concerned. She had thought that being around Devin was difficult before she had traveled to Bella Vita Isle with him. Following their day aboard the *Windsong,* she found it to be sheer torture.

By the time the boat docked at the marina in the early hours of the morning, she'd realized she had lied. She wasn't on the verge of losing her heart to him. It had happened. It was a done deal. She was toast. She'd fallen head over heels in love with Devin Santa Claus Murphy.

She believed, all right. She believed she was an idiot.

His family's arrival on the island had been a welcome distraction, and she'd happily joined Lori and Sarah on a visit to the market despite having so recently shopped until she dropped there.

It helped that Devin didn't appear to want to be alone with her anymore than she did him, and he spent the majority of his time doing activities with his brother, including building a large and intricate sand castle. In fact, once his family arrived, the two of them didn't exchange a word in private until just prior to their departure for the wedding. "Pretty dress," he said. "You look beautiful in yellow. You look beautiful in everything. In nothing . . ."

"Devin," she'd protested. "Off-limits. That's the other universe."

"Yeah. Yeah. I know. Sorry." His grimace held a bit of yearning that served to soothe her lovesick heart. He might not be one to permanently trailer his boat, but that didn't mean he didn't want her. Crumbs, true, but at this point her feminine ego would take them.

The wedding was a sunset beach ceremony on the Brogan property, a beautiful meld of traditions from the heritages of both the bride—a Minnesota native educated at Michigan—and the groom—Caribbean born, raised, and educated in the island studio of a master glass artist. Mitch made a stir when he appeared without his customary Rastafarian braids—a promise to his bride, he'd declared to the shocked assembly. She floated up the beach in diaphanous white on her father's arm, and bride and groom said their vows against a palette of orange, rose, and gold as the sun slipped into the turquoise sea.

Jenna seldom cried at weddings, and she barely knew this couple, but while watching Mitch pledge his undying love to his bride, she teared up nevertheless. Her emotions were a jumble of grief and yearning and acceptance and anticipation.

This was the worst, standing beside Devin in these circumstances. Once she got through tonight it would get better. Maybe not out of sight, out of mind, but out of sight and in Eternity Springs, where broken hearts go to heal.

She couldn't think of a better place for her to be. From now until Christmas at least, she would nurse her broken heart while she doctored the women, her new friends who were in need of her professional services.

Following the ceremony, the guests moved off the beach to the poolside garden and lawn where a buffet dinner was to be served. In the midst of all the people, Jenna was able to relax and enjoy herself. Obviously, friends and family hadn't picked up on the fact that she'd been intimate with Devin, so she need not fear facing those uncomfortable questions. She caught Lori looking at her curiously once or twice. The gaze Sarah leveled upon her son when he was looking at Jenna was downright suspicious. Such things Jenna could withstand. What happened on the *Windsong* had stayed on the *Windsong*—and for that, she was grateful.

It wasn't until Devin smoothly led her off into the

garden at the end of a dance that her tension returned. "How's your ankle doing?"

"It's okay. Devin, we shouldn't leave. They'll be doing the sendoff any time now."

"We won't be long. I just need to speak with you alone, and with the family at the house, I might not have another chance. Jenna, I've been thinking about your idea to stay at Eagle's Way. The more I turn it over, the less I like it. I think we should keep to the original plan. I'll go back to Eternity Springs tomorrow and—"

"No."

"Hear me out. I think that—"

"No! We settled this, Devin."

"But I want you to be safe. I need you to be safe."

"I *will* be safe. You know it's true."

"But I won't be there to see it!" He shoved his fingers through his hair. "Look, I'll be the first to admit that I don't understand what's happening here, Jenna. I have all these questions spinning around in my heart."

His heart? Not his mind?

"Jenna . . ." He took both her hands in his. "Jenna, I need answers, and I'm afraid I'm not going to get them in Queensland."

She closed her eyes against the turmoil his words created inside her. What if she took the risk? What if she believed—

Cam's excited voice interrupted them. "There you are. We've been looking all over for you. Neither one of you is answering your phones."

"What's the emergency?" Devin asked, frustration in his voice.

"No emergency. News. Great news. Jenna, Daniel has been trying to reach you. The FBI in Nashville has your stalker in custody."

"What? Oh, my . . ." She covered her mouth with

her hands and swayed as her knees went a little weak. As Devin caught her elbow and steadied her, she asked, "Who is he?"

"He's someone connected to the surgeon," Cam replied. "Daniel has all the details. Devin, why don't you show her to Flynn's office and she can return his call. I'll tell Zach where to find us. I know he's as curious as I am."

"But the sendoff . . . ," Jenna said. "Devin, you need to . . ."

He placed his finger atop her lips. "Mitch won't miss me. And I'm not missing this. C'mon. This way. We can reach it by going around through the garden."

Flynn Brogan's office was more workshop than traditional office space, with gleaming stainless-steel work tables and an array of tools to leave most men of Jenna's acquaintance drooling. Devin escorted her to a chair and as she pulled her phone from her evening bag—silenced for the wedding—he moved a chair close to hers and straddled it.

She drew a deep breath, and then placed the call. Daniel answered on the third ring. "Congratulations, Jenna. You can once again order a pizza without any hesitation."

"Who did this? Why?"

"Is Devin with you?"

"Yes." She glanced toward the door as it opened. "Cam and Zach too. Shall I put you on speaker?"

"Good idea. The Callahans and I are up at Jack's. You're on speaker here. Sounds like we have the whole team together, which is fitting. Jenna, I think the most efficient way to do this is to allow me to summarize first, highlighting the pertinent details. Then I'll take questions. Okay?"

"Of course."

"Your stalker is Jonathan Reid."

Jenna blinked. Her gaze flew to Devin's. The name meant absolutely nothing to her.

"He is sixteen years old. The connection to you comes through Dr. Snelling and the boy's father. Allan Reid had secured financial backing for his medical-device start-up from Snelling, and the deal fell through when Mrs. Snelling filed for divorce. Reid lost his shirt, and the family lost their home. A mention of you during his ranting in the aftermath led to his son's obsession."

"Sixteen," Jenna said. "That means he was fourteen when this started."

"Yes. Thirteen when they lost their house."

Jenna took a moment to digest that information. Stalkers were invariably disturbed individuals, and she'd expected her stalker to be young due to his use of doxxing and swatting. But . . . fourteen?

Daniel turned over the conversation to Mark Callahan, who explained how they'd tracked the boy down. Honestly, her thoughts wandered as he spoke of digital footprints and technologies about which she had no knowledge or interest.

It was over. Reilly was safe.

Reilly was safe.

She came back to the conversation and realized that Mark had concluded his explanation. Zach and Cam were asking questions. Devin was looking at her. She smiled shakily at him. She was having a hard time taking this all in.

"Do you have any questions for us, Jenna?" Jack Davenport asked.

"What's going to happen to him? To Jonathan?"

"That remains to be seen. Unfortunately, Jenna, you are not the only person he has tormented. We turned over evidence of three more victims. He's a troubled young man."

Daniel added, "Something you need not worry about . . . he won't be allowed near a computer for a very long time. And now that his issues are known, he'll get help."

"Good. That's good." Her thoughts drifted off again as she tried to imagine the Reids' reaction to their son's arrest. Then something Daniel said jerked her back to attention. ". . . to apologize for missing Jonathan Reid the first time."

"Whoa. Whoa. Whoa," Jenna interrupted. "Excuse me, Daniel. Please. I've been fighting this for two years. You guys have found him in less than a month. And you did all this . . . went to all this effort . . . just because . . . because . . ."

"You're our friend, Jenna," Jack Davenport said. "We value friends in Eternity Springs. You are part of our family."

The Eternity Springs family.

A knock on the door sounded and Gabi Brogan stuck her head into the room. "Mitch and Elizabeth are about to leave if you all can join us."

Zach nodded. "Thanks, Gabi. I think we're about done here. Last word, anyone?"

"Yes!" Jenna said. "The last word . . . words . . . are mine. Thank you. On behalf of Reilly and myself, from the bottom of my heart, thank you. You all have changed our lives, and that is a gift beyond words. So . . . thank you."

Her mind fired in spurts and sizzles just like the sparklers she held a few minutes later, ushering the bride and groom into the car that would carry them to their honeymoon bower. It was over. Over. Over.

The following day at the tiny Bella Vita Isle airport where she watched Devin hug and kiss first his sister and then his mother, the words played a litany through her mind. *It's over. It's over. It's over.*

He shook his father's hand, they pounded each other's shoulders, and then Cam pulled him into his arms for a hug. "Fair winds and following seas, son."

"Thanks, Dad. Love you, too."

Both Lori and Sarah had tears in their eyes when Devin went down on his knee to speak softly to a sobbing Michael for a few moments before hugging him long and hard.

Michael turned to his mother for comfort when Devin rose and finally looked at Jenna.

It's over. It's over. It's over.

"Well, Jenna," he said in a voice that was gruff with emotion. "Tell Reilly I know he's going to love Ms. Jenkins—she's the second-grade teacher."

"I'll do that." She worked to keep her tone light.

It's over. It's over. It's over.

"I . . . um . . ." He tossed his parents a pleading expression.

Sarah took the hint. "Michael, let's pop into the store and buy some snacks for our flight. Cam, here come the Romanos. You should go help them with their luggage."

"Why would I want to do that? Lucca is younger than me."

She hooked an arm through his elbow and dragged him off. Lori shook her head sadly at her older brother, and then turned to follow her parents, saying, "I need to buy a paperback for the flight. A romance. With a happy ending."

Devin muttered a curse. "She's such a smart-ass."

"She loves you. They all love you. You are blessed in your family."

"I know," Devin said, watching them go. "I know. My growing family." Then he turned back to her and said, "I can't tell you how much comfort it gives me to know that you'll be there to watch over them. I trust you'll take good care of my ladies."

"You have my word on it."

"I think this is why it happened . . . the wrong number. I think we were meant to help each other."

Not meant to love each other?

It's over, it's over, it's over.

"I believe you're right."

His lips twisted. "Believe. That reminds me. With all the excitement last night, I didn't get a chance to say goodbye to Celeste. Though knowing her, she's liable to be on my flight in the seat next to me."

"She's flying back with the Brogans. She told me last night. She said she has pictures of a house that is coming onto the market that she wants to show me. One she thinks I should buy.

"Oh, yeah? Are you ready to buy a house in Eternity Springs? Put down permanent roots there?"

"Maybe. We'll see. I told her I might be interested in a rent-to-own scenario. See how Reilly does in school before I commit to a house. If it's the perfect house for us, I'd hate to miss out on it."

"Where is it? In town?"

"On the lake. Next to Boone McBride's house, I believe."

Devin scowled. "Why are we talking about houses? Why are we talking at all?"

He closed his lips over hers, and just for a moment she allowed her senses to steep in the taste of him, in the firm warmth of his masculine form, in the scent of salt and sand and sea that clung to him. For just a moment, Jenna allowed herself to kiss him goodbye.

Then she pulled from his arms and put the first few feet of distance between them. "Thank you for a lovely cruise, Devin Murphy. Safe travels as you continue your journey."

Jenna turned and left him. It was time to take her broken heart home to Eternity Springs.

Chapter Nineteen

Boone McBride eyed the half-dozen boxes, each big enough to hold a full-grown St. Bernard, that were lined up in his next-door neighbor's living room. He softly whistled. "Wow. Exactly how do you code the billing for this, Dr. Stockton?"

"Oh, hush. This was a labor of love."

"Appropriate on this Labor Day.

"Hey, we are all about labors today." Jenna fussed with one of the bows, then took a step back and surveyed them with a critical eye. "I think we're good, don't you?"

"Well, little lady," he said in an exaggerated Texas drawl, "I think we're safe from getting them mixed up."

"That was the idea." All the boxes were wrapped in glossy white paper and tied with big red bows. Rather than use tags to indicate which box was intended for which couple, Jenna and Reilly had played Picasso and decorated the paper on each box with permanent markers, drawing not only names but other details to personalize each one. "I loaded one box at a time and we wrapped and decorated it before starting another box. It wouldn't do to mix them up."

"That would not be good," Boone agreed. "So, are you ready for me to start loading them into the Jeep?"

Jenna glanced at the clock. "Yes please. Thanks again for the help, Boone."

"Glad to do it. That's what neighbors are for."

As Boone carried out the first box, Jenna began gathering up the rest of what she'd need for the afternoon. She had sold her extended cab pickup along with the fifth wheel last week, and she had a nifty Jeep in her driveway and a new trailer on order to replace the behemoth they no longer needed to live in.

Boone quickly returned for the second box and then the third. He saw the tote bags she'd filled. "Those going too?"

"Yes, they're the entries we received at the clinic this week and more entry blanks."

His brows arched and then he laughed. "Brick's idea to turn this whole thing into a contest was brilliant."

"Wait until after today. He has his entire family ready to whip out their checkbooks to find out the baby news. Before he's done, Brick will have raised enough money to build an entire new school, much less fund the expansion."

All of Eternity Springs had been invited to the Back-to-School event to celebrate the beginning of the school year. The highlight of the party was to be the update on the school expansion fundraising contest that Brick Callahan had announced at the Fourth of July party and subsequently dubbed the "Maternity Springs" contest. The update consisted of a gender reveal moment for each expectant family.

Two of the couples had elected to receive their happy news in private. Three wanted to share their big moment with family and friends. Cam and Sarah were being old-fashioned about the news.

"A gender-reveal party?" Cam had repeated in a voice laced with disgust when Sarah had shared the idea with him during their last prenatal appointment. "No. That's not natural. That's a personal, private moment meant to happen when we take our first good gander at the squiggling little rat and see what sort of equipment he's got."

"I'm not giving birth to a squiggling little rat." Sarah's lips had twitched with amusement. "Gender-reveal parties have become quite popular the past few years."

"Yeah, well, so has kale. I rest my case."

Despite his traditional views, Cam had been amenable to the idea of participating in the Labor Day fundraising event. Today, they'd be opening a box filled with yellow and green balloons. Lori was going to be disappointed. She was almost as excited to find out whether her baby was expecting an aunt or an uncle as she was to learn the sex of her own child.

The past month had been a busy one for Jenna. She'd loved the house Celeste had shown her upon her return from Bella Vita, and she'd negotiated a six-month lease with an option to buy. Her license to practice medicine in Colorado was approved the first week of August and she'd begun seeing patients immediately. The joy she found in the process revealed the truth that she'd hidden from herself during their months on the road—she loved her work, loved her profession, and she'd missed it rather desperately.

She'd also missed Reilly rather desperately, but the healthy, joyful boy she'd visited at the Rocking L to share news of their stalker's apprehension had made every lonely moment worth it. Eternity Springs had certainly worked its magic on her son.

She was still waiting for that healing magic for herself.

She missed Devin. He'd cut a big jagged hole in her heart when he'd returned to Australia, and it wasn't going to heal overnight. Maybe now that Reilly was home from camp and her loneliness not so acute, the intensity of the ache would soon begin to dull.

Reilly burst into the room from the backyard, Sinatra

close on his heels. Both dog and boy raced in mad circles around the remaining boxes. The two were all but inseparable. Jenna wondered how both of them would manage the stretch of separation necessitated by the school day.

"Is it time to go yet, Mom?"

"Almost. We're loading up. Why don't you make sure Sinatra has plenty of water and put up the doggie gate?"

"Can't I take him with me? I'll watch him really close and keep him on his leash and he'll behave. I know he will. Besides, we'll be in the park."

"No, my love. You're doing very well with his training, but there will be too many people in the park today. He'll be happier here."

"But Mo-om!" he whined.

She gave him her stern mother look. "Tend your dog."

Ten minutes later, she and Reilly pulled out of their driveway and followed Boone's truck. The park was already crowded upon their arrival. The Chamber of Commerce had been set up accepting entries and donations for the contest since mid-morning. Brick and the other fathers-to-be were out working the crowd. "This is kinda fun, isn't it, Mom?" Reilly observed.

"It is."

"Michael is really excited. He hopes he's going to get a brother and a nephew." He looked at her closely then sighed heavily. "You never give away anything, Mom."

She laughed, shifted the Jeep into park, and then reached into her tote for her wallet. She pulled out a twenty. "Here, go make a donation and a guess."

"Blue or pink?"

"Your guess."

He scrambled out of the Jeep and took off. Approaching the Jeep with Zach and Savannah Turner's box in his arms, Boone asked, "Does he ever slow down?"

Jenna lifted Cam and Sarah's box from her back seat,

then smiled warmly up at Boone and laughed. "Only when he's sound asleep."

At that moment, Reilly let out a loud squeal. Alarmed, Jenna turned toward the sound—and went numb. The box slipped from her fingers and fell to the ground. Unprepared, Boone stepped right into the middle of it.

A yellow balloon bulged from the hole his foot made.

"Seriously?" Devin said, his arms full of Reilly. "I come all this way for the big surprise, and get yellow?"

All that yellow and Devin was seeing red.

He was jet-lagged, exhausted, feeling light in the pocketbook after purchasing the last-minute ticket, and hungry. For Jenna. And thirsty. For Jenna.

And she shows up all sunny and grinny with Mr. Next-Door-Neighbor. Devin grumbled, "I need a beer."

His big surprise was looking like a great big mistake.

All flustered, Jenna had barely glanced at him as she fussed over repairing his parents' box before the cat climbed any further out of the bag, so to speak. After that, the hoards spotted her and her boxes and descended, and Devin had no chance for any sort of private conversation with her at all.

His decision to travel to Eternity Springs for the big baby-reveal extravaganza had come after a phone call with his sister, during which she'd expressed her deep regret that he wouldn't be there in person to share the big moment. Then he'd called home to talk to his folks and Michael at a time when his brother's BFF was over to play.

Talking with Reilly about his time at camp and hearing his enthusiasm for life in general had made Devin feel like a million dollars. Neutralizing the threat that had been Jonathan Reid had made a significant difference in Reilly's life. While Devin had been busy patting himself on the back, the boy began talking about his mom and their new house and new neighbor. Devin learned that McBride got out and threw a football with Reilly almost every afternoon. Before Devin quite knew how it had happened, he'd been on an airplane back to the States.

He watched the box-opening spectacle with sincere interest. Brick made the whole process entertaining. The Garretts had a boy on the way, as did the Turners. A bouquet of pink balloons sailed out of the Brogans' box. It was too fun to watch his parents' reaction to the news that they had a granddaughter on the way. And Lori . . . well . . . she beamed and got teary-eyed, and if Chase smiled any wider he'd have broken his jaw. *A niece. I'm going to have a niece.*

When the family swept him into the circle for a group hug, he was truly glad he had made the trip.

The final reveal of the afternoon was Brick and Lili's box. Showman and fundraiser that he was, he whipped his family into a frenzy of last-minute check writing before opening the box. Blue balloons sailed out . . . and so did pink.

"Very funny." Brick cast Jenna an annoyed glance. Despite all his campaigning, it was obvious he was ready to find out if his child was a boy or a girl. "Now where's our real box?"

But beside him, Lili started to giggle. "This *is* our real box. Use your brain, Callahan."

It took him about ten seconds, but then the color drained from his face. Frantically, he grasped his wife's hand.

Brick's father Mark fist-bumped his twin brother, Luke, and said, "I knew it. I just knew they were having twins."

For the next hour, Devin watched and waited for his chance to talk to Jenna. That chance never came.

The woman was avoiding him. Oh, she spoke to him. She was cordial . . . friendly, even. But anytime he came close to cutting her from the herd, she managed to flitter off to another group or invite a different crowd to join her. Man, but that chapped his butt. He finally abandoned his efforts to speak to her privately at the baby party and waited at her house for her to come home. That never happened.

Turned out she and Reilly had made plans to go tent camping somewhere in Rocky Mountain National Park for the remainder of the holiday weekend. He'd completely missed them.

Devin returned to Australia with about a ton of torque in his jaw and emotions he couldn't name swirling in his gut. He called her the first time three days later. She didn't answer. He tried again the next day and again the next. Had she blocked his number? Finally out of patience and disregarding the time difference, he began calling once an hour. If she hadn't picked up by three a.m. her time, he'd conclude that she'd blocked him. Then it would be on to Plan B, whatever that was.

She picked up at two p.m. her time and spoke without preamble. "Devin, you have to stop this. I can't bear it anymore. It's bad enough that people around here talk about you all the time, and everywhere I go I see something that reminds me of you. Now after the Maternity Springs party, I'm afraid you're going to pop up unexpectedly every time I go into town. I can't even escape you at night! You haunt my dreams. Do you know how many times I've woken up in the middle of the night believing my bed was rocking because my dreams about the *Windsong* are so vivid? You can't call me, Devin. I'm trying very hard to find that Eternity Springs healing spirit, but so far the only spirit is a ghost and that ghost is you. I wish . . . well . . . it doesn't matter what I wish. Please, Devin. Stop calling me."

The call disconnected.

In the quiet of a peaceful Queensland morning, all those thoughts and questions that had swirled in his heart since even before Bella Vita coalesced into a single truth.

He loved her. He was in love with Jenna Stockton. With a capital *L*.

Okay, then. Now that he had the answer, what did he want to do about it?

On the last Saturday in October, Jenna offered Sarah Murphy a hand to help her rise to a seated position on the exam table. "Everything looks good, Sarah. Your blood pressure is a little higher than I'd like and we will keep a close watch on it. But everything appears to be right on schedule for your little peanut."

"I shouldn't have called you. This is my third time around. You'd think I'd know what I'm doing."

"You were absolutely right to call me. I want you to always err on the side of caution, Sarah."

"Because I have a geriatric pregnancy," she grumbled.

"Because you are my patient and friend," Jenna gently chided. Then, to lighten the mood, she added, "And you make the best cookies in the world."

Sarah wrinkled her nose. "Or I did until you suggested I cut back my hours. Due to my geriatric pregnancy and everything."

"I suggested you pay close attention to your body. Work when you feel like it, but have backup for when you don't."

"I had so much energy yesterday, I couldn't believe it. If this were December, I'd have told Cam to get ready. But October is too soon."

"Yes, we need your peanut to bake a few more weeks for sure."

"I was definitely baking yesterday. I made a few cakes for the Fall Festival. Quite a few of them. When I started feeling so strange today, I worried I might have overdone it. I only made one batch of cookies this morning before I started feeling weird. Celeste came over for coffee, and we talked about Maternity Springs, which led to reminiscing about the contest Angel's Rest sponsored that I won. The grand prize was a trip to Australia, and that's what brought Cam back into my life. Talking about that made me miss Devin, so I made his favorite cookies. Figured I'd send them along with the cakes to the festival tonight. Experience has proven that you can never have enough." She paused a moment, then said, "Is it okay if I go?"

"Listen to your body, Sarah. It will tell you."

"Okay, I will. You're going, I assume? With Boone?"

"Boone and I are not going together. We've decided we need to stop attending town events together no matter how convenient it is. People keep insisting we're a couple, and we're not. However, I am attending the Fall Festival. I wouldn't miss it for the world." The Fall Festival was the annual fundraising event at the school that featured carnival-type games. "I been hearing about it since Reilly and I first visited Eternity Springs."

"We are nothing if not traditional here in Eternity Springs and the full-contact cakewalk has become a prized one."

From outside in the hallway, they heard a panicked Cam. "Sarah? Sarah! Where are you?"

Jenna motioned for Sarah to remain where she sat. She hurried to open the exam room door and said, "She's fine. The baby is fine. She's in here."

Later that evening she walked the hallways at Eternity Springs Community School trailing after Reilly and Michael and other friends whose hands were full of tickets. Surrounded by new friends and acquaintances in the school, an uncomfortable melancholy filled Jenna. She recalled the love that had resonated in Sarah's voice as she'd spoken of her reunion with Cam, and the expression of devotion on Cam's face as sought his wife in the clinic's hallway. Jenna remembered how Gabi and Flynn had held hands almost the entire time during their most recent appointment. She thought back to the way that Daniel and Shannon Garrett had giggled like children when they'd watched their baby turn somersaults during one of the sonograms.

Would she ever share a moment like that with someone else?

It's really too bad that she and Boone had agreed they'd never be more than friends and neighbors. He was a great guy, and every so often, she sensed that he was as lonely as she. There was a story there, but he wasn't sharing. Guess Eternity Springs wasn't working its mojo on his broken heart any faster than it was on hers.

Despite her melancholy, Jenna enjoyed herself at the festival. After she saw Reilly off to the community center for the big children's slumber party, she prepared to join the other adults for cleanup following the final event of the evening—the adults-only cakewalk during which the Romano siblings and their friends would battle over the chance to win Maggie Romano's prized Italian cream cake.

Boone stopped her at the door as she stepped into the library where the contest was to be held. He had a strange look in his eyes as he said, "Jen . . . because you've become such a good friend, I'm prepared to make this sacrifice."

"What are you talking about?"

"He's going to hurt me." Boone then took hold of her chin, lifted her face, and kissed her.

Then he put his arm around her shoulder and escorted her toward the ring of spectators before joining the participants on the field of play: Brick Callahan, Josh Tarkington, Zach Turner, Lucca Romano, Gabe Callahan, Daniel Garrett, Chase Timberlake, Flynn Brogan, and . . .

Devin Murphy.

Chapter Twenty

"Who starts a fight at a cakewalk?" Jenna demanded before slamming her front door in his face.

Devin wasn't about to let that stop him. He opened the door and stepped inside, then followed her to the great room where she paced like a caged lioness. He glanced around. According to what he'd gleaned from the Internet, Jenna's house was a four-bedroom, three-bath, six-year-old log cabin built as a second home for an architect out of New Mexico. "Nice digs."

She whirled to face him. "You smashed Maggie's cake!"

"Yeah," Devin grimaced, then wished he hadn't. The movement hurt his swollen eye. "That was unfortunate. But since I was the winner, the only person I hurt was myself. Besides, I scored pinwheels."

"You broke Boone's nose!"

"Well, he deserved that. He put his mouth on my woman."

Jenna sucked in a breath, and then narrowed her eyes. "Your woman?" She took three steps toward him then punched him in the chest with her index finger. "Your woman! Did you just say 'your woman'?"

His mouth quirked. "Yeah."

"You arrogant, conceited, loathsome"—eyes flashing fire, she shouted—"cake killer!"

Cake killer? Good one.

"Why are you here? No, it doesn't matter. I don't care. I'm getting over you. I want you to leave."

"Not until we talk. I've allowed you to avoid talking to me for the past two months and that was a huge mistake."

"Allowed? You didn't *allow* me to do anything, Devin Murphy. What do they have in the water in Cairns that has turned you into a troglodyte? Haven't you heard? Alpha males are politically incorrect." She put her palms against his chest and shoved him hard.

"Let's keep politics out of it. This is romance."

"Romance! This is not romance. This is . . . this is . . ."

"Love. This is love, Jenna."

She went still. He took her by the shoulders and held her, his grip firm. He met her gaze with a steady one of his own. "You turned my life upside down and you have brought me to my knees. I love you, Jenna. I can't live without you. I want you to marry me. Please marry me."

Speechless, she stared up at him, her wide gray-blue eyes shimmering with tears.

"I can give you and Reilly a good life. The business is doing great. One of the reasons it took me two months to get here is that I have a deal cooking with a group of investors that will set us up to make great things happen."

"You want us to move to Australia with you?" she asked.

"I do. Not before the babies are born, of course, but after Christmas. I've looked into it. We'll have some hoops to jump through, but you'll be able to practice medicine. I want to give the ocean to Reilly like Cam did to me. I want to give him brothers and sisters."

"Plural?" she squeaked.

"I'd like at least three, but it's negotiable. Say yes, Jenna. I know you're crazy about me."

"Somebody's crazy," she muttered, not yet willing to relent.

Devin decided to tease her a little more. "This thing you have with Boone was just an effort to get over me. Maybe in time, it would have worked, but I wasn't stupid enough to give you time, and despite Big Tex's taunting kiss, I know I'm not too late. Reilly told me he doesn't sleep over."

"You did not ask him that!" She slapped his shoulder.

"No. I didn't." Devin grinned and took her back into his arms. "I didn't have to ask because I know you love me too."

"You are so conceited."

"I am so in love with you. Head over heels, until death do us part, in love. Marry me, Jenna. Say yes. Repeat after me, 'Yes, Santa.'"

"Santa?" Her lips curved.

"You didn't think this was plain old Devin Murphy who just proposed marriage, did you? I'm Santa Claus, and it's my business to make wishes come true." He slipped his arms around her and pulled her against him. Gazing intently into her eyes, he kissed her once lightly. "Believe, Jenna." He kissed her again. "Believe in me." He kissed her a third time. "Believe in us."

She hitched in a breath and licked her lips. "Yes. Yes. I'll marry you."

He gave a murmur of triumph as he closed his mouth over hers. The homecoming of the taste of her soothed away all the aches in his body and soul. "I've missed you. Oh, woman, how I have missed you. Where's Reilly?"

"A sleepover."

He drew back, and a smile of pure delight spread across

his face. "I love the boy like my own, but damn, do I have timing or what? Which way is your bedroom?"

He lifted her into his arms and carried her from the room whistling "I Saw Mommy Kissing Santa Claus."

Jenna had stars in her eyes the following morning when she woke snuggled in Devin's arms. A glance at the clock showed she'd slept half an hour later than her usual six a.m. wake-up time after sleeping very little during the long, delicious hours of the night. Now, she'd better get her sated little self in the shower and dressed because Reilly would be home before she knew it.

Ten minutes later she stood at the stove frying bacon and reliving moments of the previous night. In the middle of the night in the darkness of her bedroom, he had painted her a picture of Australia, of Queensland and Cairns and the Great Barrier Reef, so vivid that she'd all but seen the images on her ceiling. They spoke at length about his charter operation and the opportunities that had come his way in the past few weeks. His excitement was infective.

"The boats make the *Windsong* look like the S.S. *Minnow*—after it wrecked on Gilligan's Island," he'd told her around two in the morning. "We'll have personal use of one of them too. I'll take you to Tahiti and Bora Bora . . . all over the South Seas. And we have more than five hundred national parks in Australia. Reilly is going to love it."

Jenna hoped so. Reilly was the only real reservation she had. He had sunk his roots quickly in Colorado. How would he feel about picking up and moving? He wouldn't be happy about leaving Eternity Springs, but he would be getting his number-one wish in the deal—a dad. He would adjust, wouldn't he?

Hands came around her waist and lips nuzzled her neck. "Mmm. Bacon." Devin nipped her neck.

"Are you calling me a pig, Devin Murphy?" Jenna asked as a thrill ran down her spine.

"I was talking about breakfast, but now that you bring it up, your sexual demands last night might be considered excessive."

"They might be, hmm?"

"Have I mentioned how much I love bacon? Any chance I can get some scrambled eggs to go with it?"

"You'll find a carton of eggs in the fridge. Get to crackin'." When he leaned over to peer into the fridge, she swatted him on the butt with a wooden spoon, and then laughed when he shot her a narrowed-eye scowl. She'd have laughed at just about anything at that moment. She couldn't recall the last time she'd been so happy.

She started humming a certain Christmas song along to the sizzle and spit of the bacon. He cracked eggs and sweet-talked her into making biscuits.

"It's amazing how taking care of one hunger can work up another," he observed just as an unfamiliar ringtone sounded from her bedroom. "That's work. It's midnight at home. Wonder what this is about?"

"Take your time."

She had just put a sheet of biscuits in the oven when Reilly opened the front door. "Hey, Mom. How is Sinatra? Did he do okay without me?"

"He did great. I put him outside a few minutes ago and he's probably ready to come in. How was the sleepover?"

"It was soooooo much fun." He went to the back door and called his dog. A few moments later he was sitting on the floor playing with the puppy as he rattled on about the movies they'd watched and popcorn fights and on and on.

When he finally ran down, Jenna decided the time had come to broach the subject uppermost in her mind.

She rinsed her hands and wiped them on a dishtowel, then said, "Hey, hot rod. I need to talk to you about something."

"Uh-oh." Warily, he looked up at her. "That's never good."

"No . . . this is good. *Really* good. Reilly, remember when you made the first phone call to Santa a couple years ago? Do you remember what you asked him for?"

"Well . . . yeah. I told you about that. I asked him for a dad."

"Well, this is my really great news. Reilly, Devin asked if he could be your dad. He asked me to marry him."

Reilly put his puppy aside and went up on his knees. Hope filled his voice. "Devin? Devin is going to be my dad? I love Devin! This is the best news ever!"

He pushed Sinatra off his lap and leapt to his feet and threw himself against his mother for a hug. "Michael's brother is going to be my dad! So does that make me and Michael brothers? Oh, no." Reilly pulled away and looked wide-eyed up toward his mother. "He won't be my uncle, will he, like with Dr. Lori's baby? He's real obnoxious about being an uncle."

Jenna laughed. "I'll have to look into it to see what the relationship will be. I wouldn't worry about it though, Reilly."

"Okay. Oh, I'm so excited. I wanted a dad more than anything, even more than I wanted Sinatra."

"I know."

"When is Devin coming home to live in Eternity Springs? Will you have a wedding? Do I have to wear a tie?"

"Yes, we will have a wedding and yes, you'll have to

wear a tie. And no, Devin is not moving back to Eternity Springs." Jenna drew in a bracing breath, sent up a quick, silent prayer, and explained. "Devin has asked us to join him in Australia."

It took a moment, but the light in Reilly's eyes died. "You mean . . . like . . . move there?"

"Yes." Jenna told him about the five hundred national parks and the rain forest and the Great Barrier Reef. She told him that Devin loved him and loved her and wanted them to be a family. "He says his dad—Michael's dad— gave him the ocean, and he wants to give that to you too. It's his favorite place in the world and he wants to share it with you."

In a little voice, Reilly said, "But I like Eternity Springs. I don't want to leave."

"We've only been here a few months. Not nearly as long as we spent in Nashville or Tallahassee."

"I didn't make friends there. I have a lot of friends here."

"I thought you wanted a dad."

"I do. I really do. I love Devin. But why do we have to move to Australia? This is the best place in the whole world! I get to be a camel in the Christmas pageant and Ms. Gabi is going to teach me how to make a glass ornament for our Christmas tree."

Jenna's teeth tugged at her bottom lip. She'd figured he wouldn't be thrilled about moving, but obviously this wasn't going to be as easy as she'd hoped. "We won't move before Christmas, honey. It'll be sometime after the first of the year."

"I don't want to move to Australia ever! Why can't Devin move to Eternity Springs and stay here with us?"

"He can't do his job here."

"Why not? Other dads have jobs here. *His* dad has a job here. Devin could work with Cam."

"It doesn't work that way, Reilly. Look, I'm sure you'll love it there. Devin will make sure of it. You'll make new friends and the three of us will have new adventures. You just need to give him and Australia a chance."

"I don't want to! I want to stay here."

"We'll come back to visit."

"I don't want to visit. I want to live here! I hate jobs! A dad was supposed to make things easier because of you working all the time. Not make everything worse! I hate Australia! I'll be scared there. I'm never scared here! Everybody knows me here and they're not going to break my arm or point a gun at me. You go without me, Mom. You're not my real mom, anyway. You can unadopt me. I'll find another mom."

Tears streaming down his face, Reilly whirled around and dashed for the back door, failing to wait even long enough for Sinatra to catch up with him.

Jenna groaned and muttered, "That went well."

Hearing a sound behind her, she turned to see Devin standing in the great room just beyond the kitchen door. By the stricken expression on his face, it was obvious that he'd heard everything.

Jenna went to him and wrapped her arms around him. "It's okay. He'll come around."

"Hearing that ripped out my heart."

"I know." She closed her eyes and heard the echo of his hurt little voice saying, "Unadopt me." Tears flooded her eyes. Here she'd thought he'd healed. Guess she'd gotten ahead of herself.

"I can't do that to him, Jenna. He's been through so much. I can't put him through more traumas. I won't be able to live with myself."

"We'll find a way to make it work."

"How? I can't make a living in Eternity Springs. If I tried to work for Dad again, we'd be at loggerheads and it would ruin our relationship. My higher education took place aboard a boat. It's all I ever wanted. All I know."

He closed his eyes and rested his forehead against hers. "I've considered it, you know. When I learned about these babies coming and knowing I wouldn't be part of their lives, I considered my options. Family does matter. It matters a lot. That's one reason why this new deal matters so much. The deal gives me the financial resources to come home when I want. Let me tell you, three flights since June has made my credit card bill a thing of horror."

The timer went off. They stepped apart, and Jenna moved to take the biscuits out of the oven. She tossed the hot pads down onto the counter, closed her eyes, and rubbed her temples. "I suspect what we saw a few minutes ago is simply a case of too much change in too short a time. Reilly probably needs to talk to a counselor too. I wanted to do that last summer, but moving around the way we did didn't make it feasible."

"Moving around the way you did," Devin repeated. "See, that's what makes this so bad. I knew he liked it here, but I didn't realize he'd fallen under the Eternity Springs spell. Dammit, Jenna, I wouldn't have . . ."

She folded her arms and faced him. "You wouldn't have what? Fallen in love with me? Risked your heart on me?"

"Taken so long to figure it out."

"Long? We've only known each other four months."

He shook his head. "I fell in love with you long before I spotted you on the Hummingbird Lake fishing pier. I knew from our very first phone call, Jenna."

"That's sweet, but silly. You don't fall in love with a stranger during a phone call."

"Don't be betting against the Eternity Springs mojo."

"I'm not going to. That's why I'm sure we will find a way to make this work. Listen, Devin, you and I can be sensitive to Reilly's needs—we should be—but we should be fair to ourselves too. Families make sacrifices for one another. That's what families do."

"But he's just a boy and he's already been through so much."

"I know. And if he was truly in danger like before, that would one thing, but this situation is different. Families all over the country—all over the world—face this same problem every day. Sometimes, kids have to move for their parents' job. That's life. Children have to learn that the world doesn't revolve around them. Otherwise they grow up to be selfish and self-centered and narcissistic, and I want better than that for my son."

Devin took Jenna into his arms. "Reilly isn't selfish, he's scared."

"Yes, but those fears are not based in reality. Not this time. Moving him to Australia will not put him into danger. I wouldn't do it if it would. But I also won't let my eight-year-old son dictate my life. I love you. I'm not going to walk away from that. We will give Reilly some time, but he will just have to learn to deal. You asked me to marry you. I'm not letting you take it back. You're stuck with me, Devin. We will find a way to make this work."

He pressed his lips to her forehead. "I'll make him happy. I'll make you happy. I swear."

"I believe you, Devin. I believe in us, in the family we will form."

"Okay. I trust you. I believe in us too. The bad news is . . . that phone call . . . there was a fire at the marina office. This wasn't a hurricane that sank my boats, but my paperwork is a mess. I have the meeting with the investors next week. I'm going to have to recreate a lot of records. I have to go back."

"Oh, Devin, no. When? When do you have to leave?"

"Right away. I've already called the airlines, and connections are gonna be a bear." He glanced toward the back door. "I want to talk to him, but what can I say in a couple of minutes? I'm afraid I'll only make things worse. Dammit, Jenna. I don't know how I went from such great timing yesterday to such sucky timing today. I don't want to leave here, not like this, but everything I own is tied up . . ."

She rested her index finger against his lips. "You'll be back for Christmas, right? After the babies are born?"

"Yes."

"Then go take care of business, Devin. Reilly and I will be waiting here for you when you return."

"I wish . . ."

"I know. Me too."

"I'll call you from the airport. From all of them. I'll call you every day." He kissed her once, hard and quick. "Why are we always saying goodbye?"

He'd just shifted into reverse to back out of Jenna's drive when she ran out of the house with a paper bag in her hand. He rolled down the window. She shoved the bag at him. "Breakfast. And not goodbye. Never goodbye. I'll see you at Christmas, Santa. Don't forget to believe."

Chapter Twenty-One

Elsewhere in the country the day after Thanksgiving was known as Black Friday. In Eternity Springs, things were different. Here the day was known as Deck the Halls Friday, and everyone turned out to dress up the town for the holiday season. As always, spirits were high, the cinnamon-spiced cider was hot, and by noon, wreaths decorated doorways, garland graced lampposts, and thousands of twinkling white lights set the scene. Citizens pitched in to decorate the town's official tree in Davenport Park, and once the mayor and honorary Deck the Halls chairwoman Celeste Blessing placed the angel atop the tree, they dispersed to trim their family trees and put up their personal holiday decorations.

At Angel's Rest Healing Center and Spa, Celeste and her helpers had been busy little elves. When Reilly and Jenna arrived for their three o'clock appointment, she had the old Victorian mansion that served as the headquarters of the resort glistening and twinkling and glittering in silver and gold. Angels sat on every nook and cranny and post and beam throughout the house.

"Everything looks beautiful," Jenna told her as Celeste descended the staircase carrying a large canvas tote.

"Thank you. I so enjoy decorating for the holidays."

Celeste lifted a down-filled white coat from a hall tree near the front door and asked, "Where is Reilly?"

"He's outside with Sinatra."

"The boy does love his dog, doesn't he?" she observed, slipping into her coat.

"Yes." It was the one thing Jenna could count on where Reilly was concerned these days.

This past month with Reilly had been a challenge, to say the least. The first week after Devin returned to Australia, Reilly would hardly talk to her. The second, he spoke with her, but pretended their conversation about Devin had never happened. She'd gotten him in to see a counselor in Gunnison that week, but she knew better than to expect too much too soon on that front. Trust in counseling relationships took time to build. During the last two weeks, she'd begun to hope that they'd made some progress. Her son hadn't bolted from the room every time she'd brought up the subject of their future.

Devin had called daily. They'd decided to keep news of their engagement to themselves until he returned at Christmas. His family had been curious about his unexpected brief trip home, but when he'd asked them for patience, they'd given it to him. With their due dates fast approaching, the Timberlakes and the Murphys both had babies uppermost on their minds.

"I'm so glad you invited me to join you this afternoon, Jenna," Celeste said. "It warms my heart to know that you and Reilly have chosen to adopt my family's Christmas wishing tree tradition."

"It's a lovely tradition. I'm grateful and honored that you shared it with us."

When they stepped out onto the front porch of Cavanaugh House, the sound of Reilly's unbridled laughter reached Jenna's ears. She watched her son and his dog play together in the snow and a sense of peace washed through her. Everything would turn out okay. She knew that. After all, hadn't that been her wishing tree wish?

Jenna picked up the backpack she'd left on the porch swing upon arriving at Angel's Rest and slipped her arms through the straps.

"The sun has come out," Celeste observed as they started down the front steps. "Isn't this lovely? We had just enough snow to freshen everything up. I do love sparkle and glisten."

Celeste had a treat in her pocket for Sinatra, and the puppy wiggled and yipped with delight upon seeing the biscuit. As they hiked toward the forest, she chatted with Reilly about school as Sinatra raced in mad circles around them. Then as they entered the hushed cathedral of the forest, even the pup quieted and fell into step at Reilly's feet.

They'd hiked for about ten minutes when Celeste abruptly stopped. "I think we've found it. That looks like a perfect Christmas wishing tree."

In front of them stood a majestic blue spruce about twelve feet tall. Frosted with snow, heavy with pinecones, and with a beautiful shape.

"It's close to last year's tree," Reilly said. "It's right over there. See it? I can see it." He pointed toward a spot some twenty feet away where an angel remained standing at the top of the tree. "They can be wishing tree friends."

"I like the sound of that. So, let's get to work, shall we?" Celeste set down her tote and began pulling out an amazing number of trimmings for the size of her bag. For the next ten minutes she, Jenna, and Reilly draped garland and hung ornaments upon its branches. When the tote bag was finally empty, Celeste used a folding extension tool to place a simple straw angel atop the tree.

"There. We're all done but for the final touch." She reached into her coat pocket, and as she withdrew one last ornament, a small gold velvet bag fell into the snow.

"You dropped something," Reilly said, diving for it.

Celeste smiled down at Reilly as she accepted the bag. "Thank you, Reilly. I would have hated to lose this."

Then with quiet ceremony, Celeste hung an intricate woodcarving of a snowflake on a branch. The trio stepped back and observed the tree. Following a few moments of reflection, Jenna observed, "It's simple and lovely."

"Yes, isn't it?"

"I like your tree, Ms. Celeste," Reilly said. "Whose are we doing next, Mom? Yours or mine?"

"You pick."

"Let's do yours. We'll save the best for last."

"Okay. But I want you to help me pick out the perfect tree."

"I can do that."

"We'll follow you."

The path the boy led them along took them past Celeste's wishing tree from last year. Jenna was surprised to discover that the tree's decorations appeared unharmed by a year's worth of wind and rain and snow and squirrels. She spied only one bit of damage.

Reilly saw it too. "Oh no. The angel you hung last year has a broken wing."

"No problem," Celeste said in a chipper tone. "I have a few more wrinkles and creases this year, myself. But she's hanging in there, isn't she?"

"What if she'd disappeared? What if a bear knocked her out of the tree and stomped on her? Would your wish be ruined?"

"Oh, Reilly." Celeste gave him a quick hug. "Don't forget that she's only a symbol, just as the wishing tree itself is symbolic. Don't forget that what matters is what was in my heart when I hung her on that branch."

The boy continued to look at the broken angel for a

long moment. "What is in your heart matters most of all. I remember." Glancing up at his mother, he said, "I remember there's a pretty tree next to the wishing tree I chose last year. You might like it."

"Why don't you show me?"

"It's this way. I remember." Reilly headed off through the forest with Sinatra, as always, at his heels.

"How does he know where we are?" Jenna wondered aloud. "We've wandered a lot of different woods in the past year."

Celeste slipped her arm through Jenna's. "It's amazing what our young ones recall when it comes to everything Christmas."

That much was true. A few minutes later, he stopped in front of a Douglas fir just a little bit taller than Jenna. "What do you think, Mom? Do you like it?"

"It's perfect." Jenna slipped off her backpack and started unloading decorations. Yesterday after sharing a Thanksgiving meal up at Heartache Falls with the Timberlakes and Murphys, she and her son had passed a pleasant hour creating their wishing tree ornament. Reilly had made a snowman from pinecones and twigs.

Jenna would have loved to know what the snowman symbolized for her son, but she remembered the rules. Ms. Celeste said it works better if you keep your wishes in your heart.

Personally, Jenna was wearing her wishes on her sleeve these days. She'd carved a whole, healthy wooden heart from a piece of firewood she'd filched from the Murphys' woodpile, decorated it with sparkling gravel gathered from the banks of Angel Creek, and tied a leather band around it that roughly—very roughly—symbolized eyeglasses.

Reilly had looked at the ornament and then at her with

an expression that said, *Really, Mom?* but he didn't comment. He knew the rules too.

With her tree trimmed, Jenna carefully unwrapped her heart from its protective tissue paper. She hung it on the tree, and then looked at Celeste. "Because I choose to live my vision, not my circumstance."

Celeste's answering smile warmed Jenna from the inside out. "And for that, I have a little something for you to carry with you wherever you go. It's a bit easier to carry around than a snow globe."

Jenna opened the bag and removed a delicate angel's wing pendant on a chain. She knew what this was. She'd seen her friends wearing it. Her eyes flooded with sudden tears. "It's the Angel's Rest blazon."

"That it is. Awarded to those who have accepted love's healing grace."

"It's beautiful, Celeste. Thank you. But . . ." Something else remained in the small gold bag. Jenna looked again. "Two more?"

"Live in your vision, not your circumstance." Celeste looped her arm through Jenna's and spoke to Reilly. "I think it's time to decorate your Christmas wishing tree now, don't you?"

"Sure! I have one all picked out. It's right this way."

Jenna scooped up the backpack and followed her son through the woods to a spot along the forest's edge. "What do you think, Mom?"

He'd stopped in front of what could best be described as a Charlie Brown Christmas tree. Its trunk was bent but unbroken, and the branches sparse. It grew from the midst of a rocky section of land that offered little soil for roots. Despite the less than ideal circumstances, the tree survived.

Just like Reilly survived. Survived, ready to thrive.

Tears flooded Jenna's eyes. Her voice sounded a little shaky as she said, "I think it's the perfect tree."

"You couldn't have found a better choice!" Celeste agreed.

Reilly took off his own backpack, and as he began to pull out the decorations he'd assembled, Celeste snapped her fingers. "Oh, posh. Do you know what I did? I left my mittens back at my wishing tree. Reilly, do you mind getting started without me while I run back to get them?"

"That's okay."

Jenna looked down at the abundance of trimmings he'd set out. She couldn't for the life of her imagine how they'd all fit on that little tree. "Where do you want me to start, hot rod?"

"You can wrap the ribbon around it."

After much debate on what constituted "natural" as far as tree trimmings went, they'd decided that one hundred percent cotton ribbon counted. Jenna had made one loop around the tree with the red ribbon when Riley threw her a curve ball. "I don't believe in Santa anymore."

The ribbon spool slipped from her hand and landed in the snow. Her heart twisted. He was eight years old. She'd expected this subject might come up this Christmas, but she wasn't ready! "I don't know . . . um . . ."

"It's okay. You don't have to pretend. I know that you're the one who buys the Santa presents and puts them under the tree. I know you fill my stocking. Santa doesn't come down the chimney, and he doesn't answer the telephone when somebody calls North-Pole-One."

Jenna started to reach for him, but his body language shouted, *Stay away.*

"Oh, Reilly." Jenna scooped the ribbon spool up off the ground and tried to recall all the parenting advice she'd read on this subject as she made another loop. "It's true that I'm the person who puts Santa gifts under the tree, but that doesn't make me Santa. It also doesn't mean that Santa doesn't exist. Santa does a really important job because he teaches children a really important lesson. He teaches them how to have faith in something that they can't see or touch. He teaches them to believe, and that is something important to have as you grow up."

"I know."

"You do?"

"Uh-huh. It's like the Christmas wishing tree. Santa is a symbol. The real magic of Christmas isn't wishes or reindeer. The real magic of Christmas is . . . are you about done with the ribbon? I'm ready to hang my special ornament."

Jenna gave her head a little shake, glanced at the pile of decorations on the ground, and saw that while she'd been occupied with one of the traumas of parenthood, her son had decorated his tree. "Okay. Sorry."

She made one final circuit, then stepped back and surveyed the tree. Darned if he hadn't balanced his decorations in such a way that the crooked little Charlie Brown tree stood a little straighter.

Reilly reached into his backpack, but the ornament he hung on the tree was not the pinecone snowman he'd made the previous day, but a little wooden boat.

"Reilly?"

"Don't ask, Mom. You know the rules."

"Okay. I won't. Only . . . finish what you were going to say. What's the real magic of Christmas?"

"Geez, Mom. Don't you know anything? It's love. The real magic of Christmas is love."

After his father mentioned the upcoming sleigh ride during one of their calls, Devin planned his surprise with the precision of a battlefield general and kept knowledge of it strictly need-to-know.

It was the first Saturday in December and "any time now" was the phrase of the week. In a half-dozen houses across the small mountain town, mothers-to-be couldn't sleep—their backs hurt, and they had heartburn, swollen feet, and moods that swung from rage to tears to joy to despair on the basis of . . . well, anything. These were a half-dozen women who wanted to not be pregnant NOW.

And a half-dozen fathers-to-be who dearly loved their wives but whose nerves were frayed to the point of breaking. Something had to give.

Enter, Santa Claus.

The first salvo was a mano-a-mano confab to be held over cookies and milk at Fresh. Cam delivered the goods shortly after the bakery closed at noon. "Where's Michael, Mr. Murphy?" Reilly said when he spied the table set for two. "I thought he was going to be here."

"Well, I tricked you, Reilly. I said *my son* is waiting for you."

"He meant me," Devin said, stepping into the room.

Reilly folded his arms and frowned at Devin.

"Good luck," Cam said as he tipped an imaginary hat and left the room.

Now that the moment was upon him, Devin was a little nervous. "Would you sit down and share some cookies and milk with me?"

It appeared to be touch and go for a moment, but eventually, Reilly shuffled over to the table and took a seat. He didn't touch his snack.

Devin forged ahead. "Before we dive into this, I need to say something flat out so that there is no ambiguity. I love you, Reilly. I love your mother. I want us to be a family. I want to be your dad and to be your mother's husband. That's the bottom line."

Reilly dipped his head, but not before Devin caught

the sheen of sudden tears in his eyes. Was that a hopeful sign or a problem? He wasn't sure.

So he hurried on. "Everything else is open for negotiation. That's why I invited you here today. I have a proposal to make, man to man."

"Aren't you supposed to propose to my mom?"

"I did. Sort of. I have plans to make an official, more flashy one later today if you and I can come to an agreement here." Devin pushed the plate of strawberry pinwheels closer to Reilly.

Reilly picked up a cookie and took a bite.

That was something, anyway. At least he hadn't thrown it at him. Yet.

Devin breathed just a little easier and launched his argument. "I can't go back in time and change my decision to make my living from the sea. Now, because I'm shooting straight with you, I probably should mention that I'm not sure I would change it if I could time travel. You see, Reilly, I love what I do. The ocean is part of me. It's such a fascinating, amazing place, and every day offers something new. It's exciting. Going out on the ocean, diving and snorkeling and fishing, it's like visiting a new world every single day. I truly believe you will love it, Reilly. I think you'll love the ocean as much as you love national parks, and maybe even more. I want to share it with you and your mother."

"Australia is really far away from Eternity Springs," Reilly pointed out in a small voice.

"Yes, it is. It truly is." Devin paused and took a sip of milk. "I recognized that the distance between Australia and Eternity Springs was one of the main problems facing us, so I set my mind to finding a solution. That brings us to my proposal."

He picked a notebook off the seat of the chair beside them and set it in front of Reilly. It was a three-ring binder with a leather cover. Embossed across the front of the journal were the words REILLY JAMES MURPHY'S CARIBBEAN ADVENTURE.

"I can't move to Eternity Springs, Reilly, but I can move my business back to Bella Vita Isle. It's a whole lot closer than Australia. When I used to live in Bella Vita, I visited Eternity Springs all the time. Michael and my parents used to visit me a lot too. The Brogans have a home there and so do the Ciceros. People are always going back and forth between Bella Vita and Eternity Springs."

"This says Reilly James Murphy. Not Reilly James Stockton."

"Well, yes. When I marry your mom, I would like to adopt you. I want very much for you to be my son and carry my name."

"Michael and I would be like brothers."

"Almost."

Reilly ate the rest of his cookie and took a drink of milk. He opened the notebook and began flipping through the pages behind tabs that read ANIMALS OF BELLA VITA and CARIBBEAN SEA MARINE LIFE and PIRATES OF THE CARIBBEAN. Reilly paused at an illustration of Blackbeard's frigate, *Queen Anne's Revenge*, flying the skull and crossbones. "Pirates?"

Devin nodded sagely. "It's not just a ride at Disney."

"Cool!"

"I think we could make it work, Reilly. If you'll give me your permission to marry your mother and become your dad, I'll give you my solemn oath that you'll get to spend plenty of time in Eternity Springs each year."

"And Michael can come visit us?"

"Of course."

"He'll probably want to get away from the babies. Especially if they're both girls."

"Hey, we Murphy men will have to stick together."

Then, with his heart in his throat, laying it all on the line, Devin extended his hand. "So, Reilly James Stockton, do we have a deal?"

Reilly stared at Devin's hand. "Two years ago, I asked Santa to bring me a dad."

"I know. Merry Christmas, Reilly."

The boy took his hand. "Merry Christmas . . . Dad."

Devin's heart took flight.

The twenty-minute sleigh ride up to a high meadow on Murphy Mountain proved to be just the medicine her patients had needed, Jenna decided as Cam reined in the horses and the sleigh glided to a stop. To a woman, each expectant mother was more relaxed upon arrival than they'd been at the beginning of the ride. Nothing like shared misery and commiseration to ease one's burden.

The fathers-to-be had traveled ahead by other means, primarily snowmobiles, and the women arrived at the meadow to find a bonfire burning brightly. Playing with both speed and fire had mellowed the men's moods too, so everyone was relaxed and happy as hot chocolate and warm apple cider was passed around.

"It's a pretty day, isn't it, Mom?" Reilly asked her.

"It is. Did you enjoy your snowmobile ride with Mr. Chase?"

"It was *so* much fun. Michael and I wanted to go faster but he said maybe next time, because Dr. Lori made him promise six ways to Sunday not to be one bit reckless."

"Six ways to Sunday, hmm?" Jenna grinned over the top of her steaming cup of chocolate at her rosy-cheeked, sparkling-eyed son. He was one happy boy today. He'd been happy ever since last week's wishing tree outing, but today his little light seemed to shine exceptionally bright.

Wonder if he snooped and found his stash of Christmas presents?

"The sky is sure blue, Mom, isn't it?"

"It is."

"No, look at it! You gotta look at it."

The insistence in his voice caused her to follow the path of his pointing finger. Only then did she see the small single-engine plane flying high over the meadow.

And something fell out of it. *Holy cow, are we witnessing a drug drop?*

A minute after the object started falling, a parachute popped. Soon everyone in the meadow had his or her gaze glued to the sky. As each moment ticked by, Jenna was able to identify a bit more. First, she saw that it was a human, not a box. So, not a drug drop. Then she recognized what the figure was wearing. A red suit? With black boots? A snowy white beard?

"It's Santa Claus!" Michael Murphy exclaimed.

Jenna glanced around the group, wondering who had arranged for a visit from Santa. Must have been Cam since he'd put together this sleigh ride. Plus he had a knowing smirk on his face, although Sarah obviously wasn't in on the surprise. She looked as baffled as Jenna.

Santa managed a near-perfect landing some fifty yards from the bonfire. At exactly what moment she recognized him, Jenna couldn't say, but by the time he'd dealt with his chute and somehow turned a backpack into Santa's bag, her heart began to pound.

"Ho ho ho," Santa said, striding toward them, the unmistakable twang of Australia in his tone. "Merry Christmas."

"Devin!" Michael protested. "You're not Santa." He turned to Reilly and said, "That's my brother. He's just dressed up. He's not the real Santa."

Lori reached for her mother's hand. Emotion cracking in her voice, she said, "He's here. He came to be with us when they're born."

"I'm not surprised. I don't care what he said." Tears rolled down Sarah's cheeks. "Devin is such a marshmallow when it comes to family."

"Ho ho ho. Merry Christmas." Devin's cheeks were rosy and his eyes surely twinkled, and while he didn't pull off the Santa belly, he did find a booming voice when he added, "I hope everyone's been behaving because I have presents for the good girls and boys. Where's my helper elf?"

To Jenna's surprise, Reilly said, "Here I am, Santa."

"Where'd he get that elf hat?" Jenna murmured as her son ran to meet Devin.

"And ears!" Lori said with a laugh. "Look at the pointed ears."

"He was in on this," Sarah observed. She glanced up at Cam. "You were, too. You dog, you. You didn't say a word!"

"You would have worried about the skydive part of his plan," Cam defended. "You always fret when you know that he's going to jump out of a plane."

"True." Sarah glanced toward Jenna. "I think it's a stupid hobby. Why, once—"

"Gifts!" Devin interrupted loudly. "We have gifts galore." He opened the bag and fished out two small packages. "Hmm . . . this one appears to be for Baby Turner and this one"—he read the tag—"Baby Brogan."

Reilly delivered the gifts to the parents, then ran back for more. "Baby Timberlake and Baby Garrett. Baby Murphy and the Babies Callahan."

As Reilly took the gift to the Timberlakes, Lori asked, "Santa, can we open them now or do we have to wait for Christmas?"

"Whatever you'd like. Feel free to open them now if you wish."

He'd brought them each a little koala bear, and Jenna grinned at the chorus of oohs and aahs. Santa started to pull the drawstring on his pack when his little elf said, "Wait, Santa. Isn't there one more thing in your bag?"

"Is there?" Santa asked.

"I hope so," Reilly said. "Because there's one very good girl who didn't get a present."

"Oh. Well. Hmm." Santa made a show of peering into his bag. Then he said, "Aha, elf. It appears that you are right.

He reached deep into the bag and pulled out a black velvet ring box. Jenna's heart pounded like reindeer paws on a rooftop as he made a show of reading a tag. "For the love of my life." He glanced down at Reilly. "I think I'd better deliver this one myself, don't you?"

"Yep, sure do, Santa."

Finally for the first time since his arrival, Devin met Jenna's gaze and held it. He walked slowly toward her and went down on one knee. "Jenna Stockton, my love, my heart. Will you marry me?

"Yes, Devin Murphy. Of course I'll marry you. You're my Christmas wish."

He slipped a beautiful solitaire diamond ring on her finger, and his mouth had just touched hers in a kiss when his mother interrupted the moment. "I hate to do this, but Devin, I need to borrow your fiancée. It appears that my water just broke."

With his black belt discarded and his red jacket unbuttoned to reveal a plain white T-shirt, an unkempt Santa Claus paced the hospital waiting room. What a crazy day and night this had been.

His mother might have kicked things off, but it hadn't

stopped there. They'd no sooner got her down off the mountain and settled into a room at the clinic than the same thing happened to Shannon Garrett. After that, it was like dominoes. All six women . . . every last one of them . . . went into labor.

Devin wondered just what his father had put in that hot chocolate he served up on the mountain.

With so many patients involved, it was all hands on deck at the clinic. But all the rush and hurry quickly became hurry up and wait. Hours crawled by in a waiting room packed with friends and families. Devin was excited for his sister and parents and the other expectant couples, truly he was. However, would it have hurt any of them to hold things off for just a couple of hours? He'd barely had the chance to kiss his fiancée, much less share a proper hello.

He visited with the Timberlakes and Celeste and the Chamber of Commerce members who stopped by for updates on the big Maternity Springs contest. He pillowed Michael's head in his lap and Reilly's against his chest as both boys slept. At one point during the long night, his soon-to-be son looked up at him and said, "Don't worry, Dad. Sometimes Mom's work hours stink, but you'll get used to it. And from now on, we'll have each other."

Yes, from now on, they'd have each other.

Dawn the following morning broke on six inches of new snow. Devin stood at a waiting-room window watching a new day dawn over Eternity Springs, his heart full of quiet anticipation. So much to look forward to. So much to be grateful for.

His sister and his niece were born within half an hour of each other.

It was noon before he made it home and got the boys settled and fell into bed for a much-needed nap. When he heard the phone ring, he almost didn't answer it.

What phone was that, anyway? He lifted his head from his pillow. His Santa pants that he'd left pooled in the middle of Jenna's bedroom floor were ringing. Why were his pants ringing? He glanced at the bedside table where his phone silently lay.

But his Santa pants were ringing.

Devin stretched out an arm, snagged the red velvet, and tugged it toward him. Damned if there wasn't a phone in the pocket. A flip phone.

He flipped it and cautiously brought it to his ear. "Hello?"

"Santa, this is Reilly from Nashville again, only this Christmas I'm Reilly from Eternity Springs and next Christmas I'll be Reilly from Bella Vita Isle. I have another Christmas wish for you, Santa. You did so good bringing me a dad that I figured I'd better get this on record. My poor best friend Michael got stuck with two girls today. If you have any pull in the baby department, could you see about getting my family a boy?"